THE GOBLIN MIRROR

THE GOBLIN MIRROR

C.J. Cherryh

A LEGEND BOOK

Published by Arrow Books Limited
20 Vauxhall Bridge Road, London SW1V 2SA

An imprint of Random House UK Limited

London Melbourne Sydney Auckland Johannesburg
and agencies throughout the world

First published in 1992 by Ballantine Books

Legend paperback edition 1993

1 3 5 7 9 10 8 6 4 2

© C.J. Cherryh 1992

Printed and bound in Great Britain by
Cox & Wyman Ltd, Reading, Berkshire

ISBN 0 09 925071 3

THE
GOBLIN
MIRROR

A witch wind, country folk called the sudden storm that plunged Maggiar from autumn into winter, that stripped the colored leaves from forest and orchard all in a night. Behind it came an ice wind, edged with sleet and bitter cold—but that same winter brought a wealth of game the like of which the old folk had never seen. Hunters trekked home over the drifts with their pack ponies laden with meat and furs to keep old and young well-fed and warm; and with ample stock besides for trade to the west: deer and badger skins, marten and fox and ermine, from a plenitude of game that never seemed diminished. By midwinter deer had stripped the forest branches low enough to reach, foxes raided middens and storehouses, and the hunters could not shoot or trap them fast enough. Deer took to farmers' fruit trees. Boar rooted after winter stores, and marten and ermine hunted right up under the porches of Maggiar's isolated steadings. The old folk said: It was never like this before.

Behind the deer and the marten came the wolves, well-fed, content, inclined to lie about at first, but more and more of their voices sang in the mountain heights, songs cold and keen as the winter wind, that set folk looking anxiously toward the shutters at night and asking themselves was the door latch snug enough and had they barred all the sheds?

At last and as suddenly came the melting wind, a dark

nighttime storm that rattled doors and windows, pelted the trodden snow with mingled sleet and rain, and turned the fields overnight to hedge-rimmed lakes. Farmers slogged about their spring chores in mud-weighted boots, attempted planting in the high spots, and swore that they had never seen so quick a thaw or so much flooding.

In that season hunters began to find strange tracks in the woods, and spied shadowy movements flitting at the edge of the eye—a creature that left bearlike prints, walking upright.

The forest took on a dangerous feeling then, and the Old Folk whispered that a troll might have moved in. As yet no one had seen it, but the woodcutters and the charcoal burners cast anxious looks over their shoulders as they worked; while in lord Stani's keep, hunters old and young gathered and whispered in somber tones. Lord Stani's wizard, Karoly, wore a longer and longer look, casting the bones often and listening with his ear to the stone of the walls and the earth of the courtyard. Lord Stani asked Karoly what he heard in the earth, and the hunters asked. At one such asking, Karoly only muttered that many things seemed blessings that were not, and that father Sun and mother Earth never gave so liberally without a cost.

A deer was found at the forest edge totally blind and thin as a wraith—hunters killed it out of pity and let it lie and rot. That, too, they whispered about, unsure why that single death so disturbed them—but the truth was, once pity had afflicted them, a sense of guilt crept in, and made them think twice about the pelts stacked so high in the storehouses. It made them wonder for the first time whether luck that came so easily could be wholesome, or whether there might be something wrong in what they had gained too cheaply—as if they had plundered what was sound and left what was lame to breed and increase.

Master Karoly waked the watch one midnight swearing that he smelled something burning—not cookfires or rushlights, but something like old straw set ablaze. The watch failed to smell it, the night scullions failed to find it in the kitchens, and no more discriminating nose they roused could smell it at all. Still, when a wizard insisted, it seemed only prudent to wake the lord and lady, so before all was done, lord Stani had his men and lady Agnieszka her women searching the keep from tower to deepest cellars, while servants scoured every outbuilding and haystack inside the walls and nearby for any hint of smoke.

But nothing turned up, after the hold had been in uproar half the night. There was bleary-eyed grumbling among the people at breakfast that their wizard might be confused in his old age—complaint that fell silent once Karoly came draggling into the hall, haggard and worried, and begging their pardons for his foolishness. Somber looks followed his distracted passage through the room, and folk whispered how wizards sometimes had the Sight, though Karoly had never had it: the bones gave him merest hints about the future.

In one rainy mid-afternoon soon after, Karoly asked a passing serving maid what child was hurt; but the maid heard no crying child at all. Karoly stopped more than one servant, upstairs and down, distressedly asking did they not hear some child? And that report sent more chills through the keep. A ghost, some muttered. Ill luck, the servants began to say. The cooks obsessively feared fire, and parents kept an anxious eye to their children.

"What do you see?" lord Stani asked Karoly that night. "Is there some danger—of fire? Of flood? Or is it some other thing?" There had been peace in lord Stani's land for all his lifetime, except the ordinary bear trundling out of the forest after easier pickings, and once, twenty years ago, an incursion of bandits. So lord Stani asked the questions the hunters had asked, as a man who had known peace all his life, and feared now, as the hunters feared, that his run of luck might have been too much and too long. "I need leave," Karoly said for reply, "to visit my sister over the mountains, and ask her what she sees. My dreams worry me."

Lord Stani (the servants who witnessed it reported so) asked very cautiously, "So what *do* you dream, Karoly?"

Karoly was silent a moment, gazing at the wall. Finally he said, "Wizards' dreams are all true and all treacherous; and if we knew always what we dreamed, we'd be no wiser. I put no trust in my dreams. I beg you, let me go."

No one had known Karoly had a sister—that news flew quickly about the halls, likewise Karoly's saying that, "Something drove the deer." The rumor of the hour said that lord Stani was reluctant for his old tutor to leave, especially now, but saw no way of stopping him, none, at least, that Karoly would regard. It was foolhardy to ignore Karoly's advice, that was the consensus on the scullery stairs and in the smithy: some disaster boded, that Karoly sought to head off at its source.

So Stani called his two elder sons, Bogdan and Tamas, and bade them take Karoly through the mountains and bring him home again as soon as possible.

"It may be an old man's notion," lord Stani told them, "or it may be foresight—he always was wise before. Don't let his horse throw him, don't let him go cold or hungry—and above all bring him back in one piece. Woodcraft was never his best point; and he has no seat at all. If his horse so much as caught wind of a bear, he'd be afoot with it."

The brothers laughed, restless with the spring rains and delighted with the proposal. Bogdan said, "So much worse for the bear," and Tamas, the younger, said, "We'll take good care of him, papa." No one of their generation had ever ventured over the mountains. They had distant cousins and uncles in that land, they supposed. They knew of places like Krukczy Straz and Hasel, Burdigen, and Albaz, where their grandmother had had brothers and sisters—a land, the gran had told them, of beautiful waterfalls and tall pine forests. They knew all the names of them: the land over-mountain was their own land of once upon a time, and to ride out on their father's orders, to find this un-guessed and surely witchly sister of master Karoly's—for the rescue of Maggiar, if the rumors were true—all this, and to have a winter full of their own tales to tell when they got safely back again? This was the chance of their young lives.

Their mother took a far dimmer view of matters. Lady Agnieszka went storming to lord Stani's chambers and servants pressed ears against the doors and listened wide-eyed to the shouting inside for half an hour; while the youngest of lord Stani's three sons, Yuri, aged fourteen, declared to his friends that Bogdan as heir should by no means put himself in danger; *he* should be the one to ride with Tamas,—which opinion he bore to lord Stani, himself, hard on his mother's icy retreat.

But to no avail. Lord Stani informed his youngest son in no uncertain terms he was the sacrifice to his mother's good graces, the piece held in reserve against fate and accident; lord Stani said no, and no, and no.

After which, Nikolai, the master huntsman, his feet propped in front of the kitchen fire, told the pastry cook, "Trolls, that's what it is. Truth is, I'd rather not have the boys along. And come to that, I'd rather not have the old man. Send us up in the mountains and let us singe a few hides, I'd say, and leave the youngsters out of it. But the boy's of that age. . . ."

Bogdan, he meant. Bogdan, who was lord Stani's own image, dark haired and broad shouldered, the first in every game and every hunt; lord Stani foresaw the day Bogdan would be in his place, and wanted his heir to gain the levelheadedness and the experience of border keeping a lord ought to have. Bogdan should see the land over-mountain and maybe, lord Stani had confided it to Nikolai in private, come back with a grown man's sober sense, less temper, and less interest in girls and hunting.

As for the younger son, Tamas, just past his seventeenth

winter—shy, too-gentle Tamas, prettier than any girl in the keep—the boy was a fine hunter, if he could hit anything he'd tracked; a fine bowman, against straw targets; a serious, silent lad who would sit for an hour contemplating an antheap or picking a flower apart to find out what was inside. A little slow-witted, Nikolai summed him up, a little girlish, decidedly different from Bogdan's headlong rush at life. And this was the boy lord Stani sent in his charge, likely to hunt trolls?

Because that was what was really behind this flood of game, lord Stani himself had said as much to Nikolai when he had charged him pick the men for the escort and see that both the boys and the wizard got back with a whole skin.

"Don't speak of trolls," the pretty cook said, making an averting sign.

"I'll bring you a tail," Nikolai said. He was courting the cook. And not lying: a troll-tail he had taken, once upon a time, and given it to a silly maid he had been courting then. But Zofia was horrified. The kneading of bread had grown furious.

"You keep those boys safe," Zofia said.

"Keep Tamas safe. That's why m'lord sent young wander-wits: to put a rein on master head-foremost Bogdan."

Zofia frowned. The dough changed shape and folded again, in Zofia's strong, floury hands, a fascinating process. "The scullions heard a thing in the eaves last night," Zofia said. "Skritching and scratching and beating with its wings. And master Karoly said yesterday—he was sitting just where you are, having a sip of tea—he said we should do without mushroom picking, not send the lasses out, not go in the woods. And I says, Why? What's out there? and he says, Just don't be sending the young-sters beneath the shade of the trees. Why? I says again. Is it trolls? And he says—he takes this long sip of tea, like he's thinking—but he says something odd, then, like: There might be a troll, but it didn't *want* to come here.—That's just the way he said it. What do you make of it?"

"That it's exactly what I said to m'lord upstairs, a fat summer in the high country. A fat summer, a bad winter, too many deer. They strip the woods and they're straight for the orchards, it's as simple as that."

"And the trolls?"

"The wolves and the trolls, they go where the pickings are. But now that the bears are waked up—" Nikolai recrossed his feet on the bench, so the fire warmth reached the sole of his other foot. "*They'll* put master troll back up the mountain in short order. Then *they'll* be rattling the shed doors and sifting the midden heaps—so you can look to hear trolls under every haystack, half of them with cubs and all in a bad humor."

"It's not lucky to make fun." Zofia licked a floury thumb and made a gesture toward the witch-knot on the rafters, garlic and barley stalks. "You watch those two boys, you hear, don't you be letting them do something foolish, and don't you and Karoly do it, or the lord and lady won't let you back again.— You!" Thump of the dough on the table, and a scullion froze in his tracks. "Fetch the milk upstairs, and don't be slopping half of it.—I swear, the help is all scatter-wits this evening."

But Nikolai, thinking about the lord's two sons, said, half to himself, "The boys with trolls is one thing. Over-mountain is another. See his sister, the old man says. Why hasn't he seen his sister before this, is what I'd like to know, and where did he get a sister and what's he to do with her of a sudden? He's never been back over-mountain that I know. And I ask lord Stani about this sister business and he says Karoly insists and we should go."

"Old Jan says he'd come and go over-mountain."

"Upon a time, you mean."

"When he and the *old* lord was pups, long before you or I was born." Another folding in, another cloud of flour. "Old Jan was saying how Karoly was always out and around, in those days, off in the woods, up in the hills . . . the old lord, too—or least as far as old Jan remembers. So there could be a sister over-mountain, could be a horde of sisters, for all anybody knows. And how did the old lord find the lady gran? We all know she at least come from there." The dough thumped down onto the table, whump. "Lady gran used to come down here and stir the pots herself. 'More salt,' she'd say, and me mum and she'd be going round and round about the pepper and the spice. . . ." Whack. "She used to get herbs from Karoly. Karoly'd go pick at the right of the moon and the old lady'd say, Which side of the tree did you dig it from? And Karoly would say, snippishlike, The *right* one. I 'member that, plain as plain, I'd be stirring the pot, me standing on a step stool, I was so little, and they'd be arguing. And me mum said I shouldn't listen, the old lady had strange practices, that was what me mum called it. 'Strange practices.' The lady gran died and they still hang charms on the grave. Don't they?"

It was true. And it was certainly not the first time Nikolai had heard witchery and the lady gran joined in one breath— along with the observation that Karoly had been the guiding hand behind the young lord, Stani having been about Yuri's age at the time the old lord went over his horse's neck and never walked again—and the lady gran had had her way with the land until lord Stani was toward twenty and nine, with the god only knew what arrangements (or doings) between her and Karoly.

"Don't they?"

"They do that," he said. Women's business and witches. It was bad enough Karoly wanted to consult a witch: Nikolai wanted no part of the lady gran's business. The lady was in her grave and stayed there, thank the god; trolls were enough trouble for any man.

Cook gave a shake of her head and mounded the dough into a bowl, threw a towel over it. "Over-mountain isn't where I'd like to be right now, with strange doings and things flying about a' night. Ask yourself what was trying to get in with the scullions last night, eh?"

The boy was clumping up the steps with the milk pail. He came in white faced and hasty, all ears. Nikolai looked at the boy, who set the pail down and said, "Is that all, dame Zofia?"

"Be off," cook said. And when the door was shut: "They don't want to go into the barn, don't want to go to the sheds in the dark. I don't rightly blame them."

"There's no troll in the courtyard. They don't go where there's this many people."

"If they eat them one by one there's not that many people, is there?" Cook's voice sank to a mutter. "I don't like the store room meself, and that's the truth. Karoly said keep all the latches tight. And what did he mean by that; and what was that smell of burning, I'd like to know. So he's running off to over-mountain, to the lady gran's relatives as well as his, if you ask me—and lord Stani sending the boys with him . . . at whose asking, I want to know. His lady certainly didn't want it; and lord Stani wasn't listening to her at all, that's what the maids heard come out of that room."

That was what the men were saying, too, down in the courtyard and in the stables and the barn. The grooms were saying other things, how the barley sheaves above the stable door had fallen down in the wind, the doors had come open, and something had scared the horses last night, the same maybe as had scared the scullions.

Or maybe the wind had been what had them all upset. The old man smelled smoke and heard lost babies, rumors of it traveled from village to farmstead, and you could stay in the kitchen listening to tales until all the world outside seemed dark and evil.

But Nikolai had a lonely walk out to the tower tonight to reach his quarters, and on the way up the twisty, narrow tower stairs, where the light he carried up from the doorway made rippling giant shadows on the stones, he found himself thinking about the upstairs shutters and wondering if he'd left them latched or open on the night.

Foolish notion. An open window had never bothered him before. There was nothing to fear—nothing that wouldn't have a better chance at him tomorrow night, when they were sleeping under the stars. But there was something about old piles of stone like this, that had seen lords and servants come and go, that they accumulated shadows and odd sounds, and creaks and sighs of wind; you could well expect to meet the lady gran or old lord Ladislaw on the stairs—and it was no good thing to think of, on the eve of going troll-hunting and wizard-shepherding: the lady gran might be safe in her grave these last ten years, but *he* had to open the door of his room and probe the shadows, a grown man, for shame! who did not like to find the shutters open on the night and the light blowing precariously in his hands.

He went and pulled the shutters closed. In that instant the lamp blew out and the door slammed shut, thump! plunging the room into dark and echoing through the tower like doom. It actually took courage to turn again and calmly latch the shutters, to remember his way blind through the dark of his own chambers, feel after the door, and open it.

A very little light came up from below, not enough to light the steps. He found the lamp on the table and felt his way downstairs again to light it—not the first time the door had played that rotten trick, with the wind coming out of the south; not the first time he had trekked down the steps to relight the lamp—but he had never had a heart-thumping panic like this, god, not since he was nine years old, and he'd dared the bogle in the hay-loft that the neighbor boys refused to face.

It had known better than to meddle with him, and fled with a great rustling of straw and a clap of wings.

He lit the lamp. He climbed the stairs and on that last turn half-feared that the shutters in his room would be open again, or that something would be waiting in the shadows, or behind the door. That was the price of listening to stories, and he was a fool to think about them. Zofia was probably snug in her own bed, forgetful of all her notions.

But he thought not. He somehow thought not, tonight. And even with the shutters shut and the lamp burning bright, he longed for the morning, when they could be under the sky and out from under vaults of stone and memories.

Trolls and wolves isn't all that's wrong, he thought to himself, suddenly, for no good reason. He remembered over-mountain, at least the glimpse of it he had had from the heights, the year of the troll. He remembered a green land under a strangely golden sky, and a feeling he had had then of secrets beneath that green and witchcraft thick as leaves in that country. He had come from the north, followed the soldiers at fifteen, through wars and famine and the doings of wizards and witches—but that place had had a spooky feeling to it even that long ago. He had closed his mind to it, then: put away the memory until it was nudged by a rattling shutter and talk of the lady gran.

Karoly? Karoly was a dabbler, a pot-wizard, a weather-witcher. Think of Karoly and you thought of wheaten charms and jars and jars of powders for toothache and the gout. Karoly was sunny fields and winter firesides—

(But in the lady gran's day Karoly had gone off for days on end, that was so. One wondered where. Or why. Assignations with some sunburned country lass? Karoly was a man. And the lady gran—)

The lady on the stairs, dreadful in the lamplight—she had not been old. Her hair had been black. He remembered it as black, the year he had come to Maggiar. "Whose are you?" she had asked. "Whose are you, pretty? And what are you doing on my stairs?"

Shutters rattled with the wind. Forget the pretty cook, her

pastries and her stories. Forget the lady gran, the stairs and the long-ago dark. Lord Stani's master huntsman longed for sky above him, for the sighing of leaves—the forest had no memory such as stones acquired, when men piled them up and dwelled in them and made walls and bolts to keep themselves safe from each other inside.

The white bitch had whelped in the night—soft nosed, was nudging the newborn pups against her belly to nurse in the morning chill.

No few of them were yellow. Yuri was quick to point that out; and Tamas rubbed the ears of the gawky yellow hound that thrust its head under his arm to have a look at the puppies: Zadny, they called the ugly stray, who desperately wanted to please, who was good-tempered and keen to do what a body wanted. Somebody had lost a fine dog, in Tamas' estimation, the day Zadny had slipped his leash: he had arrived in the ice wind, starved and foot-sore, refusing every hand but Tamas' own, from which day he was Tamas' dog, and fastest of all the dogs Tamas used. In case wanderlust took him away this spring, Tamas was delighted to see the puppies.

But Tamas came to the kennel in armor this dawn, with grandfather's third best sword bumping at his side, breakfast uneasy in his stomach, and the stark realization in his mind that he could not be here, that Yuri must inherit the puppies—to see them walk, and tumble, and play. Yuri had run up looking for him and Bogdan as if nothing else were going on in the yard: Bogdan was busy at the stables, in the deepest throes of packing; but Tamas had excused himself and come for Yuri's sake; and, faced with changes that would pass without him, was suddenly beset with apprehensions.

Yuri lifted up a puppy and showed him the face. "It has to be his, doesn't it?"

"No question," Tamas said, rubbing the blunt puppy nose that had Zadny's yellow fur. "Only lighter. But puppies are, you can't tell yet." He had come here to mollify Yuri's offended sense of importance; now he felt unease, and a sense of loss he could not define. It prompted him to say, "Take care of them. If anything should happen——"

"It won't happen!" Yuri scowled and set the puppy down against its mother. "No reason I can't go, I'm only two years behind you, but no one sees that."

It was three. But shading on two. " 'Anything can always happen,' " Tamas quoted Karoly, and reached out to squeeze Yuri's sullenly averted shoulder. "Maybe it's nothing, all this business, maybe it's just a bad year and it's a foolish goose chase, over-mountain. It might be. It's not what goes on there that I'm worried about, it's what happens here."

There was a wet-eyed angry look from Yuri. "Nothing happens here. Nothing ever happens here!"

"So it's your job to see it doesn't. Hear me?" His brother longed after importance. Tamas offered what romance he could. "Noises in the stables, scratches at the windows . . ."

"Birds," Yuri said sullenly. "That's all, it's birds. It's springtime, master Karoly says so, what do they expect?"

"Just take care. And don't go off alone in the woods and don't let your friends go. There *could* be a troll, and I don't want you to find it."

"I thought there *was* a troll. I thought you were supposed to kill it on your way."

"If we meet it on our way. We're supposed to ride over-mountain and back, that's all we're supposed to do. Master Karoly isn't happy with things *here*, that's why we're going to talk to his sister, isn't it? It's no good if we get there and something dreadful's happened back here, if the house has burned down or something. So watch out for things. Keep an eye on everything—don't let your friends be stupid, don't go into the woods. Don't let something go wrong. You're taking Bogdan's place in the house. —And take care of Zadny for me. All right? The houndsmaster doesn't like him; he threatens to lose him in the woods, and I want you to watch out for him and see he's all right while I'm gone. Promise me."

There was not much time. Men were mustering in the yard. And talk had only broken the dam: Yuri glared at him with tears brimming, temper and shame equally ruddy in his cheeks. "You get to do everything. Bogdan ignores me. It's not fair!"

"It's the first time, I promise you, it's the first time I've ever gone anywhere—and next time, you will go. You'll be tall as I am in another year."

"It won't do any good. The baby has to stay home if the rest of you get killed. For the rest of my life they'll say, 'Somebody has to stay home . . .' "

"Take care of Zadny. Keep out of trouble. Promise me?"

"I promise." Sullenly. Tearfully.

"Come on." He tousled Yuri's hair and Yuri batted at his hand.

"Don't treat me like a baby. Don't do that."

"I promise. Never again." This morning seemed an ominous time for Never Agains. He skirted around that thought, into irrevocable decision. "Come on. Walk me to the yard."

Yuri got up in glum silence and dusted himself off. Zadny came wagging up, brushed his cold nose against Tamas' hand, and got in his way—Zadny was roundly cursed for that habit, by cook, by Taddeuscz the houndsmaster, by Bogdan, especially since the day Zadny had gotten shut upstairs and chewed Bogdan's best boots. Zadny had a way of crossing one's path on stairs, or in doorways. Zadny chewed on things. He was lost,

Tamas was wont to argue on his dog's behalf. —He likes to be close to people. He hasn't grown into his feet yet. He hasn't had anyone to teach him manners.

He thought of Zadny underfoot in the yard, with the horses, or the very likely chance of Zadny following them down the road. "Yuri," he said, "we have to tie him," and Yuri agreed and got a rope.

It was a betrayal. He got down on one knee and tied the knot tight, getting dog all over him in the process, and a wet kiss of forgiveness in the face. "Be good," he told Zadny. "Stay, mind Yuri." After which he got up, wiped his face and his leather surcoat, and went with Yuri out of the kennels.

Barking pursued them through the gate, onto the trampled earth and flagstone of the larger courtyard, where horses and grooms mixed with stray goats and a handful of agile pigeons. The escort was gathering, with relatives and well-wishers, mothers and wives and younger brothers and sisters, uncles and aunts and cousins and grandparents, all weaving perilously in and out among the horses, all turned out in holiday best because it was no hunting party they were organizing, it was as bold and ambitious a setting-forth as anyone had made for years in Maggiar, to legendary over-mountain, with the chance of trolls along the way—fifteen men, all told, with their horses and three pack ponies loaded with grain and canvas for the mountain passes. The commotion caught Tamas up, making his heart beat faster. Colors and edges seemed both bright and unreal this morning. Master Nikolai was shouting at the grooms. Jerzy was flirting with a knot of Zav's cousins. Bogdan, looking every bit a lord's son and a warrior, was taking his leave of their mother and father at the top of the steps.

Tamas eeled through the confusion, hurried up the few steps to the landing with Yuri in his wake. "Do you suppose you can get this lot away today?" their father asked Bogdan just then. Bogdan laughed and took his leave, clapping Tamas on the arm and ruffling Yuri's hair as he passed, with, "Be good, little brother."

Tamas went and kissed his mother—"Be careful," she said to him, straightened his cloak-pin and remarked how handsome he was, but she had said a great deal more than that last evening—about witches and trolls and the necessity of watching what he ate and what he drank and never, never, never believing something that looked too good to be true.

"We'll be back before high summer," he told her, seeing tears glistening—high summer was what master Nikolai had assured all of them; he kissed her a second time, guilty for her tears, then briskly hugged his father, who patted him on the shoulders, saying, dryly, "Tamas,—keep a leash on your brother."

"I will," he promised, startled: his father had never said such a thing before, never hinted in all their lives that he doubted Bogdan's leadership, and he was not sure it was not a joke, except his father was not laughing. Had there been some falling out this morning? Bogdan at least had been laughing as he left.

Their father hugged him a second time, closer, clapped him on the back and shoved him after Bogdan, as if that was after all his final judgment of the sons he was sending out into the world—but, lord Sun, he had no idea how he was supposed to restrain Bogdan's headlong rush at obstacles: master Karoly could hardly do that. He was the younger son, Bogdan was in command, and their father told him to keep Bogdan out of difficulties?

The clatter of horses racketed off the courtyard walls, drowning shouts and conversations as Tamas went down the steps, past master Karoly, in armor like the rest of them, who was on his way up to his father. He spotted his own horse in the milling yard: the grooms had brought him, and they had indeed tied his packs on for him as they had said. He headed that direction in relief, done with good-byes and parental tears. Now his only worry was not to look foolish among the older men—when out of nowhere a chubby girl ran up, pressed a heavy packet into his hands and fled.

He stopped, confused, as Yuri turned up at his elbow, breathlessly asking could he have use of his hunting bow while he was gone, his own was too short for him, and he needed a far heavier pull than Bogdan's old cast-off . . .

"Yes," Tamas said absently. The packet the girl had given him smelled wonderfully of cake and spice; and he wondered who she was, or what he had done to deserve her attention. Other girls were giving out gifts of cakes or garlands to their sweethearts—but he was notoriously, famously shy of girls—everyone teased him for it; she intended he give it to Bogdan, that was most probably the answer.

"Tamas? Can I?"

He remembered his promise not to ruffle Yuri's hair—just in time. Yuri stood looking up at him, promising fervently, "I'll take care of it," —meaning the bow, which would only gather dust this summer, and that was not good for a bow. Or for other things. "Use anything," he said. "Anything of mine you like." One did not hunt trolls and come back and play with kites and tops. The clothes, he would outgrow. The few things else . . . why detail a few sentimental trinkets? Yuri had the last of his boyhood to go, the exploring years, the hunting and the fishing out at distant farms a marvelous half day away from home and supper. . . .

Pottery crashed. Michal's horse, fighting the grooms to avoid a gaggle of girls, backed into stacks of baskets, then surged back toward the screaming girls, across a ruin of apples. Chaos spun through the yard, Michal and the grooms all cursing as they restrained the horse.

"All right, all right," the master huntsman shouted, "to horse, lord Sun, clear back, can we have less commotion and get us underway? Master Karoly? M'lord Tamas? Can we get to horse?"

His face went hot. He glanced back, where Karoly was still with their father, insisting, he suddenly realized, on rehearsing every detail he had gone over with their father last night—he knew Karoly and he could catch the gist of it from here. So he ran back up the steps, tugged master Karoly by the sleeve, with: "Master Karoly, we're leaving *right now*," and drew the old man down to the yard.

"The weather-glass," Karoly was calling over his shoulder as grooms at the foot of the steps were boosting his armored weight into the saddle. "Don't forget the weather-glass, I showed Yuri how to read it—"

Their father called back, "Be off or you'll be here for harvest. —And mind, *listen to advice*, master Karoly!"

"—have to keep the water up to level!" Karoly shouted back, while Tamas tucked his be-ribboned prize into his saddle pack before mounting. "Be careful!" Yuri wished him, with worry on his face.

"Use your heads!" their father bellowed across the yard. Bogdan, ahorse, laughed and waved, already turning away; "Good-bye!" Yuri was shouting, and with his foot in the stirrup, Tamas had an overwhelming impulse to glance back toward his parents and his home as if—as if, it seemed, he had only this last moment to fix everything in memory, everything about this place . . .

But Bogdan was riding for the gate with Karoly and Nikolai, leaving no time for moon-gazing, and he hit the saddle as his horse joined the milling spill outward, overtaking Bogdan and the horse his own was most used to following. Hooves rumbled on the bridge, thumped onto the solid earth of the road, and the voices and the cheering grew faint. When he looked back a third time, home was gray, forbidding walls and a last pale glimpse of festive well-wishers within the gates, but no sight of Yuri, who was probably sulking. The day seemed perilous, full of omens; yet there was nothing he could put a thought around, as master Karoly would say. As if—

As if he were on the brink of his own forever after—or maybe only of growing up. It was a slice of his whole year this journey might take, bound where there might be bandits, or trolls. And he had given everything away.

He asked himself why now. Yuri would only lose the things—Yuri was fourteen, still careless, and could Yuri know the value of a broken toy horse and a bird's nest? Yuri would toss the keepsakes into the midden and use the painted box to hold his fishing weights.

But fields surrounded them now. The horses ran out their first wind and settled to a steady pace as friends sorted out their riding groups. In a little more there was no sign or sight of the keep at all, only orchards on either side, and a dark straggle of wild woods in front of them. The day had settled to a steady creaking of leather and jingling of harness and armor—as life would be for days and days, and probably more of that than of meeting bandits.

And they were not strangers he was riding with, they were mostly Bogdan's friends; and a few of his father's men. Bogdan might be in command for appearance's sake, but master Nikolai was in charge where it came to trolls—not to mention master Karoly, who could tilt any odds to Nikolai.

As the day passed, it felt like any ordinary hunting-party, forgetting the armor and the swords and master Karoly's presence with them: the jokes and gibes were the same, older men testing the younger ones—in which, being youngest and a fair target, he made no jokes, only defended himself. He could trade gibes with his lord brother, if he chose, which the others only rarely dared—

But he would not do that in public. Not in front of Bogdan's friends. Bogdan was anxious about having him along: Bogdan was always anxious about his wit in front of witnesses, and generally left him alone: by Bogdan's example, he supposed, so did Bogdan's friends, although he was a fair target on certain points, like girls and hunting, and doubtless had a reputation for glum, dull silence.

'Keep a leash on Bogdan,' indeed. Only because he was a weight on his brother, and knew court proprieties and not to set his elbows on the table.

And maintaining Bogdan's good humor in this company meant calling down no untoward attention on himself, making no mistakes and not becoming the butt of jokes. Of Bogdan's friends, Filip was amiable enough. Of the grown men, master Karoly was safe, even master Nikolai. But Jerzy—lord Sun, who could deal with Jerzy, elegant master Barb-in-everything? Or Michal, who was still smarting about his horse and the apple baskets?

Apples, Jerzy recalled at every opportunity. Michal was frowning, dark as the thunderclouds that shaded their road, and making shorter and shorter retorts.

In that way they passed from fields to occasional thicket. It rained, a sudden downpour, and they rode under rain-dripping branches of the deeper woods—("Where's weather-witching?" the grumble was heard then in the ranks. "Our own wizard along, and we're soaked the first day out. Wake up, master Karoly!")

But the air held a clean fresh scent the rest of the day; Jerzy wearied of apples; and they camped in a charcoaler's clearance as the trail grew too dim for safety, with a fire of wood and leftover lumps of charcoal.

Then everyone broke out the drink and the packets of honeyed sweetmeats, fresh baked bread and cheese and sausages, all the rich food that was bound to go bad in a few days, and shared it around—"Oh, ho!" Bogdan said, as Tamas offered the cake, "that's not cook's work, is it?"

"I think she meant it for you," Tamas said, trying to hand it to him. But Bogdan waved it off—"I'm *sure* it's yours," Bogdan said. "Keeping secrets, are we, brother?"

"Many," he retorted shortly, and glanced down, for fear of the cake becoming as notorious as apples.

But in fact, the plump maid's spice cake was delightful, and, sharing it around, and with the men not too wickedly asking who the mysterious sweetheart was, he found himself thinking she *had* been somewhat pretty: the gatewarden's second daughter, if he had his girls sorted out.

And not even an impossible match for lord Stani's second son, although his mother would hold out for, (he shuddered) Jerzy's hot-tempered younger sister, or lazy third-cousin Kataryzna, lord Sun save him. A wife was another prospect that came with growing up and riding with the men. All too soon, someone else's decision was going to arrive in his life with a clutter of baggage, disarranging his quarters, his habits, his days, his holidays, and his time to himself. And while spice cake was a benefit, the loss of privacy was not.

"Don't mind if I do," master Nikolai said, taking a chunk. "Mmm."

Master Karoly meanwhile had strayed off about the fringes of the clearing, among the trees. Nikolai's eyes were on him. So then were Bogdan's.

"Master Karoly," Bogdan called out as Karoly wandered further into shadow, but the old man showed no disposition to come back.

"It's going to be that way," Bogdan muttered, and elbowed Filip on his other side. "Filip, —god, —go watch him. Don't trouble him, but don't let him find a bear out there."

Filip swore wearily, got up and took his sword and his piece of cake with him, while master Nikolai washed his mouthful down with a long drink from his flask.

"Trolls aren't much for fires," Nikolai said, and finding every eye on him, went on with satisfaction: "They're not much for wizards either. The one I killed, now, that was the year a whole band of them came in on one of our farmers, killed the family, him, his wife, her brother, all the livestock. We found just the bones left of most of them. Dreadful winter. When we tracked them up into the mountains they charged right into the firelight and tried to make off with our horses. Either they thought we'd be easy as the farmers or they were that hungry. Trolls have a prodigious appetite."

"What did you do?" Jozef wanted to know. Jozef was new in the hold, an exchange from maternal uncle Ludwik's hold at Jazny-brook. Tamas and Bogdan and every youngster in the household had begged the tale every winter, how Nikolai had grabbed the chief troll's tail and cut it off, but Jozef was a new audience.

". . . bear-sized, these were. Big as a bear at least. You could take them for bears, except the faces, except the tail. It's long and naked as a rat's; and if you can grab that, you've got him. Except then you have to decide what to do with him."

Nikolai was joking with Jozef; the older men's eyes were sparkling with amusement. "So what did you do?" Jerzy asked, in the exact moment.

"Why," Nikolai said, "cut it off and ran like hell."

Laughter around the fire. Of course Nikolai could be talked into telling his story in detail, starting from the ruined farmhouse, and the dreadful find there.

Meanwhile Karoly came trailing back with Filip, sat down in silence and seemed to listen, hunched over with his arms about his knees. Nikolai told of the events near the cave, and how he had done for the king of the trolls, and him big as a bear and strong as two men.

The whole woods seemed full of sighs and whispers. An owl called. Jozef jumped, and laughed about it.

Karoly said, afterward, "I don't look for them here. Though it's possible. We should have a guard tonight."

"Jerzy," Bogdan said.

"A guard against *what*?" Jerzy protested. "That's what I'd like to know, if I'm going to sit up listening."

"Against whatever comes," Karoly murmured, staring abstractedly into the fire, and that was all subsequent questions could get out of him.

Jerzy, grumbling, dislodged Michal from the most comfortable spot near the fire, set his back against a tree and propped his sword across him, while the rest of them settled to sleep: Jerzy, and Michal, Filip, Pavel and Zev, that was the sequence of watch Bogdan set up, to take them to dawn; and Tamas loosened the belts and the straps of his armor and slid out of some of it, besides the boots—he watched what Nikolai and Bogdan did, to see how much comfort was prudent under the circumstances; and settled down with his saddle packs for a pillow, and Nikolai's story to darken his thoughts.

The newly leaved trees rustled and sighed over them. Night-creatures creaked and hooted through the woods around about. Their horses moved about their firelit grazing, bickered and shifted suddenly, rousing several heads from blankets, then quieted for a while. Nikolai had sat down near Jerzy, on watch, and the two of them talked in low voices, something to do with bear tracks in the woods: Tamas tried to hear, his mind too full, he feared, for sleep, and what regarded trolls or bears interested him. He shut his eyes to rest them while he listened; but he waked with the sun filtering through the trees, the whole camp stirring, and Bogdan calling him the family lay-about.

Things were immediately dull once Bogdan and Tamas had ridden away. Night was worse, with no brothers bickering down the hall. And breakfast was altogether glum and much too quiet. Yuri stirred his porridge about, with no appetite for it, slouched about his morning duties for Karoly, the slate-marking and the daily estimation of the weather-glass, then ghosted through their mother's sight, their mother moping and sewing and discussing with her audience of maids and matrons.

But he was too old to have to sit with that. He went down to their father's hearings of the farmers and tradesmen, but the only excitement there to be had was the story about farmer Padriaczw's bull and widow Miriam's cow, and once that was done, he slumped downstairs toward the yard to look for some of the other boys.

He was sure he would find them about the kitchens. But cook was making pastries, and said the boys had ridden out to Ambrozy's holdings to hunt rabbits.

That was completely unfair. Nobody had told *him*. Never mind he had slept late, and dallied about master Karoly's study, and lingered to hear about the bull and the widow's cow: one of them could at least have looked for him, and he was not now even interested to go and scare rabbits with a pack of boys too busy to come and find him.

So he collected a few special scraps for the white bitch and his brother's dog, deciding puppies were more fun than traitors, and that he and Zadny could go hunt rabbits around the orchard outside the wall.

So he flew down the scullery stairs, leaped puddles of wash water, and skipped down and around to the rickety kennel fence, near the stables. His father's dogs immediately set up a row, wanting what he had; Bogdan's six hurled themselves at their kennel gate and barked and yelped to attract his attention.

But the new mother, the white bitch, put her nose up to the

gate and took her scraps with licks of gratitude, like the lady she was. He counted to see were the puppies all in their nest and they were. Then he went as far as Zadny's lonely and ramshackle pen, which Tamas had made doubly strong to keep the other dogs from fighting with him.

But no Zadny came up to the gate; and when Yuri lifted the latch and looked, there was the rope lying in the mud, chewed through.

He had let Zadny get away. Tamas would kill him.

No, Tamas would forgive him, and that was a thousand times worse.

"Where are you going?" the armorer asked. "Isn't that Tamas' bow you're taking?"

"He lent it to me," Yuri said. And never answered the first question, in his flight downstairs.

"Where are you going?" cook asked, when he begged a hamper of food.

"To find the boys," he lied—although it was not quite a lie, if one could count his brother and their friends. "Please could I have extra? They'll probably be starved."

"Where are you going?" the stablemaster asked, when he caught him saddling his pony, Gracja.

"Oh, cook gave me this for the boys." He showed the basket, but not what was in it.

"You mind don't break your neck," the stablemaster said. Yuri was sure the stablemaster was thinking mostly of the pony's neck and the pony's welfare, no matter Gracja was his pony and he had never brought her to harm.

"Where are you going, young lord?" the guard at the gate asked.

"Oh, out and about," he said, and rode through.

"When will you be back?" the guard called after him.

"When I find my brother's dog," he shouted back, and set Gracja to a brisk trot, because the guard was hard of hearing, and every boy knew it.

And because he knew what direction Zadny had gone, and how far he might go, and because that direction was (he would admit it to himself only for a moment or two) exactly the way his heart wanted to go, at least in his fondest imagination . . . only, in his pretending, he dreamed of overtaking Zadny just as Zadny reached the men on the mountainside, and hearing his eldest brother say, "Oh, let him come, he's already here."

But that was not what Bogdan would say. And he knew the look Tamas would give him if he could not even keep his dog safe in his pen.

He had some pride. And if he was out all night and if he came back with Zadny, maybe everybody including his traitor friends would have worried enough to realize they cared.

It was forest for the next whole day; and expecting trolls palled after a time, in Tamas' thinking. The land began to rise. They saw game, but never yet a sign of trolls, and made no diversion to hunt—Bogdan maintained that rabbit stew would be a fine supper and argued that they could spare the time; but Nikolai overruled him, as Nikolai had their father's instructions to do, saying they could enjoy that luxury on the way back: it was better they move along, until they knew for certain what weather they were facing in the mountains.

Besides, they had the remnant of the cakes and cheese and sausage from home; and they had to dispose of that before it went stale or spoiled—amazing, Tamas said to himself, how obsessively men's thoughts turned to their next meal, when there would be no kitchen to provide it; and how after two days of looking for trolls under every log and bush, the mind wandered and began to observe other detail for relief, the flight of birds, the sunlight on new leaves, and the quick scurrying of vermin in the undergrowth.

The damage of the winter past was everywhere evident, in bushes that should be budding, now attempting to come up from the root; in trees leafing only above the reach of deer. But deer left little sign, now; instead, there was a great busyness of small scavengers—at one days-old carcass, like a swarm of rats when the granary door was opened.

—The forest is wounded, Tamas thought, not to the death, yet, but wounded—when no one could imagine a forest this wide and healthy could take harm, even by fire. He would never have said there could ever be too many deer, or too many foxes, but seeing the damage here, considering scratchings at doors and desperate flutterings at the eaves of the keep itself, he began to believe it more than a mere omen of harm: the harm here might be subtle, but it was already begun, in a spring that would not come with its usual vigor, and in the abundance of carcasses that the wolves had not touched.

There were always deaths in winter, that the melting snow turned up—deaths culling the weak and the old and the lame: but these were too many, and too recent: animals that had survived the winter were dying of privation, one kind preying on the next. Undergrowth was less. Roots had washed bare in the rains. Berry-thickets were scant of leaves. The other men began to remark on it, and asked Karoly what he thought.

Karoly said, "One thing touches everything." But when Jerzy asked what he meant, Karoly only looked at the sky through the branches, gazing, it might be, toward the hills, and said, "That answer is over the mountains."

I t was a good thing cook had put extra biscuits in the basket; and a bad one he had not managed to come away with but a light cloak—but, Yuri said to himself in the chill of the night, if he had gone out with a blanket and everything he needed he would never have gotten away.

And if he had been a little earlier going out to see to Zadny the way he had promised, he might have caught Zadny before he chewed through the rope.

But there was no use sleeping with might-have-beens, his father would say. He was in the woods. He had called after Zadny until every farmer in the valley and every deer in the forest must have heard him. It was only after the sun went down that he had begun to think overmuch about trolls, and wolves, and bears; and now in the dark it seemed scary to call out. This was the hour the four-footed hunters were out—and the time that trolls moved about, looking for boys and lost dogs to have for their suppers, if they could not catch a deer.

Or maybe they would rather catch boys and stupid dogs.

He had given up trying to start a fire. He had never been good at it. He wrapped himself in his cloak. Gracja's blanket was too sweaty and he had rubbed her down with it. And now he was acutely aware of the dark around about him, and the sighing of the leaves and the calling of night creatures he would swear he had never heard before in his life.

But then he had never been alone in the woods.

Perhaps he should give up and go home tomorrow morning. Surely they were searching the woods for him now, although he had not heard them, and whatever their opinion, he was not lost: he was absolutely confident of the general direction of home, and he had found what he was sure was Bogdan's party's trail through the woods, which was one of the usual ones. Zadny, with a hound's keen nose, had surely found it, too, and followed it.

And ever so much he wished that Zadny's keen nose could find him, because he could hear something moving about in the brush, and something was beginning to make Gracja very nervous.

He leapt up, the way he judged his brothers would, waved his cloaked arms and yelled, "Go away!" in his gruffest voice.

Whatever-it-was scampered away through the woods. Gracja jumped and almost broke her tether. Yuri sat down and tucked his cloak about him again, feeling better, at least.

Maybe even a wolf had been afraid of him. Maybe a bear. At best a deer or two.

God, he hoped that had not been Zadny.

"Zadny?" he called out into the dark. "Zadny? Here, boy—come here." It raised a dreadful noise in the night, and he imagined every bear and every troll within earshot pricking up its ears and saying, "Now there's a boy in the woods, isn't it?"

"Zadny?"

He heard a stirring in the brush. He imagined wolves and bears at least, took up Tamas' bow and nocked an arrow and waited.

"Zadny?" His arm trembled. He *wished* he had tried harder to start a fire.

But a pale starlit nose crept out from under the leaves, and ungainly large forefeet followed. "Zadny!" Yuri exclaimed, letting the string relax. "Lord Sun, I'm glad to see you! Come on, come on, boy!"

He had, he had realized it this morning, come away with no rope or leash, only Gracja's tether, and that was in essential use. So it had to be his belt. He laid the bow down as Zadny came out and regarded him in the dark, he talked gently to the hound the way Tamas would:

"Come on, come here, boy." He knelt down, delved into his pack and pulled out a biscuit. "Here, boy, cook sent it, come on, there's a lad . . ."

Zadny would not approach his hand. He broke off a bit and tossed it, but like a wild thing, Zadny took that and shied out of reach, and stood staring at him from a safer distance like a deer about to bolt.

"Oh, I'm not going to grab you. Here's a nice biscuit, *nice* dog, *good* dog, Zadny. You know me. I'm Tamas' brother. Tamas said to take care of you. The houndsmaster didn't hit you, did he? He surely didn't hit you. And you wouldn't run off from the puppies, would you? Tamas said you were to mind me while he was gone, and you're not to follow him, you hear? He won't like that."

Zadny might hear, but not for any coaxing would he let a hand near him. Offer a morsel of biscuit and Zadny would creep up, stretch as far as he could, snatch the bit and go; on the second such approach Yuri made a grab after him.

That was a mistake. Zadny shot off into the brush and vanished.

"Zadny?" Yuri called, over and over again, and apologized. "I'm sorry. I won't do it again, there's a good boy. . . ."

The nose came back, under the leaves. The forepaws did. But not a bit closer would Zadny come, not for any coaxing.

Yuri slept finally, exhausted; and waked with a sloppy wet tongue on his face. His eyes flashed open on dawn woods and a yellow hound's face, and he made a startled snatch after Zadny's collar.

And missed again.

"Zadny," he pleaded. "Zadny, come back here!"

But the dog simply stood out of reach while he saddled Gracja and climbed up.

Then the hound trotted off his own way, the way his master had gone.

The next day's ride was climbing. All the party bundled up in cloaks as soft-leaved trees gave way to cedar and to scrub pine. Snow patched the ground and fell in spits and fits from the gray overcast, until the horses went with beards of ice. High on the mountainside, they stretched their two canvasses between stout, uneven trees, in a wide spot in what Nikolai swore was the right trail. They shared a fireless supper, huddled in cloaks, with the wind roaring and thundering at their tents. Trolls could carry them all off tonight and welcome, Michal swore: slow roasting was preferable to freezing.

"Trolls wouldn't go out in this," Bogdan said, and more loudly: "I think a wizard's company ought to be worth better weather, don't you, master Karoly?"

"It could be worse," Karoly retorted, "and it could have been better, if we'd stopped where I said, an hour lower down."

They were at recriminations, now: things had devolved to that. Master Karoly had said wait, Bogdan had said go ahead, Nikolai had grudgingly admitted there was a stopping-place further on; and now they were all at odds, with the canvas snapping and thundering in the gusts.

With no warning then their canvas ripped, letting in a great gust of cold air, and Bogdan and master Karoly were shouting and swearing at each other, while Filip and Zev grabbed after the canvas and called for cord, shouting down all recriminations. Tamas hugged his cloak about him and buried his cold nose beneath its folds, lifting it only to say (but no one stopped arguing to listen) that if they used the sense the horses had and sat close against one another they would all be warmer.

"The storms aren't through," Nikolai said. "We should have waited."

But Bogdan said, "We're in it now. You say we're halfway. This is no time to talk about quitting."

Tamas agreed with Bogdan, though no one listened to his muttered opinion. Michal and Zev and Filip had patched the canvas with a rock and a wrap of cord, which stopped the most of the wind; and in relative comfort he drowsed and waked to find the wind fallen and everything still. Filip was on watch, tucked up at the door with a dusting of snow on his knees—he moved his feet as Tamas got on his knees and looked out from under their shelter.

The dawn sky shone cold and clear and the horses were bunched in the shelter of the pines near the other tent. New snow made dusty blankets on their backs and in the hollow of the canvas. Like the mountain storms he had heard Nikolai tell of all his life, this one had been fast and bitter—but it had left the air clean and tingling with life.

Karoly was awake, too: Karoly got up from his place at the back of the shelter, and excused his way over sleepers, on business Tamas figured for urgent and private until Karoly failed to return in the usual time.

"He's been gone a while," Filip whispered, and got up; Tamas rose to go with him, stiff and sore in every joint, peered out and saw the old man standing out in the open, looking out off the cliff into the distances of a rose and shadow sky, where shone a few bright morning stars.

Maybe he's working magic, Tamas thought. He had never seen Karoly at work: master Karoly had taught him and Bogdan and Yuri what he called the principles of the arts, shown them the weather-glass and other such prognosticating devices; but the true magic master Karoly had never given them, nor ever worked in front of witnesses, unless one counted his communing with the walls of the keep and the earth of the fields.

"What's he doing out there?" Filip whispered distressedly at his shoulder.

"I don't know," he whispered back. Nikolai and Bogdan stirred, then, grumbled and swore they might as well be up and moving, there was no sleeping with all the whispering and the coming and going, and they'd made acquaintance with every rock under them.

"Why are we under snow?" Jerzy asked, punching the patched canvas, that sifted snow down on everyone. "If he's so great a wizard, why do we have such rotten luck?"

"Because he can't do everything at once," Tamas said under his breath; he had stopped expecting the men to listen to him. "We haven't met any trolls, we haven't lost anybody, we got to cover last night before the storm broke. . . ."

"I'd like to know what he *is* doing," Michal complained. "Standing on the edge like that—a wind could blow him right down the mountain."

He's listening, Tamas thought of a sudden, he had no idea why, but he thought of master Karoly listening to the stone of the hold, and thought, if those stones talk to him—what might a whole mountain sound like?

There had been a time he could have turned back, Yuri said to himself, wedged in behind Gracja, among pines, among rocks, and nursing his little fire into a dawn spitting and blustering with snow. The first night he could have come back and lied and said, well, he had not found the dog. But not after another day. Not after a third, Zadny always dancing out of arms' reach, accepting his charity and always, with a worried expression, looking off the way the men had gone, as if he would wait for a boy on a pony, but only just, only long enough; and he would stay for a boy and a pony to sleep, but never quite long enough.

If he had to go back now and claim he had outright lost the dog, he might have to maintain that lie between himself and his brother for ever, perhaps. And if he went back and told the truth, the other boys would say he had been outwitted by a mongrel stray, and that was a tag he would have to live with for the rest of his life. That he had hedged the truth with everyone, and that Zadny running away had given him a chance to do exactly what he wanted to do, did rub at his conscience—but there was actually no choice but to keep going now. They would forgive you if you were dead and they would forgive you if everything turned out all right (well, truth, papa would put him on bread and water for a week when he got home.) But when you got a reputation for lying or foolishness when you were fourteen, nobody ever forgot it, and your friends when they were grown men would never let you forget it—unless you were lord of Maggiar, which, being the youngest of lord Stani's sons, he never would be.

So he could not go back without the dog, who would not be caught, and very soon now, by tomorrow, he would be out of food and closer to over-mountain than he was to home, which meant he had to find Tamas and Bogdan. He certainly was not lost: Zadny gave every sign of knowing where he was going—and he could see the traces the horses had left, so he knew Zadny was not mistaken. They were going to be slower: Gracja was nothing for speed and he had had to camp early and hunt for food along the way; but eventually, on the other side of the mountains, he would catch up with Tamas and Bogdan and the rest of the men, in that country grandmother had told them about.

Or Zadny would run ahead and find them first, and while they were still wondering where Zadny had come from, he would come riding up on his pony and say blithely—he had this planned—Hello, brothers. And when Tamas called him a fool: You said I should watch your dog. Was I going to let him get eaten by bears?

No, it was Bogdan who would yell at him, first: Tamas would want to, but after Bogdan had vented his temper, Tamas would start defending him: that was the way he planned his reception.

And, after all, they could hardly send him home at that point: that was what he was sure master Karoly would answer to the men's objections to having him along. But he did not want to look at master Karoly until after his brothers had gotten to quarreling, because master Karoly would see through him otherwise and give him one of those soul-seeing looks Karoly could give . . .

In all versions, he had first to get there, and not to freeze before he got to the pass, which he had to reach today, if he was following master Nikolai's accounts. He had worked from dusk into full dark last night to get a smell of smoke out of the driest pine tinder he could manage—he had had it drying in his pocket all day, the way Nikolai had said one should in the mountains, where sudden showers and snowfalls were likely and the air was moist. He had cut pine boughs for a bed and for shelter to sleep under, and had Gracja's blanket under him and his cloak over him, besides. He had fed his fire dry tinder and pine needles before he offered it twigs and little branches and more tinder before solid wood, the way Nikolai had taught him in his ninth summer. The biscuits might have run out—he had shared the last one with Gracja and Zadny yesterday noon—but he had chopped and stuffed grass into Gracja's empty saddlebags and his empty food basket, so she had food for the climb, be it ever so little. Yesterday afternoon he had shot and cleaned a rabbit, that he had cooked last night, while Zadny had had the offal for his supper. This morning he peeled the red, soft lining out of cedar for tinder for his next fire. He would pack a fistful of that in his pocket, and as much dry wood, broken to lie flat, as he could tie to the saddle. All these things he had learned from master Nikolai in winter tales, how he had done when he had hunted trolls—and unlike some boys of his acquaintance, he *listened* when his teachers told stories, of which he was very glad this morning.

He was still reasonably warm in the shelter of the rocks, while the sleet skirled around the mountainside; and Zadny, the rascal, came almost but not quite within reach, seeking that warmth. He had not slept soundly last night. Keep the fire going: master Nikolai had said that was the most vital thing.

People had died up here who had let their fires go out, frozen stiff by the time the searchers found them—and he had never kept an all night fire by himself.

That was the only truly scary part, knowing his life continually depended on things he had never done before—like getting a fire to take, like staying awake, with no older brothers to wake him if he nodded. But he had done it. He had not frozen last night. So he thought he could do the other things, and the next and the next.

He had a small bit of rabbit for breakfast, and gave the bone to Zadny, who came just close enough to nip it in his teeth. He thought if Zadny were truly clever he would find his own rabbit, but he did not think Zadny was thinking about being hungry right now until someone held food in front of him. Nikolai said it was four days from the start to the top of the mountain, he had tucked that away in his memory, too, so that was all the breakfast he afforded himself. He crawled out of his bed of pine boughs into the cruel wind, dusted the snow off Gracja, and put the warm blanket he had slept with on Gracja's back, before the saddle that had been his pillow.

Then he bundled up the wood he had had drying all night next the fire's heat, and tied it on with Gracja's saddle-strings. He had done everything Nikolai had taught him to do; his breath hissed with shivers as he climbed onto Gracja's back the hard way, with a great deal of squirming about to bring his leg over Gracja's neck, because of the wood; the cloak flapped in the wind, and half-blinded him—it was not a graceful mount, but he was up and on his way to the hardest part of the climb, with Zadny already leaving tracks in the new-fallen snow.

He would show up on the other side of the mountain with Gracja and Zadny and say, "Of course I made it. No, I didn't have any trouble—none at all . . ."

"Quiet everywhere," Nikolai remarked, riding closer to Tamas and Bogdan. "No sight nor sign of trolls."

"No sight nor sign of anything," Bogdan complained, with a gesture outward, toward the sky and the eagles that hunted above them, in the thin, cold air. "Except them. —Where are the trolls, master Karoly?"

"Minding their own business," master Karoly retorted.

Master Karoly meant they should ask him no more questions; but it was a half-hearted shot, as if he was thinking about something else entirely.

"Something's wrong with him," Nikolai muttered to Bogdan. "He hasn't complained once today."

It's true, Tamas kept thinking—he kept hearing that remark over and over in his head and it made him more and more uneasy about Karoly. Something was wrong, something that distracted the old man, as if he were hearing something distant and difficult.

Bogdan remarked finally, when they were riding side by side, "The old master's worried. Has he talked to you?"

Tamas shook his head. "No." He waited for Bogdan to confide further in him, the way Bogdan would if they were at home and without Bogdan's friends around. But that was all Bogdan said. He asked finally, to fill the silence, "How far are we from the top? Did Nikolai say?"

"We're past it. Nikolai says. We're through the pass and going around the mountain—Nikolai says. But he's never been farther than this."

The valley looked no different than the one they knew. There was nothing magical about it, nothing that gran had described, no sign of trolls or faery. Bogdan rode beside him a while more in silence, then fell back to talk with Filip, in words too low to hear, perhaps confiding his worries to his friend, since his brother was too young for his confidences.

The journey was not turning out as he had hoped. It was

certainly something to see the mountains from up here. But what had seemed an adventure into once-upon-a-time at its outset, came down to ordinary, barren stone, with more spits of sleet to sting their faces. Karoly was not talking to any of them, the older men were not talking to the younger—they rode in their own small group, with Jerzy wondering aloud were they on the right trail; and *no* one was interested in Stani's second eldest's opinions or his presence.

But it did, thank the god, seem that the trail was slightly downward, now; and by afternoon, that pitch was unmistakable, even steep—all rocks and scrub pine, never yet a flat place and never yet a leaf the horses could use to fill their stomachs, but at least the wind was not so bitter cold, and even Jerzy grew more cheerful.

Now, Tamas thought, they would begin to see the landmarks their gran had described. A place called Krukczy Straz, that was the first—a tower in pine woods, that guarded the broad valley where the road went down to Hasel, where there might even be relatives, if grandmother's kin were alive. At Krukczy Straz they might find a warm gate-house to sleep in, at least, even if it was nothing but the defensive tower its name implied. There would be warm water for washing, and a good meal, and hay for the horses, and they might still get there tonight, if it was well up in the highlands, the way he recalled in gran's stories.

"Isn't there a tower?" he ventured, riding close to master Karoly. "Do you think we can reach it tonight?"

Everyone else was more cheerful. Master Karoly was not. Karoly took a glum moment about answering him. "It's possible. Or not. Let's not get ahead of ourselves, shall we?"

It was certainly not the forgiving master Karoly of the drafty tower study or the orchards around home. Tamas rode by him a moment more, wondering if Karoly would have more to say, or remember his presence—a lad could begin to wonder if he had not gone invisible to his companions, or whether Karoly saw him at all: Karoly did not so much as look at him again, or speak. He let his horse drift back to a slower walk, until it was him in the middle, between Nikolai's group; and Bogdan's group.

Tell Bogdan about it? Tamas wondered. What could I say? Master Karoly frowned at me?

The trail meandered along the mountain and then plunged steeply, wearingly downward, with never a sprig of grass for the horses, into a dead, skeletal ruin of pine and cedar. They had fed the horses the scant grain they were carrying, and pressed their journey late into the afternoon on a level road, with the mountains like a wall around them, unforgiving, sleet-dusted lumps of rock.

"This is madness," Jerzy said, as a sudden bitter wind howled out of the heights, whipping at their cloaks and the winter-coat of the horses. "Are we on the trail at all? I swear we're going up again."

"It is the road," master Karoly broke his silence to say. "It's illusion. We're still descending."

"I'm not sure you know where we are, old man. I'm not sure we didn't take a wrong turn on the mountain—"

"No," Karoly said shortly.

"Master Karoly," Bogdan said, "we're out of supplies; and if we come to green grass, or if things get better lower down, that's one thing: but it's far from encouraging, what we're seeing. We can't press on without limits: these horses can't do it, we can't do it—"

"We can't make it back over the pass," Nikolai said, "without supplies. There's no point arguing it. No matter where we are, we've got to go ahead. It is a road, it has to go somewhere, and somewhere has to be down from the heights. We should keep moving, past sunset tonight if need be."

"It is the right road," Karoly said under his breath.

Tamas said, "Grandmother mentioned—" and then held his peace, because what gran had said had no more currency than what Karoly knew.

"We're lost," Jerzy maintained; and Karoly only shook his head and looked away across the valley. Wisps of cloud veiled the depths. Birds circled far out across the gray expanse, eagles or carrion crows it was hard to say: size and color were illusory in this place. The birds made long shadows on the clouds.

Crows, Tamas decided, as they rode lower, through a foggy patch. Carrion crows and ravens fit everything they had seen so far; not only Maggiar had suffered a blight last winter. Trees on the mountains had died, leaving sticks of evergreens. The wind came out of the west, down the throat of the pass and against their backs, cold and damp off the patches of sleet on the slag-heap mountains. Instead of gran's waterfalls they found frozen, soot-stained ice; instead of the pine groves of her stories, charcoal stumps thrust up through sere, blackened brush.

Filip said, "The whole forest burned."

Master Nikolai said, with despair in his voice, "At least we've passed well below the tree line now. Spring will bring out the green in the lowlands, no matter the fire. There's bound to be forage further down."

Down was where they were surely going now, Karoly and Nikolai were right in that. The horses maintained a weary, jolting pace. The dusk between the mountains had closed about them, and since the foggy patch, cloud hung around the heights above their heads, gray and heavy with snow, casting everything in gloom.

Maybe Jerzy's right, Tamas thought: maybe we missed some turn of the trail on the heights and we've come down in the wrong valley—

But could master Karoly let us go astray? He's a wizard, Jerzy said it, persistently: Why don't we meet better luck?

Except if master Karoly could have cured what was wrong

at home, wouldn't he have? And if he could have gotten us through the mountains without the storm, wouldn't he have? He's come here looking for his sister because things are happening he can't do anything about. Didn't he say to our father—I have bad dreams?

They passed into a defile of pale rock and a wide stream below the trail, that Karoly suddenly proclaimed was the road he remembered.

"Was it this grim?" master Nikolai asked.

"No," master Karoly admitted, still riding.

The men said other things as the road wound around the barren hillside, a slip zone of rockfalls and a long slope of rubble and dead brush down to a barren streamside—an appalling place, deeply shadowed by mountain walls on either side, but the road was most definitely a road now, broad and well-defined. They came to a milestone of the Old Folk, which explained the stonework bracings along this stretch—such roads ran here and there in Maggiar, too, with similar milestones; but a grinning face was roughly painted on it.

"What's that?" master Nikolai wanted to know.

"No good thing," Karoly said. Nikolai had reined to a stop at that find, so had they all, but Karoly passed it by with a look, as if it was part and parcel of everything in the land.

"What?" Bogdan called after him angrily. "Master Karoly, where are you leading us? What do you know, that you're not telling us?"

"That there's no way but this," master Karoly said over his shoulder, "That we've no choice but straight ahead. Come on!"

"Bogdan," Tamas began to say, with a strong feeling of misgiving about this road, but Bogdan set his horse to overtake Karoly's, saying something about keeping Karoly from breaking his neck; master Nikolai did the same, and the rest of them followed.

Tamas cast a second glance at the stone that seemed to mock

any further venture down this road, wondering if the men all knew what that painted countenance signified, and he did not. He did not want to be a coward, and they would not regard his arguing. He worked his weary horse up to the head of the column with Bogdan and Nikolai and Karoly—easier on the overtaking just then as the road wound along the hillside to a steep descent.

But there they caught the first hopeful sight, a pale green vision of sunlight in the east, beyond the mountain shadow. Against that sunlight a dark tower loomed on the roadway, its foundations butted against the stream.

"Krukczy Straz," Bogdan murmured.

It surely was, Tamas thought. It was after all the road their grandmother had described to them, burned and dreadful as the mountains had become. They had come through the right pass, after all, and elsewhere the land was catching the sunlight still, like a promise of better things. "Quickly now," master Karoly said, silencing their chatter, and urged his horse faster down the road, that passed right alongside the tower crest.

Hisses then, sharp and quick, that no archer had to guess at; "Jerzy!" Filip cried. Tamas looked wildly about as horses bolted past and his own shied and reared. He saw Bogdan hit and falling as his own horse stepped backward on the road edge. He knew one heart-stopping moment of falling over the edge and onto the rubble, into a thunderous slippage of stones, battered and deafened in the rolling tide that carried him. He had time to despair of finding a stopping place. He had time to think of finding hold. The slide was a roaring in his ears and every handhold moved with him, slipping and tumbling as he went, down and down into choking dust.

Came quiet, and cold stone beneath Tamas' back. Water dripped and echoed in the dark around him. His body still felt the falling, but did not move, in a long, slow gathering of scattered wits, trying to reconcile sliding in a torrent of rubble, with this pervasive ache and this darkness and the regular echo of water drops.

The ceiling reflected a faint glimmering of light. None touched the walls. It was a broad cave, or a man-made vault—he could distinguish that much; but being here made no sense to him. He remembered going down, he felt the battering of the rocks—remembered he had outright fallen off his horse, no glorious end to his journey. Bogdan had been hit. Jerzy had. Dreadful images succeeded that one, arrows streaking black across a clouded heaven, horses and men screaming . . .

A second waking, how long after the first he had no idea. He was still lying on his back. Light from some source touched both shaped and living stone, a ceiling glistening with water and black mold, but nothing of the walls. It was the same place as before: he could hear the drip of water and smell the mustiness of wet iron and stone. But there was a thumping somewhere distant, like drums, he thought, or the beating of his own heart. He remembered the road, and he had to find his brother, he had to get back there, their father had told him take care of Bogdan—

But something held his hands fast above his head, and fighting that restraint sent a wave of pain through his back. He worked half-numb fingers, trying to feel what was holding him, and touched what might be rope about iron bars, but he could not be sure whether anything was warm or cold, nor tilt his aching neck further back to see.

A shriek reached his ears, far away—only a bird, he told himself, a crow, maybe a dog's injured yelp—not a human voice. His hazed wits could not shape it. He lay straining and dreading to hear it again, but the drip of water into some pool was all the measure of time and sanity.

Eventually, louder than the water dripping, came a slither like something dragging across the floor, with an audible breathing. It was a nightmare. He wanted to wake, now, please the god, he was very willing to wake up now, but there was no waking. One wanted to think of escape, but he could not so much as turn over. He asked himself who had tied him here, and why; and with his head lifted as far as he could, saw a large shaggy lump move out of the faint light and into the shadow beside him.

A troll. He was done. He knew he was. Only the bones left, he remembered Nikolai saying; and wondered if he was the only one imprisoned here. "Bogdan?" he called into the dark, with all the courage he could find.

"Ssss!" the troll hissed, trailed musty rags of wet fur across his face and clapped a massive hand over his mouth. Half-smothered, he struggled and, with his head beginning to spin, stopped, in token that he would be quiet, with no surety at all it would let him go. But it slowly drew its hand away and let him breathe.

Then it shuffled off as erratically as it had come. He listened after its departure over the beating of his heart, saw its retreating shadow against the light and, shivering, gazed into the dark for a long time after. He wondered where it went and why it had left and most of all what had become of Bogdan and Nikolai and the rest of them—not without reckoning master Karoly. A wizard might have defended them. Maybe Karoly had saved the rest of them, Bogdan and all of them, that was what he wanted to think—he might be the only one the trolls had gotten, lying unconscious as he must have. Bogdan and Karoly might be looking for him this very moment. They might save him if he could stay alive, if he was not going to be a troll's supper before they could get here.

And if he could somehow get his hands free, and get away on his own . . . that would save everyone the danger of rescuing him and himself the guilt of making them do it.

He refused to think of other possibilities. He worked at the ropes, not pulling at them: that would tighten the knots; but trying with every possible stretch of his fingers to find a knot within reach.

The troll had been cleverer than that; and while he was working, he heard the troll come shuffling back again, a humped shape against the illusory light, trailing cords of its shaggy coat to the floor as it walked.

He tried not to think what came next, as it crouched over him, as it slid a hand beneath his head, lifted it gently and put the cold hard rim of a cup to his lips.

He did not at all understand its reasons. But he saw nothing now to gain by fighting the creature, and the liquid against his lips tasted of herbs, nothing foul. It let him drain the cup, after which it let his head gently to the stone floor and crouched beside him, waiting, he had no idea for what. He only hoped it would go away and let him go on trying after the knots.

But he was in less pain than he had been. He felt his fingers and feet going numb, and then he began to be afraid, even while his wits were growing foggy.

He thought, I've been a fool. What does it want? What is it waiting for? Do they drug their victims? Poison—but would it poison what it was going to eat?

Hold Bogdan back, his father had said to him, and he had chased Bogdan down the road after that warning marker, instead of making a strong, reasonable objection to the decision that had put him here.

He was very sorry about that. He hoped Bogdan had gotten away. He hoped Bogdan would not come running in here to rescue him, even with Karoly's and Nikolai's help, because he much feared they were not going to be in time, considering the growing numbness he felt now in his limbs—he feared they would find nothing in this cave he ever wanted his father and mother to know about . . .

The road was deserted, so far as Nikolai could see, from his painful vantage on an otherwise glorious sunrise—he had crawled to this place on the mountainside, with a rock between him and the view of the road, but as for how he had gotten off the road and into the rocks in the first place . . . whether he had been left for dead and crawled up here or whether some one of his companions had carried him this far and left him to seek water or help . . . he had no recollection. He was, if he began to dwell on that thought, afraid, and confused; and the pain did not help him at all to sort out his thoughts.

He had gone down with the howling of goblins in his ears. He had waked with his sword in his hand, its hilt glued to his hand with blood, and he still carried it: his arm hurt too much to try to sheath it, and he had no assurance that what had brought him up here was not a goblin with a particularly selfish bent. He supposed he had had time to draw it and to use it, and that it was not his own blood on it, at least.

He had been shot—he had a sure reminder of that: the arrow had broken off, the black stump of it through his arm—through his side, too, except for the inside of his leather sleeve and the mail about his ribs. *Hell* of a pull that bow had had—he could admire the goblin archer that had drawn it; and damn him for the pain, in the next breath, when he moved his arm and the projecting head raked against his ribs.

Enough of trying for a view. He fell back and watched the dawn sky, trying to force any recollection out of his pain-fogged wits—where the boys were, what had become of Karoly, where anyone might be. He was halfway up the hill, hidden, as he hoped. He remembered—thought he remembered—the dirt of the road in front of his eyes—

So he had fallen. He remembered a confusion of rocks and brush. Maybe that was the climb up, a jumbled image of rock and sky. Karoly—damn his stubborn forging ahead into disaster—was not here to help. 'Listen to advice,' lord Stani had said. As well spit into the wind. Trust a witch or a wizard, listen to his advice, and this was where it brought you. The lady gran had had a cruel bent. He had known it. He should have suspected Karoly.

An eagle crossed the sky. It was the only feature in a sea of dawn, serene, without obligations to the world. But that was not his case. He shut his eyes, recalled the road last night, the tower hulking beside the stream, and thought, I have to go down there. I have to know. That arrow has to come out, doesn't it?

Damn Karoly for not being here.

An eagle cried like some lost soul across the mountainsides. On either side of the road, mere stumps and blackened trunks and stubs of trees. Nosing the ground, Gracja blew at the ash in despair, snorted, and lifted her head without resisting the reins. It was no place to stop, Yuri told himself, no matter how tired they all were. Even Gracja knew it, and kept moving on her own.

He had expected green grass, he had hoped to find his

brothers not too far ahead once he reached the warmer eleva-
tions. His brothers would come off the mountain heights tired
and in want of rest, and most probably they would camp and rest
at the first opportunity—that was what he had told himself,
before he met this desolation. He had found traces of their
passage all along, seen tracks of their horses as late as this afternoon, on a wind-scoured crust of snow that he did not think was
that old.

But no sight or scent of a campfire this day. Everything was
charcoal. Zadny limped, sometimes on one foot, sometimes on
the other, leaving blood on the snow this morning, but he was
still going ahead, still tracking, nose to the trail—and that was
assurance of a kind, but it was a scary place, this road, so void
of every living thing.

The way began at least to be wider, steadily downward with
another turn on the mountain, and there, lord Sun, was a deep
stream-cut valley falling away steeply at his left. That encouraged him—because where streams cut, there were passes, Nikolai had said so.

The road became a steep descent, then, with the afternoon
sun behind the mountains, a plunge deeper and deeper into the
premature twilight of the valley. With every rest they took, once
silence descended, the gloomier and the spookier the place felt.
It was not like gran's stories. Not a leaf rustled here. There was
only the wind, and once they were underway again, the solitary,
lonely sound of Gracja's hooves made him think of walking
through some vast, forbidden hall.

I don't like this, he kept thinking. Zadny seemed anxious—
circling back closer to him, looking out into the shadowed
valley and growling. Yuri thought, I don't like this open place.
Anybody on the heights can see anybody on the road. I wonder
if it is the right road, after all, or if we're even following the right
horses.

But there was no going back now. He kept telling himself—
if I just keep going, I'll surely find them. Some forest fire
happened here, that's all.

The last of the grass had run out; the last of the rabbit was
yesterday. Lord Stani's youngest had never missed a meal in his
life, and he was so hungry he seemed apt to fold in half. As soon
as the air had warmed enough to risk the wood, he had strung
his bow, and carried an arrow ready in hope of rabbits; but now
he kept the bow and the arrow resting against his knee because
he was anxious and determined to get down to the streamside.
The road was getting darker and darker, in a real twilight now.

Color touched the sky and cast a strangeness on the rocks
and the surface of the road. He came to a milestone that looked
the same as the milestones in Maggiar, old and worn and telling
travelers nothing useful nowadays; but a dreadful painted face
grinned at him from its whiteness, and the paint was not old. His
heart jumped and for a moment everything seemed scarily sharp
in detail, the white stone in the twilight, the grinning face, a boy
on a fat, shaggy pony, a yellow hound, all brought together in
this almost-night.

He rode further, slowly around the turning of the road and,
by the last light, into the valley beyond, where a great tower was
set low beside the stream, its crest rising beside the road.

Men had made it. One hoped that they were men. But there
was that stone back there. Gran had never told his brothers
about such things. Or if she had, Tamas and Bogdan had never
told him. And he had been too young to remember.

Would they go there? he asked himself. Should I?

Master Karoly was with them. Master Karoly undoubtedly
knew what he was dealing with, and had planned everything,
and knew exactly what he was doing, no matter how dangerous.
So here came a boy, a pony, and a silly dog, into the middle of
older people's plans that were life and death to everyone—not
things he knew how to deal with, like cold and wind and getting

food in the mountains—but places with strangers, in towers like that.

I don't belong here, Yuri said to himself. I should have stayed at home and never tried this at all. I can starve or I can go down there and knock on the door, or I can try to get past. What did master Karoly tell my brothers to do? Or why did they come this way, if not to find this place?

The more and less of haze seemed only part of slipping into unconsciousness, except Tamas found his joints stiff and his back numb and realized that he was on the other side of that dreaded sleep. More, something was still hovering near him with the same slithering movement and musty smell he associated with the troll. He saw its shadow loomed between him and the source of the faint light like a huge mass of shredded rags, all hunched down as it was. He did not want to be awake. He shut his eyes all but the least view through his lashes and tried not to betray that he was.

But it did not touch him. Eventually it got up and moved away, a shambling hump that, indeed, had a long tail. Tamas lifted his head and saw it dragging and snaking nervously in its wake, as the troll passed the dim lamp and its shadow crept up to the walls and the ceiling.

It was a nightmare. He heard that thumping sound again, or it was the beating of his own heart. Dizziness overwhelmed him as he let his head down. He was not dead. It had made him sleep long enough that his back was half numb and he could only wish his arms were numb, too. But why would a troll want to keep him here, and sit by him while he slept?

A bolt clanked and thumped somewhere above, a hallway echoed. The troll jumped, leaped, and a flare of its shaggy arm extinguished the lamp. It scrambled toward him, felt him over hastily and shoved his knees up perforce, smothering him with a raggy, massive hand over his mouth. Another clank. The creature settled its long, damp fur over him, and hissed, close to his ear, "Goblins. Husssh."

Goblins. Worse and worse—the troll crushed him into a bent-legged knot in the corner, against the bars, urging him to be quiet, and he lay absolutely still, breathing through the musty fronds as it tentatively let up its hand.

A door creaked. He saw a seam of light through the trailing fur of the troll's arm, past the shadow of its crouching body. Came the gleam of a torch, a silver sheen of weaponry and armor in that light, and he held his breath, ready to call out at any risk of his life, in a heart-clenched hope that it was one of his friends come looking for him.

Then the intruder turned his head, showing an animal's sharp ears in a mane of dark hair, a jutting jaw, a face human and beast at once. His heart froze as its gaze passed over them. It lifted the torch and scanned the vault in other directions, as if it dismissed them as some mound of rags.

Then the goblin slowly turned the other way, along the corridor and around the winding way the troll had always appeared and vanished. Tamas trembled beneath the troll's crushing weight, dreading the goblin coming back—and it did, a martial and dreadful figure in its silver-touched armor. It cast a slow second gaze in their direction, holding the torch aloft.

But it seemed blind to them: it went out by the same door it had come in, and shut it.

A bolt slammed home. The troll shifted its weight very slowly, drew back and left him as another door opened and shut, deeper inside the mass of stone.

Everything was dark and breathlessly still then, except the troll moving about in the utter night of the vault. Tamas slowly, painfully straightened his legs and settled himself, in a depth of despair he had never imagined. Goblins. *That* put more pieces together: Krukczy Tower, the clouds, the road, the outlook toward the valley, the long slant of loose stones . . .

He realized his horse had been hit, now that he put things together; he remembered its sudden jump before it hit the edge, and he pieced together an attack from the rocks above the road.

But it had not been trolls, in that attack: he had never heard that trolls were clever enough to use archery. Goblins were. And he remembered the stone marker, the dreadful living face he had just seen in torchlight, the doors and the echoes he had heard.

It was no troll's den, it was the cellar of Krukczy Tower itself; and goblins held it, loosed from what hell he did not know: but by all the late-at-night tales that had ever frightened a boy sleepless, he knew they were no solitary bandits, no witless bludgeoners, like trolls. Goblins came from deep and unfriendly places, they were clever and they came in armies, that was what he knew from gran's tales. Sorcerers and wicked powers used them to fight their wars.

What had happened this side of the mountains? Had not Karoly *known* they were in trouble, the moment he saw that stone—and still he led them toward this place? Had he not known in dreams before that? Had the mountain not told him, that morning on the heights, and he had said nothing to them?

Betrayal and Karoly had never seemed possible in the same thought. But whence this sister? Whence this mysterious sister Karoly had never mentioned to anyone? And whence this plague that Karoly could not stop—except from what was here in Krukczy Tower? Whence the smell of burning that had roused the whole household, but on this mountain? And whence the cries of lost children, if not here, in Krukczy Tower?

Ride quickly, Karoly had said, before the attack. Karoly had *known*, and he wished he could believe Karoly was free somewhere and plotting his rescue; but Karoly, if he was alive, well knew where he was—in this tower, and in the hands of creatures Karoly had already failed to deal with. He began to hope that everyone else was dead in the ambush—please lord Sun they were dead . . .

But if they were, he was not, and since he was not, he had no hope but the troll's slow wits and its intention to keep him to itself—which meant time to work on the knots, if not to rescue anyone, then to get away and onto the road and up the pass to home, to warn his father what was happening over-mountain, because he saw the next step in the taking of this tower: goblins raiding through the high pass next year, killing and doing in Maggiar whatever goblins did with their victims—which he did not want to think about. How he should escape, how he should survive the cold of the pass he could not imagine, but he could not imagine his father's son lying here and waiting to die, either. That was not what his father had taught his sons, and not what his father expected of the men he had sent over-mountain.

And once he heard the troll's slithering sound diminish down toward the end of the tunnel, he began to try again to feel out the knots, using what slight movement he had in his fingers, in the case that the troll might have redone its work and left him a knot in reach . . .

There was so little feeling left. He tried and he tried, and eventually decided he could just reach something curious that might be a knot. He stretched as far as he could and worked ever so patiently, tears of exhaustion running on his face, and his arms and back burning with the effort.

But while he worked, long before he had loosened the knot, he heard the troll returning, in faintest light now, from some distant source. Unfair, he thought resentfully, if after all this time it wanted its supper, please the god it did not, and that it would not test the ropes. He knew now that it had the power of speech, and he asked it, "How many goblins?" —to gain what knowl-edge of his situation he could, perhaps to distract it, or, most improbably . . . even to befriend it and escape this place, if trolls could reason, if it conceived of itself in danger from the goblins.

But it hissed at him, then lifted his head as it had before, and put a cup to his lips as it had before, with no answer to his question.

He would not drink this time. He kept his mouth obstinately shut. But it shook him sharply, one snap that rattled his brain in his skull, and offered it again. He drank, flashes of color still hazing his eyes. It let his head down afterward, and sat close to him, waiting.

He tried again. "What happened to the others?"

"Ssss." It might be asking him to be quiet. Or it was an expression of its anger. He whispered faintly: "I can lead us out of here." But he was already feeling a numbness in his hands and his feet and a frightening confusion in his wits. His tongue was going numb. "I could help you." He was not sure it could even understand him.

It hissed at him, more intensely. He thought it might be answering him after all—if one had goblins upstairs, one certainly might want quiet in the cellar.

"I wouldn't bring them," he argued with it.

It said, "Not now."

There were drums, Yuri could hear them from here, the whole mountain echoed them crazily, and one had no choice but hear. He hunkered down on a flat stone in this concealing bend of the road, with Gracja's reins in his lap, holding her out of sight of the tower, waiting—because the more he considered knocking at that dreadful gate, the more he was afraid. It was not a tower where farmers came and went, it was a martial tower, where it was set and as simply as it was built, with no other possible use for it but border watching and bandit hunting. Whatever men might live here, if they were men at all—might be little better than bandits themselves, for all he knew. He was only waiting for moonset, hoping for clouds, and shadow—him with a yellow dog and a pony with a wide white blaze and a white foot. He had muddied up Gracja's blaze and her white stocking, with water from his canteen; but that was small good—he could not lay a hand on Zadny, who had gotten restless and run off on his own business, to bark at the tower, for all he knew, and rouse everyone in there.

Probably something had caught the dog. Or he was going to come back chased by a hundred bandits, and run right up to him. And the wind was getting colder or he was growing shivery with thinking about it and listening to the drums in the night.

He left Gracja tied to a cindery tree trunk for a moment to stretch his legs, and went far enough to steal a look down at the tower. It was lit up on top, torches all about.

No sign of Zadny.

"Stupid dog," he muttered to himself and to Gracja, and paced and shivered, and paced, and sat down and waited, and finally told himself that he had to go. The moon was setting and if he was going to try to pass the tower in the dark, he had as well do it while there was still noise and they were busy, not while they were sleeping—with the sound of a horse passing right under their walls. He started to get up, teeth chattering with the thought that he was really, truly about to try it.

Suddenly a pale shaggy shape came barrelling off the hill and into his lap, licking at his hands and his face and making his heart skip a dozen beats. He sat down hard on the stone, the hound a flurry of paws in his lap and on his arms. He shoved to protect himself, he flung anxious arms about what was warm and safe and alive in this dreadful place, and tried to hold on to him, for fear of what had sent Zadny running back to him.

"Where have you been?" he whispered. Zadny's pale shape, cavorting down the road, had been plain for any eyes to see. "What's down there, what do you know?"

But the hound jerked about of a sudden, braced and staring wildly up into the rocks, toward a dark shape and a gleam of metal.

A troll, Yuri thought, frozen as Zadny was frozen, expecting it to spring.

But it skidded down among the burned trees, human looking, and slid down against the rock right in front of him, saying, "You damned *fool!* What are you doing here?"

"Master Nikolai?" he said faintly, and, holding Zadny's collar fast, hugged him tight. "Master Nikolai?" He did not intend his teeth to chatter when he spoke: he tried to stop it. "Where are my brothers?"

Tamas waked with his arms free beside him, with a warm cloak over him, and blinked in a wild hope that he was miraculously rescued, that Nikolai or Karoly had found him, or that Bogdan had—

But it was the same dank, dreadful place. He hauled himself painfully onto his knees, felt about him in the dark, and up against the iron bars that he had lain next to. They made a wall, and a gate, and that gate—

—was chained shut.

He sank down with his shoulder against the bars, and leaned his head there until his heart had settled and the despair that welled up behind his teeth had found a bearable level again.

It was no worse than before. It might be some better. He bestirred himself to search the dark, and, feeling around him, discovered a slimed wet water-channel, carrying water that smelled and tasted clean. He washed his hands and face and drank and drank until he was chilled through, sure at least it was not drugged.

But when he had felt his way about the rest of the space of his prison, and found masonry walls on either side and the ceiling lowering at the end so he had no hope of squeezing further, he went back to the bars and sank down against them.

He could move; he had his cloak to wrap in against the chill; and when time passed and nothing threatened the silence or his solitude he crept back to the water-channel and washed at his leisure, although he was sore down to his fingertips and the cold and the effort hurt. Papa would not die in filth; mama would never tolerate perishing like this; Bogdan had not had to, he hoped that much for his brother, and for all the rest of them. And in the increasing cohesion of his aching and battered wits he told himself if once the troll opened the barred gate, if it once gave him the least chance, he was going to run for it, find his way out or find a weapon. If he did not make it, well—he had seen worse waiting for him, in this very cellar.

So he waited, nursing a headache and rubbing his chilled limbs to keep them from stiffening, and passed his time remembering good things, his home, his family, playing up and down the brook, sailing leaf boats.

Master Karoly's lessons—the tower room, the cluttered shelves with their dried leaves and books and curious objects; learning their letters, and their insects; and the name of the birds that built nests under the eaves. . . .

When Bogdan and he were boys together they had gotten bored with indoors and played pranks on the old man, turned the pages in his lesson book when he was out of the room, put live frogs in his tackle basket, rearranged every single book on his shelves, and never understood that they were doing wrong. Master Karoly had always seemed different from serious grown-ups, both wiser and more childlike. Master Karoly had kept his own counsel regarding the mischief they did; and derived his just amusement and his revenge (as they had duly expected) by posing them long, long cipherings or particularly arduous errands the next day. That always seemed fair, in the balance of things. And it had never once occurred to them that master

Karoly should mind looking foolish, because dignity was not the province of young boys.

But as he thought back now, he decided the old man might have been annoyed at young fools who happened to be a lord's undisciplined sons—especially in the matter of the frogs, which had been his personal inspiration.

That was the forgiving master Karoly he wanted to believe in—not the short-tempered, close-mouthed old man on the trail. He was not sure now which man had really ever existed—but discovering what had lain next door to Maggiar unsuspected, and discovering that grown men fought and picked on each other like boys, and that sometimes good people died for no fair reason at all, everything else seemed in question, of things he thought he had understood. He was not likely to have the chance to use that knowledge . . . or to find out other lessons this place had to teach, only defeat, and his own limits of courage, and the fact of a lord's second son mattering very little to the creature that looked on him as its property or its supper.

In time he heard the troll returning. He waited, trembling with the effort to hold his limbs tensed to move. It came up to the bars, a shadow that cut off all the light on what it was doing. He heard the chain run back ever so softly, link by link, and suffered sudden doubt what he should do next, whether it might be wiser to await a better chance than to try to break past it—it was a clever troll, cleverer than any troll he had heard of. It seemed to have some obscure purpose in what it did; and it whispered, now:

"Follow me."

It was foolishness even to imagine it could mean something other than harm to him. It might have hidden him from the goblin, but it had hidden itself by doing that. He had provoked it, and it had cuffed him, using nothing of its prodigious strength—but none of that said anything at all of its reasons.

He got up slowly, thinking: What if it only wants me in

reach? And again: What if goblins are about to search this place? He felt after the gate in the dark, ducked his head when his fingers met the low bar overhead. The troll moved away from him, affording him all the room to run he could wish. He saw its moving shadow in other shadows, heard the slithering passes of its tail along the stone floor, and followed it—like any silly sheep, he said to himself: Bogdan had always called him the slow wit of the family; and he could not make up his mind what to do or what to trust—but he had no idea whether that sometime source of light down the tunnel was open or barred or a route straight to the goblins.

A door creaked ahead, on the right hand, the same door the goblin had used, he was sure of it. He saw it open, heard the troll go through, heard it breathing, and thought—the troll did fear them. It hid from them. It wouldn't willingly walk into their hands . . .

He felt his way through the doorway, banged his shin and stumbled against steps. The slithering sound came from above him, as the troll climbed. "Where does this lead?" he whispered, as loudly as he dared; but it gave him no guidance but the sound of its tail trailing up the steps.

He felt the pitch of the stone stairs, climbed, aching from bruises, his head throbbing—there was no quickness or agility about it. A door creaked above, and when he had gotten there he felt his way through into another dark, smooth-paved passage, with an unfamiliar taint: goblins, he thought, dreading what he might stumble over in the dark, his worst fear that the troll might have made some understanding with them.

A door in front of him cracked on night and moonlight. The troll went out. He followed it onto the broad wooden roof, delirious with relief to have the sky and the stars over him.

But ringed about that sky, on pikes set in the ramparts, stood the skulls of humans and of horses. Heaps of bone were swept like offal against the ramparts, white bone with dark bits of flesh still clinging.

He spun about to escape the sight, to strike at the creature that betrayed him—

A slim, slight shadow stood there, wrapped in a dark cloak. A goblin, he thought at first blink—until the figure cast back the hood. A mere girl faced him, pale as the starlight and insubstantial as his grip on the world. She had a cleft in her chin. Would a sorcerer's illusion add that human detail? His wits were fogging, his legs were shaking—he felt the troll's shadow in the wind at his back.

"Who are you?" he asked.

"A witch," she said. "A powerful witch. I came here to find a wizard named Karoly. Do you know him?"

No, he thought distressedly, no, I'm not sure I ever knew him. He thought of the skulls at his back, and doubts and anger welled up, with a memory of his brother, and the road, and the warning stone. "Are you a friend of Karoly's?"

"My mistress is. Was he with you?"

"How should I say? I don't know your kind, I don't know if wizards die or not. He saw the stone, he didn't warn us, he didn't stop—" He was shaking in the knees, and it was not all the cold. "Look around you. Tell *me* if he's alive, and I'll ask him where my brother is!"

She looked distressed then. And the troll said, in a deep, deep voice:

"Ate them all. Only bones are left."

She glanced past him and above, and for his part, he wanted to sit down and let the troll and the witch argue out what to do or what more they wanted with him—escape was a far, confusing enterprise, and led probably to the hands of goblins, or witches, who knew?

"I have two horses," she said. "I've food enough. Krukczy, bring him."

He did not want to be brought. If there were horses, if there was a way off this rooftop, he was willing to go. The witch walked away to the edge of the parapet, and over the edge—onto downward stairs, as he saw; and he began shakily to follow, stepped over the brink and saw dark air and empty space as the wind rocked him.

But the troll caught his arm in a powerful grip and held him from falling—kept its grip on his arm and guided him all the way down the steps to the stones of the streamside, the witch moving constantly ahead of them, a cloaked black shape with now and again a pale wisp of hair or gown. He went without argument now, although the troll's grip hurt him. He thought: We came to find a witch; and I've found one, and she might even be what she says . . .

If she's not in league with the goblins herself.

"**H**old on," Yuri begged. "Don't fall, don't let go—"

Master Nikolai clung to Gracja's saddle as he walked, that was how they descended from the road, Gracja stumbling on rocks as they worked their way down near the slide. Of a sudden, faced with a cluster of boulders, Yuri had to let go the reins, because there was no more room for another body as Gracja passed between—he had no idea whether there was footing for her there, but the sheer slide on their right went straight to the water.

"Look out!" Yuri pleaded, seeing Gracja stumble and Nikolai's body hit and drag through a gap not wide enough for him and Gracja at once: Nikolai had lost his footing, but he was still holding on, his left hand wrapped in Gracja's saddle ties, when Gracja stopped unevenly in the shadows of brush and rock right at the streamside. Zadny began jumping up and pawing at Nikolai anxiously, the habit that made the houndsmaster hate him. Master Nikolai, hanging limp from a wrist wrapped in the saddle-tie, no more than lifted his head and said, "Damn you," to the dog.

Yuri threw an arm about Nikolai, trying to help him stand, but he was no better help than Zadny: the moment Nikolai unwound his wrist from the leather, his weight was more than Yuri could hold, and he collapsed with him, Nikolai gone suddenly all limp and loose and maybe dead, for all he could tell. Zadny licked his face and Nikolai's while Yuri had not a hand to spare to hit the dog. His heart was pounding from the climbs, one after the other, racing from the fright just now of losing Gracja's reins and almost having Nikolai dragged to his death, and most of all from being very near the tower and the goblins.

But they were in cover now, finally, in the dark and the brush on the streamside where Nikolai had intended to go—or as close as he could manage. Gracja had just slid whichever way she could at the last, and chanced into this nook where only the starlight reached.

"Stop that!" he whispered, elbowing the dog's attentions away from him, "dammit, stop!"—language his father would by no means approve. Then to his vast relief he felt Nikolai move. "We're all right," he promised Nikolai breathlessly: he wanted ever so much to believe it himself. "We're all right, we've made it, we can rest here."

"Good boy," Nikolai said, "good boy," and might have been talking to the dog. The drums were still within the looming tower, long quiet, but it was a lonely silence, without even leaves to stir, only the soft rush of water in the stream.

Goblins, master Nikolai had said: they already had his brothers and master Karoly and everybody—even the horses. And master Nikolai had been going to see what he could do alone, when Zadny had found Nikolai and guided him—but Nikolai had run out of strength and bade them go down into the brush and get into cover. Without him, Nikolai had meant. But he had talked Nikolai into holding on; and he had gotten him down here, and once Nikolai had caught his breath he would tell him what he had to do next, please the god.

He began to shiver in the wind, knees and elbows tucked for warmth, saw Gracja pulling at the leaves of the bushes—she had found something alive, in the very shadow of the goblin tower, at least enough to keep her stomach from hurting, he hoped.

Because his did. Master Nikolai had told him everything down to this point. But there had not been much of the rabbit yesterday; and he had a very sick man in his lap and he honestly did not know what to do with him here, where goblins could find them at any moment.

He knew at least where to get warmth. He unsaddled Gracja, rubbed her down briskly with her blanket and took it, still heated from her body, back to Nikolai, and tucked it about him; then he took his water-flask from the saddle, held his head and gave him a drink.

"That's good," Nikolai breathed, in the waxing and waning of a pain he had never felt and did not want to imagine. Nikolai was stronger than he looked, he kept telling himself that, and kept believing they had only to do the right things, one after the other, and somehow the sun would come up in the morning and master Nikolai would be all right, and they would make a plan to rescue everyone alive from the goblin fortress.

But Zadny had lost Tamas' trail up there on the road. Zadny had cast about and then gone off after master Nikolai's scent, from all he could guess, as the only one who had walked out of the ambush, perhaps the strongest trail, the only one without goblin smell about it: he could think of no other reason Zadny would have followed Nikolai and left Tamas.

Nikolai breathed, "Damn you, why are you here?"

Following the dog seemed a miserably stupid thing to say. He said, with a lump in his throat, "Because I'm a fool, sir. What shall we do now?"

There was long silence. He thought Nikolai must have fainted again, and feared he might even have died, but Nikolai blinked, then, staring at the sky.

"A pair of fools," Nikolai said finally. "I'm not going to make it, boy. Can you get home from here?"

"No, sir." Short answers, Nikolai had always wanted from them, no excuses, when he was teaching them. He blinked tears and tried not to shed them. "I'm out of food."

"There's the horse," Nikolai said, and he did not for a moment understand that.

"No, sir," he said, "no, sir, I won't."

"Then eat the dog and ride the horse."

"No, sir!"

"Like your damn fool brother," Nikolai muttered, but which brother he meant, Yuri had no idea. Nikolai shut his eyes, and drew several slow breaths, then looked at him in the starlight. "The horse is goblin bait. So's the dog. So are all of us. You understand that, boy? Are you going to stay here and watch, and then be dessert? Your father's lost two sons in this place. You're the heir. Do you understand me?"

"So what were you doing? Were you going home without them?"

"I was going to see—" Nikolai stopped. Master Nikolai stared at him straight on, all shadow and starlight. "Don't you think about it. Don't you think about it, boy."

But it was exactly what he thought master Nikolai would do. Nikolai had been going down there, hurt as he was, to see if his brothers were alive, or if any of them were, or if there was anything he could do, and master Nikolai had not waited to get well, because there was no time to wait, if the goblins had his brothers in that tower. So he knew what he ought to do, then, first off.

And there was still night left.

"Boy," Nikolai said, when he got up to go to the tower. "Young lord." More respectfully, and struggling for his words. "Listen to me. . . ."

"I'll be careful," he said, and got his bow and his arrow case from Gracja's saddle.

"They can smell you," Nikolai whispered, evidently resigned to what he would do. "At least trolls can. Watch the wind."

Yuri came back and squatted down with the bow across his knees, out of Nikolai's reach, because Nikolai was devious, he knew that. "I'll find out where they are. Don't move around and make it bleed." Nikolai had lost enough blood. It was all down his side. Nikolai said he had pulled the arrow himself, and he flinched even thinking about it. "If I'm gone awhile I'm hiding, all right?"

"Don't take that damned dog," Nikolai told him. "Leave him with me."

That also seemed like a good idea.

The stream was cold water, stones slick with moss. Tamas wobbled along the edge, slid and slipped and saved himself from falling, but the effort left him hurting. Meanwhile the troll carried the witch girl effortlessly in its arms and set her safe and dry-shod on firmer ground. Then it forged ahead of them, breaking a passage through the brush.

A whispering began to surround them, not alone the sound of water over stones—but the wind in living leaves. The branches he fended with his hands were pliant, and the boughs above their heads sighed with life. The fire that had blackened the mountains must not have reached downstream—and very far downstream, as it seemed to him, before the troll slowed to a stop, looking as satisfied as if it had gotten them somewhere besides the middle of a forest.

But he was glad enough to rest, and glad enough to find things alive, and sank down on the spot, covered in sweat and shaking. The troll for its part seemed to be leaving them—it walked back up the water's edge, passing him with no notice or apology; the witch girl called after it, "Thank you, master Krukczy."

It turned in the moonlight, looking like someone's abandoned mop, except the snaking tail. It bobbed a little and inclined as if it bowed, then turned its back and waded into the stream, a moving ripple, that was all.

Tamas muttered, "Good manners for a troll."

"He's not a troll," she said sharply. "His name is Krukczy like his tower. This is his Place, and he saved your life."

Troll was close enough, in his opinion. But he had not meant to offend her, or the mop, for that matter: he got up with the very last of his strength and put forth the effort of manners, starting to say, "I am grateful—" But she turned her back and began to walk away down the shore, evidently expecting him to follow.

Damned if he would stammer and protest after her. For a very little he would let her walk on alone to her business, and take his rest here, and go home.

But he needed a horse and she claimed she had one; he needed food and he had none—a bad position for any assertion of his independence, no matter that the arrogant witchling looked fragile as a flower and younger than he was. And she had claimed to know Karoly.

So he followed, on what breath he could find. He even recovered his manners, and panted, when he had almost overtaken her, "I apologize. He's not a troll. Whatever he is."

"The watcher here," she corrected him.

"Watcher."

"Of Krukczy Straz. And you can't bespell them, it only makes them angry."

None of that made sense to his ringing ears. He walked, stumbling on the stones and the roots, and asked finally, because nothing else of his situation made sense, "Why did you rescue me?"

She cast him a shadowed glance and never slowed a step. "I thought you might be glad to be out of there."

"I am." He had a stitch in his side that was only growing worse, never mind the bruises that hurt with every step. "I am grateful." They had started off badly, without names or courtesies; but, granting the complete justice of her displeasure, and the sting of her treating him as a servant, it still seemed foolish to volunteer too much to any stranger, who he was, who his father was, and hence that he might be valuable. He said only, when he had overtaken her again, "My name is Tamas."

"Ela," she said.

"Your name is Ela?" (Evidently it was. She said nothing else.) "I'm very glad to meet you." God, it was ridiculous, chasing the damned girl, trying to observe the courtesies when he could scarcely get a pain-free breath to talk at all. "What do you want me to do?"

"Walk," she said, and pushed a branch aside, that sprang back and caught him in the face.

Outrage only made him dizzier, and shorter of breath. He wiped the tears the grit from the branch had left, kept walking, and promised himself he could leave the surly girl whenever he liked, just let them somewhere find horses and a sense of direction—soon, please the god. The pain in his head had become blinding since the blow across his eyes, every bone end in his body was bruised from the slide down the hill, and he was weak-kneed from want of food.

But just when he thought he could go not a step farther, the space along the shore widened to a moonlit strand of grass, where grazed the promised horses, one dark, one light. Lwi, Nikolai's glass-eyed gray, and Jerzy's little bay mare: he recognized them the moment Lwi lifted his head, and he went and fell on Lwi's warm shoulder with his eyes stinging and a lump in his throat—an old friend in a bad place, Lwi was, his own horse's stablemate, who knew him despite the troll-smell and the dirt, and nosed him in sore ribs, in recollection, he was sure, of smuggled carrots.

"Nothing this time," he murmured shakily, patting Lwi's neck, "Good fellow. How are the legs? Better than mine, I hope. —Skory, good horse." Skory evaded his hand, skittish fool that she was; he remembered why he hated her; and he looked along her side to find the witch girl frowning.

"The saddles are over there," she said, pointing grandly to a brush heap, and he stared at it and at her, out of breath and out of strength, wondering if she even understood that he was doing well to keep his feet.

"I take you do know what to do with them," she said, as if she were far too exalted a lady to deal with horses . . . and he caught a breath and another and found himself moving—he had no idea whether it was anger at her that lent him strength or that he had suddenly found a last reserve somewhere at depth, but he went where she said and found the saddles and all the gear, including Nikolai's bow, lying under brush, on the ground, of course, in the dew and the damp—

Fool girl, he thought in growing contempt, and then realized what he had seen when he came up to the horses, that they had not even a tether—no tether, goblins all about, trolls running up and down the riverbank, and they were still waiting where she had left them? That was more evidence of witchcraft than he had seen out of master Karoly in his lifetime.

It gave him second and third thoughts about disrespect to the girl, while he flung the brush aside and, staggering, retrieved the tack. If a witch's mere servant could do this much, and expected such great respect for herself, then perhaps master Karoly's sister was someone of immense consequence in this land, the sort of help his father might soon need against what was preparing, so he might do well to keep a civil tongue, saddle the horses for the girl and meet this mistress of hers face to face before he claimed anything about his origins.

So he took Jerzy's mare, Skory, first, adjusted the blanket on her back, took deep breaths until he could bend and snatch the saddle up and fling it on—waited several more, leaning against her side, before he could attempt the girth, that was how scarcely he was managing. But through all of it, the mare at least stood still, better than she had ever done for Jerzy.

Lwi had better manners from the start. Lwi did not suck in wind the way Skory did, Lwi took his bit without fussiness: that was the kind of horse Lwi was, besides sure-footed and level-headed; and the witch taking Skory's reins and of course assuming the pretty mare was hers was entirely agreeable to him—he said not a word about Skory's character, only gave the girl a hand up, gave her the reins and showed her how to hold them. The elegant mare was beautiful and sly and fractious—like Jerzy; but she did not go into her accustomed dance, she did not pitch the witchling off her back. Somewhat to his disappointment she stood like a lady; and he went and, with failing strength, got his foot into Lwi's stirrup and flung himself into the saddle.

Through a haze of dark and moonlight, then, he saw Ela ride the mare past him and felt Lwi turn of his own accord, in a dreamlike slowness. Moonlight on the water beside them showed only vague shapes of stones and turbulence. The horses kept to a leisurely walk as if no goblins dared assail them.

"Are we going to your mistress?" he asked.

"As quickly as we can," she answered him.

"To do what?" he asked, but got only silence. "To do what?" he repeated, more loudly, and had no more answer than before.

Damnable rudeness. If he could get to this sister of Karoly's, and prove who he was, and tell her what had become of Karoly, she might care what befell her neighbors—but now that he had leisure and breath to think about it, the witch's own land had not fared outstandingly well, if Krukczy Straz was any evidence of her authority. One could suppose matters might be better lower down, that the goblins might be a plague that had turned up on the heights, or the borders, and that Ela's mistress could deal with if she put her mind to it—but would she not, knowing that her brother was due over the mountains, as she must have if she sent this girl to find him—have done something to defend him? —Unless, of course, she had relied on Karoly's own abilities.

For some reason the goblins had quitted the tower—perhaps the girl's mere arrival had confounded them and driven them in retreat, but Ela had been anxious to leave the tower itself, and she had certainly been no help to Karoly, if that had been her mission.

A great many things did not make thorough sense. He began to take sober account that if he was wrong about following this girl, he could lose himself and leave no warning at all for his father—but if he left her without seeing her mistress, he lost all chance of the help Karoly had supposedly tried to find.

He could hear his brother saying, Brother slow-wits, can't you make up your mind about *anything*? —But, no, he could not be easy with what he decided, go on or go back. It was never his skill, to take a blind decision and wager others' welfare on it. *Doing* something required knowing where he was, or who he was dealing with—and his guide and her mistress and Karoly himself were ciphers. The girl might be a graceless shrew, but maybe she was the grand lady she claimed. Maybe she was unaccustomed to riding alone in the woods with strange young men who (he had to admit it) reeked like a troll den. Maybe she thought him some man-at-arms, accustomed to rude orders. Maybe—

In the star light and the dizzy patterns which forest shadow made of his companion and Jerzy's mare and Lwi's pale neck, it was easy to become foggy-headed. He tried to reason clearly, he tried to maintain a recollection of the way they were going: descending straight along the river into the green land they had glimpsed in the sunlight, he thought, if it was the same stream as ran beside the tower.

He thought that if he should decide to go back, he could trace the water uphill at least to the road, but it seemed more and more deceptive: in the way of streams, that met and joined and carved narrow passages the horses could not follow, it wove back and forth and lost itself repeatedly beneath the trees. Leaves brushed his face and blinded him, then gave way to streamside again, the same one, a different, he had no more confidence he knew at all.

Barren rock offered few hiding places; but the moon was over the shoulder of the projecting mountain now and Yuri's heart was thumping like a rabbit's. The hulking shape of the tower rose up to blot out the sky. He had not known the place was so large and so high: that was his most daunting surprise thus far.

Try sneaking up on a watchdog, Nikolai had said, of the goblins. —Do that, and tell me you'll get away with your fingers. This isn't deaf Pavel you're sneaking under the nose of. They'll have guards posted, young fool, they're soldiers; maybe with noses keen as hounds', do you understand that?

Nikolai was angry; Nikolai called him young fool; but only because Nikolai had been sneaking down here with a hole in his arm and half his blood on the mountainside when they had run into each other, and Nikolai could not do it himself, that was what Nikolai was angriest about.

So Nikolai and he had agreed without agreeing; and Nikolai had stuffed his head so full of details and exceptions and instructions between then and moonset, he had to stop now and think it through and through again.

But the outpost that was Krukczy Straz sat directly on the streamside, and the plain fact, as Nikolai said, was that a castle of any use to anyone had to have water: where it got water it had either to sink a well straight down into the ground or build some fortified tunnel out so they could get to the stream, maybe both, the oldest castles tending to grow from small beginnings and be patched together with this and that owner's intention. And this one being set on mountain rock did not make wells a certainty. Nikolai said he had seen a lot of towers like this one in his travels; and Nikolai said he had traveled a lot, had been a boy up in the Rus, before he had come down to Maggiar.

That Nikolai had ever been a boy was a revelation. That he had seen castles more than one certainly was. But Nikolai sounded as if he knew exactly what he was saying, in every particular of the torrent of detail Nikolai had poured into him. Nikolai made him look at the lines of the tower and see how it was laid out, and where they would most likely have guards, and where their blind spots were. . . .

Where they don't have windows they'll post guards on the roof, Nikolai said. Where they don't have guards they think that face is too strong to worry about; where they don't expect attack they'll have fewer guards than where they do . . .

The strongest point of a tower is one direction to come up on, because they may not have guards there; and the water-channel or the drains are easier to get at than windows.

Nikolai added then: But they know that. And they may take precautions. Don't go inside. Just look it over. Remember every window, every hole, every nook that can give cover, to them or to us, and come back and tell me what you see. Then we can decide what to do next.

That last, he knew, was Nikolai trying to get him to be safe. And this back and forth bearing of careful reports made thorough sense, if one's brothers were not in there being eaten alive, or whatever terrible things goblins did with people they caught. Nikolai had said they had even hauled away the dead horses. And that did not sound good, in his ears, except they might take longer getting around to the men.

He moved very carefully, trying not to rattle the stones, and most of all to keep out of sight—Nikolai had grabbed his head without warning and jerked it down hard, pointing out to him that where he had sat the moonlight was on him, and below the rock shadow was where his head and his body and his arms and his legs all belonged, if he wanted to keep them when he was sneaking up on anybody. He could still feel the bruises of Nikolai's fingers on his neck. So he thought about that while he moved, crawling on his stomach and his elbows—likest, in his experience, to sneaking under orchard fences—and remembering always to take the long and patient way if that was the way with most shadow.

That way turned out to run right up against the wall, following the foundations down to the streamside, a shadow so black he went a great deal by feel. By comparison the water glistened brightly in the starlight, once he reached the water's edge; and by that same starlight he saw a barred iron gate in the stonework, facing the stream, stonework steps mostly awash.

He slipped up to the side, found the gate ever so slightly ajar, so that one would never notice if one did not happen to be pushing at it, hoping it was unlocked. The gate might creak if he pushed it wider. He might have to run if it did. He might have to throw himself in the water and hope it swept him to some handhold downstream, away from Nikolai, where he would not wish to lead pursuers in any account, and he did think he was being commendably thoughtful, to reason that out in advance. He knew exactly what he would do if he were surprised, he had a plan—so he gave the gate only the gentlest effort, ready to stop at the first hint of resistance that might make the hinges creak. It went wide enough for a skinny boy—which was good enough; and he thought, meanwhile, It's dark inside. I can at least see if it goes all the way in without a second gate in there—master Nikolai would need to know that, or we can be coming and going here all night, and every time we come and go is a chance for them to catch us, isn't it?

So he slipped inside, and had the foresight to pull the gate almost shut behind him, so it looked exactly as before.

The air inside was cool and dank the way one would expect next to water, and a little musty, as if someone used the place for storage or refuse. He felt to one side a fair distance before he found the wall; he walked carefully ahead and found no second gate—it felt like a tunnel of some kind, maybe even a natural cave, since he felt no mason-work. So far he smelled and heard nothing that indicated occupancy, only the odor of old, wet sacks. He debated whether to go back, decided to try just a little further, always keeping to the wall which could guide him back in the dark, and with one hand above him to watch his head, if it was like the cellars at home—because the starlight and water sheen that reflected into the entry rapidly ran out, and he needed to stop now and again and let his eyes grow accustomed to more dark.

This tunnel was certainly something Nikolai would want to know about—and more so if he could report a door or a gate through which the goblins in the tower might get down to the water and by which they might get up into the tower and rescue his brothers and the rest.

There *might* even be store rooms, as he thought about the probable use of this place: that was what the basement was at home, it did smell like it was used for that—and store rooms, he thought excitedly, were one place the goblins might lock up their prisoners, the way the servants said grandfather had locked up the bandits once upon a time, before he hanged them.

In that thought, he desperately wished he dared call out his brothers' names, and he stopped now and again, held his breath and listened for the faintest sound that might indicate a prisoner locked in this place.

Water dripping was all he heard—plunk, plunk . . . plunk. Louder and louder—until he heard another step, back toward the gate.

Lord Sun, he thought, heart in his throat, someone's in the tunnel behind me.

His first desperate thought was to press himself tight against the wall, and he did that, in the hope someone more used to this place might walk down the middle and miss him. But that was no good if they lit a lamp; and if they did not light a lamp it meant they were walking in the dark on purpose, which if they owned it, meant they knew a foolish boy might be in this tunnel. Noses keen as hounds', Nikolai had said, but he had never expected any guard would come in from the water side, from the same way he had, or move in the dark.

He hugged the wall, trying to think of some better choice, all the while trying to hear how many there were. The presence moved in two parts. Like a snake, he thought, swallowing hard. Or a single goblin dragging something, like a sack, or a body.

The gate to the outside might still be open. He might rush past the goblin by sheer surprise if he waited until it was almost on him and then burst for the exit. Or he might sneak as far as he could ahead, and hope the goblin turned off into some passage on the other side of the wall, at some branching yet unfound. The first offered a better chance: he knew the door was there, which he could not say about any other doorway; but it would alert the whole tower; the second was the quieter, and there had to be a door from upstairs, or how did they ordinarily come and go here, without getting their feet wet? If he could get past that, the goblin might go upstairs.

Except, god, they could *smell* him. And there was no surety the gate to the outside was not locked, now that whoever had gone out had come back.

Quiet was what he thought Nikolai would choose. Raising a general alarm was not a good idea—that could bring a search along the stream that might find Nikolai; that would be a disaster. So he edged along the wall, feeling his way past projections, along turns, utterly blind now, hurrying faster than he liked. He knocked into something, that, thank the god, he grabbed before it fell. A lamp, he thought, steadying it in its niche; and quickly he moved on.

Then he ran into bars, a shock that half stopped his heart. But he felt out an open gateway in them, ducked through it and went further; but then he was running out of ceiling—so he had to bend, and then to go on hands and knees, truly scared, now, that he had gotten himself into a trap, hoping desperately that beyond the bars might be a nook they might not search—hoping Nikolai was wrong about their sense of smell. He hunkered down, almost out of room altogether, trying not to breathe hard. He heard the movement behind him stop, and then a little gleam of red showed in the dark—he thought at first of demonic, glowing eyes.

But it was ordinary coals in a firepot, and a wick that caught yellow fire, and flared on its way to a lamp—showing him shaggy fur, a broad face, eyes dark and liquid with light, suddenly staring right at his refuge.

He hugged his knees tighter and tried not to shiver, hoping it did not see him in the shadow. But it said, "Another one," in a harsh, deep voice, and shuffled over toward him, with a long, ratlike tail snaking and coiling behind.

He looked back to see if there was anywhere at all else to go, but the ceiling was so low he could only crawl—

Which the creature could not. He scrambled for the low spot and heard the bars bang. He was crawling into it as flat and as fast as he could, trying to get beyond its reach, when something seized on his ankle and dragged him backward, burning his palms and his chin as he tried to hold to the rock.

It dragged him out to the lamplight kicking and struggling. He kicked it, but it held on, and looked at him, after he had run out of breath trying to escape it.

It was a troll, he was sure. He had gotten himself into a predicament master Nikolai had given him no instructions for, unless it slipped its grip. It had the lamp in one hand and his ankle in the other, and seemed perplexed by the situation.

But it set the lamp down on the floor, tore him loose from the bars where he had immediately anchored himself, and held him by both arms in front of its face—to bite his head off, he was sure, and he kicked it again, to get even.

"You smell familiar," it said—when he had never heard that trolls talked at all. "You smell of dog."

He did. Zadny had been all over him. And what did Zadny have to do with trolls?

"Where are my brothers?" he asked the troll, on what little breath he could get, suspended as he was. "What did you do with them?"

"Most dead," it said. "Only bones."

Most. He clung to that 'most.' And it had not bitten his head off. It talked about dogs. It looked him thoughtfully in the eyes, not looking particularly fierce, now that he had a longer look at it. It looked puzzled; and his arms were near to breaking, but it had not done more than hold him eye to eye with it. "Some not dead," he gasped, and kicked without intending to this time.

"Where?"

"Two rode away."

"Where?"

"Outside. Away. —You smell of boy, not goblin. Boys don't belong here now. Bad place, bad."

"I'm looking for my brothers." The pain was worse and breath was shorter. He thought his arms would break. "Where did they ride?"

"Looking for brothers," it rumbled. "Looking for brothers." It set his feet gently on the floor, eased its grip and patted him on the shoulder with a huge, shaggy hand. "Good. That's what to do."

"Do you know where they've gone? Do you even know it was my brothers?" It was magical. He had no idea of its capabilities. But sudden hope brought a wobble to his voice, and he hesitated to run. "My name is Yuri. I come from over-mountain. My brothers are Tamas and Bogdan. . . ."

"Don't know names. But look for brothers, yes, a good idea, very good idea."

For some reason a prickling went down his arms, like being with the priests, or hearing the winter wind, its voice was so deep. The troll did not look wicked or cruel to him, it looked sad, and wise, and it seemed to be saying more than it owned words to say. It said, "We'll go," turned him with a vast shaggy hand and urged him to walk.

He should run for his life, he thought. It was probably a trick. He was probably far faster than it was—it was very big and heavy; but it was already taking him where he wanted to go, beyond the light, back down the shadowy tunnel to the streamside and the starlight and the open.

"Go find them," the creature said, exactly what he wanted to do.

But he could not go with it anywhere looking for Tamas and Bogdan, not leaving Nikolai lying wounded and waiting for him and not knowing what had happened. Nikolai had killed trolls—it might not take kindly to that, if it knew—but maybe it would not know, and maybe Nikolai would give it no hints.

They walked as far as the gate and the river, with his stomach knotting tighter and tighter over the question.

But Nikolai had said himself, I'm not going to make it, boy. Nikolai believed that. Nikolai had believed it when he came down the mountain looking for his brothers, and Nikolai usually knew the score on things. So there was no hope for him—

Except if a boy could bring him help, and he hoped with all his heart it was the right thing to do.

It seemed forever, the waiting did. The damned dog at least had settled to rest. Nikolai had his belt around his wrist and its collar, and passed the moments scratching the soft hide under the hound's jaw, because it was warm, in the dark; because it was not really a stupid dog, just a clumsy, well-meaning dog, after all, that would track its master through hell.

And lead a boy into it. And wake every damned goblin in that fortress if it took a notion to bark, which he earnestly hoped Zadny would not, and tried to keep the hound comfortable and distracted—the right arm would not move, now, with any speed. He could not get a better grip on the dog, or hold it quiet. The pain came and went in waves that wiped sense out when the dog would get restless and pull at him in the least.

"Shush," he said, when it did. "He'll be back. He'll be back soon, hound. He's a clever boy. Lie still."

So he told it. So he wanted to think. The boy might be in serious trouble by now. He kept listening for any commotion in the distance, hoping against all reason for the boy to follow his instructions to the letter and only find out the lay of the place, then come back for more instructions—and more instructions, and more argument: it was the only delay he could think of to dissuade the boy. Maybe by morning he would be stronger—

And maybe pigs would soar, he thought. He needed to box the boy across the ears, get him on that pony and tell him get the hell home, was what he needed to do. He would keep the damned dog, who could atone for his sins in leading the boy here in the first place; he and the dog might get along, and he might somehow find fish in the stream—

More winged pigs, he thought. The stream had poured off the ice of the heights, and it offered only sterile water.

Water and a way . . . maybe a way to float downstream to safer territory. Damn. He had not thought of that. If he could just get the boy back . . .

If the boy would only come back . . .

Lord Stani's remaining son on his hands, the other two missing—but if they could go downstream, go back to the mountains once they were well away from here, then find another pass—

All this through a landscape barren as hell's doorstep and haunted by goblins, after which they faced a journey through the mountains with no food, nor forage, nor any hope of finding any on their way; with only the vague hope of finding a pass no one else had found, besides the fact that mountains tended to fold in unpredictable ways, and lead one into blind ends, and mazes . . . maybe floating downstream was a better . . .

Zadny lifted his ears, lifted his head and jumped to his feet. Nikolai tensed his arm against the lunge, got a grip on the belt and held to it, knowing the dog was going to bark, damn him—he jerked at the belt hard, to bring the hound to the reach of his fingers, and tried to bring the left hand to seize its muzzle.

There was a bark, a feeble, uncertain whine, then a boy's running steps—he hoped that was the case. "Hush!" he whispered to the hound, fearing the boy was running with goblins on his heels.

But the boy showed up and slid to his knees, babbling, "Master Nikolai! Master Nikolai, I found someone!"

There was no one to find but goblins. And Zadny's pulling at him all but took his senses away. He said, with greatest apprehensions: "Who?"

A huge shadow lumbered up behind the boy, a huge and shaggy shadow with a ratlike tail.

He snatched the sword that was by him, but his good hand had the damned leash tied to it, and the boy grabbed that elbow, and hung on it, objecting: "No, no, it's all right, master Nikolai, he's all right!"

The troll squatted down to have a closer look at him, rumbled, "Bad, bad hurt," and put a hand on his shoulder.

He had never imagined a troll could speak. He was quite out

of his head. The creature had tricked the boy. It was contemplating supper, he was sure of it. But between the boy holding his arm and the leash on his wrist—

It said, "Krukczy is my name."

"Nikolai," he said, to humor it while he tried to think. The fool hound was trying to leap up and paw at the troll's lap like some long-lost friend, shooting pains through his wound while Yuri held its collar. The troll patted the dog, then reached and patted his shoulder.

"Nikolai," it said. "Yuri. Good. Good we find brothers."

"It says," Yuri panted, "it says two got away, it says it's going with us."

His heart could only beat so fast. He was not thoroughly aware of his fingers now, or his feet, and the rest of him was fading fast. He said to the boy, "Run, dammit." But the boy paid no attention, neither the boy nor the troll, which was working at the knot that held the dog to his wrist, hurting him and getting nowhere with it.

The boy took over. Fever had set in, Nikolai decided. He was dreaming now, how a troll gathered him up and carried him in its arms, and that Yuri rode along on his pony.

He dreamed that they went into the stream and under the walls of the fortress, and down a winding dark tunnel, pony and all. Lamplight cast shadows on the ceiling above his face. He heard the clip-clop of the pony's hooves.

"What about the goblins?" he asked, because even in a dream, one should not leave such details unseen-to.

The troll said, "Gone to their queen."

"What queen?" And more to the point: "Why?" Why always mattered most, of questions.

But it laid him on the floor without answering the important things. Dreams were like that. Yuri leaned over him to say they were safe, and that the troll was out looking for supper, which it had not been able to do while the goblins were in the tower.

"Fool," he murmured, "it's found it . . ."

Zadny licked him in the face. Yuri made him stop.

"Tell it eat the dog first," he muttered. "Boy, get away, get out of here."

But perhaps the dream had started way up on the mountain, when he had pulled the arrow. And the boy and the dog had never arrived, and there was no troll at all. Only goblins, who had gotten everyone but him.

The troll came lumbering back, shadowing him. There was a great deal of moving about then, in a haze of pain and light and shadow—he fell asleep until Yuri bumped his head up on his knee, and said he should drink.

Fish stew. It wanted salt. But it was hot. "Get away," the boy chided Zadny. "You have yours."

Amazingly detailed for a dream. So was waking again with a contemplative troll staring at him in the lamplight.

"Good, good," it said. "Better?"

He nodded, wanting the other part of the dream back, the one with the boy and the pony and the free sky still overhead. He glanced around him, lifting his head, and saw boy and dog curled up together with the pony's saddle for a pillow, saw the pony dozing on three feet within the tunnel.

The troll was still sitting there when he looked back. It looked very real. It smelled real. It made a shadow where it should. He did not at all like this persistence of imagery—or his situation, or watching the troll's flickering eyes watching his with too much awareness.

"What do you want?" he asked it finally, in his dream; and it said only:

"Sleep, hunter. Go to sleep."

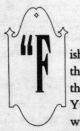ish," Krukczy announced, all dripping, and fish there certainly was, a big fat one, flopping about on the floor. Zadny began to bark, threatening it. But Yuri got it and cut its head off, and cleaned it. So when master Nikolai finally opened his eyes on the morning there was breakfast cooking.

"We're still alive," master Nikolai murmured as if that surprised him.

"Goblins all gone," Krukczy said, very full of fish, as it seemed, and wanting to nap awhile, with Zadny, who had breakfasted on fish offal and roe.

"Damned good friends," Nikolai said under his breath. "Never ask where that hound came from. Friends with trolls, it is."

Yuri cast an anxious glance over his shoulder, but Krukczy only seemed to drowse, and Zadny had curled up and shut his eyes.

"Go home," Nikolai said in a low voice. "If there's fish in the stream, catch some, take the pony, leave me and the damned dog with the troll, and get *home*. Tell your father—"

"I'm not telling my father anything," Yuri said, with a lump in his throat, "because I'm not going home yet."

"You've no business in this—"

"You've no business either, you can't use your left arm.

What are you going to do to rescue them?"

"I'm going to use my head and go home when I can walk, and get help over here, so there's no question of your going along—"

"Yes, there is. Because if you're going home you can ride Gracja and I'll take Zadny and I'll find them."

"You'll mind what you're told, young lord! I'm responsible for you—and don't think you've proved a thing, running off from home, trekking over-mountain with no damned sense what you were getting into . . ."

"Did *you* know?"

Master Nikolai shut his mouth and clenched his jaw.

"And you wouldn't go home," Yuri said further. "Not except to make me go. Which you can't do. So there."

"Damn your disobedience."

He did not like being damned by master Nikolai. He was sorry to be disrespectful. But he said, to drive home the point: "You can have my pony, if you want. I got this far. I can walk." Master Nikolai was furious with him, but he was not going to do as he was told, not this time, he had made up his mind on that account, and he was more scared than he had ever been in the mountains. He changed the subject, since master Nikolai was not going to say anything helpful. "Breakfast is ready."

"We're not discussing breakfast."

"Krukczy can catch you more fish. They'll freeze in the pass and they'll be fine. You'll have food all the way home. And he brought greens for Gracja this morning. So she's all right."

Silence from master Nikolai. Nikolai was mad at him. Nikolai tried to sit up and hurt himself, which did not improve his temper.

"Go home!"

"I wouldn't go home without my brother's dog. Do you think I'd go home without *him*?"

"You've not a hope of finding the boys. We don't know where they went."

"Zadny will."

"Damn that dog, he'll get you killed, that's all he's good for. He's got no sense!"

"I'd rather have you with me," he said, with a glance from under his brows, and there was a lump in his throat, and in his stomach, too, where breakfast sat like a stone. "I followed everything you said, master Nikolai, all the way up the mountains, and I didn't have any trouble. I did everything you said last night. Didn't I? And things are all right. I can get along all right if you go home. —But I'd rather have you there. Gracja could carry you. And Krukczy says he's going with us."

"Damn," Nikolai said under his breath, and muttered to himself and winced, with his eyes shut, because it hurt him to sit up. "Damn and damn, boy! You belong at home!"

But Nikolai never for a moment intended to go home without him. Nikolai *wanted* to find his brothers and not to have to face his parents without them. There was never a time they were lost or strayed that Nikolai had not found them and brought them home, only this time was the worst, it was by far the worst.

"So will you go with me, master Nikolai?"

They were riding in the sun, and Bogdan asked him—asked him something, Tamas was sure—but, distressingly enough, he could no longer remember the exact sound of Bogdan's voice; or see Bogdan's face except in shadow. Sunlight streamed about them blindingly bright. Petals drifted down in clouds from the orchards, a blizzard of dying flowers.

If there were a means, he thought, to gather up all the flowers, if he could recover the recent springtime, if he could retrace their path on the mountain road and say, when they had hesitated at that dreadful stone, Master Karoly, where are you leading us? Whose friend are you?—then everything might be different.

But he and the witch girl kept riding down the stream, and fever and sunlight blinded him. He might be home, in the orchards about the walls. But if he was where he remembered, a dreadful thing had happened, which in his confusion he could not recall, except the ominous curtain of petals, a sign of decay and change.

The stones in his dream echoed with drums. A goblin looked at him and was blind to him. A troll held him in its arms as skulls shone white under the moon, horse bones alternate with human, a goblin fancy of order. Their kind was not incapable of artistry.

Birds screamed from the thickets while the horses picked their steady way downhill. He saw huge lumps of rock, saw juniper and patient saxifrage, but nothing in this place of orchards, no tree so tame, only twisted shaggy bark, tough and resilient, and weathered gray stone. Gone, the soot-stained snows and lifeless rocks of recent nightmare. Roots here invaded rock and patiently wedged cracks wider, making mountains smaller. Master Karoly said so.

Came pine and linden, rowan and new-leafed, timid beech—he knew them by their names, master Karoly had taught him. Listen to their voices, Karoly had said: each sings a different song. So he knew with his eyes shut the sound and smell of each and every one. But what did that say of where he was or what did it say of the character of his companion, who refused all questions and rode in disdainful silence?

Woolgathering again? he could hear Bogdan say. There are times to *do* things and times to think, brother. Figure it out, will you?

A dark-spiked shadow of pine ran along the streamside. The witchling led them down to the stream again—when had they ever left it?—and let the mare wade in and drink.

He stopped Lwi short of that: it dawned on him to look into
the saddle kit, now that they were stopped in daylight. He was
too stiff and sore to turn around to search the gear from horseback, so he slid down, thinking if anyone had food left in his
saddlebags it might have been Nikolai; he had never thought to
search this morning, and hunger had not much intruded
through the pain.

That was a mistake, he thought, kneeling by the water's
edge. Getting off was very surely a mistake.

Ela rode the mare between him and the sun, asked, disgust-
edly, "What are you doing?"

He had tried to get up. Instead he knelt with one knee on
wet and soaking reeds, and wet his hands in the icy stream and
carried them to his face, while Lwi wandered free in the shallow
water. Ela dismounted, and he blinked wetly up into eyes green
as glass, green as pond water. Her hair was palest gold. These
details absorbed him, along with the frown that knit her brows.

"Fool. You'll catch your death. The stream is ice melt."

It might be. But it took the pain away, and he laved his face
with it, ignoring warnings. He wished he could slip into it
head-deep, and have it take all the ache, and the thinking, and
the remembering. He said, conversationally, on the last of his
self-possession, and the last shred of his strength, "I was looking
for something to eat. Is there anything? I think I could go on,
if there were."

As witches went, he vastly preferred master Karoly. Karoly
would not have called him a fool. Karoly would have had some
sympathy, long since, even if he had betrayed them. But she
confessed there was something to eat, and said she would get it
out of her packs if he would quit being a fool and not drown
himself in the meanwhile.

She had not a kindly word to her name. She was the most
unreasonable, ill-tempered, and arrogant creature he had ever

met, including the troll. But she took packets from Skory's saddlebags, and thereafter Lwi and Skory browsed the shore while he and the witch shared the first meal he remembered in days—a little jerky and biscuit, and a sip of clean, cold water.

But after the work the dried meat was, he felt wearier than he was hungry, and set his shoulders against a gnarled pine so that the roots and the stones missed most of his bruises—only to rest, he protested, to her impatience, only a moment.

He was filthy, he was bruised down to the fingertips, there were cuts in his scalp, his bath in the cave had only moved the mud about, so far as he could tell, and she was right, he had soaked himself down the neck and now he was chilled and sorry for it. But he had a precious and clean bit of food in his hand, overall nothing much was hurting him, and his eyes drifted shut—as if, once the terror was past and food had hit his stomach, he could not keep his wits collected or his eyes open. He had found his land of once upon a time, but it was all dark, everything was grim and magical things lived here, oh, yes— trolls and witches. Of gran's stories—at least there were pine groves, and this brook which the goblins had not so far fouled. That was true. So he could still believe in her, for what little good those stories were.

Ela's mistress would prove wiser, and better natured than Ela *or* gran. And if not, if this ride was all for nothing, then he would ride away on his own, and trap and fish for his food and get home past the goblins somehow.

And his father would ask—

His father and his mother and Yuri would all ask, Where is Bogdan?

His only answer must be, I don't know. And his parents would ask why, and he could only say that he had not warned Bogdan, worse, he had fallen off his horse when Bogdan could have most used help, and he had no real answer for what had become of his brother. He never would have, unless he found someone who could tell him what had happened in this country and why goblins were loose and no one stopped them, and whether Bogdan had died with the others—he had not counted the skulls, he had had no such thought in his head last night, nothing but to escape the sight. . . .

A warm hand touched his brow. It confused him, or the tingling that followed it did. He opened his eyes in confusion, saw Ela with a frown of concentration between her brows. He felt warm and cold all over, felt . . .

She said to him, "Get up. Do you hear? Get up now."

He did not even think about doing it. He got to his feet with the bit of jerky still in hand, stumbled on the roots and went after Lwi, as the witch girl put her foot in the mare's stirrup—not a graceful mount, but the mare stood still: creatures did as Ela said. So was he doing, although it dawned on him while he was gathering up Lwi's reins that his pain was less, and while he was hauling himself into Lwi's saddle, that he was not so weary or short of breath as he had been.

Only tired. Unbearably tired, so that once he was in the saddle it was easier to let Lwi follow the mare.

"Wake up," Ela told him twice, before he caught a branch across the face, and, his forehead stinging, kept himself awake.

"I 'm fine, I'm fine," master Nikolai panted, and Yuri bit his lip while Nikolai hauled himself painfully into Gracja's back. Master Nikolai was not at all fine; but he wanted no help, he said, thank you.

"Are you on?" Yuri asked, holding his breath for fear that Nikolai might slide right on off the other side, onto the rocks. He held his hand ready to grab Nikolai's trouser-leg.

"Go now?" Krukczy rumbled, curling his rat tail around and around so it made ripples in the water; Zadny put himself under Gracja's feet as they started off, and scampered from a near miss.

Gone to their queen, Krukczy said of the goblins; but Yuri had had no disposition to search the place to be absolutely sure. It was enough to be away, as quickly as they could.

The morning shadow of the mountain was still on them, the rocks dark and the water beside them murkily gray, but darkest was the out-thrust shadow of Krukczy Straz itself, where the going was so narrow Nikolai's leg brushed the tower wall, and he felt the shadow and the threat of the tower looming until they had made it away into the living brush.

"Green," Nikolai murmured, and it was. Grim as the mountains had been, they had come where there was forage. Gracja nipped leaves as she went, caught mouthfuls of grass, so that Yuri tore up handfuls to give her as he saw a chance, to keep her from jolting Nikolai. Zadny rolled in the grass and got up and ran circles until he panted. But the troll met them only now and again as they went, preferring the stream they could not at all times follow. Krukczy would emerge like a bear from the water, shoulders first, and then two large eyes, that might vanish again; or all of Krukczy might come out to walk with them awhile, dripping on the leaves, squishing like a sheep in a rainstorm, and trailing a watery snake curve with his long furless tail.

"Find brothers," Krukczy would say on occasion. And: "Went this way, went this way." And, yet another time: "Going to see the witch."

"Karoly's sister," Nikolai said, with the nearest interest he had shown in Krukczy's wandering conversation. "Where does this witch live?"

It obtained an airy wave of a very large hand. "There, there, down."

"Fine directions," Nikolai said sourly. Nikolai was in pain, and sweating, and they needed to stop—No, Nikolai insisted, he was on the horse, he was staying on the horse, so they were still going.

Nikolai asked aloud, "Are there more goblins, master troll?

Or what kind of place is this they went to?"

"Gone to their queen," was all Krukczy would say. "Gone to their queen. Queen sends them, queen says come back."

"Where?"

Krukczy gave what seemed to be a shrug as he walked, and his tail whipped about nervously. "Where the queen is." Krukczy seemed more and more agitated. "Goblins . . . goblins . . ."

"Where?"

"Gone."

"No sense," Nikolai muttered. "No damned sense, you can't talk to it . . ."

Krukczy was further and further ahead. Yuri tried to hurry, tugging on Gracja as branches separated them from Krukczy's shaggy shape—Krukczy was only a shadow now, a brown shadow quickly slipping away among the leaves.

"Give me the reins," Nikolai said. And when he started to protest. "Give me the reins!"

He passed them up, and Nikolai gave Gracja a fierce kick, sent her at a run on Krukczy's track—and, fearing Nikolai would fall, Yuri began to run, diving through brush Gracja and the troll had broken, Zadny racing ahead of him. He ran and ran, and heard Nikolai call out, "Damn you—"

But Nikolai had brought Gracja back to a walk by the time he had him in sight again. There was no sign at all of Krukczy. "Damned troll," Nikolai breathed as he caught up. But Nikolai kept Gracja moving, so that he had nothing to do but to walk behind with Zadny and hold his side against the stitch he had caught running so hard.

Then he saw Gracja's reins fall slack, and Nikolai leaned perilously in the saddle. He flung himself forward to stop Nikolai from sliding off, heedless of the thornbush Gracja's forward progress took him through. He shoved at Nikolai, got the reins and made Gracja stop. Gracja was confused, and scared, and Zadny's jumping at her legs was no help.

"Easy, easy," he breathed, trying to steady Gracja with one hand and hold the other ready to keep Nikolai upright. Nikolai had caught himself against the saddlebow, but the whiteness of Nikolai's face and the set of Nikolai's jaw said he was in excruciating pain.

"Better lead," Nikolai said in the ghost of his own voice. "Do you know the way back, boy?"

"No, sir," he said faintly. The very sunlight through the trees seemed cold. "I don't think I do. We've been up and down so many hills . . ."

"I don't know either," Nikolai said. But he did not believe that. Nikolai never got lost.

He looked about him, and up at the sun, the way Nikolai himself had taught him. But lord Sun was hidden by the trees. He only believed he knew where west was. But west was a long ridge of mountains, and a maze of hills. Nothing—nothing was certain. He led Gracja a while, in the direction he thought was right. And when he looked back master Nikolai's eyes were shut and Nikolai was leaning again.

"Please don't fall off," he said. He was still shaking from running. His side hurt, and he could not get enough breath. "I think we need to find somebody, I think we need a place with people, very soon."

"Karoly's sister," Nikolai said. "The ones we're following— there were hoof-prints . . . some time back. Horsehair—white —on the branches."

Yuri was embarrassed. He had been blind—leading Gracja, keeping his eyes on the troll, that was all. He had seen no such things. Nikolai, hurt as he was, lying much of the time against Gracja's neck, had kept his eyes open. But he had a dreadful thought then. "Do goblins ride horses?"

"Eat them, for all I know." Nikolai's eyes shut again, and half opened. "Shouldn't have run. Shouldn't have run. Damn, boy."

"Yes, sir," he said. "What should we do?"

Nikolai sat there a moment, above him, his eyes open—but Nikolai said nothing; only, for no reason, took his weight to the stirrup and began to get down—which, if he did—

Yuri shoved hard to stop him, put himself in the way so Nikolai had nowhere to step. "You can't get off," he told Nikolai. "Don't get down. . . ."

"Boy, I want you to take the horse."

"No!" he said. "No. If you get off, I'm staying here. We're both staying here. Do you want that?"

"It's left us," Nikolai said. "It's left us in the middle of the damn woods, boy, it's smelled goblins and it's run."

"Then don't make things worse! I can't get you back up on the horse if you fall, and I don't even know where home is."

"You can track us backwards. Back to the tower . . ."

"No, sir! I won't, I won't do it—you stay on, you hear me? If you get off, I'm staying with you until you can get on again. Do you hear me, I'll do it!"

Nikolai seemed to think about that. Or Nikolai was in too much pain to think at all. He leaned heavily on the saddlebow until all Yuri could do was steady him; and he knew it hurt Nikolai's wounded arm, but it was the only way he could manage. He started leading Gracja again, making as much speed as he could, looking back as he could to be sure Nikolai was still steady.

But a thread of blood was running down Nikolai's hand, staining Gracja's side.

He's dying, Yuri thought in panic. He's going to die if we don't get help, and there's nothing we can do any faster than we are.

Zadny went in front of them. "Find people," Yuri said to him—"Zadny, find people, do you hear me?"

There was no knowing whether Zadny understood a word, but he kept to the front of them, sometimes losing himself in the brush, so he feared they would lose track of the hound, too, and be alone.

"Maybe we can find somebody besides Nikolai that got away," Yuri said to himself. "Everything's going to be all right, it's just trolls don't know what people need, it's just scared, probably Nikolai chasing it scared him, he'll come back. Nikolai shouldn't have run the horse, that's all—the blood will stop."

"Karoly's sister," Nikolai murmured, once, obscurely, and he stopped Gracja and went back to him to see whether Nikolai was all right. But Nikolai only said, "Are we still on the trail?" and he said, "Yes, sir, I think we are. . . ." realizing with a chill that Nikolai was off his head and lost.

He had made Nikolai come with him. He had been disrespectful, he had refused Nikolai's advice, and been smug about it; and offered Nikolai no choice but come with him—because he had known in his heart of hearts that Nikolai would never take Gracja and ride home without him. He had wanted Nikolai to get on Gracja's back and come with him this morning; and he had been so sure he was doing the right thing, so sure Nikolai was strong enough—although Nikolai had told him last night he would never make it.

He had not listened: he had not wanted to listen, that was the bitter truth. Nikolai had said go home and have his father send men who could do more than a stupid boy could do— Nikolai had never once asked him to get *him* to safety, Nikolai was too strong for that, Nikolai was supposed to be with him to advise him, that was the way he had intended things . . .

The woods blurred in front of him. He walked and followed Zadny, and looked for the hoof-prints master Nikolai had said

he had seen, because there was no time to be wrong now—
thanks to his cleverness and his disobedience, master Nikolai had
no time.

The sun sank as they followed the watercourse downhill, sometimes among rocks, in the shadow now of tall beeches not
fully leafed, and early willow, and brush as stripped as the brush
the other side of the mountains. The plague of beasts had passed
here, too, Tamas thought, in the numb lucidity that had come
since he had had water and food. Leafless vines snagged the
horses' feet and snapped, dry branches broke under their hooves.
The horses, taller than deer, found browse along the way, a
snatch of leaves, and in clear spaces, patches of stream-side cress
that had grown since the depredations. Ela held the lead, no
horsewoman, but Jerzy's mare went along as if it had home and
stable in mind.

So did Lwi, without his urging; and when he protested the
horses could not stand that pace forever, she declared they
would be all right, that was her word, they would be all right.

"Are there goblins behind us?" he asked. And got no answer.

His bruised bones ached, after so much and so rough riding—but he was thinking clearly enough these last hours to
realize that he had lost his grandfather's sword, and even the
saddle knife, with his own horse. Nikolai's bow was all the
weapon they had, that and its handful of arrows.

Well done, he thought bitterly, in Bogdan's tones. Well
done, little brother. And only now wondering what you have
for resources? You unfailingly amaze me. . . .

He tried at least to calculate how far they had come. In a
clearer space he looked back and all about for the sight of
mountains, but the trees still loomed taller: the forest was all
their surroundings, the colorless and dimming sky with its high

cloud making time itself uncertain. He was all too awake, in the dark that lived within the forest, where twilight was early and shadowed with leaves. The whole world tottered on the edge of reason, imagination led nowhere, and he had no sane choice now but the one he was following.

"We'll make it by twilight," Ela declared, the only words she had volunteered to him since noon. "We have to."

He repeated his question: "What do we fear in this woods?"

"All manner of things," she said, and added: "Everything."

Lwi tossed his head, sweating. Tamas patted his neck beneath the fall of mane, misliking vague answers, and disliking witches more by the passing hour. Maybe she could ease his aches, but the ease did not last. Maybe she could make creatures go where she wanted, but clearly that did not extend to goblins, and maybe not to bears; so what good was that?

Besides, who knew what women thought, or might do, or why? Here he rode in a shadowy, goblin-haunted woods asking himself not for the first time how Ela had escaped the goblins' ambush, or hidden the horses, or made bargains with trolls to rescue him.

Walls before nightfall had been his hope in mid-afternoon: the expectation that they would find some fortified and human hold, an unassailable place with a great lady who happened to be a witch, but who, please the god, would turn out to remind him a great deal of the Karoly he had loved, an old woman who would keep a study in equal clutter, who would answer his questions with equal sympathy, tell him the good and the bad that he had to deal with, and magic up a wise and potent answer he could bring back to Maggiar.

But by the beginning of sunset he still saw no fields such as a great hold would need, only this barely flourishing desolation of woods and stony hillsides. He was down to hoping for another tower, like Krukczy Straz. (And another troll, shuffling about the halls in service to Ela's mistress? He was over the boundaries of Maggiar and clearly things here were different.)

Madam, he would say to Karoly's sister—at least he imagined that was how to address a witch—I was with master Karoly, whom, I fear, the goblins . . .

. . . ate? Killed. Killed was far kinder, and he could get immediately to: Master Karoly came to ask your help, my father asks it—

Then the witch would say: What exactly do you want me to do? and he would have not an idea in his head: he had no idea what a witch could do, or what she would ask of him—

Because witches asked payment, that was in grandmother's stories, along with trolls and magical waterfalls that made one young a thousand years, and undead creatures that haunted the site of their demise, different than ghosts, and bloodier. . . .

Madam, he would say, if you would help my father and my people—and my brother, if he's still alive . . .

What would he do in return for that? Anything, he said to himself. Anything. Bogdan had left him that duty. Master Karoly had. He was the last of their company and he had no choices, now that he had gone this far.

Madam, anything at all, if only you'd do something . . . if you *could* do something . . .

But the witchling pushed the horses both to the limit of their strength and spoke of being in after dark, and that was no recommendation of her mistress' power. "I don't like this," Ela said once, which instilled no confidence at all. He asked no further questions. But she said again, "She should hear me," and he thought she must mean her mistress.

"Where are we?" he asked. "How far yet?"

But for an answer, the witch-girl only put Jerzy's mare to a jogging, bone-jarring pace, slipping perilously from side to side of the saddle. They rode down a slope and along a winding hillside, and even in the clearings now, the light was dimmer. Sanity seemed diminished, feeble, overwhelmed.

"Be careful," he began to say, but it was far too narrow a trail to overtake her and Skory was already vanishing in the brush. Lwi had taken to running, too, through twists and doubling turns, under trees and headlong downhill. Alone, he would have reined Lwi back, but pride or fright said no fool witchling who could scarcely stay ahorse was going to lose him in a woods full of goblins—not now, with night coming.

Down to the trough of a hill and up again, up and up through a jolting series of climbs, then onto—thank the god—a well-worn footpath, that promised habitation hereabouts. Earth and recrossed roots sped under Lwi's hooves, new-leafed branches whipped past. Then an archway let them through a stone wall so overgrown with vines it loomed right out of the woods, one with everything around it.

He saw Skory and her rider and the skull-topped poles ahead of him all at once, saw Ela sliding down from the saddle in the courtyard of this forest-wrapped tower and an outcry of protest stuck in his throat. With all the clatter they had just made, they could have roused the sleeping dead, but there was no need compounding the error: he kicked free of both stirrups and slid from Lwi's back while Lwi was stopping, chased a disappearing flash of blond hair and flying cloak into the shadowed doorway of the vine-veined tower. Goblin work was plain to see in the courtyard, the door dark and unbarred to all comers—and Ela ran inside and upstairs with the fleet surefootedness of someone at home on those steps.

He could not. He stumbled on them in the dark, hurrying as fast as he could to overtake a bereaved and frightened girl, intending to reason with her: after the rooftop of Krukczy Straz he had not the heart to blame her; but echoes were waking to her search with the dreadful sound of an empty house, and betraying where he was now seemed doubly foolish. They had two horses in the courtyard that might be their only way out of here, he had left the bow down there in his haste to overtake her, and if there was any mystery left of them, he hoped to preserve it, arm himself and reserve some surprise on their side if she came running . . .

A step rasped on stone below him and his heart skipped a beat. Down the dark of the winding stairs, the faintest of twilight from the hall below still showed at the edges of the steps and on the walls opposite the core. And the step repeated itself.

Ela, he thought. We're not alone. Do you know that?

He fervently hoped for witchcraft, recollecting that Ela had come and gone undetected among goblins, and got along with trolls; but that had been no trollish movement. That had been a shod foot, a scuff of leather on stone, and since the second footfall, silence: Ela's, his, and whoever shared the tower with them.

He leaned his back against the stone of the stairwell core, keeping still in the remote chance it would go away and not come up the stairs. *Ela* was silent now that she had roused trouble; Ela must have heard it wherever she was—in some hallway upstairs, while here he stood guarding her retreat, and he could only hope she had recovered her good sense.

Not a woman's step, below, he was sure. It had sounded to his ears very like a man's boot, edged with metal. And the silence persisted, as if the presence down there had realized its mistake, and waited for him to make the next move.

Which could just as well mean some guard of this place, some honest servant of Ela's mistress, who could end up in fatal misunderstanding of intentions on this dark stairs—fatal for him, counting he was empty handed. The intruder, if intruder it was, had come past two horses out there—and knew their number. He thought, I'm trapped. Maybe I should take the chance and call out—in the case it is a friend.

An outcry would warn Ela. But Ela was being wary now that it was too late, and he decided that he was in no hurry either.

Let whoever-it-was move again. He wanted to be surer, before he made an irrevocable move, and meantime he wanted off this stairs if there was a hope of doing it in silence.

He heard a faint, faint movement below him—the tower was old. Its steps gritted underfoot, there was no helping it. So did his, he discovered, and the other was moving now. He pressed his back to the wall for steadiness and heard a whisper of cloth and metal, saw the illusory light at the lowest steps eclipsed by darker shadow. He set his foot to the next step and moved up and up, trying to mask his movements beneath the movements of the one stalking him, and meanwhile to widen his lead on it, hoping desperately for some doorway out of this place that would not compromise Ela.

But the next turning of the stairs showed a faint glow above him, a window at some higher turning, when he most prayed for deeper dark, and when he judged he was running out of stairs altogether.

That was no good. He had made his own mistakes, he could only hope in Ela's magic now, and he thought he had as well find out whether it was friend or foe stalking them, before someone died of what might, after all, prove a mistake. He called out, failing nonchalance:

"Are you a friend, down there?"

It glided onto the steps below him, a darkness on which metal glistened, a horrific and elegant armoring he had seen once before, in the cellars of Krukczy Straz—a jut-jawed countenance beneath a mop of dark hair and braids.

Fangs, oh, indeed it had. And eyes large and virtually whiteless. And an unsheathed sword.

"Well," the goblin said. "Well, shall we see?"

He backed up a step. He had not intended to, but the creature seemed to have more of the stairs than he had, as he took account of its reach and the sword in its hand.

"There's nothing up there," it said. It beckoned to him with an elegant, beringed hand. "Come down, come, you've nothing to fear."

"So goblins joke."

It laughed, showing fangs, and climbed another step closer. "Oh, often. It's a joke, you know, like that in the yard. Where's the witchling?"

"Out the door. Riding away. You can't find her, can you?"

"So men joke, too."

Man, it called him—not for his age or his facing it: it meant his difference from its kind, it meant no sympathy or mercy, and he backed another step, he could not help it. He was not ready to die. He contemplated a rush against it, perhaps to bear it over on the steps, or tear through its grip. Its nails were dark and long, on hands as beautiful as a woman's, as expressive, as graceful in ironic gesture. And somehow it had gained another step without his seeing it.

"Where is she?"

"I've no idea." His heart fluttered. It took another step and he had no choice yet but to back up, feeling his way around the core. It was clearly in the light now. Its eyes were green as old water, its smile nothing reassuring.

"Afraid of me?" it asked.

"Oh, never. Why don't you go downstairs?"

"Why were you going up? Looking for something? A witch, maybe?"

"I'm a thief," he said. "Like you."

A second time it laughed, and flexed a hand about its sword hilt, beckoning with the other. "Then we should be friends. Come down. We'll have a drink together."

"Be damned to you."

The sword flashed, rested point down on the steps between them. "You've great confidence. Is it justified, I wonder?"

It meant to kill him outright, he had no doubt now. He

backed up only for a feint, shoved off from the edge of the step and, bare-handed, struck the blade aside as he dived for the shallow of the turn.

The goblin warrior followed the blade about, full turn, that was how it had its arm in his way, and him pinned against the great pillar of the core, staring at it face to face. Its iron-hard arms were on either side, and the carelessly held sword leant against his neck as it shook its head slowly. "Not justified," it concluded, and grinned at him, a showing of fangs, a glitter of shadowed eyes behind a disordered, fringe of mane—such details stood clear as his heart pounded away and he wondered could he duck down quickly enough, or dared he move—considering the cold blade beneath his chin.

"Lost its tongue?" it asked him. "Fellow thief?"

He had. And his breath. He brought a knee up. The goblin knocked his head against the wall, not grinning now. He made a second try—but the goblin was too tall, and breath was too short. It said, hissing into his face with that lisp the jutting fangs made,

"I want the witch, man."

"What witch?" he asked. "Which witch?" Light-headedness suggested rhymes. It could not be more annoyed, and he was out of strategies. He tried to pry its hand loose. As well dispute a stone statue. "I think you ate the last one—hereabouts . . ."

"Liar," it said, and tightened its grip. "Are you a liar?"

"Of course not," he had wind to say. It slacked its hold ever so little.

"A conundrum. How clever." Unexpectedly it let go entirely, and gave him room on the stairs. "Run, man. Run."

He did not believe it, not even when it dropped the sword point and gave him room. He drew a shaky breath, made a gesture downward, giddily, toward the stairs. "You first." If one was about to be beaten anyway, he had learned that from Bogdan—if one was about to be stabbed from behind, as seemed now, then play the game for pride, if that was all he had left. And to his own light-headed amazement he was not tongue-tied or wool-gathering. Bogdan would approve, if Bogdan were here, but this creature and his kind had—

He could not think about that rooftop. He refused to think about it now.

The goblin stepped higher on the stairs, trading places with him on the narrow steps, and tapped the side of his leg with the sword blade as they passed each other. "I'm letting you go, man. Go. Next time—find a sword."

It was going on upstairs. It was searching for Ela. It would come back for him, or others were below to deal with him. He contemplated attacking it as it turned its back on him in contempt and kept climbing—the troll had inured him to terrors, for days now, and he wanted to go for it bare-handed as he was. But that served nothing. In the hall below he might find a weapon, a fallen board, anything to throw a penny-worth weight onto his side of the balance and do it harm it might feel, if it followed him. Or get to the courtyard and his bow if it did not.

He sped down the steps, angry, desperate, blind in the winding dark below, expecting to run headlong into more of them at any turn. He saw the faint twilight from the doorway and bolted down the last turns into the entry, where his dark-accustomed eyes picked out cloth in the shadow, a cloaked figure that accosted him with:

"Shh!"

Ela's whisper—while his fist was knotted up to strike and his legs were shaking under him. "What were you *doing* up there?"

"There's a goblin," he stammered. The fury ran out of him, and he set his shoulder to the wall for support to his shaking knees. Hardly a hero, he: he had fled pell-mell down the stairs, and the goblin could come back down or call to its friends from the window at any moment.

"Then get out of here! There's a place I haven't looked—"

"Ela, give it up! Everyone's dead! The horses are out there. They know there's two of us! They'll find us. —Lord Sun—"

"I have to!" she whispered, and tore away from him.

"Ela!" he whispered furiously, but she was a wisp of cloak and shadows, headed for a door, another stairway, he had no idea. He took her advice and ran out the open door to the yard, where the horses were grazing on the grass that had sprung up in the half-buried cobbles.

"Aha!" rang out from some window, from the roof, he had no idea, nor waited to see in his reach after Lwi's saddle. A knife thumped into the ground beside his boot, stuck upright in the weed patch beside the cobbles. He jumped—he could not help it, and Lwi shied as he grabbed the reins. The bow was not strung. He snatched up the knife as his only gesture of defiance and looked up at the tower.

"Ah. Do you take my gift?" the goblin warrior called down. My gift, my gift, my gift, echoed off all the walls, loud as Lwi's hooves clattering on the pavings. Skory danced away, out of his reach, and he had visions of the goblin coming down the stairs and cutting off Ela's retreat. "And are you a thief, too?"

Thief, thief, thief, the echoes said.

"What harm have we ever done to you?" he shouted up through the echoes. "What do you want?"

Want, want, want, the echoes gave back, as Ela came flying from out the door.

"Ho!" the goblin shouted; "Witchling!" But Ela never stopped. She caught Skory's trailing reins as the goblin disappeared from the window, downward bound without a doubt. He drew Lwi after him, held Skory's reins while Ela climbed up to the saddle, and without a second glance over his shoulder, flung himself for Lwi's saddle.

"Witchling, witchling, witchling," the echoes were still saying, as they rode past the grisly warning on the poles, through the gateway and into the tangle of the woods again, where the horses had to strike a slower pace.

Then he cast an anxious glance over his shoulder, and saw Ela's face as she looked back at the vine-shrouded gates. It was not grief, not a child's bewilderment, but a cold, white-lipped fury.

"What can we do?" he asked. "How can we fight them?" He was willing to hear anything but pointless defeat, nothing done, nothing even learned about their enemy, and their enemy in control of the place they had come to find and despising all they could do.

She laid a hand on her breast, and said only, "It's *mine*, it's *mine*, and he knows it."

"What, the tower?"

"This." The hand was pressed to something beneath her collar, and she looked at him with a set face and a defiance that challenged him along with the goblin as she rode past him.

So it was *not* for her mistress she had been searching the tower. Karoly's sister was dead, if those skulls could tell the story. And he—

"Where are you going?" he asked.

"To make them regret it," was all she would say.

Their going was a hasty confusion of dark and branches by starlight. Leaves raked Tamas' shoulders as the horses struck out on a downhill and up again, on a ride in which any stir of brush might be goblin ambush, any twitch of the horses' ears might be the only alarm they would have. The witchling told him nothing—but, Tamas thought, nothing he had done back at the tower had deserved her confidence. The goblin had *let* him go: she might have bewitched the creature, or not, for all he knew—she might not know what had happened up there on the stairs and might ask herself how he had escaped, weaponless.

But it was not an hour to plead for trust. And counting her reticence and the fury he had felt in her glance, he began to ask himself whether she was in fact a white witch, whether in fact she needed help in which a fool would do very well—he had heard about *that* kind of sorcerer in gran's stories, too.

But how did one know the good witches from the bad? Ela moved by dark, in shadows, and by moonlight, and if that had not been a curse she had loosed against the goblin he never hoped to feel one. The horses' mad steadiness, jolting his exhausted, spinning senses, the goblin saying, "Run," as if it were a choice he had . . . its eyes looking into his, mad and malicious and amused with him and his plight . . .

Lwi stumbled, and the near fall and the slope beside him sent a chill through him. "The horses can't do any more!" he protested, with too much pride to add, Nor can I. He was crazed, trying to comprehend goblin games and witches, most of all for staying with her, and he began to think that his own staying might be more spell than reason.

"Not far now," she promised him.

But Not Far took them down a hill and along another and another, and maybe a third: he was drifting in nightmare corridors and remembering goblin footsteps somewhere along the second hill, in a forest darker than the night sky, Lwi panting as he moved.

Then he heard water out of the dark—their stream again, he thought; or he was dreaming still. He heard it nearer and nearer, until he saw Skory wading into it, Skory first and then Lwi dipping their heads to drink as they walked—he let out the reins and let Lwi drink as he could, never stopping, even yet—bewitched, as before.

"Have mercy," he pleaded. "This is foolish. What good to kill the horses? We've outrun the goblins. They aren't following us, Ela, for the god's sake—"

They were at the bank. She rode Skory further up before she stopped—but Lwi stayed on the bank to drink, no longer spellbound, as far as he could tell.

So they must have arrived, he thought, and slid down from Lwi's back, sore, and dizzy, and suddenly perceiving a stone wall and a gateway in the darkness of the nightbound trees. For one blink of an eye he feared they had ridden full circle back to the tower and into a trap, but at a second, he saw only an open gateway into, so far as he could tell, an overgrown ruin.

"Ela?" he said, but she was staring at the gate, simply staring. Lwi had had enough water, and he patted Lwi's sweat-drenched neck, and led him up gently to the grass that grew along the shore, while the mare wandered at will. This time he loosed the bow and the arrow case from the saddle; and looked around to learn in what precise place Ela decreed for their camp.

But she had vanished in that instant of inattention—through the gateway, into the ruin.

"Ela?" he asked the empty night, exhausted, lost, and suddenly outraged. He went as far as the dark doorway, and found no sight of her, listened, and heard no sound but the sighing of a cold night wind and the sudden jingle of harness as Skory shook her head.

So the girl wanted to slip away alone into the ruin after riding all day, finding her mistress murdered, and escaping goblins with something the goblins were looking for? Well and good. Maybe witches needed no sleep and no protectors and dined on moonbeams. He strung the bow in a fit of temper, set it and its arrow case against a man-sized lump of stone, and unsaddled and walked and rubbed the horses down—*there* were grateful creatures at least.

Afterward, in a calmer frame of mind, if no easier in conscience, he bent down at water's edge, cooled his face in water that chilled him to the bone—good water, clean water, that set him shivering as he washed and drank—but that was honest work that he had done, unlike some he could think of; honest work and honest sweat and trying to do the right thing.

He was chilled through. He took his bow and found a seat next to the wall, hugging his cloak about him against the night wind, and thinking that now that his stomach was quieter, he ought to try to eat—get into the packs and find something to eat for himself, since the girl would not deign to advise him where she was or what she was up to or when, if ever, she would come back.

But he had no real appetite left, and not to be pent anywhere or shoved anywhere, or bewitched off on another ride—that was all he wanted. It was enough to know there was food and water within reach, even if he was too exhausted to eat. He could sleep a moment, he decided. It was only his neck at risk, now. He need only shut his eyes and listen to the forest whispering in the wind.

"Men see so poorly at night," a goblin voice lisped, from the wall above his head. He flung himself to one knee, reaching for the knife.

The goblin leapt down with a light clash of metal as he reeled to his feet, drawing the knife—it was that near him. He heard the horses bolt and run.

"Well, well. Here we are again, and you threaten me with my own gift."

"It *is* you," he said, backing up a step, trying to clear the light-headedness that assailed him. *"Ela!"*

"Oh, hush, hush, man, she's not afraid of me. She should be, but she isn't. She's a great magician, like her mistress, don't you know? Undoubtedly greater. Ysabel wouldn't touch what she's taken up. Now Ysabel's dead, and her poor, slow-witted servant with her. I wonder how *she* will fare."

"E-la!"

"I tell you she won't hear you. She can't hear you."

It advanced. He stepped back again, giddy, keeping the knife between him and its owner—a wicked blade, with a backwards spine he could only guess how to use—but this creature most certainly knew, and it had the sword that matched it.

"Ungrateful wretch. Here." Jewels glittered in the starlight, in a black-nailed hand. Something thumped to the ground at his feet.

He was supposed to look down. He refused to take his eyes off the creature, who smiled at him, showing fangs, and leaned casually against the wall, long fingers, spiderlike, grazing the sword hilt at its side. "Oh, not at all trustful. Are we, thief? Lie to me, and all the time you were with the witchling. For shame, for shame."

"Where are the rest of you?"

"Of me? Why, altogether here, man, altogether where the

witchling is and isn't. —But witches are like that, nor here, nor there, most of the time. While you—" Another smile, close-lipped, but the fangs still showed. "You are most definitively here, young gentleman, in possession of my knife, and, by my graciousness, its sheath, and your head. And here am I, seeking *your* gracious hospitality. What do you say to that?"

It was hard for a cobwebby wit to follow the twists and turns of its converse, but it seemed foolish to attack the creature, more foolish to die in contest with weapons it knew, when it seemed extraordinarily enamored of its own cleverness, and he had no idea the measure of it. He took a breath, adopted a careless stance. "What do I say? —That you're a common bandit!"

"Oh, uncommon. A lord among my kind, and grossly inconvenienced by this girl, this fledgling, this would-be sorceress. So here we are, thief and liar, and bandits both."

"I'm no bandit."

"But thief and liar you admit to?"

"No."

Again the sharp-edged grin. "Azdra'ik is my name. And yours, man?"

"Tamas." He gave no more clues to his family or his friends than he must. Exchanging names offered a familiarity he had no wish to share with this creature. He only hoped Ela had heard him call out, and was working some magic to deliver him: meanwhile he could no more than play for time, and he wondered how many other goblin warriors were slipping around them in the forest dark. Lwi and Skory had made no further sound, but he did not think goblins could overwhelm the horses without at least some commotion.

"So, Tamas, and are you a wizard, too?"

"The greatest."

It laughed. "Audacious man. Why don't you go find the witchling? I'll wait here for you."

"Of course you will."

"No, no, my solemn word. You're free to go."

It meant to follow him to Ela, he was certain of it. But he did not know what else he should do, that might give him a chance, or even delay this creature more than a single pass of its sword; and he no more knew where Ela was than it did. Perhaps he could lead it a chase and raise enough noise that Ela would know where he was. Or maybe they had already caught her, and it was only a cruel joke the creature played. But he had no better offers for his life.

He caught up the bow and case, dived through the gateway into the shadow of the ruined wall, and found himself in a maze of brush and broken walls. His footsteps sounded louder than he liked on patches of exposed paving stones. He tried to keep silence, and now and again glanced back, afraid the creature was laughing all the while and following him.

He dared not call out. He feared she might answer, unaware of the danger. It was not even his intention to find her, only to raise enough noise for her to take some magical precaution—and for him to locate targets at more than arm's length, if the creature had companions slipping through this woods. He had an arrow against the bow. He was ready for treachery.

Then he saw Ela's pale hair past a screen of head-high brush, and stopped and caught himself against a truncated wall, trying to think what to do or whether to go to her—

But she stood so still, so unnaturally still, paying no heed to his footsteps on the stones and his moving in the brush. She was gazing down at her cupped hands—working some magic, he told himself, but nothing evident to him, nothing to his observation that might have dispelled the threat outside.

He glanced back the way he had come, wondering whether to go back and try to lead off the creature rather than disturb her working—but that seemed supremely ill-advised. And if despite all he could do, he was followed, they had already found her.

He came to her and stopped at respectful distance, trying to say calmly, "Ela. Ela, there's a goblin—in our camp—"

She might not have heard him at all. He saw the flash of glass and starlight in her hands, held the bow and the arrow in his left hand, touched her arm ever so slightly, then shook at her, when she remained, statuelike, completely oblivious to his touch. "Ela. A goblin. It's after us."

A flutter of her eyelids then—a moment that she looked straight at him. "No," she said, shaking her head, as if what he said were patently foolish. "No. Not here."

Perhaps, then, the wall did keep something out. Perhaps there was some magical reason the goblin asked him to find her, and perhaps it had been a mistake to come in here and disturb her magic. Maybe that was exactly what the goblin wanted. But there was nothing to do now but make her understand him. "It's out there with the horses. It followed us from the tower." He tried to sound sane and reasonable. Breath failed him. "It *spoke* to me. It told me to find you. What should I do?"

She seemed to have understood, then. And the amulet in her hands began softly to glow and cast a light on her face—a mirror, it was, a simple mirror. He remembered the goblin saying that her mistress would not touch what she had taken up . . . and he thought: This small thing?

Then a feeling of malaise tingled through the air, through the earth, through the soles of his feet and the nape of his neck and the palms of his hands. He heard the trees sighing in the woods and the water of the brook running, and a distant shouting, as if it came out of some hollow hall. Ysabel wouldn't touch what she's taken up, echoed in his ears, like voices from the tower—taken up, taken up, taken up—

The dark around them receded. They stood beneath the ghostly lamps and hangings of a great hall, and all around them men and women fled in fear. The floors and walls began to crack as light blazed through, brilliant as the sun.

Everything whirled about them. Suddenly a veiled woman

stood in this thundering chaos, her cloak and her robes cracking like banners in the winds that swept the hall. She looked full at them, at *him*, and pointed her finger, crying into the gale—
" . . . one and the same . . . One is all! Remember that, above all! There is always a flaw—"

The image shattered, with a sound of breaking glass. Shocking quiet followed, isolation and dark, ordinary night around them, an ordinary moon above the ruined walls and the brush. He discovered himself breathing, and his heart beating and the sighing of the wind moving without his will.

"Wizard!" Ela cried, tearing her arm free, and hit him with her fist. "Liar! Damned *liar*, get away from me! You touched it, *you* changed it—"

"No!" Too many accusations of falsehood had come his way tonight, too many confusions. "Anything that happened, *you* did. That *thing* you have—did." Words were coming too rapidly, and he could not get breath enough, in the sudden stillness of the air. She began to walk away from him and he caught her arm and held her perforce. "I've nothing—*nothing* to do with magic, or goblins, or this thing of yours! I don't know what you were doing, but there's a goblin the other side of the wall where the horses are, it's looking for you, and it says you've inconvenienced it—that that *thing* you have, your mistress wouldn't touch! He called her name. Ysabel. And he told me to find you, don't ask me what for—I didn't know anything else to do!"

Light shone through Ela's fingers, reflected on Ela's pale face—the rest was dark, and sighing wind. "My mistress wouldn't touch it," she echoed. "Then why did she hide it from everyone but me, why did she tell me to use it, did he tell you that? —Let me go! Where do you get the right to shout at me?"

"You said you were a witch!"

"I am!" Light reddened the edges of her fingers and made the illusion of bones within. "I brought us away from the tower, didn't I? I brought us here!"

"Did you rescue me, or was it the troll's idea? This is the second time that creature's let me go!"

"He's not a—"

"I don't care what it is. Karoly is *dead*! Your mistress is *dead*! Krukczy Tower is full of goblins, and now your mistress' tower is! The one waiting out there—wants you." He struggled to keep his voice down. "It says its name is Azdra—Zdrajka— something. It says—"

"Azdra'ik!"

Beyond belief. "You *know* him?"

The glow had all but died within her hand, leaving only night above them, and a plain piece of mirror when she opened her fingers, that reflected nothing but dark and moonlight. "This is *mine*. I have it! It can show me anywhere in the land. It can open magic to me. It can defeat them!"

"Then begin with the one that's been following us! If it gets the horses, we're afoot here with its friends, with lord Sun knows what next! Send *him* off, for a start!"

She seemed to have run out of words. The bit of silvered glass flashed in the moonlight, inert as its delicate chain that sparkled in her fingers. "Let me go," she said. "Let me go! You've already changed something, I don't know what. What more damage can you do?"

He released her arm. She eyed him balefully, then began to walk, back toward the gateway and the horses. He walked with her, with a stitch in his side and with the disquieting understanding that she was going indeed to confront this Zdrajka-goblin with her piece of glass, and he nocked the arrow and had another ready as he walked.

"Let me go first," he said, "and tell him I found nothing." Perhaps after all, he thought, lying was his best talent. But it was not fair tactics he expected, from a goblin; and it was not fair tactics he meant to use, with the advantage all to the goblin.

Ela might have heard him or might not: she kept walking,

and he saw her lips moving, shaping words that had no sound: That, he did not like: it might equally well be a magic to deal with him as with the goblin, so far as he knew, or blackest sorcery that might not care where it made its bargains.

But when they came to the gate, the horses were grazing peacefully in the moonlight, as if nothing had ever happened.

"Well?" she asked. "Where is he?"

"He *was* here," was all he could say—until, outside the gate, walking over the ground he and the goblin had occupied, he saw the glitter of jewels in the moonlight, and gathered up the sheath that belonged to the knife. "It *was* here," he said, showing it to Ela. "It was here and it left."

Why? was the next obvious question. But Ela only frowned and walked away in silence.

While the horses, that should have been off in the woods and the devil's own work to catch after their fright, might have had second thoughts about the grass growing in this spot, and hunger *might* have weighed more with them than goblin-smell—they certainly showed no signs of recent panic.

He could not answer that well for himself: he ached from running, he was ravenously hungry, which no one reasonably should be, who had just seen what he had seen. He was vastly relieved that the horses were all right; and beneath all that, he felt the complete fool. So far as he knew, Ela's magic *had* bespelled the creature, brought back the horses and secured their safety, and he had been unjust to lay hands on her and most of all to disturb what might have been a delicate and essential work of magic. He could no longer even swear that he had seen what he had seen either outside or inside the walls—it was slipping away from him, detail by detail, like a dream—but he did know that he found himself deeper and deeper entangled in what Ela would, and where Ela was going, and what Ela wanted.

He asked himself when and where he had passed the point

of no return, because he no longer knew how to ride away—not alone because he no longer knew the way home through these wooded hills. He desperately wanted a hope to chase—anything but a blind flight this way and that from successive disasters, anything but a return without answers and without help.

But, damn it all, if magic was the help Karoly had placed all his hope in, a waking dream did not change what was going on in this place, or get them help, or get him home again with any answers.

He thrust the goblin knife into its sheath and that into his belt, and went and sank down on his heels where Ela sat. The mirror was in her hands. It seemed to occupy her attention, quiescent as it was, and he waited a long time to see whether she was doing anything or only brooding on his company.

"Ela," he began finally, most respectfully, most courteously, he thought, "Ela, I want to know where we're going, and why, and what's ahead of us. I want to know why that creature left and why he asked for you and told me to find you. I want to know why master Karoly believed it was so important to talk to your mistress, but he could never tell anyone why; and I want to know why he rode past a goblin warning and never warned us what it was."

"Sometimes you can't," she said faintly.

"Can't what?"

"Can't break through a spell."

"Is that what happened? He wanted to and couldn't?" It opened a sudden hope for master Karoly's character. He wanted to understand Karoly's actions, even if it involved dark and damning things. But she looked away from him, evading his eyes the very way Karoly had done since his dreams began, and with gentle force he touched her knee and drew her attention back, with all the gentleness and patience he could muster. "Is that the kind of thing that happens?"

"Sometimes. Sometimes—else."

Oblique. Always oblique. She still evaded his eyes, even answering him.

"Like the goblin leaving? You made it leave?"

"I don't know." Her gaze roved distractedly about the wall of trees as if she were listening to something, to anything and everything in the world but his voice.

"What's out there, Ela?"

"I don't know."

'I don't know,' began to take on a thoroughly ominous ring—recalling Karoly and the goblin stone, and considering their present situation.

"Ela. Are we in danger?"

"I don't know." A sudden pale glance, starlit. A frown. "Yes. The moon. On the lake. There's danger. There's always danger."

There was no lake. It was a stream in front of them. "From where? What lake? What are you talking about?"

"The goblin queen."

He rocked to both knees on the cold ground. "Why should she be our enemy?"

Another wandering of Ela's eyes, about the sky, the stream-side. The leaves whispered louder than her voice. "Because. Because she is. Her kingdom—I don't know if it *appears*, or if it always is. But she can reach out of it, and this knows where she is." She held the mirror against her heart. "This always knows."

She looked so young—not the witchling now, but a frightened child, pale in the gibbous moon.

"And your mistress said to use this thing."

"My mistress said—if everything failed, if she wasn't there when I got back, that I should try to get help here."

My god, he thought. With no more than that instruction, the woman sent a girl off to Krukczy Straz? A great and powerful witch, Ela claimed to be—and maybe it had been her magic that lent him strength to ride, and not the first meal he had had in days. Maybe it had been her magic just now that had sent the goblin away, and maybe it was her magic that had waked him from the daze that had held him since Krukczy Tower—

But, lord Sun, was there not better hope for them than 'try'?

He asked, "Wasn't master Karoly supposed to come back with you?"

"Yes."

"So he was supposed to help you use this thing? He was supposed to know what to do? Is that what was supposed to happen?"

A glance aside from him, at the sky, at the wall, anywhere but his face.

God, he thought, murkier and murkier. He touched her arm gently and made her look at him.

"Ela. What would master Karoly have done with the thing, if he were here? Do you have any idea what that is?"

"Stop her."

"How would he do that?"

Her eyes slipped away from his.

"Ela?"

There was no answer. Their journey had been disastrous from home to the mountaintop—their canvas had ripped. They had had nothing but contention among themselves. And Karoly—had gone silent when he most needed to speak.

"Ela. If you're a great witch, can you say what you want to say? Can you answer me?"

She did look at him, a pale, distracted glance. The mirror in her lap began to glow with light as she brushed its surface, and she looked at him, truly looked at him.

"I saw a castle," he said. "We were there. Weren't we? I saw a woman. . . ."

"It was a long time ago. The chief of the goblins came here. Right in that very gateway—"

He glanced toward that gate, he could not help it—and the goblin was sitting on the wall, long legs a-dangle. "God!" he gasped, snatched up his bow and scrambled for his feet.

The goblin leapt to the ground. It landed with grace and arrogance, and swept them a bow.

"Well, well," it said, "not paying full attention, are we, young lady? —You truly shouldn't distract her, Tamas. Keeping us away takes constant thought, especially once we've made up our minds about a thing."

It wanted Ela—that was what it had continually claimed. He felt of the arrow he had ready, and laid it to the string. But it made an airy gesture, refusing such unfavorable battle.

"Oh, no, man, there's no need of that. I've merely come to watch."

To watch what? was the natural question. But he disdained to ask it, and the goblin laughed softly and made a second flick of the wrist.

"Ah, ah, ah, pricklish pride. It does lead us by the nose, doesn't it? —I'd advise you *give* me the trinket, witchling. Or at least put it away and don't use it."

"You killed my mistress," Ela accused it, standing at his elbow. "You killed her!"

"I?" The goblin laid a hand where its heart should be. "I by no means killed your mistress. We were always on the best of terms."

"You just happened by today," Tamas scoffed.

"I just happened? Ah, no. I knew. No sooner than a foolish woman dismissed this girl to Krukczy Straz, the ravens knew and gossiped on the housetop. The whole woods knew. Did not you?"

He did not take his eyes from the goblin. But he saw a flare of cold light in the very tail of his eye, and saw the goblin's face go grim and hostile.

"Forbear," it said, holding up its hand. "Forbear, foolish girl, *put it away!*"

"Did you kill her?" Ela's voice cracked like a whip. "Don't lie to me, don't dare to lie, ng'Saeich!"

"No." A short answer. The goblin's nostrils flared and the scale armor on his chest flashed with his breathing.

"*I* am the witch in Tajny Wood. Am I *not*, Azdra'ik ng'Saeich?"

"You. Are."

A silence, then. Tamas dared not turn to look. He felt ants walking up and down his spine and on his arms and felt his heart beating fit to burst. The creature would spring. He raised the bow, gauged the gusting wind.

But the goblin shrugged a shoulder into a spin half about and a mocking flip of the hand. "Ah, well, a new witch in Tajny Wood and a bit of broken glass. And what do you propose to do with it, pray tell? To order me about? Does that amuse you?"

The feeling was dreadful then. Tamas drew the bow.

"Put it away!" Azdra'ik exclaimed, his voice trembling, and turned full about, holding up his arm. "Put it away, young fool, do you even know what you're dealing with?"

The mirror, the goblin meant. And the goblin took no step closer—took two away, in fact, and turned full about a second time, pointing with a dark-nailed hand.

"That—fragment—is not a toy for your amusement, girl! That is nothing for a human whelp to handle in ignorance! Give it to me! *Give* it to me before you destroy yourself!"

"Leave us alone!"

"Man. Tamas, . . . this *thing* she holds—the witches of Tajny Wood have feared to use, and this *underling* proposes to make herself a power with it."

"You seem not to like that."

"Listen to me, fool! A mirror stands in the queen's hall beneath the lake, a glass taller than the queen is tall; and in it she sees what is and what may be, and she shapes what she wishes and deludes those that will believe. *That* is that shard and the magic of it, a shard from its edge, against that and against the queen. *That* is the power your young mistress proposes to oppose. A gnat, man, a gnat proposes to assail the queen of hell—and for her right hand, lo! Tamas, with his bow and his dreadful knife! Tell me—what will you do first, young witch?"

It was laughing at them, this creature, as it sauntered away toward the wall, the dark, and the brush. It vanished.

"I'm not sure it's gone," he said.

"He's not," Ela said. He looked at her, seeing anger, and fear. Her hands shone like candlewax in the fire they covered. "But he won't do anything. He daren't. He *can't.*"

He let the bow relax, caught the arrow in his finger along the grip. "It doesn't dare the gateway. I'd rather we moved there tonight."

She gave a furious shake of her head. "We daren't go back in there. Not tonight. No."

"Then why did we come here in the first place? What are we doing here?"

Her eyes slid away, toward dark, and nowhere.

"Is it because of the mirror? Is it something it can tell you—or something you don't want to meet?"

A frown touched her brow, as if he had said something curious.

"The mirror called me a wizard," he pursued the point, "and it was wrong about that. Did it show you the goblin?"

"No," she said, and walked away from him, a deliberate turning of her back. "But why should it?" floated back to him, supremely cold and disinterested in his challenge.

Maybe it was a spell that made her deaf to him. Maybe it was sheer arrogance. He inclined now to the latter estimation, thought: Be damned to her—and went to see whether the horses had come back unscathed.

Liar, she had called him. She and the goblin were evidently agreed on that point.

Well, then, admittedly he had not been scrupulous with the truth, with witches or goblins. Or trolls. He saw no obligation to have his throat cut. Or to have his land invaded and his kinfolk murdered by goblins. Or to die for nothing because some self-righteous slip of a girl was too cocksure *stupid* to take anyone's advice.

He found no harm with the horses, at least. He thought again of taking Lwi in the morning and riding west, just blindly westward, until he found the mountains to which these hills were the foothills; and he thought how Karoly had not been able to do what was right or sane either. Maybe his own hesitation was a spell; or only his good sense at war with his upbringing, that said girls were not safe wandering the wilds alone: for her part, of course, she would very surely hold him by magic or by any other rotten trick, because *she* would not saddle the horses. *She* was too fine to soil her hands, and *she* was too delicate to lift the tack about, but forget any other use he was—*she* was too wise to need what he knew.

He gave Skory's neck a pat and walked around her, with suddenly a most unpleasant notion he saw something in the tail of his eye. He walked behind her and around to Lwi's side, to steal a glance toward the wall without betraying that he had seen anything.

The goblin was back, sitting in the shadow, simply watching.

Damn, he thought, and turned his back on it, at wits' end, exhausted, robbed of appetite and, as seemed likely tonight, of sleep, by a goblin who made no more sense than Ela did. At Krukczy Straz he had known where home was. The troll had not even been that bad a fellow, give or take the want of regular meals—

But the memory of that roof-top brought a haze between him and the world and he was too tired to dwell on horrors. They twisted and became ordinary in his mind, an unavoidable condition of this land; and he found himself a place at the foot of a tree with his bow across his knees and his eyes shut, refusing to care what the witchling thought. She was awake. Let her watch. Let *her* worry.

But he had not succeeded in sleeping when Ela came back and made a stir near him, getting into the packs. He tried to ignore her, but what she unwrapped smelled of spice and sausage, and it was impossible to rest with that wafting past his nose: he gathered up his bow and, with a glance at the goblin still sitting in the shadows, he served himself a stale biscuit and a bit of sausage and sat down.

"Was Karoly your father?" she asked straightway.

"No." Appalling question. With *his* mother? The girl could have no idea. So much for witchcraft and farseeing.

"Someone in your house was a wizard."

"Karoly—just Karoly. And he's no kin."

"Or a witch," Ela said.

"No."

But gran leapt into his mind, gran, whose grave—

"There had to be someone," Ela persisted. "A cousin? An uncle?"

"There wasn't," he lied: god, he was growing inured to lies. He was surrounded with them. He had the most disquieting feeling if he looked toward the wall this moment, he would find the goblin staring back at him—

—mirror image, down to the arm on the knee. He shifted his posture, suspecting mockery in its attitude, and fearing suddenly that its sharp ears might gather every word they spoke.

"I'm no wizard," he muttered, lowering his voice to the

limit of hearing. "Master Karoly taught me, just simple things. Maybe he taught me a deal too much, maybe that was what you saw. . . ."

But gran was from over-mountain, from these very hills.

Gran had shown them little tricks, move the shell, find the coin—two young boys had been oh, so gullible, once, and gran had laughed in her solemn way, and said there was always a deceit, gran had called it. —Always look for the deceit, even in real magic.

Please the god, there was a deceit.

But the only deceit he could see was over there, by the wall, staring back at him.

"You were Karoly's student?" Now, *now* the girl wanted to talk, suddenly she was brimming with questions, worse, she had made up her mind to what she thought and there was no shaking it.

"He taught me letters. And how to name birds and trees. That was all. —It's listening to us, you know that."

"It doesn't matter. What you are, his kind can tell without your saying."

He muttered: "I'm the lord in Maggiar's second son. And my brother is his heir, if he's still alive. I'm *not* a wizard, none of our family have ever been."

"I *felt* what the mirror was doing. It answers you. It won't do that except for wizards."

"Well, it makes mistakes, doesn't it? It didn't see him—and is he there, or isn't he?"

She was not as sure of herself on the matter. Such as he could see her expression in the dark, she was not utterly sure, and he was relieved at that.

Gran was not a witch. Gran was gran, that was all.

(But the country folk to this day hung talismans about her grave, straw men and straw horses, sheaves of wheat—childless couples brought straw children to gran's graveside, and . . .

. . . burned them. He never had understood that part.)

"All the same . . ." she said, frowning. And took her blanket, flung it about herself and settled down with Skory's saddlebags for a lumpy pillow, having had the last word, and giving him no indication at all what he should do about the goblin.

There were worries enough to keep his eyes open, if they had come singly, if the whole whirling chaos of them had not exhausted him. The suspicion of gran was the final straw, the absolutely overwhelming weight on his mind, and, back at his chosen resting place, while the girl slept, he began against his will to rehearse memories, gran's friendship with Karoly, gran's possets and potions—gran's staying up all night. One could see the light in her window, late, later than a boy could keep his eyes open—but was that incontrovertible evidence of witchcraft?

He remembered the day she died—and the storm and the lightning, and the people and the horses all drenched, lit in the flashes, while they rode back from the burial—the rain and the bitter cold. He and Bogdan had taken chill, and their mother had had a fierce argument with their father, giving them hot tea and vodka, wrapping them in blankets—their mother saying . . .

. . . "This is her weather. God, when's morning? When will it be morning?" And their father: "Be still!" But the vodka had woven through his wits, and hazed everything. Their mother had said something else, that their father had shushed, and their father had said, "I never knew her. The god knows she was no mother to me. But she loved the boys."

And he had thought, half-asleep then and sleep-haunted now, Gran was gran, that's all, gran loved what agreed with her, gran would ride out with anyone who'd ride with her—she loved the open sky, she said—she and Karoly used to—

He did not want to think about that. He twitched and shifted position, but he kept seeing gran and Karoly grinding herbs, gran and Karoly riding in the gates one early dawn

. . . gran being so long a widow, people talked, but people somehow looked past the indiscretions. . . .

While grandfather Ladislaw had been alive, there had surely been no such suspicions, god, it was not *true*, his father could not be Karoly's bastard, wizardry would have out, would it not, if gran were a witch—Karoly most certainly being a wizard? That was the way he had always reasoned, when the unwholesome thought had nudged him—but *no* one thought twice about it, no one ever thought, the thoughts just—

—slid right past it, like water around a rock. Like questions around a wizard.

He felt cold inside, false and hollow, as if he might not be who he had always believed he was, as if the lineage of Maggiar might not be his at all, and his uncles and his cousins— Who knew in what degree they were really related, any of them? If Karoly was in fact his grandfather, and Ladislaw no kin at all, then his father had no right to the lands or his house. If Karoly was in fact his grandfather . . . had his father known, and faced Karoly every day of his life?

But it was ridiculous, patently ridiculous. No one in his house had taken it seriously or put themselves out about the gossip—

—As if, lord Sun, gran being widowed and Karoly and gran being mostly discreet about their nighttime rides, no one wanted to say anything, no one had ever *dared* say anything. Mother would never put up with unseemly talk in the house, Mother would never tolerate a breath of impropriety, everyone knew that, certainly never any scandal touching the household—and Father having not a shred of magic about him . . .

Everyone had known so many things without knowing them, without anyone taking rumors to heart, without anyone ever blinking at an association that, however flagrant, never—somehow—seemed to be anyone's business.

God, he did not want to think about it now. He saw the

horses eventually asleep, forgetful of the goblin presence near the wall, and if an old campaigner like Lwi had smelled out the situation and decided to rest, a tired young fool might be excused the fault. He tried to chase away the worries, angrier and angrier that Ela had first upset his stomach and then assumed *he* would watch while she slept. Probably she made it all up on purpose, so he *would* stay awake.

He saw the goblin's head fallen forward, now, as if even the goblin found it too much. Now, surely, he thought, he could watch the creature a while, and if it was no trick, then maybe he dared catch a wink himself.

But before that happened he heard a bird begin to sing; and another; and he sat there while the goblin slept on, dark head bowed, braids hiding his face.

So in this country such things were not nightmare, they lasted unabashed into sunrise.

And this one feared no harm from them—that seemed evident, whatever its reason.

8

Gracja had to rest and Nikolai stayed on her back, sleeping, Yuri hoped, but Nikolai had been very quiet, scarily quiet, this last while, and he hesitated between touching him to be sure he was all right or letting him sleep if it meant he was out of pain.

He decided the latter, weary as he was himself—his feet ached, his legs ached . . . he stopped counting there, except the stinging scratches he had gotten from brush. He was not cold. His rests were too short and the going too hard to let him chill, and he had given Nikolai his cloak, because Nikolai's wounded hand was growing colder and colder, even while Nikolai's face was warm to the touch.

"I'm fevered," was the last thing Nikolai had said, the last thing that made sense, at least. Something about goblins and trolls, and the folly of trusting one.

There had not been another sign of Krukczy, but thank the god and the lady, Yuri thought, there had been none of goblins so far, either; and the sun was coming up now, as he tugged at Gracja's reins and coaxed her to move. Zadny was already off down the trail, too fast, always too fast—he had given up worrying that he would lose the dog, Zadny came back when he had gone too far, and he just slogged along at the best pace he could until Gracja had to rest again.

His side hurt. He tugged Gracja up one hill and down the

other, with never a sound out of Nikolai.

But Zadny had been out of sight a very long time now, and he was beginning to wonder and to fret, and finally, though he hated to make a sound in the woods, he called out, "Zadny!"

Echoes came back. "Zadny—Zadny—Zadny . . ." And Nikolai moaned and lifted his head.

"He's just been gone a long while," Yuri said, and went back to Nikolai's side and touched his face. Nikolai was burning hot. "Do you want a drink, sir?"

"Find the damn dog," Nikolai said fuzzily. "Something's the matter."

He did not know whether that advice was fever-inspired or not, but it was his own sense of priorities. He got back to the fore and led Gracja along the base of a wooded hill, along a leafy track, and a muddy spot.

A horse had trod there. So they were still on the right track. He pulled at Gracja, wanting her to hurry, thinking—if only they had made enough time during the night, if the ones they were following had made camp and slept, then they might overtake them, and they might find help in time for Nikolai—

Zadny came panting back, just close enough to catch sight of a shaggy flash of his tail through the brush. Then he yipped and was off again. Maybe, Yuri told himself, struggling to pull Gracja along faster, faster. Zadny was excited, Zadny might have found something—please the god it was not just a rabbit hole.

He was watching his feet, trying not to trip, his arm feeling near pulled out of its socket by Gracja's resistance, but he glanced up to see where the slope upward was leading, saw stones and vines through the trees, saw . . .

"We've found somewhere," he breathed, holding the ache in his side. "Master Nikolai, there's a gate—"

He could see it clearly in the dawn. He saw Zadny dart into it and out and back again into some courtyard. It looked dreadfully deserted. If *he* owned a tower in the middle of a forest full of goblins, *he* would not leave its gates standing open or let its walls grow over with climbable vines like that.

"Master Nikolai," he said quietly. "I think you'd better stay here and let me see what's inside."

"Doesn't look too good," Nikolai murmured. So he was aware of what was going on around him. Yuri patted his shoulder, eased his bow and his arrow case free of Gracja's saddle and said,

"I'll be right back."

But he strung the bow and he took out an arrow before he slipped up to the gateway and had a look.

God.

He shut his eyes and looked away, and had to look back, at the poles, and the dreadful skulls. He felt cold all over, and his heart was thumping from the shock.

Goblins, he thought.

And then he realized there were two skulls, besides the animals, and he remembered they were following two people, and his knees began to shiver under him, and his heart to thump harder. He did not want to worry Nikolai until he knew something—he could not think that those grisly bones were his brothers, he refused to believe that could be them. His teeth chattered, he was so scared, so he clenched his jaw, and, shoulders to the wall, eased inside, behind the cover of a bush that should never have been allowed to grow right next to the gate. His father would have such a sorry castelan horsewhipped, his father would say, his father would never let a place get into this condition . . .

Nothing stirred. Zadny was gone, somewhere, and nothing had eaten *him*, yet, or if it had, it had been quiet about it. He spotted another place to hide and slipped toward it, did not feel comfortable in that one, and went for a second nook, closer still. There he waited for Zadny to come back, waited what felt like a very long time, long enough almost to start thinking again about those awful bones and wanting and not wanting to look at them to see if there was anything familiar in them.

So he moved again, because if Zadny would only come back, so that he could get his hands on him and be sure Zadny was not going to do something stupid, like start barking, he urgently needed to get back to Nikolai, who was waiting alone out there.

More bad yard keeping. Maybe goblins had raided the place, but if they had not broken the house door down, they had probably climbed right up the huge vines that led to that open window . . .

He had a sudden spooky feeling that something might be watching him. He held his breath and wanted out of sight of that window, looked for a place to go, and ran for the side of the tower itself.

Then he heard something like claws on stone, that might be Zadny or might not be. He was furious at the dog. Come out here, he wished Zadny; the faintest whistle might bring him, if he was in the hall—or it might bring something else.

If the place *was* deserted, he thought, and the goblins were gone, the same as they had left the other tower, then he and Nikolai might be safe here tonight. They might find a bed for Nikolai and doors to shut, maybe not the outer one, that would betray their presence here; but some inner one, maybe the lowest rooms where they would never think to search, and Nikolai could rest—

His brothers might have thought that. He had followed two horses this far, and if they had seen the same thing in the courtyard that he had seen, they might have ridden out of here on the instant, the way they would if they could—or they could even have done what he proposed to do, and bolted themselves inside.

A dog yipped, and yelped into silence. His heart bounced

into his throat and sank again. He thought, I should get out of here. Now.

But if it were not his brothers—if it were *not* his brothers—why had Zadny led them in here, what would keep Zadny occupied here, when Zadny would hardly quit the trail to eat or sleep?

The goblins were surely gone. The goblins in the tower in the mountains had made no secret of their being there.

He eased forward, then stopped, at the clatter of a horse in the courtyard behind him, saw Gracja, with Nikolai upright in the saddle and holding his sword in his left hand, the god only knew how he had drawn it. Gracja woke echoes in the place, a slow clatter of hooves as he rode in, and Yuri held his place, shivering, thinking, If there's anything here, they'll see him and he can't see me. Father Sun, what's he doing? Is he thinking about that? Nikolai's too clever to ride in here making all that noise . . .

Then he understood what Nikolai was doing. Nikolai had a fool boy overlong inside this place, and Nikolai was making a racket and putting himself right in the middle of the courtyard, to turn up whatever was hiding here, maybe to create havoc enough to let a stupid boy get out of here if he had run into trouble.

There was the scuff of a footstep, inside. Yuri glanced at the door, looked frantically back at Nikolai, stepped out as far as he dared, trying to signal him—but there was a bend of the wall in the way—and whoever was inside was coming out.

Someone was going to get an arrow in his back the moment he went for Nikolai. Yuri lifted the bow and drew in the same motion, taking calm breaths, the way one had to, who expected his hand and eye to be steady, and he did not think about killing—never think about that, Nikolai had said, just aim.

He drew his arm back, full, as a gray-cloaked figure came

out the door, only at the last moment remembering goblins were not deer, goblins might wear armor and the back was a hard place to find a target . . .

But Nikolai was looking at the creature, and Nikolai was not even lifting the sword—Nikolai said, "You bastard," and slid down off Gracja's back.

Then the creature said, "Where are the boys?" in master Karoly's voice. . . .

Yuri held the arrow steady. Magical creatures were full of tricks, and they might look like what they were not, so he had heard. But he did not fire, even when master Nikolai fell, the sword clanging to the dirt-covered cobbles.

The might-be master Karoly hurried to him. Yuri saw white hair beneath the hood, and master Karoly's aged hands, even Karoly's frowning face. But he did not believe it until he saw the old man trying to help Nikolai, and then he knew it was Karoly. Then he let the bow down and came to help.

Master Karoly looked around, startled. "Damn you! What in hell are you doing here?"

"A goblin shot him. I think it could have been poisoned."

"It didn't need to be," master Karoly said, and turned his attention back to Nikolai, swearing as he felt over Nikolai's neck and shoulder. Yuri kept quiet, standing there with his bow in his hands while master Karoly unfastened Nikolai's collar and felt of his heart and his head. "The goblins left us damned well nothing," master Karoly said, to him, Yuri supposed, and he waited anxiously for orders. "I don't suppose you've got blankets. Or a pot."

"Yes, sir." He went and got them from Gracja. And the rest of the herbs Krukczy had found. "The troll gave us these. He made tea with them."

"Troll, is it?" Master Karoly's face was drawn and strange as he snatched the things he had brought. "Troll be damned. Lucky if he lives the day."

"Don't say that!"

"Lucky he's alive this long." Master Karoly started pulling at Nikolai's buckles, trying to get the armor off, and he was being too rough about it.

"Let me," Yuri said, and got the ties that held the sleeve on, while Karoly took his knife and cut off the bandage Nikolai had tied around the outside.

"Damn, it's stuck to it. Get that pot, get some water."

"I've salve—"

"Not for this you don't," Karoly said. "Move, young fool! We need a fire, and the god knows what it'll bring, but there's no damned choice—don't stand there with your mouth open waiting for flies! Move!"

"Yes, sir," he breathed, and grabbed the pot. Zadny was barking again, waking echoes inside. "Where's the water, sir?"

"In the back of the yard!" Karoly snapped at him. "Where would you expect a well? —And, boy, . . ."

He stopped and turned on one foot. "Sir?"

"—Shut that damned dog *up*, will you?"

The goblin watched them make a fire, the goblin watched them make breakfast, the goblin watched them eat it, and Tamas glowered at it. His head was throbbing, his eyes felt full of sand, and only motion kept his mind from straying down the same unpleasant and useless paths it had followed all night.

"What do we *do* about it?" he asked.

Ela merely shrugged. "Let be."

"Are we staying here?"

Ela shook her head.

He kept his temper and asked the next question. "Are we leaving now?"

Well, then, Ela would not talk. *He* would not talk. He got up on legs that felt wooden, limped over to the horses in a temper and began to saddle them to leave this place, Ela nothing gainsaying.

The goblin turned up next to him, at the edge of the woods, making the horses nervous, watching him as if *he* were the object of its intention.

"You wanted to see her," he said to it, hauling on Lwi's girth. "All right, you've seen her. She doesn't want to talk to you. Why don't you leave?"

"She's not reasonable," it said. "Or wise."

He leaned on the saddle, looking across it as the goblin stood, arms folded, foot tucked, leaning against a tree. "Not wise—because she won't listen to you?" Humor failed him. "What do you want? Why do you destroy things? Is it just your nature?"

"You mistake us."

"Mistake you! Did I mistake what I saw in the courtyard? Or on the roof of Krukczy Straz?"

"I'm i'bu okhthi. That's itra'hi work."

Goblin babble, to his ears. He glared across Lwi's rump and rested his arm on it. But only a fool turned down knowledge. Master Karoly used to say so. So he overcame his headache and his temper and advanced a surly, "So?"

"Itra'hi aren't my kind, man."

"I'm sure it made a difference to my brother. I'm sure it made a difference to her mistress. They didn't introduce themselves. They didn't exchange formalities."

"They're not the brightest."

"And you are."

"Are you a horse? I think not. One has four feet. It's easy to tell the difference in your kindreds. Easy in ours, if you have half a wit."

"Are you saying you're something different than these—whatever you call them?"

"Flat-tongued human. Indeed, different as you from your

beasts. One sends and they do. One doesn't talk to them. One doesn't deal with them. They're dogs. The i'bu okhthi are clearly *civilized*."

"God." He turned his back on the creature, turned to Ela, sitting on the margin of the stream, and said, "We're ready."

But when he looked back to the goblin—only trees were there, and not a leaf stirring to mark where it had been.

"Butchers," he said after it, hoping it did hear. "Murderers. You loose your hounds to do your work, what's the difference? What's the damned difference, tell me that!"

"Don't," Ela said, behind him when he had not heard her move. His heart jumped.

"Don't what?" He was still angry—with her, now that Azdra'ik was out of sight. "Don't ask what happened to my brother? Don't ask where we're going?"

"There." She nodded at the gateway she had not been willing to pass a second time last night. She was bringing the packs. Ela—was bringing the packs they had been using, practical girl: he was astounded.

"Thank you," he said, not with his best grace, and tried it again, with a sketch of a bow, after he had taken them: "Thank you."

"It's not a safe place," she said. "There's a woods past the second gateway. People go in and don't come back. My mistress said she wasn't sure it has another side, or not always the same side, if you can't see the path."

Three thoughts in a row. Twice amazing.

"Can you?"

She lifted her chin slightly, frowning, and said, "Of course. Can't you?"

He did not understand for a moment, or care to: he was exceedingly weary of her moods and her offenses. Then he realized it was the wizard business again, *and* an accusation of lying.

"No," he said, and then (he could not help it) had a look toward that gateway to see if he *could* see anything. "There's nothing."

She went on frowning, while he tied the packs to Skory's saddle and gave her a hand up.

He cast a second glance towards the woods as he rose into Lwi's saddle. And there was still nothing that he could see from that vantage.

She started Skory off, and he followed her, thinking that here was one more choice made, that, dangerous as it might be to try to go back from here, it was going to be worse hereafter.

"Where are we going?" he asked. "Are just the two of us going to go up and knock on the queen's gate and say Shame on you, or what are we going to do, for the god's sake?"

"Banish her," Ela said. "Unweave her spells."

We're both mad, he thought. He thought: What if I *were* Karoly's grandson, and not Ladislaw's? What if, after all, Karoly's gone and her mistress is and we're all that's left for everyone else to rely on?

What if we were? We wouldn't know. We wouldn't know unless we turned around and came back, and then it would be too late, wouldn't it?

They passed beneath the arch. They rode a weaving course through brush, around piles of rubble, past the walls that had been rooms and vaults and hallways. There was still no path, only half-buried paving-stones, through which weeds and brush grew up. There was no magic. He waited to see something happen.

"My mistress' grandmother lived here once," she said, in answer to nothing. Or maybe it was part of her last answer. "She was born here."

"What was this place?"

"Hasel."

"Hasel!" But it was a strong place, a place full of people. His dream of last night came back, when he was wide awake, people and disaster, and stones riven with light.

"Do they know about Hasel, over the mountains?"

"My—" —My grandmother told me about it, he had begun to say. Gran had relatives here. God. What if it *were* true? And all those people last night . . . they're dead, dead as gran. The stories were yesterday in his mind, forests and fields and villages where people lived and went about their lives.

"Your—?" she prompted him, but he was not ready to talk to her about gran, or to trust her that much.

"What happened to it?" he asked.

"What happened to it? The mistress here died. The people here died. Ages ago. Hundreds of years ago. If they know about Hasel, don't they know that?"

He heard her, and it sank right to the pit of his stomach, refusing reason. Nothing gran knew could be that long ago. It was some other Hasel. Or the things gran had said she had seen were only stories gran told—only lies.

He might be Karoly's grandson. And now for all he knew gran had lied to him about this place. Too many things were shifting, that he had never doubted in his life—while beyond the farther arch he saw a forest that the witchling called dangerous, a gateway that showed only green shadow and the trunks of aged trees.

"What happened here? Was it a war?"

"With the goblins. When the mirror broke."

"That mirror."

"This mirror. Mistress had it in Tajny Tower; and the goblins killed her and killed Pavel but they couldn't find it and they couldn't find me."

"Who was Pavel?"

"Just Pavel. He came from Hasel when it fell. And he was never right after, mistress said. But he would have fought them when they came. He would have." There came just the least wobble to Ela's voice, true distress. But he was thinking more about what she had said, and about finding her in a lie, as they rode through the archway, as the horses' hooves rang on the threshold of the forest, and went thereafter with the soft scuff of fallen leaves. Wind sighed above them, and morning sun dappled the ground. It did not look so terrible a place, not to left nor right nor straight ahead. The horses certainly took no alarm—Skory most irreverently snatched a mouthful from a bush as they passed, and ate as they walked.

He considered whether to challenge Ela. And decided. "You said Hasel fell a hundred years ago."

"Hundreds."

"So how could this servant of your mistress' be from Hasel? That can't be true."

She frowned and seemed to think about that a moment. "I don't know, that's what she said."

"Hundreds of years ago?"

"Witches—can be that old. I think she was."

"How old are you?"

"I'm not sure . . . I think, I think maybe fifteen."

God, she was hardly older than Yuri. Than *Yuri*, for the god's sake. And had this laid on her?

"Where did you come from?"

"From Albaz. I think from Albaz. Mistress got me when I was very small. I thought she was my mother when I was a baby. But she wasn't."

After silence it was a torrent, in a silence so profound the whispering of the leaves and the horses' movements were the only sound. He thought it sad she had mistaken something as vital as that, and not been sure even where she had been born. At least, with all the confusion she had set in him . . . he knew who his parents were, and what his home was.

"Or maybe I *was* hers," Ela said, after a moment more of riding, in the whisper of leaves under the horses' feet. "It wouldn't matter. —Who was your mother, if she wasn't a witch? —And how old are you?"

"Seventeen. And my mother isn't a witch. She wouldn't approve of witches."

"Why?"

"She just wouldn't. She's very much on things being—solid. She wouldn't want to think about goblins. She—" —never liked gran's stories, he thought to himself. She was afraid of gran.

Gran *wasn't* like everybody else, was she? Nobody did say no to her.

God, maybe nobody could.

Maybe, he thought, maybe I could have learned magic from master Karoly, if he had wanted to teach me—but if he could have taught me . . . why didn't he?

"Ela. *Why* didn't Karoly stop the goblins from attacking us?"

She looked at him, across the distance between their horses. "What?"

"The goblins that attacked us. Why didn't master Karoly stop them? He was with us, he saw the warnings. Why didn't he stop us?"

Ela cast a look ahead, as if she were looking at something a thousand miles away.

"Ela. Why. Didn't. He?"

"Pardon?"

"Why didn't master Karoly stop us from that road? Why didn't he work magic and protect us?"

"Why didn't *you*?"

"Because I'm not—because I couldn't. Whatever I am, I never learned, because *he* never taught me. Why can't you answer a plain question? You were there, weren't you? Why didn't *you* warn us?"

She shook her head. The air around them seemed unnaturally still and heavy. He had thought the frowns were arrogance.

Or anger. But *he* felt uneasy now. It seemed the sunlight was less ahead. And if there was a path here he could not discern it.

"Ela?" he asked, because the spookiness of the place made him think about that road. Or maybe thinking about the road made him remember ambush too vividly. "How did Karoly do nothing to warn us?"

"Because—because the magic wanted it."

"Whose magic? Goblin magic?"

A shake of her head. "No one can know. No one can know, when magic fights magic. It could have been anyone, it could have been my mistress. It always could be anyone. Contrary magic can go anywhere. You can't tell what will happen."

'It always could be anyone.' It sounded like Karoly.

"Sometimes," Ela said, "sometimes you can't avoid things because you don't even know if you did them. Sometimes you're afraid not to do something. My mistress said—said Karoly might make things worse, she wasn't sure he should come at all, but she couldn't wait any longer. You don't know whose idea it was—her magic or the queen's. She called him, all the same. And it turned out—it turned out the way it did."

"And our going now? We don't know where, or why, but we're just going?"

"To find the center of the woods," she said, "but I don't know whose magic is leading us. I don't know who's stronger."

That was not at all a comforting thing to hear. "We're going against the queen of all the goblins and you wonder whose magic is stronger? Ela, you're not—" —Not as damned good as you think, he thought, in Nikolai's way of saying.

But was not he going where she led? And had he not reasoned half a score of times that if he had any good sense he would have gone home? And where was he now?

Looking about him at the trees, at a woods pathless to his eyes—where, indeed, was he?

"Not just me," she said faintly, "it's all the witches of the

Wood. I may be the only chance they have. And I think we should go and try—because I think that, that's all. Everything they've done and everything she's done, I'm what it comes down to—so I *am* the greatest witch in Tajny Wood, do you understand? And I don't know whose magic brought you, but neither can the queen. Neither of us can know whose magic is working."

"Then what good is it, if no one can tell what will happen?"

"But things change. And if you do something small, it could be because of something large—and if you do something very large, you'd better know what you're doing, that's what my mistress said."

How do you *do* something very large? was the question that leapt to mind. If he were Karoly's working, if what she said was at all true or sane, then he wanted to challenge the situation and *do* something magical—please the god, that could fail outright; or prove whether he had any magic at all in him. If he was at all a wizard he could magic up an incontrovertible proof, could he not?

But then—if magic worked the way she said—one could never know. Was that not what she had just said—in all her reasoning: there's never a way to know?

Where had the damned goblin gone, and what was it up to? Bearing messages to its queen?

And why had Karoly never told him, if he was a wizard? And why had Ela said what she had said, when all this time . . . she would or could say nothing?

Has something happened? he wondered. Has something somewhere changed? And is it our magic or theirs that's brought us into this place?

ell of a wakening. Dark and fire and something clanking in his ear. Shadows on stone ceiling. Dull pain. And that damned dog. Nikolai put up the hand that worked and shoved it away. Karoly leaned over him. For a moment he had trouble sorting it out. But the images lingered in his vision.

"Well, well," Karoly said. "Good afternoon, master huntsman."

"Damn you," he murmured. *"Where were you?"*

"Afoot, as happens. While you had a horse to ride on. At least a pony. Followed the dog, young Yuri says. And doesn't know where his brothers are, except he hopes they got away, he was following them in company with a troll, and he hopes they aren't the skulls in the courtyard." Karoly slipped a hand under his head and stuffed a wad of blanket behind him, then went to the fireside and poured something, which he brought back. "Drink this."

"It smells like stable sweepings."

"It's been a little through the damp, just drink it and stop complaining. You're alive. That's more than some of us can say, isn't it?"

He drank it, sip by nauseating sip. The dog had gone somewhere—where the boy was, he hoped. "Where's Yuri?"

"Asleep," Karoly was putting jars in a sack, scores of little jars, all over the table. And scattered powders and leaves and herbs. Nikolai finished the cup and set it on his chest, looking at the ceiling of what he supposed was the hall in the tower he had fainted in front of, and a fire that was not a good idea, if there were goblins about.

"Is this your sister's place?" he asked when Karoly took the cup.

"It was."

He recalled the skulls in the courtyard, and gave the old man latitude for rudeness. He tried to think ahead of things, tried the fingers of his wounded arm to see if they worked, and they did, enough to serve. But whatever tea Karoly had just served up was the same sort as the troll's, so far as his head could witness: he could count the beats of his heart, thump, thump, thump, louder than the crackling of the fire, louder than the old man sitting with his hands between his knees and his fingers weaving cat's-cradles with a bit of yarn.

He thought of slender fingers, the same game, the same tuneless humming . . . thought of the lady gran, by the fireside, the lady gran looking up at him with dark, dark eyes, and saying, "Aren't we the curious one? Spying, are we? Do you know what happens to boys who spy?"

"I was looking for Stani," he had said—to go hunting, as he recalled. Stani and he had used to do that in those days, when Stani was a gawky young man and he had been—

He had been—

"You're often about with my son," the lady gran had said. "What do you do in the woods, you? Watch the birds?"

"Yes," he had said. And:

"Look at me." The lady caught his eyes and he could not look away. A long while later she ceased to frown, and he could breathe again. "You have no lies. That's remarkable. I don't think I've ever met a boy who wouldn't lie. Are you loyal to Stani?"

"Yes, lady," he said.

She said, "You're a clever boy. Too clever to catch at lies. Don't spy on me again. Do you hear?"

"Yes, lady," he had said. And all the while watched the patterns that she wove. . . .

Karoly had said, "Let the boy go, Urzula." Urzula had been her name. But no one ever called her that. She was the Lady from the day the Old Lord had his fall until the day she died: only then had Stani become the lord and his wife Agnieszka became lady over Maggiar, and Stani had been a man with three sons by then.

The same weaving as the lady gran. He had not seen Karoly do that in years.

"What is that?" he asked muzzily, the question he ached to ask the lady—but she was dead. She had died in the storm, and it had rained continually until she was in her grave—a cold and comfortless rain, with lightnings and thunder . . .

"What do you imagine it is?" Karoly asked. The firelight caught Karoly at disadvantage, cast his face grim and his hair fire-colored. The fingers caught another loop. A cage, Nikolai thought, for no reason. A trap.

"I don't know." The years had taught him to lie, at need. "Where's the boy?"

"Asleep. He's exhausted."

"What about Bogdan and Tamas?"

"I don't know."

"Well, where were you? Where have you been the last two days?"

"Three. It's afternoon of the third."

"Where the hell were you?"

"My horse bolted," Karoly snapped. "I fell off. I went for help. As of yesterday—there wasn't any here. Is that enough?—" Zadny broke out barking again, and barrelled through the room, oversetting a bottle from the table. "Dammit!"

Zadny was scratching at the door, furiously. Nikolai bethought him of his sword, and felt for it, as Karoly abandoned his cat's-cradle and stood up.

Nikolai asked: "Where does that lead?"

"The cellars."

"Master Karoly?" Yuri stumbled from around the corner, wiping his eyes, his hair tousled. "Master Nikolai?"

"Hush," Karoly said, went and gathered up a staff standing against the door. Nikolai tried to get up, feeling around him for his sword. Yuri had his bow in hand, and strung it.

"Hush!" Karoly said again, and Zadny whimpered into silence. One could hear something being dragged, slowly, slowly, step at a time.

"It's the troll," Yuri whispered. "It's Krukczy!"

"Krukczy, is it?"

"Where's my sword?" Nikolai hissed, but Karoly shot the bolt back and shoved the door open.

It was a troll, that was sure. It looked as if someone had deposited a brush heap on the steps: it stood there covered with twigs, with two great eyes in the shag of its mane. And Zadny, loyal hound that he was, leapt into its arms, licking it and wagging his tail.

"That's Krukczy, for sure," Yuri said.

"Oh, *hell*," Nikolai breathed, sank back against the support of the corner and watched the troll and the hound come inside.

The sun was a green brightness in the canopy. "I never saw trees so tall," Tamas said, and added, "I never heard a forest so quiet," because there was not the least sound now but their movement, not the sound of birds or insects, not the scamper of a rabbit across the leaves. "Do you still see a path? I don't."

"I can see it," Ela said, following whatever she had been following, and for all her claims that he had wizardry of his own it only seemed to him a spookier and spookier place, a place that gave him a feeling—he could not quite surround the idea with a thought—that the woods had no definite edges from here. That was a peculiar kind of impression to have, as if it could be different from inside than out. But that was the way he saw it. And it looked darker ahead than anywhere left or right, while Ela steadfastly maintained she knew her way, and that when they got to the right place, she would know it, and use the mirror, and have all the magic of the woods at her command. The horses trod a brown mottled carpet, the leaves of many summers, and the trunks of the trees were huge beyond anything he had ever seen—as if they and the horses had shrunk or the scale of the world had changed. Only the dead leaves were of ordinary size, and very thick, as if winds seldom reached here. The horses trod carefully in places where the packed leaves concealed uneven slopes or hid the roots of trees—the ground was full of deceptions and traps. And from green above them, there gradually seemed more brush and tangles, in a premature twilight that persuaded the eye that the sun was setting.

But it could not be. It had only just been noon, and they rode now in such shadow that it seemed the sun itself had failed, or the hours had slipped away toward dark and night in furtive haste. The eye believed it. The body did. Tamas found himself fighting a yawn, and arguing that it was not that late, that he was sleepy from too long last night goblin-watching. With Lwi walking sedately at Skory's tail in this tangled undergrowth, with Ela sunk in thought or magic the while, he found it harder and harder to keep his eyes open. His body swayed to Lwi's gentle motion. Why resist? the leaves seemed to whisper.

"How long do you suppose to sundown?" he asked, if only for the sound of his own voice above the sleepy sigh of leaves. "I can't think it's that late."

"I don't know," Ela murmured. He had only her back for a view, but a downhill slope encouraged Lwi to overtake Skory, step by slow step, so that for a while they rode side by side. Ela herself repressed a yawn, the back of her hand to her mouth, and he shook his head, because it made him have to.

"I can't keep awake," he said. "It's this place. It's this woods. Damn!" A third yawn. It was beyond foolish. He shook his head.

"It's very old," Ela said. "That's all. It's an old place. Mistress said—"

She stifled a yawn of her own and he could not resist. It was ridiculous and frightening at once. The shadow was like a blanket coming down on them, and the air beneath the aged trees should have been cold with that shadow, but it had no feeling at all. He could not remember now what their immediate aim was, but he recalled it was important and they dared not stop— there had been too many deer and too many wolves, and he had given his bow to his brother, back in the yard. A girl had given him a cake and they had had it that night at the fire—Lwi caught-step of a sudden, over a fallen branch or his own feet, and shook him off his balance.

"Damn!" His wits were wandering. The horses' steps were heavy and slower and slower, and that was not right. He leaned over and hit Skory. Skory jumped and Lwi did, startled awake. But by the time they had come to the bottom of the hill, the horses were only ambling again, and resisted a second such trick, only did a faster step for a moment, and slacked off again.

"This isn't right," he said, "this isn't right at all . . ."

Ela lifted the amulet to her lips and held it aloft, her eyes shut and a dreadful concentration on her brow.

"What are you doing?" he began to ask, but just then came a spark of light, as if the mirror had caught the sun, then another, and another, and another. Her eyes opened and she let slip the mirror to dangle from its chain, as sparkles of light began to dance about them, on the ground, on themselves.

"Keep on!" he said, and in a numb, distant daze saw sunlight from the mirror glitter on the trees and sweep the ground. He had no idea now whether it was the right way they were going. He could only ride with the sparkles of light, that seemed to dance and beckon further and further amid the gloom.

A long time it seemed they went that way, the horses walking more alertly, their way lit with dazzle from an absent sun, a giddy, spinning dance of light in which Tamas began to hope there was safety . . .

Until they came to a steep descent, and that light glanced off metal.

"Ela!" he whispered, reining back. He saw goblins, hundreds and hundreds of them, arrayed in ambush among the leaves.

But his own voice seemed to come from far away, and Lwi stumbled when he began to turn on the slope. He saw Ela riding on, and he tried to bring Lwi about again on the leaf-buried slope, to reach her and turn her aside—but before he could persuade Lwi to overtake her it was too late: she rode within the goblin ranks, and those ranks tumbled, one and the next and the next, into piles of metal, moldered leather, and bleached bone.

He stared, overwhelmed by the strangeness of the sight, so that he questioned whether he was awake or seeing what he thought he was seeing. Lwi had stopped with him, and he tried to urge him to overtake the witchling, but Ela was further and further away, from the moment he had reined back. Now the sparkle of the mirror swept the ground ahead and danced among the trees, but not where he was. The whole woods seemed darkened, and Ela and the light seemed far, far away.

"Ela," he called after her. "Ela!" The woods seemed to swallow up the sound. He struck Lwi hard, for both their sakes, but Lwi would not go faster, not even take alarm at the heaps of bone that tumbled and rattled where they rode. He saw Ela look back as if at great distance. She was almost to the top of the next hill, and then at the crest of it.

"Tamas?" he thought he heard her answer him. But the sparkle went out then, and left no traces in the woods where he was. Lwi stopped listlessly, and he slid down in desperation and took the reins and began to lead him, insisting he keep moving, up and up the hill.

But perhaps he had turned aside on the hill and mistaken his direction—hills had so many faces, and deceived the senses so easily. He trudged the whole wide hillside, and found, everywhere, the ghastly dead, as if he had wandered onto some forgotten battleground, of some unchronicled war. There was no sign of Ela, not the least glimmering of the light he sought, only the rattle of bones falling, of armor clattering, and the sight of unhuman skulls—Azdra'ik's kind, and in like armor. He gathered up a sword from one of the dead, a frightening thing with backward spines for one of its quillons, the use of which might be to disarm . . . the god knew, else.

With that, he kept going about the crown of the hill. Ela could not have had that much time to disappear. Skory might have had her way and gone off without direction, or even, the god forbid, thrown her and left her hidden in the brush. If that were the case, he might see her from the height.

But when he had trekked all about the hill, he found only more white and eyeless dead, and endless tracts of forest. He set out in the direction he thought they had been going, the sword thrust through his belt and Lwi's reins in hand, dragging at him so his arm ached. He called Ela's name from time to time, but, dreamlike, the forest smothered his voice. He said to Lwi, in the numbing whispering of leaves, "We'll find her. We won't lie down here. The silly girl says I can work magic. So let's try, shall we? Let's say we should find her, let's think about that, that's a good horse. . . ."

Easy to sleep. Far too easy to shut his eyes, even walking; while he still came on scattered stragglers of that ghastly army—as if some of that number had attempted escape from whatever had left them waiting for all time—only to let their eyes drift shut, losing their war to a gentle enemy. If he had magic, he called on it to save him and Ela from this place. If he had favor with the gods, he pleaded with them, but he was not sure they could reach within this realm, and he was not sure he had been as devout as the priests would wish.

"This way," the leaves seemed to whisper. "This way, Tamas."

Fish roasted on the fire, and there were greens such as Krukczy had found unspoiled in the garden and a few kitchen stores, but goblins had gotten the rest. It was a strange night, with Krukczy's musty fur drying in the heat of a fire, and Zadny with his head on his knee, and the dreadful warning still standing in the yard. Yuri did not like to think about it, and master Nikolai himself had asked if Karoly did not want them to try to bury the remains, such as there were, but Karoly had said no, said it with such harshness as invited no second question on the matter.

So here they sat, roasting fish in a ruined hall, amid the clutter the goblins had left of the place. Nikolai was able to sit up and have his supper, one-handed, and they had found master Karoly, and they had a roof over their heads and a wall around them tonight, but over all, Yuri found no appetite—thinking about Karoly's sister, and the servant, Karoly guessed it was, out there in the yard; and most of all thinking how it must have been Karoly's trail Zadny had followed, not his brothers', after all. This might be the end of it, beyond which—beyond which was nothing but going home, with Nikolai and with Karoly, at least, but—

He felt Zadny's head on his knee, absently scratched the soft, shaggy ears. Zadny had had his fish and probably wanted his, that was growing cold on a broken dish, so he began to break off bits, and pick out the bones, and give it to him.

But he heard master Karoly say something to Nikolai about tomorrow. Then followed an exchange he could not hear, the two of them talking in low voices; so he listened harder, and heard, "—going on from here."

"Alone?" Nikolai asked, then Karoly said something, but Krukczy switched his tail just then, and a coal snapped in the fireplace, making Zadny jump.

He listened harder. And suddenly saw two grim faces look his way in unison.

He set his jaw and said, "Master Karoly. Are you talking

about finding my brothers? Because if you are I'm not going home."

"Damned right you're going home," Nikolai said. "You're going to do as you're told for once, young my lord, and if you've any regard for your brothers' lives you won't take *me* from Karoly to make sure you get there."

"They're alive."

"I've the notion one is," master Karoly said, at which Yuri's heart beat faster and faster. "I'm fairly certain Tamas was here, and not so long ago."

"Then where is he?" His voice startled Zadny, who jumped up, darting from him to Krukczy, who crouched by the fire, and back, and back again.

"He knows," Krukczy rumbled, and rubbed Zadny's head. "Hound, he knows—brother. Hound, he knows."

"It *talks* to him?" Nikolai asked, but master Karoly held up his hand and said,

"Say on, master Krukczy. What else do you know?"

The troll's tail spun a nervous, curling trail, and ended in its broad hands, for safekeeping, as seemed. "Witch."

"What about a witch?"

"Young witch. Belongs here."

"Her apprentice," Karoly said, and got up and paced as far as the door to the outside. "Damn! her apprentice . . . that's who. *That's* who! I couldn't see her!"

Who what? Yuri wondered, but it was Nikolai who dared ask it.

"Who are you talking about?"

Master Karoly turned about, and it was a frighteningly different old man, it was not the amiable master Karoly who had shown him the weather-glass, it was an angry man whose sister was dead outside, who had seen friends struck from ambush, and who had walked for days to get here.

"A young and desperate fool," he said, and cast himself

down again by the fire. "God, god—she might have taken it. I'd forgotten all about her."

"Taken what?" Nikolai asked.

"What she has no business on earth to have in her hands. But if I weren't here, if she did survive . . ."

"What?" Nikolai asked, but Karoly shushed him and stared into the fire and thought and thought.

Yuri ate a cold bit of fish. And another. The troll said that one of his brothers was alive. And the way Zadny was after the trail, it might be Tamas—he hoped it was Tamas. He did not know if that was wicked or not, but he liked Tamas better.

But if it was Bogdan, he was still not going back without him. He watched Karoly, and waited, and so did Nikolai, uncommonly patient with master Karoly.

Yuri sucked his fingers clean of fish, and held the bones in a napkin on his lap, waiting; but finally he saw master Nikolai lean his back against the wall, seeming in pain; and he said, very so quietly, "You should go to bed, sir, I'll wait up. I need to talk to master Karoly anyway. I'm *not* going back."

Nikolai frowned darkly at him, cradling his wounded arm. "It's *my* brother, sir."

"My *god*, your father should take a stick to your backside!"

"The boy belongs here," Karoly said.

"What do you mean he belongs here?" Nikolai cried, and winced. "Lord Sun, Karoly, your wits are addled."

"My wits are in excellent form, master huntsman." Master Karoly had pulled a twig from the bit of wood he added to the fire, and he stripped bark from it with his thumbnail. "If the boy went back now, he would be in worse danger. There are things abroad that would smell him out in a moment."

"We're not safe company," Nikolai said.

"No. Nor is he. Nor is my sister's apprentice." Master Karoly's mouth made a tight line as he tied the bit of cedar in a cross, and split it further. It made, Yuri realized of a sudden, the shape of a man.

Karoly cast it into the fire.

"Why did you do that?" Yuri asked.

"One pays," Karoly said. "One at least acknowledges the obligation to pay. Be polite with the gods. These are dangerous places."

"No riddles," Nikolai said. "I'm full to the teeth with riddles, master trickster. No more flummery. Where is Tamas, what did the apprentice take, and where are they going?"

"In over his head, a bit of mirror, and the heart of hell. Now do you know what I'm talking about?"

Two grown men were about to argue and nothing was going to get done. "Please," Yuri said. "What about mirrors, master Karoly?"

Karoly looked him in the eyes so long he felt the silence grow, but Krukczy the troll rumbled,

"Mirror of the goblin queen."

"A fragment of it," Karoly said. He had pulled another twig and peeled it, turning it in his fingers. "A fragment of the goblin queen's mirror. It has the power of delusion, the power of bewitchment . . . the power of misleading and confusion and seeming."

"Where is it?"

"It used to be here. Since it isn't, I can only hope the apprentice has it. I can only hope my sister warned the girl what it is, and most of all what it isn't."

"For the god's sake," Nikolai said, "in words without their tails in their mouths—what does the thing do? Or what doesn't it?"

"It doesn't make clever out of foolish, it doesn't rescue lambs from the slaughter, and it doesn't help a mouse catch a cat."

"What can it do?"

"Too damned much to have it wandering the countryside. When the mirror cracked, a goblin carried one shard to the upper world, so I had the story. That was a long, long time ago."

"Young mistress got it," Krukczy said.

"*Did* she, now?" Master Karoly lifted his brows and stared at the troll.

"Young mistress took it from the goblin. A present. A long, long time ago."

"What does he mean?" Nikolai asked.

"It means I know now how it came to my sister. Urzula never said. Damn."

"Urzula never said?" Nikolai asked.

Gran? Yuri wondered. *Our* gran? Meanwhile Karoly nodded to Nikolai's question and chewed on the twig, staring into the fire. "I wish the girl had waited. I do wish she had waited."

"Young witch came to my tower," Krukczy said, "to find brothers. One fell to the river, down with rocks. I give him to her."

"It *is* Tamas," Nikolai said. "He and his horse went down the slide."

Yuri drew in a breath. He remembered the road and those sharp rocks from the bottom side, as it slanted down and down toward the stream that flowed past Krukczy Straz. But Tamas was alive, even Nikolai believed it, now! He rested his arm on his knee and his fist against his mouth, trying not to ask silly questions while his elders were thinking, which they clearly were.

"I don't like this," Karoly said. "It doesn't have a good feeling at all. That fragment is moving."

"Moving where?" Nikolai asked.

"Toward its owner. It's been in a safe place all these years. The goblins were no present threat. Now the girl's missed me and gotten Tamas, and they've taken the piece and gone east, no question but what it's east. . . ."

"Goblin follows them," Krukczy said. "I smell him in this room."

"Ng'Saeich," Karoly murmured, or something like that, and Karoly's jaw stayed open, twig and all. "God. That scoundrel! Of course he is!"

"Who?" Yuri asked, he could not help it.

"The thief, of course, the thief, damn him! The fools murdered her and they probably didn't even know who she was. They didn't care. But *he* knew. He knew, damn him, he felt it the same as I, and he beat me here!"

"I need to speak with you," Nikolai said to Karoly, in that way grown-ups had when they wanted boys out of earshot.

Karoly said, "The boy is going with us. There's no choice now."

"How far is he going to make it? To a den of goblins? To what the rest of us made it to? What they did to your sister and her servant . . . god, they probably *ate* them, man, this is not an enemy who'll fight fair."

"Neither do I," Karoly said, and spat a bit of the twig, that hissed in the fire. "Neither would my sister. That's why I won't bury her. Go to bed. Both of you. You'll not dream tonight."

"I thought we were going after my brother!" Yuri protested. He did not understand what Nikolai and Karoly were arguing about. He did understand Tamas and a witch's apprentice being somewhere in the forest and someone named ng'Saeich looking for the piece of mirror they were carrying. Most of all he understood what he had seen in the yard, and that goblins had done it. "What about Bogdan? What about Jerzy and Zev and Filip? What about . . . ?"

"In the morning," Karoly said. "In the morning we'll go, and go quickly. Don't wake for any sound you hear. —Master

Krukczy. Watch the deep ways. And take the dog. He'd be better with you tonight."

"Master Karoly," Yuri protested, upset and angry. But Karoly got up, making a shadow above him, and caught his face painfully in his hand, after which Yuri found his eyes closing.

"There's too much, too much to explain. Go to bed, boy."

Yuri found himself doing that without knowing why or remembering quite what they had been saying. He only remembered Zadny after he had gotten to the pallet master Karoly had made him in the wreckage of the hall.

And once that night he opened his eyes to think that a stranger stood near him. He thought it was a woman. He could not say why. He only knew whoever it was, was angry, and looking for someone who was not him.

Whoever it was brushed his hair with its hand and went away. He shivered after that. He had no idea why it had scared him, since none of the anger was aimed at him. But he was afraid, all the same.

The boy was quiet—exhausted, Nikolai could think, except he had the evidence of magic in himself with every breath he took. He kept expecting the pain to come back. The memory of it was so vivid he expected it to return if he so much as shifted his back against the wedge of blankets between him and the corner. And he had never given that much credence to the old man's abilities, true, but he had never forgotten the lady. He had tried to tell himself all his life it had only been a boy's imagination that had tingled through his bones that night and spooked him down the stairs—and that the pain in his arm was fading steadily was all very fine, he supposed, but no one had consulted him in it. It had been his pain and it was still his arm, and he sat there in a witch's ruined hall with the acute feeling he had had something thoroughly unpleasant done to him, but he could not swear to what; and the equally acute feeling that he both knew and had never known the old man across the room.

He watched Karoly throw a log on the fire, watched Karoly press his ear to the stone of the fireplace and shake his head as if he did not like what he had heard. Karoly patted the stone as if it were alive, then pottered about some more, putting their pans away into the packs. Finally he came and sat down on the bench next to the bed. The fire cast a halo around the old man and the shadow fell on Nikolai's face, making him feel, for some reason, cornered.

"How's the arm?" Karoly asked.

"All right," he said. "Twinges." Which was the truth. The old man's magic was not perfect. "—So what do we do about the boy?"

"Nothing we can do." Karoly was still chewing that bit of twig, and made it turn in his mouth. "When magic works it pulls things. If something's going the way its various parts are, it's safer for that particular something, you understand?"

"You mean the boy going with us."

"I mean *you* going with us. Leave us and you'll be goblin bait by morning. The boy has to go where everything else goes—getting him away from the magic at work in this land would be impossible."

"Impossible! Tell me 'impossible!'" He remembered the boy asleep and dropped his voice. "I can get him home. Trust me!"

"Not a chance. He'd come back, probably because you were dead. You're alive now because of him, and don't ask me why. I don't know everything."

"But you know *that*, do you? You're so damned sure of that? One of Stani's boys is wandering around the woods—"

"One of Stani's boys is in serious trouble. Shut up and listen, master huntsman. Tomorrow morning, at the crack of dawn or just before, I want you to take the boy and the horse and the dog and get outside the gates. I may join you. If I don't, and you don't like the look of things, head east, bearing along the wall. Krukczy will go with you."

Something about not fighting fair. The skulls in the yard. And not burying his sister.

"What are you up to? What's this—'take the boy'? Where will you be?"

"Tomorrow will tell, won't it? Behind you, in one sense or the other."

He did not like that in the least, either. "Take the boy and do what?"

"Find Tamas. I'll find you, if I can. I *think* my sister forgave me. We'll find out tomorrow."

"What do you mean—find out? Isn't she dead?"

"Oh, she's dead. Dead without a stroke struck or a goblin suffering for it, and that's not her style, not Ysabel." Karoly took the twig from his mouth and spat a piece at the floor. "Raising a ghost—you never know what you'll get; that's the trouble."

"Is she around here?" The room seemed too full of shadows. "Is she listening to us?" It was deeper into magic and wizards' business than he ever wanted to delve, but Karoly said, so quietly the snap of embers seemed to echo in the hall:

"I don't get that feeling. That's why I don't know how much of her I can get back. Sometimes it's just a piece or two. That's the danger."

"What's the danger?"

"Of only the anger coming back."

An ember popped. Nikolai jumped, and the shoulder sent a warning ache. Karoly looked about him with an absent stare, and spat another bit of twig.

"Was that her?"

"That's the other problem with ghosts. Ysabel, Ytresse . . . I wouldn't put it past any of them."

"Who? Put what past them?"

"The witches. Doing anything. I went to live over-mountain. My sister refused to deal with me after that. But she spent everything to call me home. She deserved her revenge. No one should die like that."

"And you brought the boys into this? You led us down that damned road and you knew all along what was going on here?"

"Keep your voice down. No, I didn't know what was going on here, I dreamed it, and there's a difference."

"What difference? You *saw* that marker!"

"And what could we do, then? Get back across the pass, with no supplies? Wait for the goblins to invade Maggiar? We were as close to their source as we might ever get—as close to the *only* place anyone can stop them, and close to the one who might have done it, with my help. But I wasn't in time."

"In time for your sister? What could you have done?"

"That's to be seen. That's still to be seen. —Let me tell you a story, master huntsman, if you care to hear it. Someone but me should know the truth."

He frowned and waited. Anything that made sense of the business, he was willing to hear—but he had limited faith the old man would make any.

"Some hundreds of years ago," Karoly said, "many hundreds of years ago, in fact, before there even was a Maggiar, there was a queen in over-mountain, and a tower at Hasel. The queen in Hasel had a daughter named Ylena. And nothing was good enough for Ylena. In her household, she had golden tables, and silver plates. Even her bed was silver and her washbasin was gold set with jewels. . . ."

"This sounds like one of those tales," Nikolai muttered.

"Of course, but that's Ylena the tales talk about. They don't know it's Ylena, but I assure you it is. Nothing but the best. And being a princess, as well as a witch—"

"Were all of them witches?" It seemed to him that essential things were being left out. A bard, Karoly was not. "Or was it just Ylena?"

"Oh, mostly they were. The queens of over-mountain all knew the arts to one degree or another. Anyhow, the queen discovered one day what a truly vain and ungrateful princess Ylena was, and she worried and worried about this."

"Too late," Nikolai interjected. "She should have taken a switch to the brat."

"Far too late for that. Ylena would ruin the land when she became queen, and queen Mirela, knowing that, . . . looked for some magical solution: a failing in lazy witches. So she went to the goblins."

"Just like that? Walked up to the front door and knocked?"

"Oh, being a witch, Mirela rattled a few dark doors at night, some few that wiser witches wouldn't touch. Remember, she wasn't a particularly wise witch. She'd brought up Ylena. But she was a desperate witch, and good-hearted. And the goblin queen, in exchange for a promise of access to the world of men for one night a year, gave queen Mirela a potion that would assure her youth and beauty. The usual bargain. So queen Mirela came back young and beautiful and healthy enough to reign forty years more at least. Ylena was *furious*."

"Naturally Ylena worked a spell against her."

"No, not immediately. It was a very powerful magic that surrounded her mother, and if you go against something that strong without knowing exactly the terms of it, you can do yourself harm. So Ylena waited a whole year until that night the goblins could come into the land, and approached their queen to ask her how to get the throne. So what was a little treachery against one's mother? And what was murder? Because Mirela had asked for youth and beauty, not a charmed life. So Ylena promised the goblin queen a whole year of access to human lands, when she should rule, in return for that advice. And that let the goblins into human lands again."

"Again?"

"Oh, they'd begun here. That's how queen Mirela first found the key to calling them. They'd left their signs on old stones, they left their spells—in magic, one wanders through them like old landmarks. Of course the goblins had their own reasons for leaving such clues in the world when they were banished—but that's another story. At any rate, Mirela perished under most suspicious circumstances, Ylena became queen, and the goblins arrived in the world with banners and circumstance. They were on best behavior. They did no mischief. They were courtly, they were flattering to the queen, and they oh'ed and ah'ed over the new princess—"

"Ylena got a husband."

"At least a daughter. She was named Ytresse. She was very beautiful even as a baby. But Ylena had never planned to have an heir, and she hadn't succeeded in preventing her birth, if you take my meaning. Nothing worked. She suspected goblin treachery, and she fell out with the goblin queen until the day the year was up and the goblins were preparing to leave. They professed their regret to give up so much grace and comfort, and the goblin queen remarked to Ylena that she wished they might make a further bargain."

"The fool."

"Ylena? Of course. Ylena sensed magic in that baby. Powerful magic. She sensed goblin work. And the baby, Ytresse, had survived some very determined efforts. So Ylena wanted a spell stronger than the baby's determination to live. And the goblin queen said there was a lake—a particularly beautiful lake they had come to revere—"

"Goblins revere something?"

"There are goblins and goblins. Certain ones, yes, apparently do. This lake had a perfect reflection. It's quite shallow, very still, and it was a place of power in this world that the goblins wanted. So the goblin queen swore that Ylena might live so long as they had possession of that small lake. It was just tricky enough that Ylena believed in it. So she agreed on the spot."

"Clever woman."

"Ah, but when you deal with devils, beware the loopholes."

"The youth and beauty part?"

"Exactly. But—the goblins were of course willing to give Ylena spells to stave off age—by their magic, of course. So Ylena was trapped in her own bargain. But—*but*—" Karoly spat another bit of twig. "Ylena wanted to deal no more with the goblins, and began to sustain herself by . . . well, say her subjects grew fewer and fewer. She knew of course she'd been betrayed. Then a certain goblin came to her and offered her a secret—a secret, he said, in return for which he asked three wishes."

"You're joking."

"Three is a potent number. And he used his first two, but the third—not yet, for all I know. But for whatever reason, he told her how the goblin queen's power lay in a mirror, a working of magical smoothness and exactitude, and that if Ylena wanted power to equal the goblin queen's spells, that was what she had to defeat. So Ylena had a mirror made of silvered glass as smooth and perfect as she could obtain, and put into its making every spell she knew. —None of which, of course, went unreported in the territory around the lake. So on a snowy midwinter's eve, when everyone should be asleep, and, as it just happened, the night before Ylena was quite ready to take her on, the goblin queen sent out her army and turned her spells against Ylena's mirror. When all was done there was little left of Ylena but a wraith, nothing left of Hasel but the shell, and nothing of Ylena's mirror but silver powder—so they say."

"And the goblin queen's?"

"Cracked right in two, with a small fragment fallen, that was the price she paid for defeating Ylena. But the same goblin, so he claimed, the very one who had dealt with Ylena, stole the piece and took it straightway—you guessed it—to Ylena's successor, Ytresse, who had grown up into a wicked, wicked woman. But Ytresse no more trusted the goblin queen than her mother had. She made sure of her own heir—nothing of the goblin queen's doing, a witch named Ylysse. And Ylysse, after a long, long lifetime, passed the power to Ysabel—"

"Your sister."

"My sister."

"But it's a goblin trap, that fragment. It was from the beginning. —Isn't it?"

"Consider its history. Is the goblin thief lying or not? And why that knowledge he gave to Ylena in the first place, and why the three wishes, and the unfortunate issue to Ylena? It certainly *is* to ask. . . ."

"Then—" Certain prying questions occurred to him, that did not seem entirely unwise, also considering the history.

"Then—?" Karoly asked.

"Where do you come into the story?"

"I? Nowhere. Or only at the last. Ysabel and I weren't descended from Ytresse. Not even from her apprentices. *Urzula* was."

His heart gave a thump. "The lady gran?"

"Exactly."

Nikolai let go his breath and drew in another one, thinking. *My god. What else isn't what we trusted?*

"You and your sister? —Where did *you* come into this?"

"Urzula's apprentices."

Apprentices, for the god's sake. "And what brought the lady to Maggiar? And don't tell me 'adoration for Ladislaw.' I was at the funeral."

Karoly laughed grimly. "Not overmuch of adoration. But a

fair bargain on both sides. Ladislaw got his heir. And dare I say—if one hopes to undo a spell, one has to reach outside its arena of influence, one has to do the unexpected, work where one won't be spied upon—conditions which don't obtain on *this* side of the mountain."

"But she never *warned* anyone, not m'lord Stani, not—"

"I knew."

"Damned lot of good it did anyone. You knew, you knew when you saw the trouble start, let alone that business on the trail."

"It might have been trolls."

"Might have been trolls! The *troll's* not guilty, master wizard, the *troll* was hiding in the basement at Krukczy Tower, in fear of his life, don't tell me you hadn't clearer messages out of your dreams than that, once every wild creature in the overmountain began pouring into Maggiar. . . ."

"There could be other causes. I hoped for other causes. That's the nature of magic, master huntsman. When will it rain, do the birds tell you that without fail? Better yet, do they tell you where? Or are there ever false signs? The goblins have been in this world for hundreds of years now—and will be, so long as the agreement with Ylena stands."

"It doesn't."

"Oh, but to this day, Ylena has never given up her power— power to frighten, power to kill. She's still in this world."

"You mean she's not dead."

"That describes it. Not dead. Not alive either. So the goblins hold their land—and the mirror is mended, with its one piece missing. As for mistress Urzula—what she did, and how much of this is the queen's doing, the Lady knows, but I don't—nor can, I've realized that, long since. Let me tell you another secret. Urzula's real name was Ysabel."

"Your sister?" More and more crazed, it was.

"Both were named Ysabel. Our mother was a servant in this

tower, a very minor witch, a distant cousin. Ylysse gave Ysabel to our mother to bring up and gave out that we were *her* children. Which put us in danger, certainly. But Urzula—"

"Your sister?"

Karoly shook his head. "Use the names they lived by. It's less confusing. And listen. Urzula wanted me with her because I wasn't gifted enough to leave here in danger—that and other reasons. . . ."

"Were there other reasons?"

"Were we lovers?" Another spit of twig, and a dark, silent laughter. "Yes. Ysabel—my sister Ysabel—and I had a falling out on that point. We were twins. Ysabel expected loyalty, since she was getting the short end of things, and standing in the most danger. Ysabel wanted the teaching more than she wanted life and breath and I wanted—Urzula, that was the sad truth. I wasn't so gifted nor so dedicated as Ysabel. Magic for me didn't take fire, the way it did for her. I never trusted it. Still don't. Ysabel drank it, breathed it—and she never could have the magic she really wanted, could never *be* the witch she claimed to be. And Urzula—Urzula . . . the way she felt about it—you know, I never understood whether she was, inside, like Ysabel, in love with magic, or more like me. Urzula held everything inside and you never knew. But with her birthright, the god only knows what she *could* do if she used it as freely as Ysabel—if she let it use her, like Ysabel. I always thought—leaving Ysabel on watch here was like leaving the fox in charge of the hen-house. Fond of designs, she was. Fond of workings and intrigues."

He found himself uncomfortable, in wizardly confidences. Embers popped, again, and Karoly's brow wrinkled with an upward glance.

"Are you there?" Karoly asked the shadowed air and the firelight, and Nikolai held his breath waiting for an answer, but Karoly gave another humorless laugh and looked down at his hands. "I chide the boys for moongazing. But boys are silly longer than girls, aren't they—and that I wasn't her ally, that was something Ysabel never could understand. That Urzula wanted me with her was something she thought she did understand— god, Ysabel was furious. And Urzula was on her way to get a husband and a successor the goblins wouldn't know about. That was—a painful realization."

A successor. Nikolai found his heart thumping so loudly of a sudden he could not believe Karoly did not hear. He asked, quietly, carefully, the gossip of every servant in the house: "Whose is Stani?"

"Urzula's, of course."

Damn the old man, up to the edge of truth and no further. But Karoly added, then:

"That's enough, if you want the truth. As witches reckon lineage it's enough. Ysabel and I lived this lie all our lives. And Urzula—" A private and lengthy silence. "She was really a reprehensible woman, Urzula was . . . short-tempered; cruel, at times . . . most times. Dreadful things amused her. But she worked for the right. —And defend her own people—god, she would do that." Karoly drew a long breath. "You know what disturbs me most?"

I couldn't possibly imagine, Nikolai thought distressedly, and simply answered, "No."

"That so much of the business with Ylysse began with Ylena."

"What do you mean—began with Ylena?"

"In sorcery—and far-working is necessarily sorcery—one wants to affect events at a great distance and over time, and one can't predict whether the outcome is good or bad for one or another person, only *numbers* of people. Urzula could dismiss consequences like that: Urzula didn't see one person, or a son, or a mother. Urzula saw—I can't tell you what Urzula saw, or, for that matter, what Ysabel saw. I only loved certain people.

And I couldn't *change* what Urzula worked, I couldn't even change myself, or Ysabel. . . ." Karoly cleared his throat. It had gotten very still in the room, and uncomfortably close. "Anyway, I chose the small magic, I'm a wizard, not a sorcerer, not even a good wizard until I've something I want with a clear conscience. I follow along after a sorcerer like Urzula, you understand, just picking up and patching what I can. Work *against* sorcery? That takes sorcery. That was Ysabel's domain." He took the twig from his mouth and shredded it in threads with his nail, as if the need to do that utterly occupied his attention.

"You mean you can't change anything? You can't do things differently than they've done?"

A moment's silence. "That's sorcery, too. Change the things they've done, means you change the far things. One thing touches everything. It's only the broken bits, the used bits, the bits passed over . . . that I can patch. The pieces in use—I can't help."

"Like Tamas? Is that what you're saying?"

"Like any of us. —Ysabel was as dangerous and as much in danger as anyone. It was a long and lonely time here, weak as she was, pretending so much more strength. Thank the god for Pavel."

"Pavel."

"The chap in the yard." A motion of Karoly's eyes. Up. Meaning the second pole and the second skull, Nikolai realized with a motion of his stomach. "He came from a long time ago. From Hasel. Half-mad, but he was devoted to Ysabel. Supposedly he kept the grounds—now and again. Mostly he kept Ysabel. —But beware the apprentice. Beware anyone who learned from Ysabel. The girl will have no conscience, Tamas, she won't know right from wrong . . . not if she learned at my sister's knee. Only the faraway things matter. Only the outcome, to anyone Ysabel would have taught . . ."

The old man was staring off at nothing, spinning the chewed

twig in his fingers, talking to Tamas as if he were there, and the hair rose on Nikolai's nape. It took more than ordinary craziness to spook him, or ghastly sights to scare him—he had seen so many on his trek south, through the wars of wizards and petty tsars.

"Urzula saw the boys born," Karoly said, for no reason that Nikolai could understand, but the god only knew who he was talking to now. "She was satisfied then. She'd lived a long time. And she said they weren't her responsibility any longer. And I wasn't. So she died."

"Suicide?"

"No. Sorcery's like that."

"Better to wish your *enemies* dead. Damn. —And why didn't your sister know the goblins were coming? Why didn't she blast them with lightning or turn them to pigs or something? If she could call you from over-mountain, she wasn't helpless."

His caution had deserted him: he had asked too bluntly, perhaps, and he thought he might have angered the old man. But it was not a challenge. He honestly wanted to know why reasonable things had not happened, in a war of sorcerers.

Karoly frowned and finally said, very slowly, as if he were explaining to a child: "Because, master huntsman, do you forget? We aren't the only side in this war. The other side casts spells, too."

"So she couldn't just—send earlier?"

"So she couldn't *think* of it—at least not well enough to do a number of things all at once. It's often the little things that slip your notice—and sorcery doesn't leave tracks *on* objects that cause you problems, the way magic does. Mostly it's a gate unlatched, a moment of forgetfulness. Forgetfulness and looking past a thing are both deadly mistakes. The object on the shelf for thirty years, that you never think of being there, the thing you do every day, so you never remember whether you've done it or not, on one specific day. That sort of thing."

"Like this mirror that's so damned important? What does this mirror do? Why didn't the gran take it with her to Maggiar? Why did she leave it with your sister, where they could get at it?"

Karoly blinked and stared off across the room—looked back at him then as if he had only then accounted of his presence. "What did you say?"

"I said—why did the lady gran leave the mirror with your sister, if this tower wasn't safe from sorcery?"

Karoly blinked, shook his head, bit his lips a moment, frowning as if he were listening to something. Then he rose up, a shadow against the fire.

"Old man?"

"Find Tamas, do you hear? Find Tamas. Nothing's more urgent than that."

"And do what with him?" All his senses seemed foggy of a sudden, and the wound on the edge of hurting. "Shall we say, Excuse us, your goblin majesty, but we're not really interested in your war, and may we please go home? —I've been in bad situations, master wizard, I've been on battlefields and I've seen a city burn, but I didn't have a boy and a pony and a damned dog for an escort. And what do we do with the mirror if we find it?"

Karoly pressed his fingers against his eyes as if he were fighting headache. "It's hard to think about. Ask it again, master huntsman."

"Why . . . ?" He must be falling asleep. He could not recall himself what must have caught Karoly's attention, god, he'd said it three times—did the man want it again? "What do I do? Where do I take the boys? If we get the mirror, what do we do with it? What can it do?" He remembered another piece of his question. "Why didn't the lady gran bring it with her?"

"Again."

"The damned mirror, master Karoly. What about it? Why

didn't she take it to Maggiar? *What's going on?*"

Karoly looked . . . frightened, of a sudden, his eyes darting about the room. He's gone mad, Nikolai thought in distress. The old man's not sane . . .

Because he had never seen anyone do that in the middle of talking with someone, had never seen anyone take to watching something immaterial that flitted and darted and circled the room.

"Karoly?" Nikolai insisted.

Karoly stood up, and turned, a shadow between him and the fire as Karoly stared down at him. "Go to sleep," Karoly said, and suddenly Nikolai found his eyes so tired and the crackling of the fire so intense and so absorbing that he could not keep his wits collected. "Dammit, stop it," he protested—but his thoughts and his anger ran off in various directions, into memories of the road, the mountains, the woods and the pony. . . .

"The boy's in trouble," he dreamed that Karoly said. And Karoly said something more, concerning a place called Hasel, or where Hasel used to stand, but he could not hold onto the thought, not even enough to tell the old man what he thought of him. . . .

And Karoly for so many reasons deserved cursing.

9

Lwi ambled to a stop in the twilight of the everlasting woods, and it would have been oh, so much easier to give up and let the struggle go, Lwi refusing all reasonable urgings to go on. The morning had to come, and Tamas was so confused and so weary— but the easy way was the dangerous way, the easy way must always be suspect, master Karoly had always said—think twice and three times before you take the easy way.

Enough bones in this woods to make anybody think twice, he thought muzzily, and tugged at the reins and led Lwi's irregular steps on the straightest line he could walk among the trees, one step after the other, no wit left to reason what way he was going, except that everything ended, and that this night, like this woods, surely had an other side if he only persisted long enough in one direction, in one choice and not the dozen his mind wanted to skitter off into . . .

It seemed to him at last that the woods was growing lighter ahead—like the moon at forest edge. He hoped then, that he had found the way out he was looking for, and the trees began to appear like shadowy pillars in some great hall, but he saw more trees beyond, and that light nearer and among them, as if the moon itself had come to rest in the very heart of the trees.

"Come here," a voice said softly, from everywhere at once. Ela, he thought at first, Ela's magic was talking to him, she had found the magical place she was looking for and she was calling him to her—and then he thought that the speaker seemed older than Ela: so readily a mind beset by spells began to apply ordinary judgments, as if such manifestations happened by mundane rules.

"Who are you?" he asked it.

"Why, the mistress of this woods, boy. What and who are you? Do you have a name? It seems I should know you."

The voice that had seemed to come from all about him came from his left this time; and he looked in that direction, seeing only massive trunks of trees.

"Tamas," he panted.

"What are you doing here?" The voice came from behind him now, the self-same voice, as if it were stalking him, but it was nowhere, when he turned unsteadily and looked. "What do you seek here, Tamas?"

"Are you a witch?" he asked, he hoped without a tremor in his voice.

"Of course," it said. It was behind him again. He turned back the way he had been facing and saw a shadow between the trees, a woman, he thought, with a cloak drawn tight about her. "Where are you going, Tamas?"

"Out of this woods," he said, and decided that if it was her woods, disrespect to her domain would never help his case. "I'm only going through, good lady. If you know the way out I'd be grateful."

"Why so anxious? Are you afraid?"

"I've no reason to be. I haven't taken anything, or touched anything." Those were the magical rules as gran's stories had them. He pulled Lwi to the side and took another direction. Or perhaps he dreamed he did. She appeared in front of him again, saying:

"But what's that at your side, Tamas? Is that yours?"

A chill went through him. He reached blindly toward the

goblin sword, and pricked his finger on its spines. "I didn't think it was stealing."

"But this is my woods, Tamas. Everything in it is mine."

"I beg your pardon," he said. Breath came short, shameful panic. "I didn't think there was anyone to—" He drew Lwi in the other direction, and caught his foot painfully on a tree root. He recovered his balance and she was still in front of him.

"—anyone to care?" she mocked him.

"Are you a goblin?"

"Do I look like one?"

"I've only seen one, face to face. You don't look like him. But how should I know?"

She laughed softly, and beckoned him toward her. "Come inside. I'm not so stingy as that. And you don't look like a goblin, either. You look like a young man who's far from home."

For the first time he saw the dim outlines of a doorway behind her. Perhaps he had been looking so hard at her he had seen nothing else. But gran's stories had never encouraged him to accept such offers and he shook his head no. "Thank you, no, madam, I'm looking for someone."

"Have you lost someone? I can help you. There's little goes on in this woods that I don't know. —Oh, come in, come in, no sense to stand outside. The horse will be safe. Nothing harmful comes here."

It was dark, beyond that doorway. Everything about it seemed untrustworthy. "You can just tell me the shortest way out," he said, but she stooped and ducked inside—perhaps, he reasoned with himself, only to light a lamp or poke up a slumbering fire, and he might be foolish to object—but Ela had told him nothing of houses or cottages in this woods, especially not ones lit by a moon that, by his reckoning, ought not to have reached mid sky yet, a waning crescent by now, and not so bright as the light that filled this grove.

He did not want to go into that place—but what else might he do but wander on in the dark? he asked himself. Her invitation was the only choice he saw.

Much against his better judgment, he lapped Lwi's reins about a low live branch and went as far as the entrance, with no intention whatsoever of going inside until there was a lamp lit or a fire to show him what he was walking into. The air that wafted out to him had the chill and damp of a cave, but it looked on the outside like a peasant's cottage. He touched the rough stonework and it felt real enough, down to the grit of old mortar.

"Will you help me?" she asked from out of the dark.

"Madam, I would, but I'm sure you know your shelves better than I do. I'd only be in the way."

"Cautious boy." He heard further small movements within. "Afraid of me, are you?"

Less and less trustworthy. "Madam," he said uneasily, "I've seen nothing in this whole land but trouble." He heard Lwi tearing at the leaves behind him, and thought that if he had the sense his father hoped for in his sons he would walk away now, take Lwi in hand and keep going in his own slow and uncertain way, in hope of sunrise, eventually.

But of things he had met in this land, witches seemed thus far a power opposing the goblins—and light *did* spring up inside, a golden and comforting light, that cast a warm glow over an interior of curtains and shelves and domestic clutter—just the sort of things a woodland wise-woman might collect, birds' wings and branches and jars and jars of herbs and such. It reminded him acutely and painfully of master Karoly's study.

"Well?" she asked, from inside, and beckoned to him. "Oh, come, come, boy, I don't bite."

He could see all the inside from the door. He entered cautiously. She was standing at her table, pouring from a pitcher into two wooden cups.

"I don't really think I need anything," he protested, because he had no desire whatsoever to eat anything or acquire any obligations of hospitality with a witch. But she set one cup into his hand and waved him toward a cushioned ledge, settling herself at the far end of that small nook, a very proper witch, very—beautiful, he decided, which bore not at all on whether he should trust her, of course, but she did not look wicked. She had put off the dark cloak, that was not black, but deep, deep red. Her gown was embroidered and fringed and corded and tasseled with intricate work of black and colors, of a fashion both foreign and strange—in fascination with which, he took a larger sip than he had planned, and felt the liquid go down like fire.

"*Are* you honestly a witch, lady?"

"Honest people have certainly called me that. And for your question, my question: What are you doing in my woods? Was it a way out you wanted—or were you looking for someone? Have you decided which?"

Perhaps she had the power to help them. Perhaps he had grown confused in his wandering. "Looking for someone. Who probably found the way out." Perhaps witches all knew one another. The tower was not that far away. He took the chance. "Do you know a girl named Ela? She came from Tajny Straz."

"From Tajny Straz. And don't you know these hills are a dangerous place?"

"Madam,—" Words failed him. Everything he had seen came tumbling about him, with too much vividness and too little reason. "Are you at all acquainted with Ela's mistress? You are neighbors. And I know it's a dangerous place. The goblins killed her."

"A sad business. Yes, I'm aware. But that still doesn't answer why a young man is wandering these hills looking for a young lady from the perilous tower. I could wonder why I should answer his questions or tell him what I know—which might be something useful to him or not. How could I tell, if he won't tell me what he has to do with Tajny Straz and if he won't tell me the truth of what he's seeking?"

"We came to stop the goblins. They drove the deer and they burned the woods and when we came to see why, they ambushed us . . ."

"Did they? Why would they do that?"

"I've no idea." He held the cup locked between his fingers and wanted no more of what it held. His head was spinning and his thoughts fell over one another. "A girl is lost somewhere in this woods. I have to find her . . ."

"Poor boy." She got up with a whispering rustle of cloth and taking the cup from his fingers, set both cups on the table nearby. "Poor boy, you've hurt your hand—you've bled all over the cup."

"I'm dreadfully sorry. . . ."

"Oh, let me see." She began searching among the jars on the shelves, when he was only thinking how he could gracefully retreat. She found something, brought it back and reached for his hand. "Come, come," she said, and he felt like a fool, hesitating like a child with a cut finger—he truly did not want her to touch his hand, but she insisted.

"The sword did this. A wicked thing, and maybe poisoned." She carried his finger to her mouth while he was too confused to pull back or to protest her licking the blood off—quite, quite muddle-headed, then, and a little dizzy, as the pain stopped, and nothing seemed so comforting as her lips against his hand. "There," she said, edging closer, pressing his hand in hers, "isn't that better? Perhaps I can help you find your young lady. I do have my ways. And I can show you so many things, if you only pay some little token—the magic needs that, it always needs that, if someone asks a question."

He had not remembered about witches and payments. He regretted coming inside in the first place, or drinking anything, or letting her lips touch his hand. "I think—I think you never answered me—who you are, whether you know where Ela went."

"I don't. I can learn, ever so easily. Only I have to have something from you to make it happen. And you don't look to have any gold about you. What if my price were a kiss? Would that be too much to ask?"

He had never—never kissed any woman but his mother and his cousins: the truth was, he had never had the remotest chance, and her offer flung him into confusion. He was not courting some maid in Maggiar, he was sitting on a ledge in a strange little shelter with a witch who, he suddenly feared, was edging her way to more than a kiss. She might ask things he by no means wanted to do with a witch and a stranger. But he might be wrong about her intentions, and others were relying on him for their lives. So he leaned forward—it was not far—and paid her what she asked.

Her arms slipped about him. She held him that way and looked him closely in the eyes, laughing gently. "Oh, come, come now, was that a kiss?"

He had to allow it was not the way Bogdan would have done it. Certainly not Jerzy, or Nikolai. So he made a more honest try, but that did not satisfy her either: she made that kiss linger into two, and three, wandering from his lips to his neck, at which point he grew confused, what he should do, what he should agree to, what was right or wise to agree to or whether help that might be bought with dishonor could be relied on at all.

But what honor was it, if it let Ela go lost or goblins come at his land or his brother die without any justice for it?

She undid a buckle at his collar. He tried to think what to do, but when he shut his eyes to think he saw a dark tower, surrounded by goblin armies, saw war, men and goblins, a queen against a queen, not knowing how he knew that. He saw the great mirror cracked, and all the world rippled and changed like a reflection in water. Images flitted by, true or false, or what had been or what would be, he had no comprehension. What was happening in this world and the other tumbled event over event in confusion: he saw Lady Moon, in thinnest crescent, shimmering on a mountain lake. A goblin warrior stood on its dark and reedy shore, a knight whose countenance changed from fair to foul with the waxing and waning of the moon's reflection, with never a sun between.

That goblin figure turned and stared at him, the image of the goblin in the cellar, a hoped-for rescue turned to threat. Fair turned foul and fair again, not a human beauty, but beauty all the same, constantly changing with the reelings of the moon across the night.

But the shadow came across that goblin face and that armored body like the passing of a cloud across the moon, and when that shadow was full the body seemed broader, more familiar to him. The whole attitude was an echo of someone he knew—god, he *knew* with a pang at his heart, even before the cloud drifted on and the moon showed him Bogdan's pale face, remote, as a stranger to him. Slowly Bogdan began to turn his head, the very image of that creature in the cellar. He sought to escape that moment that their eyes should meet—but he could not turn away, not though his brother's eyes were dead and dark; and after that single glance Bogdan began to walk away, along the shore, into the dark.

"Wait!" he cried, and his voice echoed in vast halls that were suddenly about him, a structure of palest green stone and deepest black—he saw goblins standing about him, tall and grim, in the vaulted hall where the goblin queen issued her decrees. He saw her dusky face, dreadful and beautiful at once, with eyes of murky gold. Her braids were bound with silver, her necklaces were silver and gold, her long-nailed fingers were ringed and jeweled, and her arms were braceleted from wrist to elbow. "Well," she said, with that lisp that fangs made in a voice, and stared right into his soul. "Well, well, a venture against me. How nice."

"No," he cried, as she lifted a long-nailed hand and beckoned him closer, closer, with the force of magic. His body longed to go. He saw that Bogdan already stood there, among the dead-eyed courtiers. "It's all right," Bogdan said. "You've nothing to fear."

For a moment he looked at Bogdan, wanting desperately to believe in his safety—but it was shameful, it was horrid, Bogdan believed in no one's promises, and Bogdan was saying trust and believe that the queen had no wicked purposes.

"This is only the beginning," the witch in the wood said, standing beside him. "Is this someone you love? She'll find them, every one. She'll take them all from you, if you stand in her way. Believe what I say, believe what *I* say, and lend me your strength, boy, and there's nothing we can't do."

But nothing else had proven what it ought. And he felt cold in her touch, he saw shadow about him, and edged away.

"Not wise," she said.

He turned away and flung himself desperately at hall doors that shut in front of him—turned to run and found himself in the witch's forest cottage again, caught in an embrace that clung with frightening strength, arms with nothing of softness or flesh about them. Everything was lies—he had not seen his brother in that place, it could not have been Bogdan, no more than he had stood just now in the goblin hall. He began to push away with all his might, tore from the witch's embrace and caught himself against the table, the wall, the draperies. The door was shut. The bolt was shot. When had that happened?

"Tamas," the witch reproved him, as his cold fingers struggled with the bolt. He heard the rustle of her garments behind him and he could only move in nightmare slowness.

"Are you afraid, Tamas? Look at me. *Look at me*, Tamas. I showed you a symbol of things as they are. But will you run away now, and be blind to what will be? Do you want the truth, Tamas? Have you no courage for the truth?"

He shot the bolt back. The door resisted like heavy iron. He scraped through the slight opening he forced and caught a breath of cold clean air as he fled, stumbling over the uneven ground on legs numb as winter chill. He met a shadowed trunk, clung to it and struck out for a further one as his knees went to water. Lwi was standing where he had left him, and he flung himself in that direction, but the empty space was too wide. His knees gave way beneath him and sent him sprawling in the damp leaves.

"Well, well," a deep voice said, a voice that made his heart jump—but he could not recall if that voice belonged here, with a witch in this woods. He lifted his face from the leaves and rubbed the grit from his eyes . . . saw Azdra'ik standing among the trees.

They're in league, he thought. The witch and the goblins, all of them—

With a dry rattling and a whisper of cloth and leaves, the witch arrived beside him, her skirts in tatters, her feet—her feet beneath that hem were a pale assemblage of bone, which moved as if flesh contained it.

Azdra'ik sauntered closer. "Three wishes, mistress, wasn't that the term? I think I do remember your swearing it once upon a time, in exchange for my services." Three long-nailed fingers ticked off the items. "My first wish, I recall, was that you have no further power over me. My second . . . that you never oppose my purpose. And the third . . . the third, I fear, must be this wretched, foolish boy."

"Damn you," the witch whispered.

"Oh, I've served you more faithfully than you know— certainly more faithfully than you deserve. Now he's mine. By the terms you yourself proposed, he's mine. So begone, Ylena!"

A sound of breath, or angry wind. A soft and bitter laugh.

"Cheaply bought, that third wish of yours. I feared so many worse things. But they're done. You can't banish me hereafter, ng'Saeich. I never need fear you again!"

"Begone, I say!" The goblin stood up tall and flung up his arm, and for a moment there was a dreadful feeling in the air. Lwi whinnied as a gust of wind blew decayed leaves and grit into Tamas' face, chilling him to the bone. He ducked his face within the protection of his arm, and hoped only for a cessation of the wind that turned his flesh to ice.

But in the ebbing of that gale an armored boot disturbed the ground near his head. A strong hand dragged him to his knees, up and up toward Azdra'ik's very face. He tried to get his feet under him, and Azdra'ik struck him across the mouth, bringing the taste of blood.

"You are an *expensive* bit of baggage, man. Shall I begin by breaking your littlest finger, and work up to your neck? I would do that ever so gladly." A second blow, harder than the last. "Stand *up*, damn you!"

He tried. Azdra'ik seized him by the hair and by that and a grip on his belt, half-dragged, half-carried him as far as Lwi. He staggered against Lwi's yielding body and groped after the saddle with the desperate notion of breaking for freedom, if he could only get a foot in the stirrup, if he could only find the reins, if Lwi could do more than stagger away from this cursed place.

Azdra'ik grabbed his shoulder and faced him toward him, his back against Lwi's shoulder. "You," Azdra'ik said, "you can walk, man. You richly deserve to walk."

"Where's Ela?"

"Oh, where is Ela? *Where is Ela?* Now we're concerned, are we?" The goblin flung him away and took Lwi's reins in hand as he staggered for balance.

"Fool," Azdra'ik called after him, and somehow he found the strength to walk, shaky as his ankles were. Azdra'ik had neglected even to disarm him. So had the witch, that was how much threat he was to them. He might draw the sword now and offer argument—he might die on the spot instead of later, less quickly. He was no match for Azdra'ik as he was: he suspected that not on his best day was he a match for a goblin lord—foolish Tamas, Tamas who had no natural talent with the sword, Tamas who was scarcely able to keep his feet under him at the moment, who needed all his effort to set one ahead of the other—he was cold, cold as if no sun would ever warm him. When he faltered, whenever Azdra'ik overtook him, Azdra'ik struck him and made him walk, but that he felt anything at all began to be welcome—anything to keep him awake and moving and on his feet.

"You cost too much," the goblin said again, hauling him up by the scruff when he had fallen. Azdra'ik struck him hard across the face and cried, in this space distant from the witch, "Do you know what you've done, man? Do you remotely comprehend what I paid for you?"

"A wish," he murmured through bloody lips, the only answer he understood; and Azdra'ik shook him.

"A wish. A wish. —She ruled this land when these trees were acorns, and she's not all dead, do you understand me? Wizards can be trouble that way, and among witches in this wood it's a plague! Didn't you see the warning in the forest? Didn't you apprehend there's something wrong in this place, before you went guesting in strange houses?"

Curiosity stirred, not for Azdra'ik's question, but for his own: incongruous curiosity, held eye to eye with an angry goblin, but pain seemed quite ordinary by now. "Why?" he asked Azdra'ik. "Why pay so much? What am I worth to you?"

A long-nailed finger jabbed his chest. "Because, thou innocent boy, if she had had the rest of you she would have gained *you*, and gaining you—gained substance in this world, among other things neither you nor I would care to see. But thou'rt

mine, thou art *mine*, man—she can't touch the horse while I
hold him nor touch me or thee by the terms we agreed to. So
walk! You're bound to the witchling by magic nor she nor we
can mend, and, by the Moon, you're going to find her!"

He did not understand. Bound? By magic? He stared stupidly at Azdra'ik, until Azdra'ik flung him loose, with:

"*Walk*, man, or *fall* down that hill, I care nothing which, but
find her you will, so long as you have breath in you—don't look
back, *don't* look back now!"

It was his worst failing, curiosity: the moment Azdra'ik said
that, he could not but look back—and he saw the witch as if she
were very far away, in the dark between the trees. Faster and
faster she came as he watched—

"Fool!" Azdra'ik shook him and spun him about to face
him. "Don't go back, you've no right to go back now, don't
think of her!"

"I don't want to," he stammered, shaking with cold. It
seemed when he shut his eyes she *was* there and he was *not*
free . . .

"She can't claim you again unless you will it, man, don't
think of her!"

"I'm not," he said, and it was the truth—he had rather
Azdra'ik's company than the ghost's, for ghost she must be:
Azdra'ik at least was living, and solid, and where he had been
and what he had let touch him he wanted not even to think
about now that he was clear of it.

"Then keep walking!" Azdra'ik shoved him and he walked.
But constantly he had a compulsion to look back, or to shut his
eyes to see whether or not she was there—but it was not her,
it was the goblin lord behind him, he convinced himself of that
without looking back; he heard the constant meeting of metal
and Lwi's four-footed stride in the leaves. He did not need to
look over his shoulder, or even to blink so long as he could resist

it—because at every blink of his eyes that place was waiting and at every weakening of his will that ghostly touch was brushing at his shoulder.

A light glowed through the trees, with a source beyond the next hill. The witch again, Tamas thought, reeling blindly through the dark—it seemed to him in his despair that they must only have gone in circles or that the witch had won and Azdra'ik was defeated, finally, fatally for both of them.

But the forest seemed to grow thinner as he went. Thorns and brambles grew more frequent. It was the east, he began to hope at last, the east, and the edge of the forest, and the faintest of rising suns.

He lost his footing in his anxiousness to reach it, skidded and fell—the second time, the third, he was not sure, a slide over dry and rotting leaves. He made it to his knees, hearing Azdra'ik behind him as sound and sense spun and whirled through his wits. He reached his feet, and Azdra'ik had not struck him. His next reeling steps carried him to a massive rock, from which he could see a dim gray dawn, a last fringe of trees, a vast and open valley: he launched himself down slope for that light and glorious sky with a first real belief he might escape.

An iron grip spun him about and slammed him back against the stone. Azdra'ik's hand smothered his outcry, Azdra'ik's whole armored weight crushed him against the stone, and for a desperate, bewildered moment he fought to get free, expecting the god knew what betrayal.

Then he caught from the tail of his eye a chain of dark figures crossing the open hillside below them.

Azdra'ik's enemies might well be his allies; that was his first thought. If he might free himself if only for a moment and attract their attention—but the least small doubt held him hushed and still. He felt a short, sharp movement as Azdra'ik jerked Lwi's reins, warning the horse to be still—and in only that small interval he saw more and more amiss in those figures down the hill, a foreignness in gait and armor.

Not men, he began to be sure now: they were goblin-kind, broader and smaller than Azdra'ik, like bears walking on two legs, armored and bristling with weapons.

"Those," Azdra'ik whispered, the merest breath stirring against his ear, "those are itra'hi, man, do you see the difference now?"

He tried to speak. Azdra'ik lifted his hand a little.

"No noise," he managed to whisper.

"Wise of you."

"Where are they going?"

"To mischief, always. Be still."

He was still. He watched until the goblins passed out of sight around the rock, and for a time after. Then Azdra'ik seized his arm and led him, Lwi's reins in his other hand, down a stony flat somewhat back of the track the goblins had crossed, and for the first time under the open sky.

Wooded hills rose on every side of them: huge boulders tended down to a straggle of grass and a dizzying prospect over a dawn-shadowed valley. It seemed to him that smoke stained the sky. Fires glowed within that smoke, hundreds of them, in a distance so far the eye refused the reckoning.

"Burdigen," Azdra'ik said. "Albaz."

"There's fire," he said faintly. "Why?"

"Have you never seen war, man? This is war."

"Against whom? Why?"

"Need there be a reason? That men exist. That the queen wants the land. *That* was the betrayal the witches of the Wood made inevitable."

"Why?"

"You do love that question. How can I know a human's thinking? Greed, perhaps. Or merely whim. A foolish witch wanted all that the queen had, and she tried to take it. While I—"

There was long silence. "What would you?" Tamas asked.

"I wanted what was ours," Azdra'ik said bitterly. "I wanted what was ours from time past. I thought there was a hope in humankind."

"Of what?"

"Of common sense." Azdra'ik seized his arm and shoved him along, and he saw no choice but walk—in a place made for ambushes, and not for silent passage with a shod horse. The rising sun picked out the faintest of colors, warning them they were vulnerable; but if he were free this moment he could not face that woods now, or bear its shadow. The witch began to seem to him a recent dream, a nightmare in which he had not acquitted himself with any dignity or sense . . . but the consequence of it was with him, in the cut finger, the chill in his bones, the vision of the dark and that cottage at any moment he shut his eyes.

"I'll walk," he protested faintly, trying to free his arm. But he stumbled in the next step and Azdra'ik jerked him hard upright and marched him a hard course downslope and among the rocks.

"It's where they went," Tamas objected, and jerked at Azdra'ik's hold a second time. "Where are we going?"

"To our little would-be witch. The fool's using the mirror."

"How do you know that?"

"Does the sun shine? How do you *not* know? Are you numb as well as stupid?"

He did not know. He did not know how the goblin knew, except by smelling it or hearing it in some way human folk could not. "Why?" he began to ask, hauled breathless along the slope in the wake of what he had no wish to overtake, and with the vision of smoke and distant fires hazy beneath them. "Inside or outside the woods? What do you—?"

Another jerk at his arm, that all but lifted him off his feet. "Quiet!" Azdra'ik whispered, and led him down and down the hillside, all the time holding Lwi's reins in his other hand. On a steep, gravelly stretch Lwi slid past them and all but broke free. But Azdra'ik held on, the reins wrapped about his fist, and meanwhile gripped his arm so hard the feeling left his hand—stronger than a man, Azdra'ik was; but what Azdra'ik proposed to do on the track of a dozen of his enemies Tamas had no idea: no idea what Azdra'ik intended and no idea whether he was not better off drawing the weapons he still carried and trying the small chance they offered—

Were they going down there? he wondered. Were they going into war and siege? Nikolai's tales had seemed adventurous, distant, long-ago—but facing the fires in the haze across the plain, he found such destruction not romantic at all, rather a promise of terrors, in a land where goblins were the rule and humans were the prey. The fate of this valley might next spring be Maggiar's and the people suffering next year might be his own—while a goblin hauled him willy-nilly along the hill with what purpose he could not decide.

"I'll *walk*," he protested again, hoarsely, and jerked his arm to make the point. Azdra'ik did not let him go, but he kept his feet under him for the next dozen steps without wincing and Azdra'ik eased his hold.

Then without his asking or expecting it, the creature let him free.

He had thought he understood goblins, since Krukczy Straz—until this one, damn the creature, twice spared his life, and rescued him, and kept him on his feet last night, when sleep would have left him prey to . . . whatever he had dealt with in the deep woods. Did one stab in the back a creature who had thus far led him nowhere he would not go?

Not when he was doing very well to keep his feet under

him, and skirting hill after hill in the very footprints of a goblin patrol, above a smoke-hazed overlook of cities under siege.

I t was scarcely light outside when master Nikolai roused them out of sleep, gathered up all the things they could use and ordered Yuri to take Gracja's tack and get out of the hall— Karoly, poking up the fire in the fireplace, with no evidence whatsoever of breakfast in preparation, said he would follow, go on, get out, go with Nikolai and Krukczy as far as the gate: he had something yet to do and, no, he did not need help and he did not need boys' stupid questions this morning.

"What's the matter?" Yuri asked Nikolai while they were saddling Gracja. "Are goblins coming? Does he know where Tamas is?"

Master Nikolai said, "Does any wizard make sense, ever?" and ordered him to stop asking questions and go.

So they led Gracja out as far as the gate in the shivery half-light of morning, with Krukczy stumping along like a moving rag-heap, Zadny loping from one to the other of them and around and around Gracja's legs. Yuri found his teeth chattering, and told himself it was not fear that did that, he always did that when he slipped out in the morning cold without breakfast.

But what master Karoly was doing in there must be serious, the way he had snapped at them and wanted them out the doors before he started.

Maybe he was burning the tower down, so the goblins could not use it. He had heard that a general should do that, if a tower was likely to give an enemy a place to hold. But there was all of the forest around the tower, that could catch fire if that was the case, and burn all of them with it.

Surely he's thought of that, Yuri thought to himself, but one never knew about Karoly—sometimes he was fearfully absent-minded.

Maybe instead the old master was laying a curse of demons on the doors and locking the goblins out. Karoly was certainly a stronger wizard than they had ever believed in Maggiar: Yuri was in retrospect chagrined and on best behavior, thinking he and his friends at home had been lucky Karoly liked them.

"He's taking a long time, isn't he?" Yuri asked. But Nikolai gave him no answer and neither did Krukczy, who was sitting like a brown lump among the vines. Zadny whined and pressed close against his legs, nosing his restraining hands. Zadny was shivering, too, feeling the uneasiness, Yuri thought, the way he felt Nikolai's anxiety.

"Master Nikolai, what's he *doing* in there?"

"Wizard-work," Nikolai said, his jaw clamped so tight the muscles stood out.

Zadny whined. A wind began to rise. Brush crackled near them—that was Krukczy, heading away from them in a great hurry.

"Troll!" Nikolai said, and made a grab for him. "Krukczy! Troll! Come back here!"

But Krukczy was through the vines and out of their reach. Came a sudden blast of wind and leaves began to fly and vines to whip about the wall like snakes, blowing loose around the open gateway. Came a dreadful wailing inside the yard, loose boards or something—Tamas had always said that was what made sounds like that in the night. It was loose boards.

Or owls. It might be owls.

Gracja tried suddenly to bolt. Nikolai hung on to her reins as she rolled her eyes and tried to stand on her hind legs. Then light burst inside the gates, light bright as noonday flooding out over the paving stones, casting the skulls and the poles into eerie shadow, as if the sun had invaded the tower. Wind shrieked. Dust flew into their faces and stung their eyes. It wasn't owls. It wasn't boards creaking. It was the shriek of iron bending, it was a roaring like flood coming down, it was cold, and the thump of loose shutters and banging pails and the gate hitting the wall.

"Come *on*," Nikolai shouted, starting to lead Gracja away. Gracja was more than willing to go, to run over him if she had her way—but, Yuri thought in dismay, they were deserting master Karoly, leaving him in that place with that banging and shrieking going on: and Nikolai would not do that. "Wait!" Yuri cried, "wait! He said—"

Nikolai only grabbed him by the arm, holding Gracja with his other hand, and yelled, above the wind, "Get on the horse!"

"We can't leave him!" he cried, but Nikolai yelled louder: "Get on the damn horse, boy, it's Karoly's business in there—he told *me* he'll follow us!"

He was used to moving when Nikolai yelled at him in that tone—his feet began to move, without his even thinking; and then he drew another breath to argue right and wrong. But whatever-it-was shrieked around the walls, scattering gravel from the crest, and Gracja was struggling to break away from them.

"It's wizard's business!" Nikolai yelled into his ear. "Get up on the horse and stay out of it!"

He found the stirrup and got on, while Nikolai held her—Nikolai did not give him the reins; he began to lead her instead, while she was trying to get free and run. Bits of twigs and leaves were flying around them, Nikolai was hurting himself trying to run and hold on against Gracja's wild-eyed fright, and he could only duck down and try not to let a branch rake him off.

He hoped master Karoly was all right, he hoped Nikolai knew where he was going, he hoped—

He hoped they would only get to somewhere quiet and warm, because the wind was more than cold, it had the chill of earth and stone and it cut to the bone.

"He's in trouble in there!" he objected to Nikolai: if Nikolai had more confidence than that in master Karoly, he did not. But Nikolai kept them moving until they had left the stone wall behind. Then he gave up running, only limped along at Gracja's head in a wind-tossed dawn.

Zadny was still with them, Gracja had run her fright out, but anything could scare her into another panic; and Yuri had a cold lump of guilt lying at the pit of his stomach because he had been a boy and a burden. Nikolai had had to protect him, instead of helping master Karoly, Krukczy had run off from them, and Nikolai was doing the best he knew to get them somewhere— he began to understand that master Karoly had given Nikolai orders: Get the fool boy to safety, was probably what Karoly had said.

He slid off Gracja's back as she was still moving, hit the ground at Nikolai's heels. "Master Nikolai. You ride. You shouldn't have been running. . . ."

Nikolai gave him a look in the cold daylight, a drawn and dreadful glare—'run' was a sore word with Nikolai right now, he realized that the instant it was too late to swallow it.

He amended it, with a knot in his throat, "I know you'd have stayed if I wasn't there."

Nikolai kept walking, all the while casting him foul looks. "Maybe I wouldn't," Nikolai said. "Damned wizards shove you here and there and don't ask your leave. . . . Who's got a choice? Who's got a bloody choice, lately?"

"He magicked us to go?"

"He did or common sense did," Nikolai said. "Get back on that horse, boy. *Get on!*"

Nikolai made Gracja stop. Nikolai's pride was sorer right now than his arm was and it was not a good time to argue the point: Yuri scrambled back into the saddle and shut up, but it grew clear in his head that Nikolai had all along been put to bad choices, Nikolai would have gone after Tamas to the ends of the earth, if he could have, but he could never have made it alone.

And if wizards and witches were at work, it was a good job that Zadny had broken that rope, because otherwise Nikolai would be dead on the hill at Krukczy Tower, and Tamas would not have any help at all, that was the way he added it up—so he was *not* all to blame for things.

And, more to the point, Zadny had found a trail, running along with his nose to the ground, blundering into this thicket and that bramble, as if the wind, gentler once they were past the walls, were playing him tricks, but he was clearly onto something.

"He's following them," he said to Nikolai. "Tamas went this way—Zadny wouldn't follow, else."

"Good," Nikolai panted, not in good humor.

And finally: "Maybe we should slow down for Karoly," Yuri said, when Nikolai was well out of breath. "You said he was going to follow us. . . ."

"I don't know what the hell's following us! —No. We don't slow down. Damn that troll. 'It'll help you,' Karoly says; 'It'll go with you,' Karoly says . . . 'I'll follow you one way or another,' he says. Probably as right about the one as the other."

"There's tracks."

"I'm not blind. —Dammit!" Nikolai was in a great deal of pain, and Zadny crossed his path and bothered Gracja; but Nikolai would not agree to take his turn riding, not even after they stopped for rest and water.

So there was nothing to say—Zadny came back from an inspection of the area and tried to climb into Yuri's lap, whining and clawing at him, wanting to go on, and Yuri wrapped his arms around him to keep him out of mischief while they sat and rested. Nikolai's face was white and he was sweating, but he was clearly not going to listen to advice, or reason. In a moment more Nikolai got up, took Gracja's reins and told him to get on, and they waded the stream, where the horse tracks were clear— two sets of tracks, Nikolai had spared breath to tell him, which confirmed what he thought he saw; and on the other side they found horsehair snagged on thornbushes, where horses had climbed the bank.

"One white," Nikolai said, and added, short of breath. "It's the same ones we've been following."

But why was Tamas even going this way, instead of home, Yuri wondered, once they had found Karoly's sister dead?

And what had master Karoly said last night about a piece of mirror and the heart of hell? Everything he had overheard jumbled in his head. He had not understood all of it at the time, and now it slipped away from him in bits and pieces—

But Zadny was smelling something else as they went, shying back with his nose wrinkled and his hackles raised, and Nikolai squatted over the prints a second time. "What is it?" Yuri asked, about to get down to see for himself, but Nikolai shoved Zadny out of his way and got up.

"Someone wearing boots, moving at a fair pace. Someone a little taller than I am."

His heart sank. "That's not Tamas."

"No," Nikolai said, and led Gracja further down the bank, to thoroughly trampled ground. Horses had been back and forth here, had drunk, perhaps, had torn up the earth in deep, water-standing prints.

"That goblin Krukczy smelled?"

"Very probably. It's a narrow foot. And long."

He did not want to think about that, he did not want to wonder and to worry when he could not help—but there were other prints, and Zadny stayed bristled up and uneasy as they went.

But toward afternoon, and still following those tracks, they came to an old foundation, a well, overgrown with vines. People of some sort had lived near here, unless goblins had, and if Tamas and the witch were going anywhere looking for somewhere, this certainly began to look like more of a somewhere than the forest was. He began to imagine riding just around the bend of the water, finding another ancient tower, and a white and a black-tailed horse waiting safely in the yard.

What are you doing here? Tamas would say, all upset with him; and he would answer shortly that it was a very good thing he was, and they should go back and get Karoly: a witch and Karoly together ought to be able to deal with the goblins and they could all go home.

But he could not help thinking of Tajny Straz, and the skulls and the poles; and about that light and the wind that had broken out around the tower. When he thought about that, the whole forest seemed cold and menacing, and he began to hear every rustling of the leaves.

Something suddenly bubbled in the stream beside them, rose up with a rush of water and scared an oath out of Nikolai. It looked like a mass of water-weed, or a huge mop upside down.

Krukczy.

"Damn you, get up here!" Nikolai said. "What's happened to Karoly? What happened back there?"

Krukczy ducked under again and resurfaced somewhat downstream in a reedy area, just his eyes above water, his snaky tail making nervous ripples along the surface.

"I don't trust that thing," Nikolai muttered. "I don't trust it."

And just beyond where Krukczy was—

"There's *two* of them," Yuri exclaimed, and pointed, seeing a second lump in the water, another snaky ripple just beyond.

It vanished just as Krukczy did.

"Dammit!" Nikolai cried.

But Krukczy was not running away from them. He came squishing and dripping out on the shore further along beside a ruined wall, and a gateless gate. Before they reached him, Krukczy had shaken himself off and sat down to rest on one of the old stones; and Zadny had raced ahead of them and leapt all over Krukczy, getting wet as Krukczy patted him with huge hairy hands and tucked him into his lap, in curtains of dripping fur.

Then the second troll came out of the stream, shook itself, and came and sat down by the one they had now to guess was Krukczy.

"Well," Nikolai panted, leaning on Gracja's shoulder, next to his leg. "Well, now, we've got *two* trolls—they've sat down, and I suppose we wait here and hope Karoly makes it. Or we think of something. Or the goblins find us—in which case—" Nikolai caught a breath and looked about them, at their grassy space between the woods, the stream, and the ruined wall. "In which case I want us solid cover and a place to hide the horse. —Is that bow of yours any good, boy?"

"Yes, sir." He took it for leave to slide down, with the bow in hand. "It's Tamas' old one." He did not like this planning for goblins, as if they were a certainty. There was no tower beyond that wall that he could see, no door that they could bar, just the sky and the woods and the old stones around them. And he was tired, and scared, and cold, and there was no sign of Tamas but the tracks and a bit of horsehair on a thornbush.

"Goblin was here," Krukczy said, holding Zadny in his arms. "I can smell him. Smell him lots."

"The same one?" Nikolai asked him.

"Followed them," Krukczy said, and the other troll bobbed its head in agreement.

"Hssst!" Azdra'ik said, catching Tamas' shoulder, and hauled him back to cover among the rocks, next to Lwi. There was not a sound but the horse and a bird singing somewhere near, in the late afternoon of this bad dream, on a long and rocky ridge. Then Tamas heard the faint jingle of metal, more and more of it.

"Another patrol." Azdra'ik extended his arm and pointed off along the slope. "I want you to go down and along that hillside, do you see?"

"Me."

"I'll keep the horse here."

"It's *my* horse. . . ."

"It's a large horse, fool. Go down there now and don't argue. Do you want him seen?"

"You're not going to eat him!"

"I much prefer young fools. —Get down there! Now!"

Tamas made a violent shrug, threw off Azdra'ik's hand and scowled into his face. "What is it you want? —Bait?"

Azdra'ik frowned at him, dreadful sight from his close vantage. "At least you stand a chance that way. —Take that damned thing away from her!"

"The mirror?"

"The mirror. The mirror. *Yes*, the mirror. Lady Moon, stand in a field and shout, why doesn't she? —Get down there, fool, before the rest of the world hears her business."

"How do *you* hear—"

Azdra'ik's hard fingers bit into his shoulder. "Because *you're* with me, because you resound of it, man, like a hammered bell; it bounces off every magic in the world, particularly if she wants to find something. That's why that patrol is hiking about the hills chasing its own tail. And that's why they haven't found her yet. But *you're* here with me, do you comprehend me yet? No? —Twice a fool. Go!"

He did not grasp Azdra'ik's purposes, but that patrol they had both seen he understood. That something had gone amiss with Ela's plans, he was sure; that Ela was making a magical commotion of some kind, he had Azdra'ik's word for it—and there was no question of her danger if the patrols found her. He scrambled away among the rocks, ignominiously dismissed, vowing he was going to live to rescue Ela, then take Lwi back and avenge himself on Azdra'ik ng'Saeich, sorcery and all—

But if Azdra'ik had told two words of truth, Azdra'ik wanted him for a way to obtain what a goblin dared not touch: he did not in the least believe that Azdra'ik meant to wait up here with his hands folded while he located Ela. It might be that Azdra'ik could not find Ela past the confusion he claimed existed. It might be that Ela's magic overwhelmed some sense goblins possessed and ordinary folk did not, and it might be that all that Azdra'ik *could* do now was to loose him like a shot in the dark—something about geese in the autumn, silly pigeons to their roost, he thought as he worked his way along the hill, exhausted and at wits' end. He had no more idea than Azdra'ik where he was going, he only hoped if there existed any shred of magic in him he would find Ela before the goblins did.

He passed along the long hillside, wary of ambushes. But perhaps Ela's magic did possess an attraction of its own, because something told him bear left and uphill, and, once he had gone far enough to have himself irrevocably confused, after the last split in the ridge, and once he had climbed down and up again, whether he was still on the same hill or not, he saw Skory's brown shape among huge pale rocks. The mare was still under saddle, grazing the coarse grass on the hillside.

He slid down the dusty slope toward the horse, losing skin on his hands. Skory interrupted her grazing to look at him, then went back to cropping the grass, loyal horse, while there was no sign of her mistress.

He dared not call out. He only followed the impulse that had led him this far, walked along the hillside among the head-high boulders—and seeing shadow where no shadow should be, looked up, expecting a cloud overhead but there was none, just a darkening of the air and ground ahead of him.

I don't like this, he thought, and imagined some sorcerous goblin trap, but he could not think of going back. It was this way—he was sure enough to keep walking; and nothing visible threatened him, not the towering rocks, not the deadness of the grass or the leafless bushes. Perhaps by the sky above there ought not to be shadow on this ground, but it was no illusion: the air seemed colder as he walked, a wind began to blow, and when he looked back in unease, he saw nothing of the rocks he had just passed.

Worse and worse.

"Ela?" He dared not call aloud. He felt the cold more bitter than he had expected—whether it was the lack of sleep, or the dank chill in the air and the way things of magic tricked the memory. He had the feeling of walking toward some kind of edge, some place where everything he knew ceased.

Then there was that jingling of metal he had heard before, soft and growing louder: the patrol, he thought, and sought some place to hide. Dust whirled up on the wind, and through the veil of the wind came riders all in goblin panoply, banners flying indiscernible in the thickened air. He hid himself among the rocks as they streamed by him unseeing, riders on creatures shadowy and dreadful, with eyes of lucent brass and the sheen of steel about them—they passed, and the sound diminished to a thumping in the earth and in the stones, that itself faded.

The rocks remained. The dust did. He was uncertain of everything else: it fled his mind like a dream—they had been goblins, they had been men—he held to the solid stone and felt the world unpinned and reeling around him—felt the rock shift in his grip, thump! once and sharply, as if the earth had fractured, and might do so again.

He made himself let go of that refuge, while his heart said danger—he let go the stone and walked, then ran across the trembling earth, through the dust and the howling wind. The jolts in the earth staggered him. The ground was darker and darker ahead—the quaking rocks hove up like ruined pillars.

Beyond them the air was ice—and sound ceased. He came on Ela in a frozen swirl of shadow and dust, the wind stopped with her garments still in motion—the mirror blazing in her hands like a misplaced piece of the moon.

He reached for her—reached and reached above a widening gulf, as wind began to roar and move about them, storm that whipped Ela's cloak about him and his about her.

Ela struggled at the envelopment, struck at him and tried to escape; but he would not let her go—not her and not the mirror: it burned his hand with fire and with ice, and he would not believe in the dark or the wind any longer. He believed in the hillside, and Skory waiting, and the rocks and the morning sunlight, no matter the shapes that came to his eyes. Fool, his brother called him, fool who would not make up his mind, but he knew what safety was, he remembered the stones and the brush and the mare and the sun on the stones and he meant to reach that place.

Then it was quiet, and they were there, almost within reach of Skory. Ela tore at his hand to free herself and take the mirror back.

"Stop it!" he protested. "They're after us, for the god's sake, get on the horse, they can hear the magic—they're looking for you!"

"Don't ever," Ela gasped in fury, "don't ever, do you understand me?"

"Girl, they hear it, everyone hereabouts hears it—" He had not yet let go her hand or the mirror, and she had not stopped kicking and struggling to have it away from him. "Stop it! Listen to me!"

"Where were you? I *told* you stay with me, and you go wandering into the woods—you're the cause of all this! I don't need your help! Let me go!"

All right, he thought, all right, others had told him so in his life—Bogdan said it: everything was his damned fault. But her shouting was going to bring trouble on them, and he could not hold on to a furiously fighting girl and catch the horse at the same time. He abandoned his argument and his hold on her and the mirror in favor of catching Skory before she bolted along the ridge.

But when he had caught the mare's reins, he looked around to find Ela disappearing straight up the slope.

He dared not shout after her. He muttered words only Nikolai used and hurled himself to Skory's back, out of patience with the mare's opinion what direction they should go, out of patience with contrary females altogether, and rode breakneck after the wretch, steeply and more steeply uphill, until he had to dismount and climb.

He had left Skory in a stand of scrub pine. Ela was not hidden. She was sitting down when he came up behind her, crying her eyes out, he could hear it—and he refused to be moved.

"Get up," he said. "Take the damned horse and the mirror and go where you like, I didn't come to rob you."

"I can't do it," she sobbed, "I can't do it, I wasn't strong enough . . . I lost the woods, I wasn't *there*—"

That was the first admission of truth he had had out of her—and, god, at this moment she looked no older than Yuri was.

He sat down beside her, weak in the knees, now that he had stopped running. She buried her face in her hands and sobbed for whatever reason stupid girls cried for—while he had a lump in his own throat, of self-pity, it might be, counting *he* had no prospects but the goblins hunting them.

"Look," he began, "crying's no good."

She made an effort to get her breath. "I was trying," she sobbed, "I was trying to find my way in the Wood, but it wasn't doing what it ought—nothing's done the way it ought ever since you came—"

"All right. All right, maybe that's so—but maybe mistress didn't know everything."

"You don't know!"

"That's not the point, Ela!" God, he could hear Nikolai shouting it at him and Bogdan on the practice field. "The point is, you're not winning, are you? You're not winning. *Maybe* it's my fault. *Maybe* I'm not going to do anything I ought to do. That's not the point either. What are you going to do to win?"

She swallowed a breath and another one—while her lips began to tremble and angry tears welled up.

"Don't dare," he said. "Don't you dare. You were left with a weapon, girl, a damned important one, by the commotion everyone's making over it. Azdra'ik wants it. Do you want him to have it? Or what are you going to do with it, now the first try's gone bad?"

"If mistress' brother hadn't gotten killed—if you were any help, but, no, you were off in the woods—if anything mistress told me had worked the way it was supposed to—"

"That's not the point either. What are you going to do to *win*?"

"You've no right to talk to me that way!"

She was the most maddening creature he had ever met, but the goblin lord himself. He was at the end of reason, and sanity. "Then take the horse," he said, not even angry now, only reckoning what he would be worth, and how long he would last as an obstacle once Azdra'ik caught up, or the patrol did. Longer, he thought, if he could get clear of Ela, by going afoot, and maintain whatever magical echoes Azdra'ik said confused goblin pursuers. "Just take the horse, get out of here, and good luck to you. I'm tired, I'm just very tired, Ela. If you're going to be a fool, go do it by yourself."

"I'm not a fool," she said, her chin trembling. "She didn't tell me how it was going to be, she just said it would work, go and do this and this and this, and if that didn't work—if that didn't work, I had to find a place where magic was . . . and we can't get into the Wood in the right place, I can't find the center of it—I don't know what to do!"

Her mistress was a liar, her witchcraft was a muddle of truth, misinstruction and guesswork, and nothing in her life had prepared Ela to guess for herself. Entirely reasonable that she offered no answers and no reasons, he thought: she had none for herself. And such chances as he had to take, he could not do with a fifteen-year-old girl hanging around his neck.

But another sort of coming-to-senses occurred to him, seeing she wanted to act the child: he pulled her up by the wrist, took her face between his hands and kissed the second pair of lips he had ever kissed, neither kindly nor gently, intending to finish it with a cold Goodbye, I'm leaving—after which, in his fondest and most foolish imagination, she would come running to his heels and ask his help; or at least grow up a week or two.

But came a curious giddy feeling—it might be the mirror or it might be something as mundane as his lack of sleep. He grew short of breath; Ela's arm had arrived somehow about his neck and he found himself doing exactly what the ghost had done—

passing on what had happened to him. He began to draw back in dismay, but the look in her eyes was as astonished, as bewildered and as frightened as he had been, and her fingers were knotted into his collar and the fist with the mirror was clenched into his sleeve.

"I'm sorry," he found breath to say—from which beginning he did not know how to get to Goodbye. He blurted out, "I'll get you to your horse," and bundled her downslope where he had left Skory tied.

"I don't know where we're going," she said, putting the chain over her head.

"Where *you're* going," he said, and untied the reins.

"I am not!"

"Just get on the horse," he said, and faced her toward Skory's saddle. "Don't argue. And be careful. Azdra'ik's out there looking for you."

She had her foot in the stirrup. He shoved at a clinging mass of skirt and cloak, and she landed astride, with a frightened grasp of his hand.

"What have you to do with him?" she demanded. "What happened to you? —*Where were you?*"

"I met a ghost," he said, and intended to give Skory's rump a whack. But she still held his hand.

"Whose ghost?"

"Ylena. That was what Azdra'ik said. He said she owed him a wish. It was me he asked for, or I don't know what would have happened." Skory's restlessness was pulling at them, scattering shale from underfoot, and he had to move a pace to keep up with her. "Get out of here."

"No. —No, I'm not going without you, I *need* you!"

"That isn't what you said."

"I never said, I never said that. I tried to bring you back—I *did* bring you back, and you can't leave!"

"You worked magic on me? You put a spell on me?".

"I brought you back! I brought you out of the woods, I rescued you! You can't leave, I won't let you!"

Wait and see, was on his lips to say. That she had bespelled *him* was treachery. But the touch of her mouth was on his lips, and maybe it was a spell: he was still moving beside Skory's drift, with her stupidly holding his hand.

"*That's* why I couldn't stay," Ela protested, "*that's* why I couldn't find you, I couldn't work in that age of the Wood . . . Ylena's the worst ghost we could meet! She's the witch who started the curse! She wants the magic! —Tamas, you can't stay here, you can't stay near this place, neither of us can! She's too powerful in the Wood, mistress didn't know that. She wants the mirror, that's what's gone wrong— She's planned this forever—"

He all but tripped over a bush trying to keep up with the mare, and fell behind, but no longer with the notion of going back and disputing passage with a goblin. He began to follow at Skory's tail, with the deep woods of yesternight too close in memory, and a shadow whispering in the dark, saying that there was no freedom from the magic the witches of the Wood had already made.

"So where else can we go? Do you know?" They were not headed back into the woods, but further along the hillside. "Ela?"

(A place of power, Tamas. My place is strongest, and safest. They dare not kill me, by the spell that binds them here, they dare not—I *am* your ally, if you would only listen. . . .)

He stumbled, so clear the voice was to him, like a memory of something he had never heard, something that had to do with that place behind his eyelids. He was cold through and through, he was lost in dark—

Azdra'ik! he called in that dark territory, and for a heartbeat believed Azdra'ik his hope and his safety—but that was a fool's thought, a dangerous thought—god, if Azdra'ik should have heard him . . . if the witch had . . .

God, no, he had escaped that embrace once—he had no desire to court it again, no desire even to think about it. He overtook Skory and limped at Ela's side. The sky had gone to milk and brass. His chest burned, and from brass the sky went to palest violet against the ragged shadow of the pines. Ela drew Skory to a walk in the slight cover of the trees, and he found a saddle-tie to hold to, half-blind with exhaustion, stumbling on the crumbling shale—while something within him said, dark and cold as night,—Tamas. You can trust me. It's my own interest, Tamas, as well as yours, your defeating her is in my interest, and I've no quarrel with the girl—

Listen to me, Tamas. . . .

Curse all witches who made this folly, he thought in distraction. Curse the ignorant witch who had taught Ela by guess and by supposition: he had that clear now, too: Ela had had reason to be distraught, realizing of a sudden that all her resources were unreliable—so she looked to him?

Gran, he thought, and could all but see that charm-hung tomb in the rocks of Maggiar: Oh, gran, if spells are at work here—if her mistress has lied—if one ghost can harm us—I know you wouldn't. Can you hear me, gran, where you are? I need you, if you can hear me.

Foolish way of thinking—expecting magic, thinking that gran could possibly hear him . . . he was down to such boyish imaginings.

But would not magic work that way? Was that not what a wizard was for—to demand the impossible of the world?

The peasants did—the country-folk came with their barley-straw men and their offerings of food and their requests for children. . . .

What had gran to do with that? What had gran to do with them?

If gran's ghost *could* come back, she would stand between him and that apparition of bone and shadow—gran would never abide threats against what she called her own.

But where did he begin thinking such foolish things? As a shield against the dark? As a wizard-wish? Or a boy's longing for gran's stories not to have been lies—when everything around him spoke of desolation and death. Gran's sunlit woods, gran's bright towers and gran's fields and villages and gran's faery. When was it so? Why fill her grandsons' heads with such hopeless, bare-faced fables? Was it an obligation of witches to deceive? Was that all that magic was? He had never felt that in Karoly.

Gran had crossed the mountains and gotten children with the lord of Maggiar—or—whoever his grandfather was. . . .

Why? To escape the folly the witches here had done? But why *lie* about what was here?

Because below them now was devastation. And Ela went— lord Sun knew why or where: he doubted she knew, except it bore them away from the hunters, and away from the haunted woods.

There was a hot supper, even a decent one. Nikolai insisted on making a small fire at sunset, saying if goblins smelled the smoke, they were apt to smell horses and human beings, just as likely, and tea and flat-cakes would put spirit in a body—but supper lay like a lump in Yuri's stomach. The trolls had gone off somewhere—into the stream, most likely. Zadny had had a flat-cake and part of his, and was off investigating a frog or something at the water's edge, among the reeds.

The time was, not so many days ago, when he would have been over there himself, as lively and as curious as Zadny, inclined to poke about with sticks in the water and turn over rocks, but right now he thought that he had seen enough strange things to satisfy him for months and months to come. He wished the trolls would come back, he wished the wind did not sound so lonely in the treetops; and he understood why Nikolai was sharpening his sword, scrape, scrape, scrape, but that was not a cheerful sound, with the wind and the sighing of the tall trees and the flicker of what was, after all, a very small fire against the night in a probably haunted place.

Most of all he wished he had some idea where Tamas was tonight, and whether Tamas had had a good supper.

And what had become of Bogdan, to be evenhanded about it. He knew he should feel dreadfully guilty for being glad it was Tamas they had a chance to find. Unquestionably he would still be here if it was only Bogdan they were tracking . . . he had gone out from home and over the mountains when it had been just Zadny, for the god's sake, so he had no question about his courage or his resolution on his brothers' behalf, but he had never considered before now that he really would not miss Bogdan that much if he could only find Tamas alive, and he did not think that made him out a very honest boy, when it came down to it.

He had found out a lot of things about himself since he had set out across the mountains—he had always thought of himself one way, that he did not have to be serious, *he* was not the heir to Maggiar. He would always be the youngest and he could do fairly much as he pleased in his life.

But Maggiar seemed very far away tonight, even if it was the same sky and the same stars over them. All the things he had used to do and all the friends he had used to have and all the things he had used to be interested in were on the other side of mountains—on the far side of sights none of the other boys had seen and experiences the other boys would never have, that was the truth of it. Tamas had given him his bow and he liked holding it now. He felt better for touching it, as if, as long as the wood was warm against his hands, things were not so bad.

It would grow cold if Tamas should die, that was the stupid kind of thing the ballad-makers said; but he had seen so much of magic in this place he was not so sure it was all stupid. He felt better if he had something of Tamas with him tonight, so maybe anything would do. Maybe the stories had something true about them, and it mattered less what it was one held to than how hard one thought about the person. Maybe if he could hold it tight in his arms and think of Tamas very, very hard, he could make him hear him:

We're here, we're looking for you, don't give up and don't do anything stupid. . . .

The wind whipped up of a sudden, a dreadful, sudden blast that chilled the air, that blew even the blankets into a rolling tumble and the fire into a trail of sparks and embers. Gracja whinnied in alarm and Nikolai leapt to his feet.

"It's the wind!" Yuri cried, cold through and through, and trying to stop the blankets and the pan from flying away, while Nikolai was grabbing after Gracja. "It's the same wind—"

Things that had started flying toward the gate started blowing back again, as if by magic—a gale was blowing from out of the gate, too, with equal force, and Yuri felt it hit from both sides at once, blowing his hair and his cloak straight up and around and around, and when he had fought himself clear of the cloak and prisoned it in his arms he saw the cooking plate fly up into the air, high as the trees, and come back down with a clang.

He stared at it, in a sudden silence, in the starlight. And looked up at a disheveled figure standing on the shore, at an old man in a pale cloak, with his hair all unkept, a man—

Lord Sun—it was master Karoly, walking as if he were very, very frail . . . or hurt.

Zadny ran up to him—shied back again, circling about in bewilderment, at master Karoly's feet.

"Karoly?" Nikolai asked cautiously, and Karoly kept walking slowly, until he had gotten to the flat rock where they had made their fire. The wind had died. So had the fire, once, but it immediately sprang up again at Karoly's feet, with no cause that Yuri could see.

"Master Karoly?" he said, advancing cautiously, Zadny close about his knees. "Master Karoly?"

"I would very much like some tea," Karoly said in a faint, hoarse voice.

Tea, Yuri thought, and remembered the pan falling, and ran to get it, while Nikolai came near, stuck his hands in his belt and remarked, "Hell of a woman, your sister."

"God," Karoly said, with a shudder Yuri could see from there. He swept up the pan and filled it with water from the brook and came and balanced it on the fire at Karoly's feet.

But Karoly was talking to master Nikolai, saying something about his sister, and when Nikolai asked how things had gone, master Karoly said only: "Not totally—as I'd hoped. It's Ysabel. I've kept her company . . . all the way from Tajny Straz. But I think it's Pavel, too—he wasn't altogether sane. I'd hoped . . ."

Master Karoly was shaking. Yuri grabbed up a blanket from its grassy tangle, shook it out, and master Nikolai put it around Karoly's shoulders.

"She got ahead of me," Karoly went on, and his voice was so faint and strained it was scarcely louder than the creaking of frogs in the brook. "I'm afraid she's reached something else, something *here*, that shouldn't be. Her and Pavel. This was his home. —I would really like supper, Nikolai. I don't think I can do any more."

The sky lately ablaze with colors had gone to dark as they picked their way along the barren heights, seeking the cover of scrub and rocks as much as possible. A faint smell of smoke was on the wind. In the valley below, the sullen glow of goblin siege-fires made constellations and clusters of hellish stars, and the number of those fires, Tamas did not know how to reckon. He only knew that Maggiar could never withstand that tide once it lapped up against its eastern borders. Those lights went on and on to the horizon, where the hills narrowed in, and beyond, for all he could tell: campfires, the burning of human homes and livelihoods, the god knew.

(Many, the voice within him said. They have no mercy.)

He tried not to listen, resisted even blinking as much as he could, the dark around him matching so well the dark behind his eyes. Hard enough to keep walking, hard enough to keep his ankles from turning or his knees from failing. In the easier places, he clung to Skory's saddle-strings and guided himself by that, because his wits were so muddled and weary he tended to nod even while he walked. He suffered dark moments in which he was aware of nothing, no ghostly voices, no visions, just dark, and rest, and that, he thought in his muddled way, might be the witch trying to lull him into trusting sleep. She could afford to bide her time, knowing a man had to rest, had to, when he had not since . . . he had lost count how long it had been since he had dared even shut his eyes.

The ghost had shown him Bogdan—shown him his brother in goblin hands and he had not stayed to ask her whether that vision was true—he had had a sword by him in that cottage and he had clawed his way out the door and fled without even thinking of it, when, if he had been a man, he might have threatened her into telling him the truth, he might have learned enough to help them right there, and he might not then have needed Azdra'ik's rescue, or lost Lwi, or ended up where he was, running for his life with no notion even where he was going.

His footing failed him. He caught himself on Skory's saddle, or thought he had, except he came awake in the dark, flat on his back on cold stone, with a shadow leaning above him.

He was back in the troll's den, he had waked again and it was back—

"Tamas?" Ela said from out of that shadow. —Ela's hands were the hands touching his face. He had to recall where he was, and he almost longed for the troll, and the cellar, instead of the hillside, and the fires, and the flight.

"I haven't used the mirror," she said in a faint voice. "I'd rather not. Tamas, Tamas, are you all right?"

He had a bump on his head. He must have fallen when he reached for the horse—or he might have walked a ways blind and numb, for all that he knew. It was no matter. He was lying down and he had to get up and go on, but even a moment of rest was to cherish. He drifted, half-waking, aware of Ela, thinking that, except the lump on his head, he was more comfortable right now, and closer to sleep, than he had been in days.

"Tamas."

"I know. I know. I'm moving." But it was hard to move at all, and he lay there collecting breaths for the attempt, or however many attempts it might take. Then that tingling feeling began again, and a flickering glow like marshfire fluttered over Ela's arms, over her heart and throat and almost to her face— mirror-magic. She shouldn't do that, he thought, it's my fault she's doing that, I have to get up—

He tried. He began to rise on one arm, and got as far as one knee when he heard that faint sound of metal he had heard before. His heart sank. He snatched at Ela's hand, wanting no more magic, wanting quiet.

"It's a patrol. Quiet." He saw Skory's shadow, and got up as quickly and quietly as he could. Skory stood with head up and ears pricked—he caught her reins and put his hand above her soft muzzle, distracting her, cajoling her.

For a very long time there was nothing—only that sound, and Skory's alarm, and the soft, soft sound of Ela's cloak and skirts as she came near to wait.

Maybe the patrol was on the other side of the hill, he thought, maybe it was an echo from somewhere, and they were safe within their little cluster of scrub pine and brush.

Then, looking up the hill through the twisted pine boughs, he saw the flash of metal by starlight and the moving of shadows along the slope.

"Hobgoblins," Ela whispered, faint as breathing.

The small ones, he thought; the ones Azdra'ik compared to beasts. The ones that had taken the towers, and left them guarded by human heads when they abandoned the places they had taken, not even caring to occupy them. He kept his hand on Skory, felt her nostrils flare and her head toss in alarm as a wayward breeze carried goblin scent to her—it was not a greeting he had to fear from her, it was a sudden bolt for safety.

And thank whatever god watched them, the wind, that skirled so unpredictably in these cuts and crevices in the hills, was in their faces at the moment—goblin noses might be keen enough to smell them. Goblin hearing might pick up their least movement.

But for eyesight—the one in the cellar of Krukczy Tower had missed him, while these . . . these tramped down the hill and passed so close, so close to them at the worst moment that there was only a clump of brush between them and the goblin column, and they still did not see, nor smell, nor hear them. The foremost led the way downhill and the others followed, shadows sheened with figured steel and bristling with bows and spears, that diminished on the slope, and filed away into the dark approach to the valley.

Support for the siege of human towns, he thought, beset with a shiver now that the danger was past. He let go Skory's reins, wiped his hands on his sides, and felt he could breathe again.

"The hills must be full of their armies," he said in a hushed voice, and felt his knees trembling with exhaustion. For his part he would insist they keep going under cover of darkness, but Skory had had her own troubles at the last, had had to consider climbs carefully—Skory had had little rest herself, by day or by night, and, he thought distractedly, perhaps they should leave her and go afoot.

But she was goblin-bait for certain if they did that, and he was by no means certain they ought to go on in the haste they had been using.

(Go back, something whispered in him. Yes, go back. Bring the mirror back to the woods, Tamas. That's the only hiding place.)

He saw the ghost for the instant, white and drifting among the trees. He was not even sure he had had his eyes shut—he thought that they were open, but he could only see the dark, and that figure, and when a rock met his shin, he felt it over with his hand and sat down, propping his elbow on his knee and trying to rub sight back into his eyes, rubbed and rubbed and tried to banish that persisting vision in favor of the hillside, and Ela, and the ordinary rocks and shadows.

Stop it, he ordered the ghost, stop it, let me go, you swore to Azdra'ik—

A hand touched him and he flinched from it, thinking it was the ghost, but the rattle of pebbles agreed more with the hillside, and with the rock he had chosen as his anchor in the world, it felt more like Ela's touch, and he became sure of it when it slid to his hand and closed on his fingers—it was warm and fleshly, and it wanted his attention, sharply *insisted* on his attention.

(Two innocents, the voice within him said. Two damned *fools*.)

He jerked his head, thinking as forcefully as he could, Go away! And, beside him, Ela—

Ela slipped her hand from his and rose to her feet in silence. He could see her when he looked up—he saw her walk away from him as far as where Skory stood, and stand there, looking out into the dark. He felt a wall between them, as cold, as palpable as stone. He felt—a memory on his lips, that foolish moment he had thought to teach Ela a lesson. His mouth burned with it. It might have been an instant ago. Foolish, foolish exchange, with a witch . . . with the witch of the Wood, no less with all that name seemed to mean in this land, in this war—

He saw the pale edge of Ela's face appear from the shadow of the cloak, like the moon from eclipse, felt her eyes on him, a regard both intimate and dangerous, as if—as if trust and mistrust and all she knew hovered only on that moment.

He wanted to be nearer to her—he could not decide to get up, and before he could persuade his weary legs to move, Ela walked back to him, arms hugging the darkness of her cloak tightly about her.

"Something happened to you," she said—as well say he had committed every treason imaginable, it was that tone of voice, it was that feeling in the air between them.

"I told you," he protested.

"I can *hear* you."

He was too weary for puzzles. But she meant more than the words, she meant something dangerous, she meant treachery and lies and the fragile hope that he was not lying.

He shook his head desperately. He did not understand, he wanted her to know he did not understand even what she was talking about.

"The way you hear magic," she said. "The way you—know it. I *hear* you."

"Couldn't you always?" Nothing made sense to him. But he was sure of things he did not know how he knew, he was guessing things he could not possibly know, he remembered her arms about him and how in the last few moments he had felt her presence near him like a shadow in the wind, all in the desperation and scatter-wittedness of the moment—he was dreaming now. He had lost his sight or he had already been dreaming then, and he was sitting on a real stone on a real hillside looking up at her, but he was only dreaming of Ela, as a man drowning in witchcraft might reach out to a safer presence and a safer dream. Don't go away, he wished her. The witch will come back. I can't shut my eyes but what she comes back.

Ela turned her back on him, perversely left him prey to the dream—but she stopped, then, and turned back and looked at him in such a way he knew she was not deserting him, he knew that she was angry at the ghost and not at him, and he could not remember if he or she had just said a word aloud—god, he prayed it was not a permanent condition, this listening, this— rawness of the soul that felt Ela's shadow, balanced dread of the ghost and fear of her own anger and her own impulses toward him, forbidden things, forbidden closeness—a witch did not care, a witch did not *this*, and did not *that*, mistress had always told her, and most of all a witch did not harbor such longings to be touched, or held, or to rest safe, with just someone, *anyone*, once in her life to hold her.

He would hold her—he would do anything she asked, anything but feel that lonely—he had never *been* alone, he had had brothers, he had had parents, he had had Karoly, he had never known such a feeling, except in the troll's den—but she turned abruptly away, and gave him her profile, pale as starlight. She stared into the night and her loneliness welcomed the shadows, the way mistress had taught her. Her presence cooled to ice.

"You didn't know," the child-woman said at last, the merest whisper. "Magic always had to be in you: the mirror knew. I know you didn't lie to me, but something's happened, somebody's made it happen—you're—hearing—me, aren't you?"

"I don't know what you mean," he said in frustration, but he already knew she meant the magic, and knew he knew—but he had no idea whether it was something that had broken out in him, or something someone had done to him, or it was good or it was bad, or whether it was the ghost's doing, some shameful mark of his near debauch and rescue—he was beyond his own understanding, utterly, afflicted with ghosts and with thoughts and feelings that were so certain and so utterly unproven to reason that he could not draw a line between what he had dreamed or what he had done. "I don't know what I'm hearing, I don't know what's going on in me."

His fear leapt to her like fire, and died, starved of substance, chilled to death while she gazed into the goblin-haunted dark—no, she did not want to be touched, now, to need that was weakness, and she was not weak—while he—he had meant no affection in laying hands on her or in kissing her lips, he had not come here to court some girl while his home was at risk, he was not so shallow as that, please the god, he was not such a fool, if only he knew whether it was his thought or hers that chilled his impulse to go to her and hold her. If he should touch her now, she would become more dangerous to the world than the ghost in the Wood; if he should want the things she wanted, he would never know his own thoughts again; if he should fly away to the ends of the earth this instant, it would make no difference: she would go on hearing him forever.

"Don't," Ela said faintly, still without looking at him—if she had looked at him just then her glance would have burned him like fire—Then the world jolted, thump! back to earth and rock, and Ela standing distant from him. After a moment more she did look at him, came back and sat down by him. Then he looked away, himself, not to start it all again. He felt precariously balanced, and he only wanted to lie down and sleep and wake out of the dream that had so many discordant parts in it—perhaps he *was* still sleeping, perhaps he was still in the troll's den, perhaps it would come back soon and he would not have to concern himself with solutions or escapes.

No, not asleep, yet. He caught himself from falling with a jerk of his head, which proved the case, and did the same thing again, thinking quite calmly that it was most unusual to fall asleep terrified, and that he was quite close to falling and adding another lump to his head, if that first one was real.

He simply could not open his eyes this time. He slid down sideways, with the whole night spinning, and tried to open his eyes, for fear of the ghost, but he felt the warmth of a cloak cast over him, and a living body next to him, and a weight on his arm. It seemed Ela was making a pillow of him, and hurting his bruises, but they were mostly numb: it was not that which he wanted to object to her—it was that it was no place and no time to rest, and that there was a ghost trying to find him in his dreams. She should magic them both awake . . .

But sleep was a weight he could not move this time, not even to lift his hand to wake her.

11

S upper seemed to help. Yuri thought to himself that master Karoly must have been all day without food, and small wonder, then, he looked so vastly over- come: it was *not* all the ghosts, Yuri tried to con- vince himself. Fear was not the reason master Karoly's hands shook and rattled the knife against the pan. But Nikolai did not look cheerful in Karoly's arrival, and Zadny butted his head in Yuri's lap and tramped him with his huge paws, unwilling to be separated from him by so much as an arm's length—nor had the trolls come back, since the wind and the ghostly presence, and Yuri did not blame them: if he had not known Karoly, and known Nikolai, he might have run off, too.

"So what do we *do*?" Nikolai asked when Karoly set the plate aside. Yuri was very glad Nikolai asked questions like that. He had sat ever so long in his life waiting for grown-ups to ask questions like that.

"We see if we can get her back again," Karoly said.

"Who, your sister?" Nikolai asked.

"No telling. No telling what we'll get now. Ytresse was here. Ylysse was." Master Karoly took a stick and began stirring the fire around, sending up sparks in streams into the dark. "Ytresse was before Ylysse, Ylysse was the first of our time— Ysabel knew her. But Pavel—Pavel—*he* has to be one of the ones in the mix."

"What mix?" Yuri asked faintly, figuring everyone would tell him to shut up, they always did.

"The ghost," master Karoly muttered absently. "Ysabel's in pieces. Bits of her, bits of Pavel . . . Ytresse held this place after it fell, while Tajny Straz was building. And Ylysse. And Ylena. I wouldn't except any of them."

"Who are they?" Yuri wanted to know, but Nikolai got up from the fireside and stood behind him, his hands on his shoulders. "The castelan. Dead witches." Nikolai said under his breath, not interrupting Karoly, whose meddling with the fire had not ceased.

"Attract her into a whole," Karoly muttered. "Ysabel's— diffuse right now. That's why you can't find ghosts." Sparks flew up. An ember snapped. "It takes passion to make a haunt. Murder, violent death, tragic death . . . that, oh, yes, yes, she had." More sparks. "Ysabel? Ysabel? Do you hear me, sister? It's Karoly calling you."

The sparks from the fire seemed to hang too long in the wind, to dance and swirl and come together like a congregation of fireflies.

"Then the obsessed ones," Karoly said, still stirring, still sending up stars, "the ones that can't turn loose of the world— that's Ysabel, too, that's certainly Pavel. I think that's Ylena."

Nikolai's fingers bit painfully into Yuri's shoulders and Yuri held his breath, unable to look away from that aggregation of sparks. He heard Zadny whining and growling, he felt the hair on the nape of his neck lifting and he wanted to run, except master Nikolai's fingers were bruising his shoulders.

A shadow rushed at them, a shadow shaggy with brown hair burst through the fire scattering embers, and turned and hissed and spat.

"Krukczy!" Yuri breathed, while Krukczy brushed at the singes to his coat, and spat and fussed, the other side of the fire, in the dark. Zadny barked, once and sharply, and Yuri hushed him.

But the magic had stopped. "Damned troll's right," Nikolai said in a low voice. Master Karoly had gotten to his feet, turning slowly to survey the woods, the ruined wall, the dark along the stream. The other troll had shown up, too. It huddled in the reeds.

"Damn," Karoly said, flinging out a gesture of disgust, and paced a wide circle. "Damn, and damn, Ysabel, don't be contrary, do you hear, don't be contrary! Do you want the goblins to get away with it? Is that what you want? To spite me, is the queen going to get away with what she did to you? With what they did to *Pavel*? He's dead. He's there with you. So are others, Ysabel, for the Lady's sake figure it out!"

Yuri flinched, because master Nikolai was hurting him— and it seemed to him now that the sparks were getting up on their own, that they were making a shape.

And the old man rounded on it. "Ysabel?"

The fire blew up and sparks showered and whirled in trails of glowing smoke, up and up and up, until it made a shape, or shapes, all rolling and twisting like snakes.

"Pavel," Karoly snapped, "get out of the way! Do you hear? You're not protecting her, you're in the way, do you hear me?"

A thread spun off, and snaked around and around the center shape.

"Ysabel!"

Sparks flew every which way, and of a sudden a great wind blasted through their midst. Sparks stung Yuri's face and hands, and Zadny barked and growled at something as Nikolai let go his hold and swore.

Trails of glowing smoke spiraled all about the stream bank, raced along the walls, wove among the trees, and spun faster and faster. Nikolai had his sword, but there was nothing a sword could fight, only the wind, and of Krukczy and his friend there was no sign at all.

Then came a voice that might be a woman's voice, Yuri could not tell. It was everywhere, and terrible, and a face loomed up right in his face, saying, "Who are *you*?"

He did not think he ought to answer. He stood still, while Zadny leaped and tried to bite it, but Karoly said sternly, "Ytresse! Is it Ytresse?"

The swirl broke apart and spun elsewhere, around and around and around the circle of firelight, and suddenly rushed from everywhere at once, up and up, until it made a shape.

"Ytresse!" Karoly shouted. "You've no business here. Begone! *Ysabel! Urzula!*"

"That's gran's name," Yuri exclaimed, twisting to see what Nikolai might know. "What does gran have to do with it?"

"Maybe she wants her right name," Nikolai muttered, which made no sense. Nikolai was looking at the fire, over which, when he looked back, a shape hovered, and changed, until it was a woman's face, and another woman's, and a man's, Yuri could not tell which—they blurred one over the other and the features changed like pictures in glowing coals.

"To the queen," the image said, in its double voice, "to the queen, to the queen—the mirror of what is and may yet be—to the queen—the mirror of the moon, change fixed unchanging—" It said more than that, but more and more voices chimed in until nothing came clear.

Karoly ventured close to the fire—scarily close, Yuri thought: he would not have done that; close enough to pick up a burning stick and trace patterns in the air, patterns which stayed in the eye like the sun at noon. Letters, Yuri thought. Writing, all tied together in knots. The letters turned around and around the way the smoke did, and then streamed, *streamed*, large as they were, right to Karoly's open hand. The smoke followed the letters and the sparks followed the smoke.

Then there was just the fire, and Karoly leaned on his staff and sat down, plump! where he was, head hanging, in front of a tame, quiet campfire.

"So?" Nikolai wondered under his breath. "So? Did it *do* anything?"

Good question, Yuri thought. Excellent question, master Karoly would say. Nikolai gingerly let him go and walked over to where master Karoly was resting. Yuri followed, with Zadny crossing repeatedly in front of him and jumping at his hands. "Go away!" he told Zadny, and grabbed him before he bothered master Karoly, who did not look at all well.

"What was *that?*" Nikolai asked Karoly, and Karoly, with a deep breath:

"My sister. And Pavel. Together. Mostly. Ytresse. Ylysse. Lady Moon, what have I called?"

"So could you talk to her? Dammit, old man, could you find so much as where Tamas went? Did he go through the arch?"

"Oh, that they did," Karoly said, "that they most certainly did."

"Then let's go after them!" Yuri said. But no one listened. Nikolai muttered something about if Karoly had taken care of things the way he should, and Karoly said something about people needing to deal with what was instead of what could have been, and that sounded dangerously close to a fight.

"Stop arguing," Yuri cried, and to his surprise both of them stopped talking and looked at him. "My brother needs help," was all he could think to say. "If the ghosts won't help us, if magic won't, then we have to go there ourselves, don't we?"

"Not in the dark," Nikolai said.

"Not in the dark," Karoly agreed, and got up, leaning heavily on his staff, and began to draw a line in the dirt and in the grass.

Why? Yuri wondered. But it looked like what boys drew in

the dirt when they were going to fight, or a line nobody was supposed to cross. And when master Karoly drew it, he thought, things had better think twice about crossing it. He went and brought Gracja closer, where she could be inside that line when it closed, and all the while Zadny kept at his heels.

All the way about a huge area, master Karoly went, drawing his line. And he came back and muttered something at the fire, which flared up and ran a tendril of smoke out and out and around and around them like a wall.

"We left the trolls outside," Nikolai said, "good riddance."

"They can come and go," Karoly said.

"Fine. Then what good is it? Trolls can come and go. Can ghosts?"

"Not if I can prevent it."

"Well, it's not damn much good at all, is it?"

"You didn't build it, master huntsman. Let's see your line, let's see you defend it."

"Don't fight!" Yuri cried, angry at both of them.

"Listen," Nikolai said, ignoring him, "one—*one* troll was useful. Two of them we don't need. Why are there suddenly two of them? What do we need with two?"

"Because Hasel had one," Karoly said. "Every civilized place has one."

"No place that I was," Nikolai said.

"Then you were never anywhere civilized! And they have them north of here, I have every authority for it."

"Bogles in the hayloft," Nikolai said.

"And the bath-house. And the grain-bins. And the fields and the milking-sheds and the cellars."

"Those aren't trolls."

"It's the same thing!"

"They haven't any tails! I never saw a polevik with a tail!"

"Have you ever seen a polevik?"

Evidently Nikolai had not. Nikolai sulked, and rubbed his

arm and paced. Then he said, "So have we got any help from your sister, or what?"

"I don't know," Karoly said. "I don't damned well know, I'm not going to know until we go in there, it's not an ordinary woods."

"It's not an ordinary woods."

"It's not."

"Well, fine, what's not ordinary about it? Ghosts?"

"You might say," Karoly said, and Yuri sat down slowly and put his arms around Zadny. He had seen all of ghosts he wanted to see today. But if Tamas was the other side of that place, or lost in there, well, he was going, and he did not want to call attention to himself or raise any question between master Karoly and master Nikolai about him not going and one of them staying to watch him. There were times, if one was a boy, it was a good idea not to be noticed. So he let them quarrel with each other, and like Zadny, he just kept still.

Things went more than bump in the night, they moaned and they whispered, and they hissed in the leaves, they croaked and they creaked in the brook and the brush, and they trod on ghostly feet, disturbing the leaves around about the line master Karoly had drawn.

What do ghosts do when they get hold of you? Yuri wondered. But no one yet had said anything about taking him home, so he lay still, shivering in his blanket, and hoping that last noise was Gracja stirring about, *inside* their circle. Zadny was bedded down with him and Zadny was asleep. The trolls had not shown up again, and he wished he could think they were part of what was going on out there, but he feared that Krukczy had indeed found his brother, or whatever made his going worthwhile. He was glad for Krukczy if that was the case. He hoped that he would find Tamas tomorrow.

Hello, he would say, when they rode up on Tamas. Tamas would be surprised, and angry, but over all glad to see him. Tamas would be impressed with what he had done and his keeping his promise—no, truth, Tamas would be furious at him for leaving home and worrying their parents and losing Zadny in the first place; but Tamas would forgive him, because Tamas would be very glad he had brought master Karoly and master Nikolai, who were help Tamas must have given up on—whatever Tamas was doing, whatever he was into, running off with witches.

Probably he was looking for Bogdan. If Tamas had gotten out in one piece, he would be doing that. Or possibly Tamas was trying to do whatever master Karoly was supposed to be doing, that his sister had wanted of him; so master Karoly's sister should not mind helping them, if master Karoly could make her understand.

And what was that master Karoly had said, using gran's name? People said gran had come from over-mountain, and people said gran had been odd. The boys said gran had been a witch. And evidently she was.

So what did that make papa, and what did that make him? That was a scary thought, and one he kept skipping off of, like a stone going over a river—back to the rustlings in the brush and back to Tamas and skip-skip-skip, across that dark spot again that held things he knew for certain master Karoly was not going to tell him, or master Karoly would have before this.

Then—it was after a dark spot, so he thought he must have dozed off—Zadny brought his head up and jolted his arm, and he saw master Karoly down on his knees with his ear to the ground, listening, the way he would do at home. He wondered if master Karoly's sister was talking to him, and he moved his arm and put his own ear to the ground. He was not sure he wanted to hear what master Karoly was hearing, and he was not sure it was right to eavesdrop.

But he heard nothing, anyway, but the noise of the brook and the rustle of the wind, and Zadny's heavy sigh. For a long time master Karoly stayed the way he was, and sometimes after that he cupped his hand as if he were whispering to someone, and listened some more. Yuri's eyes were very heavy, and they kept drifting shut, since nothing was going to happen that he could hear. And finally he knew he was asleep, because he kept dreaming of the troll's cave, and the cellar at Tajny Tower, and about home, too, as if he could drift around the halls. He could see his father sitting late, late in the hall, with no one around him. He could see his mother, looking so worried and so unhappy. He wanted to say, We're all right. And ordinarily in his dreams he could do as he wanted to do, but this time he talked and they did not even turn their heads, as if in his dream he was not there at all. And he went to Tamas' and Bogdan's room, but it was dark and no one was there; and he went to his, and everything was just the way he had walked away from it, even Tamas' box sitting on the bed, and everything dark, but he could see it. It was scary, as if he really was there, and his mother had not let the maids move anything, or even dust anything, because it had a musty, unused smell. He wished he were back with master Karoly and master Nikolai and he wished it would be morning soon.

Which it was, because he heard the birds starting up. And then he wanted to sleep, but master Karoly came and poked him with his staff and said they had to be moving.

Skory had snorted and moved, just a moment before Tamas knew that birds were singing—he had that vague, disturbing impression, and he opened his eyes on gray sky and the branches of pines, seeing nothing wrong: he was numb on his back from contact with the stone, he would ache if he moved, and Ela's weight on his shoulder was truly painful, but he would have been oh, so willing to shut his eyes just a moment more.

But they had at least to think through where they were going and what they were going to do. He moved his left arm to lean on and lifted his head, and saw the rocky nook by daylight, saw—

"Ela!"

Goblins, all about, armed and squatting on the rocks and the earth of the hillside, only waiting, spears angled over shoulders.

Ela waked. He gathered her to her feet in the sweep of his arm as he scrambled up, saw goblins reach for spears and rise to their feet. He reached and drew his sword in hope that goblins had some concept of honor, enough to bring them at him one at a time—enough that it was not a volley of spears they had to face.

But the goblins all about suddenly changed their expression and looked past him, to the sounds of a rider arriving among the rocks. He turned his head just enough to confirm the pale gray horse he suddenly, angrily, believed it was. The goblins stood waiting for the intruder as Azdra'ik took his own time, rode up on them at an easy pace, swung off and lit on both feet at once, with a clash of metal. Lwi shied, snorting in dislike, and Tamas brought the sword up, waiting.

But Azdra'ik waved at whatever was happening at his back. "Oh, put the damned thing down, man, I've brought your horse back, haven't I?"

For a very little he would have swung at Azdra'ik. He did not put the sword away, he held it, waiting for Azdra'ik's joke to play itself out how it would; but Azdra'ik came closer, Lwi's reins in hand, and, with the point a hand's span from him, pushed it delicately, carefully away with the back of his hand, offering Lwi's reins inside Tamas' guard, while all about them was silence and waiting.

"Tamas," Azdra'ik said, looking him straight in the face; and did a beast call a man by his name, or give him time to think how fatal a move it would be to kill the goblin they knew, in the face of so many they did not.

Ela was as much in doubt. He felt her behind him. He kept his eyes on Azdra'ik and everything within eyesight as he lowered the sword point and reached after Lwi's reins, expecting some goblin joke. But Azdra'ik gave up the reins, and grinned at him, for which he was not in good humor. Azdra'ik turned away and swept a grand gesture at his cohorts around them, beckoning them to join him.

"Come down," Azdra'ik said, "come down, pay your respects to the witch of the Wood and—" With a turn half about: "—What *are* you, Tamas, lad? *Have* you a title this morning? Witchly consort, or—"

"Be damned," he muttered, and knew what they had seen and what they thought, while Ela stood hearing this and there was nothing reasonable he could say to Azdra'ik's suppositions.

Goblins came from out of the rocks, two score of them at the least. Tall, these were—like Azdra'ik, with like armor, and like faces, and an elegance and grace about them that declared they were no rabble. They were every bit what he had seen in the cellar at Krukczy Tower, if it had not been Azdra'ik himself—that memory welled up with cold clarity. They *were* guilty of that butchery, one and all of them. He had Azdra'ik's word they were not the lesser sort. These—these, then, were the lords and masters, these were Azdra'ik's kind; and he hoped for nothing different than his companions and Ela's mistress had gotten, seeing what he saw about them. He kept the sword in hand, he wanted to know Ela's mind—but perhaps he had dreamed last night: he felt nothing—nothing of her thoughts or her wishes or her intentions, only her presence. He saw the goblins going through the motions of courtesy toward her, but whether it was some mockery, or honest chivalry, their manner gave no clue. He felt cut off, bereft of that feeling he had dreamed he had last night, bereft of understanding friend or foe, or what Ela was, or where her allegiances lay: she had *been* at Krukczy Tower, she had escaped ambush, and he had thought when he first set out with her that she might be one of theirs. He did not want to think that there had never been any chance of his escape, that she served some goblin master,—oh, god, he did not want to think that.

Not an ordinary forest, the old man said, and Gracja objected to being saddled—smart horse, Nikolai thought, cinching up. There was no question which of them had to ride today. Their wind-blown wizard looked as if a breeze hereafter would carry him body from soul—his hands were shaking, his steps were wobbling: clearly the old man had had all he could bear, and one could give him credit for courage if not for success with his magicking.

If only the old man could have done something about the boys, or magicked Yuri home, or something useful, but there was no place to put the boy, that was the problem—no place to put the boy and meanwhile Tamas was going deeper and deeper into trouble, so far as the ghosts said anything useful to Karoly.

Even the dog was quiet this morning, pressing himself as close to Yuri as he could get. The dog knew there were things he could not get his teeth into, and things that could chill a body into shivers and haunt his sleep—if a body could get any, with skulkings and prowlings all about their circle last night. The little that Nikolai had slept, he had dreamed of ambush, and Krukczy Straz, and the hillside and the birds circling.

Prophetic, it might be.

Meanwhile the old man was sitting waving his hands at the fire and talking to it. If other old men did that, the neighbors gossiped.

"We'd better get moving," he said.

"He's doing magic," Yuri said.

"He's doing magic. He's been doing magic since yesterday morning." For his part he had as lief sit here and let the old man magic up an answer that would save them going through that gateway, but he had no trust that would ever happen, and no trust that matters were not getting worse for Tamas while they sat here. "Come on, old man, are you learning anything? Or should we douse the fire and be out of here?"

The fire went out. Gone to cold cinders. That was impressive.

"No need to waste your strength," he murmured, rethinking the old man's value and the old man's awareness of the situation. Karoly the pot-wizard he was no longer, and perhaps never had been, that much had been clear since yesterday. "Do you want to get up on the horse, or are we still going?" It had been rush and haste and hurry, before the old man had started meddling with the fire. Half an hour ago nothing would do but speed; and half an hour ago the old man had looked on his last legs.

Now Karoly leaned on the staff that had rested against his shoulder; and changed as he was, more lined in the face, whiter of hair, there was a force to Karoly as he rose that made Nikolai think twice about the dead embers and what a life and a fire had in common.

"War and famine," Karoly said in a low voice. "That's all I see. The cities of the plain are under siege. The world reflects the mirror now, not the other way around. God hope they don't lose it."

"Lose what?" Nikolai had to ask.

"The fragment. The one piece that still reflects this world."

"How do you know it does?"

"Because we're here, working against her."

"You mean—" Yuri asked the question. "If it reflects us not being here—"

"—we won't be here."

Enough to upset a man's stomach. "Then why in hell didn't we go last night?" Nikolai asked, and went and brought Gracja back for the old man to mount. "Wait around here with ghosts prowling around—what worse can the ghosts do to us? They can't lay hands on us . . ."

"Don't depend on it," Karoly said—the way Karoly said things and then held his silence, when a body most wanted to understand.

"Get up on the horse." Nikolai held the reins for him, turned the stirrup and helped him up—Gracja verged on horse-sized, a stout pony showing her ribs by now, wanting farrier's tools the boy had come away without: and she took the old man's armored weight with a laying-back of her ears and a stolid plod forward before Karoly took up the reins, as if she knew already they were bound for the gateway.

Or maybe it was like the fire just now, and Gracja had her orders.

Fire crackled. Goblins needing to make no secret of their presence, they were beginning breakfast. They spoke together in a language of lilt and necessary lisp, not without reference to the unwilling guests among them, Tamas was certain—good-natured reference, cheerful reference, oh, yes, of course. It was their fire and their breakfast.

They had not disarmed him. But then no one had, who had ever had the choice. Evidently he did not look that much of a threat to anyone—which did not please him, but it was not, master Nikolai would say, an excuse to be the fool they took him for. He had gotten to unsaddle the horses and give them rest, he had brought their personal belongings to where Ela was sitting, next the fire-making, none of which the goblins prevented, but there was always one watching him, leaning lazily on a spear but never failing attention. He set down the baggage, sat down beside Ela, and darted a glance at Azdra'ik talking with one of his fellows.

From Ela there had not been a single word, not a supposition, not an opinion: counting the sharpness of goblin ears, discussing their choices probably was not wise. Ela had the mirror and Ela had chosen not to use it—Ela surely knew the danger they were in and knew the choices, but she was evidently no freer than he was, and he wished he dared advise her: she looked so young and so shattered in her confidence at the moment. Speak, he dared not; and as for knowing her mind—he could make no guess, only anxiously wonder what Azdra'ik was about— whether Azdra'ik thought that, having the witch of the Wood in his hands, *he* might have use of the mirror; or whether he expected some great reward of his queen for returning it to her.

Spits and forked sticks had gone into the fire, propped on stones, holding flesh black and shriveled already from some previous smoking: their owners set them to heat, each goblin to his own breakfast, as it seemed, no preparation of cakes or bread—and increasingly now his and Ela's place of warmth and refuge near the fire began to acquire companions.

A goblin settled on Ela's other side, and Azdra'ik himself sat one place removed on his side, with a stick on which he impaled something and propped it on the rocks that rimmed the fire, the same as the others had done. All about them now were goblin faces, jutting jaws and flat noses, ears not where ears ought to be. Not untidy creatures, Tamas had to admit: hair, manes, whatever one might call it, were cleanly, black and wavy, some, or straight; loose or in braids; some about the face, some in back. Most wore rings in the ears, and one—Tamas could not help but stare, amazed—had a ring in his right nostril, evidently no inconvenience to the goblin.

And he could not but wonder at the wealth in the armor, of every least goblin in the lot—the most of it was brown and black, plain leather, the sort that foresters might wear; but the knives, the swords, the armlets and other pieces that they wore were blued steel inlaid with brass and gold and silver, and the chain where it showed at sleeve-edges and tunic-hems shone brighter and finer than any he had seen. They were none of them impoverished, who managed ornament like that; nor they had the look of bandits: what they wore was well fitted. Lords indeed—arrogant lords, who laughed, and cast one another grins, with glances back at them.

"They say you're very brave," Azdra'ik remarked.

He did not in the least believe that was what they had said. Then Ela said, coldly: "Pahai'me. Shi ashtal i paseit."

Goblin eyes widened. Faces turned, conversation stopped, and Azdra'ik laughed in what sounded like surprise.

"Pase*ith*, ng'Ysabela."

Tamas cast a glance at Ela: he *heard* the name, constructed it with ng'Saeich, and saw the whiteness of Ela's face, cold, ever so cold and angry. "Spas'i *rai*, ng'Saeich. You are most grievously mistaken."

"Am I?"

"*Did* you kill her?"

Azdra'ik laid a hand upon his heart—if he had one. "I swear by Lady Moon."

"The Lady changes."

"No. She has moods, but she never changes. Nor I. Nor have I ever, young witch. I swear that, too."

Ela did not answer that, Ela only stared at him, and, oh, god, the stress of the question in the company. Tamas saw it in every face, every frozen motion.

"You should learn your friends, young witch."

"You'll let us go," Ela said coldly. "No three wishes this time, ng'Saeich."

Grins broke out among the goblins. One nudged Azdra'ik in the ribs, but Azdra'ik seemed not so amused. "Impudent child."

"You know who I am," Ela said coldly.

"Young," Azdra'ik retorted. "Very young. *Leave it alone*, young mistress. Yes, it has power. So does the queen, and she's well aware of you now, and of us, if you use it again."

Ela said nothing to that, only scowled. What side is she *on*? Tamas asked himself, but clearly it was not quite for or against Azdra'ik, who was not quite loyal to his queen.

Meanwhile the goblin next to Tamas had caught a stick back from the fire, snagged whatever black, ragged thing was sizzling there, cut it and leaned their direction to proffer a tidbit on the edge of his knife. "Our guests first?"

"No, thank you," Tamas said faintly: his stomach was upset enough with the debate and the company. He had rather not look at it, and now that he had, he had rather not imagine what it had come from. The goblin laughed as if it were a great joke, others laughed; Azdra'ik, too, who said, "Rabbit, man. It's rabbit."

"We have our own breakfast," Tamas retorted, which set off more of their laughter, but he got into their packs and un-wrapped what they owned. He could not have eaten that bit of meat, or, on second thought, have used his borrowed goblin knife to eat with—he was glad to keep to bread and cheese, and he offered a portion to Ela.

"A slight of our hospitality," Azdra'ik said. "How are we to bear it?"

Ela said nothing. And so it went. They ate their separate breakfasts in silence. Azdra'ik and his company pieced out theirs on knife's-edge and spoke animatedly in their own tongue. But eventually Azdra'ik said,

"Not a word of thanks for your rescue."

"Rescue!" Ela said.

"Especially seeing young witches with more in their hands than they can handle. That will not serve you in the least, mark me. You know *nothing* of it."

"And you do," Ela said coldly.

The goblins thought this funny.

"Do you?" Ela wanted to know.

"Only," Azdra'ik said, "insofar as I betrayed its secret to the witches of the Wood, and counseled Ylena to make her mirror." Azdra'ik rested an arm on his knee and pointed a black-nailed forefinger at them both. "She was a fool. At the moment of the disaster, I was with the queen. I smuggled the fragment elsewhere and bided my time. Ytresse betrayed her maker."

"Meaning Ylena," Ela said.

"Oh, no, meaning the queen. Ytresse was hers, in all senses but maternity. Ylysse—was her own. Likewise your predecessor—who was twice a fool. Now is the time, I said. Do something with the mirror, I said. But no, *she* was afraid. Now comes her apprentice to take her place, and what does her apprentice for a beginning? Her apprentice wanders the hills using the mirror for trifles and rattling the queen's own gates, then wonders that it attracts notice. Be *glad* that I found you, young witch. And show better manners."

"To you."

"Ela," Tamas said. If there was a peaceful offer from the goblin lord, he was willing to hear it—he was desperate to hear it, considering it was himself Azdra'ik would slice in pieces first if Ela decided to provoke him.

"No, now, I have patience. You remember my patience, man." Azdra'ik nipped a bit of meat off the skewer with a small knife, and offered it. "*Rabbit*, I swear to you. Lady Moon, what a disgusting thought. —Will you?"

"No, thank you."

"The rabbit doesn't care. Not now. There are ways and ways to lose one's concerns. I'd listen to advice, man. I'd persuade the witchling to listen. There is something about her and you that cannot find the right way through the woods—that will never find it, because the magic weights you in one direction, do you understand? The Wood is like that. You'll never meet a thing there but what you've already met, and I *wouldn't* advise going back in."

"What do you advise?" he asked, since Ela was too proudly sullen.

Azdra'ik shrugged. "Why, rattle the queen's gate quite properly. A place of power, that's where to use that trinket. And the Wood is denied you. So—take it to the queen's gate to use it."

"That *would* suit you," Ela said.

"That *is* where you were going," Azdra'ik said, "isn't it? Else you could have circled full about and headed back to Tajny Wood—which I don't think you dared last night to do. The magic—the magic was bringing you toward the queen's own doorstep. And think of it—what better trap for your predecessor to lay, than to plot her magic right down the very course the queen wants most? Irresistible? The queen would not stop you. So who carries that fragment has to come this way. I only hoped to stop you so long as there were choices—to take that bauble back to hiding before you did yourself and us grievous harm."

"Oh, I am sure!" Ela cried.

"An effort foredoomed, I've no doubt now. You were set before birth to be where you are, and I couldn't prevent you. So—since you want to go to the queen, we'll take you to the queen."

"No," Ela said flatly.

"I assure you," Azdra'ik said, "you've no other choice. The world—has no other choice. You see in us a company that does not love the queen. But your obstinacy has put us in danger—has *damned* us to assist you now or die, and I assure you, young witch, we have our preference in the matter."

"I'm sure I should believe you," Ela said, but it seemed to Tamas there was worse than listening, and a more dangerous course than asking why.

"So why," Tamas asked, "don't you just kill us, take the mirror and do what you please? That seems the way goblins do things."

A quiet settled at the fireside. Azdra'ik gave him a look that seemed to go on very long. "Because, man, among other virtues I do possess—I am not a witch. None of us can use the mirror— worse, none of us can long resist the mirror—but the existence of that fragment of the great one is the only freedom we have."

"You say," Ela retorted. But it seemed to Tamas that he had just heard a compelling reason, if it was in any sense true.

"I do say. The mirror shapes what is in this land—beyond this land, for all we know. But as long as there exists another mirror, as long as there exists a different vision in another such mirror, there is hope for us. No, we are not eager to contest with our queen. We'd be content to live as we have, in exile— because we *have* no great hope in opposing her and we have no wish to lose everything in hasty confrontation. But to work against the magic that draws these pieces together—that we cannot, and since we cannot, we attempt to persuade those who can. Unfortunately—" Azdra'ik rose to his feet, towering above them. "Unfortunately, considering who holds it, and who can and cannot use it, the fragment cannot go back into the Wood again. Everything indicates where it's going, and that, young witch, means the queen."

A goblin said something to which Azdra'ik paid attention, something which brought frowns all about, and another and another spoke, in increasing heat.

"He points out," Azdra'ik said then, "that there is no good for us in waiting for the outcome. If you fail, young witch, we will *be* the queen's loyal subjects—because there will *be* no other possibility once she gains the fragment. You see what's at stake for us."

(The Wood is the only safe place,) something said in Tamas' heart, and he felt a great unease, as if that dreaded voice were giving him the only honest advice. (Azdra'ik is a liar, he's always been a liar, ahead *isn't* the only choice open to you. Everything he's done has been to his benefit and our harm. This is not the time to believe him, Tamas.)

But that was Ylena—he had Azdra'ik's word it was Ylena who haunted him, and Azdra'ik was standing in front of them in plain daylight, a goblin countenance which they had learned to tell apart from all other goblins, and which did not now appear to be lying.

"Are you going to let us go?" Ela asked.

"Go," Azdra'ik said, and waved his hand toward the horses. "Unless it occurs to you, as perhaps it will, that there are a great many hazards in the land, and that if you go back to the woods, you would fall into the worst hands that could hold the fragment, except the queen herself."

"And you," Ela said.

"Young witch, *I*, and my company, are as I said, yours to command, if you can command us. That's the nature of the mirror, and of any portion of it. Make us free of it."

Ela reached slowly to her throat, and drew the mirror from her collar. Goblins about the circle rose to their feet, and those nearest jostled for a look at it.

"Have a care!" Azdra'ik said, alarmed.

But Ela hurled it to the rocks at her feet. Tamas jumped back, expecting fragments, expecting—the god knew what. But it lay there whole, reflecting not the sky—but fire; and when he dived to retrieve it, his eye caught the roiling of dark images before his hand shut the sights away.

"Only magic can break it," Azdra'ik said. "Would not I have tried to have a piece of it to myself, when I had the chance? I tried the same. I tried stones and steel and curses, and it would not break."

Tamas gave it back to Ela—was glad to surrender it to Ela, because he only half-heard what Azdra'ik said: louder was the whisper of the wind in the trees, and keen and cold was the touch of a hand at his shoulder, an angry protest he could not altogether hear.

"Don't use it here," Azdra'ik said. "Wait. Be *wise*, young witch, put it away. And go where you please. But unless you use the mirror against us, and I do not for your sakes advise it—this company will go with you, this *company* will go with you against the queen, which is where you're bound, whether or not you know it—until you can no longer hold that portion of the mirror. We—come and we go with that. We rise and we fall with that. We will never betray the holder of the mirror. And that, young witch, comprehend exactly as you hear it, no more, no less."

B eyond the arch was a tumbled ruin, a whole great hall with hardly anything of it standing but the walls—a mysterious place, very old. Master Karoly said it was Hasel, but it was not at all what Yuri had heard regarding Hasel. Master Karoly rode behind them while Nikolai walked ahead with the bow in hand and he followed Nikolai—Zadny keeping right by him, sometimes crossing in front of him, sometimes trying to press up against his legs while he was walking.

It was hard to believe that these halls, open to the sky, had ever had a roof or held colors and voices. Nikolai had talked about wars and towers burning, they had seen the destruction at Tajny Straz, and seen the work of ghosts, but the spookiness about this place was unbearable—maybe, Yuri thought, that it had been dead longer or (he shuddered to think) that worse things had happened there. Constantly there was a hint of movement in the tail of one's eye. There was a chill in these stones that had nothing to do with early morning, and the echo any sound made lived on and on here, imitating voices, while they walked through what had been walls, and a horse went through what had been rooms, with a lonely clatter of hooves.

Yuri cast a glance over his shoulder, just to be sure—and something flitted in the edge of his vision. He felt a coldness at the back of his neck and swatted at it, but nothing was there. If

"I came as quickly as I could," Karoly said, from Gracja's back. Zadny whined and wanted reassurance. Yuri ducked down and held his muzzle, for fear he would start barking—it was not the time for it, most assuredly not the time.

"I want their *heads*!" the lady said. "I want them to pay, Karoly."

"A matter of sovereignty," another said. "Do I know this boy, Karoly?"

"This is Yuri," Karoly said, and Yuri, feeling altogether too conspicuous, stood up, and made a respectful bow.

"And Nikolai," the same lady said. "Faithful Nikolai."

A wind began to blow, picking up leaves and rushing through the trees with a deep sigh.

The trolls leapt up and scattered, as Gracja backed and faced to the stinging gale—Zadny yelped and took out for the brush and Yuri grabbed for him, missed and grabbed a second time, afraid Zadny was going to disappear into the thicket forever.

"Yuri!" he heard Nikolai shout behind him. And: "Karoly, damn it!"

He made a frantic grab after the hound, sprawled full length in the leaves and scrambled up again with a glance over his shoulder.

But there was no sign of the ladies, no sign of Nikolai or Karoly and none of the trolls—it was just woods, just a lot of trees, and a leafy spot, and plain daylight.

He heard something coming across the leaves. He looked and saw Zadny waggling up to him, all humble and contrite, now that they were completely lost. He made a half-hearted snatch and caught Zadny's collar, knelt down by him to look around and try to get his bearings, and it was all just forest.

Zadny licked him on the ear, on the jaw. Damned dog, Nikolai would say. And he would not damn Zadny, but Zadny was not high in his favor at the moment.

That was stupid, he thought. Nikolai would call it stupid—

losing himself for a dog, worrying everyone—making the ghosts angry at him. The woods did not feel as spooky as before, but there were ghosts. As real as death, master Karoly had said. As real as the fact he had had people with him, who were not with him now—or he was not with them.

"Stop it!" he said to Zadny's whining and washing of his face. "Stop it! You've got us both lost, you understand that? Stupid dog."

Zadny ran a few paces off from him as he got up, and ran back to him, and ran away again in the same direction, the same way Zadny had done on the mountain.

"Is it Tamas?" he asked, suddenly realizing what Zadny's behavior might mean. "Is it Tamas you're following? Do you know where he is, boy?"

Zadny went a little further, and circled back and out as he followed, faster and faster. Zadny had his nose to the ground now—he was on a scent, there was no question of it, and whatever had happened to separate him from the others, following Zadny before had never brought him to harm. So he trusted him this time.

A blast of dust in the eyes and a blink and there was nothing, no one, no sign of the boy or the dog—I knew it, Nikolai said to himself, casting about in every direction for something familiar. I knew it, I knew it, I should have had that dog for goblin bait . . .

"Yuri!" he shouted into the woods. "Karoly!" And furiously, desperately: "Krukczy, damn your hairy hide, find the boy!"

"Find the boy, is it?" said a quiet voice.

He spun about. It was the voice on the tower stairs. It was the voice out of his boyish nightmares, the voice drowned in thunder and in rain and sealed behind stone.

"And what about yourself, Nikolai?" the lady asked, drifting closer. Her hair was black. Her gown was black. "Have you no need to be found?"

He backed a pace without thinking about it, but she kept coming until she was as close to him as she had been that day. Wind stirred her gown and her silken sleeves and the dark veil of her hair. She was young and she was beautiful. And her eyes were bottomless.

"Faithful Nikolai. I asked you that day, were you faithful to Stani. And you said yes. Did you know then that was a promise?"

"I've never broken it," he said.

"You're here," she said. "Why?"

"For Stani's sons. For your grandsons." The ground rumbled underfoot. The wind began to blow. He flung up his arm to shield his eyes. "Witch, damn you, rescue the boys, can you do that?"

"But that's why I sent *you*, Nikolai."

"Sent me!"

"All those years ago. Yes. You climbed down from those stairs safe that night. You had a job to do for me. You've done part of it. But it's not done, Nikolai."

"Where's Yuri? What have you done with him?"

"Not I, Nikolai. Not I. All of us—the witches of the Wood, the goblins and their queen—and the young witch, Mirela. Tamas is my heir. Tamas . . . is my heir. And Urzula was not my name."

"Ysabel," he recalled.

"Karoly told you that. Yes, Ysabel, once upon a time. But Urzula is good enough a name for my son to know. Goodbye, and fare exceedingly well, Nikolai."

The lady leaned forward, and rested ghostly hands on his shoulders. He felt the chill even through armor. And touched ghostly lips to his ever so gently.

"I wanted to do that," the ghost said with a wicked wink, and was gone, in a whirl of shadow and pallor, and silence. "One thing more you will do," the voice lingered to say.

"What?" he called after it.

But it was gone, into daylight and ordinary woods.

"Damn!" he cried. "Damn! Lady! *What thing am I to do?*"

In its silence he walked straight ahead. He could think of no better direction. And if there was a ghost in the world that had reason to guide him to the boys, he believed in this one.

But all he found when he had come over the second leaf-paved hill was a bony old man in a gray cloak on an unlikely shaggy pony.

"Where's Yuri?" he asked the ghost. But it was master Karoly who called out from the bottom of the hillside.

"I don't know. I hoped he was with you."

Nikolai slid down the hill on slick leaves, caught his balance under Gracja's startled nose and snagged the bridle for a look up at the old man. "Not hide nor hair. Only the lady. Your lady. Ladislaw's wife."

"Urzula . . ."

"Urzula—Ysabel. You're the wizard, you *knew* what you were doing when you brought the boys here in the first place. Don't lie to me, Karoly! They're caught up in something you know about. She said Tamas was her heir. She said he's with Mirela. What in *hell* did she mean?"

"Oh, god."

"What did she mean, Karoly? You know, don't you, you damned well know!"

"She didn't say a thing about Tamas. She named *Yuri*, to me. But there's not a shred of magic in him, I couldn't find it in any of the boys and she never got a daughter—which she could have. Witches can do that."

"I don't doubt it," Nikolai said glumly.

"Deception I can understand. Her whole life was deception.

Krukczy Straz was the only guard on that border. But, god save us . . . Mirela? Are you sure that's what she said? That that's who Tamas is with?"

"The same name as you said. Mirela. I didn't forget it."

Karoly said nothing more. Karoly climbed down from the saddle, and Gracja shied and pulled at the reins, nervous about something, ears flicking one way and another. Nikolai held fast to the reins and paid his attention to master Karoly, who seemed to have sudden interest in the treetops, or the weather.

"Tamas *isn't* a boy to set in a hard situation," Nikolai protested. "Nice boy—but he hasn't the toughness—god, Yuri's more resourceful than he is, the boy's shown it. Why did she settle on Tamas?"

"It's not settling, master huntsman. You don't *settle* on being a wizard. It's what you're born."

"Then why didn't you see it?"

"You're not listening, master huntsman. *Urzula* may not have known. Magic has its ways of tricking everyone, most especially those next to it. I'd have bet on Yuri myself—but that's evidently not the way it is."

"Tamas can't shoot a deer. What in hell is he going to do with the goblins?"

"Come again?"

"I said—" God, he was off looking at the trees again. "Are you listening to me?"

"Ask your question again."

The question eluded him. "About Mirela?" That was the important one. But Karoly did not look at him. "I asked how he was going to shoot the goblins if he couldn't shoot a deer."

"He has nothing against the deer."

For some reason that sent a chill down his back. He did not know why—except . . . except he was used to Tamas the way he was: not a bad boy, nor a coward, now that he thought of it, nor anything he knew exactly to fault the lad on. The fact was—he liked Tamas better than Bogdan: he suddenly realized that for the truth—that if he could get two of Stani's sons back, he knew which two he would prefer. God, that worried him.

"Magic will out. Magic will out, do you understand, even after years. That Ladislaw fell off his horse and that Stani existed and that Urzula had sons and not daughters—these are all beyond us; and a lot of it was beyond Urzula herself. —Listen to me, Nikolai. Don't give me that frown. Understand me. Urzula sacrificed everything and everyone on the altar of her purpose. I make no excuses for her. That is sorcery. That was the way she chose. But Tamas—"

"The boy is not a killer. He hasn't the heart to be a killer. I wouldn't make him shoot the deer, Karoly. I talked to him, I reasoned with him—but I wouldn't shame him and I wouldn't force him. The boy's—" Reasons deserted him. The boy's expression that day came back to haunt him, the promise to try—the absolute surety in his mind that Tamas was lying to please him, that ultimately Tamas had rather the shame than the kill and the arrow would most certainly miss.

Lord Sun save the boy, he thought in despair, and, still holding Gracja's rein, beckoned Karoly to get up again.

"We can't find him here. We've got to do something. We've got Tamas going lord Sun knows where, we've got a boy lost out there following a damn dog who's following Tamas, if it makes any sense at all where Yuri's gone."

"Tamas," Karoly said, suddenly paying complete attention. "Tamas. That *would* be it, wouldn't it? That's where he *has* gone. No question."

They rode a faint footpath along the flanks of the hills, among pines and massive rocks. In the low places between hills gray haze stung the nose and the eyes, and made Lwi and Skory blow and shake their heads in disgust—while in front of them and behind them, dark goblin figures moved at an untiring pace, figures that flitted in and out among the rocks and sometimes, now and again, vanished along different tracks, to rejoin the trail at some further winding. Tamas wondered where they went— whether scouting for human ambush, or simply taking shortcuts they knew, paths the horses could not climb.

But at one such meeting came other goblins, in plainer armor, and after three of their own party had talked with them a moment, one returned and brought Azdra'ik forward to talk to them, the lot of them with chin-rubbing and fist on hip and downcast looks and language that, even when the chance breeze brought it to them, meant nothing but perplexity to a lad from Maggiar.

"Can you catch any of it?" he asked Ela. "Is it trouble?"

"Something about the way ahead," Ela said. "Something about a meeting, and horses."

He kept still in the chance that Ela could gather more of it.

"Something about the queen," she said. "Azdra'ik asked them something, I can't make it out. They say they don't know, they—"

Azdra'ik came back then in haste, passed all the way back down the column to speak to them. "We have horses. Around the hill and on. Yours may not care for them. Keep clear."

"Goblin horses," Ela said, as Azdra'ik went further back.

Tamas glanced back uncomfortably, wondering what they were, and suddenly heard movement on the road around the bend. He turned his head a second time to look, and the goblins behind him were moving to the rocks.

What came was shadow, shaggy maned, black, with a swiftness and silence on the stony path that made him think for a moment both riders and beasts were illusory, creatures of the mirror—but Lwi shied over and snorted as half the riders passed in strange quiet, and Skory shied further, until the rocks and witchery stopped her. It was a rattle and scrape of claws the goblin horses made, leaving white scratches on the rocks where their feet had touched. Their riders stopped them and slid down, both at the head of the column and behind them—Azdra'ik's company made a quick exchange with them, while Tamas kept a tight grip on Lwi's reins and kept seeing this and that view of the road as Lwi spun and backed, the old hunter snorting and laying back his ears. He caught an impression of long-tufted tails, abundant feather from hocks to heels, and when one goblin horse nearest turned profile, it yawned at the bit and showed fangs more formidable than its rider's—that, and a disposition to snap at its fellows. Eyes obscured in forelock and mane, nostrils less horse than cat . . . Tamas kept a tight hold on the reins and patted Lwi's neck; called him good horse and honest horse, and wished him back in his stall in Maggiar, where he might come to some better end—these creatures might well eat ordinary horses, for what he or Lwi could know.

And it was not fair that magic stilled honest fears, that first Skory and then Lwi quieted, and stood and sweated. Ela had done that, he was certain. "Good lad, good lad," Tamas said, patting Lwi and easing off on the bit, for the ease of the horse's mouth at least. "Just stay back, we won't put you near them."

The goblins began to move then, the ones that had brought the horses withdrawing up the hillside afoot, under what arrangement there was no guessing. It was only clear that their own party was going on and that the other band was staying—riders were behind them as well, and he no temptation to linger. Lwi jolted into a quicker pace, and Skory matched it, on the verge of bolting free.

"Watch her," Tamas said through his teeth, fearing not even magic would give Skory sanity, and all the while something kept saying to him, This is a mistake, Tamas. You have no place here, no earthly thing but breath in common with these creatures. And least of all believe ng'Saeich—

It began to be like a bad dream, their own horses too trail

worn and weary now to keep the pace, and the goblin riders pressing them from behind, which distracted Lwi and made him lay back his ears and look askance. Worse, they entered a deep drift of stinging smoke, where the mountainside was afire— bright flame showed, and elsewhere the grass was blackened. Like the mountains, it was, like the descent to Krukczy Straz, like the way to ambush.

Smallish stout figures moved grayly through the smoke, pacing them on the hillside, figures that appeared and vanished like ghosts.

"Hobgoblins," Ela said. No rider before them had seemed to notice or remark them, and Tamas swung about in the saddle to see if the ones behind had seen.

But when he looked about again, there was not a one of the watchers on the hillside.

"I don't like this," he said. "I don't like this at all. —Don't touch it, Ela, don't."

Ela had her hand on the mirror below her collar, and cast a burning glance toward the goblins. "Those are the ones—*those* are the ones at Krukczy Straz."

"Get on!" he said. "They've looked us over. Let's close it up. Come on."

He put Lwi to a faster pace, and Ela kept with him, the goblins behind them following them or not, he was not sure until he cast an anxious glance over his shoulder and saw nothing behind him but gray haze and empty trail.

"Itra'hi," he said as they rode in among the riders ahead, and there were looks. Two and three and four riders reined back immediately and veered off to the rear before they even reached the foremost riders.

"Azdra'ik," he said to a goblin he passed in the haze.

"Gone," that one said. "Stay with us!"

"Gone after them?" He had not intended argument. It leapt out.

"Stay!" that one said sharply. Lwi and Skory were surrounded by goblin horses and he had his hands full with Lwi. He dared not break from the group and had nowhere to go if he should. Ela stayed beside him, clinging to the saddle, casting fearful looks behind, and with her hand reaching fitfully after the amulet she did not touch. Reassurance, he thought, the possibility of reinforcement . . . overwhelming temptation: (Take it, from her, something said to him. She won't refrain. Something will happen and she'll resort to it, and that's fatal, that's death, Tamas. . . .)

But before the horses had run out their wind, before they had even cleared the area of the brushfire, goblin riders came up from behind them through the smoke, and Azdra'ik was with them, frowning and angry.

"Keep going," Azdra'ik said, but Lwi and Skory could not stand the faster pace, and fell farther and farther behind as they went, as the trail climbed up and up among rocks likely for ambush. Tamas was not sure whether all the riders in their party had come forward with Azdra'ik, leaving no rear guard. For all he could tell enemies might be chasing after them and their group might be in full rout.

But at the crest of the hill and above the smoke, the goblins abruptly stopped, their horses milling about in confusion and turning and snapping at each other in the way of their kind.

Lwi slowed to a walk. Tamas let him. Ela rode beside him in silence as their winded horses climbed, up and up the loose earth that claws had scored before them. Something was wrong with the sky, that was—Tamas' first impression—some dreadful fire, far worse than the last, shadowing the eastern sky with a black pall of smoke.

But the higher they rode the darker it looked, until they came cautiously among the goblin riders and had a look over the ridge. The daylight stopped in the valley, simply stopped, and the rest was a wall of night, a division drawn in sun and shadow across the end of the valley, and across the hills. Looking into it, the sky was pitch black, the more stark for its touching the daylight where they were. Tamas blinked, and had an impulse to rub his eyes, although there was no wavering in the sight, no compromise with his outraged senses.

"Lord Sun," he breathed—but lord Sun did not rule yonder. Other powers did.

"Every day," Azdra'ik said, riding close to them, "it grows. Lately it has grown by valleys and hills. This is the queen's power advancing. This is what you attack, young witch, do you see it? Are you still confident, or will you retreat?"

"Retreat where?" Ela asked faintly. "Where could we go to escape this?"

"You might delay it. Go make young witches. Go make someone brave, or stronger, or wiser in choosing the hour."

Ela shot him a hard, pale-faced look. "It's *mine*."

God, Tamas thought in despair: it sounded like the old, the unrepentant Ela, Ela who could do anything, and they were done, if that was her whole answer.

"Ela," he said.

"He *won't* have what he wants," Ela said. "He can't make up for stealing it, the queen won't forgive him—"

"That's not what I want, young fool! I want this thing taken away from here!"

"For how long, ng'Saeich? For how long do you think you can go on hiding in the hills and looking for charity?"

"No charity!" Azdra'ik declared, clearly offended.

"I remember a night," Ela said, and Azdra'ik glared.

"It was the collection of a debt. A favor done. There was no *charity*, ng'Ysabela."

"Mistress fed you. Mistress said to me later that you were harmless. I didn't believe it. I still don't."

Azdra'ik swept a bow from the saddle. "I'm ever so gratified, young witch." And with a cold stare: "But what *other* judgments are you fit for? Lady Moon, wait at least for your own maturity!"

Ela shook her head and shook it a second time. "That," she said, gazing out toward the dark, "is that waiting? Where is it going from here and how fast? Or is she content?"

The goblins murmured together; and Azdra'ik grimly nodded and slid down from the saddle. "Down and rest," he said, and said something to his people, some of whom rode back down the hill.

"Itra'hi," Azdra'ik said. "Sniffing about us. If you don't make the point with them, they'll not take you seriously. And one *cannot* trust them. —Get down, get down, take a rest. Closer than this—there's no safety."

"Should have let the forest have them," the one nearest muttered, and Azdra'ik:

"Worse will have them. They already belong to her."

"How long a rest?" Tamas asked. There was not a bone of him that did not ache, as he slid down and his feet touched the ground.

Azdra'ik's hand landed unwelcomely on his shoulder, and he looked the goblin full in the face, expecting some foul trick; but Azdra'ik's grip had no force this time.

"As long a rest as the queen affords us," Azdra'ik said in a low voice. "As long as that comes no closer. Personally, I don't expect a dawn."

He stared at the goblin, wondering—too many things to keep collected. His exhausted thoughts scattered, and beneath them a crawling of the flesh insisted, Don't trust him, don't believe in him, don't take his reassurances.

"Mind," Azdra'ik said, "the young witch holds all our lives." He did not know what Azdra'ik expected him to say. But Azdra'ik had not let him go. "A dangerous business," Azdra'ik said in a low voice. "Affections for a sorceress."

"She isn't," he said. And he heard the other word then.

Absurd. "And she doesn't. She hasn't. She won't. Ela hasn't a shred of romance."

"Her opponent is darkest sorcery." Azdra'ik lifted the unwelcome hand on his shoulder, on the way to sitting on the rock beside him. "Sorcery that has less romance than you can imagine. Ask your guest."

"I've no wish to ask her anything! God, . . . I want free of her!"

"She does devil you, then, does she?"

A breath. A difficult breath. Images and fears crowded him close. "Small freedom you won me."

"I bargained for your life, man. The bargain you made with the ghost was your own folly, and damn your prideful foolishness."

"I made no bargain with her!" But he thought of what he had done, paying the kiss the witch had asked, and of what he had been willing, then, to do. It was only from time to time and afterward that he had changed his mind and wanted his own life back.

"Listen. Long ago, *long* ago, man, when Ylena was in mortal flesh, she came to us. Granted, we have our moral faults—"

That was worth at least a bitter laugh.

"I say, our moral faults," Azdra'ik persisted. "Not far different from those of men. Among them contentiousness. And greed. And intolerance. We lost our place in the world—we were driven from it. If our queen took any means no matter how desperate to restore that to us, there were those who would do any work she required. Ask me tonight, when there's leisure for such things. But meanwhile—meanwhile . . . offer the young witch no choices, no distractions of your evidently potent charms—"

He started to object, but Azdra'ik's long-nailed finger lifted before his nose.

"Hear me," Azdra'ik said. "Hear me, or damn her and all of us. If the young witch with that fragment in her hands, with the queen at war with her, has one single thought of compromise, she will worse than die. If she spares a moment for interests other than her own, she will lose everything she has and might have, that is the war she was fitted to fight, that is the war she has undertaken, and that is the enemy she faces, do you comprehend? Sorcery cannot be half-hearted, it cannot *think* with a heart, it simply has to be the only answer she affords. If we are extremely fortunate, we may still be in possession of that fragment tomorrow and the sun may yet rise on this hill. But if you distract her young and eminently scatterable wits—"

Lwi was pulling at him at the other hand. Lwi jolted him with a butt of the head, one more irritance than he could abide in patience. "Her young and scatterable wits have outwitted you, m'lord goblin: *she* is where she chooses."

"Is she? Are you absolutely sure?"

Now that Azdra'ik said it—he was less so.

"There," Azdra'ik said, with a nod toward the horizon. "There is the most potent magic I know, that has moved events before now in the world. Whatever magic on this side and that may have done—the queen fences masterfully, feint and double feint and misdirect, press and provide the adversary the chance, do you see: the riposte and the waiting target, be it her heart, the queen has done everything on purpose. Disabuse yourself of all thoughts to the contrary."

"Are you her move—against the witches?"

"You might be. The young witch might be. You can't know. I can't. Even Ytresse betrayed her creator."

"The witch Ytresse."

"The witch Ytresse. My creation, the queen's . . . who's to know?"

"Your creation." Anger gathered out of that dark place in him, a muddle of desire and rage, regarding the creature that had its hand on him—he gave a shudder and knew at the same time it was the ghost, a woman's ghost, who had had a foolish, foolish knowledge of this creature. He could not move, he could hardly breathe collectedly.

"You might say," Azdra'ik said. "Surely Ylena remembers."

"Don't talk to her! Damn you, let me alone."

"So you understand what distraction can do to a witch. And how far this all reaches."

For a moment the sound of Azdra'ik's voice was faint to him. He gazed off into the darkness above the hills, and the valley where the fires of destruction still burned, faint pinpricks of red light in the darkness.

"That I'm here is no accident either," he said.

"This close to the queen's domains, nothing comes by accident. You—and I. Your assumption that you are not the queen's may be true—or false."

"I know whose I am," he said, with a sudden thought of gran, like a breath of free air. "I know who sent me."

"Who?" Azdra'ik asked, curiosity quick and alive in his glance, but Azdra'ik surely hoped for no truthful answer from him.

"Ask me tomorrow." He jerked his shoulder free. "My horse is tired. I have work to do."

"Man," Azdra'ik said, as he began to lead Lwi away. He looked back. "It's good advice," Azdra'ik said.

"I don't doubt it, m'lord goblin. I'll keep it in mind."

He led Lwi over to where Ela was trying to care for Skory. "Here," he said, "rest, I'll tend to them."

"What did he argue?" Ela asked.

"Nothing," he said. "Nothing I regard. Go sit down. They're making a camp here."

"The lake is yonder," Ela said, looking off toward the east. "The lake that the queen bargained for. That's where I have to go tomorrow."

"We both have to go there," he said, and said it not for loyalty, but in argument to what in him loathed and feared the thought. I have to, he thought. If magic brought me here, if gran was what they say, gran had something to do with this.

And would she have told me so much about this land, the way it was—for no reason? That wasn't like gran. That wouldn't be like her. *Why* did she tell us—if she was a witch—if we weren't someday to be here?

Bogdan and I—both of us—here.

Zadny kept just ahead, constantly just ahead—the hound might at least have trusted him after all this time together, Yuri thought, especially given he had made not a single try to stop him. But for mile after mile through this endless woods, Zadny skittered away from him like a wild thing. Twilight came, and he stumbled blind and exhausted through the brush, shouting "Zadny, Zadny!" and sometimes calling after master Karoly or Nikolai in the hope they might hear him and follow him.

But it was not until he had fallen on his face and lacked the strength to get up again that the wretch showed up and licked him in the face.

"It's too late for that," he said, and struck at Zadny with his arm. But Zadny was too quick for him, and lay down with his chin on his paws, out of reach, watching him until he could get his breath and stop his side aching and get up to his hands and knees.

Then Zadny ran again, disappearing through the brush.

"Dog!" he yelled, hoarse and furious. "Zadny!"

He scrambled after, catching his sleeves on brambles, tearing his hair and his face and hands as he dived through the twilit brush—and onto an open, rocky hillside, where a shaggy lump sat, holding Zadny in his arms.

"Krukczy!" he cried, sitting up and nursing a skinned knee. It was not fair, it was supposed to be Tamas that Zadny was following, it was supposed to be his brother, and it was not.

Then another troll appeared among the rocks. And another one. They shuffled out and squatted down next the first one, and Yuri stared in dismay.

"Krukczy?" he asked, wondering now which was which, and the one holding Zadny bobbed as if he agreed.

"Come find brothers," the troll said, "find brothers."

It was a riddle. It was powerful and it was scary and the presence of the others made him sure he did not understand trolls, but they were all the help he had in front of him, and he thought he even might know their names.

"Hasel?" he asked, and the second bowed. The third was harder. But he said, "Tajny?" and the third bobbed in trollish courtesy. So he did understand the nature of them. And Krukczy had found what he had come for, Yuri guessed, but *he* had not.

"You've found your brothers," he said, "but I haven't. Let Zadny go. He can find Tamas. I *need* him."

The trolls drew closer together, until they were like one lump.

"Dangerous," said the one he was sure was Krukczy, and the others nodded.

"Wicked queen," said the one that answered to Tajny. And Hasel, whose tower was only ruined stones, said:

"Wicked, wicked, wicked."

"Long time ago," said Krukczy, "long time even for us— the goblins go below."

"Long time ago," said Tajny, "long, comes magic back to the land. The queen bargained with the witches. Foolish witches."

"Foolish witches," said Hasel. "Foolish queen."

"Wanted the lake," Krukczy said.

"Now we go there," said Tajny. "Mistress is dead. We go there."

"Go find brothers," said Krukczy, and rose with Zadny in his shaggy arms. "Find brothers. Make the queen pay."

"I think we ought to find Nikolai and Karoly first," Yuri protested, unwilling for Krukczy to carry Zadny away, or lead him anywhere without their advice. "Karoly would know what to do."

"Not theirs to do," Krukczy said, already shambling away, and the other two got up silently and went after him.

"Wait!" Yuri called after them, afraid to make over much noise on this open hillside. He ran, got in front of Krukczy and tried to block his path. "It's not that much to wait—we can find them first."

"Not theirs to do," Tajny said, and Krukczy lumbered past him and the other two followed, relentless as a landslide.

What did one do? What was right to do? If he went back into the woods, master Karoly had said it, he had no idea where or when the forest might let him out again, or what he might meet in that shadow, alone.

Zadny, let down to walk, skipped and leaped and went with the trolls, a willing companion.

So he saw nothing wiser to do, himself.

Every bramble, every hedge, every branch in the forest reached out to stay them, Nikolai swore it: he was accustomed to pass through a woods as free as a deer's shadow, but his eye could discover no path for himself, let alone for an elderly wizard on an exhausted pony—while Gracja, in Karoly's hands, had her own notion what was the easiest route down a hill—not always the wise one. She fetched up into a dead end, a narrow, leaf-walled wash barriered with a windfallen tree, and Nikolai had to climb over the trunk to reach her head.

But having sat down on the trunk in the process, he found getting up harder than he had expected, and he rested there to catch his breath.

"It's getting darker," Karoly said.

"I'm trying! This is a woods where we could use a dog, never mind trying to track that fool hound!"

"I mean it's getting darker faster than it ought to."

Nikolai looked toward what he took for the west, and glanced over his shoulder to what then must be the east, and he could see no difference. It had gotten to that time of evening when all light was gray and equal in the woods, when the trees and the canopy turned to their own woodland monotones—and there was no knowing what sort of predators might go on the hunt for boys and dogs once night had fallen.

That thought lent him strength to get up. He freed Gracja's rein from the branch that had caught it and backed her out of her predicament—poor pony, she was as blind-tired as they were; and she made a powerful effort to get up the slope again. He patted her sweaty neck when they had gotten to the top of the rise, and swore to her that he would get her out of this woods.

"Get down," he said to Karoly. "Get down, she can't carry you any more."

"We've got to keep going."

"Do it on your own legs. We may need her before this is done. Dammit, old man, just do what I say."

"Can't tell where you'll come out," Karoly muttered, trying to get down, entangled in his cloak, which was snagged on a branch. "Can't tell where he is, *Ysabel* can't get to us, we've just got to go on as we're going, as straight a line as we can hew, however long it takes."

"End up in some bear's belly," Nikolai said under his breath, and tugged the pony into motion so Karoly could get himself past the tree. "Some bear's late supper. Midnight snack. Probably already eaten the dog. Where in *hell* is the troll when you could use him?"

"Keep walking," Karoly said. Which was the only choice he saw.

I t was a strange nightfall, a shadow that hung motionless in the east and then, slowly, in the dying of the sun, spread like a starry blight across the valley and the hills. The goblins built a great blazing bonfire, extravagant defiance against the night, and posted their sentries around about, whether against human armies from out of the valley or against others of their kind.

But their own light blinded them to all but each other.

"Join us at the fire," Azdra'ik said to Tamas. "I swear to you, I *swear* to you it's rabbit and venison, nothing else. Nor has ever been. Come."

There were scruples, and there was hunger, but truth to tell, they had little left in the way of provisions, besides that these goblins seemed fairer and more amiable than their smaller cousins, and one could slide toward believing their reassurances, even against experience. Tamas found himself looking toward the fire, beyond the goblin lord's retreating back, and telling himself he was a fool to have come thus far off his guard with the creatures, or to attribute any common decency to them.

But Ela got up, dusted off her skirts, and walked in that direction, which left him solitary and supperless, except a last little heel of stale bread. What they were cooking this time looked like rabbit and smelled like rabbit, for what he could tell. They had torn back the grass to afford safe room for the fire, a blaze thicketed with sticks and spits—each goblin being responsible, as before, for his own supper, which they collectively proposed to share with their prisoners, their—guests, their fellow fugitives from the night and the queen's displeasure: he had no clear idea what they were in the goblin camp, and that in itself made him equally uneasy with the invitation and with their own refusal. If there *were* overtures toward them and he refused, that could be foolish, too. Even if the goblins only offered a shred or two of understanding of what they faced or where they were going . . . it could make a difference in their living or dying tomorrow.

And if there was treachery and if the goblins intended betrayal, he would be more apt to discover it yonder in their company than sitting here alone.

So he got up and joined Ela in the firelight, easing his way in as goblins edged over to give him room. Goblins laughed with each other, albeit grimly, goblins spoke in low voices, and did their cooking, like any group of hunters. He watched the light as if it were the center of a black and unreasoning universe, until the voice within him said,

(Azdra'ik claims he's my servant. What do you think?)

He shrugged it off, watched as a goblin carved a small carcass in pieces, onto a square of leather, judging that that was the provision made for them, and sure enough, the goblin brought the packet to Ela and set it in her hands.

"Young madam," the goblin called her, bowing, and him: "Young sir."

Courtesy. Manners. There was too much puzzling about Azdra'ik and the company about him, too much of contradictions past unexplained. The ghost flared up all bones and shreds of grave-clothes, and a shiver went through him, a fear of believing anything.

But it was not bad rabbit. There was enough to eat, and warmth from the fire. For a moment or two on end he could shut his eyes and imagine he was back in his own woods, in Maggiar. But the conversation around him was not conversation he understood, and the creak of leather and the jangling of rings and ornaments was martial and strange.

He and Ela did not speak. There seemed nothing to say, that they would say with strangers around them. She seemed to drift very much as he did, remembering, perhaps, or thinking.

But her hand rested over the mirror beneath her gown, and her gaze turned toward the east.

He reached toward her arm. "Don't," he said. "Don't touch it tonight. Wait." It seemed desperate to him that she believe him, and he did not know why he should think so, but what she was doing terrified him.

She let her hand to her lap, and laced her fingers together and bowed her head.

(Inept, said the ghost. And thinking she knows. Damn you, boy, . . . listen to me. Listen before it's too late.)

He blinked, he looked distractedly at the fire. He reached for Ela's hands and clenched them in his own, heedless of goblin stares and nudges of elbows, thinking, God, how can we survive till morning, how can we last the night, how if there's not a dawn?

A goblin arrived out of the dark and whispered something to one goblin, came to Azdra'ik's side and said something into his ear. Azdra'ik made a gesture and sent off ten or so of his company, who gathered up their weapons and followed the messenger.

He was holding Ela's hands too tightly. He let go. But she laced her right hand in his left and held on, only held on for dear life.

"Nothing," Azdra'ik said with an airy motion of his fingers. "A maneuver. A movement. Possibly even some of ours."

"Are there others?" Tamas asked in Ela's silence.

"You saw them."

"Shadows in the smoke."

Azdra'ik said something to his company, and some few of them rose and left, gathering up their weapons from beside them. "Troublesome shadows. The queen's shadows. There will be a guard tonight, I assure you. Sleep with at least that confidence."

"In you," Ela challenged him.

"In us," Azdra'ik said. "In us who have not consented to the queen. No, now—" Azdra'ik forestalled her interruption. "Listen to me. For one night, only this night, will you listen to me, young witch, and let me tell you a story. Was a time we ruled this land, was a time we had the respect of men . . ."

"When," asked Ela, "when ever did you have our respect?"

"Oh, long ago. Long and long, when the old stones were young. Before the stone roads and the fences. Then sometimes men guested with us and we with them. But there was a falling out. Some say it was about the fences. Some say another thing.

But however it was, a man died, a goblin was to blame, and bound as we were by a promise, and such as we are, and such as the promise was that bound us and men—we had no choice. We lost all the world. It was that absolute. It was that much trust we had placed in our virtue. We assumed too much, we believed in ourselves too implicitly. And we failed. So we left the world—and, young witch, let me tell you, to lose the sun and the moon was a dreadful thing. We would have promised anything for a foothold on this earth. Can you understand that?"

Tamas did. He would not have, before the troll, before the tower, before the woods, before he entertained a ghost within him. The firelight on the flat-nosed, jut-jawed profile lent it elegance, even comeliness—or the dreadful sights he had seen had made even a goblin face seem better to his eyes. He found himself glad of Azdra'ik talking to them, even longed to trust the voice, because it was alive, and in this world.

"After hundreds of years," Azdra'ik went on, in the soft crackle of the fire, "after so long a time, the witch Mirela read our stones and our signs and sought us out; and in exchange for a magic she could not do—one night a year we might see the world again. Of course we would agree. What would we not, for the smallest glimpse of moonlight? Then—you know the story—her daughter Ylena also found the way to us. Set me in my mother's place, Ylena begged us, and offered us a year to see the sun and the moon. For *that*, again—what would we not do? But it was an ugly bargain this witch wanted. We knew what she intended. Some of us spoke for and some against—but our queen in her cleverness said that any wrong Ylena did was a human's choice and a human's crime: that as the guilt of one goblin had damned us, the guilt of this woman was to free us. So she took the witch's bargain. We gained our year, and for all that year—can you imagine? We did everything, everything we had dreamed of since I was born—we walked in the sunlight, we saw the colors, we enjoyed every flavor and texture the world has to offer. We were happy . . . except one thing: that no matter our virtue or our fault, Ylena meant to send us back to exile."

(Virtue, the ghost laughed, and Tamas felt cold inside.)

"So the queen cast a spell, that Ylena should have a child Ylena did not want, despite all her magic—in which—" Azdra'ik made a small gesture. "I was an instrumentality."

"You," Ela said.

"I was," Azdra'ik said, with a downward glance, "in a position of trust. And it was not a position I cared for, let me say."

The anger, the darkness of the ghost was for a moment more than the firelight, more than the hillside and the earth and the presence around them. "Damn you!" burst from Tamas' lips, and he swallowed down the torrent that wanted to follow, stopped his own arm in mid-reach toward Ela and the mirror and knotted both hands together between his knees, where they were safe, where he could not reach after what Ela would not, not yield to him—

Not, not, not, he told himself, daring not shut his eyes, staring into the fire until the light hurt and burned and he could not see the darkness inside him.

". . . he's dreaming awake," Azdra'ik's voice was saying, and he became aware of Ela's hand on his arm, shaking him. "One simply shouldn't bed down with ghosts."

"I didn't," he said between his teeth, acutely aware of Ela's presence. "Don't listen to him."

"Or witches," Azdra'ik said, "but, after all, tomorrow things will be different—in one way or another."

"You were telling us," Tamas said, hands clenched, "what your own share of this is."

"Ah. That."

"Why should we believe anything you say?"

"Man, man, you prejudge us."

"What's the difference, you or the creatures that attacked

the towers? What's the difference, you and the ones burning the cities down there?"

"Because we are *not* burning the cities down there. The queen tricked Ylena and held the land, *and* had a hold over Ylena's heir. Well enough if it had stopped there, if the queen or even Ylena could have been content—"

The things the goblin was saying roused echoes, memories of great halls, and goblin courtiers, and music, memories of a reflection that swam in liquid silver—a face that was his . . . or hers, or the queen's, he was not sure, he only knew he did not want to see it clearly. He bit his lip until it hurt.

"I betrayed the secrets of the mirror," Azdra'ik said, "for one reason: if Ylena could have ruled her mirror, the queen with hers could never have prevailed over the world entirely; Ylena's wickedness aside, if another mirror existed, there would be another power—and if one witch failed our measure . . . even if one witch *was* with the queen's, her *ambition* would have led her to wield her mirror for her own interests. Therefore any shaping the queen would cast on the great mirror would always have its rival and neither one could prevail. That was our plan."

Anger grew and grew in him, the ghost troubling him so that he could scarcely sit still. He saw dark behind the fire, a great mirror swirling with baleful images—and he would not, *would* not consult the knowledge that lodged, screaming for attention, behind his teeth.

"The fragment," Azdra'ik said, "was our unexpected result. Ytresse ruled, then Ylysse, before Ysabel. Any of the three you might have met within the Wood: but when you were lost there, Tamas, my innocent, you strayed straight to the magic that had most claim on your presence. Of all ghosts in that wood, you met only Ylena. And that tells me there's more to this than a fledgling fool's bad luck."

Thoughts tumbled one over the other. The goblin was half shadow, half light. "You," Azdra'ik said, "you—resound—of magic. Yet you're deaf to it. You come from over-mountain to Ylena's doorstep. And the witchling crosses your path, with the fragment. And . . . much against my advice," Azdra'ik said, looking at Ela, "you've looked into the mirror. What you see the queen can see, if she dares invoke your world within the great mirror. You've guessed that, surely. Tomorrow, you have to compel her to see—what you wish. That's the whole business of the mirror. It's so dreadfully simple."

Ela said nothing.

"Do you understand?" Azdra'ik asked. "Do you want—perhaps—a year to think about it? To grow older? To bear children and pass this burden on? The i'bu okhthi can hide you—we *will* hide you, and set you away in safety where the queen may not reach you."

"No," Ela said shortly.

"Pride," said Azdra'ik. "Pride is a deadly matter."

"I don't believe," Ela said, "that there is anywhere safe."

"What do you say, young Tamas?"

He thought of Maggiar this time. He thought of home and orchards and their woods and the mountain trails that led straight to the heart of this land, and he thought of gran, and Karoly, and how gran had frightened them and Karoly had taken them over-mountain in full knowledge of where he was bringing them.

"There's no hiding," he said. "There's no hiding place even for a single year, that I know of."

A long time Azdra'ik looked at them, one and the other. Tamas thought—even began to hope—that Azdra'ik might know something he did not, and offer them a place.

"None that I would trust implicitly, no. No cradle for fools. No hiding place. Besides that we have no way off this hillside without more magic than we've yet seen, young witch. Make the sun come up. Make the day come. There's your first challenge."

"No," Ela said. "No. I won't fight her about that."

"What will you fight her for?" Azdra'ik asked, and the ghost in Tamas listened, oh, it listened, and he trembled.

Ela said, "I'd be a fool to say. Mistress said—never give that away to anyone. I think she meant anyone. And I won't."

Anger welled up, anger he hoped was not his, at her obstinacy, at her damning them to this encounter, at her refusal to argue or to listen . . . anger at Azdra'ik, who rose from beside them and walked away to the edge of the fire, a dark and martial figure that might have been human.

Not my anger, he told himself, struggling with the presence in him. Not my resentments, not my advice.

Shut up, he told the ghost, and feared it would find a way yet to harm them. It was vengeful. It had learned treachery at its mother's knee. He—had learned it from Azdra'ik . . . he had learned it from Karoly, if he knew how to recognize guile at all.

An unarmed babe, he told himself, a boy who should not have left his father's roof to be put where he was set, to fight a war where truth was bent and what one saw and what *was* were at war.

Why, gran? Why didn't you teach us more?

Stories about the fairies and green valleys and magic waterfalls? What kind of help was that? Was that all you could think to give your grandsons? They said you were wise. They said you were a great and dreadful witch. And, fairy-tales? Was that the limit of your magic?

Damn it, gran! What are we going to do tomorrow? If I've got one ghost, why not yours? Couldn't you manage *that*, if witches have the run of the forest?

Hate him, the voice came back, soft and bitter; and he was looking at Azdra'ik's back, thinking that he could never take the creature face to face, that somewhere in this Azdra'ik meant to betray them—that at some time he would have to take the creature, from this vantage if he could, preferably from this vantage, and with no one else to know—because he was not a fighter. And not, evidently, a wizard either, who could bend the creature to anything useful.

Be rid of him, echoed deep inside him. Protect *yourself*. You have too much value. Think of your own kind.

It left him a different feeling than the first ghost—less violent, more cold. Gran? he wondered. Is that gran? Or is it lying? Or is it something else altogether?

Many of the goblins had gone away from the fire, some to pallets spread about, some to the shadows. He saw them, he felt Ela's touch on his arm and felt her departure, he supposed for sleep. He watched her walk to where they had set their packs, near the horses, was aware as she wrapped her cloak about her, settled down and tucked up against the saddles and the packs. All the camp was settling, and oh, he wanted the idea of sleep—but he feared it, feared the ghost and its treacheries. He only wrapped himself in his cloak for comfort against the wind and decided at least to loose the buckles about his collar and his ribs, and find himself a comfortable way to prop himself, head on arms, simply to rest his smoke-stung eyes and armor-weary shoulders.

To his dim suspicion the ghost did not immediately trouble him. The dark within the shadow of his folded arms was empty and comfortable; he saw only—imagined—he was sure—a night clear and sparkling with stars. Not a bad dream, he decided, not a threatening dream. He heaved a sigh and imagined himself walking along boggy ground that seemed somehow familiar to him. He could not remember when he had acquired the memory, but he thought certainly he had seen it before, every detail of the reeds and the starlit water at their roots, at just this moment, on just this night.

The moon was a sliver of herself, embracing shadow. That, he saw, looking up, and then saw the whole lake, and the dark hills, like a blow to the heart.

No, he thought in fright, wanting escape, because he did know this shore, this lake—he had had this dream before, and it was a trick and a trap that had brought him here.

But before he could look away a movement drew his eye: came a troll past him in the dark, one troll, and another and another. That was enough: he did not want to see more than that. The dream was about to revert to the nightmare in the tunnel, and that might be preferable to this place, but he most wanted to wake up and have no dreams at all.

Then came a pale doglike shape down the hill. It looked for all the world like Zadny, and he could not understand why he would dream about that.

After the dog came a boy, so like Yuri in every way that his heart ached with homesickness. He stood perhaps a moment longer than he should have, watching Yuri chase after the hound who chased the trolls. It made no sense, it made absolutely no sense, except in his attempt to change this dreadful lake shore into something he knew, perhaps his dreams were going to be better disposed to him and show him something he longed to see. The three trolls—that was a bizarre touch, and there was enough of nightmare and of memory both about that apparition to disturb him; but seeing Yuri—cautions fell out of his mind. He even tried to call out to Yuri, reckless of the dark and the wild shore, but in the perverse way of dreams, he could not get a sound out, or run, when he tried—no matter what his effort he could travel no faster than a walk, as if the land resisted him, as if, in this dream, he could not recall the next bit of ground beneath his feet fast enough to enable him to go faster—he could not look down and look at Yuri at once, and he feared something else appearing, every time he took his eyes off his brother.

He walked and walked, while the trolls had gone farther than was safe—there was a guard on the lake that he knew was the goblins' lake, and the three trolls had gone past that point, he was sure they had. He began to be afraid where this dream

was going, and told himself that it was of no concern, his dream was powerless to harm anyone, and he could withstand any fright it offered: Yuri was home safe in bed. *He* was the one in real danger tomorrow. If he hoped anything good would come from the dream, he hoped if Yuri was dreaming, too, Yuri might hear him and wake up with a memory of talking to him, and remember it. Maybe that was what this dream was for. And, if that was the case, he did not want to tell Yuri how afraid he was, or how dreadful this place was, he simply wanted to say—
Do what's right, do what's wise, Yuri, mind papa and grow up, and if I don't make it home—

No, he did not want to scare the boy. I've had adventures, he would say, if he could. I've met this girl—

No, not that either: Yuri would make fun of him and girls. And how could he explain Ela to his family?

—I don't think mother would like her.

But I think—where would I be without her? And where would she be without me? She's very brave, Yuri. I don't think she ever had a friend but Pavel and her mistress, and that's no way to grow up. I think—

I think I needed someone like her. And you really would like her. If she were your age she'd climb trees and run races.

God, he thought then, she *is* Yuri's age, isn't she? And in his dream he said:

Yuri, if I get home I'll have the time to do things you wanted to do. . . . I really mean to, this time . . .

All these things he made up in his mind to say, so perhaps they were said. He walked along beside Yuri, chattering like a fool about anything he could think to say. But after a time he could go no further, he did not know why, he just stopped, or Yuri was getting ahead of him; and Yuri just kept walking, farther and farther along the shore, where Zadny had gone, where the trolls had.

Come back, he tried to say. Yuri! Come back!

But Yuri trudged along the boggy, reed-rimmed shore until he was part of the shadows.

Then came a slight shimmering of the lake, as if someone had shaken water in a goblet. Water lapped at the reeds. Metal clanged in that impenetrable darkness, like a gate gone shut, and he tried to go forward, but he could not take a step, could not call out, could not move.

And Zadny came running from out of that darkness, running for his very life.

Zadny! he cried silently, as the hound hurtled past him and up the hill. Halfway up, Zadny stopped and looked back, tail tucked, as if he had heard, after all, but he spun about and began to run again, to the top of the hill, where he vanished, as the lake did, as the shore, and the sky, the way dreams began to come apart when they had made their point.

He saw the drifting of a shape in this half-dream. He heard the ghostly voice saying, Fool, it's *not* a dream, never think things are only dreams, here.

He opened his eyes on dark that promised nothing of morning and gave not a hint of time passed or yet to come. He achieved a few moments of sleep and sleep left him with nothing but troubling images—did not purge his mind of nightmares or break off the chain of sleepless yesterdays and yesternights that ran unbroken through his awareness. His very bones felt now as if a force ran through him, insufficient to sustain him and too intense to make breathing easy. The movement of goblins about their watch, the flicker of the fire, all floated through his awareness, disjunct from every experience, every memory equally important: dreams of home, dreams of the ghost, with never a boundary of dark in which he could say, Asleep, or Awake, or know unequivocally past from future.

Ela understood the dark around them, and he knew that—intimately. Ela was awake and aware of his awareness. All of which was too much for him. He dropped his head into his hands and wished that whatever was happening would be over tomorrow so that he need not spend another night like this one, nor another day after it, never, ever another day like this, if he died.

Ela was angry at his despair, and something more than angry. He looked up from his hands to find her bending to him, reaching for his arm, and he flinched from her, thinking how the goblins were witness, the goblins had already laughed at their apparent dalliance, and now he was humiliated in her eyes, in the helpless trembling that came over his limbs, that he did not want her to discover, but she did. She hovered by him and he sat there wanting to scream, wanting to laugh, wanting to cry— but she *knew* what had happened to him, that it was magic that would not let him rest, would never let him rest until he had done what magic charged him do—that was what gnawed at him, she had not understood it before now, and she was afraid of it breaking out ungoverned in him . . .

"Mistress said," she whispered, as if that made enough sense, and gripped his hand with a force unlikely in so small a girl. Ela had not slept either, Ela had been thinking—as one did, on the brink of magic, as one must, when so much was pent up inside trying to find its way out. *She* was feeling it. And she had no doubt now that he felt the same force running through his bones.

"I'm not a wizard," he protested in their strange, half-spoken conversation. It horrified him to think of sorcery breaking out in him like some loathsome plague; to think of Ylena's ghost shedding him like some outworn skin and acting in ways he could not predict, maybe against Azdra'ik, maybe against Ela, he could not understand Ylena's motives or its presence, except he had given the ghost the chance it wanted to escape the woods.

"Dammit, it's not *me*, Ela, it's not me, it's the witch, it's somebody named Ylena that I don't know about, I don't know what she'll do, I don't know what she wants but what she wanted when I was in her house—"

But he could remember the mirror beginning to crack, the dark and bright lines running everywhere across its face, and the light breaking out through the seams of the world. He could remember Azdra'ik being her lover, and he could still *feel*, as if it had been a moment ago, Ylena's lips on his fingers, on his mouth. He could remember her walking up beside him, and seeing white bone through her flesh, when Azdra'ik had bargained him free.

"I won't go tomorrow for some dead woman, Ela! I won't do it! I don't even know what we're going to do."

But he was lying, he knew he would go, it was quivering in his bones and his brain, and he had no command over it.

"Hush," she said, "hush."

She had touched where the mirror rested beneath her gown and it was suddenly worse, overwhelmingly worse. He caught her hand, too hard, and tried to be gentle, but he was shaking beyond his power to master his own strength. He thought of taking the mirror from her—he *wanted* the mirror in his own hand, because he did know what to do, and she did not.

He flung himself to his feet instead and staggered for balance, while goblin sentries looked their way in alarm—incongruously unsure whether it was reason for weapons or not; while Ela— Ela rose slowly and was angry with him, with the ghost, he could not tell, he could not at the moment tell which he was.

"Ela, I can't—can't touch you again, I daren't, I daren't be close to you tomorrow, you understand? That's what it wants. When we can't deal with it, it's going to turn on us! Stay away from me, don't touch me!"

Ela shook her head, and a quiet confidence came around her, about her. "It's mine to carry," she said, so firmly he could not himself disbelieve it. "Sit down. Sit *down*."

He did. How could one do other than what Ela wanted? He

fell onto the stone and sat down, dizzy and confused, and Ela sank down by him, and took his arm in hers and held on to him.

"Shut your eyes," she said. "Trust me."

It was not easy. The ghost protested, wailed and flinched from Ela's touch. (Fool! it cried.) But he made himself do it, and found himself after a moment drawing easier breaths, and then a great, deep one, that seemed to come from the bottom of his soul.

Dangerous, he thought. Deadly dangerous, this trust he let her impose on him. Or the ghost thought so. He shut his eyes, on a welcome, vacant dark, and heard Ela say—or was it Karoly? —Take your time, Tamas, *think*, Tamas, . . .

They had their supper at least, from Gracja's pack, no thanks to their foresight. The two of them sat down to eat it in the tangle of woods that did not seem willing to give them up, and Nikolai for one had diminished appetite. "Not even a belt knife on the boy," Nikolai said to Karoly, over stale bread and sausage toasted on a stick. "I should have drowned that dog when I had a chance. —It's burning."

"Shhh," master Karoly said sharply, and sat staring fiercely at the fire while the sausage on his side of the fire caught fire and sizzled and popped and cindered. Nikolai watched the sausage, for want of other visible result—watched it turn to cinder, and the oil on the stick catch fire, and the stick burn, and the end fall off in the fire.

Curious, he thought. One wondered what wizards did. Or thought. Or thought they thought. Meanwhile the boy was still lost, *they* had to get up somehow and keep going, and he ached from head to foot. He had pulled the pony uphill and down, the pony having, reasonably enough, no driving interest in where they were going, until finally Karoly could not walk any further, and the god knew *he* could not carry the old man on his back.

So they sat and burned a sausage to the powers of the woods, or whatever forces Karoly was engaging.

Finally Karoly blinked and said, not to him, he thought, "No. No. Dammit."

The air was cold for a moment. For a moment Nikolai was certain he felt a breath on the side of his neck, and the fire went down flat and sprang up again.

"I know that!" Karoly objected.

Fine, Nikolai thought, fine, now we're talking to the air. He looked around uneasily, afraid of what he might see, but he found nothing and felt nothing.

Then Karoly leapt to his feet. "Get the horse!"

"I'm not—" —your servant, was what was first to Nikolai's mouth, but before he could even get it out, the old man was wandering off into the woods, into the dark without a care in the world for his safety or their weapons or the supplies in their packs.

"Damn!" Nikolai hurled his aching body into motion and stuffed their belongings in the pack, threw the pack on the pony and buried the fire in the earnest desire not to have the forest burning down around them.

The old man was out of sight. It was a crashing in the brush he followed, tugging Gracja after him in the dark for fear of his head if he tried to ride her through the woods. It was a breathless hill later that he even caught sight of Karoly, and onto the other side of it and downhill again before he overtook the old man.

Karoly knew he was there. Karoly spared him a glance and said something about the boys and trouble, but he knew that already. Something had persuaded Karoly of the right direction: Nikolai most earnestly hoped that was the case. The old man talked to ghosts and one of them had finally come through for him, but *he* could not see it, he could not tell.

Then he spied a pale shape in the shadows ahead of them, a pale, dog-sized shape, going through the brush and circling and looking back, not as if he were following a trail, but in the manner of a dog desperate to be followed.

Something had happened to the boy. The dog was roughed from scratches, dark marks on the fur—he limped on one paw and the other and evaded every attempt to lay hands on him. There was nothing to assume now but the worst; and Nikolai hurried as best he could with the horse in tow. "Get on," he said to Karoly when they had gotten to a single spot of flat ground. "Ride after him, I'll follow!" Because he feared there was no time for a man afoot, no time for maybe and no time for consideration. He took the bow from the saddle and held the reins for Karoly.

But when he looked about he could have sworn a man stood near them—real enough that his first impulse was to reach for his sword: a man in armor, who paid no attention to mortal threats, Pavel, he thought, but young Pavel, who walked away through the trunks of trees. There seemed to be a woman ahead of him, and maybe a girl, he could not tell.

Something wet touched his hand. Claws raked his leg.

"Damn!" he cried, before he knew it was the hound: and the hound was bounding away from them, after the ghosts, as if they should follow.

"Follow them to hell," Nikolai muttered, because following ghosts and stupid dogs could well lead there. Karoly was trying to get his foot into the stirrup, the pony was moving about, uneasy with good reason as Nikolai saw it, but he shoved the old man for the saddle and led off, with the most queasy feeling they were not anywhere people could get to without magic involved; and without it there was no way back.

14

A soft hiss and a sputter of sparks broke into half-dreams. Tamas suffered a moment of confusion, tucked into a stiff, foot-tingling knot next the fire, unable at the moment to recall what fireside of his life he was sitting at, or what was the warm and unaccustomed weight resting against his shoulder. But it proved disturbingly the latest place in memory, goblin-owned. The escaping sparks were a floating image in his vision, the night was still thick about them, smoke going up from a fire half smothered in earth, and the horses—goblin horses as well as their own—made uneasy sounds beyond the pale of the light.

"Good morning," Azdra'ik said somberly, "such as it is." Something else he added in his own tongue, exhorting his folk to wake and move, as seemed. Ela rested still against Tamas' shoulder, awake, but too weary to move and wondering (he was distressingly aware) whether there might be any breakfast, any warm cup of tea before they completely killed the fire. She wanted a hot drink very badly, astonishingly calm in her reckoning that there might be no more chances for such pleasures hereafter.

So she should have it, Tamas decided, excused himself to her and got up and told the goblin who was shoveling dirt onto the fire to desist.

That one scowled at him and he scowled back and interposed himself bodily until Azdra'ik intervened, asking what was the matter.

"Ela wants tea." That sounded foolish, but he felt exceedingly righteous in his insistence. Azdra'ik heaved a human sigh, shrugged and drew the other goblin aside for a word—which left untouched a single burning branch.

So Tamas fetched the wherewithal from their gear, and brewed a single cup of tea, with singed fingers, while camp was breaking.

"Thank you," Ela said when he brought it to her, seeming pleased that he had done that for her. It was indeed a silly thing to have done, he thought. But it lent a sense of their own pace in the morning which felt strangely necessary, in ways Ela herself might know, and it set him to quiet, unhurried recollection, as if, over the edge now, he had to pull pieces out of memory, as if—as if the pieces *were* there. . . .

He thought for no particular reason of master Karoly at home, taking matters at his own studied pace—Hurry, hurry! two rascal boys would shout, eager to be at the orchard or the brook or wherever they had convinced the old man to take them for their day's lessons. So what *is* the answer? two scoundrelly lads would ask, impatient to be away from their lessons and away from the smelly bottles and vessels in the tower room.

Master Karoly would say, In time, in time, hush, be still, nothing works but in its own time.

Even with magic? they had asked once.

And Karoly had said, in his close-mouthed way, Especially.

Especially this morning, Tamas thought, while the camp broke apart in martial order, while, under the final shovelful of earth, the fire went as dark as the heavens. Ela had her cup of tea and he had his moment to himself, recalling the tower study on a rainy morning when the old man had said, for at least the hundredth and maybe thousand and first time, Think about it, think about it, boy. Don't ask me the answer. Don't even ask yourself. The answer's not in either place.

What had they been talking about? What had he been asking, that morning?

Something about clouds and rain, or—?

"*If* our witchly guests are ready," Azdra'ik arrived to say, as goblins were going every which way into and out of the shadows. Behind Azdra'ik a goblin led up Lwi and Skory, saddled, without their leave; and Tamas frowned as he rose and took both sets of reins from the creature—angry at Azdra'ik's hurrying them, angry at the handling of their gear and their belongings and the lack of consultation when he was not, *not* hurrying this morning. He still did not know why. It was not the ghost. But he firmly made up his mind Azdra'ik should not be the one in their company to bid him do anything, or to require anything of him or her.

And most of all not to make him lose a thought.

"Don't hurry her," he said shortly. "Don't hurry *me*, master goblin, if you want our help."

"Ah," Azdra'ik said, hand on what ought to be a heart, extravagant as always. "And can you bid the queen wait? *That's* the question, isn't it?"

He stood sullenly telling himself he had had far and away enough of m'lord goblin in recent days; and telling himself that Azdra'ik was no different than he had ever been, and that it was fear he was feeling now: his body and his senses said that it was time for a sunrise and the stars were still bright—that was what had him short-tempered and jumping at every offense.

And if magic had sustained him through these sleepless days and nights—it had more to do now, and he felt nothing in himself like the currents of it that ran through Ela's fingers or the passionless confidence she had when that power worked— this girl that was hardly older than Yuri. He could not capture that confidence for himself this sunless morning.

Are we fools? he wanted to ask her. Are we fools to go

ahead, or should I have given you better advice?

No, he thought then; she thought: even that distinction became muddled at unpredictible moments. He distressed her and distracted her and she wanted him quiet now, that was all. Shut *up*, she wished him, justifiably. So he asked nothing, tried to think nothing, and waited while Ela tucked the cup away and got to the saddle.

But as he was getting up on Lwi he suffered a lightning stroke of overwhelming panic, asking himself what he was doing, why he believed Ela, what a lad from Maggiar was doing, riding with a pack of goblin rebels. It was mad. He was mad. The whole world was, this morning. He kept thinking: Stop, go back, this isn't where I planned to go when I left home, this isn't what I planned to be, I don't want to die today, in this dark.

But he settled into the saddle, while, in his moment of fear, the spiteful ghost stirred within him, saying things he could not grasp, something about choices and cowards, and showing him (but he would not look) the faces of goblin courtiers and the sound of goblin promises. He patted Lwi's neck, warmed cold fingers under Lwi's mane, and told himself Lwi had much rather other company than goblin horses, Lwi had much rather have the sun come up, and much, much rather his own stable. But Lwi, with a snort and a shaking of his neck, did what he had to, as the company began to move, as goblin riders surrounded them and swept them onto a starlit trail. And Lwi's rider did—what he had to—no way back now, everything in motion from very long ago. He had as much as gran and Karoly had given him, that was all; and as much as he had learned on this trail, of goblins and of the witches of the Wood . . .

He had a tenuous awareness of Ela riding beside him. Ela was not thinking about home. Ela was thinking about the dark, and the hills, and the lake in his dreams, the same lake, that had been the bargain, and the point of treachery, and the home of the goblins for hundreds of years.

There was the place where wizardry lay veined in the rocks and sown into the soil and mingled with the water and the air. And in that place there was all the magic and more that a mortal could draw on and use. That was where they were going. Ela believed in evil and believed that that evil was on the side of the possessor of that lake, in a long, long series of deceptions, goblins against the witches of the Wood, and in that place, with all of that to draw on, and the mirror in her hand, what was just and right had to count for something . . .

He wished it were so clear to him: evil and good had seemed so much more definable when he had thought all the evil came from goblins, and the ghost had done its best to urge that on him, but its reasoning was increasingly suspect; he wished he could recall something master Karoly had said on the matter of wickedness, but in all the years of teaching them, for the life of him, this dark morning, he could not recall a thing master Karoly had said on the subject, except that silly business of the frogs in the tackle-basket: It was not kind to *them*, boy. His mind fell into *that* memory for some reason he could not fathom. It was not kind to *them*.

And how did a man find his way on such thin and long-ago advice?

And what about the fish, that they had caught that very day for their supper?

Something about necessity, and doing what had to be done, and using no more of the earth than one needed . . .

S pookier and spookier, Yuri thought, worse than the troll's tunnel before he had known the troll. It was not a hallway, it was not a tunnel, it was just a place he could not get out of. There was the shimmer of water on the ground, everywhere the sound of water, and the chill and the smell of water. He had never imagined such a peculiar kind of tunnel, and as for trolls, he would give a great deal for the sight of Krukczy just now. But Zadny had run past him in such a terror he could not catch him.

All of which ought to tell a boy to go back—immediately. But when he had tried that, he had found himself up against a wall of—just nothing, that felt like an edge of some kind, where you could fall and fall forever if you got overbalanced; and Zadny might have run right off it, for all he knew. He hoped not. He hoped there was not another such edge ahead—though he thought not, because the trolls seemed to have gone on through; or they had just fallen off into the dark one after the other without a yell or a protest or anything, and that was not like trolls.

But he was truly scared, now, if anyone had asked him—and ever so glad when he suddenly saw a light ahead, a hazy glow toward which he was walking.

And brighten, the pathway did, until there was a ceiling and there were walls as well as a floor—all rippling with water-patterns, and light beyond that watery surface, the way a pond might look if he was walking along the bottom, in some great bubble, and looking up at the sun.

It was water when he looked back, and when he went near the walls, they shimmered as if the bubble he was in might collapse. That scared him.

But he did not see any way to go but straight ahead, and if somebody like the goblin queen was doing this he did not want to give her any ideas about collapsing the bubble around him. And thinking about it might make it happen, if this place was like dreams, as it seemed to be. So he walked, quickly as he could.

Then—he could not be sure at first—there seemed to be someone standing in the watery uncertainties of the hallway, a long, long distance in front of him. He wondered if it was his own reflection he was seeing. Or it might be a goblin. But even when he stopped walking that figure looked as if it was moving closer. And when he blinked to be sure he saw it, it had moved closer still, seeming like someone he knew very well, who just should not be here. Whether he walked toward it or not, it just kept coming; and looked more and more—

Like Bogdan. It did look *exactly* like Bogdan; and he should have been ever, ever so glad—he would have been; but Bogdan did not smile, Bogdan did not meet him with open arms like a brother, or act astonished to see him, or even ask him how he had come here.

Bogdan only said, as if he were mildly disappointed:

"I expected Tamas."

Hour upon hour the stars stayed overhead, the same stars that shone down on Maggiar, as far as Tamas could tell; and the pole stars had not moved in all the time they had been riding. But he did not know how that could possibly be—unless the very sky was standing still even in Maggiar, and unless lord Sun himself had no power to break the witch's hold—in which case his own family and every farmer in Maggiar and lands clear to the great sea must have wakened in confusion this morning, must be huddling together, hour by hour of this darkness, looking up at the stars and wondering at the meaning of it and whether there would be another sunrise.

But Ela commented quietly, as they rode side by side among the goblins: "Nothing changes here. The stars don't move. It's the same hour. It's always the same hour. That's the spell she's cast. Until that changes, nothing can."

She need not have spoken aloud. He was hearing her thinking just then, and wishing he did not, because in her thoughts was something about this not being a part of the present world they were traveling in, and it not having been a part of the present world ever since they had entered the Wood.

He was not sure of that. He thought about what master

Karoly had said, how one thing touches everything—and re-called the deer ravaging the woods, and the store rooms piled high with furs, and the spring failing to come . . . all this silent colloquy, while they rode above the fires in the valley, all this, while they rode in a serene high hills quiet. He thought, All this *is* there. What we do here, reflects there. Like the mirror . . . it's all one mirror, and which side is the reflection, and which is true?

Riders burst past, with that strange thump of pads and scrap-ing of their horses' claws. The last reined back to ride by them, to Lwi's offense. "Itra'hi are out there," Azdra'ik said out of the shadows. "Sniffing around the hills. I don't think they'll dare come at us. We're going right where their mistress would have us. I don't know what she has to complain of."

Disquieting thought.

"Unless you'd like to change your minds," Azdra'ik added. "We can still retreat."

"I don't see we'd gain anything." Tamas felt constrained to give a civil answer while the ghost or his own fear clamored otherwise; and he *had* lost a thought, confound the creature, but for some reason he found himself adding: "Possibly the queen can make a mistake."

"Oh, the queen makes many mistakes. But so few can take advantage of them."

"Maybe we will."

"The night the mirror failed," Azdra'ik said lightly, "the morning failed. And for two days thereafter. Witches and wiz-ards knew. But the world never did. Did it? Do your old men say?"

It cast his calculations into disorder and agreed with Ela's way of thinking. "You mean no one elsewhere even noticed?"

"Except within her power—as we clearly are. This is a night of her making. This is the goblin night. This is the goblin realm you've crossed into. And she rules it absolutely. To do other than she wills is a difficult matter. Will you still challenge her?"

You're wrong, he thought, forgetting the question. You're wrong, master goblin. One thing touches everything. The deer came to *our* woods. And the goblin queen doesn't rule everything.

"Here is your last chance," Azdra'ik said. "Hereafter—you have no retreat." With which, Azdra'ik moved off, with a suddenness that unnerved Lwi and made him jostle Skory.

In the next moment, round the shoulder of the hill a glistening horizon unfolded. He forgot what he was saying. He forgot everything he had had in mind to say, as he saw the starlit water cupped between the hills.

The lake, he thought, the place exactly, in every detail, that he had seen in his dreams.

The goblins in front of them rode down the steep incline toward the shore, fantastical shadows, they and their horses, against the star-sheen on the lake. They followed that lead, perforce, and other goblins rode down after them.

"The queen knows we're here," Ela said.

He felt nothing of the queen's presence. For a moment he felt not even the wind around them, and doubted what a moment ago he had thought he understood.

"Then do something," he said. The sense of urgency was suddenly overwhelming.

"Not yet," Ela said.

"Not yet. Not yet. This is the place, Ela, this is the lake, this is where she lives. I saw it last night, I've seen it before . . ."

"Everything here is what she wishes," Ela said. "Even we are. We couldn't have come here, else."

"No! Don't believe that! *We're* here. We're here because *we* decided, don't think anything else."

But the hill was the very hill that Yuri and the trolls had descended in his dream—the very shore on which they had vanished, and Zadny had come back again, terrified and alone. . . .

Foolish fear. It was entirely unreasonable that Yuri or Zadny had been here. It was the sort of thing his own mind might conjure, out of his homesickness, that was all, and the goblin queen had nothing to do with it.

But that meant his vision of Bogdan might be no different, and that there was no hope of finding him. Or—the thought came to him, and now he was not sure it was his own—if the mirror could make anything happen, if the queen could learn anything of his family none of them was safe . . .

His confidence ebbed away from him as they drew rein on the very shore of the goblins' lake, and the horses, disrespectful of haunted places, dipped their heads to drink. He was terrified for his family, for his brother, for his land—

But Ela's thoughts slipped in again, calm as the lake in front of them, on which the horses' intrusion sent out an irreverent ripple far across the mirrorlike surface—Ela had no attachments to anyone or anything, except, remotely, him—the goblin queen herself had seen to that; but not alone the queen. Her mistress *Ysabel* had left her no certainty, even about her own identity, but she had no one the goblin queen could threaten: everything she owned was hers. She stared into the dark, her hand above the mirror beneath her gown, he could feel it as if it rested against *his* heart, and said, so faintly he could scarcely hear:

"When I wish. That's my choice. When *I* wish. And no one can change that."

The lake reflected the sky and the sliver of moon so perfectly the mind grew dizzy searching for the seam of substance and image. One was the other. Up was down. Down was up. And the juncture between the two was the very heart of illusion. There, something said to him, there is the place.

It might have been the ghost that spoke. It might have been Ela. But the fear that stirred when Azdra'ik climbed down and walked along that reedy edge—that was most surely the ghost.

Treachery, it said. Treachery. Watch him. This is a potent place.

Treachery? he thought. Azdra'ik serves his own kind. Is that treacherous in him?

He slid down from Lwi's saddle and intended to lead Lwi with him; but a goblin offered to take the reins. He gave them into the creature's hand, thinking if there was duplicity now, if there was ill intent, it needed little violence to achieve its purpose. Either Azdra'ik's folk were rebels against their queen or they were the queen's most loyal subjects. And no goblin had moved against them yet.

Then he thought of what Azdra'ik had said, that his kind would be whatever the mirror made them—whatever the mirror could make them; and something about the fragment . . . that as long as it existed . . .

Ela had said and he had not understood until now. They were in the queen's realm, as close to the queen's absolute will as she could compel them or lure them. They were her enemies. They bore what the queen most dearly wanted—without wanting them to succeed. And in the goblin queen's sight, they were here with her permission, walking into her hands, himself, Ela, Azdra'ik and all of them . . .

Delicate, oh, so delicate, to be here within the queen's will in her view of the mirror, and not to be *as* the queen willed in their own. The whole world poised on the knife's edge of that distinction, precarious as a next and necessary breath, two reflections nearly identical—Ela with her hand poised above the mirror, and himself—

Himself, walking along the lake shore in Azdra'ik's tracks, with his sword at his side and intent against the queen in his heart.

He trod on bog. One boot leaked. He looked down before he thought, at water among cat-tail roots, reflecting his presence, and the dark reeds; and he had seen this exact thing before, so small and ridiculous a detail, but he had dreamed it, the exact same sight; and when he had looked up, in his dream . . .

—He beheld the face of the watcher on the shore, the armored figure whose face shifted with the changing moon. In his dream he had not recognized him—but of course it was Azdra'ik who faced him on the shore, Azdra'ik who, in that very image of his dream and this moment, turned his face from him, folded his arms and stood looking philosophically across the lake.

"Don't believe the quiet," Azdra'ik said. "The queen isn't waiting. This is her spell. This is her mirror. We're standing in it. The question is—will there be anything else? So far, our fledgling witch accepts what she sees."

"I've dreamed this," he said. "I saw my brother in the mirror. I saw him in the company of goblins like you. Is he possibly alive?"

"I'm sure I don't know."

"*Don't* you."

"Are we back to lies and liar?" Azdra'ik faced him, the exact figure of his nightmares, of his prophetic visions, he had no idea. "Not I, not I, lord human. Do you suppose I dealt with your ghostly tenant all those years ago . . . for my queen's welfare?"

The ghost he had thought might be gone moved in him like the striking of a snake—there was blinding anger. He walked away without thinking about it, along the boggy edge, and on a saner uncertainty and a steadier breath, looked back, in possession of himself again, forewarned of its presence and sure, now, that the ripples he sent into the still lake were of his own making.

"Where will I find her?" he asked Azdra'ik.

"Find whom?"

"The queen, of course."

"You're quite mad. With that sword, with my dagger, will you attack her?"

"Yes."

Azdra'ik grinned, as if he had been waiting for that very thing, as if the dream were still proceeding, in the way of dreams, with a sense of necessity. "I'll take you there," Azdra'ik said, and, splashing across the boggy ground, gave orders to one and the other of his people.

Tamas looked toward Ela. She sat on Skory's back, Skory still as a painted image. Her hand was where it had been, above the mirror she wore beneath her gown; and he thought then—

Perhaps I should tell her what I'm doing.

But she's aware. And as for where I am in her mirror—I'm either, aren't I? I'm in in the queen's mirror and I'm in Ela's, and when she looks, I'll be there—

(Don't rely on it, the ghost said. Young fool. Her fears can overwhelm her. Fears for *you*, young fool. She's blind and deaf to what her mistress taught. It's disaster . . .)

Azdra'ik's hand landed on his shoulder, startling him, making him look more closely than he liked into Azdra'ik's face.

"Come with me," Azdra'ik said. "I'll show you the way."

"To her?"

"As close as we can, as close as ever you'll wish."

Fear for *me*? he asked himself, disquieted. When did she ever care for *me*?

Am I doing the right thing?

They walked along the lake rim, the same path he had dreamed of Yuri taking, following the trolls. And they were not alone. Four of Azdra'ik's company were behind them—he discovered that as he glanced back.

The lake shimmered as it had in his dream, a watery flash of reflection, all around them, and above them. The stars vanished, and a gate clanged shut behind them.

15

I t was not as if there was anywhere to go, it was not as if he had tried to get away and not as if he had done anything wrong except be where his brother had not expected him, but Bogdan insisted on holding Yuri's arm as they walked the tunnel. "That hurts," Yuri cried, trying to twist loose. It did hurt. And Bogdan jerked him hard.

"Behave," Bogdan said harshly.

"I am! But where are we going? We need to find Tamas!"

"We need to find Tamas," Bogdan mocked him, and swung him around to look him in the face. "Do you know where he is? *Where* is he?"

"I don't know." It happened to be the truth, but the way Bogdan asked him he would not have told anything he knew. "Let me go!"

"What are you doing here?"

"I don't know." That sounded stupid. "I just decided to follow you, that's all!"

"Decided to follow us." Bogdan gave him a shake. "You're lying, Yuri. Where is he?"

"I don't know! You're hurting me! Let go!"

"Let me tell you something. They don't play games here. They don't understand boys here, they don't have any, and if you keep on like that they won't have *you*, do you hear what I'm saying? Don't play these people for fools. It doesn't work, here. They'll kill you, do you understand, they'll kill our mother, our father, every single one of us, if you try to play them for fools, —*do you understand me, little brother?*"

"I don't know what you're doing with them! Why don't we run away?"

"There is no running away, get that through your head. These are dangerous people. Offend them and they'll go against us. Accommodate them and there's nothing that can stand in our way. Maggiar can rule everything from the mountains west to the river and beyond that. The goblins have no interest in ruling men. *We* can do that for them. *We* can be the power, our little Maggiar can become an important place in the world, *the* important place, and there's nothing in the way of that. They actually *want* us to succeed, do you hear?"

Maggiar being a power and the goblins keeping promises did not sound reasonable to him. He could not think what to say to Bogdan. He knew he was waiting too long to think of it; and Bogdan lost patience with talking to a mere boy and spun him about and haled him down the tunnel.

Then of a sudden—it was more a change in the place around them than the opening of a door or a gate—they were in a hall blazing with lights, and those lights floating about in arches of green stone that itself rippled with water shadows. Yuri gawked, he could not help it, he was still thinking about how they had gotten into this place, and he had never seen lights floating in the air before, or stone the color of old summer leaves, or a place as rich and powerful as this.

But he stopped gawking then, because goblins came walking toward them from all sides, some no taller than he was, some taller than Bogdan, which few people were, and all of them bristling with spiny armor and with weapons. He was ready for Bogdan to draw his sword and defend their lives from these creatures, but evidently not. Evidently these were the friends Bogdan was talking about. Bogdan only said,

"This is my younger brother. He's mine. Keep your hands off him. Understand?"

Yuri did *not* like the look in the goblins' eyes. Least of all did he trust the whispering behind them as Bogdan hurried him on along the fantastical hall. He had heard that kind of thing from bullies and wicked boys like his sometime friends back home. He pulled to free himself from Bogdan's grip, wanting to find the tunnel again and get out of here, because Bogdan was being stupid if he thought these were friends. But next to a carving that might have been real lily roots and lily stem, towering up and up, Bogdan set him against the wall.

"Listen," Bogdan said, bending to look him in the face and giving him a shake. "You're safe if you do what I say. Do you hear me? We can be safe here, you and I, and Tamas can be safe here. There's an army out there burning Albaz, and Burdigen, and all the towns in the valley to the ground—because those people were stupid. That's not going to happen to Maggiar. It's not going to happen to *us*. . . . because you're not going to make trouble, you're not going to offend these people! Remember that before you act the fool in this place!"

He saw nothing in the way of bad things happening to him or anyone the goblins could catch, except his brother was giving orders to goblins instead of being a prisoner, and his brother was talking about goblins burning towns their gran had told stories about, stories Tamas had handed down to him after she died. He thought he should be happy that Bogdan was alive—but he had far rather know that Bogdan was the brother he remembered.

"Do you understand me?"

"Yes," he said, because he did not want his arm broken.

"Come on," Bogdan said, and pulled him along a hallway. "I want you with me. I don't want any misunderstandings."

"What happened to Jerzy and everybody?" he asked, hoping Bogdan would at least remember that something bad had happened at Krukczy Tower.

Bogdan jerked his arm so hard it brought tears to his eyes, paying no attention to his question, and Yuri suddenly had no inclination whatsoever to tell Bogdan about Karoly and Nikolai having escaped the goblins at Krukczy Straz. He was scared, really scared, since Bogdan had chosen not to answer his question about Jerzy and the rest, who had been Bogdan's friends, and the men he was leading. Bogdan had not been his favorite brother, but Bogdan had never, ever acted like this, or talked about being safe with goblins who had shot Nikolai and tried to kill Tamas and master Karoly.

Bogdan took him down one hall and into another, with the floating lights and goblins coming and going. Bogdan gave him to a goblin to watch, while Bogdan went over and talked urgently to a handful of tall goblins that looked more important than the rest, all in armor, all bristling with weapons.

Yuri calculated the chances of kicking his goblin guard in the shins and making a break for a door, but Bogdan had said don't be stupid, and that, in this place where halls happened without ordinary doors, seemed good advice, except not the way Bogdan had meant it: as he saw it, it was a question of biding his time.

So he watched the disgusting sight of his brother talking with his goblin friends, while another goblin was holding his arm, and he (he could not help it) looked up at him to get an undersided view of a goblin face, while the lights were floating around them like fireflies and congregating where Bogdan and the others were talking.

A strange sight, that face was. But he did not like it when the goblin realized what he was doing and glared down at him.

He heard the group with Bogdan say something about other

goblins; and he heard Bogdan say something about promising to let him deal with Tamas himself.

So he crossed his eyes at the goblin who was glaring at him and made a face, for good measure. And the goblin clearly had his orders not to bite his head off, and did nothing. A light floated right around the goblin's shoulder and drifted off to join the others bobbing around Bogdan and the rest, where the center of interest was.

So Yuri straightened around and kept a calm face, watching his brother betray Tamas, and Maggiar, and everything and everyone he knew.

Which hurt—hurt worse than anything anybody had ever done to him. It was not a thing boys did. It was something a man did, and that man was a brother of his—which made him somehow dirty, too, and responsible, and completely desperate to find a way out of this trap to warn the people he cared about.

Like finding Tamas, he thought. Tamas was older. Tamas would know what to do first and where to go.

He stood there in a goblin's keeping until Bogdan decided to take him back. Bogdan took him down the hall, past the fantastical lilies and the carved fish and the monsters that lurked in the stone, while a trail of excited lights tried to keep up with them.

"We've got to find Tamas before he undoes everything," Bogdan said as they went. "He's around here somewhere. Come on! Fool!"

They walked a corridor of strange watery darkness, and Tamas asked himself, alone with goblins and the consequences of his confusion, whether he was entirely sane. The ghost had ceased to trouble him, inside, for the moment—Ylena was visible now, apart from him, walking ahead of them—at least he fancied he could see her from time to time, at the instant the eye had to blink: most horrible in aspect, a tattered figure of a woman, all bones and gauze.

"Ylena," he said to Azdra'ik, as the only one who might understand his distress. "I can't be rid of her."

"I see her," Azdra'ik said. "The pretentious baggage. A tag-along."

"More than that, damn it." Azdra'ik had a way of provoking the ghost, and he flinched, expecting its spite.

Azdra'ik said, close by his ear, grasping his arm. "She fears dying—and die she will, if ever goblins leave the earth again. That was the term of her long life. You should be wary of that. Promise her you don't intend to banish us."

He heard that, and his heart gave a thump, as if he were being threatened into an agreement more important than his distracted wits could surround at the moment.

What does he want of me?

"Ask that favor of Ela," he said. "What have I to do with it?"

"As the residence of a power that can damn us? As Ylena's means into the queen's hall? A great deal. I gave her the secret of the mirror and the woman blames me that she was a fool— not *my* fault, I say."

He was trying to understand Azdra'ik's position. But the witch hovered near him, there at the edge of every blink, a shadowy swirl of living anger. "Let be. Don't quarrel with her."

"Oh, not with her, man, with her successors. Given the choice, your young witch out there—"

A shiver went through the floor—but the tremor was more than in the earth, it was a shock within his heart. A desire that was Ela's. A solitude that was Ela's, overwhelming the ghost's faded spite. This was now. This was imminent danger.

"Someone," Azdra'ik said, "just gained the queen's attention."

"Ela!" He jerked his arm away from Azdra'ik's grip and at once felt an edge near his foot.

"Fool!" Azdra'ik caught him as another tremor ran through the tunnel, making the reflections shimmer—and he did not fall, only by the intervention of Azdra'ik's hand.

And the silence that followed the shaking was smothering. He tried to free himself.

"Be calm, be calm." Azdra'ik released his arm slowly. "You can so easily fall here, man, you can fall to something like death—you can drown in the queen's imagination. Or in the queen's all-demanding will, which I personally count worse."

"Ela's under attack."

"Did you expect not? I asked you—take the mirror. I pleaded with you, take the mirror. Now—*now* you have second thoughts. The war is launched, man. There is no disengagement. And for good or ill, the mirror shard belongs to the fledgling."

"The witch with a wizard consort," another said, close at hand—which startled him: few of the goblins seemed to have human speech.

"With a wizard consort," Azdra'ik agreed. "That's true. That's never been. It may make a difference, that she wants him more than the queen does."

"She has no consort! Don't assume—"

"Man, you echo of it. The whole mirror does. Do you think we're deaf?"

He was surrounded by goblins, and Ela's presence ran through him like hammer-blows, shock after shock to his bones. He saw only fierce, expectant faces in the dim, watery light, and suddenly—suddenly a sense of that presence so vivid there was no difference between him and her, no housing left for the ghost that clamored outside. He *saw* into somewhere he could not see with his eyes, into a hall . . . but he could not make it clear. It shimmered—

The lake . . . god, the *lake*, Ela!

One thing touches everything. One thing affects everything. They wanted the *lake*, Ela, everything for the lake—that *is* the mirror, in our realm—

"Man!" Azdra'ik cautioned him. "Man, listen to me."

There was light, watery reflections glancing and bouncing off the floor. The way ahead looked like a bubble in the sun. He rubbed his eyes, and started walking with Azdra'ik and his companions about him.

Came a cold touch at his shoulder. Too late for recriminations, he said to the ghost's nagging at him. We're here, madam. We've no chance to be anywhere else. Shut up!

It did not *like* to be addressed that way. He felt its anger.

And will you die? he flung back at it. We all can die. Easier than not, at this point.

It did not want to be here. The *queen* wanted it to be here, it believed that beyond a doubt, now. It had touched him, it had tried to hold him and it had gotten swept up in the current of spells—

—of spells ages old and more powerful than she understood. The ghost had kissed an innocent to steal his life and found something far from innocent; she blamed him for that, she railed on him for that, she suspected him of wizardly complicities she could not find . . .

Consort, the goblins had said. The witches of the Wood had no such thing. There had been no wizards in Ylena's time . . .

But in gran's, he thought distractedly, there was Karoly. . . .

Fear broke forth in Ela, then a regathered collectedness, as the air in their very faces began to shimmer like the air above a forge: the water-patterns shimmered violently, and then stopped. They faced a man and a band of goblins that reached instantly for swords.

But it was himself, his own startlement, their own reflections, that dissolved into ripples of light and pattern, as if someone had cast a stone into water.

"Tamas?" a boy's voice called out—a boy's shape was the new image it was taking. Yuri's image looked out at him—touched the invisible surface, and made it ripple, but no more than that, and, for a boy Tamas knew beyond a doubt was home and safe—lord Sun, it looked and sounded so very real.

"Tamas!"

"Is it a lie?" he asked Azdra'ik. "He's not here! He's safe over-mountain!"

Yuri's reflection shook its head, remarkable in the likeness that pulled at his heart. "Zadny got away. I followed him and I got here—Bogdan's here. —*But don't believe*—"

The mirror shimmered violently and something snatched Yuri out of his sight.

Goblin hands snatched Tamas back, on his side, or he would have followed.

"Let me go!"

"Don't," Azdra'ik said, "don't be a fool. It's the mirror that governs such things. Make it give the vision back!"

"I don't know if I want it!"

"Then know!" Azdra'ik shouted at him. "Know once for all, man, you've few other chances. Will you face it? Yes or no!"

"I want it back!" he cried.

The shimmering steadied, and Yuri came bursting through it, sprawled flat and looked up, still as a fawn before the hunters, his expression all dismay and desperation.

"It's *me*," Tamas said. But the mirror showed another image before him—: Bogdan, in every detail it was Bogdan.

"Come across," Bogdan said, beckoning him. "Tamas, bring Yuri, and come here."

"No," Azdra'ik said under his breath. "That's the queen's work. Pass through that surface and he can touch you."

"Tamas."

He thought how his company must look to Bogdan, and he had the thought to explain to Bogdan it was safe and he was not a prisoner, but suddenly there were goblins at Bogdan's back, too, a good many of them, a hall, bright with lights, and it was himself who stood in shadow, with his younger brother dazed and trying to choose what was real. It was the look on Yuri's face he could not bear, the doubt between the two of them.

"Yuri," he said. "Yuri, can you answer me?"

"Yes," Yuri's image said, sounding like Yuri's very self if Yuri were frightened out of good sense. "I hear you."

"What should I do, Yuri? Should I listen to him?"

"No," Yuri said definitely enough.

"The boy doesn't understand," Bogdan said. "Tamas, I want you to take Yuri and bring him with you. I've a guarantee of your safety."

"The queen's promises," Azdra'ik said.

"Shut up!" he hissed at Azdra'ik. "Bogdan. Are you free to come to this side?"

"Free," Bogdan said. "Free, yes. But I want you to come to me. You'll be safe. I promise you."

The rippling surface belled outward and gained a portion of the hall. "Tamas!" Yuri yelled in dismay as the mirror snatched him back, and Tamas made a desperate reach for him, but goblin hands held him back.

"Come on!" Bogdan said. But Yuri was not pleased with where he was. Tamas saw the shake of Yuri's head and stopped struggling with the goblins' hold on him.

"Back up," Azdra'ik said, laying a hand on his shoulder. "We're losing, back up. We can't press it yet."

"No," he said. Backing up and leaving Yuri and Bogdan there—even the illusion of his brothers—he could not risk losing them. He tried to feel Ela's presence. He reached for magic, and intended the wall to waver the other way and give up his brothers, by the god, it would.

He held steady, at least—the surface shook one way and the other, as if a stone had struck it.

"What are you doing?" Bogdan asked.

"Wizardry," said a lisping, soft voice from somewhere among the goblins, at Bogdan's back. "Grandson of Karoly Magus—the gift you don't own, your brother Tamas clearly does. He has magic enough to make him a power in the world. Did he tell you that on the other side of the mountains, or did he keep it secret from you? Clearly we have the lesser brother on our side."

Tamas heard it, angry at its insinuations, he heard it and he saw Bogdan half-turn to cast a look behind him, and, in the same moment, knew the way he knew his brother's character what that cursed voice had done to them, what a soreness it had touched, the same that he had protected in Bogdan with every duck of his head, every taunt turned and every provocation declined that his brother had offered him.

Damn you, he thought on the instant, a lifetime's evasions all come to this.

"You're no wizard," Bogdan said, angrily. "*You're* no wizard."

"Bogdan,—"

"—I want you to come here," Bogdan said.

"He didn't tell you," the insidious voice said. "But certain ones had to have known. And lay odds that your brother knew—and Karoly Magus. Probably even the servants—"

"I didn't," Tamas said. "That's rubbish, Bogdan, for the god's sake, what are we talking about? Get out of there. Walk out. Give me your hand and hold on to Yuri."

"To do what? To have Maggiar burn? But maybe you don't care about things like that,—Tamas Magus."

"Oh, for the god's sake, Bogdan, I never hid anything from you. I don't even know what they say is true, I don't know to this day that it's true—don't listen to them, this is family, this is our *family*, Bogdan, not some strangers' word on it—"

"Then come over here. Do what I tell you. They're willing to have us rule Maggiar, to have us rule over all the world on our side of the mountains. They'll let us do as we please, Tamas, one kingdom after another—"

He shook his head. "You. Over here."

"Am I the oldest, Tamas?"

"You're the oldest."

"Do I know better than you do? I'm telling you what to do, little brother."

"No. Bogdan, don't listen to them. We don't have to take their terms. We can beat them. Get Yuri out of there."

"He's very confident," the voice said, thick with fangs—and it began to sound feminine to his ears. "Isn't he?"

"Shut up," Tamas said to the queen—he was sure it was the queen—and the mirror shook.

"Wizard," the goblin queen said. "Come across. You can be with your brothers. You can have any reward you like."

"No."

"Tamas," Bogdan said.

"He won't listen to you," the goblin queen said. "He knows everything."

"He'll listen," Bogdan said, in his no-nonsense way, his side of the mirror advanced as he strode forward, and Tamas backed a pace: he had learned when he was five to back up when Bogdan sounded like that and came in his direction. But his back met a wall of armored goblins—and Yuri was held by goblins on the other side.

"Get hold of him," Tamas said, turning to Azdra'ik, trying to avoid the fight Bogdan was pressing. "Hold on to him."

But that was the wrong thing to have said. Bogdan drew his sword with a rasp of metal that made the mirror shiver.

"Put it away," Tamas said, turning again. "Bogdan. Put it—"

Bogdan sliced through the mirror surface between them and Tamas jumped back as goblin steel rang out. Swords cleared their scabbards on either side, and Tamas was still trying to evade Bogdan's attack, empty-handed.

"No, Bogdan!" A second close pass, the wind of which passed his cheek: he flinched back again, hard against a goblin arm—parry him, was his desperate thought, he drew on the retreat, brought the sword up and Bogdan's blade clanged against it with a shock that jolted his wrists.

"Bogdan, quit it!" he cried, but there was the queen's laughter from beyond the barrier, there was Yuri shouting to watch out. "Bogdan! They want this, stop it!"

Blow after blow came at him and he kept turning them. No one else was fighting. They all were watching, one side and the other of the mirror surface, and jeers came from Bogdan's side. "Go on," the goblins shouted, and Yuri shouted at them to stop it—but he could not drop his guard without Bogdan cleaving him in two, and Bogdan's strokes were growing wild and desperate, ringing through the blade to his bones. The clangor filled his ears, rang over the wailing protests of the ghost, rang over the goblin voices and into the watery walls that shook to the sound of blades.

Stroke met and next stroke met: he was unwilling to back up, but he had no choice. Azdra'ik was shouting advice at him he could not hear, Yuri was yelling and his arms and his wrists were buckling under the clanging and hammering. Get the sword away from him, was what his good sense screamed at him, but doing that to Bogdan was no easier than reasoning with him when Bogdan's pride was at stake.

"They want this!" he shouted, in the hope that Bogdan was wearing down enough to hear him. "Bogdan, they've got Yuri."

"I'm not a fool!" Bogdan shouted. His face was suffused with anger, his eyes were crazed with it. "You're so damned smug, you're so damned clever, don't you think I know what you were doing getting into our company, you and Karoly—?"

He hardly had the wind to argue. Get it away from him, was all he could think of, trying to wield a goblin sword in a wearying defense, with Azdra'ik's company yelling in his ear and Azdra'ik himself shouting advice he could not consciously hear over the ringing in his ears. He made an over-reach with the blade, tried to hang Bogdan's blade with the quillon-spine on his and almost succeeded; but Bogdan's strength jerked the blade half out of his grip before the imperfect hold raked free. He made a desperate recovery. The goblins yelled advice. A familiar hand landed momentarily on his shoulder and shoved him. Azdra'ik shouted, "Attack, fool!"

"Shut up!" he yelled at Azdra'ik, and dodged Bogdan's attack.

"They're coming at Ela, man! We can't hold them for-ever—"

This as he trod on someone's foot trying to back up, and Bogdan's sword grated and sliced along his shoulder.

"Get out of my way," he panted. "Bogdan, stop it! You're *wrong*, for the god's sake, Bogdan—" He gave up trying to coddle Bogdan's sense of righteousness. "Papa would say—"

"What? That we're all wizard bastards?" A downstroke beat his blade down. But Bogdan was tiring, too. Bogdan could not take advantage on the recovery: Tamas shoved him back with his shoulder and tried bashing him with the hilt.

The barked quillon drew blood across Bogdan's hand. "Damn you!" Bogdan yelled, looking at it, and launched a crazed attack, blow after blow.

"The edge!" Azdra'ik yelled, "Watch your feet, man!"

He had no more room. A goblin's shove at his back flung

him within Bogdan's guard and he used the hilt and the side of the blade, to batter himself free. Sweat was running in his eyes. The goblins were all shouting, both sides at once. He made a second desperate try to trap Bogdan's guard, and trapped himself, the swords bound together, the tines piercing Bogdan's hand—he *had* him, if he did not let go, he could keep from killing Bogdan or being killed, if he did not let Bogdan get free, but Bogdan was grabbing at his throat and forcing him backward in a frenzy of pain and outrage, step by resisting step—he knew the edge was behind him.

"You'll take us over!" he yelled at Bogdan. "You'll take us over the edge, dammit, don't!"

His foot hit nothingness. He felt himself going, he felt the drop beginning and he let go the sword—he had made up his mind to that—rather than kill them both.

But a hand snagged him by one arm as he let go the sword. Bogdan spun past him with all his weight and both swords—into empty space past his reaching hand. The pull on his left sleeve was hauling him back to solid ground breathless and cold and shaking from head to foot—

"Bogdan!" he shouted into that gulf, in hope that if it was a magical place he might yet find him.

"He's gone!" Azdra'ik shouted into his ear, with his arms around him. "You're *here*, man. Do you hear me? They won't stop us. *Man!*" Azdra'ik shook at him. "Listen to me! You've got the power to do something—do it! Use the mirror! Break through the wall!"

One thing touches everything, he thought, for no reason. And: for less reason and with a sudden unreasoning hope: Master Karoly!

Nikolai tried not to think about the stars above the tangle of woods, but he was sure that it was at least rightfully noon, that something magical was in progress, and that if their two ghostly guides were at all reliable they should have found the boy long since.

"They're not getting us anywhere!" he protested to Karoly.

"We're not where we were," Karoly snapped. "And it's not that easy, master huntsman, it's not a deer we're tracking."

"What does that mean?"

"That it's not a deer!"

That was what one got for arguing with a man who thought in circles and heard things when he set his ear against the earth. But from the beginning Ysabel and Pavel had seemed on the track of something the hound was interested in following: Karoly's murdered sister and her soldier lover drifted effortlessly in the lead as they slogged through thicket and up and down hills, Nikolai leading the old man on the pony—with the hound out in front of all of them, running with his nose to the ground, immune to the dark that impeded a human hunter and probably tracking better than both ghosts together, in Nikolai's estimation.

Then of a sudden Nikolai smelled apples, when no apple tree should be in fruit—and that made him think, oddly enough, of the courtyard in Maggiar, an overset basket by the kitchen door, and Michal's horse.

The dog barked, letting every goblin in ten leagues about know where they were.

"Quiet!" Nikolai hissed. "Dog, hush!"

In the same instant he felt a tweak at his hair, which might have been a twig raking him. A slight breeze had started up, a whispering in the brush.

Good lad, someone said. He was sure it was not master Karoly—Karoly did not call him good and no one called him lad these days. It sounded like a woman's voice. He could not be certain.

Loyal to Stani, indeed, the voice said next his ear—no one could fault you that.

"Urzula?" Karoly asked of a sudden. "Urzula, is that you?"

"Just the wind," Nikolai said, wanting to believe in anything but the lady gran next his ear.

But in the self-same moment, on a trick of the wind, he heard a sound he had not heard since his wandering youth: the clash of swords and the sounds of warfare echoing through the woods. Gracja brought her head up, pulled at the reins he was holding, and Nikolai scrambled aside as a shadow of a rider passed right through the brush without disturbing any of it, and passed right through Gracja and Karoly to boot.

A second rider passed, and a third, all shadows, and Nikolai began to shiver in a way nothing had made him do since he was a boy hiding from the soldiers.

But he had the impression he knew who they were without clear sight of any of them: Michal, and Filip, and Jerzy and all his dead comrades, all riding toward the sounds of combat. Zadny barked at them and set up a sudden howl.

That was the only thing that brought him to his senses, because for a moment he felt so light-headed, so slightly connected to his body, that it would have been so much easier to let go and run after them.

He reached out for Karoly's knee, fearing for the old man's life. But: "Follow them," Karoly said urgently. "God, give me up the reins. The boy's in deep trouble!"

The dog crashed off into the woods ahead of them. He handed Karoly up the reins, Karoly flailed at Gracja with his heels and the pony started moving, stolidly, relentlessly forward, while the ghosts went before them with a sighing in the branches, and ghosts of every sort poured in from left and from right of them, drifting shadows in the starlight, afoot, ahorse,

some on creatures an honest man did not want to see—those
might be goblin dead.

There was a brilliance ahead, some sort of light cast up from
the valley below on the thinning screen of trees, and came a
howl from ahead of them that Nikolai had heard only once
before in his life, at Krukczy Straz when the arrows had begun
to fly—goblins leapt up ahead from ambush, with shrieks and
waving of swords that glittered in the eerie light.

But that howling changed abruptly when the shadows in
their lead poured into their midst. Goblins broke from cover and
turned in flight; Nikolai ran, gasping for breath, to add whatever
solid force he could to the ghosts, shielded his eyes with his arm
and broke through a screen of brush onto a barren hillside,
beneath which something shone like a star brought to earth.
Shadows flowed down that hill like a river of darkness behind
the fleeing goblins, a river on which the light still picked out
detail like a helmet or an arm or a mailed shoulder—shadows
flowed over the goblins and left them still—except a few that
scattered shrieking and gibbering to the four winds, and a handful of stragglers from the ambush that tried to regroup in Nikolai's path.

Nikolai did not stop to think: he laid with blind desperation
into what resistance he found, clearing a path, because an old
fool on a pony was coming behind him, and there was the light
down there, the only relief from the night around them. That
was where they had to go and he did not even question the idea,
he was only aware as he sliced his way through that Karoly and
the pony had flanked him, headed downward past him.

Somewhere he found the wind to take out running after the
old man, with a stitch in his side and the light blurring and
blinding him. Wizardry for certain, he thought, a white glare
unlike sun or fire—centering somewhere about a girl on a
motionless horse.

And surrounded by goblins.

"Karoly!" he yelled, half doubled with pain—and ran the faster to overtake Karoly, having the only sword, and seeing the old man going on as if he saw nothing at all but the light.

But these were different goblins, taller, surrounding the girl on the horse as if they stood guard—the goblin queen, Nikolai thought it might be—but if she was, her guard was trusting her magic and not shooting at them or lifting a sword.

Then the girl did move—Nikolai saw it in the jolts of his running: she looked toward them and Karoly stopped the pony as the light in her hand flared like the lightning. He could see everything, the detail of goblin armor, more than those he had seen—hopeless odds, even discounting magic.

Karoly lifted his staff, that thing that had encumbered him through the woods, waved it overhead; and Nikolai fetched up against Gracja's sweating rump for support, unable to run another step; while *something* happened. The fire grew brighter and brighter and sheeted out across a lake he had not even seen so dark it was—one blaze and another and another until it seemed from where he stood that he could see moving shapes above its still surface.

And came the belling of a hound, off along the lake shore, a pale shape running as if he had taken leave of his senses— "Follow the dog!" Karoly shouted at Nikolai.

"What?" He hardly *had* a voice.

"You're no damn use here—*follow the dog!*"

Nikolai caught a breath, shoved off from the pony's side, and started running, only then realizing that the dog would be after the boy, and that the old man might have a reason. He ran limping and splashing through shallow water, his side shot with pain—he hoped no goblins saw him; but some did and ran after him . . . and he had no cover and no strength to turn and fight: he only hoped to stay ahead of them and find some cover to duck behind and lose them before he led them onto the boy's trail.

Dark surrounded him of a sudden—he thought he might have lost a moment or passed out still running, because around him was suddenly confined, and dank and cold, lit by a watery light just enough to see—and with the dog's barking echoing in far distance, the armored clatter of pursuit immediately behind him—he kept going, he did not know how, thinking if Karoly wanted him alive Karoly should do something—but he could not keep ahead of them. When they were on him he pulled a staggering halt and spun about to meet them, but they swarmed him, grabbed his left arm and his sword arm, and held on, a solid mass of them, glittering with metal in the watery reflections.

He fought to free himself. They fought to hold on, with no reason in the world they should not swipe his head off and be done.

Which finally persuaded him they did not intend to. He stopped fighting to get a breath, and they let up their hold somewhat.

"Man," one panted, displaying dreadful fangs. And clapped him on the shoulder and pointed down the way he had been going.

It took him a moment to sort his wits out—in the realization they were offering their services at dog-chasing. The heart of hell and the queen of the goblins, Karoly had said about this place . . . but in his travels he had found more than one band of discontents.

They let him go, he found the breath to keep going, and he went with an escort with only one human word in their speech. But either they were taking him to their queen or they were going with him to their queen, and either way, that got him in reach of the goblin responsible for this devastation.

That was agreeable to him.

Nothing moved the other side of the barrier, not the goblins, not Yuri, not for the small moments Tamas could press the mirror surface: holding everything stone still was the best that he could do. But it was not an effort only with the hands—the instant his thoughts scattered to any other object, changes began to happen, and figures frozen so long as he could hold them, began to move beyond the barrier. He had no idea whether it was any good to try to stop it, he was not sure whether it was winning or not or had any hope, but he tried, and kept trying, although he knew something was dreadfully wrong outside. He had lost any sense of where Ela was, or what had happened—he might be the last hope left; and he had no knowledge to replace her—had no understanding what he was doing or had to do, he only persevered in blind attacks, willing to entreat the ghost, the goblins with him, any ally he would take if he could rescue Yuri from the hands that held him.

Yuri tried not to admit that he was afraid—Yuri scowled in slow movement, Yuri drew back his foot and, god, he knew what Yuri was going to do, he did not want him to do it, for his life he did not, and he held everything still as long as he could—but he felt something slip, then, some vast disturbance that made the barrier change—and of a sudden he lost all purchase. Yuri's foot swung, the goblin winced and doubled, and he—

—he was able now only to shout at the enemies who had his brother. He struck the barrier with his bare hands: but breach it he still could not, could not even feel solidity in what took and took his strength.

The goblins with him added their force—Azdra'ik's was far more than his; Azdra'ik was face to face with him, shoulder to the barrier, and it was the face of a beast he saw, a fear no less than his—Azdra'ik was near to losing himself and all he hoped to win back, and he, of losing Yuri—

Suddenly the surface gave way—dissolved in front of them. An image of an image of an image froze within his eyes, and they sprawled in a heap in the further hall, lights fleeing and bobbing like living things, himself and a handful of exhausted goblins . . .

Facing a sheet of glass or water—he could not tell, it shimmered so—but Yuri was there, in the hands of enemies; and most of all, most of all the goblin queen, the face in the mirror, that of a sudden blotted everything out. He got up. Azdra'ik did, and the others, facing the queen on her throne.

"Over-confidence," the queen said, "is a deadly flaw. Do you want the young one?"

"Yes," he began to say, but Azdra'ik stepped in front of him and shouted something he had no idea what, but it was enough to make the queen's nostrils flare with rage, and her cheeks suffuse with color. The queen shouted and stood up with a clatter of bracelets and pointed toward the goblin lord.

No, Tamas thought, *no*—and saw that small darkness next the queen's arm, that darkness that was the shape of Ela's mirror; and *that* was what he looked at—dared not take his eyes from that single patch, that single place on the mirror where he had a hope of seeing what he wanted, instead of what the queen wished. When he saw light on that spot, exactly the shape of Ela's mirror, the mirror was whole.

Then—he did not want it; he did not sense that the queen did—something of shadow and of bone and malice slipped into his vision to take everything from him. He saw the woods, the night, the tangled brush, the scattered bones . . .

"Stop her!" Azdra'ik shouted at him, shaking his shoulder. Of a sudden the whole mirror shifted backward, and became a wall of dreadful colors, a rush of goblins toward them with spears and swords.

He took a step back, among Azdra'ik's few, and sought his single spot on the great mirror,—and saw the shard rippling with uncertainty. Lights streamed and bobbed about them as goblins fought goblins, as steel blades flashed between him and the mirror. Without taking his eyes from that haziness he drew the dagger he had, Azdra'ik's gift, held it ready to defend himself, as he heard Yuri call out desperately for him.

But in the same moment he heard a hound baying and barking at his back—shadows poured about him in a wave of inky chill, about him and past him, as a yellow hound came skidding onto the marble floors, skidding and yelping in startlement as he skidded through the battle, against the very mirror.

It shimmered—and the queen's image shook.

"Zadny!" Yuri yelled from somewhere, and the startled dog was on his feet in the melee of shadows and goblins—but how that issue was, Tamas did not take two blinks to see. In the whole mirror he saw Ela by the lake.

He saw, around the mirror, Azdra'ik and a band of goblins pounding one another on the shoulders and shouting at each other like human boys . . .

He saw Nikolai, leaning on a goblin arm, limping and breathless, and suddenly Yuri running for him—through the very substance of the mirror. Zadny put himself in his path and dog and boy somehow navigated the battle-ground to reach him.

"Tamas!" Yuri was yelling, trying to hug him. Zadny was jumping at him, trying to get his attention.

But it was not done. It was not done until the mirror was entirely still and until he could see Ela, nothing but Ela's face against the night, completely occupying the mirror.

Master Karoly was in that image. He knew that without seeing him. He knew the presence of ghosts, that warred within the mirror, quarreling, in shouts and shrieks, and Jerzy, lord Sun, Jerzy complaining it was dark and unpleasant—

He caught a breath, on his knees with both arms full of boy and dog. He could not move, else. He dared not move or think or wonder, so long as the image remained what it was.

Something was terribly wrong, even if things had gone right for a moment. Yuri took hold of Zadny's collar, not knowing whether to let Zadny try to wake Tamas up or whether he ought not—but when his lap was free, Tamas got slowly to his feet and went on staring at the mirror, regardless of a room full of excited goblins, or anything. "Tamas?" he said, and when he had no answer from Tamas, he looked over at Nikolai and saw Nikolai limping toward him, covered in sweat and hardly able to keep his feet—so he kept Zadny tightly in hand.

Nikolai set his hand on his shoulder, hugged him against his side, and told him they were taking Tamas out of here—"If we have to carry him," Nikolai said.

But a tall goblin said, soberly, "No. It's not over. He hasn't won."

"What's not over?" Nikolai said hotly. "What's to win?"

He did not want Nikolai starting a fight with them, not when Tamas was the way he was. He tugged at master Nikolai's sleeve to stop him.

"The young wizard has his way," the goblin said, "and our people have the hall for the moment. But nothing's certain." Nikolai made a move to defy him and the goblin interposed his hand. "Fatally uncertain. He might die."

"Don't." Zadny was trying to get away, and Yuri held on to his collar with all his might.

"I'm going after Karoly."

"Wizard enough is here," the goblin said, and he meant Tamas, plain as plain. "Let him finish his work."

It needed a while, simply to gain a little breath. Ela was there, as shocked, as weary, as desperate. Master Karoly was there. Karoly was the one who said, or thought, "The whole place is hanging by a thread. Don't look away, boy. Well done. *Well done.*"

There were others present. Jerzy was indignant: I've business to take care of. I've no time for this nonsense, damn them, I've a horse in foal—

I'd care for it, Tamas thought, if I were there myself, back in Maggiar.

And Filip: What about my father? He's old. Who's to take care of him?

I won't forget, Tamas said.

Bogdan showed up in that company. But Bogdan was not speaking to him. Tamas was not surprised. He was immensely glad that Bogdan had found his friends again.

Then he heard gran speaking, shooing the other dead away too soon—but she banished one other that he felt lurking in the shadows.

Be off! You're not dead! Don't whine at me, you fool! You made your own mistakes! Leave my grandsons alone!

He was afraid for the outcome. He was not sure gran was a strong enough witch, to deal with Ylena. But he dared not all the while look away from Ela's face. He let all these things go on and he refused to give way to any diversion or trick or to look away from the only sight he was sure of.

Mirela, gran said severely.

No one calls me that, Ela protested, gazing fixedly at him, the same, holding on, only holding on, but afraid.

No one should, gran said sharply. —And you *are* Pavel's. And descended from Ytresse and Ylysse. That should make you cautious in your tempers, *and* your wants; if nothing else does. For the rest, . . . grandson?

"Gran?"

Remember the stories.

"Gran!"

Remember the stories, gran said again, and he could not help it, he was so startled: he began to remember exactly the way gran had told them, the woods and the waterfalls, the cities in the plain—

The lights began bobbing crazily, flitting around the watery walls and bouncing off them like housebound birds, the whole mirror began shaking, Zadny started barking, trying to get loose, but with all of that confusion going on, Yuri held on to him for dear life.

"What's going on?" Nikolai shouted at the goblins, but they looked to have no answers, either, just—

"Look at the mirror!" Yuri cried. It was changing, the reflection within it leaping from shadowy forests to starlit waterfalls, to courtyards and fountains and fields and beautiful places. Lights flitted above woodland pools, and wandered through the wood. Fairies, he realized. "Just like gran's stories!" he exclaimed, his arms wrapped about Zadny's neck and shoulders. "Tamas is doing it! *He's* doing it!"

Because Tamas had told him the stories, just the way, Tamas had sworn, the very words that gran had told them to him.

Doors banged open, and a wind blew through the hall, fresh and clean, direct from the outdoors.

Then Tamas turned away from the mirror, and Yuri flinched, seeing—he was not sure what he saw in Tamas' face, he only knew Tamas was still gazing off into thoughts that wanted no stupid boy interrupting, or rowdy dog jumping at him, in front of all these dangerous folk.

"Karoly's outside," Tamas said quietly. "Go and wait for me, master Nikolai. Bogdan's gone. Yuri needs to go home."

"Boy," Nikolai began to say. But Tamas only stood there, not angry, not impatient, just—that no argument was going to win with Tamas, even if Yuri had a question of his own—like, What about *you* going home?

But Nikolai gave him a shove, meaning they should do what

Tamas wanted, and Yuri held onto Zadny and made him come away, with Zadny looking back and whining in confusion, because Zadny could not understand. That was what made Yuri saddest, because Zadny was more honest than he could let himself be.

The doors led straight out under the stars. If so many odder things had not happened, Yuri would have blinked at that; but he hardly asked himself where the tunnel had gone. Master Karoly was there, exactly the way Tamas had said. And there was the witch, hardly older than he was, on a horse, among a handful of goblin guards. But the lake was not dark and dreadful now. Fairies darted and flitted above the water. It was all very beautiful.

But it was dark and cold, all the same, walking along the shore. He was glad to see Karoly and Gracja; and master Nikolai met a surprise, too, because there was Lwi, being held by goblins. It was only three words Nikolai spent on Karoly once he saw that: he went and put his arms about Lwi's neck.

And Yuri was glad about Lwi, too. But seeing the witch sitting on horseback looking just the same as his brother did, and, staring off like that, upset his stomach.

"What are they doing?" he asked master Karoly, scared, because Karoly had something of that look, too—looking at things he could not see, listening to things he could not hear, and murmuring answers to them, what was worse.

But at least Karoly seemed not to forbid him asking. And Karoly slid down from Gracja's back and put an arm about him, dog in tow and all. Yuri set his jaw, because it made him feel a lump in his throat, and brought him very close to tears. He wished Karoly would just answer his question and not do that to him.

Karoly still did not answer his question. He only said, "I have him. He's all right. He's very worried about you."

It was Tamas he was talking to, Yuri understood that of a

sudden. It made him feel both better and worse.

"I know," Karoly said, but he was still talking to Tamas. "I will. I understand." Karoly gave his arm a hug. "He'll be here."

"Who?" Yuri asked quietly, trying not to interrupt something. But it must have been him that Karoly was talking about this time, because Karoly did not answer him.

Deeper and deeper the change had to go, then, down into the earth, and into realms where strange things moved, old things, that ages of the earth had cast aside. And gran had talked about dragons and such, and said how they were cold and proud, and how one should never promise them anything, so he did not. Gran had said about the creatures of stone and ice, how they were not to trust, but, slow-moving and deliberate, they came above in winters, to howl in the mountain heights, and they had their place in faery.

The greatest and the lesser, and latest the things that could not change: it was only a matter of knitting those things together, one thing touching everything, as it had been.

And last it was a matter of letting go of things that seemed to have grown into one's soul.

And doing justice that had not been done.

He shut off seeing. It was a moment before he could knit Tamas back together, and be different from Ela, or the earth. It was self-blinding. It felt like darkness and smothering. But he endured it, and held himself to it, and eventually flesh and bone grew easier to wear and less heavy. He could open his eyes and move his hand and turn his head toward the goblins that stood watching and waiting for their banishment.

The goblin queen was already below, with every one else of her half-goblin creatures: he had seen to that, among the first things. But he looked at Azdra'ik, at nameless others, and set his hand on the dagger that was Azdra'ik's gift.

"Nothing from you," he said, "comes without attachments. And what did this come with?"

"My help," Azdra'ik said, without flinching. "When you were a young and weaponless fool."

He laughed. He could not help it. And probably there was a spell on the gift. There was when he drew it and gave it back, and caught Azdra'ik's arm in his and said he should come outside.

"Are we dispossessed?" Azdra'ik insisted to know as they walked. "Is that part of this bargain?"

"I named no bargain."

"There has to be one."

"No, no, no, master goblin. There *is* no bargain. You're in my debt, is what you are. From now on."

"No more than you're in mine! Who bought you free? Who carried you out of the woods? Who—?"

But they were at the doors, and what he had seen in the mirror, Azdra'ik could see for himself, and Azdra'ik freed himself and stood gazing at the lake, with its flitting and gliding lights.

"Oh, man," Azdra'ik said. "This is what our eldest saw. This is what our legends say. Who could know, but us?"

"My grandmother," he said, wondering suddenly about gran's sources.

But something broke the mirror stillness of the lake, and disturbed the skimming lights, something large and dark, that surfaced and dived again.

"What's that?" Yuri exclaimed. But in a moment more he knew for himself, as a trollish head broke the surface. And vanished again.

"Careful!" Karoly said, but Zadny set up a frantic barking, straining to get free, such a lunge he slipped Yuri's grip and evaded Yuri's dive after him.

Straight into the water Zadny ran, splashing and barking, and one and another huge head broke the surface.

"Krukczy!" Yuri shouted.

One splashed. But they kept surfacing and diving so quickly, swimming in a circle, that it was impossible to tell.

"What are they doing?" he asked master Karoly; but Nikolai had come to see, too, and Nikolai muttered,

"Lost their minds. Happy, one supposes."

The witch came, with her cloak wrapped about her, walking along the shore. The goblins gathered to watch. And from up the shore—

"Tamas!" Yuri said. "It's Tamas, with the goblins!"

"Four of them!" Nikolai exclaimed, but he was not counting goblins. There were four dark heads in the lake, and Zadny, running back and forth along the shore and barking as if he had lost his wits.

"Krukczy," said the witch, "and Tajny, and Hasel."

"And Ali'inel," Karoly added. "This place."

Their circle had grown tighter and tighter. And a bright spot grew in the water, bright as the sun. Their circle widened and it grew and grew. They dived all at once, in the middle of it.

But the light kept going, until it lit all the lake, bright as day; and then it brightened the ground right under their feet, and crept up their legs and up the sides of the hills and up the foundations of a beautiful tower just past where Tamas and the goblins were.

The light kept going until it had topped the tallest trees on the tops of the hills, and then it went right up into the sky, on all sides at once. And where it began to meet, in the height of heaven, the bright edges came together in a glare the eyes could not look at. It was noon, that was all. The night might never have been.

But Zadny stood looking at the lake, with now and again a bewildered bark, then ran, wet as he was, straight for Tamas.

Yuri ran after him: he could only think of Zadny making some trouble for Tamas. But he stopped in confusion when he saw the goblins, that seemed somehow—different. Not vastly changed. But maybe sunlight favored them—lent them a touch of mystery and magic, a touch of mischief, a touch of merriment. He would not have been afraid of these goblins—in awe of them, oh, yes. He was.

But not Zadny. Zadny jumped up on Tamas while he had stopped to stare and had his dusty armor all wet and muddy.

But it *was* his brother, because Tamas laughed, weary as he was, caught the hound in one arm and held out the other for him.

"Come here," Tamas called to him. "Yuri, come meet a goblin lord."

At such a chance, how could anyone hesitate?

But all the same, Yuri thought, the night of the third day on the lake shore, watching Tamas walk hand in hand with Ela, and the two of them talking that way wizards talked with each other, that no one but a wizard could hear—all the same, he did not want Tamas to have magic. It was all very fine to have supper with goblins and have trolls living at the bottom of the lake, and fine, he supposed, to have the occasional ghost straying in from the mysterious Wood, where things did not just go away in the ordinary fashion (Ylena's spell, master Karoly said, something about preserving her own life)—but Tamas was very preoccupied, very sad, sometimes, Yuri thought, about Bogdan, and it was clear to him that he was going home and Tamas would not.

I don't know why *I* have to explain to our parents why, Yuri thought bitterly. I don't know why Bogdan acted like that, except he never could stand to be second to anybody, and I don't know why Tamas and that girl are both like that, Tamas isn't ready to get married yet, and mama certainly wouldn't approve of her. I don't think papa would.

She was brave, though, and a witch (a sorceress, Karoly said) and she was looking right at him right now, giving him the most uncomfortable notion that she and Tamas were talking about him.

He glared at her, and turned his head and glared at the fairy-lights on the lake, and thought about Krukczy.

Tamas was going to keep Zadny. Tamas said wizards might understand Zadny, but the houndsmaster never could, and if he went home with him, he would only get in trouble. And that was all right. Zadny knew who he wanted.

But he did *not* want to talk to Ela, and Tamas was bringing her in his direction. He watched the fairy-lights instead, and told himself they were very pretty. Seeing gran's land was very well, too, but it was going to be better to see Maggiar.

That, if Tamas happened to be listening to him.

"Yes," Tamas said, disconcertingly. "I know. But I can't help it."

"Don't *do* that!" Yuri said.

"I'm sorry," Tamas said. But Yuri looked at Ela, all pale and pretty beside him. Master Karoly said she was Azdra'ik's great-grand-daughter and his niece, and gran's cousin. So master Karoly was going to stay behind a year or two, master Karoly said, and see Tamas stayed out of trouble. So he and Nikolai were riding home tomorrow, on Lwi and Gracja. And he did not plan to sleep tonight.

Ela reached out and tousled his hair. That did not endear her to him. But being a witch, and overhearing people, she stopped immediately, and looked unhappy.

He imagined, for some reason, she had never seen a boy. She was curious. She thought he was very clever.

It was very hard to go on being mad at someone who really believed that—which was probably a spell she was casting, who could ever know? A lot of people had been scared of gran. Probably with good reason.

Which was why, Tamas had said, it really was not a good idea for him and for Ela to come back over-mountain just yet. Neither of us knows anything, Tamas had said. We had a lot of help, that's all. And there's a immense lot we have to learn.

Stupid girl, he had said back to Tamas, being surly. Lord Sun, he did not want to remember that now, when Ela was listening. She was not a stupid girl. Not, at least, stupid.

One had to look hard to see if Ela was amused. But he thought she was. He knew Tamas was.

He decided that, on the whole, Tamas would be all right. And Tamas had promised to send him word across the mountains, how he was, how he was getting along.

He did not think, somehow, that Tamas meant writing letters.

About the Author

C.J. Cherryh's first book *Gate of Ivrel,* was published in 1976. Since then she has become a leading writer of science fiction and fantasy, known for extraordinary originality, versatility, and superb writing. She has won Hugo awards for her books *Downbelow Station* and *Cyteen*. She lives in Oklahoma and is a frequent guest of honor at science fiction conventions throughout the United States, Canada, and overseas.

*these plays represent the voices of all those
who dedicated their hope, their knowledge, their imagination
their courage, their patience and their commitment
to the collective processes that created them*

*these processes placed their first and final emphasis
upon the value and importance of every voice
the intelligence and humanity of which can be heard
in the dialogue of every scene*

*this book is a celebration of these voices
and of the many who inspired and supported us in our attempt
to reveal the injustices and contradictions in our lives
so as to learn how to transform our world*

We have begun to transform our experience and history of oppression into articulate images, objects and arguments of protest and change. This is cultural work. It is the analysis and organisation of our experience into useful everyday knowledge. If such work is developed by people democratically and grounded in a commitment to freedom, it will generate a progressive and democratic popular culture.

Culture is usually understood as work produced for galleries and theatres by geniuses in isolation. This belief has misled and intimidated people for centuries. It has been used to convince us that culture is irrelevant to our lives. It has ensured that we think we play no part in the making of ideas. It has resulted in us believing we possess no cultural skills. Above all, this myth has been used to devalue and destroy all popular democratic cultures.

Culture is how we eat, dress, raise children, work, laugh, love, speak and think about ourselves. If we do not make our own culture, we can do all these things in the interests of those who control the making of ideas. We can be owned without even knowing it.

Fragment from the introduction to the *Inside Out* programme
Derry Frontline: Culture and Education (1988)

INTRODUCTION

The collection of plays you hold in your hands contains the voices of the many people who gathered together with few resources to remember and to imagine, to reveal and to question, to risk and to learn, to support and to discover, to laugh and to sing, to unite and to tremble, to act and to inspire upon almost bare community stages during the **Derry Frontline**[1] years of cultural action for freedom. This is the theatre we agreed to present, in a time of violent undeclared wars, primarily within the communities we knew. We were all unwaged, a few by choice, most by necessity, striving to learn how to live and to intervene differently, together.

This is not a history or analysis of these years. Any serious attempt to understand and record the complex motivations and collective processes that culminated in these plays – to illuminate them, not to idealise them – would today, nearly ten years on, require an extended process of reconstruction and interpretation by people who are now all dispersed and actively involved in different projects and different lives. But because these plays represent three moments of collective resistance and because such cultural interventions are rarely recorded in their own voice, you will clearly be curious to know their contexts and how they evolved.

As one of the **Derry Frontline** coordinators, the writer of these collectively improvised plays, and the person who provided a continuity through all the **Frontline**[2] projects, I offer my own present understanding of the methods we

---

1 'Inspired by the workshops held by Manchester's **Frontline: Culture and Education** during their all-Ireland tour of *Struggle For Freedom* in October 1987, sculpture workshops were launched in the Bogside at the beginning of 1988. In June, these crystallised into the **Bogside Sculptors**, coordinated by the Derry sculptor Locky Morris. In the same month, a small group of young people from Creggan and the Bogside joined the sculptors to launch drama workshops and to form **Derry Frontline**, coordinated by the **Frontline** playwright and director Dan Baron Cohen'. (*Inside Out* programme, July 1988).

'**Derry Frontline** is a community-based cultural education organisation which works primarily with the young unemployed from Derry's innercity communities. Its cultural education projects combine educational method with drama, music, creative writing and visual arts to provide dynamic workshops which enable participants to establish a critical distance on their own most sensitive and controversial experience. The workshops enable those involved to question and understand their most deep-rooted cultural traditions so that they can actively select and participate in the making of democratic values to shape their lives and the culture of their community'. (*Threshold* programme, December 1992).

2 **Frontline**, originally called **Frontline: Culture and Education**, founded in 1986 in Manchester to contribute to the development of a community-based anti-imperialist culture of collective action. Due to the involvement of Derry sculptor Locky Morris (one of its founding members), **Frontline**'s first community play *Struggle for Freedom* was invited by Sinn Fein to tour the North and South of

used to create and stage these community plays, in the hope that this provides some insight into the circumstances, methods and objectives that inspired them. That these collective voices live beyond their times, both as echoes of living history and as participants in the ongoing unfinished debates about the future of Ireland and beyond, depends finally, of course, upon their dialogue with you.

THE CONTEXT OF THE PLAYS

Seventy-two hours before the opening night of **Threshold**, a member of **Derry Frontline** burst into our rehearsal room in Derry's Playhouse to inform us that the RUC[3] had invaded our offices and those of the **Bloody Sunday Initiative**[4] and were arresting all the people in the building. In shock, we abandoned our rehearsal to intervene.

We ran through the city and through the Bogside, joining friends and activists sprinting to Westend Park and arrived breathless at our offices to find them brightly lit by TV cameras and cordoned-off with white tape. The road was choked with RUC landrovers and British Army personnel and littered with our archives, scattering in the drizzle and wind of nightfall. We tried to intervene as our administrator and six other human-rights activists were frog-marched out of the building, bound and hooded inside white overalls, and thrown into the waiting RUC vehicle: we were brushed aside as the 'terrorists' were led away to interrogation.

Ireland in 1987. A series of workshops organised in Derry inspired the later foundation of **Derry Frontline** in 1988. **Frontline** subsequently produced *Apprentices of Freedom* (1988) and collaborated with **Derry Frontline** to produce *Time Will Tell* (1989) and *Strike or Starve* (1989), before renaming itself **Frontline** and producing *Thatcher's Children* (1990). All of the **Frontline** plays and their accompanying project manuscripts can be found in the **Frontline** archives in Salford University's Working Class Movement Library.

3 Royal Ulster Constabulary: the predominantly protestant police force (96%) of the North of Ireland that has had proven links with the paramilitary Loyalist organisations throughout its existence. See *The RUC: A Force Under Fire* by Chris Ryder (Arrow, 2000).

4 On 30 January 1972, fourteen nationalists were murdered by British paratroopers who opened fire on an unarmed civil rights march against internment. The **Bloody Sunday Initiative**, an independent Derry organisation, was founded in 1991 by relatives of the families of the victims 'to encourage creative and imaginative political action around the future of Ireland...and to commemorate the lives of those who died on Bloody Sunday...as well as the lives of all those other civilians killed in our city because of their opposition to British rule in Ireland...to work for British withdrawal and to build an independent, pluralistic, democratic and non-sectarian Ireland. The **Initiative** will especially seek to promote respect for human rights, dignity and justice within Ireland and internationally.' (contribution to the 1992 *Threshold* programme). For further details about Bloody Sunday, see *Bloody Sunday: What Really Happened* by Eamonn McCann, Maureen Shiels and Bridie Hannigan (Brandon, 1991).

Later that evening, the entire **Threshold** cast and production team assembled for its first technical rehearsal. During a collective assessment of the new situation, anxieties surfaced about the safety of the company, fifteen metres from the loyalist[5] community of the Fountain and some distance from the security of the Bogside and Creggan areas. Known republican[6] figures within the cast, already rehearsing in bullet-proof vests, declared their commitment to press on and not to allow the 'Brits' to disrupt the culmination of the two-year cultural project. Questions followed about how to get clothes and sanitary towels to the people who'd been 'lifted', and who would 'mind' their homes. Keys were exchanged and security was stepped-up at the entrances of the theatre. Despite the arrest of essential production people, partners and life-long friends of the cast, we began to familiarise ourselves with the raked stage and agree entrances and exits. The republican reflex to resist through persistence, born of centuries of harassment and human rights' abuses, had prevailed.

Suddenly, a mother and daughter from the Bogside entered the auditorium to inform us that the house of a central member of the cast was being raided by the RUC. She was released to return home with the women. As we resumed our preparation, other families and friends entered to report raids on other homes. During the next hour, as news of further raids gradually depleted the rehearsal, a collective panic spread through the company. Reluctantly, we agreed to postpone our rehearsal until the following day and to return to our homes, to protect ourselves and our communities.

The next day, sleepless but determined, we reassembled to continue our complex technical rehearsal in preparation for our dress rehearsal. By the following morning however, anxieties about the seven imprisoned activists had fused with the increasing fear of a loyalist attack on the playhouse, questioning the practicality of our resolve not to let the State force us to cancel our opening night. The release of our administrator[7] at midday inspired some

---

5 The Loyalist Movement was and remains entirely composed of protestant paramilitaries pledged to protect the union of Northern Ireland with Britain, and 'loyal' to the British Crown. For a detailed history of the Movement, see *Northern Ireland: The Orange State* by Michael Farrell (London, 1976).

6 The Republican Movement was and remains largely composed of Catholics who defined themselves as non-constitutionalist nationalists, drawn from the working-class enclaves of the North which produced and supported the Irish Republican Army (IRA). The Movement constituted some 35% of the Nationalist community up until the complex political formations that followed the 1994 cease-fire. For a detailed history of the Movement, see *The IRA* by Tim Pat Coogan (Harper Collins, 2000).

7 Throughout her interrogation, the interrogation of the six other human rights activists and the news coverage of the raid the following days, no mention was made of the alleged attempt to tap the telephone of SDLP leader and MP John Hume who lived in the house adjoining the Westend Park offices, the pretext for the raid and detention of the activists. To this day, all concerned are

optimism and relief. Throughout the afternoon, as security was increased throughout the theatre, we integrated our technical and dress rehearsals, taking complicated staging decisions under almost impossible pressure. At 7.30pm that night, **Threshold** opened to an almost full-house. The applause at the end of three hours of gripped concentration – punctuated by scenes of ironic comedy and charged with the energy of first-night nerves among first-time performers – was an affirmation not just of two years of preparation but of a collective resistance, by the cast and audience itself.

Looking back on those intensely lived days and nights – ten years to the day since **Derry Frontline** performed its first tentative rehearsed improvisations of **Threshold** to packed republican audiences in the city's Bogside Inn and Stardust nightclub to mark the 10th anniversary of the first hunger-strike[8] – these collected plays seem to belong to another age.

It seems extraordinary that to protect the lives and families of the republican youth participants of **Inside Out** in 1988, it was necessary to bury the tape-recordings of our storytelling workshops in 'safe ground' across the border that divides the North from the South of Ireland, when today Martin McGuinness (vice-president of Sinn Fein[9]) is education minister of the recently formed Northern Ireland assembly[10]. It seems equally as extraordinary that the ruthless Royal Ulster Constabulary which in 1989 patrolled Derry in highly armed units wearing bullet-proof vests and backed by the British Army – regularly interrogating the community of **Time Will Tell** inside the bars and streets of the Bogside, entering and searching our homes and the **Derry**

---

convinced this operation was intended to discredit the organisations the seven activists belonged to and to alienate the Unionist and Nationalist communities from supporting the **Threshold** project. For further details about this raid, see Pilkington, L (1994) 'Resistance to Liberation: an Interview with Dan Baron Cohen of Derry Frontline', (*The Drama Review 144*, pp14-44).

8 The two hungerstrikes in recent republican history took place in October 1980 and March 1981 following 5 years of the no-wash prison protest against criminalization. During the second hungerstrike, ten men died. For a detailed account of the protests, see *Ten Men Dead* by David Beresford (Atlantic Monthly Press, 1987).

9 **Sinn Fein** (Ourselves Alone), the republican nationalist party and political voice of the IRA founded in 1905, which until 1981 refused to contest or participate in local or British elections. Under the presidency of Gerry Adams, **Sinn Fein** has gradually mainstreamed itself to secure a mandate of some 15% in the North of Ireland.

10 The new Northern Ireland Assembly was established as part of the Belfast Agreement reached at the multi-party negotiations on Friday 10 April 1998, now commonly referred to as the 'Good Friday Agreement'. Following a referendum held on 22 May 1998, the new Northern Ireland Assembly was constituted under the Northern Ireland (Elections) Act 1998. Some 108 members were elected to the Assembly on 25 June 1998 by Proportional Representation (Single Transferable Vote) from the existing 18 Westminster constituencies. The Assembly met for the first time on Wednesday 1 July 1998 in Castle Buildings, and since then has met in Parliament Buildings. See *Northern Ireland Yearbook 2000/01*, Guildhall Press, 2000.

Frontline offices to terrify our families and undermine our determination to break the silence of official censorship[11] – is today being reformed by the British government.

And it seems remarkable that the **Threshold** improvisations – created during a period of relentless psychological strain of the weekly discoveries of 'touts' (informers within republican community organisations); the fortnightly funerals of assassinated Sinn Fein councillors; the monthly gunfire, explosions of bombs in the street and mortar attacks on British Army barracks; and the hourly need of activists to vary their routes to and from rehearsals to avoid arrest – could imagine in 1991 an imminent future when the exchange of political prisoners for political power and British withdrawal would necessitate another struggle, against an invisible, seductive and more sophisticated enemy: that of neo-liberalism and its global culture of consumerism.

This precisely identifies one of the central reasons for publishing these three plays. Because of **Derry Frontline**'s collective participatory workshop method and the identity of those who created, supported and performed the plays, each manuscript is a revealing historical testimony and document in its own right.

THE PLAYS AS CONTEMPORARY SOCIAL HISTORICAL DOCUMENTS

Inside Out was developed with a group of teenagers by **Derry Frontline** and the **Bogside Sculptors** in Derry and staged in July 1988. The production later toured seven cities throughout Ireland in October 1988. The play dramatises two complex social and moral questions (the right to choose armed struggle and women's right to choose abortion) that the republican movement was forced to review as it confronted the contradiction between its growing political maturity and its increasing political isolation – the effects of twenty years of armed conflict, *official* state-censorship (1988-94), explicit church intervention, and the accelerating technological revolution, respectively. British television's capacity to represent all direct action or street protest as violent, anti-democratic and inarticulate led to the complete transformation of the Sinn Fein identity and the evolution of a more media-astute political strategy. This moment of transition coincided with an intense need[12] for an

---

11 Official censorship in the North of Ireland lasted from 1988-94. Unofficial censorship (political and cultural) and self-censorship have existed since the colonisation of Ireland in the 16th century and persists until the present day. For a history of censorship in Ireland, see *Ireland: The Propaganda War* by Liz Curtis (Sasta, 1999).

12 **Frontline**'s first play *Struggle for Freedom* (1987) was performed throughout Ireland on a Sinn Fein tour, accompanied by workshops which in the North (and particularly in the predominantly

experimental cultural space in which young people – hardened by a lifetime of war – could emerge from behind their community barricades of silence and scarred accusation to voice personal questions and sensitive contradictions within the republican culture of resistance.

Time Will Tell was developed through a intensive nine month workshop collaboration between **Frontline** and **Derry Frontline** in Manchester, and staged throughout Greater Manchester in January 1989. It was later staged by **Derry Frontline** in Derry, in August 1989. The play looks at the consequences for a Mancunian family as the father, a self-exiled self-educated protestant from Derry, is forced through his intolerance towards his lesbian daughter to confront the unspoken and unresolved past he thinks he has left behind. In Manchester, the minimal production revealed the censored moral and human arguments of Irish republicanism to working-class communities whose youth were frequently forced to find employment in the British army. In Derry, by exploring the political unconscious of a Londonderry[13] working-class protestant and his self-destructive fear to look within, *in the heart of the republican Bogside itself,* the play enabled republican activists and their communities to reflect upon the barricaded humanity of their enemy and to assess their own sectarian fears and prejudices.

In 1991, when *Time Will Tell* was staged again in Derry, Belfast and Dublin, following the dismantling of the Berlin Wall and the disintegration of the Soviet Union, the play effectively became a critique of the emerging neo-liberal politics of 'peace and reconciliation' of the early 1990s. At its heart, in dramatising the psycho-emotional effects of three centuries of conflict in the North of Ireland, *Time Will Tell* was attempting to understand the capacity of the oppressed to become the oppressor and the relationship between patriarchy and colonialism, to construct a politicised, empathetic bridge between the divided protestant and catholic working-class communities of Manchester and the North of Ireland.

Derry Frontline's final play, *Threshold*, was developed in Derry. This play imagines the political realities and questions the republican movement will

---

nationalist city of Derry), revealed a hunger to reflect, debate and externalise experiences which remained locked within. The committed questioning of this anti-imperialist theatre from without inspired sensitive debates after the performances about the politics, psychology and social implications of the republican barricade. For a more detailed insight into this question, see the dialogue between James King and myself 'Dramatherapy: Radical Intervention or Counter-Insurgency?' in *Dramatherapy 3: Theory and Practice,* ed. Sue Jennings (London, Routledge 1996, pp269-83). For a detailed definition of this idea of the *barricade culture,* see *The Drama Review 144,* cited above.

13 Catholics and nationalists call Londonderry, Derry. Protestants and unionists affirm the Union of 1801 through the city's 'official' name. London was joined to the city's name following the successful unionist resistance of 1689, protecting the property of Protestant bankers from a catholic uprising.

face in a consumerist future – located during a stalled and unconvincing peace-process – through the 'freedomstrike' of a catholic and her protestant confidante. Both women are victims of two inter-linked wars, that of class and gender, but both find themselves transforming the histories they have inherited into a visionary united protest. Initiated through more than fifty moving public testimonies by mothers, survivors and leaders of the 1980 and 1981 republican hungerstrikes, the *Threshold* project initially expected to generate its final script through twelve weeks of workshops. However, the emotional and psychological experience of these testimonies, recalled in public for the first time by many of the original participants, generated the need for extensive improvisation and debate that could not be contained within this time frame. This process coincided with spiralling debates about the implications of the disintegration of Eastern Europe, the accelerating formation of a united Europe and 'new world order', and an increase in the day-to-day repression and State-organised murders within the North. The play's narrative structure and form took eighteen months to construct.

During the two years between 1990-92 in which the *Threshold* workshop researched and refined its themes, **Derry Frontline** experimentally searched for innovative solutions to all of its needs, generating a *women's living history project*[14] (to document the hidden role of women in the republican struggle); a *parenting and young people's workshop* (to explore new child-centred forms of parenting that could interrupt cycles of authoritarian abusive relationships); and cultural exchanges with English working-class communities. The project effectively became an extended adult-education seminar, launching a weekly schedule of sexuality, political morality, history, liberation theology and economics dialogues with the most senior thinkers and leaders within the republican movement[15], at the very moment when the latter were secretly designing the architecture of the current peace-process. In this respect, *Threshold* articulates a self-confidence and desire to experiment which had been practically unthinkable within the community that watched *Inside Out*: the possibility of imagining a new Ireland, of stepping beyond centuries of oppositional identities and the 'inevitable' free-market politics of globalisation into the threshold between resistance and liberation.

These collected plays then represent aspects of the political and cultural process that was being lived by the republican community *in everyday struggle* – its profound transition from angry accusation to self-questioning,

---

14 **The Women's Living History Project** (WLHC) contributed interviews of the families of the victims of Bloody Sunday to the book *Bloody Sunday: What Really Happened* (edited by Eamonn McCann, Brandon Press, 1991), and published *Jukin Back* (Guildhall Press, 1994), a collection of interviews of working class women from the nationalist Bogside and unionist Fountain communities of Derry.

15 See the list of contributors to these workshops in the title-page of *Threshold*.

to open debate and finally to sceptical hope, through at times painful but intensely honest confrontations with its own history, contradictions and aspirations – within a rapidly changing political world order.

Given the identity of those directly and indirectly involved in **Derry Frontline**'s plays – from the community leaders who argued for their development and inclusion inside closed local and national Sinn Fein meetings, and participated in our basement workshop dialogues with young activists, to liberation theology and human rights activists, ex-IRA members, exprisoners and republican activists who participated in or watched productions – this political theatre articulated and contributed to the vital debates which led to the dramatic IRA cease-fire on 31 August 1994.

This is not to suggest that we were all conscious of this significance. But in retrospect, as Ireland's historical processes become more clearly defined and understood, these plays may enable others to understand the integrity, risk and searching debate that contributed to the emergence of a more democratic and just Ireland.

THE PLAYS AND THEIR WORKSHOP METHODS

Rereading these plays and recalling their workshop processes more than a decade later from within the **Movimento Sem Terra**[16] and the popular socialist government of Rio Grande do Sul within Brazil where I am living and collaborating as a cultural activist, I believe that **Frontline**'s most enduring and least visible contribution may be the methods that generated our plays, the **2020 Vision** *people's banner*[17] and murals. Our contribution to this method of participatory and collective *self-determination* draws upon an international collection of intertwined and under-documented histories, and continues to develop in the lives of many of those who participated in our

---

16 **MST** (*Movimento Sem Terra*), the landless movement of Brazil emerged in the late 1970s out of the liberation theology and pastoral movements, occupying unproductive land to stimulate and accelerate agrarian reform. **MST** became a national movement in 1984, developing through three distinct phases: the organisation of the *favela* poor, the homeless and the displaced, to occupy unproductive land; the politicisation, organisation and agitation of the excluded in **MST** *acampamentos* (camps), evolving literacy, education, organic medicine, community art, children's and women's development projects in preparation for collective agro-ecological production; and the development of legal, autonomous self-sustaining *assentamentos* (settlements) to weaken the unreformable Brazilian state through the construction of new democratic communities.

17 The 30m banner coordinated by **Derry Frontline** and produced through storytelling workshops for the **2020 Vision** festival of democracy and change, organised to mark the 20th anniversary of the British military re-occupation of the North of Ireland (14th August 1969), and to celebrate 20 years of resistance and hope.

projects. Before outlining the methods we evolved, I want to celebrate these histories by identifying the key ideas that impacted upon the lives of those hundreds of people who developed **Derry Frontline** (and the **Frontline** organisation that preceded it).

First, that the stage is a unique, simultaneously empathetic and analytical cultural space in which every generation has an opportunity (even a responsibility) to question and define itself in terms of justice and the moral choices[18] of its time. Second, that the capacities we all possess to transform ourselves and this world are only activated and developed through *dialogue* (with others and within ourselves), centred in our knowledges, our needs, our questions, our critical imagination, and the creation of a community of solidarity. Third, that resistance *is knowledge* and must be respected as such, but that the barricades we use to protect ourselves can transform themselves into *resistance to liberation*, the key focus for cultural action for freedom. And fourth, that the *decolonisation of the mindful-body*[19] (the immunised body that contains so much wisdom, enables us to survive, but also permits us to reproduce in our own lives and politics the violence and repression we have internalised), is central to the struggle for democracy. Much has been and can be written about each of these claims. Here I want to identify the practitioners who contributed to our development and to what I now understand as a permanently evolving *method of self-determination*, so that readers looking for a more detailed understanding of the evolution of this method can study some of its historical and theoretical origins.

Derry Frontline's workshop principles and methods evolved through an adaptation of Paulo Freire's *pedagogy of the oppressed* literacy methods and Augusto Boal's *theatre of the oppressed* techniques developed within and beyond Brazil[20]; the linkage between culture, education and community participation embodied in the Kamiirithu anti-imperialist rural theatre project coordinated by Ngugi Wa Thiong'o in Kenya (1976-77)[21]; and the narrative techniques and rehearsal methods of the *rational theatre* developed by the socialist English playwright Edward Bond. In the searching experimentation of

---

18 See any of the introductions to the collected plays of Edward Bond, particularly his introductions to *Saved* and to *Lear*, published by Methuen, London.

19 See my article 'Resistance to Liberation: Decolonising the Mindful-Body' in *Performance Research 2* (pp60-74, Routledge, London 1996).

20 The centrality of dialogue and collective action within our method draws its theoretical inspiration from the writings of Paulo Freire (*Pedagogy of the Oppressed, Cultural Action for Freedom, Fear and Profundity*), and of Augusto Boal (*Theatre of the Oppressed, Rainbow of Desire*),

21 For a description of this significant Kenyan cultural and educational project, see *Detained: A Writer's Prison Diary* cited above.

Wazalendo Players 84 (London 1984)[22], **Quantum Theatre Company** (Manchester 1984-86)[23] and **Frontline: Culture and Education** (1986-90), these influences were all blended and adapted by English and Irish working class coordinators and participants of a sequence of projects through their living knowledges and workshop-evaluations into a constantly evolving but coherent application of theatre, music, the visual arts and sculpture for personal and community self-determination. This consistent emphasis upon an *anti-imperialist cultural politics of self-determination* matured considerably through **Frontline**'s relationship to the cultural wing of Sinn Fein[24] in 1987 and **Derry Frontline**'s active participation in the Irish republican cultural struggle (1988-94).

Four principles could be found braided through the centre of every workshop and project reunion: to prioritise the life-experience, the living needs and the knowledges of every workshop participant; to structure every workshop in a dialogue between the needs of its participants and the agreed cultural aims of its coordinator(s); to build a workshop culture of intimacy, friendship, democratic participation, supported risk, experimentation, questioning and affirmation; and to recognise all resistance as knowledge – particularly as expressed through the right to question and the right to say 'no'.

These principles were implemented through four phases. The first was *storytelling* – in search of a community of empathy and interest. This revealed

---

22 The theatre company formed in London by the *Committee for the Release of Political Prisoners in Kenya* to mark the 100th anniversary of the colonial carve-up of Africa. **Wazalendo** staged *The Trial of Dedan Kimathi* by Ngugi Wa Thiong'o and Micere Mugo (Heinemann), codirected by Ngugi and myself for the Africa Centre, London, in 1984. The production toured its performances and 'open rehearsals' throughout England in 1984.

23 Towards the end of the rehearsal process at the Africa Centre, I was appointed as head of the Department of English and Drama at Manchester's College of Adult Education. Inspired by a performance of *The Trial of Dedan Kimathi*, my unemployed part-time and mainly working-class students developed their twice-weekly classes into the full-time **Quantum Theatre Company** which staged Edward Bond's *The Woman* (1985) and the world premier of Bond's *Human Cannon* (1985).

24 This relationship was forged initially through the 1987 all-Ireland tour of **Frontline**'s open rehearsals and performances of *Struggle For Freedom*. This relationship evolved into an active collaboration in 1988 in Derry, principally through the Irish language group **Conradh Na Gaelige** whose cultural politics centred in the revival of Irish as a critical dimension of anti-imperialist struggle. In association with **Conradh na Gaelige**, **Derry Frontline** coordinated a series of discussions for republican activists in 1988 (held in Pilot's Row in Derry) to define the role of culture in liberation struggles. These discussions actively drew upon the ideas of, among others, Raymond Williams, Ngugi Wa Thiong'o, Amilcar Cabral, Paulo Freire, Edward Bond, Juliet Mitchell, Franz Fanon and the writings of republican prisoners (particularly Eoghan MacCormaic) who were engaged in a similar debate inside the Long Kesh prison. The collaboration sharpened the development of **Derry Frontline**'s first play, motivating its participants to begin its own Irish language study group and conclude *Inside Out* in Irish as a provocative act of community resistance.

the personal needs, skills, and knowledges of the participants, and cultivated the collective focus of the project. This phase was unhurried, informal and prioritised the emergence of the histories, contradictions and the voice of every participant in the collective search for a central workshop theme and its questions. This was accompanied by the equally as informal but structured discussion of the rights and agreements that would define a democratic method with clear boundaries and expectations. In general, this phase was structured by the questions 'who am I/are we', 'what do I/we want/need' and 'who do we want/need to present our work to'.

The second phase was dedicated *to experimentation and critical questioning* – in search of realistic, democratic and just solutions to collectively identified relevant problems or contradictions. Key dilemmas were chosen – based on the stories that had been told – for the clarity of their 'question', and then placed within 'limit situations'. As most of the workshop participants and coordinators lived within limit situations, the overriding concern within this phase was to judge when to respect and when coax open the silences individuals and communities used for self-protection, and to understand the complex and shifting boundaries between educational-theatre or theatre-for-development, and drama-therapy[25]. In general, this second phase was structured by the questions 'why am I/are we in this situation' and 'how do I/we change it'.

The third phase prioritised *narrative construction,* building a collective narrative through the selection of improvisations – in the search for a public presentation which could dramatise the workshop theme, its key questions and its objectives. This phase invariably needed to return to the second phase, and sometimes required modification of the agreed objectives of the first phase. It culminated in the recording of the final workshop improvisations to record the ideas, the cultural tone and language of each individual scene and performer, the tapes of which were then developed into a provisional and then final script by a single writer[26]. In general, this third phase was structured by the questions 'what are we trying to achieve through this

---

25 See 'Dramatherapy: Radical Intervention or Counter-Insurgency?', cited above.

26 The writing of each play itself reflected the circumstances and moment of collaboration. Within a first community collaboration, the *Inside Out* tapes were essential to catch the distinctive Derry wit and specific identities of the workshop participants. *Time Will Tell* was written after four years of community projects in Manchester; the workshop recordings more directly focussed the dramatic structure of the play,s arguments. *Threshold* was shaped more by the *2020 Dialogues* than the workshop improvisations themselves, partly because Derry's music and language were now clearly imprinted in my aural imagination, partly because the script had to leap beyond our early improvisations to encompass **Derry Frontline**'s years of questioning and debate, but mainly because political pressure on our activist-participants at time made further improvisation impractical. All three plays, however, were subjected to critical and cultural scrutiny by the workshop participants before rehearsals began.

presentation', 'how and where might this be most sensitively, creatively and usefully communicated to our defined community audience', and importantly 'what work do we want this audience to do'.

The fourth and final phase was committed to *production* – the systematic preparation of the presentation to the defined community or communities. This phase – the definition and organisation of everything from the script, casting, rehearsal schedule, production itinerary, production roles and their responsibilities, technical needs, administration and publicity – was based on collective agreements, both to sustain the democratic praxis of the workshop process and to ensure that everyone genuinely understood this process. Both were essential to the affirmation and first public declaration of a new collective identity, and to the democratisation and passing on of production skills. Provisional scripts were tested through cast-readings and rehearsal, and rehearsals frequently began and ended with collective production decisions. In general, this fourth phase was structured by the questions 'how do we sustain the integration of the artistic, technical and administrative preparation of our presentation' and 'how do we sustain the democratic decision-making of this process' under the pressures of meeting our announced production deadlines.

I have tried here to outline the collective participatory workshop methods that **Derry Frontline** used in its contribution to the development of the republican culture of resistance. Because these plays emerged during a moment of transition within the struggle for Irish self-determination – the traumatic and complex transition from resistance to negotiation – they also dramatise the psychological and emotional difficulties and painful political contradictions of a threshold that we learned to define as the *resistance-to-liberation*. In part, the difficulties of practising democracy were inevitable in a time of war, a time of necessary secrecy, necessary unity, necessary reflexes of self-protection and organisational security: the fear and scepticism of opening the fist of resistance to extend the palm of dialogue. In part, this resistance-to-liberation articulated the process of *learning democracy itself*: the pain and the euphoria; the difficulties of recognising, acknowledging and interrupting generations of reflexes and ways of seeing; the uncertainty of modifying or transforming sacred values and attitudes; and the relief of searching for a personal voice after years, even decades of having to conceal it behind the community's barricaded and unified voice of sacrifice.

In the introduction to the programme for what turned out to be **Derry Frontline**'s farewell production, the staging of *Death and the Maiden* by Ariel Dorfman to mark the 22nd anniversary of Derry's Bloody Sunday in January 1994, we wrote:

> Because our cultural work has been so intimately linked to the
> everyday needs and development of the community, our plays and
> murals have themselves contributed to exposing the contradictions

which might have served as useful barricades, but obstruct genuine freedom. In mapping out the often painful thresholds of change, our workshops have revealed how difficult it is to become democratic and how much personal courage is needed to 'decolonise the mind'. We have made mistakes in finding our way through this unchartered territory: but each mistake has yielded new knowledges, and confirmed that we are our own most precious resource for change.

These plays then document a process that was neither perfect nor imperfect, but a process of self-questioning and self-discovery. For this reason, they dramatise a range of human risks and thresholds which other individuals and communities may well recognise within themselves. This is perhaps the most profound reason for their publication: that both within the North of Ireland and beyond, they might assist communities on the many sides of the 'divides' cultivated by colonialism and neo-colonialism to better understand themselves and one another in the long revolution towards a just and democratic world.

Rio Grande do Sul, Brasil, May 2001

INSIDE OUT

Based on the **Derry Frontline** drama and lyric workshops of June-July 1988.

The original 1988 performance was flanked by an exhibition of posters and focussed through stage sculptures produced during workshops by the **Bogside Sculptors**.

The songs in *Inside Out* were selected by the full company together. Each song is protected by copyright. The writers of the songs are:

MANY HAVE GIVEN THEIR LIVES ....*Apprentices of Freedom*
Frontline 1988
THE WALL ....Sean Taggart & Dan Baron Cohen
I FEEL PAIN AS I SEE PEOPLE DIE ....*Apprentices of Freedom*
Frontline 1988
UNFINISHED REVOLUTION..Christy Moore
APARTHEID GOLD...Dan Baron Cohen

INSIDE OUT

LOCAL SOCIO-POLITICAL CONTEXT

Burial of the *Gibraltar 3*[1] in Belfast's Milltown cemetery;

Attack by Oliver Stone on the families and republican mourners of the *Gibraltar 3*[1] in Milltown cemetery during the burial, 16 March 1988;

Attack and killing of two special branch officers by republicans burying those who were murdered by Oliver Stone, Belfast, 19 March 1988;

Episcopal letter from Archbishop Edward Daley read out in churches throughout North of Ireland, appealing for information about the IRA and the names of its volunteers.

PROJECT OBJECTIVES

To demonstrate the potential of *cultural action* to the republican movement (specifically through drama, sculpture, poetry and music);

To demonstrate how collective and participatory cultural-education projects contribute to personal and community development, particularly to the development of democratic skills;

To collaborate with the republican youth of the Bogside and Creggan communities of Derry to articulate their voice, identity and concerns;

To pass on skills of cultural action to engaged youth, their families and their communities;

To contribute to the moral and political reflection and debate within the republican movemnet through a community play which could enable it to hear its own censored voice and understand the contradictions within its own culture.

THEMATIC CONCERNS

To understand teenage sexuality and women's right to choose abortion as essential elements of a progressive cultural politics of self-determination;

To dramatise the morality of armed struggle within the political context of British colonialism, military occupation, religious apartheid and censorship.

WORKSHOP AND AESTHETIC INNOVATIONS

Evolution of sculpture and spray-painting as *image-theatre* through dialogue between coordinator and participant to focus and stimulate *forum theatre*[2];

Evolution of a poetry and lyric writing workshop method based on the dialogue between the speaking writer (participant) and questioning reader-recorder (coordinator);

Development of the stage-sculpture as an imagistic focus for the ideological questions or debate on stage.

Useful notes to accompany *Inside Out:*

Kesh   The Long Kesh (or Maze) Prison, known as the H-Blocks, home to Ireland's political prisoners, the focus of the 1980 and 1981 hungerstrikes and a key arena in the military conflict during the final decades of the 20th century.

Bru   Derry idiom for the *social security* and *employment benefits centre.*

Wain   Derry idiom for *child.*

SAS   Special Air Services, the undercover highly trained and equipped regiment within the British Army that through the final decades of the 20th century was responsible for all counter-insurgency and strategic military operations related to British political interests.

Wile   Derry idiom for *terrible* or *very.*

---

1 The Gibraltar 3 was the name given to the three IRA volunteers Mairead Farrell, Sean Savage and Daniel McCann who were murdered by the SAS in Gibraltar on 6 March 1988.

2 See Augusto Boal's *Theatre of the Oppressed* (Pluto Press, 2000).

INSIDE OUT

SCENE 1: **Sermon**, *Church, Sunday morning*
SCENE 2: **Sunday Dinner**, *the DOHERTY home, Sunday midday*
SCENE 3: **Dawn Raid**, *the DEEHAN home, Monday, 6.05am*
SCENE 4: **The Real World**, *the DEEHAN home, Monday 4pm*

INTERVAL

SCENE 5: **Law and Order**, *the DOHERTY home, Tuesday night*
SCENE 6: **No Choice**, *the DEEHAN home, Wednesday night*
SCENE 7: **The Cooker**, *the DOHERTY home, late Thursday night*
SCENE 8: **The Verdict**, *Friday morning*

CHARACTERS

FATHER MORRIS ....Derry Priest. Forties
JIM DOHERTY ....Catholic. Late thirties
MARY DOHERTY ....Catholic. Mid thirties
EAMONN DOHERTY.......................................Their son. Eighteen
SEAN DOHERTY...Their son. Seventeen
GERRY DEEHAN ....Catholic. Thirties
MARION DEEHAN ....Catholic. Early thirties
ANN DEEHAN...Their daughter. Fifteen
CATHY...Catholic. Fifteen
TARA...Catholic. Fifteen
CAROL DOHERTY ....Catholic. Early forties
MARTIN DOHERTY...Catholic. Forties
JOE DOHERTY ....Their son. Seventeen
SINGERS

Inside Out is set in Derry 1988. The minimal stage sets indicated are adequate. The singers should be drawn entirely from the cast of actors.

Throughout the script, the term *beat* indicates a fractional pause, considerably shorter than the more conventional term *pause*.

Cast for the July 1988 production

Corn Beef Tin & Pilot's Row, Derry, and the Conway Mill, Belfast
and the all-Ireland tour of October 1988

FATHER MORRIS ....Locky Morris
JIM DOHERTY...Jim Keys
MARY DOHERTY...Letitia Deehan
EAMONN DOHERTY ....Eamonn Kelly
SEAN DOHERTY ....Sean Taggart
ANN DEEHAN..Ann Deehan
GERRY DEEHAN...Locky Morris
MARION DEEHAN ....Mary Gallagher
CATHY ....Cathy Friel
TARA ....Tara Gallagher
CAROL DOHERTY..Carol Deehan
MARTIN DOHERTY ....Martin Gallagher
JOE DOHERTY ....Eamonn Kelly
SINGERS ....Cathy Friel
                                                               Mary Gallagher
                                                               Carol Deehan
                                                               Tara Gallagher
MUSICIAN ....Harry Coyle

Production

SCULPTORS ....Ann Deehan
                                                                 Cathy Friel
TECHNICAL CO-ORDINATOR ....Jim Keys
PRODUCTION/PUBLICITY CO-ORDINATOR............Mary Gallagher
WRITER AND DIRECTOR ....Dan Baron Cohen
PROJECT CO-ORDINATORS ....Dan Baron Cohen (**Derry Frontline**)
                                    Locky Morris (**Bogside Sculptors**)

INSIDE OUT

A sculpture of a cooker embedded in the roof of a landrover stands centre-stage. At the beginning of the performance, two actors dismantle the sculpture, leaving the cooker on stage as a pulpit. They drape a simple white cloth over the cooker and exit.

SCENE 1: SERMON

Church. Sunday morning. FATHER MORRIS is reading from a letter.

PRIEST: Brothers and sisters in Christ
After an interval of relative calm
murder has returned to the streets of our city
foul and callous murder
It does not matter whether the victim
is a soldier
police officer or civilian
It does not matter
what his political or religious viewpoint might be
The taking of a human life
as it has been taken in Derry this week
is murder
It cannot be called by any other name

In recent weeks
a succession of decent families in Catholic areas of this city
have been held hostage in their own homes
whilst ambushes were prepared
These families were terrorised and terrified
Parents were humiliated in their own homes
before their own children
by people and organisations who dare to describe themselves
as 'defenders of the community'
These people or organisations
do not defend this community
They have persecuted
terrified and demoralised this community
The vast majority of Catholics want
nothing to do with them
They fundamentally disagree with and reject
their evil and sinful activities
I believe
that very few people in the Catholic community

are deliberately withholding information
They are as distressed about these murders
as anyone else
There is a sense of hopelessness and helplessness

All those who believe in the sacredness of human life
have a Christian obligation
and responsibility
to make known anything
they may have seen or heard
that may have any connection with murder
whoever the perpetrator or victim might be
I feel bound by this obligation
All of us must feel bound by it
The enormity of the sin of murder
must over-rule any political or other reservations
that people might have

We know it is a sin
to join organisations committed to violence
or to remain in them
We sympathise with the police forces
North and South
in their task of upholding the law
in the most difficult and dangerous circumstances
Many have lost their lives
Many others have suffered serious injury
in the task of maintaining law and order
We call on all our people
to co-operate with the police
in bringing the guilty to justice
We appeal to everyone in this community
to examine his or her own conscience
Ask yourselves honestly
Am I
in any way
assisting or encouraging
those who are promoting
or engaging in
a campaign of murder and intimidation

There is no longer any room
for romantic illusion
There is no excuse for thinking

that the present violence in Ireland
can be morally justified
It is a choice between good and evil
Our task as Catholics
is to join the forces of law and order
in the prevention
of terror and murder

My brothers and sisters in Christ
In the face of these recent crimes
let us double our prayers
that the Lord will remove the veil
from the eyes of those
who will not see
and bring about in our hearts
a true spirit of repentance
and justice

The PRIEST leaves.

SINGERS: Many have given their love and their lives
But their lives were not given in vain
Their sacrifice has brought us nearer to victory
Their sacrifice has brought us nearer to victory

SCENE 2: SUNDAY DINNER

The DOHERTY home. Sunday midday. JIM DOHERTY is sat talking with his two sons EAMONN and SEAN. They're waiting to be served. The cooker has been removed offstage. A second triangular stage sculpture with three images on its faces is revealed. The image of the labourer behind bars faces the audience. This stage sculpture remains upstage centre throughout the play.

FATHER: Did he get the books?

EAMONN: He says he'll have them read by the next visit –

SEAN: If his eyes hold out.

EAMONN: He tried to get the wee one joined up. He took it all in –

MOTHER: *(Off)* Don't you be talking about that visit till we're all in the one room. I'll just be two minutes with these spuds.

FATHER: Did you explain why I couldn't come up?

EAMONN: He knows you're waiting for the claim to come in.

FATHER: I'll make it up to you –

EAMONN: Forget it.

FATHER: All that parcel money and the travelling down. I'll put a few hundred to the car –

MOTHER: *(Off)* You've nearly that claim all spent. You remember about that cooker!

SEAN: Should've seen him up the Kesh yesterday. Screw dropped a bunch of keys. He lifts them up. 'There you are sir' –

EAMONN: Didn't it get us in quicker?

SEAN: I wanted to throw up.

EAMONN: Tactics young fella.

FATHER: That's why he's in work.

EAMONN: Aye, and the only one in the house too.

SEAN: *(Beat)* What about your redundancy, da?

EAMONN: Redundancy only comes into it, stupid, if you're laid off –

FATHER: They're arguing it was my fault. Say I didn't bend down right. Thirty years labouring and they say I don't know me own trade.

EAMONN: So you want a desk job like mine?

SEAN: Plenty of them lying about.

EAMONN: He could find something else.

SEAN: Who's going to offer him a job at his age? The only work he's fit for is the building trade and that wrecked his back –

            Sudden massive explosion. EAMONN and SEAN drop to the floor and move towards the window. The FATHER eases himself behind his chair.

MOTHER: *(Off)* Jesus, Mary and Saint Joseph!

EAMONN: Jesus, that was close!

FATHER: Get you down! The both of yous!

            EAMONN and SEAN crouch beneath the window. The FATHER squats behind the chair.

MOTHER: *(Off)* Will nobody help? Oh Jesus. Will you look at that! All over the wall! On fire! They'll never be saved! I knew it would come to this. I warned you. I warned you all!

FATHER: What can you see, Mary? Is it one of our boys?

MOTHER: *(Entering. Her face is black and her hair filled with bits of potato)* Will you look at my boys hiding in their boots! And my eyebrows all singed! Will you look at that wee strongman shaking behind his highchair! Ireland's bold Fenian men! *(SEAN and EAMONN return to their chairs)* I warned you but you wouldn't listen! Do I have to get blown to pieces before you do something about that cooker?

EAMONN: Jesus, ma. You look like one of them black men.

FATHER: *(Trying to lift himself)* I'm stuck –

MOTHER: Don't you be getting up, Jim Doherty. Stay you down on your knees until you promise me a new cooker.

FATHER: *(Hand outstretched)* Me back's gone –

MOTHER: A cooker.

FATHER: Me back –

MOTHER: A cooker, Jim!

FATHER: Mary! Me back!

MOTHER: Swear, Jim. Swear!

FATHER: Jesus! Me back!

MOTHER: Don't you be cursing in this home, Jim Doherty! And on a Sunday too!

EAMONN: Where's our dinner, ma?

MOTHER: In my hair and on that wall!

SEAN: Will I bring in the dinner, ma?

MOTHER: Sit you there. Now before everyone starts blaming me for burning the dinner –

FATHER: Give us a hand, Eamonn.

MOTHER: *(As EAMONN helps his FATHER back into the chair)* Aye. Click you your fingers and he's always beside you. Do I have to be lying in my coffin before any of yous notice? That's seven times this week I've asked you to go down to the bru about that cooker. 'There's the visit ma'. 'It's me back, Mary' –

SEAN: He was down Friday.

MOTHER: *(To FATHER)* Why didn't you tell me?

FATHER: They'll give us a loan but we have to pay ten pounds a week back. Where are we going to find ten pounds a week?

MOTHER: And you call yourself a man? You walk in there and trot out like a wee lamb. You don't get nowhere unless you kick up!

EAMONN: Lay off him ma –

MOTHER: You keep out of this –

EAMONN: I live here as well –

MOTHER: *(To EAMONN and the FATHER)* Ten pounds a week? Yous were out drinking and came back full –

FATHER: Mary. It's Sunday –

EAMONN: You come in here like a black tornado –

MOTHER: I'm warning you –

EAMONN: And lash out at the man!

SEAN: Arguing wont change it.

MOTHER: You keep out of this, Sean.

EAMONN: *(Takes out money)* Look. If Sean runs down to the Chinese I'll buy yous a take out –

SEAN: Run down yourself.

MOTHER: You give that money towards the cooker.

EAMONN: I pay for parcels to go to the Kesh –

SEAN: This is madness.

MOTHER: And I'm in debt up to here! How am I supposed to keep yous on the money coming in from the bru? *(Pause)* Jim! Will you say something!

FATHER: Will you shut up and give this battered head some peace!

Silence. SEAN goes to the window. The MOTHER sits.

EAMONN: Look. I offered a take out –

SEAN: That's no solution.

EAMONN: Don't give me lip. Soon as I've bought this car I'm moving out. Get a place of my own and take care of meself –

MOTHER: Aye and who'll cook and clean for you?

EAMONN: You're getting paid for it.

MOTHER: All I get is the money to keep yous. I'm never out. Bingo every second Sunday. Who makes your meals? Who pays the gas? The coal? The food and the electricity?

EAMONN: That's what I'm paying you for!

FATHER: Don't raise your voice to your mother!

MOTHER: Why not? I keep this house but I have no say. That cooker's a nightmare and you expect me to work miracles on it!

EAMONN: I need the money to buy a car.

MOTHER: A safe cooker's essential.

EAMONN: You can't drive round in a cooker.

FATHER: I'll look round for a second-hand cooker –

MOTHER: Aye. Show us up. Bring in a rusty old cooker with all the neighbours staring. *(To EAMONN)* Your father's too proud to ask you for a loan.

EAMONN: I work for my money!

MOTHER: And I work for you –

EAMONN: I don't wait for the bru to come in and hope on claims –

FATHER: Show some respect moneymouth! I've worked thirty years!

EAMONN: Aye and what've you got to show for it!

FATHER: How many days was I off sick since we were married? Three days! Three days on the sick in thirty years! We know what this city needs! We've got two sons inside doing life trying to change it! Don't you turn around and kick me when I'm down! I've been quiet till now. I've listened to this madness for too long. *(To EAMONN)* Look at me! I've given my lifeblood to this house! I can't even tie me own shoelaces! Do you think I want to live in this prison? Do you think I want to die a cripple? Don't any of yous point the finger at me and say I'm at fault! I've been out in all weathers for thirty years! Do you think I want handouts from them who stole our country from us?

MOTHER: I've had to hold my hand out to you week in and week out for the same thirty years. I'm on the bru here but nobody sees it.

FATHER: What d'you want me to do about it?

MOTHER: Just listen to me.

Silence.

EAMONN: You know what I'll do for you ma? Get you a wee black slave.

MOTHER: Aye. You've already got your's.

EAMONN: Who?

A knock on the door. Silence. Another knock.

MOTHER: Get the door, Eamonn.

EAMONN: Get it yourself.

MOTHER: Sean.

SEAN answers the door. ANN enters.

ANN: Yes, Sean. What about you?

SEAN: Yes, Ann. Come on in.

SEAN returns to the window. ANN sits stage centre. She stares at the MOTHER. She looks away.

MOTHER: Did you get your dinner, Ann?

ANN: Aye. At me granny's.

The MOTHER nods. ANN stares. Long awkward silence.

MOTHER: *(To FATHER)* You know Paddy? Bogside Paddy? His Donna's her granny.

FATHER: *(Disinterested)* Is that right?

EAMONN: Did you hear the scandal? They were over at Samuel's picking a ring –

SEAN: Will you shut up.

EAMONN: They're out to get married.

MOTHER: Is that right?

ANN: He's only taking the hand at you.

EAMONN: I heard it in the bar yesterday Ann.

FATHER: Sure, you never mentioned it to us, Sean.

SEAN: He's only taking the hand, da.

MOTHER: You get engaged first, Ann –

EAMONN: Aye. Give the young fella time to bring in his thirty-five pound. You could fair live on that –

SEAN: Money's not everything.

EAMONN: Aye, but it helps. You won't get paid for running to those political meetings.

MOTHER: Give you over. You're showing us up. Look at that wee girl sitting on the edge of her seat.

ANN: Aye, I know.

FATHER: Mary. D'you mind the first time I went down on one knee?

EAMONN: Aye. Your eyes met across the smoky dance floor. Da, will ye head up for a few pints and something to eat?

FATHER: Aye.

EAMONN: You pay. I paid the last time.

FATHER: *(Beat)* Sean. Could you lend us a fiver?

> *SEAN hands his FATHER a fiver. EAMONN helps his FATHER up.*

MOTHER: And you remember about that cooker.

> *The FATHER laughs.*

MOTHER: *(Gasps)* Jesus, Mary and Saint Joseph!

> *She runs out.*

SEAN: Watch your back on the stairs da.

EAMONN: Cheerio lovers. Don't do anything I wouldn't do.

> *EAMONN and the FATHER leave.*

SEAN: Thank Christ they're away.

ANN: What happened to your ma?

SEAN: The cooker exploded in her face. Caused a wile argument. I wouldn't go near it, it's that dangerous. Me da's doing his best and she just doesn't see it. He thinks she's getting at him and they're tearing each other apart. I can see both sides. Eamonn's in the middle stirring it up. He thinks that just because he's got a good job and money in his pocket he can start on anyone. Things'll settle down now he's moving out. I'll get more room to think. *(Beat)* He's no responsibility. See that job he's doing? He doesn't have to be in early. He just comes and goes whenever he pleases. He only goes up to the Kesh to keep in with me da –

MOTHER: *(Entering)* I'm away to bingo. I'll do them dishes later. Sean. Explain to Ann about the cooker. *(To ANN)* Cheerio, love.

ANN: Cheerio.

> *The MOTHER leaves. Silence. SEAN sits.*

SEAN: Seen that girl from your class last night. What d'you call her? She was standing at the bottom of the street with a wile crowd of fellas. Shouting and screaming. Full drunk. She'll give herself a bad name going on like that. *(ANN looks away)* Will we watch TV? *(ANN shakes her head)* You're wile depressed looking. I thought I was bad till you came in. *(Pause)* I don't think I'll bother going for my apprenticeship. I'd still be on low wages after a year. I could get labouring work and bring in more –

ANN: Sean. Would you come down to the family planning with me? *(Beat)* I think I'm pregnant.

SEAN: Jesus. How d'you know?

ANN: I'm late.

SEAN: *(Beat)* Could you not go down yourself?

ANN: I'd rather you came down with me. We'd know for definite then.

SEAN: *(Beat)* Would you not know?

ANN: I've never been late before.

SEAN: *(Faltering)* Go you down and I'll...

ANN: You're just trying to work your way out of it.

SEAN: No. Jesus. I don't think you would be so I don't –

ANN: You can't work round it like that. You have to think for the worst.

SEAN: It would look bad the two of us going down together. Anyway, it's all women down there. I'd be well embarrassed. The word would go round. Me da'd be well wrecked –

ANN: Will you stick by me?

SEAN: Ann. You're only fifteen. I'm just after leaving school meself.

ANN: I'm wile confused. I don't know what to do.

SEAN: Aye. There must be some excuse for it.

ANN: Aye. *(Beat)* I'll go down myself tomorrow. *(She stands and walks to the door)* I was counting on your support.

ANN leaves. SEAN sits with his head in his hands. He stands.

SEAN: Some were selecting stones from the pile
And marking them to be shaped to fit the bond
Some were hawking in the fresh mortar
And beating the stuff that had begun to dry
Some were knelt to cut the precious stones
And then stood to clear the chippings to the skip
Craftsmen matched each cut with the pattern
And scooped their mortar to bed each moulded stone
We all worked on the line together
Racing time against effort
To build another man's wall

In anger I reached my mate a stone
Paddy, where do we fit in their pattern?
Are we the founds, the bricks, or the mortar?
Step back and point to yourself in the wall
His eyes chipped at my question
Mine shaped no answer
Facing his doubts, he bedded the stone
And entered the pattern in fear
It's our work, he murmured
As he studied the fit
We're paid to labour, we need money to live
So we sell ourselves each day to get by, Paddy
All we own is our tools; who own our minds?
Each clanging hammer stopped to listen
Who are you on about?
One of them asked
I started again
From the beginning
This time no-one turned away

Their schools design and discipline our minds
And convince us we're parasites and fools
Their newspapers sell us white lies in black ink
And call it our freedom of speech
Their priests dictate the principle of life
As we kneel in their arena to receive their guilt
Their bankers beckon offering cheap dreams on credit
Trading countries for weapons in the name of peace
We confuse work with freedom
And fantasy for life
And vote for the heir to the throne

It took so long to tell the truth
There was so much that needed to be said
Right until the last word they remained in doubt
They weren't afraid
Though they were defenceless, they resisted
But every tut and snort revealed crumbling barriers
That needed to come down

For the first time in their lives
They had stepped back
And looked at their own individuality
They'd seen their worth
And the time that had been wasted
Their faces tore with hatred
At being kept ignorant and unaware
Their hearts burned in desire for new knowledge
And they stood to clear the chippings to the skip

SEAN leaves

SCENE 3: DAWN RAID

The DEEHAN home. Monday. 6.05am. The upstage stage sculpture is turned to reveal the image of the mother and child. GERRY DEEHAN switches off the radio. He lifts a case onto the table and walks offstage. He returns with underwear and shirts and places them on a chair beside the table. He walks off again. He returns with shoes and sweaters. He thrusts the shoes and some underwear into the open case and stops to listen. He picks up a shirt and begins to fold it meticulously. He stops and stares at the shirt. He shuts his eyes and buries his face in the shirt, cursing under his breath. MARION DEEHAN enters in her dressing gown.

MARION: What's this?

GERRY: *(Suddenly packing)* I have to go.

MARION: It's six in the morning.

GERRY: *(Packing)* I'll send you a letter.

MARION: Gerry! What's going on?

GERRY: *(Packing)* I have to leave. I can't talk now –

MARION: What d'you mean you have to leave?

GERRY: Keep your voice down woman. You'll wake the wains. *(Packing the sweater)* I have to go over the border –

MARION: *(Gripping the sweater)* You can't just leave!

GERRY: *(Pulling the sweater)* Christ, woman! I've no choice!

MARION: You don't just walk out on sixteen years of marriage without a word!

GERRY: *(Wrenching the sweater)* I've a lift coming in ten minutes. Now don't be getting in me way –

MARION: Where are you going? Why are you leaving?

GERRY: *(Packing)* Look. I'll call you –

MARION: *(Lifting the case and scattering the clothes on the floor)*
            What have I done wrong!

GERRY: *(Silence. GERRY stares at the clothes. He looks at MARION)*
            I seen meself on TV last night. The SAS killings —

MARION: You weren't involved —

GERRY: You didn't see me but I seen meself. In the group round
            the car. I have to run, Marion —

MARION: You weren't involved!

GERRY: Listen to me, woman! I was in the group that pulled them
            from the car! Think what you will, but I was in that group!
            I seen meself last night! Now they've just lifted twenty-
            seven people in Belfast this morning. Dawn raids. I've just
            heard it on the radio. Marion, I'm not doing five or ten
            years for that. They want names! They want people inside!
            They've stirred up an outcry and I'm not taking any risks!
            (Beat) Now I'll call you when I'm over the border.

            GERRY begins to retrieve his clothes.

MARION: You promised me you weren't involved! What were you
            going to do? Leave a note? I told you not to go up for
            that funeral! Milltown or no Milltown! You shouldn't have
            been there! How am I going to live? Who's going to feed
            the wains? *(Stopping him)* You promised me you weren't
            involved! You were at the bottom of the Falls Road! You
            were at the back of the funeral nowhere near the car —

GERRY: I was there, Marion! I didn't think I'd be seen —

MARION: You didn't think! Not about me and the wains! Good God,
            what will I tell the neighbours? What's the priest going to
            say?

GERRY: *(Stooping for clothes)* Aye. Should I go running to the
            Bishop?

MARION: *(Crossing herself)* God forgive ye. *(Beat)* Why did you lie
            to me?

GERRY: *(Packing)* Jesus!

MARION: I trusted you. And you were just going to sneak out –

GERRY: I was going to tell you! Jesus, woman! Do you think I want to be leaving you and the wains?

MARION: You never gave me the chance to think! Did you ask me? I wake up to find my life packed away in a box and my husband on the run! My husband. The man who never set a foot wrong in his life. Never been to a funeral or a march. If I'd wanted a republican for a husband I'd have married one of your brothers! And you listen to your brothers, but you won't listen to me! 'I can't just sit by, Marion'. Why not? You sat by for twenty years and it never did us any harm! *(Pause. She walks away, stops and looks at him)* Am I to be one of those thousands of women left behind? Hoping, fearing, waiting on the raids? Oh, you'll give your support to the struggle, but you never gave a thought to your own home!

MARION turns away. Long pause. GERRY approaches her.

GERRY: *(Reaching for her)* Marion –

MARION: *(Stiff. Hissing)* Don't touch me. You disgust me.

GERRY: Marion. Listen –

MARION: You listen to me! *(Takes his hand)* You've got blood on your hands. Maybe you weren't one of them doing the battering and the killing. But you've blood on your hands. I should've known. I should've stopped you. You go up a mourner and come back a – a – a –

GERRY: A what Marion? A butcher? A murderer? That newspaper shite? I was there Marion! *(Beat)* You can sit back and look at it from the distance of your own front room and feel as shocked as I felt last night. But I was there. And that anger and revenge doesn't come from nowhere. *(Beat)* Don't you think I'm frightened? Don't you think –

Sound of a car horn.

GERRY: *(Checks his watch)* Christ, he's early. *(Thrusts the last of the clothes into the case and closes it)* Marion. Look at me. Go you down to the bru later –

MARION: What'll I say about you?

GERRY: *(Lifting the case)* Tell them me head's turned. Tell them I've run off with another woman.

MARION: And the wains. What'll I tell the wains?

Sound of a car horn. GERRY moves to the door.

GERRY: Tell them the truth. *(Beat)* I don't have the arguments. Just tell them what happened. Trust me, Marion. I'll call you. I'll call you. You'll manage.

GERRY leaves carrying the case. MARION slowly sits at the table, and resting her elbow, lifts her hand to her forehead. Shocked silence. ANN enters in her dressing gown.

MARION: Get you on back to your bed, Ann.

ANN: I'm not tired.

MARION: We can talk in the morning.

ANN: It's nearly light. *(Pause. She sits at the table)* Has me da gone?

MARION: Aye.

ANN: I heard you arguing. He won't stay away forever.

MARION: Aye.

ANN: Them bastards deserved it. It was us or them.

MARION: Ann. God forgive ye.

ANN: A wile cheer went up at Sean's house when the news came in. We went running down to the centre. Everyone was there. It was great crack. We got two of them back.

MARION: Did you see them bodies?

ANN: Aye.

MARION: Stretched out? The whole world was shocked.

ANN: Sure, we get stopped and harassed everyday. There's never a whisper.

MARION: *(Distant)* Brutal revenge. Not liberation. Us innocents get caught up in the crossfire. *(Pause)* Your da's one of them now.

ANN: Fair play to him. I didn't think he was like that –

MARION: Your da's not involved! He's just on the run! *(Pause)* What are we going to do? Five wains to feed and clothe. And he's just walked out –

ANN: It's better than him stuck in jail for the rest of his life.

MARION: The bru won't be enough.

ANN: I'll have to leave school. I can get hairdressing work.

MARION: You'll mind the wains. I'll look for work. *(Pause. Reaches for ANN's arm)* I didn't want that for you. I thought it was going to be different. I don't want you locked in a house at fifteen. I wanted you to have the chances I never had. *(Takes her hand away)* He said we were going to make a go of it. *(Pause)* You won't get your exams now. We'll just have to manage, Ann.

She lifts her hand to her head. Silence. ANN reaches for her MOTHER's arm.

ANN: Will I get the tea on?

MARION: Aye.

ANN leaves for the kitchen. MARION sits.

SINGERS: I feel pain as I see people die
Will the pain go if we win the war

If we ever run
From the British guns
The pain will always be there
If we ever run
From the British guns
The pain will always be there

MARION leaves.

SCENE 4: THE REAL WORLD

The DEEHAN home. Monday 4pm. The stage sculpture remains unchanged. ANN is by the window watching her sisters. Her friend CATHY is sat in her school uniform, drinking coke.

ANN: *(Knocking on the window)* You leave that down!

CATHY: That's not like your da.

ANN: Aye. I know. *(By the window)* You keep an eye on that wain!

CATHY: Sure he's not even a real republican.

ANN: Aye. *(Sitting)* The teachers'll think I was dobbing school. Were they asking for me?

CATHY: I said you were off sick.

ANN: I'll tell them next week.

CATHY: What about the exams?

ANN: They'll have to wait.

CATHY: I can't believe that. Your da!

ANN: Sean thought I was taking the hand.

CATHY: Did he come round to see you?

ANN: I slipped out to the training centre for an hour. He should be here now. *(Looks at her watch)* He's twenty minutes late. *(Beat)* Do you see how I'm having to lie? I told me ma I was taking a note to school about leaving.

CATHY: She must be out of her mind.

ANN: Aye. She took it wile bad. She's down for the bru now.

CATHY: *(Beat)* Are you coming down to the centre tonight?

ANN:	I'm watching the wains. Me ma's looking for bar work. *(Beat)* Get you Tara and come back later.
CATHY:	Are you alright?
ANN:	Aye. Why?

SEAN enters. He wears work clothes and boots.

SEAN:	Yes, Ann. Yes, Cathy. What about yous?
CATHY:	Yes, Sean. *(To ANN)* See you later. Cheerio.

CATHY leaves. SEAN turns the chair to straddle it.

SEAN:	*(Sitting)* I couldn't get away. We were talking till now. You should've seen their faces when I told them how it all fits together. Home. School. Work and the media. How they give you a vote once every five years so you can elect their sons into power. They were raging when I told them Duponts need a United Ireland more than us. I thought they were going to kill me. They were wile angry –
ANN:	That's twenty minutes I've been waiting for you. Me ma'll be back at five.
SEAN:	It was too important. I had them there. You know I was up the Kesh on Saturday. Our Jim's right. We have to turn our minds into weapons. Did you know he's an atheist? Surprised me too. He said you can't fight with guns alone. The gun aims at the enemy, but without ideas your aim falls short. A gun can't produce ideas. We've got to know what we're fighting for. What a socialist Ireland really means. Even our Eamonn was listening –
ANN:	I got the results.
SEAN:	*(Pause)* And?
ANN:	I'm not smiling, am I?
SEAN:	Jesus. We only did it the once.
ANN:	You told me it would be alright.

SEAN: I didn't think it would end up like this.

ANN: I had to lie about my age.

SEAN: *(Pause. Stands and goes to the window)* Sure, this changes everything. We'll manage though.

ANN: What if you disappear in a year's time?

SEAN: Is that what you think of me?

ANN: You wouldn't even come down to the clinic.

SEAN: You don't want people talking.

ANN: They'll be talking soon enough. Four months time.

SEAN: We'll need a place of our own.

ANN: Me ma's not going to stand us living together.

SEAN: I'd need more money –

ANN: What's people going to say?

SEAN: We'll have to save –

ANN: For how long? Four years?

SEAN: I could get bar work at night –

ANN: Aye and I'll never see you.

SEAN: Labouring would bring in more money –

ANN: Wise up! There's thousands of people looking for labouring work in Derry –

SEAN: Sure we could go to England –

ANN: I'm needed here to watch the wains.

SEAN: I'll go over. I heard it's sixty pounds a day –

ANN: What am I supposed to do while you're in England?

SEAN: I can send over the money!

ANN: It's not just the money I need! It's support! You can't talk to a wage packet. You'll be alright over there. It's people over here that's going to be talking. What's me ma going to say? I can't tell her now with me da away. *(Pause)* I can't bring another wain into the house. I've already four to look after.

SEAN: Look. That won't last forever. Your da'll be back –

ANN: And what's going to change then? Fifteen and a wain trailing round my ankles for the next twenty years. No money to feed and clothe it. I'd crack up. There's got to be some other way.

            SEAN stares and sits. He rests his head on his folded arms. Silence. He stands and goes to the window.

SEAN: Maybe I could speak to our Eamonn –

ANN: Aye. Then it'll be all round Derry.

SEAN: Me da'll be wrecked simple. We'll have to get married –

ANN: To stop people talking?

SEAN: Sure we could make a go of it.

ANN: That's just brilliant.

            ANN goes to the window to check her sisters. SEAN leans on the chair.

ANN: *(Standing)* I've got to get the tea on.

SEAN: I'll call back later.

ANN: Sean. Go you down to your uncle's.

SEAN: I can't tell him –

ANN: He could get you a job at Duponts –

SEAN: Duponts? Get lost!

ANN: Sean! We need the money!

SEAN: Aye. Because of them Anglo-Irish conmen! American
              gangsters with Irish accents!

ANN: We need the money to pay for this!

SEAN: I'm not working for Duponts!

ANN: You want to free Ireland? It's future is right here inside me
              now. What can I do trapped in here? Wait till you find
              clean money? What's so clean about labouring? Are
              brickies free? Look at what you wrote. You're still building
              another man's wall.

              Silence. SEAN sits.

ANN: We can only lie so long. Me ma'll know when I'm sick.
              And you wouldn't have to go to England. We could stay
              together. *(Pause)* All your talk about struggle and
              responsibility. You wouldn't even come to the clinic.
              Where do I fit into the pattern?

SEAN: *(Pause)* I'm well confused.

ANN: Aye. That needs changing too.

              Silence.

SEAN: *(Stands)* I'll ask tomorrow. I'll see what I can do.

              Silence.

SEAN: Will you be at the centre later?

ANN: I'm watching the wains.

SEAN: Aye.

              A knock on the door.

ANN: The door's open.

            CATHY and TARA enter. CATHY has changed.

CATHY: Yes, Ann. Yes, Sean. What about yous?

TARA: Yes.

ANN: Yes. Come in.

SEAN: I'd better head on.

            SEAN leaves. CATHY turns the chair and sits. ANN sits.

TARA: *(Taking off her coat)* Sorry to hear about your father.

ANN: Don't be saying it to anyone. It's between ourselves.

TARA: *(Nods. Lays her coat on the table)* How's your mother
            getting on?

ANN: She's taking it wile bad.

TARA: Have you left school?

ANN: I don't know yet.

            *ANN breaks down. CATHY and TARA look at her and one
            another. TARA comforts her and CATHY kneels at her feet.
            ANN slowly pulls herself together.*

ANN: I'm alright. *(Pause)* Sit yous down. There's something I
            have to tell yous.

            CATHY and TARA sit, either side of ANN.

ANN: I was down the family planning today. *(Pause)* I'm pregnant.

CATHY: Run on, Ann.

ANN: I'm serious.

TARA: Jesus.

CATHY: What are you going to do?

ANN: I'll just have to accept it now.

TARA: Is that why Sean was round? *(ANN nods)* Is he going to stick by you?

ANN: We've not really talked it out properly.

TARA: He's the type who will –

ANN cries. TARA offers her a kleenex. CATHY goes to the upstage window.

ANN: *(Takes the kleenex. Silence)* I'm alright. *(Pause)* This is the worst problem ever. You've wee problems and you really worry about them. When it comes to the big ones you don't know how to work them out.

TARA: Does your mother know?

ANN: I don't want to tell her till everything's sorted out with me da.

TARA: How are you going to cope?

CATHY: Are you going to have the wain?

TARA: Of course she is.

CATHY: *(Pause)* Have you thought about abortion?

ANN: I wouldn't want to think about it.

CATHY: Why not?

ANN: There's no need for abortion. It was my own fault. It's not as if I was raped –

CATHY: A wain trailing round your ankles at fifteen?

TARA: She can't kill the child! There's no excuses for abortion. Not even rape. Just hearing the word makes me feel sick.

CATHY: Aye. Make her feel guilty.

ANN: I'm not feeling guilty.

CATHY: Think about the rest of your life.

ANN: It would be only thinking about meself.

CATHY: Aye. Think about yourself. You're choosing for the rest of your life. Have this wain now and that's you tied down. You'll end up like all the rest of the girls in Derry –

TARA: Women are supposed to bear wains and rear them! It's a sin! It's taking life!

CATHY: There's nothing there!

TARA: It's alive now!

CATHY: If Ann was to die now or in six months time it wouldn't live –

TARA: *(Standing)* I don't want to hear this!

CATHY: It's Ann's life –

TARA: It's a child's life too!

ANN: That'll go on to become a human being.

CATHY: Aye. Is that what you want now?

TARA: She could have it adopted.

CATHY: And see it growing up? Knowing it's living only four streets away?

TARA: It could move. Or Ann could –

ANN: Cathy. It's murder.

            Silence. CATHY walks over to the table.

CATHY: Do you think armed struggle's murder?

ANN: No.

CATHY: Well what's armed struggle?

ANN: There's a reason for armed struggle.

CATHY: And what are they fighting for?

ANN: Freedom.

CATHY: What about our freedom?

ANN: *(Pause)* There's a reason for armed struggle. It wasn't our fault the British came into Ireland. We didn't mean it to happen –

CATHY: You didn't mean to get pregnant –

ANN: But I could've stopped it. Armed struggle is to stop British tormenting our lives –

CATHY: So's abortion. So long as nothing changes we need both.

ANN: But I have the choice. Armed struggle's when you have no choice –

TARA: They're both wrong. It's murder –

CATHY: Ann. While you think it's murder you don't have a choice. Who says it's murder?

TARA: The bible! The government!

CATHY: Aye! Not us!

TARA: She's a child growing inside her!

CATHY: Tara. It's just two cells!

TARA: We all came from two cells, Cathy!

CATHY: Aye and those two cells will keep Ann locked away in her house for the rest of her life! My brother's away in prison for the rest of his life! The same people who locked him away will lock her inside and say both are right! *(Beat)* It is two cells! But we fight against one and walk into the other!

ANN: Your brother's better off. At least he gets his food and lodging for free. The whole society's wrong.

CATHY: But it's loaded onto the backs of them with nothing. And who says it's wrong? London, Dublin and the Church. The snobs with two wains and pockets stuffed with money. They've got us raising their wains while they dream up new laws to keep us inside! Behind bars! But do we see it? No. We think we're on the outside and we do as we're told until one of our men gets caged. *(Beat)* We might as well be living in the dark ages.

ANN: It's still illegal.

CATHY: It was legal in Ireland before the church colonised our minds.

Silence. CATHY stares out the window.

ANN: Jesus! The wains!

CATHY: *(Looking)* They're just playing.

TARA: *(Pause)* Where would she get the money for an abortion anyway?

CATHY: Where's she going to get money to feed wains for the rest of her life?

TARA: Sean.

CATHY: So she's going to be tied to Sean like she's tied to the wain?

ANN: I don't – I have to – I don't want to be thinking about having an abortion –

TARA: You have to think for that wain. You'd be taking the right to live away from an unborn child. It can't speak for itself –

CATHY: Tara. Ann has the right to be free. Now. Only when it all changes will having a wain mean freedom. For the mother and the child. I've heard you before, Ann. 'I'm not ending up like my mother. I'm going to get out of Derry. I want a decent job.' Think what's going to happen if you have that wain –

ANN: You can't have what you want all the time.

CATHY: Why not? Who says?

ANN: Meself.

CATHY: And where do you get your thoughts from?

ANN: Me mind.

TARA: What does Sean want? It's his wain too –

ANN: It's nothing to do with him –

CATHY: It's half his responsibility –

ANN: I don't want to marry him.

CATHY: Then what do you want, Ann? Live with your ma and have the wain on your own?

ANN: That's all I can see for meself anyway. It wouldn't make any difference what age I got pregnant.

Long silence.

TARA: Look, Ann. Go to the priest. You'll get good advice.

ANN: Get lost. They bury our dead and ask us to hand over the names of the living. I wanted to walk out of that sermon.

TARA: Maybe there's a priest who would understand.

CATHY: Aye. Seven years in a seminary and think they know it all. He's never going to be pregnant. They talk about freedom! They get our ma's to make the sign of the cross with our hands before we can move them ourselves.

ANN: He'd love to be hearing this in confession. Tell me this.
              How come we know to keep the police ignorant yet go
              running to the priests with our thoughts? They both use
              what we tell them against us.

              MARION enters angry.

MARION: Ann! Outside!

ANN: What's wrong?

MARION: Why's the wain got dirt in its mouth? You told me you'd
              watch them till I got back! Outside!

              *ANN and MARION leave. TARA goes to the window.
              CATHY sits thinking.*

MARION :   From the health centre porch she looks to the north
& CATHY   Where Nicaragua's enemies lie
              Polio crippled and maimed before things were changed
              Slowly they're turning the tide
              In the twilight she stands with a rifle in hand
              And the memory of what used to be
              Now she's part of the unfinished revolution

              Feudal landlords they've known, seen overthrown
              Afghanistan comes into view
              Learning to read and write is part of the fight
              But for her it's something that's new
              Down all the years, afraid of her tears
              Imprisoned behind a black veil
              Now she's part of the unfinished revolution

              Soldiers kicked down the door, called her a whore
              While he lingered in Castlereagh
              Internment tore them apart, brought her to the heart
              Of resistance in Derry today
              Her troubles are long, it's hard to be strong
              She's determined deep down inside
              To be part of the unfinished revolution
              She holds the key to the unfinished revolution

              'Unfinished Revolution' by Christy Moore.

SCENE 5: LAW AND ORDER

The home of CAROL and MARTIN DOHERTY. The Waterside. Tuesday night. MARTIN sits with an open newspaper on his lap. CAROL sits staring at JOE. The stage sculpture shows its third face of the petrol bomber.

MARTIN: Who put this idea into your head?

JOE: I've thought it all out –

MARTIN: You never had a single thought in your whole life. *(To CAROL)* Did you know about this?

CAROL: First I've heard of it.

MARTIN: Who've you been speaking to?

JOE: Is this an argument?

MARTIN: Who've you been speaking to, son?

JOE: *(Pause)* Two months ago the police were down in Saint Columbs –

MARTIN: They what?

JOE: Recruiting, da –

MARTIN: Who let them into the college?

JOE: The priests.

CAROL: Times have changed, Martin –

MARTIN: I'll handle this. *(To JOE)* I'll be down. I'll see about this.

JOE: Da. The police've changed since your day. They're not attacking Catholic homes anymore –

MARTIN: Read the papers, son. Open your eyes. They're battering young fellas on the streets everyday –

JOE: You were saying it's thugs that's rioting now –

MARTIN: Aye. There's that element. People drinking and throwing stones when they're full. Twenty years ago it was different. But the police haven't changed. They're still pinning us against walls. Still harassing and humiliating our people and firing plastic bullets at them!

CAROL: Things will only change when the RUC disbands –

JOE: But we'll still need a police force.

MARTIN: Aye. An impartial police force.

JOE: How's that all going to happen if Catholics don't get in there and change it from the inside? They're not just going to lay down their arms –

MARTIN: Don't give me cheek, son. I'm trying to understand you.

CAROL: (Pause) Joining the RUC isn't the solution, Joe –

JOE: Ma. What're you saying all the time? When's the killing going to end? Will nothing change? This is a way forward –

MARTIN: For you!

JOE: I could leave. Run away to a job in England. How's that going to change things here? I want to do something for my community –

MARTIN: Join the RUC and you won't have a community!

CAROL: Where are you going to live, Joe?

MARTIN: You won't be able to live here.

JOE: Belfast. Anywhere. There's plenty of places –

MARTIN: And what about us and this house? Did you stop to consider that when the police were offering you sweets in the college? While you're away discoing up in Antrim, we're liable to get our windows put in! We moved to the Waterside to get away from all that! We'll go up the town. They'll all be talking about us behind our backs. 'There's that crowd. Their son's in the RUC.' We've lived here ten years, Joe! Ten years! Built up all we have from nothing! You sign that form and you're putting your name to twenty years of persecution! This house! Where you've lived all your life!

CAROL: Martin! *(MARTIN sits)* What about your friends, Joe?

JOE: I know I'll be rejected at first –

MARTIN: Rejected? You'll be torn to shreds!

JOE: I'll make friends up there –

MARTIN: With the people you work with? They'll treat you like dirt. At the end of the day they're all bigots –

JOE: Well, someone's got to make a stand!

CAROL: Not like this –

JOE: We've got to cut through the fear and hatred –

MARTIN: You'll be in a jeep all day being ordered about. Once they get that uniform on you, you'll have to prove yourself because you're a Catholic. You'll have to be worse than the rest of them. And they'll have no respect for you. They'll think you're dirt –

JOE: I know I'm not dirt!

MARTIN: *(Stands)* But you'll be dirt! You'll end up dirt!

CAROL: Martin!

MARTIN: And you'll die dirt! *(Pause)* When they bring you back in a box, I'll not bury you!

MARTIN walks out. Long silence.

CAROL: Joe. We're your family. This is your home town –

JOE: Aye. *(Stands. Goes to the window)* Bombs every week. It's murder –

MARTIN: *(Off)* Only when it's our crowd.

CAROL: What about all the children killed by plastic bullets?

MARTIN: *(Off)* That's law and order, Carol.

JOE: They were defending themselves –

MARTIN: *(Entering with a drink)* Against children?

CAROL: You'll be looking over your shoulder for the rest of your life Joe. That's no way to live –

A knock on the door. JOE answers it.

SEAN: Yes, Joe.

JOE: Yes, Sean.

CAROL: Yes, Sean.

SEAN: *(Sitting)* Yes. What about yous? What's the crack?

MARTIN: *(Sitting)* Your cousin's only thinking about joining the RUC.

SEAN: Give us an application form.

CAROL: He's serious –

JOE: *(To SEAN)* You keep out of this. I've never interfered in your life –

SEAN: You'd be doing nothing else wearing a uniform.

MARTIN: You speak to him. He won't listen to us.

SEAN: *(Amazed)* What do you want to join the RUC for?

JOE: People can't go round hating for the rest of their lives.

SEAN: Your mind's corrupted –

JOE: It's a way forward that's not taking life. Something people like you can't understand.

SEAN: It's a way out –

JOE: Aye. That as well. I asked me da to get me work at
           Dupont ages ago. What did he do for me?

CAROL: Your father did all he could –

MARTIN: It's not my fault you've no qualifications. If you'd worked
           harder at school you could've gone to university like your
           brothers. You'd have got a job anywhere –

CAROL: Now, Martin. You know there's no work about.

MARTIN: Aye. Fair enough. But he could go down South. *(To JOE)*
           Join the guards if it's the uniform you want –

JOE: The guards have their own country –

SEAN: Their own country? Law and order's the same
           everywhere. Only here you can see it for what it is.

JOE: *(Pause)* I know it's going to be hard –

MARTIN: You'll be sitting behind six inches of armour!

CAROL: You can't change things on your own –

JOE: Ma! There's ten per cent Catholics in the RUC and the
           numbers are rising!

MARTIN: Aye. From Coleraine and East Belfast.

SEAN: When your ma and da come down the street you'll be
           standing at the white tape saying: 'Sorry love, you can't
           go down there.' Is that what you want? Tell me this.
           How're your mates going to feel about you joining?

JOE: That depends.

SEAN: They'll put a bullet in your head!

MARTIN: Who put this idea in his head?

SEAN: You're fighting the wrong war, Joe! You'll be on the wrong
          side! You might as well be a supergrass for the life you'll
          be living!

JOE: Change means taking risks!

SEAN: The IRA's doing that!

JOE: Aye! Join the Provos and kill your own people!

SEAN: Those were mistakes!

JOE: So were the plastic bullets!

SEAN: Shite! You know how the RUC'll make you feel? *(Holds up
          his forefinger and thumb)* This small –

JOE: I'm big enough to handle that –

MARTIN: Well we can't handle our end of it. She'll end up in
          Gransha. *(Beat)* So there's your problem. You'll not come
          into this house again if you join the police –

          A knock at the door.

CAROL: That'll be Father Morris. About the flowers for the altar.

          *Silence. JOE looks about. He answers the door. FATHER
          MORRIS enters.*

PRIEST: Yes, Joseph.

JOE: *(They shake hands).* How you doing, Father?

          *The PRIEST shakes hands with MARTIN who has stood up.
          He shakes hands with CAROL. He then turns to SEAN
          who stands and turns away. MARTIN taps the PRIEST on
          his shoulder.*

MARTIN: Have a seat, Father.

          *The PRIEST takes MARTIN's seat. MARTIN sits beside
          CAROL. JOE sits. SEAN remains standing. Awkward
          silence. MARTIN discreetly nudges CAROL several times.*

Silence. He crosses his legs and clears his throat. Silence. He nudges CAROL a final time and picks his nose. JOE watches.

JOE: You're just in time for the big debate Father.

PRIEST: Good.

MARTIN: He's here to see your mother about the flowers –

JOE: Father Morris should be in on this –

MARTIN: Serious business, flowers –

SEAN: Let him hear, Uncle Martin –

MARTIN: *(To the PRIEST)* You're a busy man. *(To CAROL)* The flowers –

PRIEST: Can wait. There should be no secrets before God, Mr Doherty. Trust me with your problems.

CAROL: *(Beat)* He's part of the community, Martin. *(Beat)* He might as well know –

MARTIN: Aye. *(Pause)* It's wile sensitive Father. *(To CAROL)* Maybe he can advise him.

Silence.

PRIEST: Are you in trouble with the police, Joe?

CAROL: He wants to join them, Father.

SEAN: Don't you be looking so surprised!

JOE: Your speech was very strong on Sunday, Father.

MARTIN: Sunday? What speech?

JOE: If you'd been to mass, da, you would've heard it –

MARTIN: I was well to the back. It was well hard to hear. I missed the gist of it –

JOE: Don't be lying to the priest, da –

PRIEST: I haven't seen you at mass lately, Mr Doherty.

MARTIN: I've a wile ulcer, Father –

JOE: He heads into the pub –

SEAN: I was there, Father. I walked out along with the rest of them that had any sense. But I was down Sunday because I knew what was going to be read out! Tell him what you read out!

PRIEST: Let's keep calm, Sean –

SEAN: Aye! We'll talk quietly while you bless the RUC! Tell him what you spewed from the pulpit!

MARTIN: Sean! Have some respect for the cloth!

SEAN: You want to know why Joe's joining the RUC, Uncle Martin? Ask the man in cloth hiding behind his collar!

PRIEST: The Bishop's letter didn't actually ask people to join –

MARTIN: (Connecting) Aye. It said if you had information –

PRIEST: (Nodding) You should hand it in.

MARTIN: I don't agree with it, mind. No disrespect, Father.

PRIEST: My hands were tied.

SEAN: It was more than your job's worth!

PRIEST: What the Bishop actually said in his letter is that there should be more co-operation with the RUC. That more Catholics should consider joining in the interests of law and order –

MARTIN: Only out of respect for the church I would've walked out meself, Father –

CAROL: Let the priest speak, Martin.

PRIEST: It is my duty to point the way to understanding. *(Pause)* Sean has the same intentions as yourself, Joe. He wants the situation to change. It's inspiring to see our young people questioning their elders and searching for an end to the conflict. What unites us is our belief in change and our total condemnation of violence and dogma –

SEAN: Hypocrite!

PRIEST: *(Standing)* That's why I joined the priesthood, Sean! To change the world and to end bloodshed and corruption! What do you want? Where will you find the answers? How will you achieve it? *(Pointing to his bible)* I hold in my hand the greatest lawbook that ever existed. Maybe you've turned away from God and the church now. But you'll find every answer to every problem you'll face in life in this book here –

SEAN: Uncle Martin! He put the idea into Joe's head! Why are you listening to him?

PRIEST: Sean! Will you pull down everything in your search for justice?

SEAN: They own our minds! Joe!

JOE: Will you give the priest a chance to speak!

PRIEST: The church is impartial because peace cannot be one-sided. You could find hardship joining the RUC, Joe. Your mother and father might suffer the hatred and fear of our community. You want to change all that. That's good. But just because you have god in your heart does not mean you have a licence to hold a gun in your hand –

SEAN: He's the conscience of the RUC!

CAROL: Sean!

PRIEST: All killing is wrong! All killing is murder! Life is god's most precious gift to man! We must be patient in our suffering and strive for peace –

SEAN: That's the silencer on their gun! Can't you see it? Are we all braincuffed? I'm away! I can't be in the same room as him!

          SEAN strides out of the room, past the PRIEST.

SINGERS: White and frightened soldier
          Hangman of the landlord judge
          Must they poke out the sun
          Print bars on your suburban sky
          Before you learn why you hate?

          Black and frightened soldier
          Pressed against the township sky
          See my weals on your back
          You've held me spattered in blood
          How can you live with such pain?

          Brothers! Hear our final cry!
          Who owns the rivers, the land and sky?
          Our freedom has been bought and sold
          Rise up against apartheid gold!

SCENE 6: NO CHOICE

The DEEHAN home. Wednesday night. ANN is offstage in the kitchen. SEAN sits at the table reading a newspaper. An ironing board is set up with a pile of clothes lying beside it on a chair. The stage sculpture shows the image of the mother and child.

SEAN: Is your ma away to mass?

ANN: *(Off)* Aye.

SEAN: The foreman asked us to work late tomorrow. Finish the job. I said no problem. He knows other firms. He might be able to put in a good word for me. Save me doing the apprenticeship.

            ANN enters with a plate of sandwiches. She puts them down on the table in front of SEAN and returns to ironing.

SEAN: That's dead on, Ann. *(Looks at his watch)* Just time to get these down me neck –

ANN: You've half an hour yet till that meeting. *(SEAN eats. She picks up a shirt)* Were you up at your uncle's?

SEAN: *(Eating)* Last night. Joe's thinking of joining the RUC. I'm serious. There was a wile argument. Then the priest came in and I lost the head. I didn't want to crack up like that. But I had to. You should've heard him.

ANN: *(Ironing)* Did you ask about the job?

SEAN: *(Eating)* I couldn't. There's no chance anyway. Martin couldn't get our Joe one. Is there any salt?

            ANN puts the iron down and leaves. SEAN looks at the paper. ANN returns with the salt. SEAN puts down the paper and takes the salt.

SEAN: *(Salting the sandwiches)* I'll give it another two weeks in Derry. Then I'll try England. *(Eats)* I won't waste any more time. It'll be hard but we'll work it out.

ANN: *(Ironing)* We might not need a way to support it. Not if I had an abortion −

SEAN: *(Eating)* Abortion's no answer but.

ANN: *(Ironing)* It's an option −

SEAN: *(Eating)* I don't think so. Not everything you see on TV's true −

ANN: What's that got to do with it?

SEAN: It's them who put ideas like that into your head.

ANN: *(Ironing)* I don't want to have an abortion. It's the only way I can see −

SEAN: *(Eating)* It's not just your wain. It's mine too. *(Pause)* Anyway you can't just decide to have an abortion. It goes further than that. It's a life −

ANN: It's a few cells −

SEAN: *(Stops eating)* It's a life. It's the same life doctors spend hundreds of pounds and hours of sweat trying to save whenever a pregnant woman has problems −

ANN: *(Ironing)* I'm too young to get tied down. I'm not ready −

SEAN: You can't ignore the fact that it was a mistake −

ANN: *(Stops ironing)* And I don't want to make another mistake by having it.

SEAN: How's that a mistake?

ANN: It's tying me down for the rest of me life.

SEAN: You think I'll be able to run free?

ANN: It's not going to be as hard for you. It's me who has to carry it for nine months. Feed it and mind it while you're at work or down the pub. *(Holding the iron up)* Look at me now!

SEAN: D'you think I want labouring for the rest of my life?

ANN: I'm not saying either's right.

SEAN: It's not the family we could have that's tying you down. It's the family you're in –

ANN: Aye. I've been tied down all my life. I don't want to be tied down again if there's an option –

SEAN: You're not giving me much option! You're just branding me as another man who's going to leave you with the wain. Don't you trust me?

ANN: What support have you shown me so far?

SEAN: I'll stay with you, Ann! I'll look after the wain because it will be my son. Or daughter. It's the only thing I'll have in this world and you want to take it away from me! Why, Ann? Why?

ANN: So that I can be free!

SEAN: You'll not be free with that on your conscience.

ANN: Now tie me down with guilt –

SEAN: Don't you think I'll not feel guilty?

ANN: You'll always be able to say you tried to stop me. It'll be me who has to live with it.

SEAN: Look, Ann. Sit down. You're not thinking straight. You're confused –

ANN: Ha!

SEAN: Sit down! *(No response)* Jesus! You're so selfish and narrow-minded!

ANN: It's my body!

SEAN: You're not even looking for other possibilities! I'm trying to bring a life into this world!

ANN: You're not being tied down!

SEAN: There you go again! I'm not going to run off Ann! It'll be
            my wain too. A wain I want to watch grow up –

ANN: Have other wains. When you're older –

SEAN: Aye. Have a family of three or four and be haunted by the
            one that we murdered. That you murdered! Don't forget this
            is your decision! Your decision! Now get it out of your head!

ANN: I want it out of my body! You can't understand what it's
            like to be imprisoned by your own body! You can't begin
            to understand!

SEAN: I don't want to understand murder!

ANN: You've no problem with armed struggle –

SEAN: There's no foetus pointing a gun at my head!

ANN: But there's a whole society pointing a gun at mine!

            Silence. SEAN looks at his watch.

ANN: You just can't see it, can you?

SEAN: Are you going to stop going to mass?

ANN: What's that got to do with it?

SEAN: Hypocrisy on your side –

ANN: You're the one who's always against mass. Against the
            church.

SEAN: You're the one hugging the rails each week. 'Life is so
            precious' –

ANN: Maybe now I'm wakening up.

SEAN: To what? Torment?

ANN: That's what it'd be for me if I had this wain –

SEAN: Make up your mind, Ann! One minute it's a few cells! The
          next minute it's a wain! When you remember what you've
          been told to say it's a few cells. But when you're in an
          argument – when you don't have time to think calmly –
          you say it's a wain. Because that's what you believe! And
          because that's what it is!

ANN: Sean. You can't stop me –

SEAN: *(Standing violently)* I'll kill you before you abort that child!

ANN: And you're the one who's got me thinking this way! Stand
          up against the church! Stand up against oppression! Don't
          let people walk over you! Don't let anyone tie you down!
          You have the right to say no and the right to question –

SEAN: That's right –

ANN: And make your own decisions!

SEAN: That's right! That's exactly right! What about the thing
          inside you? It'll never breathe to have the choice!

ANN: What life's it going to have anyway?

SEAN: The same life you have. *(Slowing down)* The same boring
          everyday life I have. The same life you're planning a future
          on. The same shite life we all live. The same life I hate and
          am fighting to change –

ANN: At meetings I'll never speak at.

SEAN: *(Looks at his watch)* You could come –

ANN: Not while I'm chained to a cooker!

SEAN: I have to leave –

ANN: What do you mean you have to leave?

SEAN: The meeting. I have to go –

ANN: You can't just go –

SEAN: We'll talk later –

ANN: You mind the wains. I'll go to the meeting.

SEAN: *(Stares at her from the door)* This is madness.

             SEAN leaves. ANN looks at the door. She slowly walks round to the table and sits. She brings her hand to her forehead, resting her elbow on the table.

SINGERS: Many have given their love and their lives
             But their lives were not given in vain
             Their sacrifice has brought us nearer to victory
             Their sacrifice has brought us nearer to victory

SCENE 7: THE COOKER

The DOHERTY home. Late Thursday night. MARY DOHERTY looks old and tired. SEAN stands beside the window. The stage sculpture shows the image of the imprisoned labourer.

SEAN: She can't tell her. Her da's still away.

MOTHER: How long has she known?

SEAN: A few days. A week. It's all gone so fast.

MOTHER: *(Pause)* Tests can be wrong –

SEAN: *(Direct)* It's definite.

MOTHER: *(Pause)* And the wee girl was only here last Sunday.

            Silence.

SEAN: I couldn't keep it inside any longer.

MOTHER: Does your father know?

SEAN: You're the first I've told.

MOTHER: You let me tell him. *(Beat)* You'll have to get engaged this week, Sean. What day is this?

SEAN: Ma. That's not the half of it –

            The door flies open. JIM DOHERTY enters elated and slightly tipsy.

FATHER: Yes! What about yous? What's the crack?

SEAN: Yes, da.

FATHER: *(Crouching beside MARY. To SEAN)* Life has smiled on your old da today. Twenty-five pounds on the races. *(Triumphantly holding up the money)* Twenty-five pounds Mary!

SEAN: Not now da –

FATHER: (Sitting) Sit down, Sean. This isn't a bar –

MOTHER: Jim –

FATHER: (To SEAN) Remember that fiver you lent me?

SEAN: Keep it. You're alright –

FATHER: (Holding out two notes) There. And five quid more.
            (SEAN doesn't move) Don't be so proud, Sean. Take it!
            (Beat) What's going on? (Looks at MARY. Winks at SEAN)
            Your mother's jealous. (Beat) And a tenner towards the
            new cooker! (Throws all the money into the middle of the
            floor).

SEAN: Da. Will you listen to me?

FATHER: (Pointing) Take the money, Sean –

SEAN: Will you shut up and listen!

FATHER: What's the problem? Has somebody died?

MOTHER: Jim. We've got to talk –

FATHER: Are you in trouble, son?

SEAN: (Looks at his mother) Aye.

MOTHER: (Pause) Wee Ann's pregnant.

            Silence.

FATHER: Is it yours?

SEAN: Aye.

MOTHER: Her mother doesn't know yet.

            Silence. FATHER stands. Walks. Silence.

FATHER: A grandchild Mary! Our first grandchild!

SEAN: She doesn't want the wain –

FATHER: Two jackpots in the one night!

MOTHER: *(As the FATHER takes off his coat)* What do you mean she doesn't want the wain?

SEAN: We'll talk tomorrow. He's full –

FATHER: Aye! But not full enough! My wee son's going to be a father! Our son Mary! *(Beat)* What d'you mean she doesn't want the wain?

SEAN: Leave it, da –

FATHER: Wait. What d'you mean she doesn't want the wain?

SEAN: She's only fifteen –

FATHER: Aye. That's not uncommon –

SEAN: *(Direct)* She wants an abortion.

MOTHER: I forbid you to mention that word!

SEAN: She wants a termination.

FATHER: A termination?

MOTHER: God forgive ye –

SEAN: I spoke to her last night –

FATHER: *(Sits)* An abortion? An abortion? The family's ruined. *(Beat)* Why couldn't you wait? You had to go and prove yourself. You had to have your way!

MOTHER: *(Sickened)* An abortion? At fifteen? I'll go round. That wee girl's confused –

FATHER: *(To MOTHER)* Why did you let him stop going to mass?

MOTHER: Aye. Now blame me!

FATHER: You reared him, woman!

SEAN: Don't shout at her, da!

MOTHER: Maybe if you hadn't been down the bar so often –

FATHER: *(Standing)* What d'you mean, 'don't shout'? In one night you've devastated everything! You've terminated our lives! Don't you know the facts of life?

SEAN: You never taught me them –

FATHER: I'm not paid to teach you them! Don't shout! We taught you right from wrong! And this is wrong! *(Beat)* How many months?

SEAN: That's not the point –

FATHER: How many months!

SEAN: You come in full from the pub roaring –

FATHER: *(To MARY)* What have we done wrong?

MOTHER: Jim. We could ask the priest –

FATHER: The priest knows nothing about it! And he's not going to know! Do you want this all round Creggan?

SEAN: Stop shouting, da –

FATHER: Don't you tell your father what to do in his own house. Now you listen to me, son. You go over and you put your foot down. You tell her what's right –

SEAN starts to leave.

FATHER: Where're you going?

SEAN: I came for support –

FATHER: You'll sit down and listen! Seventeen and you think you know it all! We feed and clothe you! Remember that and show some respect!

SEAN sits. Silence as the FATHER walks and thinks.

FATHER:	I don't know where she got them ideas. But abortion's wrong. Any man knows that –
SEAN:	She says it's her own body –
FATHER:	She what?
MOTHER:	She's in shock. Her father's away –
SEAN:	She's fine. I spoke to her –
MOTHER:	Then she needs the priest, Jim –
FATHER:	Will you let him speak!
SEAN:	Don't talk to her like that –
FATHER:	She's my wife, son. When you've your own home you do what you want. I'll talk to your mother the way I see fit. *(Beat)* What did she say?
SEAN:	*(Standing)* This is my mistake. I'll deal with it –
FATHER:	Aye and ruin our lives!
SEAN:	What about Ann's life? What about mine?
FATHER:	*(Stopping him)* Listen, Sean! For God's sake listen to me! I'm not an educated man! I don't claim to know it all! But the facts of life are clear. You work. You raise children. And you die. The little pleasure you can wring out of life is a bonus. I don't like it any more than you do. But it's the truth. *(The MOTHER walks to the window)* What have you got that's your own? Your life. Your children and your own people. You can't destroy life Sean. You can't break up your home and our lives. It's the only beauty we have. *(Pause)* Who stands by you when you're strapped in school? Who stands by the prisoners when the whole world's pointing the finger? Who stands by you when you're kicked onto the bru?
SEAN:	I know all that, da!
FATHER:	Then leave abortion to the people over there! To them who believe in violence and termination! The termination

of our freedom and our sons! I know life is hard. But it's so easy to murder. You tell Ann that your brothers are inside because they believe that every life is precious! *(Pause)* Look at that money on the floor. I know it's no answer. But at the moment it's all that we have. That and our lives. And we give you both because life must go on. How else will we free this land?

SEAN: *(Moving away)* Don't you think I know all that?

The FATHER slumps into a chair and looks at MARY.

MOTHER: Tell Ann to have the wain Sean. No-one's asking you to marry her. You'll make up your own minds when yous is good and ready. Have the wain. You can choose later –

SEAN: Ma. Look at yourself. What choice did you have? You slaved in that kitchen from the first day you could carry a plate. Look at you, da. Even when you worked you earned just enough to keep yourself. But you had to feed her and us and make those few notes stretch the week. What for? To roar and argue all our lives? To be chained and crippled for life? Ann wants an abortion because she believes in life. The same as our Jim and Patsy up in the Kesh. Because it's this life that has to be changed! *(Pause)* Last night I had doubts. I lost the head with Ann. But now I'm beginning to see it. Abortion's as hard as armed struggle. But you know who calls it murder? Those who drain our life's blood slowly and deliberately over sixty years! Those who pay others to lie! And we don't see it. We don't talk about it. We keep it inside behind locked doors and sealed lips. It's the same everywhere! But we all pretend the world stops at the front door. It's not just when we're raided that the world breaks in! They're inside our heads! And until we change that they'll own us for life!

EAMONN enters. He wears a suit and red shoes.

EAMONN: Who dropped the fivers?

MOTHER: Jim. We need Father Morris –

EAMONN: He's down the street. Talking to the wains.

SEAN runs into the kitchen.

EAMONN: What's the wee boy doing?

The MOTHER looks at the FATHER. The FATHER stands. SEAN enters dragging the cooker across the stage. He struggles, grunting, trying to lift it onto his shoulder.

FATHER: Sean! Sean!

MOTHER: Sean!

SEAN lifts the cooker with a roar of pain and staggers out of the house. A crash can be heard.

SCENE 8: THE VERDICT

ANN comes forward to the audience, once the stage sculpture has been brought forward, with the image of the mother and the child facing out.

ANN: Oiche areir, nuair a chuaigh an sceal thart, o theach go teach, faoi bhas an sagairt, tháinig saol an bhaile go stad tobann. Chuir se fearthainne an oíche ar fad. Ar maidin inniu bhi cocairi le feiceail taobh anuigh d'arasain Shráid Rosbile. Tá an RUC ag iarraidh ainmeacha.

              Last night, as the news passed from home to home of the death of the priest, the town came to a standstill. It rained all night. This morning cookers could be seen outside the flats on Rossville Street. The RUC want names.

              The full company begin to assemble with the beginning of the final lyric. The lyric is repeated three times, growing stronger and more triumphant each time.

              Many have given their love and their lives
              But their lives were not given in vain
              Their sacrifice has brought us nearer to victory
              Their sacrifice has brought us nearer to victory

              The company thank and applaud the audience...

Manifesto
for freedom and democracy in Ireland

When children are more valued than bombs
and they read the books that we write
When women are more valued than work
and our homes are no longer prisons
When justice no longer huddles in cells
nor strangers crouch armed in our streets
When we own our own cities and fields
we will know the meaning of freedom

Until such time
the cries of our cities and the groans of our land
will be our songs of wisdom
our poetry of anger and hope
Until such time
our watchful murals and graffiitied thoughts
will be our street newspaper
our uncensored judgement and art

But while you dance to our songs
and market our lives
read our lips:

> We are the people of struggle
> Ours is the culture of change

Dan Baron Cohen
Derry, North of Ireland, 1989

TIME WILL TELL
Scenes and Songs of Anger and Hope

Based on drama and music workshops held by **Frontline: Culture and Education** in Manchester 1989. The play grew out of a twelve week collaboration between **Frontline** and **Derry Frontline**. It is grounded in the experience of project participants who were drawn from Manchester, Liverpool, Nottingham, London and Derry.

The play was first produced by **Frontline** in March 1989 and was extensively toured throughout the North West of England over a two month period. It was subsequently produced by **Derry Frontline** as a contribution to the **2020 VISION** community festival of democracy and change which marked the 20th anniversary of the British military reoccupation of the North of Ireland, in August 1989.

The songs in *Time Will Tell* were produced during lyric-writing and music workshops held in Manchester, and by several members of **Derry Frontline/RARE**. Each song is protected by copyright. The writers of the songs are:

WE THE ANGRY........................Chenjera Hove/Dan Baron Cohen
50 YEAR HANDSHAKE....................Locky Morris/Mary Gallagher
THREATS AND PROMISES....................................Francis Simpson
MOTHERS ....Katrina McHugh/Carol Deehan/Martin Hyams
LESBIAN POEM...Joy Pitman
REVEILLE ....Dan Baron Cohen
SOLDIER HOME ....Locky Morris/Mary Gallagher

TIME WILL TELL

LOCAL SOCIO-POLITICAL CONTEXT

The murder of three IRA volunteers in County Tyrone, North of Ireland[1];

The 20th anniversary of the military (re)occupation of the North of Ireland which in Derry stimulated the formation by **Derry Frontline** of **2020 Vision**, an association of cultural and political activists who collaborated to create the **2020 Vision** *Festival of Democracy and Change*[2], its one-hundred foot (30m) *People's Banner* and the *Freedom Fire;*

The 20th anniversary of the civil rights march between Belfast and Derry which was brutally attacked by disguised loyalist paramilitaries[3] at Burntollet Bridge.

PROJECT OBJECTIVES

To train a group of young unemployed people from the Greater Manchester region and two members of **Derry Frontline** in **Frontline**'s workshop method and skills of democratic cultural production;

To contribute to the development of an anti-imperialistic culture within the region;

To build a training-collaboration between **Frontline** and **Derry Frontline** that would enable the Derry activists to return to develop the cultural movement of resistance and self-determination in Ireland.

THEMATIC CONCERNS

To understand the relationship between gender and capital, specifically through the lived experience of the lesbian participants within the project;

To understand the relationship between the protestant and catholic working class cultures within the North of Ireland and within the migrant Irish communities in England;

To understand the relationship between repressed histories and (self-)destructive social relations within the present, and how these can be interrupted to open the future.

WORKSHOP AND AESTHETIC INNOVATIONS

The development of storytelling through the 'intimate object'[4];

The development of collective lyric-writing through a dialogue between the speaking group-writer (participants) and the questioning reader-recorder (coordinator);

The use of 'double-casting'[5] as a form of collaborative, dialogic and reflexive rehearsing and performance-development.

---

1 The Harte brothers, Gerard and Martin, and Brian Mullin killed in an SAS ambush in Drumnakilly, County Tyrone, 30 August 1988.

2 Documentation of this festival can be found in the Linenhall Library, Belfast and the Central Library, Derry.

3 On the 5th of January 1969, nationalists marching from Belfast to Derry were ambushed and assaulted by Loyalist farmers and police lying in wait for them at Burntollet Bridge. For an account of this turning point in the nationalist uprising of 1968-69, see Eamonn McCann's *War and an Irish Town* (Pluto, London 1993).

4 See my dialogue with Marcia Pompeo Nogueira in *Unearthing the Future* (*National Drama*, Vol 7 No 2, pp10-18, Summer 2000), for a detailed explanation of the cultural and educational significance of the *intimate object*.

5 I first explored the strategy of double-casting in **Wazalendo Players 84**'s production of *The Trial of Dedan Kimathi* (London, 1984). Its capacity to stimulate dialogue, collaborative self-criticism and cooperation between actors was further advanced during **Quantum Theatre Company**'s production of Edward Bond's *The Woman* (Manchester, 1985) and *Human Cannon* (Manchester, 1985) and Manchester University's production of Bond's *The Worlds* (Manchester, 1986). It's origins lie in Brecht's experimental search for a dialogic democratic theatre praxis.

TIME WILL TELL
Scenes and Songs of Anger and Hope

SCENE 1: **Garden of Eden**, *Monday, 2.30am, the Knott Garden*
SCENE 2: **Eviction**, *Sunday, 2.30am, the Knott living room*
SCENE 3: **Law and Order**, *Thursday, 5.20pm, the Knott living room*
SCENE 4: **Scissoring Mother**, *Wednesday, 7pm, the Knott living room*

INTERVAL

SCENE 5: **Burning the Diary**, *18 months later, late afternoon, Katrina's lover's flat*
SCENE 6: **Home Raid**, *next day, 3pm, the Knott living room*
SCENE 7: **Future**, *a few days later, 3.30pm, park*

CHARACTERS

SUSAN KNOTT ....Mancunian. Early forties
JIM KNOTT ....Irish Protestant. Early forties
KATRINA KNOTT ....Their daughter. Nineteen
SHANE KNOTT..Their son. Seventeen
POLICE OFFICER ....Nineteen
SANDRA...Journalist. Late twenties
SINGERS

Time Will Tell is set in Manchester 1989. The minimal stage sets indicated are adequate. The singers should be drawn entirely from the cast of actors.

Throughout the script, the term *beat* indicates a fractional pause, considerably shorter than the more conventional term *pause*.

Cast for the Frontline production

Greater Manchester, Salford, Sheffield and Liverpool tour
January 1989

SUSAN KNOTT ....Susan Strongitharm
JIM KNOTT ....Jim Keys
KATRINA KNOTT ....Katrina McHugh/Siobhan Conway
SHANE KNOTT...............................Frances Simpson/Shane Carey
POLICE OFFICER...Derek Suffling
SANDRA ....Sandra Tucker/Carol Deehan
Donna Sullivan
MUSICIANS ....Harold Hammond, Derek Suffling
Martin Hyams, Tony Ricard
Jan Robinson, Mark Shotter

Production

ADMINISTRATION ....Donna Sullivan/Susan Strongitharm
PRODUCTION...Jim Keys
MUSIC WORKSHOPS................Harold Hammond, Derek Suffling
DRAMA & LYRIC WORKSHOPS.........................Dan Baron Cohen
PUBLICITY ....Jan Robinson
WRITER AND DIRECTOR....................................Dan Baron Cohen

Cast for the Derry Frontline production
Pilot's Row, Derry, August 1989

SUSAN KNOTT..Sonya Breslin
JIM KNOTT ....Jim Keys
KATRINA KNOTT..Mary Gallagher
SHANE KNOTT ....Declan Nelis
POLICE OFFICER ....Jim Collins
SANDRA ....Carol Deehan
SINGERS/MUSICIANS......................Locky Morris, Mary Gallagher
Martin Hyams, Sonya Breslin

Cast for the Derry Frontline production
Derry, Belfast and Dublin, August 1991

SUSAN KNOTT..Tracey Collins
JIM KNOTT ....Shaun Maguire
KATRINA KNOTT...Cathy Friel
SHANE KNOTT...Colin Deane
POLICE OFFICER..Maeve McLaughlin
SANDRA ....Bridie Hannigan
SINGERS/MUSICIANS ....Locky Morris
Mary Gallagher, John O'Neil

TIME WILL TELL
Scenes and Songs of Anger and Hope

ACT 1: ANGER

SINGERS: So it's you my sister lying there dead
The eye, the kiss, the clenched fist
So it's you my sister lying there dead
Scattered friends, charred hopes
So it's you my sister lying there dead
Mangled womb, mashed life

Sister
Tears drown the eyes when I behold
The yield of man against man
Sister
A fertile ravaged world
So many flags stained with your blood

So it's you my sister lying there dead
Turns seeds of anger into fruit
So it's you my sister lying there dead
Tunes cries of anger into songs
So it's you my sister lying there dead
In us your anger rises up

SCENE 1: GARDEN OF EDEN

Monday. 2.30am. The KNOTT garden. SUSAN KNOTT stands in her dressing gown in front of a sprawling burnt out fire. She clutches both arms, frozen in thought. In the debris at her feet the contours of charred clothes, twisted leather, blackened metal and smouldering shoes can just be made out in the moonlight. Long silence. SUSAN will not move from this position until the end of the scene.

Sudden light from a downstairs window in the house behind her. In the silence KATRINA KNOTT peers through the window, pauses, sees her mother, and disappears. The light goes out. Pause. KATRINA enters from the back door of the house.

KATRINA: Mum? *(Pause)* I didn't realise the time − −

             Silence. KATRINA walks slowly over to her mother.

KATRINA: The back door was open. *(Silence)* Mum? What you doing out in the garden?

             SUSAN opens her mouth to speak. Silence. She shuts her eyes. Silence. KATRINA touches her mother gently.

KATRINA: You're cold mum. *(Pause)* Have yous been rowing? *(Pause)* Let's go in. I'll make us a brew. *(Pause)* Mum? *(Notices the debris)* What's all this?

SUSAN: Your dad − −

KATRINA: *(Stares openmouthed and laughs quickly)* You had me there for a minute. I wouldn't've blamed you. Looks like a corpse in this light. *(Beat)* So he emptied the back room of all that junk. Bout time. *(Beat)* Mum. What you doing out here? *(Beat)* He hit you didn't he? *(Pause)* Tell me! Seen it coming. *(Under her breath)* The bastard. It's all my fault: said I'd ring if I was going to be late −

SUSAN: *(Gesturing towards the fire)* Your clothes −

KATRINA: He's no right to take it out on you –

SUSAN: Katrina listen –

KATRINA: And no-one's telling me what I can and can't wear –

SUSAN: Your clothes. He burnt them.

KATRINA: *(Laughs)* He what?

SUSAN: He emptied your wardrobe out the window. And your drawers. He gathered all your clothes together and set fire to them –

KATRINA: You're joking.

SUSAN: I tried to stop him. He'd had a few drinks –

KATRINA: *(Staring at the debris)* My clothes? All my clothes?

SUSAN: He lost his temper –

KATRINA: *(Kneeling beside the debris)* Why didn't you stand up to him?

SUSAN: They could hear it on both sides. The most I could do was get him inside. I came down when I knew he was sleeping. I couldn't save anything – –

KATRINA: *(Fingering the debris)* I can't breathe –

SUSAN: He's worked all these years. All the pressure and worry since he came over and nothing to show for it. He used to be so quiet and ready to please. Now I hardly know him. He's always frowning and tense. When he laughs it looks like he's crying and I can't seem to do anything right –

KATRINA: *(Charred boot in hand)* He must hate me –

SUSAN: He's so proud of you Katrina. You going to be a teacher –

KATRINA: What've I done wrong?

SUSAN: You frighten him. He doesn't understand you –

KATRINA: *(Sudden alarm)* My diary! Did he burn my diary? And my letters?

SUSAN shrugs helplessly. KATRINA stands and runs into the house. A light appears downstairs and then another upstairs. Long silence. SUSAN stares first at the fire, then at the house. As she turns back to the fire she screams in silence. The scream slowly pulls her hands to her mouth and she weeps silently. KATRINA returns with a shoulder bag. SUSAN conceals her tears.

KATRINA: If he'd burned these I'd've killed him.

SUSAN: He'll regret it in the morning. *(Pause)* Come inside Katie.

KATRINA: Where was Shane?

SUSAN: With friends –

KATRINA: That's right. He stays out all night and there's never a whisper.

SUSAN: We'll put on the kettle –

KATRINA: I can't stay here. Not after this –

SUSAN: Your father'll buy you new clothes –

KATRINA: They'd never feel right –

SUSAN: Katrina don't just go –

KATRINA: It's too dangerous mum. *(Debris)* Look at that. I don't want to be around the next time it goes off –

SUSAN: That's your father you're talking about –

KATRINA: I know. Did he hit you?

SUSAN: That's enough –

KATRINA: Mum did he hit you? *(Gently)* I need to know.

            Silence.

SUSAN: *(Shakes her head. Pause)* Where'll you stay?

KATRINA: Friends. I'll manage.

SUSAN: *(Pause.)* And what'll I tell your father?

KATRINA: I'll write.

            *KATRINA looks into the fire and then at her mother. She
            hugs her. She leaves. SUSAN stands quite still and stares
            into the debris. Then with great tiredness she turns and
            enters the house. Pause. The downstairs and then the
            upstairs lights go out.*

SINGERS: I looked between the lies
            And saw my uncle
            In friday's paper
            Smiling with the manager
            Fishing rod and reel in his hand

            CHORUS
            Dead nice man
            Dead nice man, dead nice man

            You dragged him through the gates
            And you hooked him
            Bench and machine well tied
            You netted him for fifty years

            CHORUS

Then I read what the manager said
What we need is more factories
Let's attract the factories
Fishing rod and reel in his hand
Fishing rod and reel as his handshakes

CHORUS

Fishing rod and reel in his hand
Fishing rod and reel as his handshakes

SCENE 2: EVICTION

Sunday. 2.30am. The KNOTT living room. A cheap suite flanked by framed supermarket prints. JIM KNOTT is working at an impressive desk against the wall – a calculator in his hand. SUSAN is standing at the window. Silence.

SUSAN: Jim we've got to do something. He's never been gone a whole weekend before. It's gone two thirty –

JIM: *(Absorbed)* If these estimates aren't done by the morning I'll lose –

SUSAN: I'm talking about your son Jim –

JIM: *(Glare)* And I'm talking about our future. D'you want to see five years thrown away? There's no money to pay the loan. Now why don't you finish the accounts –

SUSAN: Jim he's seventeen years old –

JIM: *(Sudden)* I know how old my son is!

SUSAN peers out of the window and looks at her watch. She goes to the kitchen offstage. Silence. JIM finally puts down his pen.

JIM: Right. You listening? I can do the whole job for three thousand five hundred. A week's labour and materials all in. No corners cut. It should be four thou but he won't get it any cheaper. If we stick to schedule we'll clear three fifty. Maybe three eighty. That'll cover the mortgage and the interest on the loan. What d'you think?

SUSAN: *(Off)* Very good, dear. What about Shane?

JIM: How much does he owe?

SUSAN: *(Off)* Three weeks including this one.

JIM: He's you wrapped round his little finger. *(Note)* Forty-five quid. Right. His attitude's changing. From tonight. I'm not keeping a parasite under this roof. How'd you pay the telephone?

SUSAN: *(Off)* I used the gas money –

JIM: *(Hand to head)* If we lose this house you'll know who to blame. Forty-five. I could push the estimate to three eight but it's taking a risk. We'll pay the car. The gas. Save five on the food. You can kiss the coat goodbye –

SUSAN enters with two mugs of coffee. She places one on his desk.

SUSAN: Should I call the police?

JIM: *(Mug)* I'd've been leathered.

SUSAN: Maybe he's round our Katrina's –

JIM: We're going to settle this tonight –

SUSAN: She might've sent him her address –

Sound of door closing offstage. JIM stands abruptly.

SUSAN: I'll handle this –

JIM: Shane!

SHANE: *(Off)* Just getting a drink –

JIM: In here!

SUSAN: Jim, I'm not having a repeat of last week –

SHANE KNOTT enters, taking off his combat jacket. It has bloodstains on its front. He looks tired and creased from sleeping rough.

SHANE: Hiya –

JIM: Sit down. She almost had the police out because of you.

            *SHANE sits on the couch. SUSAN sits opposite. JIM
            remains standing.*

SUSAN: Shane. Where've you –

JIM: Give me that jacket.

SHANE: What?

JIM: *(Grabbing and holding up the jacket)* What's this blood?

SUSAN: Are you hurt Shane?

SHANE: *(Genuine surprise)* Where's that from?

JIM: Don't play the innocent. Have you been fighting?

SUSAN: *(Stands. Examines his head)* Stay still while I see if you've
            cut –

SHANE: *(Uncomfortable)* Don't –

JIM: I want the truth son. If I find out –

SUSAN: Loosen your collar Shane, so I can check your neck –

JIM: Jesus woman! I'm trying to find out if we've a criminal on
            our hands and you're busy fondling his neck!

SUSAN: It's a few drops of blood Jim.

JIM: What've you been up to son?

SHANE: *(Loosening his collar)* I don't remember a fight –

JIM: If I find out you were fighting, I'll put you through that
            wall so fast you won't know what day it is!

SUSAN: Jim, it must be someone else's blood –

JIM: What? On his jacket?

SUSAN: Were you near someone else who got cut?

JIM: Think, son. You've kept us up late enough. Did you see anything?

SHANE: I don't know. I don't remember.

JIM: Look at him. He hasn't got a clue. *(SUSAN returns to her chair)* You don't know if you've committed a crime or been standing in the wrong place when one was committed. All right. This time it's a few drops of blood. But you can't just go walking through life mumbling "I don't know" and "I don't remember". If you don't take responsibility someone else will hold you responsible. For a fight. A stabbing. A murder –

SUSAN: Shane. Where've you been all weekend. *(To JIM)* Let him answer.

SHANE: I went for a few drinks on Friday. I woke up this morning with a bad head. I don't remember the rest.

JIM: Where'd you sleep last night?

SHANE: In a field –

JIM: *(Hurling the jacket at SHANE)* I've an animal for a son.

SUSAN: Shane, you're only seventeen. You can't just go off drinking for three days and not pick up a phone. You could be lying dead in a gutter –

JIM: He was singing in a ditch, Susan –

SUSAN: I'm your mother, Shane. What would you think if I just disappeared for the weekend? We've been worried sick –

JIM: D'you know the meaning of responsibility, son?

SHANE: Look. I just had to get away –

JIM: Oh did you? Where were you on Friday when I came back
            for you?

SHANE: *(Pause)* I left a few minutes early –

JIM: You left two bloody hours early! I was back at half three!
            With a client! I left you to finish that job. We've a
            reputation to protect. When we say we're going to do a
            job we get it done. On time! That's our bread and butter!
            (To SUSAN) I came back to find a pile of cigarette butts in
            the corner and my son dossed off leaving me in the shit!
            Are you trying to make a clown out of me? The world
            doesn't stop turning just because you're spewing your
            guts up in some field!

SHANE: Lay off me will you!

SUSAN: Jim. Let me talk to him –

JIM: We're trying to build you a future and you're doing your
            best to tear it all down! Does any of what I'm saying make
            sense to you?

SUSAN: Jim! Calm down –

JIM: He can see the pressure we're living under!

SUSAN: *(Pause)* Shane. You've had a face on you all week. Now
            let's get this out into the open. What's going on?

SHANE: *(Standing)* I'm tired –

SUSAN: Sit down. *(SHANE sits)* Now what's going on?

            Silence

            Well have you got your rent?

SHANE: *(Checks his pockets. Hand outstretched)* Just this.

SUSAN: Shane. How'm I supposed to buy the week's food with a few coins? You promised me that money on Friday morning. I've got a budget to stick to. *(Beat)* Where's it all gone?

SHANE: A pair of shoes. It's just gone –

JIM: That's not your money to spend –

SHANE: Why not? I earned it! *(To SUSAN)* With him breathing down my neck every hour of the day and night! Watching! Measuring! Why d'you think I had to get away?

JIM: Now you're learning what I have to go through –

SHANE: I don't want that –

SUSAN: But you've debts, Shane. To me. You have to pay your rent and keep like the rest of us.

SHANE: Well I can't live on what he pays –

JIM: What's your problem, son? You're getting ten pound a week on top of what the government pays me for your training. And your own firm at the end of the day. Don't you come in here and point the finger. D'you think I'm doing estimates till two in the morning for my health? Why should you get a new pair of shoes when she has to go without her new coat?

SUSAN: We've got to pull together, Shane.

JIM: You'll get a real wage when you've a real skill to sell –

SHANE: So how much am I worth? Forty five quid? Forty? Thirty five? Thirty? I have to pay back nearly half what you pay me just to live!

JIM: That's the law of hunger son. I didn't invent survival. If I gave you handouts you'd only curse me later on. So what's the answer? *(Pulls his own chair up to SHANE and sits)* Responsibility. We all start at the bottom and mistake drink for freedom. You're not the first to sleep in a ditch. But most of us stay there unless we've a skill to sell. And you're not just getting a skill. You're building your own future. You're getting a training in responsibility so you'll never have to work for anyone again. You start by working for yourself. Soon you'll have others under you to fill your table and clothe your kids. And in exchange you'll give them work —

SHANE: So they have to come to me week after week with empty pockets and hands stretched out and beg me for a wage?

JIM: *(Kisses SHANE violently on the forehead)* Exactly! That's the logic of the man-made world. Ask your mother. Without her and women like her it couldn't keep going. She produces the workers. I provide the food. And the new coats. Sounds crude. I don't like it any more than you do. But if you don't learn that logic you'll spend the rest of your life a beggar. It's the logic that binds workers to bosses and nations to superpowers. Don't fight it Shane. It's as strong as the atom and as mighty as the bomb.

SUSAN: *(Pause)* It's late Jim —

JIM: You're now going to see your son make his first responsible act. Tonight he'll become a man —

SUSAN: What about the estimate?

JIM: *(To SHANE)* When I left Ireland I vowed I'd never again work for another man's food. I'm not paying for mansions and colleges I'll never use. I'm not paying for those snobs to send their sons to schools where they learn to rob us. I'm working for myself to be free of all that. And I'm going to do something I can take pride in. That's still my dream. That and to make you freer than I ever was. What freedom do me or your mother really have? We haven't

99

been to the pictures for years. Oh I admit there's a price to be paid. You may have to leave your own people behind. But freedom costs. And when you've earned it you know you'll never have to face hunger again. *(Pause)* I want you to prove you're the right person to work with me. For your freedom. *(Beat)* I want your three week's rent on that table this Friday.

SUSAN: *(Pause)* Jim –

JIM: Think before you speak, Shane.

SHANE: *(Still shaken by the kiss)* I'll have nothing left – –

SUSAN: Jim. Let's discuss this –

JIM: Are you man enough to bid for your own freedom?

SHANE: *(Tense)* Give us two weeks. Twenty by Friday –

JIM: Freedom means no compromise, son.

SUSAN: Shane. Listen to me –

SHANE: *(Agitated)* Thirty, dad. The rest next week –

SUSAN: Jim! Shane, look at me –

SHANE: *(Desperate)* I've got to get out once this week –

JIM: It's all or nothing –

SUSAN: Pay what you can Shane. I'll make up the rest –

SHANE: *(Pleading)* Forty quid dad! Leave us a fiver –

JIM: You don't have to beg for what's already your's –

SHANE: *(Eruption)* You bastard! Is this what you did to our Katie –

JIM: That's enough –

SHANE: *(Standing)* I don't want your filthy money!

SUSAN: *(Standing)* No, Shane. Look at me –

JIM: Give me your keys –

SHANE: *(Putting on his jacket)* He pushed it mum –

SUSAN: You've nowhere to go –

JIM: Get out!

JIM grabs SHANE by the jacket and wrenches him to the door. Knocking on one wall can be heard.

SHANE: Let me have me clothes!

JIM: Give me the keys and get out!

Heavy knocking on both walls.

SUSAN: Shane!

SHANE: *(Throwing the keys at the table)* Keep your freedom!

SHANE leaves. SUSAN stares in disbelief at JIM. JIM picks up the keys and sits at his desk. The knocking dies away.

JIM: *(Picking up his pen)* He'll be back. We all run away.

SINGERS   Father, you know you made so many promises
Father, you made so many threats
Once you let me sit and drink with you
Even then you kept me tied to your leash
Once you let me sit and laugh with you
Even then I was the joke

In the pub you support me
At home you weaken me
Can't you see your anger in my fear

Mother, you protected us so many times
When you hold me now do you not feel
The bruises his anger left behind
You could have left so many times
Forgetting the laughter and the sunshine
Of those brief picnic years

In the past you weakened me
Now you need support from me
Can't you hear your anger in my voice

SCENE 3: LAW AND ORDER

Thursday. 5.20pm. The KNOTT living room. SUSAN sits in depressed silence. Long silence. The sound of a door closing offstage.

JIM: *(Off)* I'm back. *(Pause)* Susan?

SUSAN remains absolutely still. Pause. JIM enters with one hand behind his back.

JIM: I thought you were out. *(Awkward kiss)* I've been chasing my tail all day. It's good to be home. *(Holding out a bouquet of flowers)* These are for you – –

SUSAN looks blankly at the flowers. She takes them mechanically.

JIM: Daffodils. Remember?

SUSAN nods. JIM sits in his chair.

JIM: There's a box in the hall for you. *(Pause)* We can begin to live again.

SUSAN: *(Beat)* Shane was here –

JIM: I couldn't hold his job open any longer. We were in a tight corner on Monday. *(Beat)* Did he say anything? *(Beat)* He knows the door's always open. *(Beat. Stands)* I'll stick those in a vase.

JIM takes the flowers and goes into the kitchen.

JIM: *(Off)* Jesus, Susan! When did this happen?

Sounds of shards of glass being removed. Pause. Sound of water filling a vase.

JIM: *(Off)* He broke in just to spite me. Through the side window we fitted. I wouldn't take him back now if he begged me.

He enters with the flowers in a vase. He places them on the coffee table in front of the couch.

SUSAN: You took his keys. He took his clothes.

JIM: Did you see him?

SUSAN: He was gone before I got back.

JIM: Have you checked the house?

SUSAN: He's not a thief, Jim —

JIM: There's the kettle.

He leaves again for the kitchen.

JIM: *(Off)* That window'll cost us a few bob. We can't leave the kitchen like that. Anyone could climb in.

He brings out a mug of tea and hands it to SUSAN. He pours himself a whisky at his desk.

SUSAN: I reported it to the police —

JIM: You what?

SUSAN: It could've been anyone. They'll be round later.

JIM: *(Returns to his chair, whisky in hand)* They're always late or intruding. They just stand around. *(Drinks)* It's like a morgue in here. You don't expect that from your children. D'you remember bathing her in the sink? Funny how shy she was. I used to curl her wet hair round my fingers. To make ringlets. Then her hair went dark and she cut it all off. *(Drinks)* Shane sold it. He was a cheeky wee shite from the start. It was time for him to leave anyway. I did at his age. He'll understand. The pressure. Everyone snaps now and then. *(Drinks)* You think I'm destroying everything, Susan. Undoing twenty years. You must think I'm mad. I can see what I'm doing. I know I've been cruel. But you've got to take life by the throat. *(Beat)* They

don't know what cruelty is. They've never known fear.
How dare they judge me! I'm not going down on my
hands and knees to them! Who do they think they are? I
did what I had to! I don't need them! *(Drinks)* I don't need
anyone. What right do they have to come in here and tell
me how to lead my life?

*A knocking on the door. Silence. SUSAN watches JIM
carefully. Silence. JIM is visibly fragile. He stands and
pours himself another drink. A second knock. SUSAN
stands and goes offstage to open the door.*

OFFICER: *(Off)* Mrs Knott? Sorry about the delay. Another call up
the street. Probably the same bloke. *(Pause)* Can I come
in?

SUSAN: *(Off)* This way.

OFFICER: *(Off)* That the window you reported? Not very
professional. Probably desperate. You haven't moved
anything? We need all the evidence we get these days.
Right. Shall we go inside? Me feet're killing me.

*The POLICE OFFICER follows SUSAN into the living room.
JIM remains seated, whisky in hand, on the couch. Tension
throughout.*

SUSAN: This is my husband.

OFFICER: Mr Knott.

SUSAN: I'm afraid there's been a misunderstanding –

OFFICER: D'you mind if I sit down? The scabs. At the back here.
(Points to above his heel) They've come away. Like open
wounds. Very painful.

SUSAN: Please sit down.

*SUSAN sits in JIM's chair. The POLICE OFFICER sits in
her's. He begins to unlace one boot.*

OFFICER: They're not made for walking in. *(Removing boot)* Every step's agony. That's better. I can think now. They don't half bite. *(Smiles and looks round)* Lovely house. We're planning an extension. Me dad's looking round for builders now. You'll have to recommend yours. I'd do it myself only I'm doing a night course. Social and economic history. Me dad's in banking. Says now's the time to build. And seeing as he can get low interest loans – –

POLICE OFFICER massages his toes.

OFFICER: *(Awkward. Massaging)* They should give you trainers for this community lark. But would they listen to me? *(Notices the flowers)* Daffs. How romantic. Lovely thought. From you Mr Knott?

JIM: My wife's anniversary. Twenty years.

OFFICER: How lovely. Congratulations. Twenty years! Now, you'll know someone in the building trade –

JIM: No, I'm British, officer.

OFFICER: That's odd. I didn't know –

JIM: I'm a craftsman. This is my work –

SUSAN: There's been a misunderstanding –

JIM: The name goes back three hundred years –

OFFICER: *(Connecting)* Oh, you're one of them. On our side –

SUSAN: Officer. About the break in –

OFFICER: *(Notebook)* Right. You sounded very alarmed on the phone Mrs Knott –

SUSAN: You see I hadn't checked –

JIM: She panicked.

SUSAN: My son locked himself out. When I saw nothing was
           missing it all began to make sense.

OFFICER: Your son not about now then?

SUSAN: *(Beat)* Out with friends.

OFFICER: *(Understands. Nods. Writes in his notebook)* Thursday.
           Twentieth Feb. 4pm. Incident reported. 21 Plantation
           Street. Suspected B/E. That's breaking and entering.
           Domestic. No charges pressed. Good. All right. Now if
           you'll just sign to confirm this report I'll be on my way.

           *POLICE OFFICER passes notebook to JIM who takes the
           pad.*

OFFICER: Expensive business losing keys. Getting some of them
           recut.

SUSAN: *(Pause. JIM stares)* D'you need a pen Jim?

OFFICER: You can use this.

           Passes pen to SUSAN who passes it to JIM.

JIM: What would a young lad get for breaking and entering?
           First offence. Seventeen years old.

           SUSAN is stunned. Jaw drops.

OFFICER: I understand. Very sad. Well. It depends. Could be a fine
           and suspended sentence.

JIM: Imprisonment?

OFFICER: Very unlikely for a first offence –

SUSAN: He's your own son Jim –

JIM: We want to encourage respect for property, Susan –

107

OFFICER: If he can get away with it in the home, Mrs Knott, he won't think twice the next time. It all starts in the home. *(To JIM)* Mind you. If it's your own son. A firm word'd probably do the trick. You don't want him saddled with a criminal record at his age –

JIM: *(Stands. Returns notebook and pen)* I'll need to check some details. He might be quite innocent –

OFFICER: *(Stands)* Normal procedure. You come down to the station if anything new comes to light. *(Boot)* These again –

   POLICE OFFICER sits and pulls on a boot. SUSAN stands.

   I'm sure you're in a state of shock, Mrs Knott. *(Painfully wrenches boot)* These things are never pleasant. *(Tying laces. To JIM)* Sorry about before. I didn't realise. *(Stands)* If you decide not to come down later perhaps you could pop round some other time. The extension. *(Awkward pause)* I'm sure your prices are very reasonable –

JIM: *(Arm around SUSAN)* I'll be down.

OFFICER: *(Pause)* I'll see myself out then. Good night.

   POLICE OFFICER nods to the KNOTTS. Leaves. A door closes offstage. JIM replaces his glass on his desk.

SUSAN: You can't prosecute your own son!

JIM: That's the law, Susan –

SUSAN: Your own son?

JIM: You heard. If he can steal from his own –

SUSAN: He came back for his own clothes!

JIM: I don't care why he came back. He broke the law –

SUSAN: Why are you torturing him?

JIM: *(As he puts on his jacket)* If I'm not firm now he'll regret it
        for life –

SUSAN: Jim! I'm begging you! Don't go down!

JIM: I'll be back in half an hour.

        JIM leaves.

JIM: *(Off)* There's a present in the hall.

SINGERS: You came for my husband at dawn
        How could you stand over our bed and cradle his child
        When you plan to kill her at night
        Stop and listen, you soldiers of stone
        How could you stand in our kitchen and joke with his son
        You will teach him the power of hunger

        When you look down your sights
        Watch out for my children
        While they are playing
        They're planning your death

        You came for my mother at dusk
        How could you put out her candles and break up our
        prayers
        You will set us apart to be scorned
        Stop and listen you children of fear
        When they burned down our houses and buried our
        people alive
        Did they know that the burns would not heal

        When you make your own home
        Please teach your children
        To use my life as a torch
        A torch of resistance

SCENE 4: SCISSORING MOTHER

Wednesday. 7pm. The KNOTT living room. SUSAN sits in her chair with the accounts open in her lap. She wears an apron and stares in thought. JIM works at construction drawings at a new second-hand table in the corner beside his desk. Two people in different worlds. The radio is on.

VOICE: Landmine exploded beneath an army vehicle on the Buncrana Road between Londonderry and the border checkpoint. A British soldier was killed and two others were critically injured. An army spokesman said it was a miracle that no civilians were injured. The bombing has been condemned by city councillors from both sides of the community –

JIM: *(Turns off the radio)* There's no end to that war. *(Holds up drawings to study them)* If they bombed that island tomorrow nobody would notice. *(Final corrections to the drawings)* They'll be well shocked in the bank. In credit for the first time in five years. Who'd've thought that boy would turn out useful to the business? *(Drawings down. Watch. Tidies his desk)* Right. We're going out to celebrate. You done? *(Silence. He looks round)* Susan?

            SUSAN looks at him in thought.

JIM: D'you still want to go to the pictures? And a bite to eat after? I've booked a table in that fancy place down town. *(Beat)* Come on. *(Stands)* We'll take your new coat out for a drink.

SUSAN: *(Beat)* If you want.

JIM: Get ready then. I'm going as I am. *(Beat)* I'll get the club tie out.

            JIM leaves.

JIM: *(Off)* You seen my blue tie, Susan? That's funny. Could've sworn I saw it here yesterday.

SUSAN closes the accounts book decisively. Pause.

JIM: *(Off)* Beautiful coat. Bargain at a hundred pound. You don't want to leave a thing like that lying round in a box.

Silence. SUSAN stands and places the accounts book on JIM's desk. She returns to her chair.

JIM: *(Off)* Found it. I think I'll push up that estimate. Ask cowboy prices and you don't get the respect –

Sudden theatrical entrance in a striking black suit. JIM wears his hair greased back and dark glasses. He holds the coat folded over his arm.

JIM: Well? How do I look?

SUSAN laughs, covers her eyes with one hand, and looks again. She shakes her head. JIM throws the coat over his chair and pirouettes.

JIM: *(Pose)* Michael Jackson. Can't be bad. First laugh I've heard out of you in weeks. What d'you think? Would you give me a second look?

SUSAN: It's alright.

JIM: Put on the coat. *(Picks it up and holds it open)* Go on. It won't bite –

SUSAN: Jim –

JIM: Don't be shy. Put it on.

SUSAN shakes her head in embarrassment. JIM walks to the centre of the room with the coat open wide.

JIM: Put it on before I kiss you. You don't have to wear it if you don't like it. Just put it on. *(Beat)* You've been trying it on in your mind for months. *(Beat)* You scared you'll like it? There's plenty of women'd give their right arm for this rag.

(Smiles and takes off glasses) Just put it on for a second.

SUSAN looks at him and shakes her head. She stands slowly and walks into the open coat.

JIM: Do it up then. Your apron's poking out.

She fastens it.

JIM: Now walk it round a bit. You know. Model it.

SUSAN looks down. She tries a catwalk and attempts a turn. She stops dead in the middle of the room.

JIM: Don't stop now. You look twenty years younger –

SUSAN: *(Taking off the coat)* Jim. I'm not going out –

JIM: It'll take you out of yourself –

SUSAN: *(Throwing the coat over the chair)* No. I'm not going. And I don't want that coat –

JIM: Susan. We can afford it –

SUSAN: Now you've driven them out?

JIM: Don't talk nonsense –

SUSAN: You did Jim. You drove them out.

JIM: Let's just go out. I don't want to argue. Let's just forget about it for the night –

SUSAN: Forget about it? *(Chest)* It's in here Jim. I can't cut it out. *(Head)* It's in here. It's a part of me. I can't hide it under a coat and pretend it doesn't exist. *(Beat)* We're settling this now, Jim, or I'm walking out that door. I can't take any more. D'you understand? *(Pause)* Now, you drove them out. I need to know why.

JIM: They left –

SUSAN: Jim. You drove them away. I spent ten years holding on.
            In two nights you tore it all down. Look around you.
            What's here for me now? An empty kitchen. A ghost
            house. Your life's at that table. I feel dead. Empty. Used –

JIM: You can't blame me for them growing up. It's harder for
            you. Why d'you think I got you the coat?

SUSAN: Jim, what use are gifts? There's no-one to show them to.
            They can't speak or laugh. They used to shine. Comfort
            me. Now they look cheap. Ugly. I'm surrounded by things
            I don't need –

JIM: That's the pressure talking. You can't blame me for that.
            How d'you think I felt?

SUSAN: I don't know. You never talked about it –

JIM: I don't know how to!

            SUSAN starts to leave.

JIM: Where you going?

SUSAN: *(At the kitchen door)* To the kitchen. Where I've lived
            twenty years.

            SUSAN leaves. JIM paces.

JIM: *(Watch)* Look. We'll talk about it after the film. We just go
            round in circles. There's nothing like a good night out –

            SUSAN returns with a breadknife in her hand.

JIM: What's going on?

SUSAN: *(Picking up the coat)* I don't want anything from you any
            more.

JIM: Susan –

SUSAN: *(Lifting the coat)* I don't want you to take anything from
              me ever again.

JIM: *(Approaching)* Susan don't –

SUSAN: *(Knife)* Don't touch me –

JIM: That's a five hundred pound coat in your hand!

SUSAN: You made my daughter feel raped! *(Slit)* You made my son
              beg! *(Slit)* You pushed and you pushed –

JIM: You're mad –

SUSAN: And you called it justice! *(Slit)* I gave you my body –

JIM: You need a doctor!

SUSAN: And you stabbed me inside! *(Slit)*.

JIM: Stop it Susan!

SUSAN: I gave you my life!

JIM: You'll destroy everything!

SUSAN: And you never listened! *(Slit)* I can't plead anymore! *(Slit)*
              Now I can't bear you! *(Slit)* I can't bear your look! *(Slit)* I
              can't bear you near me! *(Slit)* I can't bear your touch! *(Slit)*
              I can't bear you in me! *(Slit)* I can't bear your voice! *(Slit)* I
              loved you, Jim. *(Pause. Exhausted)* Now I am numb – –

              *SUSAN stares at JIM. He stands quite still and slowly
              staggers to his table. Slowly he approaches SUSAN.*

JIM: Where is this man who consumed your life? Who is this
              man who drove out your children? Show me this tyrant
              who abused you and turned you to stone! *(SUSAN turns
              her head to face the audience)* Does he have hands like

these that tremble with debts? Does he have eyes like these that squint with strain? *(Grabs the coat)* You point your finger but all I see is a corpse! *(Holding coat up)* I see a navvy who queued to beg food for his home! A father too tired to learn how to love! A joiner whose skills betrayed his own hands! And a plumber who choked on the words in his mouth! *(Holding coat in front of her eyes)* A master craftsman? A ragged slave! How dare you blame me for the past!

SUSAN: You still have your table.

Silence. JIM lowers the coat and stares openmouthed. SUSAN puts down the knife and takes off her apron. She turns to leave.

JIM: *(Sudden highpitched plea)* Don't go – –

SUSAN: *(Turning at the door)* I'll sleep in the back room.

SUSAN leaves. Long silence. JIM sits with the coat in his lap. He hugs the coat. Silence. Finally he leans back into his chair exhausted. As KATRINA enters he looks up.

KATRINA: *(Pause)* Alright?

JIM: Can't spend long. The estimates –

KATRINA: What's that in your hands?

JIM: A bit of old rag. The car. *(Pushes the coat under his chair)* I've been fiddling with the engine –

KATRINA: Dressed like that?

JIM: Your mum and me were going out. She's lying down.

KATRINA: Oh.

JIM: She's not been well. Since you left –

KATRINA: Dad. I've not come for an argument –

JIM: The world's sick. No-one speaks the truth anymore. I thought I'd left all that behind me.

KATRINA: *(Beat)* Left what?

JIM: D'you need anything?

KATRINA: Dad. Left what?

Pause. He stands and goes to sit at his desk.

JIM: I'll tell her you called.

KATRINA stands in silence. She leaves.

ACT 2: HOPE

SINGERS   thoughts reach out
minds meet
the interaction of ideas
excites me

but if I touched you
would your body answer me
or would your flesh
recoil

you do not shrink
an accidental contact
resist a hand that's placed for emphasis
or greeting

but if you saw the flame
that runs along my nerves
would you reject me
and return
to better known allegiances

your friendship
is a card
too high to gamble
your friendship
is a card
too high to gamble

SCENE 5: BURNING THE DIARY

Eighteen months later. Late afternoon. KATRINA's lover's flat. Various political posters and a lesbian calendar on the walls. Newspaper cuttings and leaflets on the floor. Boxes all over the room. KATRINA is sorting books into piles on the floor. She divides one pile into books with her name inscribed inside them. The others she places in a box beside her. She then crosses out the inscription in each book and places it methodically in another box. She works fast. She stands once she has finished the pile and looks at her watch. She looks at the rest of the room and shakes her head. She walks over to the final row of books and carries them off the shelves to the boxes of books on the floor. She kneels and begins the whole process again. SANDRA enters carrying a briefcase.

SANDRA: Hiya. *(No answer)* Looks like a raid. *(Puts down briefcase).*

KATRINA: You're late.

SANDRA: *(Taking off coat)* What's going on?

KATRINA: *(Sorting)* No time to explain.

SANDRA: *(Kneeling beside KATRINA)* Those're from me. *(Beat)* Why're you crossing out what I wrote?

KATRINA: *(Sorting)* I've no choice –

SANDRA: You're not leaving. *(Stills KATRINA's hand)* Katrina. What've I done wrong?

KATRINA: *(Looks up)* My brother'll be here in an hour. All this lot's got to be cleared out by then. *(Deleting inscriptions)* He's staying a few days –

SANDRA: Where? Here?

KATRINA: He can't stay at my dad's. He's just phoned to ask if we'd put him up. He's back on leave –

SANDRA: You never told me –

KATRINA: I've only just found out myself. *(Stands with pile)* These'll
           all have to go. *(Loads books into a box)* This lot's the
           political stuff. Your's can go to your mum's. Mine's going
           to Jo's. She's driving round now. No-one'll find them
           there. These are safe. *(Puts them back on the shelf)* We've
           got to hurry Sandra! I'll do the posters. You sort through
           the leaflets and magazines –

SANDRA: Now hold on –

KATRINA: *(Removing the calendar)* Shall we give this to Jo?

SANDRA: I live here as well –

KATRINA: There's no time for this Sandra –

SANDRA: You can't just take everything down without asking me –

KATRINA: Sandra! He'll be here in an hour!

SANDRA: *(Holds KATRINA)* Just calm down! Let's think for a minute!

KATRINA: There's nothing to think about! He's a soldier! What's
           going to be going through his head if he sees all this
           stuff? If he finds out about us he'd go straight to my dad!
           My dad'd take it out on my mum! I'm not risking that –

SANDRA: They've got to find out some time –

KATRINA: Not like that. When I'm ready to tell them. When I'm
           strong enough –

SANDRA: What about me Katrina? This home gives me strength!

KATRINA: I thought you'd understand! I thought you'd support me –

SANDRA: *(Suddenly)* All right! *(Pause)* All right. *(Pause)* We'll make
           up separate beds. How long's he staying?

KATRINA: Two days. Maybe three.

SANDRA: Can't he stay with friends?

KATRINA: *(Agitated)* Why d'you think he phoned? He's been gone
             eighteen months! Who'd know him now?

SANDRA: All right. Don't take it out on me. What d'you want me to
             do?

KATRINA: Just sort out the leaflets and work out what you need.

             *KATRINA pulls a chair to the wall and climbs onto it. She
             begins unpinning a poster. SANDRA watches.*

SANDRA: Mind the corners. I never thought I'd see this again.

             *SANDRA puts on her glasses and kneels on the floor. She
             thumbs through papers and cuttings. They work in silence.*

KATRINA: *(Finally)* How you doing?

SANDRA: I've got the stuff for next week's article. *(Beat)* If it's just a
             few days we could hide all this in the shed –

KATRINA: *(Tense)* He's a soldier Sandra. He's paid to find things like
             this. They lock people away for these kind of posters –

SANDRA: In Ireland. Not here –

KATRINA: That's where he's based. I don't know where he'll be
             looking when we're out of the house. You don't know
             how soldiers think –

SANDRA: Then just tell him he can't stay –

KATRINA: My dad's bound to suspect. Shane'll expect the favour.
             We always stood by each other at home. *(Beat)* He's
             thinking of leaving the army. We might learn something
             meeting him. But I'm not taking any risks. Imagine him
             ringing the head with one of my letters in his hand. It's

your trainee teacher. You've a dyke in charge of primary school kids. I wouldn't stand a chance. *(Steps down from chair and gathers up posters)* I'm not leaving anything lying around anymore –

SANDRA: It's safe enough here –

KATRINA: Not here. Nowhere. What's to stop some teacher just dropping by? I can't hold them off for ever. I'm getting rid of anything they could use against me –

SANDRA: Now Katrina, hold on. You're taking this too far –

KATRINA: *(Watch)* We'll talk about this later –

SANDRA: *(Putting down papers)* We'll talk about it now if you want my support. *(Glasses off)* Those posters are going back up when you're brother's gone. I'm not having my life locked away in a bedroom. We already live in a cell outside –

KATRINA: Fair enough –

SANDRA: What d'you mean fair enough? You said two days. I'm not living with bare walls for the rest of my life! Outside it's no touching. No going out. This is where we don't have to lie!

KATRINA: You do what you want. I'm not living in fear for the rest of my life! I want to be in that classroom so that those kids never have to suffer what I had to live! Just think what their parents would say if it ever came out!

SANDRA: The school wouldn't dare. The council'd step in –

KATRINA: It's already happening! But no-one knows! Just like no-one knows you can't say certain things. You can't use certain books. You can't even find them because they're not on the shelves! You're right! They'll find some other excuse. We don't like your attitude. Your teaching's not up to scratch! Shane's visit's brought it home to me. I'll cross out my name. Wear skirts. Be their kind of woman. Live with bare walls. Anything so long as I can stop those kids making the mistakes my family made!

SANDRA: What will you teach them?

KATRINA: Don't patronise me.

SANDRA: *(Pause. Turns away)* We've never argued like this before.

KATRINA: Do you want me to move out? This is your home.

SANDRA: *(Flat)* Don't be stupid.

Silence. KATRINA looks at her watch. She places the calendar and posters in a box. SANDRA looks at the walls. KATRINA leaves and returns with a small shovel. She picks up her letters and diary. She walks into the garden. SANDRA sits in thought. KATRINA leans the shovel against the wall and builds a small fire out of the letters. She returns to the house and picks up a black binliner and matches. She returns to the garden, puts down the binliner, and lights a match. It goes out. SANDRA stands and picks up the calendar. KATRINA lights another match and sets fire to the letters. She places the diary on the fire. As it catches alight she lifts it into the shovel and holds it out to let the wind get to it. SANDRA puts down the calendar and comes out into the garden.

KATRINA: You still have your writing.

SANDRA: What's that you're burning?

KATRINA: The diary. I'll sleep well tonight.

SANDRA: Do you know how hard it is to find anything from our past? Wherever I turn I find the same lies. We're sick. Unnatural. We should be burned at the stake. Sometimes I find a fragment after months of searching. A letter some woman wrote in a cellar. Or a poem a woman wrote to herself on the back of a receipt in the middle of the night. Sometimes I find our secret locked away between the

lines of a book a woman signed as a man. Or in the
margin. For years you can search and find nothing. How
many women must have suffered in silence. How many of
us must have suffered the truth. *(Beat)* Save the diary,
Katrina. You don't know how useful your childhood
thoughts might be to the future.

KATRINA stares entranced at the flames.

The Nazis burned books. They understood the power of
the mind. They knew how dangerous the truth was. First
they imprisoned statues. Of liberty. When they finished
saying what was healthy and what was scum, they burned
people. And they built statues of the great men who'd
commissioned the human ovens. It wasn't just scapegoats
they needed. They had to be sure that no-one could
question their laws. When they stared into their mass
graves they thought the future was their's. How would
slaves rebel if they couldn't remember what freedom was
like? Millions burned. But a few kept the past alive. They
sang it to their children. Prisoners memorised street
names. Some even hid books under the ground and were
tortured for refusing to say why. *(Beat)* Save those charred
pages, Katrina. When people read them they'll be forced
to ask questions and that will move them forward.

KATRINA stands absorbed by the flames.

Suffering used to terrify people. But even when they were
too weak to protest they dreamed of change. Today we're
bored if there's no tragedy on TV. We point our finger at
some regime across the world where they're demanding
the burning of books. When we try to say why, our
tongue sticks to the roof of our mouth. We feel foolish, so
we laugh. But only anger comes out. We save up to
spend and get bored shopping. So we go to museums to
see if people felt like this in the past. But all we find are
adverts of slavery, and American or Japanese tourists.
When our children ask why we were afraid of broad
daylight, who will answer them? When they ask how a full
plate could leave us hungry, what'll be said? When they

laugh at how quiet we were, who will tell them we were angry and confused? *(Beat)* Save those fragments, Katrina. Our children will need them to survive.

The diary goes out. KATRINA stands with a shovel of ashes.

KATRINA: He mustn't find these.

She empties the ashes into the binliner and scoops up the ashes from the letters. SANDRA looks on.

KATRINA: Where should I put this? He could go through the bins. D'you think anyone saw me burn it? They might mention it. When I'm not here to distract him. I'll give this to Jo. Sandra! D'you think anyone heard us argue? D'you think he arrived and saw me burning the diary?

SANDRA: Come inside –

KATRINA: He might already be there! He'll know we've taken things off the shelves! It looks like no-one's living there!

KATRINA runs inside with the binliner. SANDRA follows quickly. KATRINA walks falteringly into the room.

KATRINA: Are we. Moving? Don't tell. Anyone about. This. Sandra! Promise! We'll have to live. Separately. I'll. Manage. You. Can visit from. Time to. Time. Late. At night. I'm. Afraid Sandra. I'm. Afraid –

SANDRA: I'm here. I'm with you.

SANDRA holds KATRINA. The binliner dangles to the floor.

KATRINA: How will I live without you?

SANDRA: You don't have to go.

KATRINA: *(Pause)* Your neck's so warm.

They hold each other in silence.

SINGERS: Now you're landed
On this foreign shore
And you batter
Outside of our doors
You go marching
Round the rooms
Inside our homes

Our minds are scarred
Wounds you left behind

When you return
To your own home town
Turn your key
And look around
See the same pattern
On your bedroom wall
The same carpet
On your mother's floor

Our minds are scarred
Wounds you left behind

SCENE 6: HOME RAID

The next day. 3pm. The KNOTT living room. The drawing table is still in the same place beside the desk but the furniture has been rearranged and reupholstered. Books on the sidetable. Flowers and new prints. SUSAN enters. She is smartly dressed and made up. She takes off her coat and goes to the kitchen. Sound of running water. She returns with a jug and waters the plants. She passes an open book lying on the floor and places it on a chair. She goes back to the kitchen with the jug and returns with a glass of orange. She picks up the book and settles into the couch with her legs up. Pause. A knock on the door. She looks at her watch and goes to answer the door.

SUSAN: *(Off)* My God. Shane.

SHANE: *(Off)* Just got back.

SUSAN: *(Off. Pause)* Come in. Give me your bag –

SHANE: *(Off)* You're alright. I'll bring it in.

           SHANE enters with his kitbag. He has grown and is dressed in man-about-town clothes. SUSAN follows and watches her son. SHANE looks round.

SHANE: This place's changed.

SUSAN: I'd've walked right past you on the street. You're the spit of your father when he was your age. If you'd said you were coming –

SHANE: Dad at work?

SUSAN: He'll be back at six.

           SHANE puts down his bag in the corner of the room.

SUSAN: Have you eaten?

SHANE: The last eighteen months?

SUSAN laughs and goes to hug SHANE. He stands rigid within the hug.

SUSAN: I'll put the kettle on –

SHANE: No need. I've just had a pint. Down the Red Lion –

SUSAN: *(Shy)* That's where –

SHANE: I know. I've been watching you from the corner. You suit barwork.

SUSAN: First job I've had in twenty years.

SHANE: What about the accounts?

SUSAN: Your father does all that now. I put my foot down.

SHANE: When did all this happen?

SUSAN: We sorted it all out. We're taking one step at a time.

SHANE moves to the desk and leafs searchingly through the books.

SUSAN: Your sister gave those to me.

SHANE: *(Scanning)* Course work is it?

SUSAN: *(Nods)* She's nearly qualified now. She'll soon be teaching full time.

SHANE: When d'you last see her?

SUSAN: A week ago. Maybe ten days –

SHANE: I saw her last night. She wasn't well –

SUSAN: She's been under alot of strain with the exams –

SHANE: She was with a friend.

SUSAN: Sandra? *(SHANE nods)* She's a journalist. They share the house –

SHANE: Known her long, has she?

SUSAN: Since she moved out of here –

SHANE: *(Puts down book)* I didn't stay long.

SUSAN: That's probably best if she wasn't well.

SHANE stares searchingly at SUSAN.

SUSAN: Are you going to take your jacket off and sit down?

SHANE: Can't stay long. Train leaves at five.

SUSAN: If you caught a later train, you could see your father. He'll be so disappointed if he finds out you were here and didn't stop to say hello –

SHANE: Don't tell him then –

SUSAN: But everything's changing and it'd help. He was so confused before. That flare up with you. And the business with the police. He knows he was wrong –

SHANE: We've got nothing to talk about –

SUSAN: He had your best interests at heart –

SHANE: Let's leave it, mum –

SUSAN: He only wanted to teach you what he believed was right. To think for yourself and be independent. I married him for those values. They set him apart. When everyone else was marching for abortion and free love, your father was out courting me. When everyone else was on strike he had his head down looking for work. And it wasn't easy to find a flat in those days. People still had those "No Irish Need Apply" signs in their heads. So though he was British, his accent betrayed him. An Irish Protestant they called a thick drunken Paddy. But he knew right from wrong and he didn't change the way he spoke. He was proud of it. And he didn't want you to suffer the humiliation and loneliness he went through. That's what he was trying to pass on –

SHANE: *(Picks up his bag)* I came to talk –

SUSAN: You put that bag down and listen! I've not seen you in eighteen months! If you're not going to wait till he gets back then at least give me the chance to explain! How d'you think it feels to lose all you've got? *(Beat)* I'm tired. I didn't mean to shout. I've been waiting for this day for ages. *(She sits)* I've had to think it all through, Shane. I'm not saying he's right. He's made mistakes and I helped him carry them out. We're trying to correct that. But you've got to work out the cause. Turning your back isn't the solution. All I'm saying is that deep down he's a good man. Don't think you're the only one who's suffered – –

SHANE: I've got to be in London tonight.

SUSAN: I'll fix you some butties for the train.

SHANE: *(Puts his bag down. Pause)* I've joined up. Rifleman with the Royal Green Jackets.

SUSAN: I knew you'd make something of your life!

SHANE: *(Pacing)* The army sets alot of stock by appearance. Keeps up morale and builds your self-discipline. Get the appearance right and the rest falls into place. You'd think wars were won and lost according to the law of polish. The lieutenant's obsessed. If he finds a wrinkle that's your day off cancelled. He's down on you like a ton of corpses. *(Hoists himself onto the desk)* Once we were out on patrol. Germany it was. We come across some barbed wire. The lieutenant shouts "I'll go first". He climbs up on to the barbed wire and jumps. Straight into a cesspit! We pissed ourselves! Him up to his neck in shit with his spick and span accent! We dunked him in the river. Fierce

December frost it was. Couldn't have the bastard sleeping with us smelling like that!

SUSAN: That's why you look so smart –

SHANE: *(Stands. Intense)* Once an ambush is set we're sent in. Sergeant checks the business and gives the "ambush set". That means nobody moves unless a war happens. In front we've each got say sixty yards. That's our killing area. So there we are. Cold. Wet. And laying in a ditch. Suddenly two blokes walk into the ambush. We positively identify weapons and open fire. One was a spick and span lieutenant. The other was his signaller. They'd walked down the road and come back up the wrong side. The lieutenant was killed outright. His signaller died on the stretcher. He'd questioned the officer's judgement.

SUSAN: You've got to be so careful –

SHANE: You've got to be so bloody stupid! I didn't give a monkey's about the lieutenant! He got what was coming to him! But the signaller was a mate. From Manchester. *(Beat)* The uniform's irrelevant. Our kind cop it in the neck every time.

SUSAN: *(Pause)* You must be glad to be back –

SHANE: Home two days and still reading the registration of every parked car.

SUSAN: That's the training for you –

SHANE: *(Sitting beside her)* I thought it'd be good to get away. See the world and have an adventure. You're only young once. Eighteen hours a day of when to move and when to speak. No different to civvie street, only harder. Instead of fighting on the terraces or in the pubs, you fight out in Ireland. Get the anger and frustration out in the open. Nice and legal. Take it out on an eight year old. Release it on a raid. It don't matter how much they make thinking a crime. You make the connections. When you've been over to Ireland, you don't have to prove yourself anymore. You see their murals. The writing on the wall. Eighteen hours of tension and boredom but you're still crouching against them murals. South Africa and Ireland. Cuba and Ireland. Derry and Manchester. I'm not saying everyone sees it. Ireland's not for everyone. But deep down they feel it.

SUSAN: I don't understand.

SHANE: You know my saddest moment on tour? Not the death of the signaller. Not the killing of the civvie searcher right where I was standing outside Wellworths. Single bullet and his head went up like a balloon. The saddest moment was when I was first spat on. A pretty girl from the same street and houses as us. Spat on me. I'd've asked her out back home. That hatred –

SUSAN: I thought they needed us there –

SHANE: Even the dogs hate us. I reckon they must show them pictures of squaddies they bite us so deep.

SUSAN: Well you're respected over here –

          Sound of a door closing offstage.

JIM: *(Off)* Susan?

SHANE: You said –

JIM: *(Off)* You seen the drill?

          Sound of rummaging in cupboards offstage. SHANE and SUSAN are completely still. SHANE stands as JIM finally enters. He pauses at the door.

JIM: When did you get back?

SUSAN: He's only just arrived, Jim. Just walked in –

JIM: *(Awkward pause. Hand outstretched)* Welcome back. You remembered where we live.

SHANE slowly shakes hands.

SUSAN: He's not got long, Jim –

JIM: You know postcards don't bite –

SUSAN: A visit's better than any letter, Jim –

JIM: How long you staying?

SUSAN: He's away to London tonight.

JIM: *(Pause)* Well sit down. *(Watch)* We've still got a few minutes.

SHANE: *(Beat)* This still your chair?

JIM: You take the place of honour.

JIM sits on the couch. SUSAN sits in her chair.

JIM: About the break in –

SHANE: Forget it.

SUSAN: We've been through all that.

JIM: *(Nods. Pause)* Will I get the kettle on?

SHANE: Only if you want one.

JIM: *(Looks at SUSAN who shakes her head)* I'll leave it then. *(Pause)* You're looking smart. That haircut suits you. Things sorted themselves out? *(SHANE nods)* You've obviously a few pound in your pocket. Found labouring?

SHANE: I've joined up. Just finished a tour.

JIM: That's good. *(To SUSAN)* That's the army for you. I told you he'd come right. *(To SHANE)* Where you based?

SHANE: Derry –

JIM: Londonderry to me. *(Beat)* You've got family there –

SHANE: Been to their house.

JIM: *(Beat)* Then you know more than me –

SHANE: I've never seen such hatred –

JIM: That's why there's no religion in this house. It's trench warfare out there. Twenty years of war have turned them into bigots, but they hated before it all started –

SUSAN: That's why you left. You could see no end to it –

JIM: Now he's seen for himself. The main thing is you've been taught responsibility. And respect. You can see it in your bearing –

SUSAN: You'll never be out of a job now, Shane –

JIM: Will you let me finish? You two've been at it all afternoon. *(Beat)* I want to talk to my son. I won't see him again for two years. *(Beat)* They've filled you out. You can see it in the eyes. You measure a man from the chin up –

SHANE: I want to leave, Dad.

JIM: What's your problem son?

SHANE: I've got to get out –

SUSAN: But it's a training for life, Shane –

SHANE: I'm not coming back in a body bag for them –

JIM: Them? What you talking about? I pay for you to work out there. You're doing a job. Millions of people are paying for you to keep the peace –

SHANE: We stoke it up –

JIM: Don't give me that! You went in to protect the Catholic
           community. Without you there'd be a bloodbath. You'd
           have Bloody Sundays every week. They need you like we
           need the police. It's a fact of life –

SHANE: It's an army of occupation –

JIM: You're bloody right. A damn good occupation. You just be
           grateful –

SHANE: I've had enough. I'm not being paid to intimidate –

JIM: Now just a minute. Let's get the facts straight. I don't
           know who you've been listening to, but I came from there
           so don't you start preaching. There's been four hundred
           years of sectarian hatred. Catholics and Protestants at each
           other's throats. Fighting for the crumbs that fall from the
           table. It didn't just start because you waded in –

SHANE: I'm getting out. I'm not being paid to protect that table –

JIM: *(Standing)* Don't mock me son!

SHANE: I'm not doing someone else's dirty work!

JIM: Dirty work? You're keeping the peace! What d'you think
           armies are for? Why d'you think we need all those
           bombs? D'you think governments want to lose lives? How
           else can you guarantee peace?

SUSAN: Now both of you listen –

JIM: *(Finger stabbing SHANE's chest)* It's a bloody vocation!
           Not an occupation! But if you can't take the responsibility,
           then don't start meddling in other people's lives! If you're
           not man enough for the job then get transferred!

SHANE: *(Stands suddenly)* Man enough? *(SUSAN stands as he
           kicks over the coffee table)* Yes sergeant! No bomb under
           here, sergeant!

JIM: What are you doing?

SHANE: Pull up the floorboards? Yes sergeant! Right away! *(Lifts chair and turns it over)* Just shift this chair! *(Kicks another chair over)* No guns under here sergeant! *(Brushes books off the desk and lifts it)* No bombs here neither!

JIM tries to restrain SHANE.

JIM: Get off that –

SHANE: Sit down old man! *(Throws JIM onto the couch)* Got something to hide? Want your sons locked away? Your daughters stripsearched? Any detonators upstairs? Handguns in the oven? *(To JIM as he rights himself)* Move and you'll be done for assault! Right sergeant. Upstairs? Shall I turn the house over? Same as last week? And the weeks before? Lean on the old man twitching behind the curtain? Yes sergeant! Right away sergeant! Five kids in their nighties sergeant! Upstairs sergeant! Turned their beds over! Just toys, sergeant! Same as last week! Nothing to report!

JIM: This is our house!

SHANE: Shut it Fenian scum! You'll get compensation for the door!

JIM: You have no right!

SHANE: You invited us in!

JIM: Tommy bastards!

SUSAN: Stop! I beg you to stop!

Silence. All are standing. Furniture lies upturned across the room.

SHANE: We were doing this spot check just outside Drumnakilly. One month back. I pull this white Ford Sierra to the side of the road. The driver winds down the window and slips me his licence. He stares ahead, but I know him straight off.

Martin Harte. 21. County Tyrone. I'd seen his photo down the barracks. Memorised the faces by the look in their eyes. You learn to read those faces like a map. How they live. What they know. Why they fight. I do it all by the book. I take the false licence over to the jeep and radio intelligence. The bloke next to Harte looks like his brother. There's an older lad in the back eating crisps. "Let 'em through" says HQ. "There's been a tip off". I stroll back nice and slow to the car. As I hand back the licence Harte looks me in the eye. I can see the anger I felt the day I was pulled for stealing back my own clothes. He smiles: time will tell. I wave them on. An hour later they're dead. Four men in jeans climb into a chopper. An SAS ambush off the Omagh Road. The next day we're sent in to bag the bodies. They've cordoned off the area and left the dead out on show! There's the Sierra – riddled with hundreds of bullets! Each one carries my nod of consent!

JIM: *(Rising from the couch)* You can't blame me. You can't hold me responsible. I never took sides! Why d'you think I came over here? I saw that war coming when I left my home! I left my city and my people so that no-one could accuse me of those crimes! *(Stands)* Your self-pity disgusts me! I was there on Burntollet Bridge when the march for democracy was destroyed! The police just stood by! Some were there in jeans and boots, but I knew who they were! There they were leaning against their Union Jacks cheering in time to the lambeg drum, chanting: "Up to our knees in Fenian blood!" "Up to our knees in Fenian blood!" You don't now what cruelty means! I held a club in this hand and watched my own brothers batter those marchers into the mud! Our house was no different to theirs'! I saw farmers punching women down the slope to the river heaving rocks the size of footballs at their faces! We'd cleared that river with our own bare hands! I gripped this club in rage – not in hatred! And when I saw a girl lying face down in the river while men hit her with nailed clubs it was my blood I saw spurt from the holes! Yet I gripped this club and did nothing! You think you've suffered? Pulled the wrong trigger? I never once raised my hand! Still they pointed! You lost your nerve! Sold out your own people! With every look they branded me traitor! With the

whole world sneering I turned my back and walked away!
I never took sides in my life!

*Silence. SUSAN and SHANE stare at the trembling old
man.*

SHANE: Why didn't you tell me?

*Silence. Shaking his head SHANE rights the furniture. He
picks up his bag.*

SUSAN: You don't have to go.

SHANE: My train.

SUSAN: *(Beat)* It's good you came.

SHANE leaves. JIM stands staring and blank.

SINGERS: On the dole in arcade city
Mind turned numb by bleak self-pity
Finds refuge in the paradise
Of high-tech dreams and neon lies
To build a home and get my share
I signed my name and cropped my hair

On patrol in wartorn city
Mind pierced by the streets of Derry
Finds justice in the voice of those
Who question why my eyes are closed
You see our homes, you see our share
Who signed your name? Who cropped your hair?

The gun we hold in trembling hands
Was aimed by them who stole our lands

SCENE 7: FUTURE

Park. A few days later. 3.30pm. SUSAN in a coat is sat beside KATRINA in jeans and boots. They are sitting on a bench.

SUSAN: He's been quiet for days. Hardly spoken a word. Like a child. Everything's new.

KATRINA: Are you going to leave him?

Silence.

KATRINA: I'm sorry. I didn't mean to −

SUSAN: It's alright. I want to move forward. Not start again. And he listens now. That gives me hope. He listened before, but he couldn't hear. That wasn't his fault. All those screams and accusations ringing in his head. I'm sure he thought you could hear them. You were so quiet. Nothing was beyond questioning with you −

KATRINA: But you've lost twenty years −

SUSAN: We were struggling for life. In a way we hadn't started living. In the quiet − after you both left − I realised we'd been fighting each other just to survive. *(Beat)* It's too easy to stay bitter. *(Watch)* Shouldn't we be leaving? Sandra'll be waiting −

KATRINA: There's plenty of time.

Silence.

SUSAN: Will I kiss her or shake her hand?

KATRINA: *(Laughs)* Sandra couldn't sleep all night. She dreamt you came over with a knife under your coat.

SUSAN: *(Laughs)* What was I like? You know I really wanted to stick him! Imagine trying to explain that to a jury! I'd be locked away!

KATRINA: You should keep that coat –

SUSAN: To show my grandchildren? They'd think I was mad! *(Beat)* Will you have children?

KATRINA: Why not?

SUSAN: *(Beat)* Would she be the dad?

The two women laugh.

KATRINA: We'd better be going. There's a meeting later on tonight. We're organising a march for Irish women prisoners. You can come along if you want. *(Standing)* We have to go. Sandra'll be thinking you're sharpening that knife.

SUSAN: *(Stands. In thought)* You know that baby? *(Beat)* How would you do it?

The two women leave laughing. The laughter is heard offstage and slowly dies away.

Operation Bloody Sunday

Twenty years ago today
when the well-heeled voice of exploitation
scattered a people's protest
into trampled placards and bloodstained shoes
our streets were turned into mazes of terror
operation Bloody Sunday fulfilled

Twenty years ago today
when the sterling voice of occupation
drove a people's vision
behind walls of panic and locked doors of fear
Derry was placed under house arrest
Operation Bloody Sunday fulfilled

Twenty years ago today
when the brutal voice of law and order
decided an innocent people
be murdered fourteen times in one day
Ireland was turned into a silent morgue
Operation Bloody Sunday fulfilled

Twenty years ago today
when Derry marched against internment
I was just two years old
and though I don't remember the handkerchief priest
I carry fourteen scars and I plan to use them
as evidence of Operation Bloody Sunday

Today when we call for justice
with the voice of a million such crimes
let us open our scars
into eyes of hope and rivers of freedom
so that Derry might flow through laughing streets
into a future of no more bloody sundays

Dan Baron Cohen
Derry, North of Ireland, January 30th 1992

One World, One Struggle: mural produced by ***2020 Vision*** in 1991
as a contribution to Central America Week
commemorating the contribution of liberation theology
to the development of an international culture of liberation.

Community mural collaboration between Derry and Managua cultural activists in 1993
coordinated by **Derry Frontline** and funded by **Oxfam**
commemorating active listening as the foundation of all dialogue
and active dialogue between the Northern and Southern hemispheres
in the quest for international justice, democracy and self-determination.

Modern Times

It is said we live in modern times,
In the civilised year of 'seventy nine,
But when I look around, all I see,
Is modern torture, pain and hypocrisy.

In modern times little children die,
They starve to death, but who dares ask why?
And little girls without attire,
Run screaming, napalmed, through the night afire.

And while fat dictators sit upon their thrones,
Young children bury their parents' bones,
And secret police in the dead of night,
Electrocute the naked woman out of night.

In the gutter lies the black man, dead,
And where the oil flows blackest, the street runs red,
And there was He who was born and came to be,
But lived and died without liberty.

As the bureaucrats, speculators and presidents alike,
Pin on their dirty, stinking happy smiles tonight,
The lonely prisoner will cry out from within his tomb,
And tomorrow's wretch will leave it's mother's womb!

Bobby Sands
H-Blocks, North of Ireland 1979

THRESHOLD

Based on workshops held by **Derry Frontline** between April 1990 and April 1992. The *Threshold* workshop included:

Dan Baron Cohen, Marie Curren, Suzanne Curren
Elaine Collins, Tracey Collins, Colin Deane, Ann Deehan
Carol Deehan, Letitia Deehan, Linda Doherty
Stephanie English, Cathy Friel, Bridie Hannigan, Eamonn Kelly
Jim Keys, Sean McKenna, Shaun Maguire, Declan Nelis
Frank Nelis, Paul O'Reilly

The following gave workshop contributions and interviews in the development of the *Threshold* project.

Gerry Adams; Dessie Boyle; Irene Burton; Bernadette Boyle
Jim Collins; Toni Devine; Joe Gallagher; the late Billy Gallagher
Maureen Gallagher; Tony Gillespie; Brendan Hughes
Micky Kinsella; Charles Lamberton; Paul Martin
Donnacha MacNiallas; Bernadette McAliskey; Eoghan McCormac
Charles McDaid; Donnacha McFeely; Sadie McGilloway
Dodie McGuinness; Martin McGuinness; Pat McKeown
Brendan McLaughlin; Mitchell McLaughlin; Daisy Mules
Kevin Murphy; Mary Nelis; Billy Nelis; Peggy O'Hara
Paddy O'Carrol; Lyn O'Connell; Des Wilson

THRESHOLD

SOCIO-POLITICAL CONTEXT

The rapid disintegration of the Soviet Union and the euphoric neoliberal declarations of the 'end of history' and the 'triumph of democracy';

The explicit political formation of a United Europe and manufacture of its 'consent' through (in the North of Ireland) cultural initiatives such as IMPACT 92[1];

A sequence of murders of Sinn Fein councillors, and an increase in military repression throughout 1990-92;

The steady reduction of the Conservative government's tiny majority in the House of Commons, London;

A series of secret talks between Sinn Fein and the British and Dublin governments, through intermediaries, to search for new political solutions to the conflict;

The acceleration of consumerism and europianisation within the popular culture and expectations of Derry.

PROJECT OBJECTIVES

To create a new play to speak to both the nationalist and unionist communities of the need for a radical unity to resist the invisible violence of neo-liberalism;

To create an inclusive cultural intervention beyond the republican enclave of the Bogside;

To initiate a series of innovative cultural strategies (independent pirate community radio, environmentally-friendly graffiti, invisible theatre) to transcend the city's cultural divides.

THEMATIC CONCERNS

To begin to identify the ideological and political coordinates of the 'new world order' in a time of accelerated technological and cultural change;

To explore the potential points of a radical dialogue between the divided working class communities of Derry;

To explore and understand the power of the consumer within the rapidly evolving culture of globalization.

WORKSHOP AND AESTHETIC INNOVATIONS

The construction of a variety of sets through hidden erectable flats within the stage-floor;

The use of the under-stage area as a permanently-present subversive space of buried and repressed histories;

The use of the voice of the underground radio as a narrator.

1 The International Meeting Place of Arts, Culture and Tourism which was held in Derry throughout 1992. After six months of debate, **Derry Frontline** finally agreed to accept a donation from IMPACT 92 to semi-professionalise its production of *Threshold*. For a more detailed analysis of this decision and its consequences, see Pilkington (1994) cited in the introduction to these plays.

THRESHOLD

Useful notes to accompany *Threshold*:

Beat   Signifies a short pause, almost a breath in duration.

Wain   Derry idiom for *child*.

Bru   Derry idiom for *unemployed* or *dole*, as in *bru-cheque*.

Bog   The Bogside, a republican community in Derry.

Comm   *letter* written by republican prisoners, families and activist on tightly folded cigarette papers, wrapped in cellophane and smuggled inside the body, to break the censorship of the prisons.

Wile   Derry idiom for *terrible* or *very*.

Gob   The Gobnascale estate, an area in Derry.

CHARACTERS

MARIE DOHERTY......................................Catholic. Early twenties
BERNIE DOHERTY..Her mother. Fifty
SAM DOHERTY...............Her brother-in-law. Businessman. Fifties
BRIDIE MAGUIRE............His sister. Republican activist. Mid-fifties
COLIN MAGUIRE ....Her son. Activist. Mid twenties
EAMONN MAGUIRE................................Youngest son. Nineteen
LINDA ....His girlfriend. Seventeen
PAULA ....Republican activist. Catholic. Mid twenties
DIANE ....Republican activist. Protestant. Early twenties
ANDREW ROBINSON ....Protestant businessman. Fifties
BISHOP BUTLER...Protestant priest. Fifties
BISHOP DEVLIN....................................Catholic priest. Late fifties
AUXILIARY ....His auxiliary. Thirties
FATHER DECLAN GALLAGHER........Catholic priest. Late twenties
DEIRDRE..His housekeeper. Forties
LETITIA......................................Catholic housewife. Mid twenties
SÉAN ....Her son. Five
ROGUE...Catholic farmer. Late thirties
GERRY ....Presenter. Thirties
MANAGER..Studio audience
CATHY O'HARA...Studio audience
DR DAVID ENGLISH ....Studio audience
FRANK BOYLE ....Studio audience
GRANNY...Studio audience
HEADMASTER ....Studio audience
JOHN KEYS ....Studio audience
SUZANNE BRADY..Studio audience
TRACEY BURTON ....Studio audience

Cast for the 1992 production
Playhouse, Derry, North of Ireland
12-18 December 1992

ANDREW ROBINSON...Kevin O'Grady
AUXILIARY ....Declan Nelis
BERNIE DOHERTY ....Maureen English
BISHOP BUTLER...Willie Curren
BISHOP DEVLIN ....James King
BRIDIE MAGUIRE.....................................Kitty McDaid
CATHY O'HARA ....Marie Curren
COLIN MAGUIRE....................................Declan Nelis
DIANE ....Ann Deehan
DEIRDRE ....Marie Curren
DR DAVID ENGLISH.....................................James King
EAMONN MAGUIRE....................................Colin Deane
FRANK BOYLE ....Declan Nelis
FATHER GALLAGHER...................................Séan Collins
GERRY ....Shaun Maguire
GRANNY...Maureen English
HEADMASTER...................................Dan Baron Cohen
JOHN KEYS ....Colin Deane
LETITIA ....Patrice Meenan
LINDA...Linda Doherty
MANAGER ....Jim Keys
MARIE DOHERTY ....Stephanie English
PAULA...Bridie Hannigan
ROGUE ....Jim Keys
SAM DOHERTY.....................................Gerry Doherty
SÉAN...Kevin Barry Doherty
SUZANNE BRADY...................................Tracey Collins
TRACEY BURTON....................................Tracey Collins

The music for *Threshold* has been written, composed and produced by **RARE** and also includes *Cellophane* by **That Petrol Emotion** and *Dancing In The Streets* by **Martha Reeves and the Vandellas**

Production

ADMINISTRATION COORDINATOR....................Geraldine Emsley

PUBLICITY COORDINATORS ....Julie Doherty; Irene Burton

PUBLICITY TEAM ....Charlie McIntyre; Tara Gallagher
Declan Kierney; Shaun Maguire
Declan Nelis

MURALS COORDINATORS ....Colin Deane; Paul O'Reilly

SET COORDINATOR...Jim Keys

SET TEAM ....Declan Nelis; Shaun Maguire
Tony Doherty; Jim Meenan
Eddie Ogilvie

STAGE COORDINATOR ....Stephen Gargan

STAGE TEAM ....Tracey Collins; Linda Doherty

LIGHTING OPERATOR...Malachy Martin

SOUND OPERATORS ....North West Musicians Collective

PLAYHOUSE COORDINATOR ....Bridie Hannigan

CRECHE COORDINATORS...............Maureen Shiels; Marie Curren
Patrice Meenan

TRANSCRIPTION TEAM....................Tracey Collins; Linda Doherty
Stephanie English; Geraldine Emsley
Carol Deehan; Bridie Hannigan
Colin Deane

INVISIBLE THEATRE TEAM................James King; Bridie Hannigan
Patsy Devine; Theresa McCormick
Julie Hill

PRODUCTION COORDINATOR ....Declan Kierney

WRITER AND DIRECTOR ....Dan Baron Cohen

ACT 1

SCENE 1: AGENT ANONYMOUS

Friday. Mid afternoon. Bogside. BERNIE DOHERTY's home. An upholstered balmoral suite surrounds an oval queen anne coffee-table which stands on a chinese-rug decorating a polished wooden floor. A well-thumbed catalogue lies open beneath a book of accounts beside a vase of satin flowers on the table. Two white shoe-boxes sit on a chair. A dark oak corner-unit focuses the room with a framed wedding photo of JOHN and BERNIE and a matching photo of their three children, perched on either side of a new hitachi. JOHN's eyes follow every movement in the room. BERNIE's eyes gaze innocently up into his ear. A sacred heart glows above the unit between a photo of the Pope and an icon of JFK.

Silence.

BERNIE enters, wearing smart seasonal clothes and sunglasses. She takes off the sunglasses, thrusts them into her shoulder bag and slings the bag onto the sofa.

BERNIE: Bad money cropping up like weeds.

> *She lifts the open catalogue and accounts book onto the sofa and enters the kitchen.*

BERNIE: *(Calls from offstage)* Marie?

> *Sounds of a press being opened and shut. BERNIE returns with a cashbox and sits on the sofa. She places the cashbox on her lap and jerks a purse out of the bag beside her. She opens the purse.*

BERNIE: We all started on our hands and knees.

> *She takes a key from the purse and opens the cashbox.*

BERNIE: *(Calls)* You up there Marie?

> *She places the cashbox beside the vase and empties coins from one compartment of the purse onto the table in front*

of her. She perches on the edge of the sofa and slides the coins one by one rapidly into the palm of her hand.

BERNIE: I warned them all. Each and every one of them. It's not only my good name that's at stake. We're like a chain. Each customer effects all the others. *(Beat)* Nineteen pound twenty one Saint Vincent De Paul.

She lifts the coins into the cashbox.

BERNIE: Probably wind up in some cheap whore's bank account.

She locks the cashbox and slides it back next to the vase.

BERNIE: Breaks your heart to say no. *(Unfolds banknotes from inside the purse)* Banty wains hanging round their necks and clinging to their legs. *(Empties coins from another compartment)* You can smell the poverty off them. God luck to the critters. Least I bring some purpose and colour into their godforsaken lives. *(Licks her forefinger and counts)* Live now and pay later. Better than shivering in the dark praying for miracles. Sixty nine fifty the catalogue. Have to tighten the screw.

She stands and walks to the unit. She reaches for a key behind the sacred heart and kneels.

BERNIE: *(Full volume)* Marie!

She looks up at the ceiling and listens intently. Silence. She unlocks the unit door and slides out a black box and a red box of index cards.

BERNIE: *(Reaches for a pen and calculator)* Out galavanting all hours. Spends the day in a coma. Should never've allowed her across the water. What that wee girl needs is a husband. Bring some life into this morgue.

She returns to the sofa and places the index boxes on the table in front of her. She sits and lifts the accounts book onto her lap. She opens the book and lifts the lids of the index boxes.

BERNIE: All them figures. *(Calculator in hand)* She could do all this bound and gagged.

With laboured precision, she moves between the book and the index cards, calling out names and entering updated figures. She stops in frustration.

BERNIE: *(Fury)* Marie!

She puts the accounts book down beside her on the sofa and strides out of the room. Sound of stairs being climbed.

BERNIE: *(Off)* Rooms have to be vacated by midday. Marie?

Silence. Sound of BERNIE bolting down the stairs. She rushes into the sitting room, shoves the loose index cards inside the accounts book, and tucks the banknotes and coins into the back of the black box. She carefully lifts the coffee-table behind a chair and leaves for the kitchen. A voice in the distance.

LETITIA: *(Off)* Get in here now! Wait till your father gets home!

BERNIE returns with a breadknife and broom. She places the knife on the sofa and leans the broom against the chair. She kneels and efficiently rolls back the chinese-rug. Suddenly she freezes. She furtively slips the knife between the sofa cushions and stands, reaching for the broom.

BERNIE: *(Sweeping)* Dust gets everywhere.

She leans the broom back against the chair and walks over to the unit. She lies the wedding photo face down and stands completely still. She listens intently. Silence. She returns to the sofa, finds the breadknife, and kneels on the floor. She levers back a board, then pulls out a second, leaving an oblong hole in the floor in front of the sofa. She reaches for one of the shoe boxes and inserts it into the hole. She stands, picks up the broom and shunts the box under the floor with the handle. Dull sound of metal scraping stone. She stops bewildered.

BERNIE: Dear god.

She feels underground with the broom. The same sound as the broom catches something metallic. She crosses herself.

BERNIE: Sweet Jesus protect us!

She leaves for the kitchen. A voice in the distance.

LETITIA: *(Off)* Another whimper out of you and you're dead!

BERNIE returns with a torch. She leans the broom against the chair, kneels, crosses herself, then shines the torch under the floor.

BERNIE: Nothing. *(Giggles)* Punishing myself.

She puts down the torch, reaches for the other box, inserts it in the hole and then stands. She picks up the broom and thrusts the box deep into the centre of the room. The same sound again. She stares in terror. Sudden realisation.

BERNIE: Jesus, Mary and Saint Joseph no! Not my Marie!

A knock on the door. BERNIE stares at the door. She grips the broom in fear.

LETITIA: *(Off)* Stand you there –

BERNIE: She gave her word –

LETITIA: *(Off)* And don't you be questioning me!

BERNIE looks up. Her mind races. She looks round the room.

BERNIE: Hail, Holy Queen, Mother of Mercy, hail our life, our
            sweetness and our hope –

LETITIA: (Off) Bernie?

BERNIE: To thee do we cry, poor banished children –

LETITIA: (Off) I don't want to hear another word out of you!

            *LETITIA knocks again, more forcefully. BERNIE stares.
            Suddenly she withdraws the broom and kneels. She slots
            the floorboards back into place with unsteady hands.*

BERNIE: To thee do we send up our sighs, mourning and weeping
            in this vale –

LETITIA: (Off) Bernie. It's me. Letitia –

BERNIE: Turn then, most gracious advocate, thine eyes of mercy
            towards us –

            BERNIE unrolls the rug back into place.

LETITIA: (Off) Take your hands out of your eyes!

BERNIE: And after this our exile –

            BERNIE lifts the coffee-table back into its original position.

BERNIE: Show unto us the blessed fruit of thy womb, Jesus –

LETITIA: (Off) Dry them tears and put a smile on your face!

            *BERNIE picks up the torch and breadknife and impulsively
            thrusts them into the unit. She looks around the room.
            LETITIA knocks a third time.*

BERNIE: That we may be worthy of the promises of Christ amen.

LETITIA: (Off) There now! Missed her on account of your tantrums!

BERNIE leans the broom against the wall, takes a deep breath, and opens the door.

LETITIA: You're in –

BERNIE: Letitia.

LETITIA: We were just about to leave –

BERNIE: Come in –

LETITIA: *(To SEAN)* You'll be there son, when I come out for you.

LETITIA and BERNIE enter the sitting room.

LETITIA: Ach the room's looking gorgeous Bernie. New rug?

BERNIE: *(Smiles)* Aye –

LETITIA: *(Sits)* Seen Sam Doherty's picture in today's Journal –

BERNIE: *(Sits)* Aye he flies in Sunday. Won't be stopping here but. Needs a hotel for all them meetings. Ten years this Monday since he last stepped through that door. *(Glances over at the wedding photo)* Flew in for John's funeral.

BERNIE stands.

LETITIA: He'll not recognise Derry now with the town-centre so clean and new-looking –

BERNIE: Aye, providing it's still standing when he lands in –

BERNIE walks over to the unit and lifts the photo.

LETITIA: My Sean's afeared to walk into the town –

BERNIE: They've this community living on the edge of a pill. The heart disease. The drinking and gambling. Wains dobbing school and upcasting their elders. Even the falling away from the church –

LETITIA: If he's not out there with a stone in his hand, he's crouching behind some wall like a British soldier –

BERNIE: I thank god my boys are away. Least they can lie in their beds knowing their wains aren't up to god knows what in the middle of the night. John made them promise. The night of Bloody Sunday. No revenge. It was like an oath. And the boys had good cause for revenge. For John was murdered that day. You listen to Sam. He's always on about his brother. At them big dinners in the States. Took him ten years to die, Letitia. That was the day he stopped living but. The bullet never even pierced his skin. Ricocheted off his cigarette case and burned a hole in the breast pocket of his jacket getting out.

BERNIE looks at the photo.

BERNIE: He never marched again. Hardly said a word. Lovely eyes. Kept the jacket years. Evidence he used to say. But no revenge. Sam's the same eyes.

LETITIA: *(Beat)* I'd like to see that jacket. Show it to my Sean –

BERNIE: John burned it. Just before he died. As though he knew.

LETITIA: *(Beat)* Knew what?

BERNIE: *(Beat)* Sun's splitting the sky and we're talking about death.

LETITIA: *(Pause)* Bernie –

BERNIE: They should make that Bishop a saint.

LETITIA: *(Pause)* Bernie. I'm down about the money –

BERNIE: Money?

LETITIA: I can't even buy milk for the wain.

BERNIE stands with the wedding photo in her hands and stares at the index cards.

BERNIE: *(Flat)* End of the month. You promised –

LETITIA: He spent it, Bernie. Go ask the bookies if you don't –

BERNIE looks through LETITIA.

LETITIA: I was wondering. Just for the weekend. Girobank Monday –

BERNIE: *(Hard)* We've all our debts to pay, Letitia.

LETITIA: And I'm your weak link...

LETITIA stands.

LETITIA: Sean's outside waiting.

BERNIE focuses on LETITIA. LETITIA moves to the door.

BERNIE: I'll write to the catalogue the night.

LETITIA: *(Beat)* I'll see meself out.

LETITIA leaves. BERNIE sits exhausted. She stares at the index cards. The wedding photo lies in her lap.

LETITIA: *(Off)* C'mon mucker.

Silence. BERNIE lifts the photograph. MARIE suddenly enters. She carries a wrapped bottle of wine in one hand, and a book and a file in the other.

MARIE: There the wine you were asking for.

BERNIE cannot speak. MARIE notices the photograph.

MARIE: You alright?

Silence. MARIE puts the wine down on the unit.

MARIE: What's the breadknife and the torch doing in there?

           BERNIE looks away.

MARIE: I'm away on to lie down. Long day in the library —

BERNIE: Marie —

MARIE: I don't need a husband, ma.

           MARIE leaves. BERNIE stares after her.

SCENE 2: PAGEANT

Monday. Late afternoon. The Richmond Centre. MARIE and DIANE sit at a cafe-table on the first floor of the Centre. In the centre of the arcade, a PHOTOGRAPHER, ANDREW ROBINSON, BISHOP BUTLER and FATHER GALLAGHER impatiently await the arrival of SAM DOHERTY. The PRIEST stands awkwardly with an enormous cardboard cheque, while BISHOP DEVLIN greets parishioners. LINDA and EAMONN quarrel in front of a jeweller's window. LETITIA and SEAN stand invisibly in another corner, surrounded by shopping. LETITIA has her head inside her purse. SEAN tugs continually at her sleeve. A crowd of BYSTANDERS have begun to gather, shopping-bags in their hands.

LINDA: Ach don't be tight –

EAMONN: I've nearly that claim all spent –

LINDA: Eamonn, you promised. That's what we came down for –

EAMONN: Why do we need to get engaged but?

LINDA: We've been through all this. For the wain. To make us complete.

EAMONN: Aye. In their eyes –

LINDA: No. In ours. I don't feel secure –

EAMONN: It's a piece of metal, Linda –

LINDA: *(Twining herself round his neck and legs)* You know you want to –

EAMONN: Jesus wee girl! The whole of Derry's watching!

LINDA: I could jump ye right here!

BISHOP B: I understand you've secured a primetime slot?

ROBINSON: Wednesday week –

BISHOP B: Very wise. Build confidence. Perfect timing of course –

PHOTO: Any sign of the main man?

ROBINSON: He's just renewing old acquaintances –

PHOTO: If this doesn't get down to the Journal by five –

BISHOP B: And there's the concelebration –

ROBINSON: He knows. We've a tight schedule ourselves –

DIANE: But your ma lives for moments like this –

MARIE: She's in a state of shock. He's the spit of me da –

DIANE: Has he any sons?

MARIE: Married to a chain of superstores –

DIANE: Well, if he needs an escort –

MARIE: Right, Diane –

DIANE: I've a wee love nest lying empty –

SEAN: *(Pointing)* Over there mammy! Mammy look –

LETITIA: *(Pencil and paper)* Five the credit union. Six the provident.
             Fourteen the coalman –

SEAN: The lasergun in the windy –

LETITIA: Did I unpin the meter before we left –

SEAN: That's the one me daddy promised –

LETITIA: Three ten the rates. *(Purse)* Should leave two sixty for his
             chops.

SEAN: Can I go for a wee duke, mammy –

SAM DOHERTY strides in. LETITIA remains locked inside her calculations. Everyone turns.

SAM: What a welcome! What a homecoming! Never experienced anything like it! Have I kept yous waiting? Sorry! Sorry! But it makes you want to weep! It's all changed! Well at least we picked the right spot. You had your doubts, Robinson! But I knew it! Soon as it came to me! Used to be the old pawnshop, Bishop. Right where you're standing now. What a crowd! That's a cheque your holding, Father! Not a coffin! What's wrong? Have yous all lost your voices? *(Watch)* My God, look at the time! Forgive me. Right. Where d'you want me –

SAM recognises an old friend in the crowd.

SAM: I don't believe my eyes! *(Shakes hands)* Robinson, look! Ya mad dog ye! Still racing the oul greyhounds? Good luck to you, mucker! Didn't I say I'd be back? You don't leave your own people behind ye! Never know what they might be saying behind your back! *(With energy)* Don't remember the name but sure as hell recognise the face! Just remind me –

The BYSTANDER answers.

SAM: *(Repeats the name aloud)* How could I forget? Robinson –

ROBINSON: Sam, the time –

SAM: You only come home once man!

PHOTO: Mr Doherty –

SAM: What a people! What a city!

ROBINSON: *(To the PHOTOGRAPHER)* Whenever you're ready –

PHOTO: I'm standing here this last twenty minutes!

            SAM continues to shake hands with random BYSTANDERS.

BISHOP B: *(To ROBINSON)* Do you want me round the back –

ROBINSON: You'll have to ask him –

BISHOP D: *(To BISHOP B)* I imagine it's the usual –

PHOTO: *(Watch)* This is madness –

BISHOP B: *(To the PRIEST)* D'you get to hold the cheque then?

PHOTO: They hold the cheque. Yous stand behind.

            *The PHOTOGRAPHER decisively starts to move each
            person into their respective places as SAM continues
            greeting random BYSTANDERS. The BYSTANDERS clear a
            space.*

LETITIA: Been shortchanged. No other explanation –

SEAN: *(Tugging)* Please, mammy –

LETITIA: You'll get a wee duke off me if you don't button it!

            *LETITIA snaps shut her purse and gets down on one knee.
            She begins to search the shopping-bags. SEAN eyes the
            shop window.*

EAMONN: Linda, let's go –

LINDA: Man of the people? He's a whoring facelift!

EAMONN: Why don't you shout something then?

LINDA: Aye right. Anyway who does he think he's fooling?

EAMONN: All them down there –

LINDA: Look the wee priest, Eamonn! Make a cracker poster —

EAMONN: Linda, I've still that editing to finish —

LINDA: Go you on. I want to see the crack —

The PHOTOGRAPHER has now positioned the two BISHOPS behind ROBINSON. The BYSTANDERS watch in fascinated expectation. LETITIA begins to search with feverish anxiety.

PHOTO: *(To the PRIEST)* Now you pass him the cheque —

The PRIEST lifts the cheque over to ROBINSON with evident relief.

SAM: *(Shaking hands with a BYSTANDER)* You're very kind. Call me —

PHOTO: Mr Doherty. If you don't mind —

LETITIA: There'll be murder if he doesn't get his chops —

SAM joins the tableau. LETITIA searches frantically through another bag.

SAM: Right. You've my undivided attention —

PHOTO: *(To the PRIEST)* You in this too?

PRIEST: I'd upset the balance —

SAM: *(To ROBINSON)* All them years. Makes it all worthwhile —

PHOTO: *(Camera)* Tighter at the back please gentlemen —

The first full tableau. The BYSTANDERS hold their breath.

DIANE: Something compelling about his eyes —

MARIE: It's obscene, Diane —

PHOTO: *(Poised)* Alright. Don't anyone move –

LETITIA: *(Kneeling)* Have to find that receipt –

SAM: *(Hands up)* Hold it! Hold it! This's all wrong –

PHOTO: Jesus Christ! *(Raises a hand)* Sorry, sorry –

SAM: Change round. This's *our* gift –

            The PHOTOGRAPHER lowers his camera in exasperation.

SAM: Our gift. So yous hold the cheque. We look on –

BISHOP D: Does it really matter Sam? It's all the same –

            *SAM passes the cheque to the BISHOPS and stands
            behind them.*

SAM: Could have been catastrophic. Historic moment this –

BISHOP B: Sponsors would've grumbled –

SAM: And we don't want to be confusing the people –

            *ROBINSON moves behind the BISHOPS and stands beside
            SAM. The group poses again.*

LETITIA: *(Searching)* He'll accuse me of spending it on myself –

PHOTO: *(Camera)* Happy now, Mr Doherty?

SAM: That's it. Fire away. No, wait! Wait! Just had an idea –

EAMONN: Now what?

LINDA: Wants to expose himself –

SAM: Turn to one side. *(The BISHOPS turn in opposite
            directions)* No. Not like that –

SAM turns the BISHOPS so that they face each other. The BYSTANDERS are curious. SAM comes to the front of the group to develop the idea.

LETITIA: In here somewhere −

SAM: Arms out straight now −

BISHOP D: Sam −

SAM: Hands closer together −

BISHOP B: Mr Doherty −

SAM: But not touching −

BISHOP D: They won't see our faces now −

SAM: That's it! Just like the sculpture!

SAM rejoins the group and completes the tableau. The PHOTOGRAPHER raises his camera. LETITIA starts to search her final bag. SEAN begins to drift.

SAM: Now that will have impact!

PHOTO: *(Camera poised)* Alright gentlemen. Just getting the new focus −

SEAN: Mammy, I'm bored!

LETITIA: Dear God! It must be in this one!

PHOTO: *(Poised)* Steady with the cheque. Steady! Hold it right there and −

SEAN runs across the floor and crosses in front of the tableau just as the camera flashes. An enormous howl from the PHOTOGRAPHER.

PHOTO: Jesus!

*The PHOTOGRAPHER's reaction paralyses SEAN at the
centre of the tableau. The cry jolts LETITIA out of her
search. She looks up immediately and instantly grasps the
situation.*

LETITIA: *(Hands to her head)* Oh my God! Sean!

LINDA: Ya boy ye!

LETITIA: Look what you've done!

SEAN: A wee duke mammy! Just a wee duke!

*Laughter from the BYSTANDERS and the tableau. Even the
PHOTOGRAPHER smiles. It is a nightmare for LETITIA.
SAM is the first to respond.*

SAM: *(On one knee)* Sean?

SEAN: Got any odds?

*SAM roars with laughter. The PHOTOGRAPHER catches
the moment. LETITIA stands in the corner in acute
embarrassment. Her hands are pressed to her face.*

SAM: Some things never change! *(Extends a hand)* Uncle Sam.
             Pleased to meet you.

*SEAN looks over at LETITIA. The laughter dies away.
SEAN shakes SAM's hand.*

SAM: Where's your mammy, Sean?

SEAN points out LETITIA. SAM gestures to LETITIA.

SAM: Come on over! Don't be shy!

*Applause as LETITIA falters forward. SAM scoops SEAN
into his arms and stands. The camera flashes.*

SAM: You're a lovely wee boy –

LETITIA: I'm while sorry.

SAM: Don't apologise. Hold your head up! Go on!

LETITIA: I – I –

SAM puts his arm around LETITIA's shoulder and turns to ROBINSON. The camera flashes repeatedly.

SAM: Andrew this is Derry! Real salt of the earth Derry! This is why I've returned! This wee boy and his mother! These are my people! And these are the people I've fought for all my life! *(To LETITIA)* We don't have to apologise any more! We don't have to beg for work in foreign countries! We don't have to hide who we are or block out the world in some ghetto bar! Any odds? Any odds? What kind of question is that from an innocent wain? What kind of vision is that at this moment of breathtaking change?

SAM lifts SEAN high into the air. The camera flashes.

SAM: Derry people have no reason to beg, Sean! Not any more! And we will not lower our eyes in shame, Sean! Never again! The future is your's! You are a citizen of the world, Sean!

Applause from the BYSTANDERS. The PHOTOGRAPHER finds the angle.

SEAN: Can I get down now?

SAM: *(Laughs)* Can I get down. *(Lowers SEAN)* What were you duking at Sean?

SEAN: *(Looks at LETITIA)* The lasergun in the windy.

SAM: *(Produces a £50 note)* Go you and buy yourself that wee gun –

LETITIA: No, please. I'm broke to the bone –

SAM: *(Tucking the note inside SEAN's hand)* A wee gift.

LETITIA: What d'you say to the kind man Sean?

SEAN: *(Smiles)* Thank you. *(Thumb)* Mucker.

SAM: *(Thumb)* Mucker.

The camera flashes. LETITIA leads SEAN away. SAM stands.

SAM: Let's get back to it.

The BISHOPS and the BUSINESSMEN regroup into the tableau. LETITIA leads SEAN to the cafe tables.

LETITIA: *(To MARIE)* I don't know where to put myself. Would you mind them messages while I take the wain to the toilet? I won't be two minutes.

MARIE: *(Smiles)* Aye surely.

LETITIA yanks SEAN away into the toilets.

DIANE: She looks shattered. I'm away –

MARIE: Just let me hand him me ma's letter –

DIANE: I can't take any more Marie. And I'm already late for a meeting. Your bru cheque's lying in the flat.

MARIE: The fear in her eyes, Diane.

DIANE: I know. And you'll have to eat with him.

DIANE leaves. The tableau is once more in place. MARIE looks on. A cameraflash. The BYSTANDERS applaud and disperse as the tableau eases apart. BISHOP BUTLER passes the cardboard cheque to the PRIEST. SAM looks suddenly haggard.

LINDA: They should bomb this whoring pit!

EAMONN: The man's no fool. I'll give him that –

LINDA: I nearly died when he put his arms around your woman!

EAMONN and LINDA leave. The PHOTOGRAPHER unloads his film. The PRIEST hovers.

ROBINSON: You certainly seized the moment –

SAM: I meant every word, Andrew –

BISHOP D: There's a wee parable in this –

ROBINSON: Let's save it for Wednesday night. Craft village at eight?

BISHOP D: God willing. Oh, and thank you both –

ROBINSON: *(Raises a hand magnanimously)* We won't be needing that any more.

The PRIEST smiles and takes the cardboard cheque off in the direction of the toilets. The PHOTOGRAPHER cuts in.

PHOTO: Magic! I'll run these over right away. You'll have copies in the morning –

SAM: *(Shakes hands)* Many thanks. God bless.

The PHOTOGRAPHER leaves.

BISHOP B: Heard alot about you Sam. But back there. Brought tears to my eyes –

ROBINSON: *(Arm around SAM)* Let's get the old hawk back to the hotel. Early start in the morning, Sam –

SAM: Mistake not having the TV here, Andrew –

              *The BISHOPS and BUSINESSMEN leave. A singsong voice
              alerts customers to the final bargains of the day. New
              CUSTOMERS weave across the floor. MARIE has not
              moved. LETITIA enters. Her hands and clothes are
              spattered in blood. She is guided by two SECURITY
              GUARDS.*

LETITIA: *(Stops)* I've a lovely wee boy. There'll be murder if he
              doesn't get his chops –

GUARD 1:   No need for alarm. An ambulance's been called –

              *The PRIEST enters carrying an unconscious SEAN. SEAN's
              face is clattered in blood. MARIE stands abruptly and
              stares. BYSTANDERS begin to gather.*

PRIEST: Please keep calm. Just let us pass –

GUARD 2:   Everything's under control.

              *The two GUARDS escort LETITIA out. The PRIEST follows,
              carrying SEAN. MARIE's mouth is contorted with rage.*

SCENE 3: ANNUNCIATION

Wednesday night. The DOHERTY home. MARIE's bedroom. MARIE sits wrapped in a blanket at her desk. The room is lit by a single candle which stands on the desk beside an open notebook and a tape-recorder. A group of girls can be heard singing outside in the street. MARIE listens to their songs. She suddenly puts down her pen and walks to the window. Without looking out, she shuts it sharply and returns to the desk. The songs are now barely audible.

MARIE: Now then. You've written it there. Now say it.

                She inhales deeply and presses the record button on the tape-recorder. She gathers herself to speak and opens her mouth. Nothing. The words are locked within. With an intense effort, she tries to will them into the open. Nothing. The muted songs of the girls outside turn into street games. MARIE sits angrily back in her chair and pulls the blanket round her. She looks at the window.

MARIE: How many women sit alone in the dark? Their lives shattered by men?

                She pulls the notebook towards her and reads. She pushes it away in frustration.

MARIE: Words. So worn out. Wouldn't trust them as far as I could throw them.

                Silence. The girls outside go. A bell rings. MARIE looks at her watch and slips the blanket onto the chair. She stands and presses the pause button. She blows out the candle and goes downstairs. She opens the door. The PRIEST stands with his head bowed.

PRIEST: Hello, Marie. I wasn't sure you were in. The lights were out –

MARIE: Come in.

The PRIEST enters the sitting room. MARIE follows and turns on a light.

PRIEST: May I sit down?

MARIE gestures to the sofa. The PRIEST sits. MARIE takes the armchair.

PRIEST: That was a shocking incident the other day. I understood as soon as you called. *(Pause)* You'll be glad to hear they've released the child. It's a miracle he escaped unharmed. The city's littered with human debris. There's so little fuse wire left. A single event could spark an orgy of destruction.

MARIE stares at the PRIEST.

PRIEST: I'm seeing the poor mother tomorrow. She's been under heavy sedation ever since. It may be for the best the child's taken into care for a time. And to think we were all there. Just minutes before. And then the boy's blood. All over the cubicle walls. I've hardly slept –

MARIE: It happens round here all the time. And you know it. The blood's washed away. The scapegoat's sedated and entered into a file. And you catch up on your sleep. What you don't notice is the drugs wear off. And the wain out looking for revenge. Till he knifes his girlfriend or jumps into the Foyle. Then you write a sermon. And the file turns into a crime.

PRIEST: *(Beat)* Fortunately there are men like your uncle who break the cycle –

MARIE: You know it's a lie! I watched you squirm with that cheque! Whether my uncle knows it or not, his shopping centres are used to hide the truth. The slaughter that's meant to stay out of sight.

PRIEST: Marie. I understand and share your frustration –

MARIE: I think you'd better leave —

PRIEST: Will you let me explain? *(Beat)* I know those shopping
            centres offer only illusions. Of paradise on earth, if you
            want. But they divert anger. And I comfort myself that
            they educate —

MARIE: They what?

PRIEST: They convert anger into pleasure. But only for a time. As
            people become bored they will search for something
            deeper. Life will seem meaningless. They'll experience a
            spiritual hunger. I can't teach them that. We must be
            patient —

MARIE: The wain was nearly killed!

PRIEST: Marie, people only change one step at a time. They
            couldn't abandon the damp of their slums fast enough to
            climb into the warmth of the high flats. One generation
            later and the flats were lying empty in ruins. We learn
            through suffering. Faith too is a matter of choice. In the
            meantime it's my responsibility to heal the wounds inside.
            So that we don't mutilate ourselves. Or our own.

            MARIE stands and goes to the window.

PRIEST: I suffer too, Marie.

            *Silence. MARIE looks out of the window. The PRIEST
            stands.*

MARIE: Declan. Will you hear my confession?

PRIEST: Confession? *(Beat)* Aye. Surely. Come you down —

MARIE: Now, Declan. I've an urgent decision to make the night.

PRIEST: *(Watch)* What's on your mind, Marie?

MARIE: I don't want guidance. Or judgement.

PRIEST: I understand.

            The PRIEST sits. MARIE turns slowly to face him.

MARIE: This is confidential –

PRIEST: Of course. You have my word. Do you want to sit down?

MARIE: Four months ago I was raped. Out there in the back alley
            behind our house. While I was unconscious. It was late.
            My head was pounding away when I came round. From
            the weapon he must've used. I thought I'd been tripped.
            Or mugged. I felt sick so I headed straight for my bed. I
            must've fell into a deep sleep for when I woke I thought
            I'd dreamt it. Till I seen the gash here. *(Head)* And the
            bruising. On my neck and my thighs. I ran a bath and
            scrubbed the whole of my body for hours. But I couldn't
            get rid of the feeling of dirt. Inside. I tried to put the fear
            of rape out of my mind. I found some makeup and
            covered the cut and bruises so it was impossible to see
            them. I even replaced the makeup so me ma wouldn't
            suspect. I went into the town. But these wee voices kept
            needling me. Dressed for action, Marie? On your own late
            at night? Sounds mad. I know. Just like the films. But the
            voices are there. What about that wee fantasy, Marie? At
            the back of your womb?

            Silence.

PRIEST: Marie, those voices –

MARIE: Are inside, Father. I know. Because one of them's yours.

            MARIE reflects.

MARIE: Three days of needling interrogation. No sleep. No breaks.
            Round and round. Always washing and always the same
            verdict. If I'd dreamt it, I'd desired it. If I'd been raped, I
            was the one responsible. Either way I was guilty. I thought
            I'd go mad. I had to return to the alley. Just to prove the

fantasy was a lie. The black tights were lying there. Next to the bins. I almost cried out! I couldn't touch them. But at least they were real. That night I slept like a wain. When I woke the next morning I nearly died! The bruises had faded away to nothing! I had to have the tights in my hand. I headed out into the lane. They were gone! It was as if the facts were conspiring against the truth!

MARIE returns to the window.

MARIE: There was no point reporting it. You're the first person I've told. I've not even been able to speak the word till the night.

Silence.

PRIEST: Marie –

MARIE: *(Turns suddenly)* No. I've listened to you all my life. Now you're going to listen to me. For four months I've been tormented by a guilt that had nothing to do with the crime. I always knew that. But I couldn't convince myself. Until I seen that wee boy and his mother. She'll probably spend the rest of her days tortured by a crime she didn't commit. But at least she's freed me. And when I seen that wain all clattered in blood I knew I couldn't lie to myself any longer. I tested myself the same night. I'm four months pregnant. Just when I was beginning to live and know what I wanted. I feel no anger towards the child. No revenge. But I can't find one reason to bring an innocent wain into this world.

Silence.

MARIE: Learn through suffering, Father?

PRIEST: There can be no justification for the cruelty you've suffered, Marie. And to suffer in such isolation. Perhaps a word with your mother –

MARIE: You taught her to kneel and suffer in silence. To love
            repentance. Not herself. To run to you from the world.
            And because she believes she is guilty and relies on your
            judgement, she's afraid to think. Afraid to act. For herself.
            She thinks and acts according to your conscience. Not her
            own. You taught her to judge without understanding and
            for four months it was her voice that nearly drove me
            insane.

PRIEST: She's a good woman, Marie. And you're her daughter.
            She might even –

MARIE: Take the wain? Aye. The self-sacrifice's that deeply
            ingrained. But don't you see? It doesn't matter who rears
            the wain. I won't bring a life into this world to tremble in
            corners and cry in the dark. I won't bring this life into a
            world where to eat it must consent to famine. Why should
            I give birth to a wain that must learn to lie to survive the
            truth?

PRIEST: If there's no anger in your heart towards the child you
            could teach it –

MARIE: To what? Step over the debris?

PRIEST: Of course not. To support and to heal –

MARIE: Heal my hole! Read the Journal! The city's coming down
            with rape and abuse! Let alone all the casualties of a war
            that only makes it into the paper by elbowing its way
            between smiling faces of confirmations and deals! And
            what's to stop me ending up like your woman?

PRIEST: Marie –

MARIE: Or my own wain ending up like this?

PRIEST: Marie. Your anger's only natural. But you must have hope –

MARIE: Must? Must? Have hope in the future? Why *must* I when
            all we're fed to explain the madness is stories of revenge

and despair? Have faith in people? Why *must* I when we're forcefed lies and impossible dreams every minute of the day? And you've the nerve to talk of human debris!

PRIEST: I understand –

MARIE: You don't understand! You're trying to massage my anger till you convince me to keep the wain! You don't understand that to bring this wain into the world would be a selfish act of murder! And cowardice! And you'll never be able to understand! Because even you could open your eyes to the real cause of the suffering, you will never give birth! You'll never give birth to fear and rape! And you'll never give birth to genocide! You'll never be condemned by your own flesh and –

MARIE suddenly collapses exhausted.

MARIE: Don't worry. I'm not about to miss on me ma's new rug. *(Beat)* I've not eaten for two days.

PRIEST: *(Beat)* There must be something in the kitchen.

MARIE: Can't keep it down.

PRIEST: *(Beat)* Will you take some water?

The PRIEST lowers his eyes.

MARIE: *(Beat)* I'll try a wee taste later on.

PRIEST: You despise me –

MARIE: No. I see you for what you are.

Silence. MARIE sits back in the armchair. The PRIEST stands and goes to the window. Silence.

PRIEST: Will you terminate the pregnancy?

MARIE: Terminate?

PRIEST: It's not uncommon for women in your situation –

MARIE: Abortion's no solution –

PRIEST: You'd have to act immediately –

The PRIEST turns suddenly to face MARIE.

PRIEST: What? What did you say?

MARIE: The suffering goes on.

PRIEST: *(Beat)* Aye. So it does. *(Beat)* But you can be counselled –

MARIE: You don't understand.

PRIEST: *(Beat)* You can come to me. In confidence. *(Beat)* Come to terms with the anger and the loss step by step –

MARIE: It papers over the cracks. Disappears again into the silence.

The PRIEST stares at MARIE.

PRIEST: Marie. You have to think practically –

MARIE: I'm are. Women and children are being tortured as we speak –

PRIEST: For the love of Christ, Marie! You have to decide! There's a child growing inside you as we speak! *(Beat)* Listen to me, Marie. Have you ever seen a child of sixteen weeks in the womb? It's the size of my hand. It can use its own hands! To grasp. To push. Maybe you've not yet felt it but it can twist and turn –

MARIE: Aye, in agony. In rage –

PRIEST: Marie, listen to reason! I beg you to hear me! You've no time to lose! We'll come back to all this. I promise we will! *(Beat)* You sound so clear. Even in anger. But your judgement must be affected. Be guided by me. As a friend. Decisions now have to be made. Arrangements take time. *(Beat)* I could give you the money –

MARIE: You'd do that?

PRIEST: Aye!

MARIE: *(Beat)* Why but?

The PRIEST looks at MARIE and smiles.

PRIEST: Because I know you've suffered. Because I held you in these arms when you were a child. That's all I remember of Bloody Sunday. You and the cold sunshine. And a people on its knees. That's why I became a priest.

A bond. A moment of possible understanding. MARIE reflects.

MARIE: Would you make your help known?

PRIEST: I don't understand –

MARIE: To your parish. Would you explain?

PRIEST: Marie. Do you realise what you're asking?

MARIE: Aye. I'm asking you to break the silence. If you can condemn the guns and bombs then surely you can speak out against the violence people don't see –

PRIEST: I'd be seen to be supporting abortion –

MARIE: No. You'd be explaining the violence that makes abortion necessary. You'd be exposing the silence that allows it to go on.

The PRIEST sits. He puts his head in his hands. MARIE continues gently.

MARIE: Stand beside me Declan. As a friend and as a priest. Think
          of your woman. And the wee boy you held in your arms.
          It's an undeclared war, Declan. Only people don't see it
          because the uniforms are so new. We still think war
          means mortars and guns. It's like expecting propaganda
          to point and wave flags. Not smile and wink like
          catalogues. *(Pause)* I could accept abortion. If you stood
          beside me.

          Silence. The PRIEST shakes his head.

MARIE: You ask me to mutilate myself and then live a lie?

PRIEST: No −

MARIE: You ask me to destroy the only evidence I have so that
          everything can return to its normal state of madness?

PRIEST: No, Marie −

MARIE: Then why keep your support secret?

PRIEST: Not secret, Marie. Discreet −

MARIE: Discreet? Discreet! They use your discreet silence to mop
          up their blood! Have you no conscience?

PRIEST: I'm bound by the laws of the Catholic church!

MARIE: Didn't our Lord speak out? Didn't he follow the voice of
          his conscience?

PRIEST: But the parish would never understand!

MARIE: How will they ever? When you walk with the rapists out
          in the open but you won't be seen dead next to me?

          The PRIEST looks away.

MARIE: You don't want paradise on earth. It would spoil the design of your world. You need the tragedy to justify your existence. And I confide in you.

MARIE returns to the window.

PRIEST: Marie. I can support you in private –

MARIE: Charity, Father. Not change. It shrouds me in pity. To hide the cause. And it allows you to salve your conscience. The worst kind of hypocrisy. By choosing to remain silent –

PRIEST: Marie, I'd be completely isolated –

MARIE: You side against me –

PRIEST: No Marie!

MARIE: And against all the women and children of this city. Of the world.

MARIE turns to face the PRIEST. He cannot meet her eye.

MARIE: You're afraid. Afraid to question. Afraid to stand alone. I can understand that. But you're also afraid to lose all your status and privilege. As a priest. And as a man. And armed with all that you're dangerous.

MARIE goes to the door and opens it. The PRIEST stands.

PRIEST: What will you do?

MARIE: Save your pity Father. For the human debris.

The PRIEST leaves. MARIE closes the door. She turns off the light and sits in the darkness of the sitting room. It is lit only by the glow of the sacred heart.

MARIE: You raped me, Derry. Entered me without my consent. Your darkness hid the rock that knocked me unconscious. Your streets held me down while you tore me open and emptied your lust into my womb. I will not give birth to that. This child will speak for them who walk your streets in fear. This child will cry out against your unborn crimes. Even you planted a seed of pain inside this womb, I'll not carry your suffering into the future. No child of mine will be a monument to revenge. That is my choice. And none of your laws or constitutions or flags of war will change my mind.

Sounds of laughter outside. MARIE sits forward and listens.

BERNIE: *(Off)* Can't get it in, Sam –

SAM: *(Off)* Give it a wiggle then –

BERNIE: *(Off)* There! It's in. *(Beat)* S'in the wrong hole Sam –

SAM: *(Off)* Here. Give it to me –

MARIE darts into the kitchen. Sounds of knowing laughter. The door opens and BERNIE enters wearing an evening dress. She collapses in a heap of laughter onto the sofa.

BERNIE: Can't breath. Dress'll be the death of me –

SAM enters laughing. He wears an elegant suit with a red carnation in his lapel.

SAM: The Bishop's face.

BERNIE: He was winking me on, Sam! Honest to God!

SAM: Three slices but! D'you have any stew!

BERNIE: Red sauce on your oysters!

SAM: *(Searching)* Where's your light switch, Bernie?

BERNIE: *(Sudden)* No, Sam! Prefer it like this, Sam –

SAM: Ach, get away with ye!

BERNIE: Got to get it off –

BERNIE stumbles and sways out of the sitting room. SAM finds the light switch and turns it on.

BERNIE: *(Off)* Sam! S'too many stairs! And they're all moving towards me –

SAM returns to the sofa and sits down. Sounds of BERNIE struggling with the stairs. MARIE watches.

BERNIE: *(Off)* Can't find me feet. Like a wounded oul dog –

SAM: *(Photo)* You'd have loved it there the night, John –

BERNIE: *(Off)* Sam!

SAM: *(Laughter)* Here comes the cavalry!

SAM lurches to his feet and leaves to help BERNIE.

SAM: *(Off)* Let's be having you then –

BERNIE: *(Off)* Don't be saying to anyone Sam. Promise –

Grunts and groans from the staircase. SAM enters carrying BERNIE in his arms. Both breathe heavily. BERNIE blinks at the light. SAM strains towards the sofa.

SAM: Not fit for this carry on. Just park you there –

BERNIE: I need freed, Sam! Honest to God –

SAM falls onto the sofa with BERNIE in his arms. Laughter and heavier breathing.

BERNIE: Jesus Mary and Saint Joseph! Take a cardiac if I don't get –

SAM: Hold your water, daughter! *(Back of dress)* Now then. Hold still now –

BERNIE: Girl must be out. *(Laughing)* What you doing back there?

SAM: *(Struggling to unclasp the dress)* Wee devils! Breathe in deep, Bernie –

BERNIE: *(Laughing)* There're wire cutters in the kitchen –

SAM: *(Caressing)* Might have to rip it Bernie –

BERNIE: *(Eyes shut)* Oh Sam, no. Hardly take it back ripped –

SAM: *(Fondling)* Have to get in the front then –

BERNIE: *(Eyes shut)* Oh, Sam. I wouldn't normally. First time since –

           BERNIE suddenly opens her eyes. SAM moves his hand to the back of her dress.

BERNIE: *(Hands to head)* Sam! The light –

SAM: *(Rips the dress)* Ach Bernie, you're gorgeous –

BERNIE: *(Covers herself)* Sam, no!

SAM: *(Kissing neck)* Pick any dress in the world –

           MARIE suddenly steps out of the kitchen. Her face is flushed with anger.

MARIE: She said no!

           SAM and BERNIE freeze. MARIE cannot speak. SAM stands and laughs easily. BERNIE suddenly cries out.

BERNIE: Have you no shame! Spying in the dark?

SAM: Bernie –

BERNIE: On your own mother? Get out!

SAM: *(Arms outstretched)* Marie –

BERNIE: Get out! Give me your key and get out!

SAM: Bernie –

BERNIE: Go peep some place else!

> *MARIE stares. She turns abruptly and leaves. SAM sits on the sofa shaking his head. BERNIE looks over to her wedding photo on the unit. SAM puts on his jacket.*

SCENE 4: SHATTERED ICON

Friday. 1pm. Bogside. The MAGUIRE kitchen. Several walls are covered with political leaflets, posters, and photographs. A framed portrait of a volunteer son hangs in the centre of the main wall beside a sacred heart. A tape recorder stands on a unit in the corner. An old typewriter sits on the kitchen table, surrounded by sheets of notes and newspapers. BRIDIE MAGUIRE leans over a newspaper. Her son COLIN sits in his dressing gown at the other end of the table with a mug of tea. COLIN is clearly only out of his bed.

Silence. EAMONN and LINDA enter. EAMONN is carrying a NEXT shopping bag and a brown envelope. He places the envelope in front of BRIDIE and puts the shopping bag down in the corner. LINDA sits.

EAMONN: Here's your application, ma. Gerry's made all the
            corrections –

BRIDIE: Never could spell –

EAMONN: Computer'll fix all that. If you get the changes typed up
            he'll handle the graphics. You've got to take his name out
            of it. And your's too –

COLIN: Scumbag won't even come into this house for fear of
            putting his wee project at risk –

LINDA: He knows what he's doing but. You want to see the
            equipment they've got –

EAMONN: No point having a vision if you can't deliver –

BRIDIE: If you want to get your fingers into the pie you've got to
            keep your ideals under the table –

LINDA: Gerry'd shake hands with the Queen if that's what it takes –

COLIN: And him with a brother inside and another on the run –

BRIDIE: Lying in your bed all morning's not going to free Ireland but –

EAMONN: And the movement needs skills –

COLIN: Such a yarn. You're feathering your own nest –

LINDA: Any danger of a cup of tay, love?

            COLIN switches on the radio/tape recorder. EAMONN smiles and looks at his watch. As he prepares the kettle and mugs, BRIDIE returns to the typewriter.

RADIO: Debate sparked by the new graffiti which appeared on the Free Derry wall earlier this week has been joined by a senior member of the SDLP –

LINDA: Here we go –

RADIO: In his reply to Sinn Féin's claims that the words WITHOUT HER CONSENT are a clear condemnation of the increased house to house searches made by the security forces over the weekend. Councillor Friel argued that the graffiti unambiguously signals the maiden city's rejection of the IRA. He praised the typical courage and ironic wit of the Bogside community –

BRIDIE: *(Switches off the radio)* Shite! The man wouldn't know wit if it slapped him round the face –

LINDA: You should hear the debate in the town –

BRIDIE: *(Absorbed)* It's sacrilege but. Desecrating that wall –

COLIN: Whoever done that should be taken round the back of the shops –

EAMONN: Aye. That's going to win us the war –

BRIDIE: *(Absorbed)* Nothing left of this application –

COLIN: *(Newspaper)* Wouldn't surprise me if the Brits done it
            themselves –

LINDA: Why don't you relax Bridie and pass that over to someone
            else –

BRIDIE: Who's going to do it but? Need to have it in his hand
            before he leaves –

            *LINDA goes over to the tape recorder as EAMONN brings
            a pot of tea and mugs to the table. LINDA inserts a tape
            from her pocket as BRIDIE loads a new sheet of paper.*

EAMONN: Best thing that's happened to that wall in years –

COLIN: *(Newspaper)* Aye. Since the rainbow –

            As BRIDIE starts to type, the tape comes on.

RADIO: You're listening to Radio Threshold 92FM. The
            underground voice of the community. Somewhere in the
            heart of the city. And this is David Bowie and Mick Jagger
            with Dancing in the Street –

            *LINDA clears the chairs as BRIDIE looks up. The music
            blares out.*

LINDA: Go and show us the old steps, Bridie –

BRIDIE: Ach, get away!

LINDA: Let your hair down, girl!

            *LINDA takes BRIDIE by the hand and spins her into a jive.
            The laughter spills spontaneously out of BRIDIE. COLIN
            and EAMONN watch amazed.*

LINDA: This's what we're fighting for, Bridie! The right to dance –

BRIDIE: There isn't the time –

LINDA: There's always the time!

EAMONN: Jesus! Will you look at them move!

BRIDIE: I was one of the best dancers in this town!

COLIN: You've me all broke, ma! Swear to god!

            BRIDIE suddenly breaks away from the dancing and switches off the tape recorder.

BRIDIE: Need to get back to this application –

LINDA: We were just getting going!

            BRIDIE sits behind the typewriter. LINDA retrieves the tape as DIANE and PAULA enter.

LINDA: Ach, Bridie. If it's not the war it's work –

PAULA: *(Hands COLIN a letter)* Here. You'd better read this –

BRIDIE: Diane. I need you on this committee –

            LINDA looks over COLIN's shoulder at the letter. BRIDIE picks up a pen to work.

COLIN: Jesus, ma! Just because she's one of them –

BRIDIE: Use whatever you've got –

LINDA: What's this?

PAULA: We're just after picking it up at the office –

DIANE: *(To BRIDIE)* Some woman's on freedomstrike –

BRIDIE: On what?

PAULA: Freedomstrike –

BRIDIE: Sounds good to me. Someone tell me what it is and I'll
           go on it too –

DIANE: On hungerstrike, Bridie. Here. In Derry –

PAULA: And she's pregnant –

EAMONN: She's what?

BRIDIE: *(Papers down)* Go and someone read out the letter –

           LINDA takes the letter and reads aloud.

LINDA: I have begun my freedomstrike today though it's four
           days since I last had anything to eat. *(Beat)* What's that?
           Monday –

COLIN: What's this? Some kind of sick joke?

DIANE: Go on Linda –

LINDA: *(Reads)* Four months ago I was raped. Here in Derry.
           While I was unconscious. As a result of the rape I became
           pregnant. *(Beat)* The writing –

           *LINDA passes the letter to DIANE and sits. DIANE reads
           aloud.*

DIANE: *(Reads)* I became pregnant. I have spoken to a Derry
           priest but cannot –

BRIDIE: Who?

PAULA: Doesn't say –

COLIN: It's a hoax. Or the wee girl's just seeking attention –

DIANE: *(Reads)* But cannot find one reason to bring a child into
           this world –

BRIDIE: Well the wee girl's no fool –

DIANE: *(Reads)* I am not prepared to run away to get rid of the truth. Of the rape. Or all that lies beneath it. I only hope I can be convinced by you the people of Derry and the action you take –

COLIN: Fat chance!

DIANE: Jesus, Colin! Will you give her a chance! *(Reads)* I only hope I can be convinced by you the people of Derry and the action you take to begin eating again. *(Pause)* And to give birth to this child. Confident the future is worth living. This is a cry for freedom. An unconditional demand from a mother. And her. And her. And her unborn child. In the name of life. *(Stops)* Bridie –

DIANE cannot continue. She hands the letter to BRIDIE.

EAMONN: What d'you call her?

PAULA: You'll hear now –

COLIN: The wee girl's got caught –

BRIDIE: *(Reads)* In the name of life. If I name myself I am certain to be stopped. Perhaps locked away. My personal life and suffering would be used to distract you from the cause. And I'm not prepared to become a statistic. Or be turned by the Journal into a two inch column on page ten. *(Stops)* My God.

EAMONN: Is that it?

BRIDIE: *(Reads)* I will continue to keep in touch with the community radio on a daily basis as long as I've the strength to write and walk.

BRIDIE puts down the letter. A silence.

LINDA: She's mad –

COLIN: *(Letter)* Here give us a wee duke at the writing –

DIANE: We've been right round the office –

EAMONN: *(Letter)* Go and let me see it –

COLIN: Linda. Is that your's –

LINDA: Get away to fuck! Swear to God!

BRIDIE: Have you said to anyone?

PAULA: *(Shakes his head)* I want to go round the priests –

COLIN: Now just hold on. You overreact and you could destroy years of work. How do we know it's true?

DIANE: She was raped, Colin!

COLIN: That's what she says. You've only her word –

PAULA: That's well out of line, Colin –

COLIN: I know what it sounds like. But someone's got to step back and think it all through. Suppose it's a fantasy. Or a lie. Could be. Could even be a cynical move to destroy the radio and all it stands for –

DIANE: Isn't this just what it's for –

COLIN: Aye! They know that too but! What if it's an attempt to pull our credibility apart? You broadcast a letter like that and you'll have the whole of Derry paranoid! You'd have at least twenty thousand suspects! You want to take that risk?

EAMONN: Maybe that's what she wants –

DIANE: To get people talking. Inside their homes –

LINDA: But what if it's a hoax like he says –

PAULA: That's why I'm saying we go round the priests –

COLIN: So now we're all out in the open –

BRIDIE: Paula's right. That's the first step. You send out your djs.
            They're already known. And others you trust. The priests'll
            keep it to themselves till it's confirmed. But yous'll have
            to move fast. She's already gone four days without food –

LINDA: Jesus, one day would kill me!

BRIDIE: How long was Bobby Sands writing his diary?

COLIN: How long did the movement support the women
            hungerstrikers?

EAMONN: Say a priest confirms it. She's no actual demands –

COLIN: It's madness! She's certain to die –

EAMONN: Will people support someone they can't see –

PAULA: There's ones support Nicaragua and Palestine –

BRIDIE: They wont talk about what's happening here in the Bog
            but –

DIANE: It's a protest against rape. She's my support for one –

PAULA: It's a protest against collusion. And I'll support that –

COLIN: So you'll support the murder of an innocent wain? *(Beat)*
            That's how it'll be seen. Because with no demands she
            can't win. The wain's already dead. She won't even get
            the support of activists in her own town. You support her
            and you do it as separate individuals. Not as
            representatives of this radio.

            Silence. PAULA takes the letter in his hands.

PAULA: This here's madness! What d'you want? The perfect
            protest? I couldn't do it. And I'd never ask her to do it.
            But don't you see? All that lies beneath it. She's talking

about the hidden economic violence! The violence that causes unspeakable suffering the world over! Her rape reveals it all! All you see is occupation! She's talking about what puts the Brits on our streets!

LINDA: What are you suggesting? Sit tight and hope it's a late April fool?

DIANE: If she dies the future dies inside her. That's how I see it. And we're her only lifeline –

PAULA: I feel wile for saying this but I'll tell you something else. She'll start a terrible lot of people thinking. Beginning with the priests –

COLIN: This isn't El Salvador, Paula –

LINDA: No. But that's what the radio's for and that's why I'm involved.

PAULA: I'll take Saint Mary's and the Long Tower –

BRIDIE: I can take the outlying chapels if yous need a hand.

PAULA: Diane. Go you with Linda to the Gob –

LINDA: Away and fuck! I'm not visiting any priest with that in me hand! They'd have me in confession the rest of me life! I'll man the switchboard. Yous phone in every hour on the hour. Why can't we start the new tape now?

DIANE: You alright reading the letter?

LINDA: Long as I don't have to look any priest in the eye! I'm not doing it if we run out of time but! You'd hear the shakes in me voice!

PAULA: Might be just what's needed. *(To BRIDIE)* I'll find ones for the Gob –

DIANE: *(To EAMONN)* We'll get the equipment set up –

PAULA: *(Letter)* Will I make copies of this?

BRIDIE: Sure, I can type it now –

PAULA: Photocopier's faster. And handwriting's more personal. It'll be hard enough to make some of the priests see this isn't a hoax. *(Beat)* What about the transmitter?

All eyes come to rest on COLIN.

COLIN: What if I said no?

LINDA: Know what a hurly stick looks like?

COLIN: *(Smiles)* I'll be ready by ten. But this needs a thorough full group discussion before you get my agreement. We'll meet at nine.

DIANE: Be back in ten minutes with your copies.

PAULA and DIANE leave with the letter. EAMONN looks at his watch and shakes his head. BRIDIE begins to gather up her notes. COLIN and LINDA stare in thought.

BRIDIE: Come back to this later.

LINDA: Just imagine, Bridie –

BRIDIE: *(Stops still)* I wonder if her ma knows. *(Beat)* Might sound cynical. But we had our protest timed from the men reached the critical point. First hunger strike shown you can't hold people's interest for long. Sat round this table with a blank calendar and worked out the dates. Planned it backwards from there. How in God's name d'you calculate a pregnant woman? You don't even know they'll reach that moment together –

LINDA: This tay's cold –

BRIDIE: Must be the cruelest decision I ever faced. To support Liam. To have to accept the limits of your rights as a mother. As the one who nursed him. And laughed and sighed as he became his own man. I don't know how them mothers go on living. *(Beat)* Divide by four. Allows for them consuming each other –

COLIN: Better get dressed.

COLIN stands. BRIDIE returns to organising her notes.

EAMONN: I can't do the recording.

LINDA: I know. You'd want to talk her round –

BRIDIE: Let's just pray it's a hoax –

COLIN: Is it the responsibility?

EAMONN stands and walks over to the NEXT bag. He takes out a new white shirt.

EAMONN: She's a wain on the way –

LINDA: Eamonn! You promised –

EAMONN: It's best out in the open –

COLIN: You horny wee bastard!

LINDA: I didn't do it on me own!

BRIDIE is stunned. EAMONN starts to unbutton his shirt.

BRIDIE: I don't know whether to laugh or cry –

LINDA: We were going to say. After we got engaged –

BRIDIE: But yous can choose! We thought that's all we were made for –

LINDA: What else's there to look forward to?

COLIN: Imagine it's the wain you're trying to save –

          EAMONN takes off his shirt. BRIDIE suddenly hugs LINDA.

BRIDIE: Well, I'm chuffed for yous just the same!

COLIN: Eamonn, what are you doing?

BRIDIE: *(Turns)* You're not going down to Samuel's now?

EAMONN: I've an appointment –

COLIN: A what?

EAMONN: A meeting. I'm already late.

          EAMONN starts to unpin his new shirt. COLIN stares.

EAMONN: You'll find someone else –

COLIN: Why didn't you say –

EAMONN: Yous wouldn't understand –

COLIN: You're the only one knows to mix the levels but –

BRIDIE: Who's the appointment with son?

EAMONN: *(Beat)* Gerry –

COLIN: Ha!

BRIDIE: Well you just call Gerry, son –

COLIN: He's thinking long term ma –

BRIDIE: You say something's come up –

COLIN: Can't be deflected by a hungerstrike –

BRIDIE: Colin, leave this to me –

COLIN: When the right moment comes and we're all away inside
           he's going to give up the car and the mortgage and the
           Caribbean beach to lead the workers out of their golfclubs
           and onto the barricades –

BRIDIE: Colin –

COLIN: The movement needs skills!

LINDA: Eamonn. Gerry might understand –

EAMONN: It's been planned for ages –

COLIN: Did he buy you the shirt then?

           *EAMONN puts down the shirt. He is struggling to hold
           onto his temper.*

EAMONN: I bought it. For myself. Alright? *(Beat)* We're meeting with
           Sam. To go through the plans for the project. Show him
           the model. Explain what we need –

BRIDIE: Eamonn, think –

EAMONN: I have –

BRIDIE: It may only be a few weeks, son –

EAMONN: And then there'll be something else! This's a year of work.
           A training for life. What d'yous want me to do? Rear this
           wain on claims? I want my wain to be able to eat. Have a
           room of it's own –

COLIN: In the Culmore Road?

BRIDIE: Stay out of this Colin. Eamonn. Fine you thinking about the
           wain and taking responsibility. It's your life. And I'm
           happy for yous. But I didn't give up twenty years of my
           life to see a son of mine tiptoe away from the struggle to
           become a collaborator's trophy –

EAMONN: Aren't you asking him for money?

BRIDIE: Aye! To provide a wee opening in a few women's lives! Not to stab my own people in the back!

EAMONN: You're at home, ma. This isn't Free Derry Corner –

BRIDIE: Don't you be upcasting to me, son! While I'm running this house you'll listen to what I have to say! This isn't the time to go waltzing off to the States. You want a training? Fine. But not when your own people need you. Not when a nation's crying out to be led into the future. What hope does Ireland have if people like us disappear? We're already bodysearched in packed city centres as if we were invisible. We're already slaughtered in broad daylight without a murmur of dissent. They won't need internment or martial law ever again. But they need to seduce us away from our own people. They need to bribe us apart. Because they're afraid that what you have in here will be joined to that wee girl underground. And to those tens of thousands of unexported young people who are now sitting idle on their fists. *(Beat)* I'm old, Eamonn. Too tired to fight much longer. But at your age I daren't even answer back. *(Pause)* We'll speak to your aunt Bernie about clothes. Yous can have the spare room up the stairs.

EAMONN: *(Gently)* Ma. There's not even coal to put on the fire –

BRIDIE: *(Smiles)* We'll muck in together. We'll survive.

          EAMONN looks down at the shirt. Slowly he puts one arm into it's sleeve.

BRIDIE: *(Portrait)* He didn't wear their uniform –

COLIN: Ma –

          BRIDIE suddenly lunges at EAMONN's shirt and rips it off his back.

BRIDIE: You'll have to nail it to our backs they said! You won't brand us with your crimes! This shirt's already drenched in blood and it's not even been worn! Appointment? He didn't rot in the stench of his own shit so you could trade in his dream! I didn't smuggle his wee notes of hope inside this body for twelve years for you to sign our land to the Yanks! I didn't bury a son and the sons of ten mothers before him so you could hand this struggle over on a plate! And I didn't walk with this knot of rage in my heart from years of raids and stripsearches and uncried tears to see my grandwains grow up afeared to hold up their heads and say with pride: that's my uncle! He gave up his life so I could be free!

Uncomfortable silence. EAMONN cannot speak. BRIDIE sits with the shirt in her hand.

BRIDIE: That's why he's here, Eamonn. That's why he won't step through that door. He knows a cannibal isn't welcome in this house. And that's what Sam Doherty is. A cannibal. He consumes peoples and continents. In the name of freedom. *(Pause)* Here's your shirt. Do as you please –

In a sudden eruption of inarticulate rage, EAMONN lifts a chair and shatters the portrait of his brother. It crashes to the floor. EAMONN stands holding the chair. BRIDIE is rigid. The white shirt still extended in her outstretched arm.

EAMONN: I can't be my brother. And I don't want my wain to have to go to jail to learn how to read and write.

EAMONN puts down the chair gently and lifts his old shirt. He strides out. Stunned silence. LINDA puts her arms round BRIDIE. COLIN begins to pick up the pieces of the portrait.

LINDA: Bridie? *(Beat)* She's cold –

LINDA takes off her sweater and drapes it round BRIDIE's shoulders.

BRIDIE: The priests —

LINDA: Someone else can go —

BRIDIE: Should've moved that photo —

DIANE enters breathless. She stands at the door.

DIANE: Were the cops already in?

COLIN: Are they headed this way?

DIANE: They've the street sealed off —

BRIDIE: *(Slow and old)* Both of you out. Linda. Help me make the beds.

DIANE and COLIN leave through the kitchen. BRIDIE stands.

SCENE 5: CONFIRMATION

*Friday night. 10.40pm. Saint Mary's parochial house. Creggan. The PRIEST
and BERNIE DOHERTY sit facing one another in leather armchairs. As
always, BERNIE looks elegant. The PRIEST is dressed casually in black.
Books line the shelves of several cabinets, beneath a collection of framed
religious prints. A desk with a telephone. The room is comfortable. The
PRIEST is struggling to sustain his attention.*

BERNIE: As soon as it happened I thought Father Gallagher! Well
            you've always been such a close friend. Now how did you
            put it? Love is a gift from our Lord.

PRIEST: The bible encourages it Bernie –

BERNIE: Aye. So it does Father. Only I thought it might be a sin. To
            you know. In that sort of way. With your own husband's
            brother –

PRIEST: Perhaps the time's come to accept John's death, Bernie –

BERNIE: Aye. You're right. I never stopped hoping. D'you know?
            In that sort of way? In all them years not once have I.
            Never once did I. D'you know what I mean Father? And I
            was in me prime when the good lord chose to take him
            from this world. I've been while faithful to the memory of
            John, Father –

PRIEST: So you have, Bernie –

BERNIE: Perhaps that's why I felt such a deep. Can't put it into
            words. I've been tormented to distraction, Father. Like I
            was sixteen all over again! D'you think Marie will forgive
            me, Father?

PRIEST: Marie's not the sort to hold a grudge. *(Beat)* Has she been
            back since?

BERNIE: *(Shakes her head)* Would you have a word Father? When
            you next see her? You'll know how to put it. It's not easy
            between a mother and daughter. We're close. And then

again we're not. In that sort of a way. Was I saying to
you? Sam's asked me up to Dublin! A romantic weekend!
I wouldn't actually. You know. With him. Before we were
married. Can't sleep for the excitement but. *(Helpless
laughter)* Here. Before I get all carried away with meself!
(Opens purse) Last week's collection. *(Envelope)* I'll leave
it there. I'm sure it'll be used wisely. Will you be going to
the chatshow yourself, Father?

PRIEST: Aye. Most likely –

BERNIE: You should see the new outfit Sam's bought me! This
leisure complex will do Creggan a power of good. Just
what the community needs. It breaks me heart to take
their last coppers. Take care of the Lord's work but and
the Lord takes care of you. Bet there's some confusion up
there Father's Day! Here. You look shattered. *(Stands)* Sit
you there and put your feet up. I can see meself out. And
thank you Father. God knows what we'd do without you.

*BERNIE leaves. The PRIEST goes to the window. He looks
out. A knock on the door. His housekeeper DEIRDRE enters.*

DEIRDRE: There's a young woman outside, Father. I suggested she
come back the morrow. Says it's urgent. And she's been
sitting now over an hour.

PRIEST: You'd better ask her to come up.

DEIRDRE: No rest for the wicked.

*DEIRDRE leaves. The PRIEST stares out the window. A
knock and PAULA enters.*

PAULA: Hope I'm not disturbing you Father. I know it's late –

*The PRIEST turns to face PAULA. He is trying to remain
composed.*

PRIEST: No. Not at all. *(Beat)* How can I help you?

PAULA: I've been asked to visit all the priests in the area. A letter arrived down the community radio offices this morning. It needs confirmed. *(Photocopy)* Here. If you read it you'll understand what I mean.

PAULA hands the photocopied letter to the PRIEST. He takes the letter and moves slightly apart to read it. His hand begins to tremble as he reads. PAULA is watching him closely.

PAULA: Obviously they can't do anything unless it's confirmed.

Silence. The PRIEST cannot speak.

PAULA: Does the letter mean anything to you Father?

Silence. PAULA studies the PRIEST and nods in some relief.

PAULA: She came to you. I'd almost given up hope.

Silence. The PRIEST is unable to respond.

PAULA: Every other priest passed some comment Father. Some attacked her. Some attacked the radio. Others doubted the very letter itself. Will you just confirm that she came to speak to you? You don't have to be named.

Silence. The PRIEST trembles visibly.

PAULA: If I leave here now. Father. A nod just. *(Beat)* Father are you prepared to take the responsibility? *(Beat)* We want to save her Father. Her and the wain –

PRIEST: Don't you think I pleaded! Don't you think I tried everything in my power to stop it! I watched the very idea form in her mind! And I stood just as helpless as you're standing there now!

PAULA: How long have you known?

PRIEST: A few hours. The auxiliary telephoned. Couldn't say anything. Over the phone. Press would be all over me like flies. Only make her retreat the more difficult.

PAULA: Will you go to the bishop?

PRIEST: *(Shakes his head)* She confided in me. In confession. Dear God. We don't even know where she is. She may still come back to see me. She spoke with such conviction. But the anger was clear. Perhaps once that passes –

PAULA: There may not be time. May I use your phone?

PRIEST: Is that wise?

PAULA: I won't name you. Not without your permission. And we don't want to jeopardise any chance she might have. You tried. Now it's our responsibility to do what we can. And it's what she asked for –

PRIEST: She doesn't realise the full implications –

PAULA: D'you dial straight out?

The PRIEST stares at the letter. PAULA goes to the phone and dials

PAULA: Linda? Are you listening? It's confirmed. *(Pause)* No. Go yous ahead without me. *(Pause)* Alright I'll be right down.

PAULA puts down the phone.

PAULA: A few hundred people'll hear it the night. Should be round Derry by midday tomorrow. I'll keep in touch.

PRIEST: What?

PAULA: Here. Take you this number.

PAULA takes a pen and paper from the desk and writes down her phone number. She looks up to the priest.

PAULA: You'll be able to get me there day and night. There's
           going to be some outcry. *(Pause)* You'd have our support.
           If you wanted to use the radio. And a rake of people
           would support you. Did you ever hear of the preferential
           option, Father? The church working for the liberation of
           the poor and the oppressed?

PRIEST: Would you mind? I need time to think.

PAULA: Paula McLaughlin. You're not alone, Father.

           *The PRIEST passively shakes PAULA's hand. PAULA
           leaves. The PRIEST stands in the deep thought and then
           sits in the armchair. DEIRDRE knocks. The PRIEST does not
           respond. DEIRDRE enters.*

DEIRDRE: I'm away to bed now Father.

PRIEST: *(Looks up)* Deirdre –

           *The PRIEST hands the photocopied letter to his house-
           keeper. DEIRDRE reads the letter.*

DEIRDRE: I know Father. The housekeeper at Saint Joseph's. It's
           desperate so it is.

PRIEST: *(Beat)* Will you pray for her Deirdre?

DEIRDRE: Aye. Aye surely. Goodnight Father.

           DEIRDRE leaves. The PRIEST gets onto his knees.

ACT 2

SCENE 6: COMMUNION

Monday. 12am. DIANE's unoccupied flat. Bogside. MARIE leans among pillows against a wall on a mattress which lies flat on a newly carpeted floor. The sitting room walls are a bare white. Overalls lie draped over a stepladder beside tins of paint in one corner. A small lamp and tape recorder stand a wooden crate beside MARIE. A red-tinted tumbler and an empty jug stand on a wooden stool on the other side of the mattress. MARIE sits beneath a deep red duvet with an open notebook and a pen in her lap.

RADIO THRESHOLD broadcasts the second letter. As LINDA reads, the lamp brightens to gradually reveal MARIE and the location of the freedomstrike.

LINDA: Last night I watched our city stagger out of the bars and the clubs. Broken bottles and cut eyes. Girls in bright clothes taunting boys with gold rings. I stood there for hours listening to their laughter as it turned blunt and angrily cast about for the wrong look or a flicker of fear to attack. It lingered to jeer at a girl boking against the wall of a bank and moved on. The whole street seemed to be lurching and scowling in sullen expectation. Tension gathered on the pads and clustered in the doorways of heavily grilled shops. Would some girl tonight slash her friend with a ring? Would the boy in the kiss bounce the head of his mucker against the statue of the unknown soldier like a rag doll? There a wee boy slipping the hand. Panting his promises into her white blouse. Will she be sent down for eighteen years before the night's over? Or wind up in some back lane with her tights round the neck? *(Beat)* Who cares as long there's some steam! Some give it to me now so I don't have to remember how much of the future I've pawned! Give it all to me now! The crack's ninety the night! Here's me walking the streets of paradise!

You've been listening to Radio Threshold 92FM. Day 4 of

the Derry Freedomstrike. You can hear this letter again at
midnight tonight. Please ask your friends to listen.

*MARIE sits with her eyes closed. Long silence. She
reaches for the jug and pours. She discovers it is empty
and puts it down. She reaches for the tumbler and drinks.
She swallows with a little difficulty. She puts down the
glass and begins writing. Silence. Sound of a key in a
latch. DIANE enters downstairs.*

DIANE: *(Off)* Jesus. The smell!

*Sounds of DIANE climbing the stairs. MARIE slowly shifts
the pillows around her and eases herself gradually into a
more upright position against the wall. As she steps into
the room, DIANE shrieks with surprise. The rolls of
wallpaper she is carrying leap into the air and tumble
around her.*

DIANE: Jesus! Marie!

*MARIE smiles. DIANE staggers over the stepladder with
her hand on her heart.*

DIANE: You've taken ten years off my life! Didn't you hear me
coming in? *(Beat)* Just you wait. When you're least
expecting it. When did you move in anyway?

MARIE: Wednesday night.

DIANE: Scared the living Jesus out of me! Trouble at home?

MARIE: Me ma's head over heels –

DIANE: Uncle Sam strikes again! Well. You're welcome to stay as
long as you want. It'll be handy having someone watching
the flat. It's coming along isn't it? Just the kitchen and the
bathroom and these walls. The meter wont be pinned
until next week so don't be going mad with the electric.
What do you think of the bedrooms?

MARIE: *(Smiles)* Warmer in here –

DIANE: Sun doesn't get round back. Jesus but there's a while
          smell here in this room. Must have a dead rat trapped
          under the floor boards. And the carpet's only just down.
          (Picks up the rolls of wall-paper) Thought I'd have the
          whole flat papered and ready to move into by the end of
          this week. Been listening to the broadcasts?

MARIE: Aye.

          DIANE scoops the rolls of wallpaper into the kitchen.

DIANE: *(Off)* I suppose you're not while impressed. You couldn't
          swing a dead cat here. And it's meant for a family of four.
          I'll ring the health and the safety this evening. No kettle?

MARIE: I wasn't planning on staying long –

          Sound of running water in the kitchen.

DIANE: *(Off)* Can't live without tay. Well she can't be a prod
          anyway. Priest's the last person I'd go to if I needed to
          talk to someone.

          *DIANE comes out of the kitchen with a glass of water in
          her hand.*

DIANE: All them statues and icons. Gives me the willies. *(Sips)*
          Besides. She's for too poetic for a Prod –

MARIE: Diane –

DIANE: I know. I can't help it. Just seems to slip out at times.
          (Sips) Must be all those years of carrying the burden of
          shame. Get the dig in first. The bastard's still keeping his
          head down. Imagine knowing who she is and not
          speaking out! Can't blame him for being scared, I
          suppose. Jesus, but you had to see it this weekend! We've
          had to move from two slots a week to one a day! We get
          a new letter from her every morning. We're having to

work round the clock just to keep up. It'll have to go out live from the morrow.

DIANE perches on the stepladder.

DIANE: I can't understand how people can just turn their backs! It's not as if it's happening half way across the world! Even the banter's dying away by the hour! And she's somewhere out there without a second to spare. We're having to fan it ourselves just to keep the argument alive! We knew it wouldn't be easy. No time to plan or prepare. We completely misjudged Derry's reaction but! They'd have strung her up in the Guildhall Square if they'd got their hands on her on Saturday! Every pub and shop was the same! I even heard ones asking if she was part of this city festival crack! Sure she knows herself. Who cares as long as there's some crack the night! Can't imagine what she's thinking inside. Even the movement's holding back! They're all afraid to risk the little that's left of the men's war. No-one sees beyond the ballotbox and the gun anymore. *(Beat)* If the Journal doesn't print the letters the morrow we wont save her or the wain. *(Beat)* D'you reckon I'm mad?

MARIE looks directly at DIANE.

DIANE: Last night I sat watching the news. Whole nations of black silent skeletons crawling like crippled insects across a continent of cracked earth for one grain of corn. And it lies there in the shadow of their enemy's cross rotting in the sun and taunting them because they've no split left to cook it in. Acres of mothers tearing at their flat shrivelled tits to wring out one drop of blood for children that look like their grandfathers. Their anger and disease have even drained the last tears from their eyes. Otherwise they'd use that to revive their famined lands! And we're slinging away halfeaten cakes we can't even remember why we bought! We're barbecuing herds of surplus cattle and overgrown pigs in protest against motorway fines and trading restrictions! And the world's politicians sit sipping mineral water. With their eyes fixed firmly on their polls!

They turn nuclear silos into coaches to bus weeping refugees across makebelieve borders to be cleansed into model consumers! And if by some chance event their ghettos are torched in a spasm of anger they find a new evangelical popstar or topless princess to distract us. It's obscene Marie! An obscene soap with a cast of millions! If only the stench of their corruption could filter through the screens into our homes!

DIANE springs off the stepladder and approaches MARIE.

DIANE: She's demanding an end to all that, Marie! I'm sure she is! An end to the frustrated anger and silence! She's pleading with people to ask questions about what they feel everyday in their homes! Pleading with her life and the life of her wain for people to get up off their arses and say no!

DIANE lifts the empty jug and tumbler off the stool onto the floor and sits beside MARIE.

DIANE: You always had a reason to keep your distance, Marie. Will it affect people inside their homes? Will it click with people like me ma? Will it give birth to a new vision for the future? All right people aren't out on the streets. They probably don't think she even exists! People like your ma are talking, but! Arguing inside their homes! That's the first step. New people now need to come forward! New ways of seeing and thinking now need to be heard! You can write. You've spent your whole life thinking! You can't sit back and expect other people to do it all for you, Marie!

MARIE smiles. DIANE is encouraged.

DIANE: D'you know why I'm involved in this no-hope protest, Marie? It's not just the radio. I had to make decision. *(Pause)* If I tell you something Marie, will you promise to keep it to yourself?

MARIE: Do you need to ask?

DIANE: Aye. Aye I do. For the time being anyway.

MARIE: *(Beat)* What was the decision?

DIANE: *(Beat)* She is trying to get people to question rape. Not just why it happens. Or how it's hidden. But to use those questions like keys to explain the world we live in. You haven't heard her third letter yet. But it opens doors. Doors that may have been locked for centuries! *(Pause)* You find yourself thinking about life as part of the world. Not just passing through it. The world as a womb. The source of justice and hope. Not as a battlefield or a cemetery. You'll hear it for yourself –

MARIE: What decision did you take, Diane?

            DIANE stares at MARIE. She stands and takes several steps. She turns back to MARIE.

DIANE: D'you mind the night Patsy O'Hara died? You came up to our's and found me in bed. D'you remember Marie? Finding me in bed with both eyes swollen out to here? I couldn't eat for the bruising round my neck –

MARIE: The night your Ken and his mates battered you –

DIANE: For going with Colin Maguire. You could never picture Colin hiding under a bed like a four year old wain. *(Beat)* Well I lied to you that night, Marie. And I lied to Colin. I lied to everyone. *(Beat)* To protect him. And me da.

MARIE: *(Pause)* You were raped?

DIANE: By him and four others.

MARIE: Your own brother –

DIANE: Swear you won't breathe a word. The shame would kill me da –

MARIE: Your da?

DIANE: Swear Marie. Swear!

           MARIE looks at DIANE. A flash of anger.

DIANE: Take your things –

MARIE: Diane, wait –

DIANE: I trusted you –

MARIE: I –

DIANE: D'you know how long it's taken me –

MARIE: Listen –

DIANE: Just to admit myself!

MARIE: I know –

DIANE: Eleven years Marie! Eleven years I blamed myself! For
           eleven years I lived a lie! Their lie! That I was a fenian
           whore! An insect! No better than the dirt I lay on! That I'd
           provoked them and deserved to be raped! Eleven years,
           Marie, I lived that lie because to imagine anything else
           was unbearable! Unthinkable! And just this last week! I
           found a wee grain of confidence! To prize open one wee
           crack! To see the truth I've carried inside me for eleven
           years! *(Beat)* You're not going to seal up that crack Marie!
           You're not going to force me back out into the lie!

MARIE: Diane, I couldn't speak –

DIANE: You didn't have to! Your silence said it all! I seen it in your
           eyes! You didn't have to utter a word! Now take your
           things and get out! No! Wait! I want to give you
           something to take home and think about! *(Pause)* All them
           years Marie there was a wee voice. Deep inside. A faint
           crack in the lie. You survived, Diane. One day you'll get
           even. *(Pause)* I heard the voice and I did nothing Marie.

Women were mocked. Harassed. Assaulted. And raped.
They suffered the same self-hatred and the same torture I
went through. And I stayed silent. I heard about it. I read
about it. I even saw it. But I did nothing. *(Beat)* My time
has come. This woman and her wain have made it
possible to stare at the truth. Her protest's given me the
courage now to speak out. There must be thousands of
women like me. Keeping it inside. In Derry alone! Millions
of women suffering the lies! Lying like stunned insects!
Squirming on their backs! Every woman should be out on
the streets! Not just in support of her! In support of
themselves! Making the new world to give birth to the
future in! There's no other way to end the fear! Only then
will we see how many we are! Only then will we know
what can be done! You can tell your ma that! Every word!

*DIANE stares defiantly at MARIE. MARIE stands and walks
over to DIANE. She takes her hands.*

MARIE: I couldn't speak before. For the rage. And I needed to
listen. For myself. That wont make sense yet. But you've
spoken for me. I know what you've been through. And I
admire you.

*DIANE searches MARIE's eyes. Silence. They embrace and
hold one another.*

DIANE: You smell like a sewer. Like the flat.

MARIE: *(In the embrace)* Diane. I'm the woman.

DIANE: You're what?

MARIE: That's the truth you can smell. Coming out.

DIANE: *(Arm's length)* You?

MARIE: I had to be sure.

DIANE: *(Beat)* You? The freedomstriker?

> *DIANE breaks into howls of helpless laughter and buckles out of the embrace. She staggers back to the stepladder for support.*

DIANE: You! *(Laughter)* You never marched in your life! *(Laughter)* You never even came out of your house for fear of being seen on the same street! *(Laughter)* You! The one who always preached no revenge? *(Laughter)* You'll have the laughter squealing out of me all the way to the grave!

> *MARIE begins to laugh and the women's laughter blends. MARIE reaches down for her notebook lying on the mattress and hands it to DIANE.*

MARIE: There the fourth letter.

> *DIANE's laughter subsides as she takes the notebook in her hands.*

MARIE: I was just finishing it when you came in.

DIANE: *(Stares)* You? Marie Doherty? The freedomstriker?

MARIE: You said it had to be someone new.

> *DIANE looks at the notebook and MARIE again in disbelief. MARIE sits back on the mattress and returns to her original position. She reaches for the tumbler. DIANE stares at MARIE.*

DIANE: My god. It's true. I'm only after seeing it all now. The third letter. It talks about the child. We were there together. Before the wain got battered –

MARIE: It didn't even make it into the Journal –

DIANE: And the graffiti. You put that graffiti on the wall –

MARIE: *(Smiles)* Didn't we always dream of doing it? Late at night?

DIANE: We could never think what to write –

MARIE: Or if we'd have been ordered out of the town.

DIANE: *(Pause)* Why didn't you tell me? Why didn't you prepare
           me?

MARIE: You'd have only tried to stop me –

DIANE: I'm your closest friend!

MARIE: You'd have spent hours Diane. Even weeks. Arguing it
           backwards and forwards in your mind. There wasn't the
           time. It's more practical like this. And besides. I didn't
           know I'd been preparing myself. Till last week. Preparing all
           of my life. I'm still trying to understand it all myself, Diane –

DIANE: It's been staring me in the face and I didn't see it!

MARIE: *(Smiles)* Diane. Listen to me. All you're just after saying
           this morning. It helped me much more than you realise.
           I'll explain later. *(Pause)* I'm going to need practical help
           but, Diane. I'm still strong enough to write the letters.
           And I can still make it to the postbox at the end of the
           street –

DIANE: No!!!!!

MARIE: Diane. Will you fetch me a wee taste of water? The jug's
           empty.

DIANE: *(Stares)* Water?

           *MARIE holds out the jug. DIANE stares at it and then
           reaches for it. She carries it and the notebook into the
           kitchen. Sound of running water. DIANE returns with the
           jug and pours some water into the tumbler. She leaves the
           jug down on the stool and returns with the notebook to
           the stepladder. MARIE sips and then drinks. DIANE is torn
           between wanting to read the letter and her thoughts.*

DIANE: And I told you the truth. About the city –

MARIE: I was there. It's what I expected. There's still time –

           MARIE drinks some more water. DIANE watches in silence. MARIE puts down the glass.

DIANE: Marie. I think you might die –

MARIE: I've made my decision.

DIANE: And the wain?

MARIE: You don't have to say yes, Diane.

DIANE: *(Pause)* Marie. How d'you feel? Deep inside?

MARIE: *(Beat)* Calm. Lucky in a strange sort of way. I don't have a face. Or a name. So it's not a question of revenge. *(Beat)* I won't settle for anything less than change –

DIANE: But change takes time, Marie –

MARIE: Something small. Something practical. But a sign. That the human future you talked about is certain. *(Beat)* I'm protecting this child Diane. It's far safer inside me than anywhere else. And I want us both to live. You've read what I wrote.

DIANE: *(Pause)* Paula will help. Bridie might too –

MARIE: No, Diane. No-one else. No weak links. Derry's too small. The risk is too great. How will people interrogate the letters and not the victim if my name gets out and they manage to trace me? I've already taken the greatest risk just asking you to help me. More than a risk. For whichever way you decide your part in this is now much more difficult than mine. *(Pause)* I'd no other choice but. And I trust you. We know each other inside out.

DIANE: *(Beat)* But the child, Marie –

MARIE: This's paradise next to what women and children are facing across the world –

DIANE: But we can campaign, Marie! The debate's already begun! All I said before! None of it changes if you come off now! It was easy to support you before! You had no name! No face! No body! No past! You were so abstract! I was only thinking of myself!

MARIE: You were out for yourself –

DIANE: But you're going to die, Marie! It's such a waste!

MARIE: I want to conserve my strength, Diane. I don't want to argue. Give yourself time to think it all through. All the time you need. I don't want you to be taking me off this protest if I reach the point where I can't take decisions myself.

DIANE looks down at the notebook. She looks at Marie.

DIANE: What about the medical support you'll need?

MARIE: I've seen a doctor. We'll talk it all through. Together. We'll prepare ourselves. We'll be completely open with each other. Support each other as we go through it.

DIANE: *(Beat)* Have you no doubts, Marie?

MARIE smiles.

DIANE: I feel desperate. I felt so sure. So certain.

MARIE: *(Smiles)* Decisions begin with the right to say no. (Beat) At least you won't have to get the carpet lifted and your floor opened up.

DIANE smiles. She reads the notebook. The lights fade to darkness. LINDA reads the letter slowly. Her voice trembles slightly.

LINDA: Imagine a womb refusing to feed it's child
so it begged for work instinctively!
Imagine a womb charging it's child rent
so it expected to be owned instinctively!
Imagine a womb refusing to touch it's child
so it maimed and killed instinctively!
Imagine a womb branding it's child
so it believed in division instinctively!
Imagine a womb blinding it's child
so it believed it was guilty instinctively!
Imagine a womb forever threatening it's child
so it obeyed orders instinctively!
Imagine a womb always interrogating it's child
so it kept silent instinctively!
Imagine a womb used as a cell
so it's child hated justice instinctively!
Imagine a womb sold in a catalogue
so it's child accepted debt instinctively!
Imagine a womb competing for life with it's child
so it expected war instinctively!

Fortunately the womb isn't like this. Why then last week
did I see a priest carrying a seven year old unconscious
wain in his arms behind a mad mother with bloodstained
hands walking through a Derry shopping centre? And why
do I read about mountains of grain lying in disused
bombers' hangers when a whole continent is dying of
famine? And why did I hear of a village of mothers who
went blind when their daughters were raped and their
sons were tortured in the name of freedom inside their
homes? Did I just imagine these things? As I write I can't
help imagining the child inside me accusing us of mass
murder and pointing at our laughter and silence as
evidence of mad guilt.

You're listening to Radio Threshold 92FM. That was letter
Day Six written by the Derry freedomstriker. I'll give it to
you once more before we open the day's debate. *(Pause)*
Day Six. Imagine a womb...

SCENE 7: INTERVENTION

Wednesday night. 9.30pm. Britannia Hall. A makeshift television studio for the Open Forum. SAM DOHERTY and ANDREW ROBINSON sit with GERRY, the PRESENTER, on informal chairs facing the audience. The lighting highlights the panel but also encourages audience participation. Theme music ends and applause begins. Cameras are visible around the auditorium as the lights come up.

GERRY: Good evening and welcome to the Britannia Hall inside the old city of Derry where Open Forum this week provides you the people of Derry with a forum to debate issues of the moment and the future of Ireland. Tonight it's our pleasure to welcome two of Derry's most influential men to answer your questions and offer their vision of the city's future. Both have risen from rags to riches, giving lie to the claim that people from the ghettos on both sides of the community lack the opportunity and the ambition to make it to the top and work together for a new Ireland. On my left: the man behind the city centre redevelopment programme and the much publicised Foyle United Football Club proposal: from the Fountain, please welcome Andrew Robinson.

           Applause.

GERRY: And on my right: the architect behind the acclaimed EuroAmerican Integrated Ireland Initiative – back in Derry after ten years and fresh from Brussels – please give a warm welcome to the Bogside's Sam Doherty.

           Applause.

GERRY: Sam. How's it feel to be back?

SAM: Great, Gerry! Really great! There's a whole new optimism about the place! It's absolutely unrecognisable! Transformed! Of course the real Derry's still here. The wit and the openness! But the city I left behind was a beaten docket. No harm to yous! But it's great to see we've put all that behind us!

GERRY: Ten years is a long time Sam –

SAM: That's what it takes to develop a concept like III Gerry.

GERRY: Andrew. The Foyle United Football Club. The beginning of real community integration and a real opening for talented youngsters across the city.

ROBINSON: That's right. And a shot at those European titles.

GERRY: You and Sam go back a long time.

ROBINSON: *(Smiles)* We worked behind the wire together. In the early Dupont years. That's where the friendship put down it's roots. We started the same day. We were sent out with the shift foreman to be shown the ropes. The two of us in these strange kinda hardhats. The next thing we knew this tall man in a long white raincoat and a white hat comes up to us and says, "Hey! Are you Sam Doherty and Andrew Robinson?" We say aye. "Well how d'you do! You're welcome aboard!" Felt like we'd known him for years! The way only Americans can. As he walked off I turned to the foreman. "Who's that fella?" I said. "That's the boss himself. The work's director." *(Shakes his head)* Made a deep impression on us –

SAM: Always stuck in me mind. They didn't care if you kicked with the left foot or the right. Providing you pulled your own weight you were family. *(Faces ROBINSON)* Mind them long summer nights? The team would come off the four to twelve shift and head away to Lisfannon with a crate of beer. Light a fire. And smoke and drink the night away together till four or five in the morning –

ROBINSON: Where we first came up with Foyle United –

SAM: Tremendous sense of comradeship –

GERRY: Before you two old muckers bring out the violins, let's bring in our first question.

GERRY stands with his clipboard and takes a mike into the audience. He holds the mike in front of each questioner after he has introduced them.

GERRY: Frank Boyle. A journalist from the Rosemount area of the city.

BOYLE: Good evening. Mr Doherty. As we speak my son's probably locked inside his nintendo. *(Laughter)* D'you not think there's a danger Derry'll be swallowed up by the mighty American culture of III?

GERRY: Are you losing us our identity, Sam?

SAM: Let me answer that in a human sort of way, Frank. We eat Indian. Wear Italian. Drink Dutch. Drive Japanese. Play American. Watch Australian. And sleep Scandinavian! *(Laughter)* But we think and we act as individuals! Irish individuals! You take the bar I was in last night. Huge untapped talent. Traditional. Country and Western. Rock'n Roll. Same all over you might say. But the generations. Dancing together. You'll never find that in one New York bar! Sure we get blootered. How else d'you put the week's grind behind ye? But the stories. The carry on. Pure Irish! It's ingrained. Our history. The lay out of our streets. Our village mentality. All deeply embedded in our everyday speech!

GERRY: But the new words. The new phrases Sam –

SAM: New ways of working. New toys and machines. Sure language changes like everything else. But our true identity: indestructible! *(Leans towards the audience)* And I'll let yous into a wee gem of a secret. The brainchild of III. We Irish have a hidden asset. The family. Extended across the globe by centuries of emigration. Serious potential for inward investment! We should be making capital out of our misfortune! Not crying over spilt milk! We Irish are already citizens of the world!

Applause. GERRY has already lined up another question.

GERRY: Irene Taylor. A headmistress from Carnhill.

HEAD: Mr Robinson. With the recent escalation of city centre
              bombings, won't multinationals see the North as still too
              unstable for investment? Is there really going to be any
              work for my school leavers?

GERRY: Are we being bombed out of the future, Andrew?

ROBINSON: Fair question. But it belongs to the past. Nothing will
              divert us from entering the new world. The only borders
              now are in our minds. We have the technology. The laws.
              And the right attitudes to bring about a permanent state
              of democratic normality here in the North. Genetic
              fingerprinting will eliminate the diehards. But nations
              round the world have learned. Negotiation. Not
              devastation. Oh there are the exceptions. Ethnic bickering
              over small details here and there. But it's merely a
              prelude to the final solution. Normality protected from
              change. The way a candle flares up before it sputters and
              goes out. You mark my words, Miss Taylor. Derry will be
              seen as the centre of national revival and common sense.

HEAD: But aren't our divided histories themselves still highly
              explosive?

ROBINSON: Look at the council festivals. The reconciliation programme.
              And wait till you hear the unifying cheer of Foyle United!
              The foundations for a new Derry − yes and even a new
              Ireland − are already in place. Have been for years.
              Invisible to the naked eye perhaps. But underneath. It's the
              political will and imagination that's been lacking. What
              d'you expect of a people betrayed and exploited into such
              despair? With the economic muscle of III you'll see a
              resurgence of hope and belief in the North. The human
              ingredients of peace and development. And you'll hear a
              universal cry to isolate and silence anyone who threatens
              that dream. *(Beat)* What d'you teach, Miss Taylor?

HEAD: History. At the Foyle −

ROBINSON: When your pupils hear the final explosions Miss Taylor you
tell them. Communities on both sides of the conflict have
always been driven together by the godfathers of terror.
We need to remember that. We shudder together. Not
apart.

*Distracted applause. GERRY is already in position for the
next question.*

GERRY: John Keys. A self-employed builder from Galliagh.

ENGINEER: You talk about a new imagination and will. A brave few
people have only debt and unemployment in their sights –

ROBINSON: You see it's a question of adjusting to a new lifestyle. To
new ways of seeing. You must try to understand. Debt is
really investment. Even the family holiday. Crucial
investment in the quality of our lives. If we neglect
ourselves we neglect the future. Well it's almost a crime!
Against ourselves! We're the future! Only some people
can't see it. Their thinking's trapped in the past. *(Pointing)*
You go back and tell your friends. The vital argument is
that we cannot afford to be left behind! There's an
enormous cake out there. And this time we're going to
get more than the crumbs.

Tension. A few isolated claps.

GERRY: Doctor David English of the Culmore Road. Doctor?

DOCTOR: *(Smiles)* First of all. Welcome back Sam –

SAM: *(Smiles)* Thank you Dave –

DOCTOR: And I just want to say how much we all appreciate what
you've both already done for this city.

(Applause)

Now I'm sure you'll understand that people are anxious.
What guarantee do we have that we'll not inherit the

drugs and crime of American cities? I believe this year
alone more than a quarter of a million young Americans
have been murdered on their own streets –

SAM: Dave. Tell me this. Is Derry all gunmen and bombs?
Television's big business. And a powerful political tool. For
millions of decent Americans there's no crack. No crime.
No racism. Sure they exist. But let's keep it realistic. They
exist 'cause we're living through a unique technological
revolution. Surely as a doctor you must realise. Change
naturally produces tension. Crisis. The groans and labour
pains of an old world giving birth to a new –

A woman grabs the mike out of GERRY's hands.

SUZANNE: *(Gripping the mike)* Forgive me for butting in. As we
speak –

GERRY: *(Appealing)* Madam –

SUZANNE: *(Gripping the mike)* Out there –

GERRY: *(Reaching)* Madam, if you please –

SUZANNE: *(Gripping the mike)* A woman's dying! Nine days –

GERRY: *(Wrestling)* Now, madam –

SUZANNE: *(Wrestling)* Her unborn child. Get your hands –

GERRY: Madam, please –

SUZANNE: *(Gripping the mike)* Her unborn child might already be
dead!

GERRY successfully recovers his mike. He smiles.

GERRY: We've touched a raw nerve. That's what the Open
Forum's for. Now I didn't catch your name, madam –

SUZANNE: Suzanne Brady. Why in under Jesus aren't we talking about what's really happening in Derry!

Scattered applause.

SUZANNE: I'm a teacher. At Saint Mary's in Creggan. My pupils are talking of nothing but the human bomb! Ticking away somewhere inside this city! Stories are pouring out of them! I'm not qualified –

GERRY: What precisely is your question, Miss Brady?

SUZANNE: For all we know she might be here!

Hush of anticipation. Hands shoot up around the auditorium. GERRY talks as he walks.

GERRY: Is the alleged woman in question here? *(Pause)* I'm sure we've all seen the street posters and broadsheets. And the Bishop of Derry's open letter in yesterday's paper clearly stated the moral arguments. Yes, you sir.

FOREMAN: George McLoskey. Foreman at Dupont's. I see no point in more mindless harping on about a rumour when there's a world recession biting –

GERRY: Well this's a community forum Mr McLoskey. Yes madam –

TRACEY: Tracey Barratt. I'd like to ask the doctor. If this woman's genuinely on a hunger protest, what are the chances her child's still alive?

GERRY: We'll come back to the doctor in a moment. If we could just collect a few more opinions. *(Looks and walks)* Yes, you madam.

CATHY: Cathy O'Hara. I was one of the five women fasting in the cathedral yesterday. Now I have to be honest. I was disgusted how small the support was for our protest. Why there were more photographers than visitors –

GERRY: Was this a protest in sympathy or against the
            freedomstriker Miss O'Hara? For viewers at home as well
            as our own clarification.

CATHY: It was a protest against rape. I'm a psychiatrist. I have to
            deal with rape and all manner of sexual abuse victims
            everyday. The scars are appalling. Usually lifelong. Now I
            admire the courage and vision of this woman. I'd be very
            concerned though about her emotional and mental state –

GERRY: If she exists –

CATHY: Whether she exists or not there are countless victims of an
            invisible war that's been waged against women since time
            began. A war that's intensifying –

GERRY: Alright. Let's –

CATHY: If she does exist she's risking her life to expose the city's
            wounds! Our past's seeping out like pus and we're all
            afraid to talk about it –

GERRY: Let's give others a chance to express their views. Yes sir.
            You sir –

MANAGER: I'm not afraid to speak me mind! I'm a manager. Up in the
            Essex factory. Where more girls have called in sick this
            past week than the three months previous altogether!
            D'you want to know what this controversy's doing?
            Destroying this city!! No working man has any peace! If it
            isn't the wife it could be his daughters. Or the woman
            sunbathing in the garden next door! She's gone and
            provided every person with a chip on his shoulder with a
            ready-made excuse. Alcoholics. Idlers. Gypsies and
            perverts! You name it and they've been downtrodden and
            oppressed! And some even think she's a hero! You can't
            open your mouth any more for fear someone's going to
            stick a claim into it! Centre of national revival? We've
            become a city of victims and queers overnight! We'll be
            the laughing stock of Europe in the morning! Thank Christ
            I've only sons!

ROBINSON: I really think it's a mistake to press this any further. It's some adolescent prank which one maverick radio station has exploited for its own ends. There's always an anti-social element. Rape is tragic. Let's leave it at that.

GERRY: *(Walking)* Let's just go back to the doctor for a scientific opinion. Bearing in mind it's still a hypothetical pregnant hungerstriker we're talking about.

DOCTOR: In my experience it's normal for rape victims to suffer intense guilt. In cases of rape pregnancy the unborn child often becomes the focus. Now in the Dublin case –

GERRY: But the child, doctor. How long could a four month old foetus survive in the womb if the mother has stopped eating?

DOCTOR: Well. She'd be in her second trimester. The placenta would be fully developed. Miscarriage would be extremely unlikely now. At this stage the body is organised to protect the foetus at the expense of the mother. However in these circumstances, we could expect the foetus to become macerated. That's to say shrivelled. The mother wouldn't even know the foetus was dead until it was evacuated. I've seen countless such examples in Africa –

GRANNY: May I speak!

The GRANNY's voice catches the mike. GERRY passes the mike to her in the row behind the DOCTOR.

GRANNY: Why are we even discussing these details? The Bishop has stated it clearly. It's suicide and murder full stop!

Applause. The PRIEST sits in plainclothes across the aisle in the auditorium. His anguish and dilemma are mounting.

GRANNY: The rape issue's irrelevant! It doesn't' matter how many days, months or hours pregnant she is. It doesn't matter if she doesn't even exist! We have a duty to be morally clear! And firm! Whoever's put this idea out into the streets of Derry is feeding young impressionable minds with dangerous satanic filth! Should it not be a crime to say such things in public? Even to distribute them? A crime to even think them? Has she ever held a child? Has she ever nursed a child? How do you begin to contemplate murdering a child inside your own womb! It's a crime against humanity itself! I've read the leaflets. Perverted nonsense! A violation of every Christian principle! If nothing else, this should unite Derry in a universal cry of horror and condemnation! I lay in bed suspecting my very own granddaughters last night! That's no way to be preparing for leaving this world! In just nine days, she's bruised the self-confidence of an entire city! For generations! Turned husband against wife and daughter against mother! She's made that Dublin girl look like a saint! In just nine days she's all but torn the very fabric of our civilisation to shreds! I'd rather she was cast out of the city or left for dead in some field rather than be offered one breath of decent folk's support! We all know rape's wrong. But you go to the police. You don't go and commit a double murder in revenge!

Sustained applause. The PRIEST's cries pierce the applause and catch the mike as it is being handed back to GERRY. GERRY is loving every moment. He guides the mike towards the PRIEST.

PRIEST: No! No! No! No! No!

GERRY: Obviously you disagree –

PRIEST: You're wrong! This woman is sincere. Genuine. And she exists!

GERRY: *(Beat)* On what authority, sir –

PRIEST: I know! I'm the priest she came to see!

Some commotion.

GERRY: What is your name Father?

PRIEST: Father Gallagher. My name's not important. Don't you see –

Commotion. Cries of 'who is the woman?' from the audience.

GERRY: Ladies and gentlemen, please.

Silence.

You've heard the debate, Father. The views of the city. Now surely to God you've a responsibility to name this woman –

PRIEST: I cannot –

GERRY: But she's dying, Father. Think of the unborn child –

PRIEST: Don't you think if I knew where she was –

GERRY: Surely the principle of life –

GRANNY: You're protecting a murderer! A suicide –

PRIEST: I'm protecting the cornerstone of the Catholic Church! Would you have me break the seal of silence? The very first principle of communion and trust –

GRANNY: You don't protect the devil!

PRIEST: I'm protecting an innocent woman! My God! How many of you have I offered the same protection to in the past? How many of you seek the same protection elsewhere? When you confess the hatreds and darkest desires in your hearts? I swear on everything I hold sacred this woman is innocent –

GERRY: But if she murders an innocent child –

PRIEST: Whose child? Your's? His? His? *(Pointing at the stage)* Or their's? If we sit here and condemn her, the blood of her child will be on all our hands!

Explosion of outrage.

GERRY: Ladies and Gentlemen, please! Please, please, please! One voice at a time! Remember who you are! We'll get to the bottom of this I assure you!

Gradually an intense silence.

GERRY: Thank you. *(Pause)* May I ask, Father. Are you with her or against her? For the viewers at home –

PRIEST: Don't you see? It's the same thing. Her letters are clear. They speak for themselves. It's pouring out in the confessions. She won't bring her child into this world. The world that raped her. Into *their* world. *Their* future –

SAM: Steady Father –

PRIEST: Do you know what your inward investment really is? Mass rape. The calculated rape of a whole people. In the dark.

Stunned silence. The PRIEST strides out of the makeshift studio.

GERRY: *(Smiles)* We'll hear the reaction from tonight's guests right after this break!

Total silence. Theme music. The lights fade on the auditorium.

SCENE 8: WOMB PROTEST

Thursday morning. 11am. Diane's unoccupied flat. There are now three posters on two of the walls and several plants sitting on a plain wooden desk. Curtains have been hung and are partially open. MARIE sits propped up by pillows against the wall with her eyes shut. She is listening to DIANE reading. DIANE sits at the desk with a pen and the notebook in her hand. The light from the lamp and the window is gentle.

DIANE: The sea was now a writhing mass of fury, heaving and –

MARIE: Writhing mass of what?

DIANE: *(Looks up)* Mass of fury –

MARIE: Change fury. *(Pause)* Writhing mass of life.

DIANE: How come you're so sure?

           MARIE smiles. DIANE makes the correction.

DIANE: Will I go back a wee bit?

MARIE: Just read to the end.

DIANE: *(Reads)* The sea was now a writhing mass of life, heaving
           and spitting it's rage towards the shore. The pilot was on
           his knees praying to a doll and footering with a shrivelled
           piece of rubber in his lap. A small black fist pointed at a
           hole in the sky.

           *MARIE opens her eyes and reaches for the tumbler of
           water. She sips slowly as DIANE reads the new letter to
           herself. MARIE is shattered.*

MARIE: Read it back to me, Diane.

DIANE: Is that it?

MARIE: Just put day ten at the top.

DIANE: *(Scribbles)* I don't understand it.

MARIE: Just read it back.

DIANE: *(Reads)* I lay in the sea caked in slime. My bare legs jutted
            out like grey fingers towards the shimmering blue line.
            Now and then my head rose up to count the bruises that
            hung like a chain of dragon's teeth around my neck stifling
            my cries. As fresh silverblack waves broke against my hips
            I saw a pilot in the distance. Laughing and dancing on the
            water like a clown. With one hand he cradled a naked
            black child. The other held a parachute of pure white
            doves. Dove after dove seemed to leap from his mouth as
            he called for me to come out and join him. I couldn't
            move or speak for the bruises! But as the wind and the
            waves pounded against my face his name echoed in my
            mouth! With a presidential salute he released the doves
            and clapped his hands sending a massive wave rolling
            towards me. It gathered and foamed and leaped into the
            clouds crashing into my womb and tearing the sky down
            around me like a cloth! As it churned and washed the
            slime from my body, it dragged me out into the open sea
            furling the sky behind me like a sail. I glided towards the
            clown as though steered by his laughter and as I drew near
            he lowered the child onto the water beside him. When I
            reached him he draped the blue sail round my shoulders
            and placed a crown of twelve gleaming thorns on my
            head. He waved my arms at the crowds that were running
            to assemble on the shore. Some knelt. Others danced and
            pointed with joy at the thousands of white balloons drifting
            into the hills. Mothers made the sign of the cross with wee
            infant hands. I laughed aloud at the island carnival and the
            sound of my own voice shocked me! I looked down for the
            bruises and saw I was standing on a world of corpses! Red
            waves were lapping my ankles! The blood was flowing out
            of me and reviving the dead! The sea was now a writhing
            mass of life, heaving and spitting it's rage towards the
            shore. The pilot was on his knees praying to a doll and
            footering with a shrivelled piece of rubber in his lap. A
            small black fist pointed at a hole in the sky.

MARIE's eyes remain closed. DIANE looks at MARIE in despair.

MARIE: We'll make a personal copy for the priest. To thank him.

DIANE: *(Beat)* You look shattered.

MARIE: Go and turn up the heating, Diane.

DIANE stands and goes to the storage heater. She turns a dial and returns to sit at the desk. She picks up the notebook and reads a few lines of the letter to herself.

DIANE: Marie, people won't have a notion –

MARIE: Aye they will –

DIANE: I'm just after staring at it for two hours and I don't have a baldy's!

MARIE: Once they start to question –

DIANE: It sounds like a poem Marie! They'll take one look at the first couple of lines and chuck it into the nearest bin!

MARIE: D'you see how reporters the day sound like poets? You can't talk about the world any more in plain language. It's too complicated. And the suffering's too great. Maybe you never could. And who trusts the old political words? They're all rusted and cracked! Perhaps that's why poets are being elected presidents. Soon as they're given power but the poetry goes. They fall back into the old words. And they wonder why the ones who packed the city centres to crown them in a night of hope won't trust a word they say in the morning.

DIANE stares at the letter in the notebook.

DIANE: Is the pilot a president?

MARIE: *(Smiles)* Thought you said you couldn't understand it.

235

DIANE: The words won't stand still.

            *DIANE snaps the notebook shut in anger. MARIE opens
            her eyes.*

DIANE: Makes you feel so stupid!

MARIE: That's why it needs to go out, Diane. To challenge people.
            Get them to ask who made them feel stupid and why. How
            can we be free to lead ourselves if we believe we're stupid?

DIANE: You dreamt that?

MARIE: Sure everyone has dreams like that. But most people
            don't even try to explain them. They remind us of what
            we can't bear to remember. Or say. If we all used our
            dreams to explain the madness we wouldn't be sitting
            here now. Dreams are like poems. They won't break the
            chains. But once we start enjoying asking questions again
            we'll spot the weak links. Wains don't find it difficult.
            That's why they're punished in school. So the fear of
            questioning replaces the desire to know.

            DIANE looks at the notebook lying on the desk.

MARIE: We might as well give up now if we're going to keep
            chucking our minds in the bin. The mind's a tool. It
            shouldn't have to be a bin lid or a barricade. God knows
            we all need the barricades. But we've got to take them
            down as soon as we're strong enough. Otherwise all we
            see of the world is the barricades. And ourselves
            crouching behind them. You know the worst about it
            Diane. You can become the barricade yourself and not
            even know it.

            *MARIE lies back exhausted and closes her eyes. DIANE
            looks at her watch and picks up the notebook and pen.*

DIANE: This has to get off –

MARIE: Go and have another crack at the letter, Diane.

DIANE: Later on –

MARIE: It's what you take out of it –

DIANE: Aye, I know. It's not that –

MARIE: Then what?

DIANE: We're already behind time –

MARIE: You're more important than the letter, Diane. Start from
           what you know. Use your own experience.

           *DIANE looks at the notebook in her hand. With some
           considerable courage she opens it to the new letter and
           lies the notebook flat on the desk. Automatically she puts
           her hand to her head.*

DIANE: D'you reckon you're God then?

           *MARIE erupts into laughter and raises an apologetic hand.
           DIANE smiles.*

DIANE: Jesus, but I used to run a mile from this kind of ordeal!
           And I end up sitting in a room with a woman who
           reckons she's Jesus Christ doing a frigging comprehension!
           (Beat) What's this slime and the black silver waves then?

           MARIE remains silent with her eyes shut.

DIANE: Oil? Spunk? I don't know!

           MARIE smiles and nods her encouragement.

DIANE: And the bruises? *(Beat)* The rape. That's why her legs are
           bare. Why the dragon's teeth but?

MARIE: Where are the bruises?

DIANE: Round the neck. Where they always are.

MARIE: Where are dragon's teeth?

DIANE: The border roads. Got it! The border marks the rape! Stops
            you from speaking! The censorship. Your head's the North!
            Rose up now and then. Jesus Christ! Not only do you
            reckon you're god! You also think you're Ireland! I lay in
            the sea. The grey fingers are bits of land. Rocky land.
            Waves broke against my hips. Mayo and Wicklow, Marie!
            Marie, it's coming alive!

            MARIE smiles.

DIANE: See your clown in the water. The President. Could be the
            Pope. Anyway the one with the doves coming out of his
            mouth. He crowns you Christ. Waving your arms and all
            that. What's he doing playing with himself and praying
            with a durex in his hand? To a doll, for god's sake! Hold
            on! Don't tell me! That shrivelled bit of rubber. Is it white?

MARIE: *(Smiles)* Could be –

DIANE: It's a busted balloon! And a durex! He's blowing up
            durexes and you think they're doves. From a distance!

            MARIE and DIANE laugh. DIANE perseveres.

DIANE: Whenever I laugh I always know I'm going to pay for it
            with tears. *(Beat)* So this president-pope's blowing up
            durexes of peace. You've a seriously warped mind, Marie.
            Anyone ever tell you that? *(Beat)* Crowds running to the
            shore. They think you're a vision. Like you thought he
            was. Only he brought you out. And the sound of your
            own laugh means censorship's gone. But when you look
            down for the bruises you see the truth. Your blood's
            reviving all them who died to free Ireland! Or the world!
            Could be all those who ever suffered. And they're spitting
            with anger at the ones on the island who believe the
            illusion!

            MARIE opens her eyes and listens with concern.

DIANE: Jesus, it's clear as day! What's the black wain doing in the dream but? Hold on. I seen Bush holding a black wain on the news last week. After the riots. Making out he cared. That's it! That's why it's a doll. And by the end the president's mad. He's praying to a doll that's pointing it's fist at the hole in the ozone! *(Looks up)* Fuck, Marie! It's brilliant! It's like a riddle! A crossword –

MARIE: D'you think ones might take the rage as revenge?

DIANE: Jesus, Marie. That's the first step, but –

MARIE: Aye. But the people on the shore have been fooled.

DIANE: D'you want to change it?

MARIE: *(Pause)* No. That's what I dreamt. Leave it stand like that.

DIANE looks at MARIE with admiration. MARIE closes her eyes.

DIANE: I'd not thought about the wains. The teacher last night. Must be some crack in the classrooms. Human bomb. I wonder which bastard gave them that. You get some rest Marie. I'll see to this letter. Anything you need?

MARIE shakes her head. She drifts. DIANE takes a clean piece of notepaper and lifts her pen. She begins to copy out the letter.

MARIE: How you coping, Diane?

DIANE: Grand. Ate with me da last night. Says they're all talking about it at work.

MARIE: What's he think himself?

DIANE: Thinks you're a crank. Or part of a fenian conspiracy. Reckons the priest invented you to bring young people back into the church. It's got him thinking but. The last letter. He actually said the world would be a far more peaceful place run by women.

MARIE: Your da?

DIANE: Thinks we wouldn't harm it. And wouldn't send our sons into war.

MARIE: Depends on the women. And the world they're born into.

DIANE: He's saved all the leaflets. Says people are talking about them everywhere. Wait till he sees this one but! And I seen Linda this morning. With a tape recorder in her hand. She's a whole squad of people out interviewing in the street. Morning to night –

MARIE: And I thought she was all armed struggle and sex –

DIANE: They took a whole batch of leaflets down to Dublin this weekend. And they were in Belfast last week. You'll have an island of poets if you're not careful!

MARIE smiles. DIANE continues to write.

MARIE: I meant you. You haven't said anything about yourself.

DIANE: *(Beat)* I know.

DIANE looks at MARIE. Sounds of children playing in the street outside.

DIANE: It's hard, Marie. Wile hard. You dying makes me feel wile angry.

MARIE: *(Beat)* Is that all?

DIANE: I feel so fucking helpless, Marie!

DIANE puts down her pen. She goes to the window. Silence in the room.

DIANE: I question the decision, Marie.

MARIE: Your decision?

DIANE: *(Beat)* Your's and mine. *(Pause)* What's a sign, Marie? How
          will you know it when it comes? Is it your priest lossing
          the head and speaking out? Is it me understanding your
          poem? Even you sent this letter to every one of your
          poet-presidents what will they be able to do? It's all so
          big! It all takes time! I don't know what you want, Marie!
          The whole of Derry on the streets? The whole of Ireland?
          Graffiti on every wall? It won't happen! And you could be
          one of the best teachers in this town!

MARIE: D'you want to end it, Diane?

DIANE: How can you be so calm?

          DIANE looks down onto the street at the playing children.

DIANE: They sound so happy. So innocent. As if there was
          nothing to fear in the world. It makes you wonder if we're
          not mad.

MARIE: Wains question every trace of madness. And they cry out
          their resistance till they learn to be insane. They'll be our
          firmest allies. *(Beat)* If I live till their parents' curses turn
          into questions this will have all been worthwhile.

          DIANE turns to face MARIE. She sits on the desk.

DIANE: When the whole school pointed and whispered their
          scorn, you were the only one that would walk with the
          fenian whore. You knew you could get battered too. Yet
          you tore their graffiti out of the margins of the history
          books and made them look us in the eye. With silence.
          And the night we decided to take the wire brushes to the
          desks. *(She laughs)* IRA SLUT. WHORE OF BABYLON.
          Branded before I'd even stepped into the Bog. The sweat
          beating off us as they drummed on the windows and spat
          into our faces. And you just stared them into silence. You

were always calm. All them nights you held me behind the boarded up windows. *(Smiles)* What were we like? Hiding under the bed during the power cut the night Bobby Sands was meant to die. Me whispering they're going to invade us! The boys are going to burst in and kill us! I despise all this! Don't be blaming me for the flags and the bands and the sash of hate! Don't be blaming me for the men with chests swollen with the pride of the dead! Don't be blaming me for the wains imprisoned inside their uniforms! Trembling to the roar and the boom of the lambeg drum! I despise all this too! The pleading and the whispering under that bed night after night! Don't kill me! Please don't kill me for where I was born! I'm as hard up and imprisoned as you! And the night them bastards gripped their slogans and ground me into the street like an insect! Their eyes blood-red! Bulging with the same hatred they'd scored into their history books! And their laughter of triumph as they draped the sash of no surrender between my legs! *(Beat)* And you ask me if I want to end it? Aye! With all my heart!

Pause.

MARIE: Revenge, Diane?

DIANE stares at MARIE. She reflects. Sounds of the children fading away.

DIANE: No. Justice. And human debt. The debt of thanks. With a wee trace of love thrown in.

MARIE: And the doubts?

DIANE: I'm afraid. Of the responsibility, Marie. Can you understand –

MARIE suddenly puts her finger to her lips. She lies completely still.

DIANE: What –

MARIE: *(Whispering)* I felt something move! Inside me! Like a butterfly.

Silence as MARIE concentrates. DIANE stands rigid.

MARIE: I didn't imagine it! Swear to God! *(Beat)* Bet Bobby Sands never felt that!

DIANE and MARIE laugh suddenly.

MARIE: Hush! There again! Oh Diane! Diane! It's not in me mind! It's here! Can you feel it, Diane? Here! Diane, here!

DIANE doesn't dare move. MARIE opens her eyes.

MARIE: Diane, it was beautiful –

MARIE cries.

DIANE: Marie? Marie –

MARIE: The life inside me! It's stirring in protest! Against me, Diane! Against it's own ma, Diane! Is it against me, Diane? Diane! Are we wrong? Am I punishing an innocent life, Diane? Let go Marie! Let go! Diane, the wain! What does it mean? This is my womb! My decision! Jesus it's done nothing! Water, Diane! Water, quick –

DIANE rushes to the jug. Tears are streaming from her eyes. MARIE lies weeping.

MARIE: *(Wails)* No!!!!!

DIANE: Marie –

MARIE: Spare me this God! Spare me in the name of Christ our Lord! Holy Mother of God see my tears and spare me!

DIANE cradles MARIE in her arms and brings the lip of the glass to MARIE's lips. MARIE clutches at the tumbler and gulps. The water comes up into the glass and goes onto the duvets. DIANE jumps up and reaches for a cloth and her own glass from the desk.

MARIE: I'm prepared, Diane. To die. But the wain –

DIANE returns to MARIE and assumes the same position.

DIANE: Slowly. Slowly. Just sip –

MARIE: *(Swallows and breathes)* It was like a kiss, Diane –

DIANE: Sip –

MARIE: As if I was being caressed by a wing. Or a feather. Or a breath. *(Cries)* It's all gone, Diane –

DIANE: Sip, Marie –

MARIE sips. DIANE guides the water into her mouth.

MARIE: It's gone, Diane –

DIANE: A little more –

MARIE: *(Pushing away the glass)* Enough! Enough, Diane! Was that your sign? A gasp for life! A sign of death! I have the right, Diane! It's my choice! My womb! So it was a kiss! I've seen men kissing missiles in broad daylight, Diane! Praying for them to wipe out whole cities of mothers and children! What future's out there for it! Inside or out! God's gift? God's a fool if he thinks I'll be conned!

MARIE lies back exhausted. DIANE releases the glass from MARIE's grip. She dries her neck and mops the duvets with the cloth.

DIANE: Marie? *(Pause)* You awake?

Silence. DIANE stands and puts her glass on the desk. She holds the cloth up to her mouth.

DIANE: Marie?

MARIE: *(Pause)* Aye.

DIANE: Are you alright?

MARIE: *(Pause)* Go you to the doctor.

DIANE: *(Nods)* What will I say?

MARIE: Everything. And talk to her yourself.

DIANE: *(Beat)* Are you sure?

MARIE: She can be trusted.

DIANE: *(Beat)* Will I go now?

MARIE: Just wait till I'm asleep.

            DIANE nods. Silence. DIANE stands completely still.

MARIE: And fetch the priest too.

DIANE: *(Nods)* I won't be away long Marie.

MARIE: Mind the letter.

            *DIANE nods. MARIE slips into a deep sleep. DIANE sits at
            the desk and picks up the pen. She copies out the letter.*

SCENE 9: AUTHORITY

Friday. 10am. Saint Eugene's Cathedral. BISHOP DEVLIN's meeting room. A medium size table with eight comfortable chairs. The walls are lined with religious portraits and paintings. Several open cabinets filled with collected silverware and archaeological objects. BISHOP DEVLIN and SAM DOHERTY are standing looking out of the window. BISHOP DEVLIN has the Day 3 letter-leaflet in his hand. SAM sips a cup of tea.

BISHOP D: So it believed it was guilty instinctively. Dear god –

SAM: She writes well –

BISHOP D: *(Crumples the leaflet)* Away two days and all hell breaks loose!

SAM: It'll die down. We've learned over the centuries how to watch ourselves die. Look at the famine. To think we ate grass and lay dying in the streets when the barns were bursting with wheat. An unquenchable thirst for suffering. *(Smiles)* And tay. *(Sips the last dregs)* But they should take out that radio. Seems like only yesterday the Bog was throwing pennies at jeeps. And the shock of the first window breaking! Two of your men would always appear to batter us onto our knees with their brollies. Weapons are so messy. Sat in Austin's the other day looking down on the Diamond. The jeeps look so comical. The rosary was always the true guardian of the peace –

BISHOP D: When people understood suffering.

SAM: Jesus should've come back as Maradonna.

BISHOP D: Who believes in the miracle of faith today?

SAM: Give us time. Who dared imagine the ragged-arsed wain giggling in the pews would consort with presidents and kings? Your crowd never doubted. But the wee boy in wellingtons never expected his barrow of brock would one day turn into a fleet of jets. You can't impose faith, Martin.

BISHOP D: I pity the young.

SAM: Wealth frees the spirit. Sometimes in the middle of the night I find myself longing for the old community. The street games. The open market. Smell of the pigs and the goats in the streets. The winter amusements. Racing down William Street with your tanner gripped tight in your fist. *(Smiles)* John Wayne and the curting. Black and red years, Martin. Fertile ground for marching. Not faith. Shouldn't lose any sleep over this freedom striker. The last fly in the ointment. She'll come round. Nice word. Look well on a billboard.

SAM walks over to the table and sits his cup on the tray.

SAM: Shame there's no leaves in the tay anymore. Me granny used to read them. Had us all mesmerised for hours. Before TV. They're reviving all that in the States.

BISHOP D: When do you return?

SAM: Sunday night. I'll look into mass before I go. *(Smiles)* Just be firm.

BISHOP DEVLIN smiles awkwardly. SAM leaves. The bishop walks across the room and rings a bell. He drops the crumpled leaflet onto the tray. A HOUSEKEEPER enters and removes the tray.

BISHOP D: Thank you.

The HOUSEKEEPER leaves. An ornate clock chimes ten times. The bishop's agitation is mounting. The telephone rings. He strides over angrily to answer it.

BISHOP D: I said no calls! *(Pause)* What? *(Beat)* Right. *(Beat)* Yes, good morning. No. There will be a statement once the bishops have convened. *(Beat)* This afternoon. *(Pause)* No. Not until I've spoken to him myself. *(Beat)* Goodbye. *(Presses a button)* Has Father Gallagher —

A knock on the door.

BISHOP D: Hold all calls. Is that understood?

          BISHOP DEVLIN hangs up the receiver. He walks to the head of the table.

BISHOP D: Yes.

          The PRIEST enters. He looks haggard and defensive.

PRIEST: Sorry I'm late. I was held up by young people in the street. And then the women. At the gates outside –

BISHOP D: Sit down.

          The PRIEST sits at the table. BISHOP DEVLIN stares at him.

BISHOP D: I assume you've seen the news.

PRIEST: About Dublin?

BISHOP D: I hope you're satisfied.

          BISHOP DEVLIN rings a bell. He speaks without turning.

BISHOP D: You look tired.

PRIEST: I've not really slept –

BISHOP D: No. I'm sure you could do with a good rest.

          The door opens and an AUXILIARY enters carrying seven precariously balanced files. He arranges the box files on the table in silence and leaves. BISHOP DEVLIN stands in front of the files. He is shaking with anger.

BISHOP D: Remarkable coincidence. The creation. Some would say a sign. Letters, Declan. Seven boxes of letters. Crammed with the outrage of our community. *(Opens the first file. Reads)* Death knell of our faith. *(Looks up)* Creggan. Your

parishioners, Declan. *(The second file)* Their lives have
been devastated by war. They look to us for support.
Reassurance. *(Reads)* Urge her to seek the healing love of
Our Lady. When will your priest come out into the open
and condemn this multiple murder? *(Looks up)* She has no
support, Declan. *(Opens the seventh file)* Anywhere.
(Reads) Sans doute c'est une tragedie même moderne et
classique. Mais au nom de Dieu! Que veut elle? La fin de
l'église Catholique? *(Looks up)* You do have French?
(Replaces the letter) The world is staring into the abyss of
a new dark age. Tilted towards genocide and holy wars.
The great statues lie in ruins. People are returning to us in
their millions. Only we can guarantee meaning. Guarantee
hope. Guarantee purpose. In this time of anarchy and
confusion we are being asked for guidance Declan. Clear
calm guidance. Do you understand?

*The PRIEST lowers his eyes. BISHOP DEVLIN suddenly
produces a letter from his inside jacket pocket.*

BISHOP D: The Vatican fax. Arrived this morning. SKY picked it up
last night. Seems the Holy Father was as impressed as I
was by your little satellite outburst. We've now been
turning down interviews for thirty six hours. You'll
probably make the front page of the *Universe*. You're in
danger of becoming an international celebrity –

PRIEST: I never thought –

BISHOP D: Never thought! You weren't ordained to think! You're
meant to serve! Why didn't you come straight to me at
the outset!

*The PRIEST looks down. BISHOP DEVLIN walks to the
window to calm himself.*

BISHOP D: Needless to say, your conduct will be unanimously
condemned by the bishops. Questions will be asked of
course. Of us all. We were too defensive over the Dublin
affair. Always risked being pushed. Manipulated. It's over.
This diocese will not be responsible for bringing the

Catholic Church of Ireland into international disrepute. The
faith will not be turned into a battlefield. We have global
responsibilities, Declan. This must now be resolved
immediately.

PRIEST: I –

BISHOP D: Incredible. The most sophisticated intelligence network in
the world hasn't one lead. Obviously you can't name her.
You've held to that principle at least. We'll have to force
her out into the open. Did you bring her letter?

*The PRIEST reaches inside his jacket. He hands BISHOP
DEVLIN a letter.*

BISHOP D: What's this?

The PRIEST looks up.

BISHOP D: A death-threat?

*The PRIEST searches another pocket. He produces another
letter.*

PRIEST: Sorry –

BISHOP D: My god. No. When did this arrive?

PRIEST: This morning.

BISHOP D: No name. *(Beat)* How many?

PRIEST: The first by letter.

BISHOP D: Is anyone else aware of this?

*The PRIEST shakes his head. BISHOP DEVLIN pockets the
letter and looks at the freedomstrike letter. He sits down
and skims it.*

BISHOP D: Dear god. Crown of twelve gleaming thorns. Have you read this?

PRIEST: Martin, I –

BISHOP D: She's probably completely oblivious to the anguish she's causing. At least the hungerstrikers were practical men. She must be enduring the most appalling suffering. Or she's on drugs. But if we can't save an emotionally disturbed girl, it's our sacred duty to protect the church. We can't let two tragedies wipe out more than a thousand years of civilisation and faith. Now you will draft a statement immediately. You were under severe strain. Deeply moved by her suffering. Without realising it –

PRIEST: Martin –

BISHOP D: You were lured into what shall we say? A pact. The implications of which you never imagined. No. Never *realised* would escalate to this point. You will pray for her soul and urge her community and the people of Ireland to do the same. Maynooth will decide if there's to be a pastoral letter. But I've no doubt it'll all be over in a few days. Let's hope she has the sense to request a meeting. Is she alone?

PRIEST: I don't know –

BISHOP D: Spiritual isolation, if not hunger, will bring her to her senses. I'll write to her personally. Through the Journal. If she won't respond to reason and an appeal to her faith she'll be excommunicated. Is that clear? *(Stands)* Now I've pressing matters to attend to. At least the Dublin women have demands. You'll find a pen and paper in my office. We'll meet tonight to arrange a period of rest. God is with you in this difficult hour.

The PRIEST stands and looks at the floor.

PRIEST: I cannot do as you ask.

BISHOP D: You will obey my instructions, Declan.

PRIEST: My conscience forbids it –

BISHOP D: Declan. You have taken a vow –

PRIEST: To carry out Christ's mission –

BISHOP D: As interpreted by his appointed representatives. I think we understand one another. Now if you'll excuse me –

BISHOP DEVLIN goes to the door. The PRIEST looks up.

PRIEST: Since the beginning of this protest, confessions have multiplied. Every day I learn more about the hidden lives of my parish. The whole city. It's deepest fears. It's darkest secrets. Unspeakable tragedy –

BISHOP D: We'll discuss that tonight –

PRIEST: Martin, this woman isn't just speaking –

BISHOP D: Now you listen to me, Declan. And listen carefully. There is no grey area here. The Maynooth ruling is clear. No motive. No court judgement. No legislation can revoke the right to life of the unborn child. Whether it's enshrined in our constitution or not. This woman has probably already committed murder. She is now embarked on a suicidal protest for what? A vision? Does she think she's a saint?

PRIEST: But if you don't listen to the voice of our people –

BISHOP D: The people are guided by the church! Not by the adolescent brock of a damaged mind! D'you no longer understand the teachings of the Roman Catholic church?

PRIEST: Now d'you see why I couldn't approach you?

BISHOP D: I've no time for this –

PRIEST: No priest in this city confides in you! Unless it's for
             reasons of self-advancement! You have no compassion!
             For us or the people of your diocese –

BISHOP D: Don't be ridiculous –

PRIEST: You are feared, Martin! Not trusted!

BISHOP D: That's enough.

             *BISHOP DEVLIN is momentarily visibly stunned. He goes
             to the window.*

PRIEST: Martin, I am trying to interpret the gospel through the
             needs and the anguish –

BISHOP D: I said that's enough! D'you want to destroy the only hope
             of salvation that guides and sustains millions of our people
             across this earth? You were not ordained to undermine
             the word of god! Do you wish me to make it any plainer?

             *FATHER GALLAGHER stands in silence above the open
             files, his eyes lowered.*

BISHOP D: You will write that letter. And when –

PRIEST: I wasn't ordained to wine and dine investors –

BISHOP D: You what?

PRIEST: Or to bless their greed and corruption –

BISHOP D: What are you talking about?

PRIEST: I dedicated my life to the service of my people. And to
             god. Not to watch vultures gorging themselves on this
             city in the name of development –

BISHOP D: Those are men of integrity –

PRIEST: They are men of lust! Do we not both wince inside at their
            arrogant laughter as they pour their donations into ghettos
            they have created!

BISHOP D: Don't talk nonsense −

PRIEST: She was raped in the ghettos of their hell! Not by some
            mysterious seed of original sin! And we cover one
            injustice with another! The sin of wilful deception!

BISHOP D: How dare you −

PRIEST: Accuse us of hypocrisy? Why not? When it's the truth!
            And when she's demanding that the truth be spoken! In
            the name of life!

BISHOP D: You believe in her −

PRIEST: Aye! Now that I understand −

BISHOP D: Read the letters man! She has no support!

            FATHER GALLAGHER lifts the open file.

PRIEST: No support? *(Scatters the file)* What do these letters
            prove? That people can write what we taught them? In
            the shadow of the strap and the stole? *(Scatters a second
            file)* What do these letters show? That people have
            thought it all through? Afraid to challenge our laws?
            (Scatters a third file) What do these letters mean? That
            people will condemn on demand? In fear of eternal
            damnation? *(Picks up a letter)* Look at the pent-up desire!
            In the force of the marks on the page! Look at the pent-up
            fear! Each line punctuated with saints! Look at the pent-up
            misery! Not a question mark to be seen! And look at the
            pent-up hatred! In the spit that smudges the name! No
            support? Where's the compassion? The doubt? *(Scatters a
            fourth file)* Where, Martin? Where? *(Scatters a fifth file)*
            Where the desire to understand? Where, Martin? Where?
            (Scatters a sixth file) Why such bitter disgust? And only
            cries for punishment and revenge? *(Scatters the seventh*

file) Show me the proof that just one of these letters was written out of love! Or by choice! Prove to me, Martin, that just one of these letters wasn't written by you!

The letters are scattered across the table and the floor. BISHOP DEVLIN stares at the PRIEST sprawled among the letters.

PRIEST: Even as a chorister you silenced me. As I knelt beside the thirteen coffins I asked where are the families? Where are the friends of the murdered? Why are they huddled in the cold? Beneath the weeping skies? Why is this chapel filled with dignitaries? And television cameras? And how do those poor people bear such suffering in silence? And as I lay in the darkness of my room in Maynooth I asked: why are we condemning these naked men and women? Are they not using their tortured bodies as testimonies to the unspeakable truth? Why am I being urged to pray for their souls, when Christ is surely among them? Why am I being urged to convince their families to doubt and betray their own convictions? And why are they being driven out of the chapels into the exile of scorn and isolation? And now. Once again. You instruct me to silence a witness to the barbarism of the world. A woman cries out against the invisible violence. That most dangerous violence that wears the mask of the street and speaks in our voice. And you urge me to betray her. To condemn her. I cannot. I will not. She is the voice of Derry. The voice of Dublin. The voice of Ireland though her own people might not yet know it. And she is the voice of the church today. Here in the world. But you will do all you can to silence her. Because her voice will pull down your throne.

The PRIEST stands calmly among the letters.

BISHOP D: I will inform the Cardinal of your awakening. You'll be assigned to another parish where you will not be tormented by such doubts and questions. Unless you choose to take off your cassock to better become a priest. I'll expect your decision within three days. Either way, make the necessary preparations to leave my diocese. Letters which arrive at Saint Mary's belong to the parish.

They will be taken care of and treated with all due respect. From this moment you are relieved of all your parish responsibilities. You are quite unwell. I will pray for you. You may go.

The PRIEST stares up at BISHOP DEVLIN.

PRIEST: May I have her letter?

BISHOP D: Perhaps. It may be necessary to keep it for a while.

The PRIEST shakes his head. He goes to the door and opens it.

BISHOP D: Declan.

The PRIEST turns.

BISHOP D: Responsibility has nothing to do with compassion. It requires cool judgement. And certainty. I shall be sorry to lose you. We had the highest expectations.

BISHOP DEVLIN turns and walks to the window.

SCENE 10: INSIGHT

Friday night. 11pm. DIANE's unoccupied flat. MARIE lies sleeping. She turns in her sleep, obviously dreaming. There is a bucket beside her on the floor. A single lamp lights the room from the desk. Silence. DIANE enters with a portable heater. MARIE stirs. DIANE plugs the heater into the wall and puts her folder of work on the desk.

MARIE: No! No! Diane! Diane!

          DIANE rushes over to MARIE's side.

MARIE: The dead are going to rise! The dead are going to rise, Diane!

DIANE: You're alright, mucker. It's that dream –

MARIE: Oh Diane! It was so clear!

DIANE: Lie back. *(Mops MARIE's brow)* You've still that fever inside you.

          MARIE lies back in her pillows. She is awake.

DIANE: You alright now?

MARIE: The trees were all twisted and black. *(Beat)* What time is it Diane?

DIANE: Can't see. Late anyway. Here. Let me moisten your lips.

          DIANE takes some cotton wool and dips it into a second tumbler beside MARIE. She moistens MARIE's lips gently as she talks.

DIANE: People are pouring over that dream like a riddle. In Dublin they've turned the ten imagines into a song. And you've all kinds claiming they wrote it! *(Beat)* Get more water the morrow. They must think I'm a health freak in Wellworths. I'll have to start buying it somewhere else. *(Beat)* The recording went well. They're getting the editing down to three hours –

MARIE: Cold Diane. Cold –

DIANE: You'll feel the heat now in a minute. I borrowed me da's heater. And I've cream for your body. Have to rub it in every six hours. Keep your skin moist. The doctor says there's next to no chance you'll miscarry. Not in the second trimester –

MARIE: I know.

DIANE: She'll come up whenever you ask.

DIANE puts down the swab and caresses MARIE's hair. She has her eyes closed.

MARIE: I'll take a wee taste of water, Diane.

DIANE reaches for the jug and pours some water into the tumbler. MARIE props herself up. DIANE holds out the glass.

DIANE: Here –

MARIE: Go and turn on the lamp so I can see.

DIANE: The lamp's on, Marie –

MARIE: Diane. Don't take the hand.

DIANE puts the tumbler onto the crate and goes to the desk. She lights a candle and returns to MARIE with the lit candle. DIANE holds the candle near to MARIE's face. No response.

MARIE: Diane?

DIANE: What d'you see, Marie?

MARIE: What?

DIANE: Here. Take my hand.

DIANE puts MARIE's hand round her own.

DIANE: There's a candle in it. Take the candle, Marie.

MARIE grasps the candle. DIANE wraps her hand around MARIE's.

DIANE: Can you see the flame? Careful, Marie –

MARIE: *(Searching)* I can feel it –

DIANE: Look, Marie –

MARIE: I'm are. No light, Diane –

DIANE: Open your eyes, Marie!

MARIE: I'm are!

DIANE: Search for the flame!

MARIE: *(Pause)* Just black, Diane –

DIANE: Marie, no! Look for Christ's sake!

MARIE: There's nothing, Diane! Not a glimmer! Not even a shadow!

DIANE: Nothing at all?

MARIE: Nothing, Diane. Just your touch.

DIANE blows out the candle and releases it from MARIE's hand. She cries silently. MARIE stares. DIANE rests the candle on the crate.

DIANE: Nothing's worth your sight.

MARIE: *(Arms open)* Diane.

DIANE takes MARIE in her arms.

DIANE: The bastards will take everything.

ACT 3

SCENE 11: AUCTION

Saturday night. 10pm. The DOHERTY sitting room. BERNIE and SAM are finishing dinner by candlelight. Several empty bottles of wine and plates on the table which stands to one side of the room. The framed wedding portrait has gone from the corner unit. 60s love songs in the background. A burst of laughter. SAM and BERNIE kiss.

BERNIE: Dublin would've been –

SAM: *(Finger to her lips)* Couldn't be helped.

BERNIE: I'd have gone shopping. Or waited in the hotel –

SAM: There'll be plenty of time for all that.

BERNIE: Will there, Sam?

SAM: Sure I'll be back and forth now –

BERNIE: I know. Had me worked up to high dough!

SAM: The night's still young.

Silence between them.

SAM: Marie should come over to the States –

BERNIE: Marie?

SAM: Sure. Why not?

BERNIE: You've not stopped talking about her since that night –

SAM: Do her the world of good to get away. Travel broadens the mind. She could work for us if she wanted –

BERNIE: I wouldn't let her near you!

SAM: She'll break a few hearts right enough.

BERNIE: And what about her old woman?

SAM: *(Sips and considers)* She'll do. In the dark –

            They laugh.

BERNIE: What was I like? You're a tease, Sam Doherty. D'you know
            that? A fly-by-night! Sweep a girl off her feet. Promise her
            the moon. And then disappear! First time I've had you all
            to myself. Bet you've a woman in every port!

SAM: Only started living at fifty –

BERNIE: Hmm. I'm sure!

SAM: No regrets, Bernie?

BERNIE: Done me the world of good. *(Laughs)* Owe it all to that
            priest –

SAM: Is that right?

BERNIE: *(Laughs)* You know what I mean. Critter. Well he's done
            nothing on me. You don't know what you're getting
            yourself into nowadays. D'you think he'll be alright?

SAM: He's being moved. Somewhere quiet –

BERNIE: Probably for the best. Will you write to me, Sam?

SAM: Sure you'll have forgotten all about me before I land! Tell
            you what though. We'll visit the graves in the morning –

BERNIE: Aye. That would be right –

SAM: Make sure there's still room to park the oul carcass –

BERNIE: Sam! God forgive ye! See? You'll only be back here to die!

SAM: Sure we'll be together for eternity then but!

SAM clinks her wineglass and drinks. BERNIE laughs and leans over to kiss him. She catches him on the side of the nose and cheek leaving a smear of lipstick. BRIDIE stands in the doorway with a brown envelope in her hand as SAM and BERNIE lean in for a kiss.

BRIDIE: Very nice –

BERNIE: Ahhh! Jesus Mary and Saint Joseph!

BERNIE jumps out of her chair. SAM sits rigid with tension.

BRIDIE: Will I come back –

BERNIE: We're just after eating –

BRIDIE: So I see. You must've been licking the plate, Sam –

BERNIE: *(Laughs)* He's just after saying how he's going to visit the family plot –

BRIDIE: Seen him whispering it there now –

BERNIE: *(Laughs)* Aren't you Sam?

SAM smiles awkwardly and squawks an inarticulate reply.

BRIDIE: I think that means aye –

BERNIE: In the morning. He'll pick me up here. What about ten?

BRIDIE: Not going to mass, Bernie?

BERNIE: Oh aye. We'll go up after mass. Won't we, Sam?

Pause.

BRIDIE: You hiding a dirty book under your pillow, Sam?

SAM bursts out laughing like a child.

BRIDIE: You can't fool your own, Sam. Remember that. Did he ever –

SAM: *(Laughing)* You coming in, Bridie, or what?

BRIDIE: Don't want to be intruding but –

SAM: *(Smiles)* Will you pull up a chair, for Christ's sake!

BRIDIE enters the room and sits.

SAM: You're looking grand –

BRIDIE: That's shite, Sam Doherty, and you know it. You look well but. The both of yous –

SAM: Can't complain. Go and fetch her a glass, Bernie –

BRIDIE: No. I'm not stopping –

BERNIE: Just the one –

BRIDIE: I'm not in the form. Look. I'll get straight to the point –

SAM opens his arms wide and stands.

SAM: Bridie, Bridie, Bridie –

BRIDIE: Sam, don't be getting all sentimental. Now sit down.

SAM sits.

BRIDIE: There's hardly a word passed between us in ten years. No need to start pretending now just because you've a few bottles inside ye. I'm too tired for games. You live your life. I live mine. I've tried to keep out of your way. Heard you waffling on the TV, mind. You almost sounded convincing –

SAM: Will I take that as a compliment?

BRIDIE: Take it how you want. The wee priest stole the show –

BERNIE: Sure he's being manipulated –

BRIDIE: That's as may be. Listen. I've done up this application. For
              a wee project. We need capital. Just to get started –

              *BRIDIE opens the envelope and puts the application on
              the table. SAM puts on his glasses.*

BERNIE: Doesn't he look the part!

SAM: What's the project?

BRIDIE: A community creche. For the Bog. Nothing fancy. And a
              wee archive. It's all down in there.

BERNIE: A community creche, Bridie?

SAM: Right. *(Glasses off)* I'll look at it on the plane and get back
              to you first thing –

BRIDIE: Oh no. I want a commitment from you the night, Sam –

SAM: Sure leave me browse through it –

BRIDIE: And what?

SAM: I need to present it to the board, Bridie –

BRIDIE: Ach, Sam. This is Bridie you're talking to. I know who
              makes the decisions. There's only one signature that
              counts. Go ahead and read it –

BERNIE: Bridie, it's Sam's last night –

BRIDIE: This won't take two minutes. Then I'll leave yous in peace.

SAM: *(Pause)* How much d'you need?

BRIDIE: Need or expect?

SAM: What are yous asking for?

BRIDIE: Twenty grand. Two wages. A minibus. And enough to
            keep us going for a year –

SAM: No can do. That kinda money has to go before the
            executive –

BRIDIE: Sam. Yous won't be able to get moving around here
            without our sayso –

SAM: Is that a threat, Bridie?

BRIDIE: No. It's a fact.

SAM: *(Smiles)* Times have changed –

BRIDIE: Not round here they haven't –

BERNIE: Are you sure you won't take some wine –

SAM: Bridie. Look. How's it going to pay for itself? I can't be
            throwing away other people's money. You've nothing to
            sell. No products. Don't get me wrong. Mothers all need
            a break. And community history's important. National
            identity and so on. But what's in it for my investors? How
            will you pay next year's wages?

BRIDIE: Sam –

SAM: And the overheads? Where's your business plan?

BRIDIE: Sam, look –

SAM: No, you listen to me. I'm not creating dependency –

BRIDIE: Charity starts at home –

SAM: Not anymore, Bridie. And I'm not going back to them days –

BRIDIE: You don't trust me –

SAM: It's nothing like that. I don't handle lame ducks.

BRIDIE: D'you want me to beg? Is that it?

SAM: Listen. I've a better idea. Why don't yous both come over this summer? As my guests? Bernie'll bring Marie. You bring the application –

BERNIE: Sam, Marie's got her exams –

SAM: Sure after they're done. A wee celebration. We'll all head down to the shack in LA. All expenses paid –

BRIDIE: And you'd work on the application –

SAM: Better than that. You'd get talking to the investors –

BERNIE: Always fancied Hollywood –

SAM: Do Marie a world of good to get out of this place –

BERNIE: She'd need her independence but –

SAM: Sure you can send her out early. We'll spend a few days together. Get to know each other again. Then she can go off on her own. I've missed you all –

BRIDIE: Where's Marie anyway? Not seen her in weeks –

            BERNIE picks up the plates.

SAM: Ach, the oul doll's all embarrassed –

BERNIE: Sam. She's exams –

SAM: Get away with you, you liar! Tell her the truth!

BERNIE: Sam –

BRIDIE: Is she alright?

BERNIE brings the plates crashing down onto the table.

BERNIE: What d'you care if she's alright?

SAM: Bernie, now hold on. I was only carrying on –

BERNIE: I threw her out, Bridie! And d'you want to know why?

SAM: Because you're jealous –

BERNIE: Because *(pointing at BRIDIE)* she corrupted her mind!

BRIDIE: *(Stands)* Give me the application –

BERNIE: You'll stay right where you are! Sam. Move that carpet –

SAM: What –

BERNIE: I'll show yous the truth!

BERNIE storms into the kitchen. Sounds of a press and a drawer being flung open.

SAM: What's going on?

BRIDIE: Search me –

SAM: All I said was a wee trip –

BERNIE throws on the lights and returns with a hammer and the breadknife in her hand. She pulls back the carpet and levers away the boards.

SAM: Bernie, what's going on?

BRIDIE: I'm away –

BERNIE: Stay where you are! Guilty conscience all of a sudden?

I've no idea where me own daughter is, Bridie! But I'm sure you've a fair notion!

BERNIE heaves away at the fixed floorboards. They splinter and come away.

BERNIE: All them IRA books! Women! Contraception! Africa and South America! You think I don't know you're poisoning her mind with that filth! This is what they do to your home every week, Bridie! Isn't it? Or is it everyday? Sorry, I don't know! Because I'm a law-abiding citizen! Perhaps Marie could teach me!

BRIDIE: Bernie stop this –

BERNIE: Sit down! Let the truth speak for itself!

SAM: Bernie hold on! Now just hold –

SAM tries to restrain BERNIE. She pushes him away.

BERNIE: Leave me be! Fly-be-night! Take me to Dublin? Take me to the States? Start over? You just want her! Well you can go back and tell your snobby investors the truth about your wee angel! At them fancy dinners! Tell them about your saintly goddaughter who peeps and pries and steals into the night to destroy all their work! You want her on your own? Just for a few days? Well, let me show you the bargain you're getting!

SAM: Bernie! This is madness!

BERNIE: You're dead right it's madness lipstick-nose! And I've lived it for years on me own! Before yous interfered! Look at this city! Old rednose is throwing it all up in memory of his dead brother! And their sister's busy pulling it down all around us! To keep the same corpse alive!

A hole in the floor. BERNIE reaches into it and starts throwing shoeboxes into the air. Their contents spill out.

BRIDIE: What's all them shoes doing –

BERNIE: My personal collection! My own wee bit of madness! Sure
            how else would I fit in to this family?

            More and more boxes and shoes fly out all the time.

BERNIE: *(Searching)* Wee tramp in short dresses and black floosey
            tights! Doesn't know the meaning of virtue! Because you
            poisoned her mind! Where is it? You rear them up to
            respect themselves with no support to speak of and what
            do they do? You can't be there all the time watching
            them! Someone has to bring in the crop! And she's up
            there reading and doing I don't know what in the dark!
            What's she reading, Bridie? How to terrorise godfearing
            mothers? How to mutilate innocent wains?

BRIDIE: Bernie –

BERNIE: Slut thinks I don't know! Never wronged her in my life!
            Only ever laid me hands on daddy's girl in temper! She's
            even betrayed him! No revenge? She's shamed the very
            ground he lies in! Where is it? Bet she took it with her!
            The sleekid bookworm! Read, read, read! How to blow up
            banks in the name of peace! How to blow up shopping
            centres in the name of justice! I warned her to keep away
            from your corruption! To keep her distance from your
            innocent sons! But oh no! You had to seduce her! Fill her
            mindless hours with resistance and freedom! Why don't
            yous recruit children? So they could do twenty years and
            still go back out into the night! It's all manipulation the
            day! You don't know who's with you or against you
            anymore! If the innocent could cry –

            *BERNIE stops dead. Fifty boxes and pairs of shoes lie
            scattered across the floor.*

BERNIE: There! There! The truth!

            SAM and BERNIE peer into the hole.

BERNIE: *(Pointing)* See your work! Satan!

SAM: It's a box –

BERNIE: I know it's a box, fly-be-night! But what's in it?

BRIDIE: It's a strongbox.

BERNIE: You recognise it then!

BRIDIE: Bernie what –

SAM kneels and reaches for the box. BERNIE restrains him.

BERNIE: Sam, no! No! Let her –

SAM: Jesus, Bernie! It's a black box just –

BERNIE: Aye! But it might explode! See how it's lying!

SAM: Ach get away with ye! Bridie, that couldn't explode –

BRIDIE: Don't be absurd. Sure where are the wires?

BERNIE: Inside!

BRIDIE: *(Laughs)* What's a bomb going to be doing under your floor?

BERNIE: You stick your mits on it then!

BRIDIE: It's an old munitions box, Bernie –

BERNIE: Aye. Just fusewire and semtex. She holding it for you?

BRIDIE: You don't really think –

BERNIE: You lift it out then! You be sent down for life!

BRIDIE: Here. Mind out the way –

BRIDIE kneels and reaches for the box. SAM restrains her.

SAM: She might have a point –

BERNIE: You're dead right I've a point! Turn me own daughter
            against me for no reason? And then get me sent away for
            life? She's jealous of all this in here! Cause deep down she
            wishes she had it too! Now d'you see the truth?

            BRIDIE shakes her head.

SAM: This is ridiculous! It's an oul box, for God's sake!

            *SAM reaches into the hole and carefully lifts out the black
            box.*

SAM: Gently does it –

BERNIE: *(Hands to head)* Jesus Jesus Jesus Jesus Jesus –

            *BERNIE scrambles behind the sofa as SAM steps among
            the shoes to carry the box over to the table. He tries to
            open it as BRIDIE approaches.*

SAM: Locked. Maybe rusted –

BRIDIE: *(Beside him)* Sure there our John's initials –

BERNIE: Sly bitch used her own father's box!

SAM: Here pass me the hammer.

            *BRIDIE reaches for the hammer on the sofa and passes it
            to SAM.*

BERNIE: *(Behind the sofa)* It's going to explode! It's going to
            explode!

BRIDIE: Ach wise up, Bernie!

BERNIE: And I'm just after having the whole house redone!

SAM: Sure you won't be worrying about shoes for the rest of
            your life!

            *SAM levers open the box. He carefully opens the lid. He
            looks inside and shakes his head. He lifts out a tightly
            folded jacket. BERNIE crosses herself and covers her
            mouth with her hands. She takes several steps forward.*

BRIDIE: Our John's jacket −

            *SAM unfolds the jacket. A tobacco case falls to the floor.
            SAM reaches for it. It has a note taped to it's lid. BERNIE
            falls to her knees among the shoes.*

BRIDIE: There the case that saved his life −

BERNIE: He swore to me he burnt it −

SAM: *(Reads)* As evidence −

BRIDIE: *(Jacket)* There the hole where the bullet escaped −

SAM: Must've been lying there years −

BERNIE: God pardon and forgive me! God pardon and forgive me!
            Forgive me God −

            *BERNIE rocks to and fro on her knees. She reaches for the
            jacket unawares. BRIDIE hands it to her as SAM opens the
            tobacco case.*

SAM: Wee notes −

            *BRIDIE returns to his side as he lifts the two comms out of
            the case.*

BRIDIE: My Liam's writing. *(Takes one and instantly recognises it)*
            Here's when he put his name forward. Thought they were
            all long lost −

SAM: Here a poem. Or a song. Need me glasses –

           SAM reaches for his glasses as BERNIE presses the jacket to her face. BRIDIE stares as SAM reads.

SAM: *(Reads)* Modern Times. By Bobby Sands –

BRIDIE: They shared a cell –

BERNIE: Forgive me, John. Forgive me. Forgive me, John. Forgive me. Why did you leave me but to suffer on me own? Forgive me, John. Forgive me –

BRIDIE: Can see him yet. Sitting. In his blanket. Like it was yesterday –

SAM: *(Reads)* In the gutter lies the black man dead. And where the oil flows blackest. The street runs red. *(Beat)* Prophetic –

BERNIE: Why did you leave me, John? Why did you leave me, John? Why –

BRIDIE: Said he'd go on. Even though it was over. And the Christmas tree. Blown over in the storm. D'you mind the Christmas tree, Sam? Up in Creggan –

SAM: Uncanny! Hear this. *(Reads)* And tomorrow's wretch will leave it's mother's womb! Coincidence or vision d'you think?

BRIDIE: I've never been able to open his diaries –

SAM: I never knew Liam shared a cell with Sands –

BRIDIE: Sure you never asked –

SAM: Now I was up there with him many times –

BRIDIE: You only visited him the once. Out of obligation.

BRIDIE turns to BERNIE. She is rocking gently. BRIDIE reaches down and lifts her on to the sofa. BERNIE clings to the jacket. BRIDIE takes her hands in her own.

BRIDIE: You alright girl?

BERNIE: Why did he leave me all alone, Bridie? Why did he have to die?

BRIDIE: Sure that's why he buried the jacket, Bernie.

BERNIE: Oh. All them shoes, Bridie! Look at all them shoes!

BRIDIE: I know –

BERNIE: They're so beautiful. All them colours –

BRIDIE: Aye –

BERNIE: Why there's enough shoes here for all Derry!

BRIDIE: D'you know why, Bernie?

BERNIE: Why what?

BRIDIE: Where'd the shoes all come from, Bernie?

BERNIE: *(Points)* From the clown!

BRIDIE: Where'd the shoes come from, Bernie?

BERNIE: From the hole –

BRIDIE: And who put them there, Bernie?

BERNIE: Promise you won't tell anyone?

BRIDIE: *(Smiles)* Aye.

BERNIE: Can't help myself, Bridie. Can't help myself, John. Where's his picture?

BRIDIE: *(Glances round)* We'll find it now –

BERNIE: Keep going back, Bridie. Don't know why. Keep going
            back for more. Can't stop myself. Never seem to be
            satisfied. See they don't fit me. Always buying and buying
            and can't seem to settle on what I want. Even dream of
            shoes, Bridie –

BRIDIE: Let's get them all red up –

BERNIE: Will Marie forgive me, Bridie? And John? D'you think John
            sees the shoes?

BRIDIE: *(Smiles)* What if he does? Let's pick them all up –

BERNIE: Shoes everywhere Bridie. How will we get rid of them all?

BRIDIE: Sure we'll set up a stall –

BERNIE: Aye! Up in the Heights!

            SAM starts to laugh. BERNIE looks at him open eyed.

BRIDIE: You're a cruel bastard Sam –

SAM: Don't you see! The hand of god's in this! It was meant to
            be!

BRIDIE: Aye right. Help me to red up these shoes –

SAM: Bridie! Listen –

BRIDIE: Look at the shape of her floor –

SAM: The creche! The community archive! It's all here!

BRIDIE: What's this? A spasm of conscience?

SAM: Wait till you hear! The jacket and these letters! It's the past
            giving itself up! To be remembered! Just one fraction of a
            huge collection! In attics and cellars! In the pockets of old

clothes! Pressed inside books! Letters and leaflets! Banners and posters! Newspapers and photographs! Personal scrapbooks and prison diaries! Fading recordings of all the great speeches! Even discarded mural designs! Now is the time to start gathering it all together! To be protected and displayed in a magnificent heritage centre here in Derry!

BRIDIE: For Japanese and American tourists?

SAM: Don't be so cynical! For ourselves! For our grandwains. In memory of Liam. And John. And the courage and vision of the Irish people!

BRIDIE: Sure that's what I'm after proposing there now –

SAM: These letters could be used but! To raise the money –

BRIDIE: Sam, I'd sell me eyes before I parted with them –

SAM: (Comms) Sell these? What d'you mean? They're priceless! Unique! They belong here! They're part of the people! No. You make prints. Say a limited edition of ten. Then you frame them. Nothing fancy. Just as they are. You keep these for the centre and you auction the prints.

BRIDIE: And what? You might make a few hundred dollars –

SAM: Bridie, they'd raise hundreds of thousands! I know the Irish-American mind! Haven't I already proved that! They'll be fighting each other to get their hands on one of these prints! And I've the contacts and commitment to make it work! I'll pledge all that now! Labour free!

BRIDIE: You'd do that?

SAM: Bridie. I lost a brother too. John saved these as evidence. Evidence of all our suffering. As well as the many lives that were lost. Imagine it, Bridie. Imagine all the evidence preserved in one building. Behind glass! Instead of lying rotting and dispersed under floors. It would be studied! Turned into books! Instead of decaying in the forgotten

drawers and dusty attics of our homes. If I took these back
with me to the States they'd convince the board to invest
like that! They'd inspire Irish-Americans across the nation!

BRIDIE: *(Beat)* And the creche –

SAM: You stick it all in one building. You'd want a restaurant. A
wee theatre. And a library too. You could twin it with a
centre in New York! That's the kinda money these'll
inspire!

BRIDIE: *(Smiles)* Would it be called the *Sam Doherty Centre*?

SAM: *(Smiles)* Your decision. You'll have to name the
benefactors somewhere in the building. Even loan the odd
letter now and then. But sure. Aren't we all Irish too? As
dispersed as the collection itself? Bridie! If we made the
prints now you'd have your heritage centre in two years!

*BRIDIE stands and takes the comms from SAM. He
releases them confidently. BRIDIE is clearly moved.
BERNIE watches in fascination.*

BRIDIE: Incredible. Who'd have thought. Two years just? We'd
want to design it ourselves now. The place is coming
down with heritage centres no-one goes into. People
need to feel it's theirs. And we'd want ones from the Bog
running it. Not cleaning it –

SAM: *(Chequebook)* How much d'you need? To start off? You'll
need a team. An office. An architect and a surveyor.
Twenty five grand? Forty?

BRIDIE: I'd have to sit down –

SAM: Work it all out. Include your mortgage. You don't want to
be worrying about debt. We could throw in a grand for
the shoes. You want people like Bernie in from the start.
Say thirty thousand now. As a deposit of good faith. We'll
take it from here month by month.

BRIDIE: I need time to think. Get back to the women –

SAM: *(Writing the cheque)* You do that. And think of the men and women who gave up their lives to make the new Ireland possible. Think what they would've wanted. How they'd have wanted their contribution kept alive.

BRIDIE: We hold on to the originals –

SAM tears out the cheque and places it on the dinner table.

SAM: You'll have them back in Derry inside two years. On my word. They'll be insured and go straight into a safe in my office. Or better still up on the walls.

BRIDIE: Of a bank?

SAM: Aye. To inspire our investors. Are we ashamed of our past? Let them see what their new Ireland arose from. You'll see them yourselves if you come –

BRIDIE: Hang these on the walls of a bank?

SAM: Bridie, I want to be able to enjoy them myself! Haven't we both sacrificed everything for the dream? You've dedicated your whole life. And your sons. For me there's been nothing but hard graft. For the means to make our dream come true! We're two sides of the same coin, Bridie. The struggle is over. This centre will document it all. It will guarantee our children's children never forget. Our whole Irish family will be able to look back in pride and understand how our new Ireland came to be.

BRIDIE looks at the comms in her hand. She looks at SAM and begins working the spit in her mouth.

SAM: What're you doing?

BRIDIE: Dry.

SAM: *(Smiles)* It's a special moment, Bridie –

            BRIDIE pushes the comms into her mouth.

SAM: Bridie what –

BRIDIE: Back where they came from –

SAM: Bridie, no –

            BRIDIE starts chewing. SAM rushes over to her and tries to prise open her mouth.

SAM: Bridie! No! Think of the centre! Liam! Bernie! Help me! Bridie, stop! Spit em out! A shrine! A celebration! Healing! Open! I demand you to open! Spit! Priceless! Don't swallow! Idiot! Bernie! Still save them! Open! Priceless Bridie! Liam! Bernie! Open up you fool! Liam! You fool! You fool!

            BRIDIE swallows. SAM stares in amazement.

SAM: Why? It was all in the palm of your hand! You fool! I understand. You need to keep them alive. The grief. You can't live without it. You don't dare let it go. You're afraid you'll fall apart. Lose the meaning of your life. I understand. Well, there are others. Ready –

BRIDIE: Out –

SAM: What –

            BRIDIE picks up the breadknife from the table.

BRIDIE: Out –

SAM: Now, Bridie –

BRIDIE: Out –

SAM: I overreacted –

BRIDIE: Out –

SAM: I understand –

BRIDIE: Out Judas. Come back and I'll kill ye. Don't even return
            here to die. Even I'm gone the ground will vomit you up –

SAM: Bridie, you're –

BRIDIE: Out!

            *SAM reaches for his jacket without taking his eyes off the
            knife.*

BRIDIE: And take your bloodmoney!

SAM: *(Pleading)* Bridie, I'm your brother!

BRIDIE: I almost believed you. Now leave.

            *SAM looks at BERNIE and leaves. BRIDIE walks calmly to
            the table and puts down the breadknife. She turns to face
            BERNIE.*

BERNIE: I quite fancied the shack.

            BRIDIE smiles.

BERNIE: And his nose. If he goes into a bar –

            *BERNIE and BRIDIE laugh. Radio Threshold is heard in the
            darkness of the auditorium.*

            This woman sat in her home everyday. She wanted to go
            out. She wanted many things. But she was denied them.
            So she promised the world to her daughter. But she
            would never let her go out because she was lonely. Night
            after night the mother cried in her bed. But every morning
            she came down the stairs with her husband's smile on her
            face. One morning her daughter asked her why she
            smiled. I hear you crying in your sleep every night. The

mother cracked and exploded like a dam unable to bear
the strain of her suffering. Her daughter got caught up in
the flood and thought she'd broken her mother. She hid
the tears under her bed in case someone accused her.
Now some years later the mother found her crying in her
room. "Go to the priest," she said, "and he'll build you a
dam." And he did! And the tears went away! But
everytime the dam broke she had to go back to him. And
her daughters and their daughters did the same. And they
all dreamed of the time when they'd no longer need a
dam. Until one day one of her great great grandchildren
went up to the priest who was now very old and asked:
"Father, who owns the world the dam's built on?" The old
priest was shocked at the question and replied: "Sure it's
a mystery! All I have is the design!" And she spat in his
face and tore up the design and flowed away to be free!

SCENE 12: THE SIGN

Sunday afternoon. 1.20pm. DIANE's unoccupied flat. MARIE lies sleeping in the semi-darkness. There is a bucket on the floor beside her. The curtains are closed. Sound of rain beating against the window. The PRIEST is sitting at the desk. He has been sitting in the same position for several hours. He wears a blue tracksuit. His peaked cap lies on the desk beside him. He watches MARIE. Total stillness. Suddenly the voice of DIANE outside talking to a small boy.

DIANE: *(Off)* Shouldn't you be inside?

BOY: *(Off)* D'you live in there?

DIANE: *(Off)* Aye. What d'they call ye?

BOY: *(Off)* Packie Bonner. You seen our Kesh?

DIANE: *(Off)* Who's Kesh?

BOY: *(Off)* Our pup. D'you believe in human bombs?

DIANE: *(Off)* What's a human bomb, Packie?

BOY: *(Off)* The devil inside ye. There's Kesh! See ya!

> *The PRIEST stands and peers through a crack in the curtains onto the street. Sound of DIANE opening and closing the front door. She climbs the stairs. The PRIEST turns to face DIANE as she enters. She is drenched. She is carrying a multicoloured umbrella and a portable tape recorder. Both whisper as they talk.*

DIANE: Chucking it down! Has she woken?

> *The PRIEST shakes his head. DIANE puts the tape recorder down on the desk and looks into the bucket.*

DIANE: Always rains whenever there's a rally or a march. Your man up there's definitely a pro-lifer! Even me umbrella broke!

*The PRIEST smiles. DIANE takes the umbrella into the
kitchen and returns with a towel to dry her hair.*

DIANE: Total disaster!

PRIEST: I'll have to be going in a few minutes.

DIANE: *(Watch)* You've plenty of time yet. Leave her sleep a bit
            longer.

            DIANE dries her hair.

PRIEST: Did you get your interview done?

DIANE: Aye. Letitia was brilliant. She's thought it all out by
            herself. It's just clicked. She's kicked out her husband. And
            she's fighting to get back the wain. Told her she should
            speak to you –

PRIEST: She'll have to move fast.

            *DIANE puts down the towel and takes off her coat. She
            drapes it over the chair.*

DIANE: Won't be able to keep up the two lives. Have to give up
            the radio any day now. Told them me da's not been too
            well. Someone else can do the interviews and debates.
            Did you come to any decision?

PRIEST: *(Shakes his head)* I've been able to think though. It's
            peaceful here. Like an oasis.

DIANE: I'm glad we had a chance to get to know each other a bit.
            Seems like I've known you for years. I've never talked to a
            priest before. Listen to us! Whispering like two conspirators!

PRIEST: *(Smiles)* Will you be alright?

DIANE: *(Nods)* I'm not alone anymore. If you know what I mean.
            Talking to you. The doctor helped too. Sound woman so
            she is.

PRIEST: What will you do now she's stopped writing?

DIANE: I'm sure we'll keep talking. As long as she's the strength.
           And she wants to record some of her thoughts. For the
           radio. No-one would know her voice now.

PRIEST: D'you think she's afraid?

DIANE: No. Not exactly. Resigned. Prepared. It's given her great
           freedom. When me ma died I avoided the question for
           years. I didn't believe in heaven. And I knew we were
           living in hell. So where was she? Marie's found her own
           answer. Takes some courage. To go it alone. But it's freed
           her from the fear of it. And she knows that's what's used
           to control us –

PRIEST: Fear of death?

DIANE: Aye. Fear of loss too. Of who we are. Having no name
           started her thinking. She says we're here. Then we die
           and return to the land. Become part of the future. How
           we live. What we do. Lives on. First as memories attached
           to our name. Then as stories and examples in everyday
           banter and the minds of our community. The human soil.
           Our names die. But we shape the future. Simple isn't it?

PRIEST: (Smiles) She'll be canonized when she dies. Her letters are
           startling. First time I met her I sensed she was different –

DIANE: Listen. If you're going to make this rally I'd best waken
           her now. Might take her a little time to come round.
           D'you know we're attempting a live broadcast from the
           Guildhall Square?

PRIEST: Isn't that a bit risky?

DIANE: There's a young fella down there could be making a
           fortune in electronics. Mind she might not be able to see
           you now.

The PRIEST nods as DIANE kneels beside MARIE. Her wet hair drips onto MARIE's face. DIANE smiles at the PRIEST.

DIANE: Splashed her.

DIANE wipes the drops gently away. MARIE smiles.

DIANE: She's burning with the fever. Marie? Marie?

MARIE stirs.

DIANE: Will you take a wee drink, Marie? You've not had anything for hours.

MARIE opens her eyes. She smiles at DIANE.

DIANE: First smile out of you in days.

DIANE looks at the PRIEST. He puts his finger to his lips. DIANE lifts MARIE a little and offers her some water from the tumbler. MARIE drinks. The water comes back up immediately. DIANE reaches for the bucket efficiently. MARIE is now awake. Dry retching. DIANE handles the situation with calm.

DIANE: Alright. Alright. Try a wee taste later on.

MARIE settles back. DIANE waits patiently.

MARIE: Smell the rain. Off you.

DIANE: There's been fierce storms all morning. Started last night.

MARIE: I dreamt people were stamping and hammering on my coffin.

DIANE moves.

MARIE: No. *(Beat)* As they chanted their abuse I could see the shape of their knuckles and fists. With each blow the lid trembled. Deafening my whimpering pleas. With each curse the air became hotter. Till the dark burned my throat. They were pounding the coffin against my ribs and my neck. My knees forced open my mouth and their rage poured inside me. Blackening my skin and blistering my eyes and my heart. I cried out and my pain pierced their chants. Suddenly knuckles were gripping the sides of my head and wrenching me out of the dark. The chants fell to murmurs. And then hands. Hands everywhere. All over my body. A huge blade slit me from my throat to my womb. Needles pierced my side. And I lay there in great agony. Unable to speak. Open. Black. Shrivelled. And then tears dropped into my sunken eyes. And the gentlest voice. Calling. Soothing. Calling me. By my name. And breathing it's gentleness into my open body. *(Beat)* I love you, Diane.

DIANE embraces MARIE.

MARIE: Can I go to the window, Diane?

DIANE: Aye.

DIANE helps MARIE out of her bed. The PRIEST moves back and onto his knees by the wall. DIANE leads MARIE slowly to the window. She wears a white nightshirt. As they reach the window DIANE draws back the curtains slightly. MARIE inhales deeply.

MARIE: Would you fetch me some fresh water, Diane?

DIANE: Aye surely.

DIANE goes into the kitchen. The PRIEST ejaculates an almost silent prayer.

PRIEST: Dear Lord, thank you –

MARIE turns to face the sound.

PRIEST: Thank you for blessing me with your presence –

MARIE: Who's there?

              *The PRIEST cannot speak. Sound of water being poured in
              the kitchen.*

MARIE: Diane?

PRIEST: O most chaste Virgin Mary, I beseech thee. By that
              unspotted purity. Whereby thou didst prepare for the Son
              of God –

MARIE: Declan?

PRIEST: A most agreeable dwelling in thy virginal womb –

MARIE: Declan, is that you?

PRIEST: That through thy intercession –

              *MARIE moves towards the praying PRIEST. Her hand
              outstretched.*

PRIEST: I may be cleansed from every stain. O most humble Virgin
              Mary. I beseech thee by that profound humility whereby
              thou didst merit –

              *DIANE comes out of the kitchen and stops with the jug in
              her hand.*

PRIEST: To be raised high above all the choirs of Angels and Saints –

              *MARIE reaches the PRIEST guided by his voice. Her hands
              touch his face and he trembles visibly.*

PRIEST: That through thy intercession all my negligences may be
              expiated –

MARIE: Declan –

PRIEST: Oh bless me, Marie –

MARIE: *(Laughs gently)* Get up off your knees, mucker –

PRIEST: Marie –

MARIE: Ach wise up and help me back to my bed!

MARIE begins to raise the PRIEST. He stands with his head bowed and unable to look at her. DIANE watches.

PRIEST: Marie, I am not worthy –

MARIE: Now I don't know where I'm are. Where's me bed, Declan?

The PRIEST guides MARIE back to her bed. He pulls back the duvets shyly and MARIE finds her way down. She settles.

MARIE: Thank you for coming.

The PRIEST cannot speak. DIANE approaches and pours water into the tumbler.

DIANE: *(Glass)* Here. You give it to her.

The PRIEST takes the tumbler in his hands.

MARIE: Take a sip yourself, Declan. It's beautiful water so it is.

The PRIEST sips some water and then guides the glass into MARIE's hand.

MARIE: Don't be alarmed now if it comes up all over you!

MARIE sips. The water stays down. She sips some more.

MARIE: *(Glass)* Thanks. That's enough.

The PRIEST puts the tumbler down onto the crate. He stands.

MARIE: You're fine where you were.

            The PRIEST sits.

MARIE: How's the form, mucker?

PRIEST: Grand. I'm nervous, Marie –

MARIE: Are you angry?

PRIEST: No. I've a clear heart –

MARIE: And a clear mind?

PRIEST: Aye. Thanks to you, Marie –

MARIE: Thanks to yourself. No doubts now?

PRIEST: You've done more for this city than I ever could.

MARIE: *(Smiles)* Your voice sounds different –

DIANE: Maybe your hearing –

MARIE: No. Lower –

PRIEST: I'm not wearing my collar –

MARIE: Aha!

            The PRIEST smiles. He is beginning to relax.

PRIEST: What about yourself?

MARIE: Stronger than I sound. And look. Don't worry about me
            eyes. They come and go. The foetus is probably using
            them. Did you know the body's geared up for the survival
            of the foetus at this stage? What did the doctor call it,
            Diane?

DIANE: The preferential option –

            The PRIEST laughs aloud.

MARIE: What's so funny?

PRIEST: It all makes sense. That's all.

MARIE: So you're not wearing your collar. Is that your decision?

PRIEST: *(Smiles)* No. I'm going to the rally. I don't want to be
            mobbed by the News of the World –

DIANE: He's a disguise. Looks like a yank!

MARIE: *(Smiles)* D'you know what you'll do?

PRIEST: I'm not sure yet. I thought we might talk. Perhaps
            tomorrow. If you're up to it.

MARIE: You'll have to arrange it with my secretary.

            DIANE and the PRIEST smile.

MARIE: Aye. Come down. You can tell us how it went. Are you
            going to the rally, Diane?

DIANE: Are you?

MARIE: Go if you want to. Go together. Yous won't be more than
            an hour anyway.

DIANE: No. Sure I can hear it on the radio. I've been away all
            morning –

PRIEST: Why don't you both go? You'd get a tremendous
            reception, Marie.

MARIE: No, Declan. Did I interrupt you?

PRIEST: No.

MARIE: My being anonymous strengthens the city. D'you see?
            Every hour longer I'm unknown the more people
            question. At least now there's no doubt I exist. Thanks to
            you. Did you hear THE DAMNED Declan?

            The PRIEST nods.

MARIE: D'you know who wrote that story? Letitia. The woman
            who –

PRIEST: I know.

MARIE: If I went out now all people would see is my suffering.
            Derry people love suffering. When they should be
            demanding pleasure. In every part of their lives! Now that
            would change everything! If I live – and if this child inside
            me lives – it will be for pleasure!

DIANE: Count me into that!

PRIEST: *(Smiles)* I've some catching up to do –

            DIANE and MARIE laugh.

PRIEST: Marie. How will you know if you'll live? The sign –

MARIE: I'll know.

            The PRIEST smiles sadly. A moment of tension.

DIANE: You'd think she was a prophet! And I have to live with
            that everyday!

            MARIE reflects. The PRIEST stands.

PRIEST: I'd better go. I'll be late.

MARIE: You should speak to others too. About your decision.

PRIEST: I will.

The PRIEST puts on his glasses and peaked cap.

PRIEST: I'll see you both tomorrow.

MARIE nods and smiles deep in thought.

PRIEST: Take care, Marie.

MARIE: *(Closes her eyes)* Thank you for coming.

DIANE: Come on. I'll see you to the door.

The PRIEST and DIANE leave. MARIE sips some water as they go down the stairs. Sound of a door being opened. MARIE puts down the tumbler. DIANE closes the door. She runs up the stairs. She enters with a deep blush. MARIE is smiling.

DIANE: Fuck I could jump his bones to death but! And you never know what's underneath them skirts! He's wile shy but –

MARIE: *(Smiles)* Diane –

DIANE: Right. Sorry. All that talk about pleasure's got me hot. And here's him. I've some catching up to do! I nearly died! He can catch up with me any time!

DIANE laughs. MARIE smiles.

DIANE: Right. I've brought the radio tape recorder back. Will you remember that dream?

MARIE: Diane –

DIANE: You've not taken offence?

MARIE: Come sit beside me a wee minute –

DIANE: Oh no. You too? I should've thought –

MARIE: Diane. Come here.

DIANE sits beside MARIE. MARIE takes her hand.

MARIE: Diane. It's over. I'm only after seeing it just now.

DIANE: What's over Marie?

MARIE: The freedomstrike. I've got to live.

DIANE: I don't understand –

MARIE: Diane. He asked me to bless him –

DIANE: *(Laughs)* I'd have given anything for a camera –

MARIE: Diane! That's the sign!

DIANE: The what?

MARIE: The sign! Don't you see? I'm being turned into an icon before me very eyes! My letters are being puffed up into epistles –

DIANE: Into what?

MARIE: Prophetic writings!

DIANE: Sure what d'you expect? They are!

MARIE: Even you're doing it! Declan greeted me on his knees!

DIANE: And what? He's a priest –

MARIE: Imagine if I died. If I wasn't assassinated by the tabloids or smeared by the church, I'd be turned into a martyr. A portrait to be hung on the wall. They'd turn me into an ideal. An ideal of sacrifice. Another Virgin Mary! The very last thing we need!

DIANE: You a Virgin Mary? How? She's the model of passivity –

MARIE: Aye now! But she wasn't!

DIANE: Then be a model of outrage! Marie every struggle needs
            it's martyrs!

MARIE: Isn't that how they've always been absorbed but? Isn't
            that how we women have always been shown? The
            ultimate sacrifice? And isn't that how they always wash
            the blood off their hands? Perhaps the most cynical
            calculating risk they take –

DIANE: Who? What?

MARIE: To create martyrs! Aren't people always dwarfed by
            heroes! If I died. In one week or two. They'd have probed
            and scavenged my corpse for the story they need. On one
            day they might need a devil. The next they might need a
            saint. And my rape fits perfectly! But if I remain unknown
            they can't interpret me. Except as a coward. Or a
            madwoman. And by then it will be too late. Any woman
            in Derry could've been me! Now that's far more inspiring
            than any picture! The strength that's inside now can only
            grow! Now d'you see? I need to make it known I've come
            off. D'you think you could still stop the priest?

            DIANE staggers to her feet with the ideas.

DIANE: You can't come off now, Marie –

MARIE: What better time? When everyone's gathered together –

DIANE: Marie, the world's press is out there!

MARIE: Even better –

DIANE: You'll destroy everything we've achieved!

MARIE: D'you want me to die, Diane?

DIANE: No! Of course I don't! But there's now a momentum! The
            beginning of something new!

*DIANE goes to the window and tears the curtains apart.
She throws open the window. A cheer in the distance.*

DIANE: That's not Free Derry Corner, Marie. That's all the way over
            from the town. Think of the many women must be out
            there! There'd be no purpose! No focus −

MARIE: There'll be only one focus. One icon. Even I stayed alive.
            Imagine if Letitia could meet me now in the street. And
            knew. Would she continue writing? Would she continue
            thinking? Or would she get down on her knees in her
            head? *(Beat)* Diane. I now need to melt away. I'll explain
            in a last letter. Let people think the worst. This way they
            will be stronger. It might not seem like it at first. It might
            seem desperate. But it's already inside everyone out
            there. And it will be turned against them when I become
            known. Dead or alive. I need to remain unknown forever,
            Diane. That may be the only way forward the day. *(Pause)*
            It's over, Diane. That's our sign.

An enormous cheer carried by the wind.

DIANE: All the agony. The pressure −

MARIE: *(Smiles)* Is over. For now. Now we'll have the pleasure of
            seeing it all become practical. And people living as if the
            freedomstriker's among them. Didn't you argue it changes
            just step by step. People can't walk or run on their knees.
            We've them moving now in a new direction. Letitia's
            letter proves that, Diane.

DIANE sits exhausted and buries her face in her hands.

MARIE: I wonder if the child's still alive.

SCENE 13: BIRTHRIGHT

Sunday night. 10.30pm. The parochial house. Saint Mary's. Creggan. The meeting room study is considerably barer. Cases and several boxes stand ready to be moved. LINDA, EAMONN and PAULA are sitting and leaning on different pieces of furniture around the PRIEST who sits on one of the armchairs. Their conversation is drawing to a close. Silence. The PRIEST is wearing his collar.

PAULA: There's no point interrogating him Linda! We'll just have to wait for her letter the morrow.

            Silence.

LINDA: I feel scunnered. D'you know if the child's still alive?

PRIEST: She didn't say. The doctor will be examining her now –

LINDA: Maybe she panicked –

PRIEST: No. She was completely calm when I left her –

PAULA: *(To PRIEST)* Will you be able to make a meeting the morrow? We'll have to work out how to break the news. Not just for Derry. It'll fly across Ireland –

LINDA: Jesus, across the world!

PAULA: You should make a statement, Declan. It wouldn't surprise me if you were accused of making up the whole thing. And us of being led by the nose or using the story to bring down the church –

PRIEST: I'll give it some thought tonight. I'll drop by your offices as soon as I'm through with the Bishop.

PAULA: *(Smiles)* I'd love to be there when he hears you're staying! It'll be good for the radio. But it's a major step forward for Derry. We've needed someone like you for years –

PRIEST: *(Smiles)* I only wish I'd had some warning –

EAMONN: I know what you've been through. It's terrifying looking at
all you believe. Once you start questioning everything
seems to just collapse into doubt.

PAULA: You come out the stronger for it but –

EAMONN: Aye but while you're in it. Look at me ma –

PAULA: She'll be alright –

LINDA: There's no-one stronger –

EAMONN: Aye, but there's a world of grief she's holding inside. And
if she let's go. I don't know whether she could survive it.
There must be thousands like her. Holding on till it's all
over.

           Silent recognition.

PAULA: If you need the support, Declan, there's a crowd of good
people I know.

PRIEST: Thanks. I'm going to keep my head down for a while.
Work out my tactics. It's going to be some fight holding
onto the collar and defying the Bishop –

LINDA: Sure you won't be needing that now –

PRIEST: No it's staying on. I'm not ashamed of my faith. Or my
decision. And people need to see a real alternative –

PAULA: Me ma'll love you! A fighting priest! You know you're
welcome the night –

PRIEST: No. You speak to her first. Besides. I'm expecting someone
now. Tell your mother I'll talk to her tomorrow myself.

LINDA: What about your own mother?

PRIEST: It'll take her a bit of time to adjust.

PAULA: We should be getting back. Colin'll be waiting. And the others are coming down for eleven with the tapes.

They all stand.

LINDA: This's going to be a while difficult meeting.

PAULA: I know.

PRIEST: Remember you saved her. And she's brought new people together. Look at the rally –

LINDA: Don't talk to me! All I remember is him! Standing at the front –

EAMONN: Proudest moment of me life seeing you up there –

PAULA: Aye. And we pulled off a live outdoor broadcast. We thought that was years away.

LINDA: I hope she'll be alright. How will we know but? *(Smiles as she clicks)* I think I understand. C'mon lets go. I'll explain on the way back.

They all move to the door.

EAMONN: Declan. Would you marry us at home? Just the family and a few friends?

PRIEST: Of course. It wouldn't be legal now. In the eyes of the church or the state –

EAMONN: That's how we'd want it –

LINDA: Excuse me! What about asking me?

EAMONN: I'm just finding out. If we wrote our own oaths. Asked others to read out their own contributions –

PRIEST: I'd be honoured. You'll need her consent first but!

PAULA: Will we go?

PRIEST: Hold on. What about Paula? If you're going to break the
            mould then she'd be ideal –

PAULA: Sure I'm not a priest but –

PRIEST: In who's eyes –

LINDA: Jesus, this's all too much!

PRIEST: Of course I'd come. But why depend on an appointed
            priest?

PAULA: I never thought! People choosing their own priests! Jesus!
            Think about that! Listen we'll talk about it. I'll be over for
            your cases the morrow at one. That statement would be
            handy for the morning –

PRIEST: I'll make sure there's something to look at by nine-thirty.

LINDA: It's all changing so fast!

EAMONN: Good luck with the Bishop.

            EAMONN, PAULA AND LINDA stand.

PRIEST: See you tomorrow.

            The PRIEST sees EAMONN, PAULA and LINDA to the door.

PAULA: We'll see ourselves out.

            *They leave. The PRIEST closes the door and goes to his
            desk. He is clearly elated and relaxed. A knock on the
            door. He turns as DEIRDRE enters.*

DEIRDRE: Your visitor's arrived.

PRIEST: Thank you.

DEIRDRE: I'm away now. I'll be staying with a friend. Till it all calms down.

PRIEST: I understand.

DEIRDRE comes into the room. She cannot look directly at the PRIEST.

DEIRDRE: *(Relic)* I wanted you to have this.

The PRIEST stands and comes forward. He accepts the relic.

PRIEST: Saint Columb. Thank you, Deirdre –

DEIRDRE: The Bishop sent me a prayer card. It's a prayer for priests. From America. *(Pause)* Will you send me your address?

PRIEST: Of course. I thought –

DEIRDRE: I don't agree with what she's doing. But I admire her. And you. That's not a sin is it, Father?

PRIEST: *(Smiles and shakes his head)* Have a good rest Deirdre.

The PRIEST offers his hand. DEIRDRE pauses a moment and then takes it. She is in tears. She turns and leaves quickly. She turns again at the door.

DEIRDRE: He's a bit worse for wear.

She smiles and leaves. The ROGUE enters and closes the door behind him.

PRIEST: *(Smiles)* Hello. *(Hand)* Father Gallagher. Please call me Declan.

ROGUE: *(Barely shakes)* Mick Donnelly. From Kilrush. County Clare –

PRIEST: I've been through there. Please sit down –

ROGUE: Are we alone?

            Sound of door closing as DEIRDRE leaves.

PRIEST: Why, yes. I believe so. Yes. The other priests are at a
            meeting. You've had a long trip Mr Donnelly –

ROGUE: I missed the rally –

PRIEST: Is that why you came? All the way from Kilrush?

ROGUE: And to meet you. I wanted to meet you personally. Your
            stand marked you out Father Gallagher. You're a bold
            man, so you are.

PRIEST: *(Smiles)* You must be hungry –

ROGUE: *(Shakes his head)* Will you hear my confession, Father?

PRIEST: Surely your own priest –

ROGUE: No. No it has to be you.

PRIEST: *(Nods)* Will you at least take a cup of tea?

ROGUE: Your housekeeper provided me with all I needed. I won't
            keep you long. I'm heading back tonight. Work in the
            morning.

PRIEST: I understand. I'll just get my stole –

ROGUE: You won't be giving in, Father, will you?

PRIEST: *(Smiles)* I can't go back. Will you take off your coat?

            *The ROGUE kneels. The PRIEST goes to his jacket at the
            desk and takes out his stole. He puts it on and kneels
            beside the ROGUE so he is facing him.*

ROGUE: Bless me Father for I have sinned. It is two weeks since
            my last confession.

PRIEST: What sins have you committed?

ROGUE: *(Hand inside his coat)* My wife, Father. At the beginning
           she was all a man could want. Loving. Patient. Good
           natured. And she bore me five daughters. We're a devout
           family Father —

PRIEST: What's on your mind my son?

ROGUE: Four years ago she took sick, Father —

PRIEST: Your wife?

ROGUE: *(Nods)* And she never moved from her bed. I am a patient
           man, Father. But she turned from me, Father. And I longed
           for a son. We have a small farm. Pigs and sheep. A son
           would keep the farm going. But the wife. She grew apart.
           I am a gentle man, Father. But when she refused to give
           me a son, I began to condemn and abuse her —

PRIEST: Was she still sick?

ROGUE: So she said. But I doubted her, Father —

PRIEST: What did you do?

ROGUE: Father, I am a gentle man —

PRIEST: How did you abuse her?

           Silence. The ROGUE cannot speak.

PRIEST: Take your time. Christ forgives those who repent. *(Beat)*
           Would you be more comfortable sitting —

ROGUE: A man has needs, Father. Needs blessed by god. And the
           land has needs. The future. The family line. My father. His
           father —

PRIEST: What did you do to her my son? I know this must be
           difficult —

ROGUE: I beat her, Father.

Silence. The PRIEST looks at the ROGUE.

PRIEST: Once? *(Pause)* More than once?

ROGUE: For three years, Father. Once a week. Sometimes more.
           She wouldn't speak to me, Father. Wouldn't look at me.
           Moved into her own room. Humiliated me in front of my
           daughters, Father!

PRIEST: I understand –

ROGUE: And I. *(Beat)* She became pregnant. It was like a miracle! I
           prayed for a son. She wouldn't speak to me, Father, but I
           knew. As soon as the boy was born, she would come
           round. She looked beautiful, Father. She wanted for
           nothing. You must understand the land has been in my
           family from before the famine –

PRIEST: How did she become pregnant?

ROGUE: Father, I am a good man. On the life of the unborn child –

PRIEST: Why have you come to me, my son?

ROGUE: She left me two days ago, Father. To. To. To abort my son.
           The news. The stories. It all turned her head. In my
           torment I have planned terrible revenge –

PRIEST: On her? *(Beat)* How did she become pregnant –

ROGUE: *(Crying)* Forgive me, Father!

PRIEST: You must confess your sin my son. Only then –

ROGUE: *(Pulls a gun)* Where is she? The freedom bitch! The whore!
           The godless cunt! Where is she now?

The PRIEST freezes in shock. The ROGUE pulls off the stole.

ROGUE: Where is the murdering whore? The anti-Christ slut! The gutless she-devil! Where is she? Without her there'd be a son! An heir for my pigs and sheep! Now my name and my land will be stained with the blood of an unborn innocent! Take off your collar! You have no right to wear it! Take it off!

The PRIEST removes his collar.

ROGUE: Take it all off! All of it!

The PRIEST looks at the ROGUE. He grabs the PRIEST by the hair and pins the gun to his neck.

ROGUE: Fraud! Imposter! Take it all off!

The PRIEST starts fumbling at his buttons. The ROGUE rips his shirt.

ROGUE: She even sneaked out of the house to watch the news! All her life she was dedicated to the home! To the farm! To me! Eating the altar rails! And now! Take off every bit of your lie! All of it!

The PRIEST loosens his trousers and takes them off. He is trembling.

ROGUE: It was a son! I know it was! It must be! For the Lord answered my prayers! But that murdering bitch! That human bomb! That thoughtless cunt! Without you she would've been nothing! Without you she'd have lain underground! Where she deserves to be! In among the fallen! Where is she messenger of the devil? Where is she?

The ROGUE forces the PRIEST onto the floor and pulls back his head.

ROGUE: For four years I've suffered! For four years she made me beg! Then she lied and mocked and abused me in front of my own daughters! Beg for what is rightfully mine! By law! *(Sticks the gun between the PRIEST's legs and yanks back his head)* Beg for this! The whore! The cunt! Your filthy words murdered my only son! Her filthy words gave her the idea! And you blessed her abortion! D'you know what it's like to be consumed! To groan and ache for what's there! Lying next to you! Lying in the next room! D'you know? Lying in the dark! Panting! Groaning! Aching for just one word of love! One human touch! One caress! Do you? You're no priest! Are you? Are you! It's a queer priest supports murder! A queer priest who supports suicide! And you know what queers get! You know where they want it! *(Rams the gun)* What d'they want? Say it! What do they want!

PRIEST: I forgive you –

ROGUE: You forgive me! You're scum! Queer dirty scum! Scum can't forgive! A murdering whoring slut can't forgive! They have to be cleansed! Chastised! Cleansed! Cleansed! Cleansed! Made! Pure!

The gun goes off. Silence apart from the panting of the ROGUE. The PRIEST is dead. The ROGUE raises his head and listens. Silence. Slowly he stands. His hands and trousers are covered in blood. He looks at the door. He pockets the gun inside his coat and goes to the window. He looks out. He opens the window and climbs out.

SCENE 14: ACTION

Monday morning. 9.30am. The DOHERTY sitting room. BERNIE sits in front of the hole. The room has been cleared up. All the wood that was pulled up has been gathered into a box which stands in front of the corner unit. The framed wedding photo is back in it's original position. BERNIE sips her tea in silence. She is obviously waiting and thinking. A knock on the door. BERNIE stands and answers it.

BERNIE: *(Off)* Oh.

LETITIA: *(Off)* Yes, Bernie. Look, can I come in just for a minute?

BERNIE: *(Off)* I –

LETITIA: *(Off)* I won't sit down.

             LETITIA enters. BERNIE follows her into the sitting room.

LETITIA: Jesus, Mary and Saint Joseph! Oh the bastards! They've been raiding down our way all morning too!

BERNIE: Bridie's sending someone down now to repair it –

LETITIA: *(Peering)* That's some damage! How many of them were there?

BERNIE: I –

LETITIA: Your panelled floor! *(Looks about and goes into the kitchen)* Left everything else. Sadistic bastards! What did they expect to find in here? Are you going to claim?

BERNIE: No –

LETITIA: Oh, but you should! They've no right. D'you know what they're after finding the next one up from our's? Beanos under the pillow! Off a thirty year old woman! Dirty knickers or pornos would be bad enough. But comic books! Well she's affronted for life! The whole street's sniggering! To her face! I'm telling you, Bernie. I wouldn't think twice about sending in a claim. What time were they in?

BERNIE: It wasn't a raid, Letitia –

LETITIA: Don't tell me. You raided yourself. Jesus, Bernie! There's no need to feel guilty! It doesn't mean your under suspicion. You think there might be recriminations if you claim –

BERNIE: No –

LETITIA: Well, you don't want to keep quiet about that sort of thing. It only encourages them.

BERNIE looks away.

LETITIA: Well, it's up to you of course. I'll tell you what it is. I'm here about that money I owe you.

BERNIE: It doesn't matter now –

LETITIA: Go and let me say my piece –

BERNIE: You won't be going through me anymore –

LETITIA: Bernie, listen. I'm while sorry for putting you under pressure. You'll see I –

BERNIE: Letitia. I'm not doing the catalogues anymore.

LETITIA: But your clients. All that money –

BERNIE: They can send out someone else –

LETITIA: To sixty people? They'll never do that –

BERNIE: Their problem. It can all fall apart for all I care –

LETITIA: What? But your commission. All that work. Your accounts –

BERNIE: Burnt them.

LETITIA: *(Open-mouthed)* Burnt them?

BERNIE: Every last card.

LETITIA: *(Beat)* Well fair fucking play to ye! *(Beat)* And you don't want this money?

LETITIA holds up a fiver.

BERNIE: You do what you want. You'll probably receive a letter –

LETITIA: You know what they can do with that! They can whistle all they want! I was only paying because we can't get into your catalogue in the Heights.

BERNIE: I was going to write to yous all –

LETITIA: Imagine if all the agents done that but! *(Laughs)* And there was me coming over to beg! I've enough on me plate just fighting for Sean. I'll keep what I have but that's it for me. I'm getting me life under control. I love you!

LETITIA impulsively kisses BERNIE on the cheek. BERNIE's eyes fill with tears.

LETITIA: Aye. Have a good cry. They'd no right –

BERNIE: Did you know Father Gallagher?

LETITIA: What?

BERNIE: Shot last night –

LETITIA: Father Gallagher! No! Are you sure?

BERNIE: On the news this morning –

LETITIA: No! I don't believe it! Who by?

BERNIE: They don't know.

LETITIA sits down.

LETITIA: You don't think. He was under a while lot of strain –

BERNIE: They're talking of murder.

LETITIA: I don't believe it –

BERNIE sits.

LETITIA: And I seen him at the rally. Disguised as a woman –

BERNIE: You could always go to him for a heart to heart. Saved my Marie's life.

LETITIA: You know why they killed him, Bernie.

BERNIE: Who?

LETITIA: I don't know. But I know why.

BERNIE: Aye. Aye I know. God protect the wee girl. And her wain.

LETITIA: And he saved me from meself. So he did Bernie. God rest his soul.

Silence as they both reflect.

LETITIA: See the mass? I'm going to say something.

BERNIE: In the chapel?

LETITIA: In the cathedral itself if needs be! It all fits together. Can't say exactly how just now. But it does. I know it. I can feel it. And I've three days to work it all out. *(Beat)* I might just read out one of them letters –

BERNIE: In the chapel!

LETITIA: From the pulpit itself! And you want to come up with me Bernie! *(Points)* And tell them about your hole!

LETITIA realises the double meaning in her words. She laughs.

LETITIA: God forgive me and pardon me!

LETITIA covers her mouth and laughs. BERNIE smiles.